PAINT

THIS

TOWN

RED

A.J Kirby: Writer

By

A J Kirby

Cover Art by Nick Button

www.nickbutton.co.uk

A Wild Wolf Publication

Published by Wild Wolf Publishing in 2012

First print

ISBN: 978-1-907954-22-1

www.wildwolfpublishing.com

"For Lily, in celebration.
For George, in memory.
And for Eric.
The original black panther."

PAINT THIS TOWN RED

Prologue

The magpie was, for sorrow, on his own. And he was rather pleased about that, because he'd seen something interesting. Something which, had he, for joy, been hooked up in a twosome, he'd have had to share. And the magpie didn't like sharing. Didn't like doing much of anything with any other birds, save for a bit of the other. And even then, he hated the boring post-coital chirpery.

He was perched on a road sign which read: WELCOME TO LIMM ISLAND. TWINNED WITH ALSFELD, GERMANY. Not that he could read it, but he could sense the meaning of it. The cold metal driven into the dirt. Meant he was close to a town. Meant he was close to people. And he didn't want to share what he'd seen with people, either. People, he knew from painful experience, were even more selfish than he was. Even more greedy. And if they saw what he'd seen, they'd want it.

But he'd seen no sign of any people since he'd landed here. And indeed, it looked as though people hadn't been round here for a while either. It was strange, even though there was a road and a road sign, the people didn't seem to have gone further than that to put their stamp on the terrain. The dense woodland had been allowed to grow thick, encroaching on the road now, almost hiding the sign. Weeds cut through the concrete, causing fault-line cracks to run across it like veins. The muddy grass on the roadside was long and unkempt.

The magpie cocked his head. Regarded the interesting, luminous thing with his beady eye. Hopped from side to side to get a better view, his claws *riiinnnggg*ing against the sign's metal. He was a little confused. The thing appeared to be floating about six feet away for him and yet it had no wings. And there was nothing

1

holding it up. And it wasn't making a sound to suggest it was powered by anything. Nothing human anyway. Their dirty great stink wasn't all over this thing.

He cocked his head again. Something told him he should simply spread his wings and fly away because although the thing wasn't human – didn't stink of *anything* in fact - it was still dangerous in some way. Ah but it was beautiful too, though. The way it caught the sun's early-morning light. The way it seemed to cast out *more* light of its own. Light from somewhere else. *Older* light.

The thing was circular. About two, three inches in diameter. So about the size of a small apple. But it didn't look like any apple the magpie had ever seen. Didn't look like food at all. In fact what it looked like was a large button or a valve. The magpie thought he'd better investigate. Gingerly, he flapped his wings, wondering if the thing would simply float away if he startled it. But nothing happened.

Stop being so hesitant. Just go get it. It's there for the taking.

The magpie gave in to the temptation. He allowed his desire to rule him. He took wing, covered the six feet which separated him from the thing in little more than a few flaps. And then he hovered. Not beautifully as a hawk would, but hovering all the same. Close up, he could see how shiny-smooth the thing was. But strangely, he couldn't see his own reflection in it.

He investigated, woodpeckering his beak against it, to see what would happen. Part of him thought he'd burst the thing, part of him thought the thing would electrocute him as a farmer's fence had once. Another part of him thought it would turn him the same golden colour *it* was. But all that happened was his beak hit it – *thunk* – and bounced off it, practically straining his neck in the process. Practically causing him to lose his hovering stroke.

He investigated it by landing on it now. And although there wasn't much purchase for his claws, he managed to stay upright. And just as he was lowering his head – slowly, surely this time – to look again, he felt a strange pulse coursing up through it and into his legs, into his hollow bones. Filling his hollow bones. He felt the pulse flowing through him and encircling his heart, starting to stifle it. And then, just as quickly as he'd felt it, it went away.

And then the magpie *knew* he should simply spread his wings and fly away. Because if the thing pulsed again, it would surely kill him. But now, when he tried to flap, his wings seemed to have forgotten their aerodynamism. His bones felt too heavy to take off. He felt as though he'd become gravity.

And if so, why hadn't he brought the floating thing crashing down into the grass?

Scared now, the magpie tried his first line of defence. He started to peck at the thing. More aggressively now. Desperately now. He pecked – *thunk* – pecked – *thunk* – and pecked again. And then he felt the pulse once more. And this time, even though he didn't like to admit it to himself, he felt it *before* it happened. He anticipated it. He smelled it. And yet he didn't move. He *let it* course into him.

And this time the pulse was stronger. Angrier. As though he'd dislodged something within it through his desperate pecking. Suddenly, all around the valve, the air started to become hazy. Hell, it became rippled, as though the magpie was looking at it through a film of water. Or as though the air *was* a film of water.

The magpie pecked at the valve again, and this time when his beak connected with it he heard a distinct *clunk.* As though the thing's inner-machinery, whatever that was, had made its final click into place. As though it was a lock, finally relenting and opening.

Now the magpie heard what sounded like a great, gasping exhalation of air. A *whoosh* like a plane at take-off. And the air around the thing didn't just ripple, it *melted.* And as it did so, the magpie began to melt too. His claws were *dribbling* into the valve, disintegrating from the feet up.

A black hole yawned open around him, buzzing with energy. He heard the crack and creak of timber. Heard so many branches snap away like brittle bones. The earth, the grass, scorched. Burned, but with no flame the magpie could see.   And then, as the magpie started to take his last breath, he heard something else. Something growled. And the magpie had the very real sense that whatever had growled *wasn't yet here.* That it was in transit. That it was still halfway over from the other side, from wherever this black hole buttoned onto. And in that moment, in that moment when he *sixth-sensed* that he was taking his last mortal breath, he was actually glad it was his last breath. Because another breath would give whatever was making that growling noise more time to get here. More time to materialise. And the magpie didn't want to see the thing. Because it sounded big. And it sounded hungry.

It sounded like death.

Two things were born of the valve that first day. The first, that growling thing which the once-curious, now-fried magpie had heard just as he was taking his last breath, was already moving when it was spat out. It hit the ground running, landing in the charred grass around the battered WELCOME TO LIMM ISLAND. TWINNED WITH ALSFELD, GERMANY road sign. But there was nothing sleek about the way this visitor moved, despite its lithe, blue-black body. It hit the ground running, but it was a scrabbling kind of run. The run of something desperate. Its ears were pressed back flat against its head, the silky fur along its spine was standing to attention, everything spoke of it being a creature *waaaaay* outside its comfort zone. Paws barely touching the ground, it moved out of the liquidy air around the black hole where the golden valve had been released as though its life depended on it.

The first visitor, our distinctly feline friend, gained the protection of the woods, perhaps looking for somewhere to hide amongst the longer, less scorched grass. It began to claw at the trunk of a tree, thinking to climb it, thinking to get away from the cursed ground, but discovered the tree was hollow and cold and as white as bone. The panther withdrew its claws, wrinkled its nose and sniffed at the bark. Then pulled sharply back as though it had smelled something unnatural.

It moved on, slinking low against the floor now, belly scraping through the accumulated leaf mulch and broken branches. It circled some of the other trees which made up its new surroundings, slowly coming to understand that *all* the trees within firing range of the black hole looked similarly, chalkily skeletal. Too brittle to hold its weight. And it was right, most likely, this solid shadow. For it was all taut muscle, coiled sinew; force-of-nature heavy. The big cat was born, *borne*, into this land already complete, already full-grown and at the height of its powers. And although it was hard to measure the panther, because of its constant movement – its head tick-tocking from side to side in a faintly reptilian way despite the cat being so obviously a mammal; its paws twitching in turn after touching the ground, as though it didn't want to be swallowed up by it; its tail scything back and forth with the frenzy of a conductor's baton – it had to be six feet long.

Now it moved with a frightful silence. A crepuscular secret made flesh. Every few paces it paused and sniffed the air and then moved on, always moving further away from the point of origin, the valve. Moving away despite the fact there was easy meat back there, in the form of the dead bird. Moving away because its every nerve, its every brain cell was screaming out to it to get away. To find a hidey-hole where it could bed down and regroup. Whenever it caught another sniff of the black hole on the breeze, it shivered.

And then, without warning, the panther broke into a run, crashing through the undergrowth, scattering the small woodland creatures in its path, sending flocks of grounded birds back into the air. It careered deeper into the woods, so deep that it became hard to pick it out amongst the dense vegetation. So deep that for a while, it could only be seen by proxy, by picking out the other creatures which it sent scurrying and flapping away. And then it was gone. Gone, but not forgotten. From somewhere in the hidden heart of the woods, it gave a furious, blood-curdling growl, that same growl which had sent the poor magpie off into the afterlife. The growl seemed to echo up as though from the very bowels of the earth.

And then it was deathly quiet.

Back at the valve though, something else was happening. Preparations were starting to be made for a second arrival. The ground seemed to crackle as though full of static electricity. The liquidy air around the black hole wriggled as though it was alive. The wind picked up, forming a localised tornado. And once again, there was that same pulsing, only this time it was louder. Heavier. Growing stronger. So strong that more branches cracked and heaved off the broken trees. The midwives to this second birth were all at the point of collapse, as though there wasn't enough energy in this universe to contain what the valve was to deliver.

And then everything stopped. The wind ceased to move the dead branches in the trees. It was as though some great power had suddenly squashed the pause button with a great sausage of a thumb. And then a new sound started to break in to the eerie silence. The new sound was very close to the sound effect used in cartoons when something heavy was dropped from a great height. Starting off barely perceptible, the sound grew and grew until it became a definite *wheeeeeeeeeeeeeeee.*

Something was coming. Something big. But it didn't appear as a vague dot in the sky, falling. It appeared four, maybe five feet off the ground, filling the exact space where the golden valve had been, seconds earlier. It appeared as though from thin air, as though it was some wondrous magician's lifetime's work of a trick. It appeared four, maybe five feet off the ground, and yet, as it

5

inevitably dropped to the ground, as normal forces like gravity started to act upon it, it bounced. The second thing bounced back up into the liquidy air as though it was nothing more than a bouncing ball. And for a long moment, it seemed as though it would remain there, suspended, *hanging*. But it didn't. Inevitably it dropped again, and this time as it dropped, it smashed through the battered WELCOME TO LIMM ISLAND. TWINNED WITH ALSFELD, GERMANY road sign as though it wasn't there, *smithereening* the damned thing. It bounced again, and then skidded off on its side, surfing across the scorched grass until it cracked into one of the half-dead white trees, its long neck ending up at a peculiar angle, its dorsal fin dog-legged.

The second thing tried desperately to waggle its tail fin, tried wildly to flap open its mouth and breathe. But this was about as far from its natural habitat as it was possible for it to be. The old deserted road on the outskirts of Limm was no place for a huge, blubbery great white shark, no matter how much it refused to believe that fact. No matter how much it gnashed its teeth, drawing its own blood. No matter how much it tried to swim through the liquidy air which surrounded it. No matter how close the sea smelled. The shark was broken, grounded, crash-landed. It reared up off the scorched earth, twisted its great neck, tried to drink in the atmosphere. Then it bucked, flipped, thrashed again. Already its skin was starting to dry, to become encrusted with dead leaves and broken branches. Already the thrashings were starting to lose energy.

Soon the shark could do little more than lie and shiver, and occasionally vomit the watery contents of its stomach onto the ground. And soon even that was too much for it. Soon the shark stopped moving at all. When a tiny fly, attracted by unusual salty-fishy stink which the shark was giving off, landed on its taxidermist's button of an eye, the shark could do absolutely nothing about it. And by the time the fly started to lay its eggs inside the still-damp eyeball, the shark didn't even feel a thing. The portal's second birth was still. But there would be some life inside it.

Day One

1: Cursed

Kirstie was convinced everything was going to be fine until the green car in front hit the goose. And it was all her fault. She'd been ragging it, going right up the old bugger's arse, cursing and gesticulating so he couldn't have failed to see her if he happened to look in the rear-view. But old buggers never seemed to care whether they were holding anyone up; they thought the whole world moved at their pace. All the dramas of their lives were over; nobody would want to see them so desperately that they needed to drive fast. And so they hogged the road, trundling along at something like twenty miles an hour, despite the fact it was an A road and everyone knew the cameras didn't work anyway.

The further up the coast you got the less dual carriageway there was. Some of the older people were forever complaining about the single-lane road and all the accidents they reckoned it caused; they wrote stiff letters to MPs in London and to the local papers. They started petitions. But in reality it was *them* causing all the accidents, on account of their painstakingly slow driving. The old bugger in front had been going so slow, Kirstie felt confident enough to fire off a few texts while she was driving. Even stole a few looks in the mirror to check whether the streaky mascara still trailed treacly-black down her cheeks. Even had the time to check whether her dark hair still looked all right. She'd promised herself she wouldn't take her eyes off the road, not for a minute, but with *him* in front, there seemed to be no real need to check for tight bends, obstructions and the like.

She hadn't stolen the car. Not really. She'd seen the keys on the counter-top in the caravan, and Rich hadn't been answering his phone, and time was pressing. So she'd just borrowed it. She'd been careful not to litter the front seat with Maccy D's wrappers like she did her dad's car, and she certainly hadn't smoked. But now, despite all her careful planning, she was going to get caught out because of the bloody menace to the road in front in his beat-up old - what was it? - Skoda or something. Rover, maybe… Tortoise? It was certainly tortoising along.

Rich's car was a Gunner. Mint condition, he proudly told her. In fact, so proud was Rich of the car, he'd even given it a nickname, although it wasn't a girly one like some of the girls in college used to call *their* cars (Stacey's Clio had, ridiculously, been called Bambi). No: Rich called his Gunner 'The Millennium Falcon' because like Han Solo in *Star Wars*, he won his ship in some bet once, only Rich had won the Falcon from his brother Mike, not Lando Calrissian.

Rich had a lot of rap music CDs in the Falcon. All of them angry, all of them aggressive. He hadn't let her put any of her own CDs in, and she hadn't had the time to pick any up earlier, so instead, she was tuned in to Radio Coast. It was pretty good, apart from the bits in between the songs when the DJs rattled on about nonsense and the constant advert breaks for silly little tourist shops in Norsea or crappy pubs in Charnley. When they played Cheesemonster, with its mind-hammering beats which *just hypnotised* you into driving fast, she'd rammed her foot down on the pedal hard, had been breezing-it. But then she'd come up behind Mr. Doddery.

Cheesemonster was going into the 'Take me awayyyyyyyyyyyyyyyyy' chorus bit, a bit which never failed to make Kirstie's stomach lurch like she'd just come up on a pill, when she saw the goose. Or rather, family of geese. They were up ahead about fifty metres away, waddling along in single file like in one of her old kids' books. Mammy Goose, Daddy Goose and three ickle Babby Geese who she could barely make out. Mammy Goose was bringing up the rear, and kept lowering her beak and gently pecking at the bums of her fluffy, feathery brood to chivvy them along.

As soon as she'd seen the geese, Kirstie had started to slam on the anchors, but the old juffer in front took a little more time. He probably needed glasses or something. Or else he was going quicker than he felt comfortable with, on account of her grinding away right behind him like one of those sleazy blokes at Ritzys for the past three miles, meaning he *couldn't* slow down. On the road, Mammy Goose finally became aware of the danger. She paused, looked round to see this beat-up old Rover closing in on her and her brood. Then she started walking more quickly. For a moment, Kirstie relaxed. The geese were going to escape. They'd be fine.

Even when the edge of the Skoda's bumper hit Mammy Goose's neck, Kirstie thought everything was going to be okay. It seemed only a glancing blow. Mammy Goose's neck bent and billowed, as though it was a piece of long grass in the wind. It was ever so graceful, like an Egyptian belly-dance.

The goose was going to be okay. Her neck was engineered to withstand things like that...

It wasn't. When a few ounces of flesh and feather come into contact with hundreds of pounds of hard metal and plastic, moving at a rate of sixty miles an hour, well, *nothing* can withstand a blow like that. The neck cracked. Mammy Goose slapped down across the camber of the road, unmoving. And although Kirstie wrestled with the wheel, skidded, *almost* made it, she soon heard, *felt,* the horrifying bump as she drove over the goose's poor body. *Th-thunk.*

She managed to correct the car before she drove it into a ditch at the side of the road and then started to drive on, but almost immediately stopped again. Right in the middle of the road. White with shock, she stared in the rear view mirror, saw the roadkill she was responsible for. Saw the brood of poor goslings that'd just lost their mother start to waddle back to her broken body.

Why didn't the father stop them? Why didn't he do something?

Evidently, he wasn't bothered. He'd made it all the way across the road now and disappeared through a small gap in a hedge. In a sudden fit of pique, Kirstie hoped there'd be a fox lying in wait on the other side of that hedge, ready to gobble him up for being a *typical male.* The old bugger's car, the one which had struck the first blow, had also disappeared now over the crown of a low hill. Unconcerned. He probably hadn't even realised what he'd done.

Kirstie breathed deeply, tried to regain control of her body which was trembling all over. Then she took the key out of the ignition and stepped out of the Gunner. In a daze, she started walking back along the road, not caring if another car happened to be coming or what would happen to her if one did. In her mind's eye, she could picture what would happen to the fragile flesh and bone of her own body if she was hit. How far she'd bounce. How much of her would fall apart. Whether anyone would stop for her.

9

The dead goose was surprisingly far away. At least three hundred metres. Despite the cold and the shock, Kirstie had stopped shivering. Or stopped noticing she was shivering, at least. She crunched along on the loose gravel, hardly aware of the woods which flanked the road or the silence in the air. The dead goose was all she could concentrate on. The dead goose and her brood. As she drew nearer, she started to clap her hands together, shouting 'shoo' at the top of her voice. 'Get out of here.' The goslings didn't move. They just fixed her with questioning looks and then returned to nuzzling at their mother's bloodied feathers.

And then she heard the truck. They all heard the truck. They heard it at least twenty seconds before they saw it, lumbering into view, surrounded by a cloud of black smoke. Through the smoke, Kirstie could make out the flashing lights in the driver's cab. She imagined someone called Wayne was driving, and Wayne had his name up in lights. He'd be on the CB thingy, probably, talking to someone whose handle was 8Ball, or something similarly stupid, and wouldn't even be looking at the road. There was only one way to respond to Wayne, and that was to stand in protection over the goslings, waving her arms above her head.

The truck didn't appear to slow. Now, she thought she could make out the vehicle's livery. Big yellow letters on black. She knew those colours. They were the colours of the small mead brewery over on the south side of Limm Island, Combs' Mead. Her dad worked at the brewery. In a brief moment, Kirstie became the small child who read books about families of geese. She became the small child whose daddy could do anything in the world. She reached into the pocket of her jeans for her pink mobile phone and was about to call his number; he'd be able to stop the truck. He worked at the brewery after all. But then she realised the phone wouldn't even have time to connect before the truck was upon them.

She started to scream nonsense words, just sounds really, but even then, she knew it wouldn't be loud enough. The truck sounded its horn. First, a few sharp blasts and then later, one long powerful note of warning. Kirstie stood firm. The truck continued to make progress. The goslings still crowded around their mother. And in that instant, Kirstie knew the whole thing was an omen. She was sure it was an omen. *This is how cruel nature can be;* the truck's angry horn seemed to be saying. *No matter how much control we may pretend we have, what happens to us is random, malicious even.* At that moment, she knew exactly what the results on the ten tests she'd bought from the chemists in Norsea would say. And that would be her life. *Bang,* just like that. She'd be on Limm Island for the rest of her days; she'd become like everyone else, beaten down by circumstance. She may as well have been lying dead in the road.

At the last, instinct took over. *The maternal instinct?* With the grating, Brachiosaurean groan of the truck's brakes flooding her ears, she dived into the ditch at the side of the road, splashing into road run-off water a foot deep. The whoosh of the truck gunning past matched her shoulder jarring against something; a rock, a sat nav thrown out of the window by some motorist finally tired of being told what to do by a machine, a hub cap? Everything went black for a moment. She feared she was about to pass out, but could do nothing about it.

And then reality closed back around her. She was aware of the oily residue on her hair, the pain in her shoulder, the way her lungs burned for air. She struggled up into a sitting position and then forced herself to look back onto the road, sure she was going to see three smaller bodies next to the now flattened body of their mother.

There was only one body on the road. Kirstie blinked once, twice. Looked again. Couldn't see the dead goslings. She gave out a low sob, suddenly realising everything was in vain. The shivering started again. Her jeans were wet through from the muddy water of the ditch. Her shoulder was *killing.*

And then she heard a little chirping sound coming from the small grass verge which separated road from ditch. She turned to see all three goslings, alive and well, chattering away to each other in whatever nonsense language geese have. A warm feeling of righteousness spread through her; felt like she'd pissed herself, she'd later think.

But then she heard a voice: 'Oi! Slag! What the fuck you think you're doing?'

She turned to see the driver of the truck – Wayne? - marching down the same stretch of road she'd walked along only minutes earlier. He was a big man, cap pulled low over his face. As he walked, he swung his powerful arms back and forth as though he was mixing records on two decks. Kirstie could only stare at him.

'You silly slag!' he bellowed. 'That your fucking car up there?'

He was getting close now. Waving his arms around ever more wildly. Kirstie almost let herself slip back into the muddy water of the ditch, before thinking better of it. He'd already spotted

11

her. He was already *this close* to his revenge. And his revenge would be brutal. She knew that by the way he almost trod on the dead goose which had already been run over three times.

And if he didn't kill her? If he didn't kill her something worse was in store for her. Urgently, she looked away, back up the road, suddenly fearful the truck had run into Rich's car. Suddenly understanding what she'd done had been the actions of a lunatic, a madwoman. The truck was jack-knifed across the road so she couldn't see Rich's darling Gunner, but it was *bound* to be totalled. And how the hell was she going to explain that to him if she did survive? This wasn't Maccy D's wrappers on the front seat or the tangy whiff of cigarettes on the upholstery.

The truck driver was standing on the grass verge overlooking the ditch. He glared down at her, ignoring the goslings. 'I said; what the fuck did you think you were doing?'

Kirstie looked back at him with pleading eyes, but couldn't find the words to explain. She gestured to the goslings. The truck driver stared at the trio with contempt. For a second, she feared he was going to kick them right into the ditch with her, but he didn't.

'I'm going to miss the fucking road now, you silly slag,' he sighed. Evidently his anger was quick-burn. She'd seen Rich more angry than this when she burned the bastard toast. Her dad too. *She'd* been angrier than this when she missed the road one time.

'I'm sorry,' she breathed.

The truck driver said nothing, but was now regarding her with more than a little interest. Suddenly, he bent down and offered a thick, sausage-fingered hand to her. Without knowing what else to do, she stretched out and allowed him to pull her up.

'I'm sorry,' she said again.

The truck driver continued to stare at her, head cocked to one side now: 'Say, aren't you the Shay girl... Mal's daughter?'

Kirstie nodded and then finally collapsed into tears. And then it all came out at once. 'Don't-tell-me-dad-please-and-don't-tell-Rich-I-only-borrowed-his-car-one-day-and-I-was-going-to-bring-it-back-and-then-an-old-bastard-got-in-front-of-me-and-I-thought-I-was-going-to-miss-the-road-and...'

The driver gave her an understanding look. 'We'll go through the in's and out's later. Right now, no harm done. But we're lucky. No cars coming either way yet. Will be soon. And my truck's all to cock over the road. *Your* car's parked across the white lines. First thing we do is move them. You okay to drive?'

Kirstie didn't even feel okay enough to walk. Her legs had turned to goose-fat, her arms a great mass of goose-pimples. The woods which flanked the road looked hazy, far-off. The jack-knifed truck was in another world altogether; Rich's car didn't even exist. The driver nodded. Reached into the back pocket of his jeans and pulled out a battered packet of Dorchester and Grey cigarettes. They looked as though he'd been sitting on them from as far away as Southampton. He shook the pack in front of her face.

'Take one. Stay here. Have a smoke. Give me your car keys. I'll move the car and the truck onto the side of the road. Your dad'd never forgive me if I let you drive in your state.'

Kirstie took a cigarette with a trembling hand and clamped it into her mouth. Then, as something else occurred to her, she started to cry once again. 'Please,' she gurgled. 'Ignore what's on the back seat. Don't say anything about it... Don't even look.'

The truck driver narrowed his eyes, but apparently knew better than to press matters further. Instead he gave a wide, obviously fake smile. 'What happens on the A24 stays on the A24,' he said, pulling out a red plastic lighter and flicking at the wheel a couple of times to get a flame. Kirstie moved closer, sucked deeply, and heard the satisfying crackle as the cigarette caught.

She sunk down into a half-crouch as she watched the driver walking away back up the road. The cigarette *was* calming her down. Restoring some form of normality. She hadn't realised how gasping she'd been. Maybe everything would still work out okay; she'd been *so* lucky the truck driver was so understanding. Maybe the world wasn't as cruel as she feared. But then, the fact he knew her father was another thing which could come back and bite her on the arse. Especially if he looked in the Salvadore's Chemists bag on the bag seat. And another thing: she'd let the cat out of the applecart about Rich, hadn't she? Nobody knew about her and Rich, and there she'd been, telling him all about how it was Rich's car. What with the stuff on the back seat and everything else, it wouldn't take an Inspector Morse to work out what was going on. And then, what if she missed the road? What if she couldn't get back for another eight hours? What if people started to look for her? What if the truck driver also missed the road and called ahead to the brewery to warn them and just so happened to tell them he'd almost run into foreman Shay's daughter on his way?

It didn't bear thinking about none of it did. And now, even the bloody goslings had deserted her. They weren't anywhere to be

13

seen on the grass verge, nor were they in the ditch. Thankfully, they weren't on the road though. She took another contemplative drag of the cigarette and then suddenly chucked it into the ditch where it disappeared into the water with a hiss. If the tests did turn out positive, then smoking would be the first on the long list of pleasurable things she'd have to do away with. Cigarettes, fun, drinks, pills, maybe Rich.

Three hundred or so metres away, the driver started trying to correct the truck. Back and forth, back and forth he moved the cab. Inching, inching. Somewhere far away, a car horn beeped. It sounded weak, piddly after the bellow of the truck's horn which still reverberated around somewhere in the back of her head. She imagined a long queue of cars waiting for the truck to move so they could get past. She imagined how she'd ruined so many people's days with her own self-obsessed craziness. She imagined the police. The police would want to know what had happened. And they'd take one look at her wild hair and her treacle-mascara and know it was all down to her...

When finally the truck moved out of the way, only two cars steamed through. The driver of the second car was so irate as to stick his head out of the window to yell more abuse at the truck driver, even as he increased his forward momentum. Poor truck driver. None of this had been his fault, and now madmen in cars were out for his blood. But he didn't seem bothered in the slightest. She watched him climb down from his cab and walk over to the Gunner, which she now saw was horribly skewed across the road where she'd abandoned it. Thankfully, it seemed unharmed. He got in, revved the engine and then threw the car into a tight U-turn and then, in seconds, he was back with her, arm leaning out of the driver-side window just like Rich did, telling her to 'get in.'

She obeyed his command, slipped into the warmth of the Gunner and let him drive her back up to where he'd left the truck. When he looked in the rear-view mirror before pulling over, she thought he was looking at the Salvadore's Chemists bag, but then told herself she was being stupid.

'Right,' he said, his hand still resting on the key, but the car now stopped. 'We've stopped a ten-car pile up now.'

Kirstie gave him a weak smile by way of response.

'But you've got some explaining to do,' he continued, lifting his bum off the seat and reaching into his back pocket for his

14

cigarettes. 'Why were you standing in the road? Why did you abandon your car?'

'Please don't tell my dad,' said Kirstie, bowing her head, pretending she was studying the mud which caked her jeans.

'Don't you think your dad would want to know?' he said, pausing to light his Dorchester and Grey. This time he had to flick the lighter's little wheel about six times before it produced a weak flame. Kirstie didn't have the heart to tell him *nobody* was allowed to smoke in Rich's darling Gunner. 'Don't you think he has a *right* to know? I mean, do you go around doing stuff like this regular, like?'

'Shouldn't we see whether we can catch the road before the tide comes in?' asked Kirstie.

'Hold your horses, duck,' said the driver through a mouthful of smoke. He hawked up a throatful of gob and spat it out of the open window into the ditch as though to summarise his feelings on the matter. 'I need to think about this a minute... I can't let you drive in your condition. And I can't afford to drive you over and come back for my rig... No time. Let me see...'

Kirstie wanted to shake him. They needed to go. Now. Limm was a tidal island, separated from the mainland by a causeway. When the tide was in, it was umbilically linked to the mainland, but when the sea dragged in, it became cut off. Cast adrift. Unreachable except by boat. And there was no arguing with the sea when it decided to come in. The sea wouldn't sit around waiting while they debated the whys and wherefores. The sea wouldn't listen to excuses like 'I had to check on some geese'. The sea came in with or without you, like, marooning you one side or the other.

The driver spoke, finally, scratching at his stubbly chin: 'Let's see now. We're going to have to get your car off the road and come back for it tomorrow. I'll take you in the rig now, just to make sure you're safe.'

'Rich's car,' said Kirstie.

'Sorry?'

'I told you, not my car; Rich's car.'

'This Rich that chef bloke who works at the Castle?'

A new wave of panic hit Kirstie's stomach right where the Cheesemonster tune hit her. 'You know him too?'

A grin. 'Sure I know him. Pretty much, anyway.'

Kirstie nodded, before quickly saying, 'but nobody knows. He wants it kept secret. Least 'til his divorce is through. You won't say anything will you, Mr... Mr...' She realised she didn't even know her roadside saviour's name. Realised she hadn't even bothered to ask.

'Joe,' he said, extending that same sausage-fingered hand that had lifted her out of the ditch. 'Joe Friar, like the monk. So which are you? I know you're a Shay, but Mal's got three, hasn't he? I'm terrible with names, but let me see, there was Rachel... uh... Dawn... uh...'

'Kirstie,' she said. 'But most people call me Kirst. I don't like it because it sounds a bit like, you know, *cursed.*'

Outside, the landscape was starting to look cursed. Colours and shapes were starting to morph into shadows. The sky bleached and then murked into a dishwater grey. Trees and hedgerows started to look like monsters. When the occasional car whizzed past, it came heralded by headlights.

'Reckon we have been cursed today, duck,' said Joe, finally releasing her hand and taking a long drag from his cigarette which seemed to make him spit out of the window again. He was like a cigarette-bulemic, Kirstie reckoned. 'Now, I'm gonna be in a load of trouble if I do miss the road, so we'll get the car somewhere safe and then we'll go over to my rig and we'll make a move. How's that sound?'

'But...'

'No buts. If we carry on messing about here, we'll miss the road. And if we do, that means I'm gonna have to come up with some kind of story for my boss. In fact, *you're* gonna have to come up with some kind of story for my boss. And I'm sure you're not gonna want to mention anything about *that* in what you say.' He jerked his thumb back to indicate the bag from the Chemist's in the back seat.

'So what you're saying is...'

'What I'm saying is we're in a pickle, and leaving *Rich's* car is the least of your worries at the moment. I can see you've got enough on your plate as it is without me sticking me big beak in, but we need to go now, and I ain't leaving you here, or letting you drive... Shall we make like trees?'

'Eh?'

'Leave?'

Kirstie sighed. Nodded again. Feeling like she should have put up more of a fight, but at the same time, knowing she really had no choice in the matter. She'd been railroaded by a man *yet again,* but now wasn't the time to worry about it. She said nothing as Joe started up the Gunner, slipped back onto the A24 and cruised along for about two hundred yards before pulling into a lay-by which dog-legged off the main road, a crescent shaped haven separated from the road by a line of trees. Had there not been decent lighting, a decrepit-looking snack van (bearing the legend 'JAX SNAX' in runny-eggy yellow paint on the side) and two monstrous lorries parked up, Kirstie might have been worried about exactly what kind of deserted spot he was taking her to.

'It'll be safe as houses here,' said Joe, indicating one of the lorries, 'this is a rigger's rest point. There'll be rigs coming in here most of the night, catching their scheduled breaks. Nobody'll touch the car.'

They both climbed out and started to walk back to Joe's truck, Kirstie having to dart back twice to check whether she'd locked *all* the doors properly, Joe waiting patiently as she did so. Once they'd moved away from the artificial lights of the rest spot, they were plunged into a darkness which was as thick as it had been quick to arrive. And Kirstie found herself walking as close to her roadside saviour as possible without actually linking arms with the man. Little conversation passed between them, but that didn't mean everything was quiet. Joe's constant coughing, hawking, and spitting saw to that.

At the rig, Joe quickly hoisted himself up into the cab with a practiced ease: *one-two-three and you're up, the rigger's triple-jump.* He seemed so high above her now as he sat, sparked up *yet another* ciggie, and fiddled with something on the dashboard. She saw the couple footholds she was supposed to use to climb up to join him and when she made a scramble for the first one, she realised just how difficult the climb to the cab actually was. She tried again. Tried to flex her leg high enough so it would reach the first of the footholds, but her jeans felt too heavy, too wet, to stretch properly. And her now-freezing hands couldn't get proper purchase on the handhold.

'Joe!' she called, knowing she was being a pathetic *girl,* but not caring any more. Knowing she was going against everything her dad had taught her about doing things for herself so men didn't try to do them for her and then want something in return, but not caring about that either. 'Will you help me?'

No response. She craned her neck to see if he'd heard her cry for help. Saw him, silhouetted by smoke, with a faraway look on his face.

'Joe!' she called again, this time hoisting herself up some with the handhold so she could *just about* reach up and slap her palm against the bottom bit of the door. Which she did, and felt the metal cold and unforgiving against her hand. It gave a muffled *blunk* as she hit it.

Joe finally responded. He cranked open the door and offered her a sheepish smile. 'Sorry,' he said, and then obligingly reached out a hand to help her aboard. She winced, remembering the pain in her shoulder, but allowed him to take her weight. She scurried up the side; it was completely unladylike, completely *like a rat up a drainpipe.*

'Thanks,' she puffed, as she gained the cab and found herself faced with a new problem; trying to find a space for her arse amongst the various discarded crisp-bags, empty cans of Red Bull and faded newspapers on the springy passenger seat.

Joe shook his head, as though to say *nuthin to it, ma'am.* He whacked on the heaters, and keyed the engine, and then she felt a huge roar of power from beneath her. It felt thrillingly comforting. Felt like, even if the tide *was* creeping in, the lorry'd still be powerful enough to plough on through it. And then, as they pulled away, he flicked on the lights at the front of the cab; those same lights she'd first seen back on the A24 when the truck had been bearing down on her and her brood of goslings. Since then, Joe had shut off the lights, as though out of respect for the dead goose but now they blazed out into the darkness. Neither of them spoke as the truck lumbered up past the lay-by where they'd left the Gunner, or even when they passed the first of the signs indicating the turn-off for Limm.

'So what do the lights say?' she asked, trying to fill the silence.

Joe exhaled as loudly as a tidal wave. Even though he wasn't smoking, his breath fugged. 'Says The Charnley Kid,' he said, croakily, not taking his eyes off the road. 'Always told me mam I'd have my name up in lights one day...'

They both laughed rather too heartily for rather too long. Then stopped. Kirstie waited for him to expand on the anecdote, but to no avail. 'You from Charnley then?' she said. 'That why I've not seen you on Limm?'

'Aye,' said Joe. 'Work on Limm. Sometimes drink there, but live in Charnley aye.'

'And you know Rich though?'

'Aye.'

'And...' She couldn't think of anything else to ask him. Couldn't think of a question which would elicit a response bulkier than a simple 'aye'. It seemed he wasn't used to actual human company up in his cab. But every thirty seconds or so, he'd reach out to his bastard cockpit of a dashboard and he'd *adjust* something. He'd flim-flam with the CB-radio tuning or he'd dog-leg with the sat nav or dilly-dally with the speed-camera monitor or any manner of other gadgetry. The only thing he didn't have to fiddle with was his Bluetooth headset thingy, which remained clamped to him like it was the only thing keeping his brain ticking over.

Even the way he turned the wheel was starting to get her goat. It was as though he'd been a driving instructor in a former life (before he became a mead delivery boy) and now couldn't rid himself of the good habits that everyone else forgot about within a few seconds of being in a vehicle on their own. He threaded the wheel like it was a rope that he was gathering in, using one hand to push and one hand to release.

Why oh why was he plodding along so steadily? Did he want to miss the road after everything that had happened, just because he was a careful driver? Even though he was a Charnley man, surely he knew anything, even a speeding ticket in the post, was better than being caught on the wrong side once the tide dragged in and covered the road. If it did, then they'd have eight hours to wait until the road emerged and Limm became reachable by car again...

But maybe it was her karmic punishment. Maybe it was her cosmic come-back-to-bite-you-on-the-bum for the goose. Even now, even above the clogged whirring of the cab's heaters and Joe's reciprocal spluttery breathing, she could hear the *th-thunk* of the Gunner squashing the Mammy Goose into the A24. She felt like she was starring in her very own Aesop's Fable, *The Local Girl Who Killed the Goose*. She just wanted to get home now. Get home and wipe away the blood, the oil, the memories. They went over a bump in the road – a *pregnant* bump – and she felt like screaming. But that would have made her *The Girl Who Cried Wolf* as well as *The Local Girl Who Killed the Goose* and so she kept schtum. Let karma, cosmic-shit, whatever it was, just get on with it.

19

Finally, they swung off the A24 and slipped onto the tighter B road which led down to the causeway. Kirstie felt her legs pistoning up and down now. She felt a heady mix of desperation, frustration and the need for speed coursing through her veins. Knowledge that she could do nothing to change the course of her fate, that *everything* was in Joe's hands felt, like, vaguely sexual, like submission, like giving in, finally, to Rich's advances had been. She choked for another cigarette but cranked down the window instead.

The road took them down a steady slope to the shore. Sea air salted through the open window and she felt it sandpapering away at her hair. She'd never get it as silky smooth as the adverts, not until she left these shores for good. And yet somehow, the sea air comforted her somewhat. Told her that there were bigger fish to fry, that she was nothing but a tiny crack in the nail-polish of some giant compared to the might of the sea. She stuck her head full out of the window and closed her eyes and let memory guide her along.

As the dip became more pronounced, she opened her eyes and finally picked out the road, the causeway. A slick of lighter grey against the otherwise uniform blackness. She could see the sea starting to spill out onto the road in the middle, and it looked like the beginning of an eclipse. Soon, it would eat up more and more of the tarmac. Soon the puddles and rock pools it left behind with each incoming wave would grow, increase in volume. Spill out. *Drown* their escape route. It was as though Limm Island grew itself a moat when the tide dragged in.

That was all it was, a moat, she told herself. A narrow channel. Limm didn't look *that* far away. Despite the dark, she could pick out the shadowy outline of the decrepit monastery (which to her eyes had always looked like the huge rib-cage of some long-forgotten sea-monster.) She could pick out the lights which were starting to pop on in the town and she could pick out the plume of smoke which came from one of the chimneys of the mead brewery right over to the south of the island. They were so close she could almost read the signposts on the other side – on the safe side – which showed the tide tables. They were so close they were going to make it. But then, every year, at least five sets of bungling idiot tourists felt the same thing. And she'd seen the terrifying pictures of cars having to be air-lifted out of the sea by the coastguard after attempting to navigate the road too close to the point of no return;

the pictures were tacked up on the same notice-boards which hosted the tide-tables.

'Nearly there!' she said, and only after she'd said it did she realise she'd said it out-loud.

Joe shot her a warning, *don't count your chickens, or your geese* look and she saw how pale his face looked. Almost moon-white in the gloom.

Still, they passed the small tourist's car park which was pretty much the last thing *land-side* before the causeway. In summer, this car park was invariably filled with tourists who'd printed off out-of-date tables off the net, who were sitting, steaming up their cars, eating their cheese and pickle sandwiches and drinking tea from flasks as they waited for the sea to do its business and release the road. She'd always been rather amused when she'd seen their faces, pressed up against the windows. That look of surprise which was always there, as though they thought the sea would make allowances for them, seeing as though they'd driven all the way up from Kent, or London or whatever. Now she wondered whether her face looked as theirs did.

They passed the small tourist's car park, which now, in February, only contained one vehicle; a National Trust landie, which didn't appear to contain anyone inside (and even if there was, she doubted the National Trust went in for dogging much, which was the car park's *other,* out of season use). She noted the big, luminous banner which was draped over the entrance/ exit barrier. It was advertising Limm Island's TALENT-STRAVAGANZA!!!!!! as they called it. When they'd announced the thing, Kirstie had been half-thinking about entering. Going along and chancing her arm at singing. But so much had happened to her recently, she'd barely given a thought to the competition for *weeks.* Now, she was surprised to see the talent show was going to be on tomorrow. Outside, in cold, wintery February. It seemed a typically small-minded Limm thing to do. To make it as inaccessible to outsiders, to tourists (and other off-island potential winners) as possible.

They passed the small tourist's car park, passed the signs bearing the tide-tables, passed the sign which bore the kinda 'End is Nigh' style sign which said 'This is the Point of no Return.' And suddenly they were on the causeway. Kirstie could *feel* they were on it because of the difference in the road surface. The sea's wear and tear made the causeway a veritable lunar landscape of bumps and bruises, dips and valleys. And for about the first time since she'd been a little girl, driving with her dad, she actually enjoyed the bone-shaking bouncing up and down, side to side, as they ploughed on through.

And for the about the seventieth time, she allowed herself to think *we're gonna make it,* and for the first time, she allowed herself to believe it. She peeked out of the window and saw the rig's tyres now starting to create the kind of splashes which Rich always liked to create with his Gunner on rainy days when he saw people queuing at bus stops, and yet her faith was not shaken. She saw the white-knuckles with which Joe was gripping the wheel, and yet she refused to stop believing.

She let her head hang out the window, revelling in the moment, not caring if she looked like a dog in doing so. Not caring if her knotty hair got in an even worse tangle. She flicked her head back, to look back at the land-side, back to the tourist car park where they'd most likely have had to spend the night (if they hadn't called one of Crabbie's boat taxis, and she wouldn't have done that, no matter how desperate she was; the boat taxi-men all drank in the Ship, like Rich and like her dad. The boat-taxi men couldn't keep their mouths shut.) She looked at the tourist car park and she saw the National Trust landie growing smaller and smaller and she considered what a wonderful thing perspective was. And as she swung her head back round to look upon her home once again, she thought she saw something. She caught a kind of red flash of something in the far extremity of her eye. She thought she saw something, but whatever it was she'd seen was so far out of left-field it had to have come out of that same part of her brain-eye make-up which formed the point liars often looked to when they were looking for an excuse or an alibi.

She thought she saw eyes. Cat's eyes. Big cat's eyes, reflecting the blood-red rear lights of Joe's truck right back at them like a curse. She thought she saw eyes fixed on them. Eyes which were moving. Bounding up and down.

Chasing eyes.

Immediately, she swung her head back round. Peered into the gloom. Tried to pick out those same piercing red bulbs. At first she didn't think she could see them. At first, she'd almost convinced herself she'd added another Aesop's fable to her rapidly increasing list. At first, she'd been looking in the wrong place. For now she saw the red eyes much closer. Much, much closer. Gaining on Joe's rig as though it was trying desperately to hitch a ride.

22

And now she'd picked it out, her brain wouldn't let her explain it away. Her brain wouldn't allow her to think that this was simply a lost house-cat who'd suddenly happened upon a cheetah-like turn of pace when confronted with the alternative of being drowned like the road. Her brain wouldn't allow her to think that because of that wonderful thing called perspective again. Because although the – what was it, a *thing?* - was close, it wasn't *that* close. For the thing to have been a house-cat, it would have to have been virtually sitting on her lap for it to have been that big. And it wasn't, it was still running behind the lorry, in its slipstream, this huge looming, hulking shape which immediately brought to mind the word *werewolf.*

Except this was no wolf, and it was nothing from a fairy-tale or a horror yarn. It wasn't a, well, what other big animals did they have round here? It wasn't a goddamn cow, wasn't even a bull. But it could well have been bull-sized. Bull-*shit,* it was bigger than a bull, surely. And yet it didn't move with the unwieldy clip-clop of a hooved animal, it moved as though it was fluid. Exactly like a cat. And its eyes were exactly like a cat. The thing was huge, but it was a cat. Distinctly, it was a feline.

And it appeared to be feline fine, keeping up with the – she chanced a glance at Joe's speedo – forty mile an hour pace the rig was setting. The causeway was a twenty zone and yet the rig and this beast from beyond were firing across it, neither showing much sign of slowing. Both now creating waves rather than splashes as they moved. The sea was slotting in fast now, and yet, strangely, she no longer seemed to be worried about it. Oh she would be if they became stranded, of course, but it wasn't necessarily drowning here in the cab which concerned her; it was a wholly different form of death. And that death came in the form of nature's own cosmic karma. It came red in tooth and claw *(and eyes).* And it came for her. For the goose.

She couldn't speak. Could barely move. She trickled an eye over to Joe in the driver seat. He looked right back at her. She tried to make her eyes communicate her fear. But he simply smiled, at last said something more than an 'aye', consoling her with a useless, 'nearly there now, duck.'

Nearly there now goose. Your goose is nearly cooked.

It took every ounce of strength which she still had to wind the window closed. She wound it closed despite the fact her shoulder was now screaming in pain. She wound it closed and immediately it fogged up. Joe smoking again and the heaters on full blast saw to that. Frantically, she wiped a sleeve on the window, desperate to see her hunter. But when she could finally look through the window once more, the beast, her stalker, her hunter, was no longer there.

'Did... did you see that?' she gasped.

And Joe turned to her again, the cigarette clamped in the corner of his mouth as though he was playing at Clint Eastwood. 'I know,' he drawled. 'Close, huh? Sea near ate us up but we made it.'

'Not the sea. Did you see *that thing?*'

Joe gave her a concerned look now, removed the ciggie from his mouth. 'What are you talking about, duck?'

'That... thing... Following us.' She jerked her head round to peer out of the window again. Could see nothing but the familiar now. Could see only Limm Island, just as it had always been. No black panthers. No beasts from beyond. She shook her head. 'But I...'

Joe's hand reached over the gearstick. He touched her shoulder (not the bad one). He started to stroke, to soothe. 'You've had a scare today, duck. Must've done what with my rig barrelling down on you like that. Ending up in a ditch and all. But we're across the road now. You're home. Get yourself some sleep eh? You look... You look a little, um... you know.' He reached up and pulled down the sun-visor to reveal a small mirror on its back side as though that would be a better, more tactful way of making his point. And over and above her shock at the fact they actually had mirrors on the back of visors in trucks (she hardly expecting there to be much demand for checking your lippy whilst up there in the cab) was the shock of seeing her own scared face in the mirror and the harsh truth it told. It summarised the story of her day very accurately, from the black bin bags under her eyes which testified to the sleepless night she'd had the night before, to the mud and oil and grease which she'd evidently shampooed her hair with in the ditch. She looked like a mad girl, one who'd see things, beasts from beyond, chasing them across the causeway.

But she wasn't mad. Only looked it. And she knew in the very core of herself that what she'd seen was real. What she'd seen was visceral revenge made flesh. And it was coming to punish her.

2: Photos of God

Yoghurt Rhodes had been peering vacantly into the muddy water of the stream for over a minute. He was in one of *his stares,* as his mother called them. He knew he was, and yet no matter how hard he tried to force his eyes away from the water, they refused to move. He'd tried to discuss the matter of *his stares* with God on more than a couple of occasions, describing them as *like I've switched myself onto stand-by,* and God had told him, well, not told him, more sent this Ready Brek glow into him which was supposed to convince him that they weren't worth worrying so much about. Still, he didn't like the way they made him feel. As though he wasn't fully in control of his body. And God knew what would happen if he got into one of *his stares* when he was riding his bike. Really, he felt he should inform the relevant authorities about his condition, like you had to if you were epileptic and wanted to drive a car. But the thing was, he was scared they'd stop him from doing the cycling proficiency classes if he did. And running those classes was almost as important to him as photography. And photography was his life, his way of praising God.

It just wasn't fair. It was like The Darkness was playing a cruel trick on him over and again. *Testing him.* Annoying. And the most annoying thing was, once he stopped panicking about being in one of *his stares* in the first place, once he just relaxed into the stare and rode it out, it was easy as pie to snap out of it. Easy as clicking a button on a remote control and hey, ho he was away again acting like normal, everyday people. It was like that now. Soon as he stopped worrying about the amount of time he was spending, eyes burning into the half-blurred, weed-clogged water, he was out. Just as quickly as he'd dipped into the stare, his eyes went back to the way they were supposed to be and he found he could re-focus on the thing which had caught his attention in the first place.

What he'd been looking at wasn't even in the water at all. It was on the bank. In the mud. A footprint. A large one. Belonging to a *massive* animal. He'd propped his bike against the fence and gone down for a proper look, muddying up his Clark's in the process (which his mother wouldn't be very happy about; if he'd been younger, he would have been facing The Shirt when he got home) and he'd been just about to start snapping away at it with the Nikon (getting a photie of the footprint *would* make her happy) when he'd started *his stare*. Now he got back to it with a renewed urgency. He unclipped the lens cap, lifted the camera, allowing it to become his eyes. Focus. Zoom. Click. He got into the zone. He clicked off a few more pictures after adjusting the light filter and then hunched down into what he thought of as his *proper photographer* pose. A kind of 'Z' shape with one knee tucked under his body, the other raised up, supporting his arm which was holding the camera.

Already, he was starting to think of Trevor Knox, the local National Trust man, how amazed he'd be when he saw the images. Trevor was mad about nature. It was why he'd taken the National Trust job in the first place, only he kept getting distracted from all the birds on the wetland around Limm and all the wildlife in the southern woods by the need to be up at the monastery, showing uninterested school-kids around the ruins and the like. Which he hated. When Trevor saw these images, he'd be Glad All Over. He'd be able to get the funding he was after. Funding which would allow him to set up the motion detection cameras and discover exactly what indigenous wildlife there still was along this rather remote stretch of the north eastern coastline. And as Yoghurt's mother always used to say, *never in a month of God-come Sundays* would Trevor Knox have expected the indigenous animal would turn out to be something like this. And sure, Yoghurt had heard from Trevor all about how wallabies had escaped from some circus or wildlife park and run rampant in some areas of the Peak District and even on a tiny remote island in Loch Lomond in Scotland so it might not have been something indigenous at all. But...

But wallabies weren't a patch on this. A wallaby wouldn't have even fitted in the *hail, praise Him* footprint of whatever this thing was. Because this thing was big. And it wasn't like any other footprint Yoghurt had seen on his photography rambles along the north east coast. And, thanks to Trevor, he had at least a basic, rudimentary understanding of how to read nature. This wasn't the print of a hoofed animal, or a shoe-shod animal. It certainly wasn't the print of a fox or a badger, though that was edging closer, in species at least. In fact, what the print reminded Yoghurt of most, though he was rather ashamed to admit it, was the paw-print on the back patio. His mother had gone to the trouble of mixing, then pouring the concrete and had given him the task of watching over it whilst it set, shooing away any of the neighbourhood animals which might have chanced upon it. It was, it proved, a task which was beyond his concentration. He'd been distracted by something, he couldn't remember what now, course he couldn't, but the mark of his sin, of his negligence, remained there to this day. Next door's cat must have snuck through the gap in the fence and was already trying to walk through the lumpen, custardy cement when Yoghurt got his mind back on the job. When he looked back on that incident, he realised he was most likely in one of *his stares,* and hence not distracted (or sinful) at all, but at the time, being six years old, he'd been frantic. Dragging the ginger Tom, Tiddles he was called, out of the cement by the nape of his neck was the least of his worries; trying to smooth over the paw-prints was more than a match for him. And when his mother returned and saw the mess he'd made, as well as the one remaining print, she'd given him The Shirt for a week. To date, it was the longest he'd had to wear it. But worse than that was having to look upon that cat's print every day for the next fifteen years as he ate his breakfast.

Foolish as it may have seemed, he realised he'd already decided the print looked very much like that paw-print. Same palm-type splodge in the middle. Same four extended, smaller spots haloed over the top, extending out from it. The claws.

Another thought struck him: if that was how *he* saw the print, then that was likely how Trevor Knox would see it. And Trevor didn't have the benefit of being here; couldn't appreciate the sheer scale of it. No, if he showed a photo of this to Trevor, Trevor would think he was having him on. He'd think he was messing about, even though it was a wholly *un*-Yoghurt thing to do. What was needed was perspective. Some other object, sitting right next to the print, just to show it wasn't trick photography.

Yoghurt tried out a few pictures with his leg extended so his Clark's trainer was right there in the mud alongside the print. But for some reason, the whole context didn't seem right. Yoghurt knew he had whopper feet – *clown's feet for clown's shoes,* they used to say at school – but Trevor didn't have size thirteens like him. So that wasn't the right kind of perspective either. He toyed with the idea of

27

getting a bit more of himself into the shot. Fiving a hand alongside the print or even laying out his luminous cycling proficiency vest next to it. But it still wasn't *just so*. And photography had to be *just so*. That was the only way it was allowed. His mother said that in order to make a good photo, the photographer must first acknowledge that each stolen image was like taking a brass-rubbing of the face of God. Therefore you had to be loyal to the sanctity of the image. It wasn't about getting God's face in the right light or anything like that, it was about capturing the truth of what was right there, staring you in the face. Putting himself in the frame along with the paw-print was definitely not truth.

Yoghurt was under no illusions about how he looked and hence certainly not conventionally arrogant. Despite the fact there were exactly no photographs of him in the house, he knew that when the camera caught him, he didn't come across well. The primary school class photograph bore testimony to that; his mother had written him a note to excuse him from the picture, but the teacher had simply told him 'a class photo isn't a PE lesson. You can't write a note for this.' And Yoghurt had been there, the truth blazing out of him, standing at the end of the back row, towering above the rest of the kids of his age, *sore-thumbing* out; an outlandish scarecrow amongst all the other cute little faces. He was tall and gawky. Too pale and too weird-looking. His hair was too wiry-springy. And so Yoghurt definitely didn't want to be the scale by which the print was measured. He would distract the eye of the beholder, simply by dint of his circus-freak appearance. No, he needed something else. Something of a uniform size. Something...

His eyes had wandered back to his bike which was leaning against the farmer's fence. Already he was considering using the handlebars... But no, that wasn't quite right. If he used the handlebars, it might look too much like he was trying to be deliberately *arty* with the shot. Like he was saying, *here is the print of nature and here is the print of man, but look, don't the handlebars look like antlers?* And the wheels weren't right either. Too much open space between the spokes. Too much room for interpretation.

Which left the water bottle which was affixed to the lower axle. A bottle which, even though his mother had scrubbed off the L'O label, was still definitively a L'O bottle. Still bore that distinctive, trademarked shape. *Everyone* knew the dimensions of a L'O water bottle, even those who didn't drink water (plenty of those sinners on Limm). Everyone would be able to look at a picture of a

L'O water bottle lying next to a paw-print and even if they were *an unfortunate* when it came to mathematics, would be able to judge just how big that print was.

Yoghurt chanced a smile. All in all, in spite of *his stares,* it was starting to shape up to be a lucky day for him. He fair trotted back to his bike, with not so much a spring in his step as a whole summer. Even the speedometer, flashing red, telling him *get back to cycling now, lazy boy, you've not covered your full twenty miles yet,* couldn't distract him. He unclipped the L'O bottle. For some reason decided that it would be better if it was an *empty* bottle. Poured its contents over the other side of the hedge. Was about to saunter on over back to the paw-print when he caught a whiff of something. More than a whiff, a full-on *body-blow* of something. Some horrible stink which had to be coming from something which was about as far away from good luck as it was possible to be.

He gagged, tried to cover his nose. Tried not to let The Unholiness enter his nostrils. But already it was as though the acrid, burny smell had somehow seared itself into the lining of his nostrils. Had insinuated itself onto those tiny – and sometimes not so tiny – hairs which were inside him. Immediately he wished he'd not poured the water away. Water washed away all kinds of sin.

But where was this sin coming from? Smelled as though it was bubbling up from the very bowels of the earth. Smelled as though it wasn't so much drifting on the cold breeze as cloying on it. Rotting on it. Yoghurt let his Nikon drop; let it hang by its cord around his neck. He peered back over the hedge. And at first he saw nothing. Just more mud. Just more trampled grass. Just more countryside. But the smell got decidedly worse. It increased in volume, got whacked on to full-blast, started to fill his brain. Confused him. Sponged out all of his normal, careful-does-it thoughts and left... And left just curiosity. Pure, simple curiosity.

Before he could stop himself, Yoghurt was pushing his way through the raggedy hedge, elbowing little tendril branches out of his way, kicking through the hedge's thickness. And then, just as he was starting to think he'd got himself trapped inside the hedge, he plunged out, onto the grass, hearing a slight rip from his fleece as he did so. And such was the force with which he had been forcing himself against the hedge, Yoghurt didn't stop there. Now there was nothing pressing back against him, he was free to totter forward on scarecrow legs and clown's feet. Free to stagger forward directly into The Unholiness which he could now see was the cause of the

29

stink. Free, and unable to stop himself from stepping right in it. Free, and unable to stop The Unholiness from soaking up and over his Clark's. Free, and unable to stop The Unholiness from creeping up the bell-bottoms of his flare-style jeans. Feeling its cold, blubbery wetness against his unguarded skin.

When he finally brought himself to a halt, Yoghurt felt a torrent of emotions coursing through him. First there was a wave of goose-pimply sickness; now he'd trodden in The Unholiness, it seemed to have increased its malodourous volume to almost impossible levels. He'd stirred it up. Then there was disgust; he could feel The Unholiness creeping up his leg. He'd forgotten to put on his cycling clips and now, just as his mother had told him, it would be the death of him, only he wasn't sure that it was this particular kind of death she'd envisioned for him. (But then, there was no telling *what* his mother could envision.) He also felt rage, impotence, and regret too. Felt it like he felt The Shirt. He could feel it prickling all around him, coating him with static electric charge. And as he felt all of these things, he also felt something else. He felt, he *knew*, he'd been wrong earlier. He knew he'd been tricked by The Darkness when he'd managed to be convinced that today was to be a lucky day. Because treading, running headlong, *dancing* in a pile of vomit as big as he had could never be described as lucky.

It looked like how his mother had described the gentlemens' toilets in The Ship. As though some ten, fifteen men had ploughed glass after glass of The Darkness's juice into their bellies over the course of an evening, and then all gone off to exorcise their demons all at the same time all in the same spot. There was so much vomit there it looked as though someone – something - had been turned completely inside out. The vomit was mostly sludgy-grey, but there were streaks of red in there too. And there were half-eaten remains of body parts in there too; a jelly-like mess which looked vaguely like a brain, a rubbery, purple thing which could have been a heart.

Yoghurt choked for breath, his lungs screaming for clean air. He knew he had to get away from The Unholiness. Knew he had to stop it infecting him. This time, instead of pushing through the hedge, he scrambled, scurried, *swam* over it, such was his desperation to be away. And once he was over the other side, he had no thoughts for capturing that final to-scale image of the paw-print in the mud by the stream. He bore it no mind. Instead, he frantically jumped aboard his racer, pedalled like fury, and only stopped once the speedometer showed him he'd put a good two miles between him and The Unholiness. Then he called Trevor Knox, his fingers trembling as he tapped in the familiar numbers.

As soon as he heard Trevor's voice, he spoke, for the first time in his life interrupting an adult. A breathless: 'Trev... I saw a footprint... big pile of vomit... There's something... evil...'

He took a rasping breath. Heard Trevor's dull voice bumbling onwards as though he'd not heard Yoghurt's sheer panic. 'And if your call is urgent, then please leave a message after the tone and I'll get back to you as soon as humanly possible...'

Only when the phone bleeped did Yoghurt get it through his ThickSkull that he'd actually been talking to an answerphone message. It took him some time to compose himself before he left his message, in the end settling on: 'Trev, it's me, you have to call me, there's something very bad in the fields off the 24, something evil and... well, please call me... Oh, it's Ely Rhodes... Yoghurt.' And although Trevor's answering service gave him the option of re-recording his message, he knew he'd already said what needed to be said. What he felt in his bones.

Desperately, he stared at his phone. Willed it to light up with Trevor's name and number on the display. But the phone wouldn't respond. In fact, when he now pressed a couple of buttons and the screen lit up, he saw that the reception bar was hovering between a half bar and no bars. He shivered, and it wasn't only the cold. Trevor might have been trying to get back to him right now, but the coverage was so bad along this stretch of the coastline that Yoghurt would probably only know about it tomorrow, when a lagging text message would sneak through, informing him that he had 3 missed calls. It had happened before. That he'd even managed to get connected in the first place was, he understood now, some sort of miracle. One last piece of luck on a decidedly back-luck day.

And that luck was about to get worse. As Yoghurt pocketed the phone and prepared to start pedalling for higher ground, he heard a terrible noise. He didn't just think he heard a terrible noise, he heard it, clear as day. And he heard it close. From the bushes not ten feet away. Rasping breathing. Raggedy, *evil* breathing. It sounded like a blocked vacuum cleaner only far, far worse. It was a clunky, bestial sound which could only have come from The Darkness himself. Him or that big evil creature that'd made the print and the vomit. Or else they amounted to the same thing. And now Yoghurt was fully attuned to the sound, he decided it sounded nothing like a vacuum cleaner. Because vacuum cleaners didn't sound as though

31

they were salivating. Vacuum cleaners didn't sound as though they were hungry. Vacuum cleaners didn't sound as though they were getting ready to pounce.

He rammed his feet down onto the pedals, churned for an awful, heart-lurching moment between gears as he tried to attain a high gear too soon, but then he was away. Racing downhill instead of uphill, racing away from higher ground, racing away from the hoped-for phone reception. But not caring. Just cycling. Cycling fast despite the uneven ground and the mud. Believing, more than he'd believed in anything in his life, that something huge was on his tail. Was leaping, bounding, swallowing up the earth after him, just as it would swallow him up soon. And yet again, he felt that crackly feeling in the air around him, as though he was already wearing mother's Shirt. As though its hairy roughness was already rubbing him up the wrong way, making it impossible to sit, think, or breathe still. Making it impossible to do anything other than pray. Certainly making it impossible for him to remember everything he'd learned, and now passed on to others, and especially to his star-pupil, Lewis Dowsing, in cycling proficiency.

The path downhill had probably been created by cattle, moving between pastures and their cowshed, somewhere too far away to contemplate now. It was badly rutted, too zig-zaggy to be taken at such a speed, even on a mountain bike, and Yoghurt wasn't on a mountain bike. Even the speedometer started to have what his mother would call a *screaming hissy fit*, flicking between distances and mileages like a fruit machine, flashing red. Its panic starting to match Yoghurt's, beat for beat, skid for skid. He came into yet another 'S' shaped bend at something approaching his all-time record speed, and he didn't even have the time to scream before the front wheel stuck in the mud and he was thrown over the handlebars.

And then it felt as though he was flying. Or falling. He screwed up his eyes, imagining the pain he'd encounter when he hit the ground. Anticipating how his head would crack like an egg. Like he was Jack, in that nursery rhyme, he was going to break his crown. And that wasn't even the worst of it. Breaking his crown would be *hail, praise Him* fine, if it didn't have to mean that it left him lying there, broken, unable to protect himself from what was chasing him.

He landed, finally, and began to roll. How far, he had no way of knowing because he still had his eyes screwed resolutely closed. He hadn't broken his crown after all, but his knees, elbows, ribcage jarred against the ground. The Nikon thudded up and down into his chest, ripping the remaining air out of his lungs. Even when he finally rolled to a halt, he didn't dare open his eyes. He coughed, once, twice, and winced at the sharp pain which was coming from his side. Tried to listen for that same raggedy, hungry breathing from before he'd started his descent.

But he couldn't hear anything. Literally he heard nothing. Which was strange. Terrifying in its own way. Because there was always *something* making a noise on the coast, be it the sea-birds squawking as they turned tricks in the sky or the crows as they moaned in the trees, or the faraway lowing of cattle or the distant hum of a tractor. He should have been able to hear the traffic from the A24 from here, or the hiss of the sea.

Unable to resist, Yoghurt creaked open his eyes and was immediately convinced he was in hell. Because if looking upon a paw-print of some huge dangerous animal was bad, if staring into a pile of vomit containing brains, guts, blood and all kinds of other unholiness rocked his world to the very core, then what he looked on now was impossibly worse. Yoghurt, sheltered as he knew he'd been most of his life, reckoned that even the hardiest of Limm sailors couldn't have looked upon the dead, mutilated cow and managed to keep a leash on their terror. Because the cow wasn't just mutilated, wasn't just butchered, wasn't just mauled. It was smashed to pieces. Had been pulled limb from limb, bone from flesh, sinew from sinew. He was lying face to face with one of the cow's eyeballs, but the socket it had been torn from was lying a good three feet away. And yet the connecting cord was still there, stretched horribly. Its neck had exploded. Half of its back leg yawned open to the elements. The other leg had been ripped away and was nowhere to be seen.

Blood was everywhere. It soaked into the green grass, turned the whole scene into the rough approximation of a child's drawing, a child who wasn't too picky what colour crayon they used. Had plumped for red, red everywhere because red would do. Only, no child Yoghurt had ever met could ever have created a scene as dripping with death as he looked upon now.

And yet, something within Yoghurt wanted to keep on looking. It wanted to continue to lie there on the battlefield earth and give in. It wanted to say, *here I am. Come get me. Get this over with...* He tried to give voice to these rogue thoughts, cracking open his suddenly parched lips, ready to offer up the invitation to The Unholiness, but instead of words, all that came out was a scream.

33

And the scream seemed to energise him. Reminded him that he still existed. He scrabbled to his feet, feeling the pain in his side and in his knees and ribcage but *using* them now. In a lurching half-run, he started to climb back up the slope to his bike, which he could now see was bent at a dog-leg angle, wedged into the mud. At any minute he expected to see that dark shadow, The Unholiness, melting into the corner of his eyes. Becoming flesh. Leaping for him. But it never came. He reached the bike, picked it out of the mud and set it back onto the path. Tried to ride away. But the back wheel was warped, didn't run true. Kept trying to take him back off the path. And when he tried to keep the thing steady, the handlebars screeched in complaint, loosened, and then lost all control.

He threw the bike down to the ground. Stared at it in mild incomprehension. Never in all the time he'd had it had it played up so badly. Never had it been so Shirty with him, in both senses of the word. He could feel panic starting to edge around him again. Circling him. And he could feel that, this time, if he lost it, he might not be able to get it back again. He pulled his phone from the pocket of his fleece again, knowing he had to do something. Anything. Seeing the reception hovering between half and no bars almost made him give up. But something half-remembered came to him. He'd done some research into mobile phones before he'd finally bought one (despite his mother's express wishes for him not to; well, he *was* twenty-one now). In his reading, he'd found out some pretty interesting stuff. Like, for instance, the fact that even if your phone was completely out of juice, it was still programmed to work if you tapped in the 999 emergency number. He wondered whether that would work if the phone was out of reception too. Wondered whether it would work even if he called the local police number.

Nothing for it but to try. He scrolled through his rather meagre phone book until he found the number for the station in Charnley. Hesitated a moment, his thumb hovering over the call button. Mouthed a rapid prayer. And then he called. Diddly-squat. The phone didn't even look as though it wanted to *try* and work. It simply returned him to the phone book screen.

But then another thought struck him. If his own phone didn't work, at least he could try for another. They had emergency phones scattered up and down the A24 for emergencies. If he could only reach the road, at least he could try to call for help. And now his brain was at least a little calmer than before, now he wasn't lying at

34

the bottom of the hill (in hell) he thought he could pick out the sound of traffic. And wondrously, it sounded much closer than he'd hoped.

Picking up the bike, Yoghurt started to run. The Nikon (which looked remarkably unscathed) bouncing against his solar plexus. His thighs burning. The bike making a worrying juddering sound. Yet he ran and did not give in running. He ran over fences, through hedges, around large, metal basin feeding troughs. Across rutted and muddy ground. Until finally the exhaust fumes from the road tickled his throat. Until he could hear the unmistakeable sounds of real people in real cars, going about their day. Until, at last, he actually saw the A24. He dropped the bike and rushed to it.

There wasn't an orange emergency phone box in sight. On either side of the road. Still panting, he weighed up his options. It would be dark soon and he wanted to be as far away from this place as possible once everything became shrouded with the north east coast's customary air-raid blanket thick blackness. Because he thought that if he heard that raggedy breathing again and it was dark, he'd probably slump down into one of the ditches which flanked the road and never come back out again. Besides, the causeway would be impassible soon...

He set off walking alongside the A24. And almost as soon as he did so, he heard the steady chugging of an approaching car. And to Yoghurt, it felt like a just reward for deciding to be brave. He stuck out an arm, thinking to flag it down. Thinking if anyone saw him, bedraggled as he was, by the side of the road, they'd definitely stop. Thinking whoever stopped was *bound* to have a mobile phone.

Gradually, he picked out a small shape on the horizon. A dot of green against the emerging grey-blackness becoming a splash, becoming a car, definitely a car. Muted headlights told him that. The shade of green told him that; it was British Racing green. His favourite colour. Felt like fate. The car edged closer and closer, keeping to its unhurried pace. Yoghurt started to wave his arms in the air, as though he was bringing a plane into land. The car dripped closer, and he started to worry that maybe the driver hadn't seen him. That maybe he hadn't picked him out in the gloaming light. Certainly the car wasn't slowing at all. Not speeding up either, just cruising at that same unhurried pace. He waved harder. The car was getting so close he could almost read the number plate now, and yet the driver was still not braking.

Yoghurt's heart dropped like a stone. Suddenly he knew the car wasn't going to stop. Time seemed to stretch out as the car passed; Yoghurt able to pick out detail even the Nikon probably couldn't as it did so. First he saw the make and model of the car, and he was able to process a full thought - *that's an old model Rover, just like Solomon used to have* – before he moved on to the next detail. The front grille, bumper and number plate. All slicked with blood and speckly brown feathers. Yes, he could even pick out the fact that the feathers were speckled, like eggshells. Then, the windscreen. The old man inside. A desperate look in his eyes. A *gotta get home, now,* look. An *I've heard too many horror stories about stopping for hitch-hikers at the side of the road* look.

And then the Rover was past him. Blood-red rear lights flooded the road, then stained it, then became two red eyes, then dots, and then, it was over a pregnant bump in the road and gone. Yoghurt gave a choked cry and then it was silent. As the grave. So silent that he almost jumped out of his lumpy-porridge skin when a new sound trilled into the dusky air.

His mobile. A text message. Reception. He reached for the phone again, discovered the text message from Aircom Mobile informing him that he had 4 missed calls from Trevor Knox's number. And instead of immediately calling Trev back, he scrolled through the phone book and discovered the number for the local police in Charnley once again. And this time when he pressed call, it connected. Yoghurt felt an overwhelming sense of relief as he heard the familiar *brurp-brurp.* Felt something approaching joy when someone picked up the phone and then that same someone started to speak in a thick north east accent, kindly informing him that he had dialled the right number. Immediately, he launched into the story of what had happened that afternoon.

'Are you playing silly beggars with us?' said the man, once Yoghurt had finished his garbled tale.

'No. It's serious. There's a… a wild animal,' he gasped, even now finding himself jerking his head, looking over his shoulder, expecting to see a big shadow creeping over the fence or up through the ditch.

'I'll send a car down for a recce. Can you wait there sir? We'll need a statement from you…'

Suddenly the cold reality of the situation seeped in through the fabric of his cycling proficiency vest, through his fleece and through his jumper. Suddenly he realised how stupid it all sounded. Suddenly he realised his mother might find out about this. Words like statement, sir, and recce; they spoke of worlds in which a great hulking, raggedy-breathing shadow could not exist. They spoke of him not being believed.

'Sir?'

'I'm still here... Uh, a statement, you say?'

'Well, yes. We have to take reports like this very seriously. What with all the farms and that...'

'I can... How long's it going to be? You see I have to catch the road before the tide comes in and...'

'You're from Limm Island are you? That explains a few things.'

'Yes, I'm from Limm and... and I'm supposed to be back home tonight and... The road!'

'Okay, okay, stop panicking. We'll get someone out to you right away. Check out this wild animal of yours.'

The man at the other end of the line replaced the receiver, but obviously not fully. He didn't end the call. Yoghurt heard him give this long, exaggerated sigh. And then, faintly, Yoghurt heard him speaking to someone else, using an even stronger north east accent, if that were possible.

'Another fucking loonie from Limm,' he said. 'Fucking wild animals this time. Honestly...'

There was a mutter of response Yoghurt couldn't understand (although he could understand the laughter) and then: 'Why'm I sending the car out? Because sometimes you can only cry wolf so many times. We've had loads of calls from people on Limm, usually it's because they've missed that road of theirs. It's time we started making an example of these chancers... Yeah, I know. In-bred bastards.'

Yoghurt pressed the red off button on his phone, calmly replaced it in the pocket of his fleece, and then started walking. Already, he'd come to the conclusion that on no account would he ever tell anyone what he'd seen, and heard, and smelled in the fields off the A24 that afternoon. Telling anyone, he decided, would be worth a month in The Shirt.

3: The Grape and the Grain

T he 'shoes off at the door' rule was already becoming a cause for concern for Adrian Devonish. Despite the rich home-cooking smells from the kitchen, the stink of his feet was a distinct note, obvious like a soprano in a choir. Brenda hadn't mentioned it yet, nor would she, but on her last orbit through to the front room bearing nibbles, there'd been a definite wrinkling of her nose, a deliberate arching-away of her head as she leaned down to deposit a bowl of cracking nuts on the coffee table. He wanted to be relaxed enough in her company that he could tell her 'smelly feet is a real Devonish man trait, I'm afraid,' demonstrating his point by wiggling his toes in those incredibly thick, incredibly scratchy woollen socks; socks whose click-clack knit creation was a real Devonish woman trait. But it was too early for such a level of understanding to be reached and so they engaged in a different game, both pretending the smell wasn't really there at all. To that effect, when she'd disappeared back into the kitchen, he tried burying his feet deep in a shag-pile rug so heavy it could have still been alive and grazing atop the rain-drenched hills of the north east coast, hoping the rug would camouflage the smell. Hoping that *wet sheep* was an aroma her fat nose had grown accustomed to.

Even though Adrian had grown accustomed to whiling away the hours in rooms which could best be described as dull, Brenda Boyle's front room seemed impersonal to the point of insanity. The rug was about the only thing with any character, everything else could have been picked out of the latest bargains section of the Ikea catalogue. Billy (the uncluttered bookshelf containing such epic tomes as the Norsea and District Yellow Pages and the rent book), Anders (or whatever they called the wholly undramatic centrepiece coffee table of light wood), and Freddie, (the function over form chest of drawers which evidently contained the good crockery) were *ever so 'umble* Swedish accountants at a mid-afternoon tea party.

38

They were on speaking terms, but only about crap like work. None of them dared say anything out of the ordinary. All probably raged inside against the injustice of a world so devoid of life. They could have been rocking-horses or hockey sticks, chess Kings, but instead they were the no-mark pawns of the furniture world.

Perhaps the strangest aspect of Brenda's front room however, was the fact there was not a single picture of family on the walls or on the poor mantlepiece (Sven?). Adrian didn't like to boast, but he'd been in a lot of women's houses over the years, and the one common denominator of your Susan's who lived in city centre flats in Newcastle, or your Tina's who stayed in a ramshackle end terrace in Charnley, was their desire to graffiti their homes with *proof* that they had friends. Brenda, it seemed, had no friends, or else, wasn't that bothered about showing them off. Or perhaps Brenda simply liked the temporary, as Adrian did. Living in a hotel for the best part of twenty years had made him extremely cute when it came to other people's houses and what they put in them. If he ever quit the hospitality game and bought his own place, part of him reckoned it would probably look a lot like this. Only with furniture bought from somewhere a bit more upmarket than Ikea.

Brenda trundled back into the front room. Her wide face was flushed, perhaps from the heat of the kitchen, or more likely from the promise of *dessert*. She looked as though she'd not had much dessert for a long time. Nobody who was accustomed to regular sex would have made the elementary error of wearing an apron like that; a plastic monstrosity which featured a perfect-woman's bikini-clad body, a body which clearly wasn't remotely like hers. Hers was a lumpen, functional body, like furniture. Like a sofa. The apron accentuated every bulge; fat was crawling out and over the top of the tied string like a soldier out of the trenches. And the time for Adrian to make some joke about the 'comedy' apron, or at least some gentlemanly remark about it, had long passed. Instead, the apron, like his feet, had passed into the catalogue of silences between them.

'Like another drink, Ade?' she asked, wiggling a can of Fairhurst's Light at him as though it were a prize in a game show.

Ade again. What was it with these people? He bit back his ire. 'So, when we gonna see this wonderful culinary creation of yours?' he said instead.

Brenda flashed him a bashful smile. It came out a little too sheepish for Adrian's tastes. This woman wasn't innocent, she was hard, no matter how much she tried to hide it. He could see it in her sea-grey eyes. 'Sorry it's taking so long. I should have tried something a bit simpler. But I wanted to impress you... I mean, your ad made sure to mention you liked good home-cooking...'

Ah that ad. That ad had been a major miscalculation. Due to unforseen circumstances, Adrian had stopped hitting the north east coast club circuit (such as it was) with the same energy as he'd formerly displayed. It wasn't so much that he was getting older, but rather, the girls were getting younger. On his last three visits, he'd had to spend at least half an hour's good chatting-up time on the forlorn search for a girl who *wasn't* the daughter of someone he knew, or wasn't so obviously jail-bait. Sex-hungry and mind-numbed by drink one night, he'd penned the fateful ad for *The Tide Piper's* Two Hearts column. Being drunk had enabled him to overcome the objections put forward by his own mind, but it had also played havoc with the text he'd eventually had to phone in because he couldn't even read his own writing. For some reason, perhaps because he was in need of a kebab, or *anything* in fact to soak up the alcohol, he'd opened his ad with the phrase, 'North east captain of industry WLTM a good home-cooker who can rustle up a decent DESSERT.' He'd followed this up with the ill-advised, 'GSOH desired, but GOOD BODY a pre-requisite,' something which the organisers of the Two Hearts column had blamed for his lack of responses after a month. Brenda was his second response (the first hadn't shown up), by which time, Adrian had decided 'GOOD BODY' wasn't as important as pulse, and thus here he was.

'Smells like pie,' said Adrian, picking up the nutcracker and a walnut and then putting them back in the bowl. He didn't want to risk not being able to crack the nut in front of this woman. Not when she looked as though she could headbutt the things into submission and then feed them to him from the mezzanine level of her breasts.

'It's a surprise!' she squealed in mock-annoyance. 'Naughty Ade; don't go guessing before it's served up!'

Adrian half-hoped she'd continue in this vein; perhaps promising him a 'smacked bottie', making it impossible for him to do anything else but run for his life before he gave in and put the woman out of her misery by shagging her, doubtless on the fuggin shag-pile. That's what it would be when it came down to it; a *shag-pile*. A mass of writhing stomachs and gelatinous thighs. A bonfire of pie-belches and chip-farts. Nothing like the early '80's porn collection he owned, in which the sex act always took place in some log cabin, in front of a fire, on an altogether more tasteful rug. He took a long gulp from his can of Fairhurst's Light, wishing she'd plumped for the stronger version, the 9% tramp-juice which rendered the drinker unconscious after three cans.

'Go on then,' he said, shaking his now seven-eighths empty can at her. 'I'll have that other can please *Brend.*'

'Brend-a,' she said. She flapped across the bare wood floor in her ridiculous pink rabbit slippers (the type you have to describe in a child's voice; *fwuffy bunny wabbit*) and handed him the can. As she did so, she let her hand linger against his a little longer than was comfortable. Part of him feared she'd stroke his pinkie with her huge rolling-pin of a digit. Part of him feared he'd like it.

'Don't snatch!' she said, through a gibbering shipwreck of a smile. And suddenly Adrian realised the woman was drunker than he was. Clearly she wasn't cuckoo-clocking in and out of the kitchen to 'check on the veg' or to 'finger the pie', as she kept claiming, but rather, to partake in seaman's gulps from a bottle of voddy or fizzy wine, or whatever it was she had in there amongst the broiling broths and simpering stews. Now she was standing in front of him, blocking his view of the telly, he could see she was swaying like an oak in a hurricane.

'Why don't I put some music on?' she said, noticing his neck was bent so he could look round her at the telly which was on silent, but still a better option than looking at her. It clearly wasn't a question which required an answer, for before he could decide whether music would be the worst idea in the world (what if she was so drunk she wanted to *dance,* and hence dinner would be spoiled? At the very least, he wanted a proper dinner out of this disaster, and Brenda, at the very least looked as though she looked as though she could cook a good dinner) or whether it would be something to cover the awkward silences. She fiddled with the buttons on her relic of a hi-fi for far too long, staring at them through one eye as though that was the only way she could properly focus. Adrian knew he should have offered to help, but also knew that being in such close proximity to her was dangerous now.

Finally, she managed the feat of switching the radio on. She had it tuned to a local radio station, Radio Coast. Adrian knew it because they always had it on in the kitchens at the hotel. It played dance music of the kind which was always tinkling tinnily out of the mobile phone speakers of the local teenagers. All speeded-up vocals and bloops and whines which sounded like a rudimentary sonar system on a fishing boat, set against a deep thudding bass. It was the

41

type of music which was starting to take over the north east club circuit; dance music which was impossible to dance to.

'I love this song,' said Brenda, staring at him with wounded-buffalo eyes. 'It's Cheesemonster. You know he's from Charnley?'

'I didn't know that,' said Adrian, staring at the dancing bear on the front of the Fairhurst's can. *Cheesemonster.* What a name! Still, it was a fitting name at least, because his tune appeared to be made from pure Stilton. It had none of the class of the late '90's dance Adrian preferred; didn't boast the addictive sax of a Guru Josh or the rhythmic intensity of a Black Box.

Brenda started moving to the music. She started slow; head-down, indie-style foot-shuffling. Then she began hefting her shoulders up and down like she was engaging in a rigorous bout of shrugging. And then her arms started to move, much like chicken wings. Finally, she attempted an out-of-context spin which almost sent her spiralling out of all control.

'I think I'd better sit down for a minute,' she said, holding on to Sven for dear life. Sven appeared to be resisting though, because her knees buckled, and Adrian feared she'd land right on top of him. Luckily, she managed to transform her slip into a reasonable attempt at an emergency landing as she flopped down onto the couch next to him. Adrian thought, *that's what they call Skyscraper dancing.* Her falling was like Fred Dibnah had set explosives under her. For a moment it looked as though she'd fall every which way but loose, but in the end, no damage done.

'You okay?' he asked, absently scratching at his beard.

Brenda looked as though she was going to throw up at any minute.

'Can you turn the music down?' she whimpered.

Adrian nodded, craned himself out of the couch's grip and then shuffled over to the hi-fi. When he couldn't work out which button to press to stop Cheesemonster's relentless gibbering, he simply kneeled down and removed the plug from the socket. 'That better?' he asked. 'Can I get you a drink of water or something?'

'I'm sorry,' she blubbered. 'Think I had a funny turn, that's all. Very hot in the kitchen... Think it just went to my head.' She was fiddling with the knot at the front of her apron, trying to take it off. Adrian didn't want to see what might be released once the tie was undone and so sloped off into the kitchen to fetch the water.

The kitchen was a typical tight terraced-house affair where all the utilities and equipment were cramped together like the contents of Brenda's bra. The work surfaces were covered with empty tins, used mixing bowls, a butcher's steel and two long rusty knives, discarded recipe books and *two* open bottles of white wine (wine of such a quality its name appeared to be WINE.) There were no wine glasses out, so it appeared that Brenda had either been supping it from the bottle, or else, with a nod to propriety, she'd poured her measures into one of the empty tins of carrots. Because of the mess, it took Adrian some time to find the sink, buried as it was under a pile of newspaper. Part of him was offended when he noticed the top newspaper was open at the Two Hearts column where *three* adverts were circled, and then graded. According to the evidence, Adrian was in fact only Brenda's second choice. But then, he reflected, it really was a terrible advert he'd placed; said hardly anything about his status in the hospitaliy trade on the north east coast, just the simple, misleading comment about him being a 'captain of industry.' Anyone could be a captain of industry. Not many could claim to have basically *invented* hotels on Limm Island.

It took him an age to discover where the glasses were kept. He tried three poky cupboards, containing, variously, a pile of dirty washing, some inexplicable implements which could have been sex toys, and seven or eight loaves of bread. The fourth cupboard contained two plates, one wine glass and a child's plastic beaker which had a *fwuiffy bunny wabbit's* face moulded onto the front. The beaker was now so old and so well-handled the rabbit's face looked like a gargoyle. Adrian decided against using the beaker (in case it dredged up bad memories; children taken away by the social and the like) and instead opted for the wine glass. When he turned on the tap, water only drip-dropped out, so he increased the pressure, and then, in vengeance, it flooded out, filled the glass and then sprayed all over his new shirt. 'Fugg,' he gasped, dropping the glass into the sink, where it smashed into about seven hundred pieces.

Brenda sloped into the kitchen after him, leaning provocatively (drunkenly) against the jamb. The apron was now hanging round her waist like some new-fangled half-skirt. Set against the kitchen's sickly green wallpaper, she looked seasick. 'Oh!' she gasped, about twenty seconds too late to fool anyone she hadn't had her eyes put out by the paint-stripper WINE she'd consumed. 'You've wet yourself...'

'Your bloody tap just erupted on me,' snarled Adrian.

'I should have told you about the tap,' muttered Brenda.

'Bleeding right you should have,' said Adrian, about to launch into an invective about how he wasn't just some common or garden *second choice* desperado, but a true Man in Full. But Brenda stuck out her bottom lip and cut him off at the pass.

'Don't be nasty-wasty, Ade,' she said. 'Look, I have some old shirts upstairs – my ex-husband's, hardly ever worn. You can get changed into one of them if you like...' She must have seen the naked fear in his eyes, but misread it, and added, sulkily: 'Don't worry, they're clean.'

Adrian looked doubtful. By way of an answer, she rammed her man's fist against her blubbery hips, shook her head and then lumbered round back into the front room with all the grace of a jack-knifed truck. He had no choice but to follow her up the narrow staircase to the top floor, the *bedroom* floor, trying not to listen to her raggedy breath as she struggled, trying not to look at her wobbling arse eclipsing the light thrown out by the naked bulb at the top of the stairs. She indicated the bathroom with a flustered wave, apparently unable to speak such were her exertions.

'The shirt?' he asked.

'I'll leave a couple outside the door. I'd better go down and check on the pie.'

'So we *are* having pie?' Adrian winked. But the time for jokes had well and truly passed now, and Brenda simply shrugged and pushed through another door. As she did so, the unmistakable smell of sex emerged. That room stunk like the jetty on Limm Island. Adrian slipped into the bathroom and closed the door behind him. He checked frantically for a lock but found none. Had to make do by pushing another small Freddie drawer-set against the door. After his discoveries in the kitchen, he didn't want to look what was inside these poor drawers, but at least they'd offer some protection.

The bathroom was as small as the kitchen below, and was also papered with that same sickly green wallpaper. There was a three-quarter size bath (*surely* Brenda couldn't have fitted in there) which contained one of those impossibly complicated shower-tubes which are fitted over the bath taps. On the edge of the bath was a single, decrepit rubber duck; the only nod to individuality in the whole room. Adrian picked up the duck and took a seat on the toilet while he waited for Brenda to go back downstairs. No way was he letting her in here while he had his shirt off. No way was he letting her have a sneak-look before he even knew whether he'd be awarding her the main prize (likely he wouldn't.)

44

There was a light tapping at the door. 'Ade?' Something in her voice suggested she feared he'd climbed out of the bathroom window and escaped. 'Ade?' she said, louder.

'Here,' he sighed, wishing he'd brought the Fairhurst's up with him. 'Leave the shirts outside. Be down in a minute.'

'Okay love,' she replied, the confidence edging back into her voice. Now she knew he hadn't gone walkabout, there was still a chance for her. 'Hurry down though; dinner'll be nearly ready.'

Adrian couldn't respond. He was too busy staring at the mass of dark hair clogging up the sink. It was as though a mountain gorilla had had his pre-dinner shave in there. If that was an indication of how hairy she was going to be, then there was no way he was going there...

Nevertheless, when he heard her creaking down the stairs again, he started to feel better. Carefully, he removed the chest of drawers, poked his head around the door, and found the three shirts crumpled on the bare wood floor on the landing. He grabbed them quickly and then darted back inside.

Brenda's divorce had clearly taken place in the early seventies, judging by the shirts her ex hubby had left behind; one of them was a frill-necked number, lizard-brown and scaly to the touch; the second had seemingly been torn off a deck-chair and was bright pink, pockmarked with deep yellow flowers; the third looked the type hired by a Swedish accountant who was trying to show he was 'up for a laugh' at the office party. It was sequinny, sparkly, and wouldn't have looked out of place in the Winter Olympics Ice Skating events. The shirts were all uniquely bad and were all about three sizes too big. It was obvious even without trying them on. But the front of his shirt was soaked, and denim was notoriously slow to dry, and besides, there'd be some mileage in the story when he told his mates down the Ship later that evening, when the worst was over.

He pulled off his shirt and then caught sight of himself in the cloudy mirror. For a moment, he was actually confused who this other person was, standing in the too-small bathroom with him. For the man in the mirror looked older than he ever remembered looking. Worn. His thick black beard, which had once been his pride and joy, now looked scraggly, as though Quentin Blake had drawn a scribble on his chin; he looked like one of *The Twits*. Traditionally, Adrian 'wore' the beard, as though it was the final piece of his hotelier costume. He'd always felt the beard lent him a kind of maverick aspect, and Adrian had always liked mavericks. Go-getters who didn't quite play by the rules (*no, they invented the rules*). But recently, he'd heard the stifled laughter. One particular guest had remarked – within hearing range, the cheeky bastard - that the beard made him look like 'the bearded guy in the 1970's version of the *Good Sex Guide.'* And while he had quite liked the idea of being seen as a – come on, there's no other word for it – soft-porn star, he wasn't so sure about the 1970's reference. Not at all. That was a little too close to some of the recent criticisms about his hotel, and *the management* of the hotel; the ones which were generally populated by words such as 'timewarp' and 'outdated'.

What's more, his body was no longer anything to shout about either. He'd always been chunky, but now he was bordering on fat. He was faced with a constant dilemma whether to pull his jeans up high, over his paunch, or leave them low, which tended to provide him with some overhang. That was the problem with being five foot eight and a half; there just wasn't enough body to properly share the flab out. A night on the tiles meant pounds on in piles. And he knew for a fact some of his mates drank and ate far more than him, and yet never seemed to get that middle-aged spread he had.

He sighed, picked up one of the shirts and tugged it over his head, delighted to find that it swamped him. He regarded himself in the mirror and shot himself a couple winning smiles, to make sure he'd still got it. Then a sneer. Sneering looked especially good with a beard. Even more menacing. What did it matter what he looked like? It was what was inside that counted, and what was inside him was pure masculine drive. Women never failed to spot that in him. They wouldn't simply stop seeing it now he was carrying a bit of extra timber. Form was temporary, class was permanent.

And Adrian had class. He had class enough to carry off a frill-necked shirt without looking the fool. He looked a little like the Benicio Del Toro character in *Fear and Loathing in Las Vegas*, he realised. It was the eyes what did it, your honour; those fiery, determined brown eyes, which actually set off the shirt quite well. The eyes had star-quality. So did the beard. He cursed himself for ever doubting the leonine intensity of his beard. *Fuggin' Brenda. It was her fault he was in such a changeable mood. Her and her leaky tap. Now, like a lion on a blazing day on the African savannah, he'd go back downstairs and show the fat bastard who was boss.*

He pushed the chest of drawers to one side, then stepped out onto the landing. Such was his determination to get downstairs, his woolen-socked foot almost slipped on the stairs, but he managed to stop himself by grabbing the banister. He entered the front room just as Brenda was mid-wrestle with her fold-up table. She appeared to be winning; one leg was bent backwards, another was screeching in agony. He shouldered her out of the way. 'Here, let me,' he said. 'Man's job this one, Brends.'

Erecting the table wasn't as easy as it looked – was about as easy, in fact, as getting an erection after a night on the Fairhurst's Super – but Adrian managed it after a few well-placed kicks and a number of muttered warnings under his breath. Once he'd finally maneouvred it into position, he realised it was leaning hazardously to one side, but he placed the TV remote under one of the legs in order to balance it. Then he sat back down on the couch, took a massive gulp from his can, and surveyed his handiwork. Brenda looked equally pleased, staring at the table as though it were a completed jigsaw puzzle way beyond the comprehension of a simple woman. She sighed happily, pleased to have a man about the house again, and then went back into the kitchen, doubtless ready to celebrate by downing another tin can full of WINE.

All was well at 24 Dewar Street. Adrian allowed himself to sink into the couch; tucked two hands behind his head. This was how weekends in February were supposed to be. The woman in the kitchen preparing lunch; you in the front room with your feet up, ready to gobble it down before getting a gobble for dessert. Perhaps they'd have the footy on later too, and Adrian wondered absently whether Brenda had Sky. He doubted it, but you never knew with desperate women like her. Sometimes they even got ESPN just to make sure whatever bloke they had round didn't scarper to the pub as soon as the sex was over. Would there be sex? Adrian wasn't sure yet. But that was the best position to be in; holding the aces.

From the sounds of it, Brenda was shunning the WINE and even, heaven be praised, starting to serve up. He heard the whoosh of the oven door opening, the clatter of metal baking trays, a few high-pitched curses as she burned her rolling-pin fingers, and then the slam of the fourth cupboard door as she retrieved the two plates. His stomach growled in appreciation. He downed the rest of his can of Fairhurst's and then took his seat at the table. After a few minutes unbearable tension, she finally staggered into the room, buckling under the weight of a huge, Desperate Dan-sized pie. 'Ta-daaah,' she groaned before slamming it down in the middle of the table. The table moaned in complaint.

'Well, Ade,' she said, 'this is goose pie. It's a speciality round our way. I don't know if they have it on Limm Island where you're from, but it used to be real popular round here.'

Adrian couldn't help a flicker of disgust from crossing his chops.

'It's got turkey in it and all,' said Brenda, quickly.

In for a penny in for a pound. 'Want me to just dig in, like?'

'I'll serve you,' she said, hacking into the pie crust with a large metal spoon which was bent in the middle. The crust seemed rock-hard; eventually she had to use the edge of the spoon like a hacksaw to break it. It took her another minute or so to work her way round the edge of the pie before she had enough for a portion. Unfortunately, when she then tried to transfer this portion to Adrian's plate, most of it landed on the plastic table. What did end up on the plate was upside down, with the mass of lumpen gravy swamping the heavy crust. 'I'll have that one,' she said, breezily, starting the whole rigmarole again. Adrian sighed and looked out of the window onto a cobbled street which could have been in any north eastern town in any era. The only car parked up was his own.

Finally they had two platefuls of pie and Brenda sat down opposite him. She made ominous signs as though she was about to start to say grace, but then clapped her hands together and exclaimed: 'What am I like? *Drinks!* What'll you have?'

Ah, that eternal conundrum. Whether to appear somehow refined by drinking wine with dinner or whether to simply stick with what you were good at; drinking beer. Mind you, Adrian had seen the WINE, and as such, it was an easy choice. 'Another beer, if you don't mind,' he said. 'But while we're eating, I'll have it out of a glass.' *All bases covered,* he thought. Until she returned with his half of lager in the blue plastic beaker with the *fwuffy bunny wabbit's* gargoyle face on the front.

They tucked in. The front room was alive with the noise of knives and forks being scraped across plates, of the sawing noise as they tried to cut through the crust, and the slurping of gravy. It was the sound of weekend roasts up and down the country; the sound of contentment. It didn't matter that the carrots were limp and lifeless, and that the chips were burned and that both of them appeared to be leaving every piece of meat which looked as though it had been carved from a goose. It didn't matter that neither of them seemed capable of starting even the most banal of conversations. But once they had finished, silence reigned supreme once again.

'So, you're in the hotel trade?' asked Brenda, nervously.

Adrian cracked a smile, pulled at some stringy meat from between his teeth, and still more from out of his beard, and then sat back. His favourite subject. 'You could say that. You could say I was in the hotel trade like you could say Alan Shearer was in the goal-getting trade. You could say I was in the hotel trade like you could say Jimmy Nail was in the singer-stroke-acting business. You could say I was in the hotel trade like you could say Fairhurst's brewed a good drop. I don't mean to blow my own trumpet, but there's some round our parts that are like, *that Adrian Devonish pretty much invented the hotel trade on Limm Island*. Before me...' He waved his arm in a dismissive gesture, almost knocking over his beaker of beer. 'Before me, there was squat-diddly on the island.'

'Very nice,' said Brenda, mindlessly.

'Heard of the Castle Hotel?'

'Errr... no. Can't say as I have,' she said, staring into her cup of WINE. Where she'd found the cup was anybody's guess. 'That your hotel?'

Adrian nodded sagely. 'That's the one. Of course, I don't own the place. It's owned by the town mayor, Manny Combs; heard of him? No didn't think so. Anyway, what he knows about the hotel trade you could write on the back of a postage stamp and still have room for the full recipe for goose pie. No: I *run* the place for him. I'm the manager. And he's never there, always off doing town and island business, whatever that may be, so I suppose you could say it's my hotel. Certainly it's my head on the chopping block if anything goes wrong.'

'Lovely,' said Brenda.

'Thirty-five rooms, thirteen staff, our own trophy cabinet... Here,' he said, pulling his wallet out of his pocket and opening it up, thrusting it out for her to see the picture of his hotel in order to illustrate his point. The photograph was a recent one; Adrian regularly updated it with the professional shots taken for the tourist brochures each year. It showed the hotel in its best light, on a summer's day when the three-tiered Georgian manor house seemed *less grey* than usual. It was taken from the front of the hotel and took in the blossoming trees which flanked it, whilst also managing to cut out the garish 1960's extension (nicknamed the Arse) out back which contained most of the smaller, more cost-effective rooms, or 'family' rooms as they were termed.

'Very nice,' said Brenda. 'But don't people usually keep pictures of their wives and families in their wallets?' She nodded down at his hand. At the wedding ring which had remained obdurately there, no matter how much he'd buttered his finger up, lathered it in goose-fat, soaped it up with shower gel or sometimes Fairhurst's (known to clear out even the hardiest of blockages). He could have paid to have it cut off, but he was damned if *she* was going to cost him another penny.

'Ex-wife,' he confirmed, coldly.

'You know, there's something I've always wanted to know about living on Limm Island,' said Brenda. 'I always wonder how people get to work. I mean, the causeway's closed for half the day making it completely separate from the real world like it's got some kind of restraining order. So how do folk get to work, like? Say if the tide times change and they can't get over to the real world in time... Are people always getting sacked?'

'It's a problem,' he admitted, thinking *I bet she knows all about restraining orders*. 'But for those so desperate to work off the island, there's always ways and means of getting across should the tide be in. Heard of a thing called a boat?'

'Ah, yes. A boat. So do you own a boat, Ade? 'Magine us two together sailing around the island in the summer. It'd be like being in Greece or something. Me at the front like one of them angels or whatever you call 'em, you being the boat driver. *Bliss.'*

Adrian noted the surreptitious moves her big hand was making across the table. The loose part of her blouse was trailing in spilled gravy now, but she didn't seem to notice, or care. Nervously, he fingered the frilly collar of the lizard brown shirt and wondered whether Brenda was now so drunk she'd slipped into the world of memory and believed him her husband.

'And the recession's not bothering you?' she asked.

Adrian smiled. 'If you've managed your business properly, you can ride out this storm no problem. It's all about preparation; the six P's: *proper preparation prevents piss poor performance.'*

'The six P's,' she repeated, voice trailing off a little.

Adrian nodded, hoping to be quizzed further on one of his favourite subjects; how to run a business properly. It was a subject which would have made a fitting book, or, preferably, a corporate video, starring him in all his glory (minus the frill-neck shirt).

50

'So did you not like your dinner? You've not said nowt about it,' she said, changing the subject, but there was only flirtation in her tone. *In a minute she was going to start talking about dessert.*

'Very good,' he said, carefully. 'A hearty, distinct flavour. Warmed the cockles.'

Brenda must have thought he said 'cock', because a look of pure lust crossed her face, rippled those rouge-tinged cheeks with all their broken vein-endings, and carried on to somewhere else within her body like some terrible, unstoppable electric charge. 'Shall we retire to the couch?' She fluttered her eyelashes like an elephant.

Adrian wasn't sure. But she was up out of her chair and wobbling over to him before he could think of a single relevant objection. She was dragging him up by the arm before he could dive out of the way. When she pushed him down onto the couch, she tipped him a saucy wink and then kicked off her *wabbit* slippers as though indicating the time for childish stuff was over. Now for the X-rated, adult fun.

'You know, I was very surprised you wanted this first date at your house,' said Adrian, playing for time. 'Not that I've ever done anything like this before, but usually, I would have thought the woman would prefer to have the blind date somewhere more... *neutral*. You know? Just in case she didn't like the man or found out he was an axe-murderer or something.'

Brenda stopped struggling with the knot at the front of her apron for a moment and raised an eyebrow. 'You're not an axe-murderer though, are you Ade?' She towered over him. He wasn't sure whether her look was supposed to be threatening or sexy. Certainly she was breathing very loudly through quivering, extended nostrils like a dray horse come to collect the barrels on a hot day.

'It's *Ad-ri-an!*' he snapped. 'Not A-a-a-a-d-e.' His last word transformed into a heady concoction of surprise, desire, and then hatred; of her and of himself. She had reached down roughly manhandled his crotch through his jeans. He felt himself stirring.

'You like that?' she asked, in a new, gruff voice.

Adrian thought, *I like a gruff voice. On a guard dog. Not on a woman who's doing th-i-i-i-ssss.* He couldn't speak though. Not now disgust had become part of the equation; not now his stomach was bubbling dangerously and he had to force his arse-cheeks together to stop himself from farting. Brenda must have taken his discomfort for pleasure, and rather too much pleasure at that. She must have thought he was about to come too soon, for she stopped

51

kneading his crotch (as she'd failed to do properly to the pastry) and moved up to his face. Where she slapped a wet-fish of a kiss. He tasted ripe onions and the tang of WINE on her tongue and wondered whether he could risk asking her to clean her teeth before she attempted something like this kiss again.

'That beard's all tickly,' she said when she came up for air. Then a thought occurred to her: 'Wonder if it'd tickle *down there.*'

Adrian closed his eyes to stop himself from retching. He felt better almost straight away, despite the fact he could hear the liquid in Brenda's belly shifting around as though she were a water butt.

'Ade?'

He opened his eyes. After a good thirty seconds they finally focused. And he saw Brenda standing on the shag-pile rug in front of him like some vision of hell. While he'd had his eyes closed, she'd somehow managed to pull off her tent-jeans revealing her sand-dune coloured, rippling-stretch marked legs. She'd wrestled herself out of her gravy-soaked blouse and even her bra. Her breasts spilled out like kicked-over sandcastles. All that remained between her and total, unbridled nakedness was the apron which was still resolutely tied round her waist like a red flag on a beach confronted with an incoming tidal wave. 'Hello, love,' she said. 'Dessert is served.'

And Adrian grinned. His decision made, he tugged at his belt buckle. After a second's hesitation, Brenda joined in, and between them, they managed to snap it open. She yanked his jeans down and tossed them over the back of the couch and then she carefully laid herself on top of him. He groaned in response to her weight, but when she leaned in to kiss him again, this time there was no hesitation. He reached down, underneath her chassy and felt... and felt... He felt only plastic apron.

'Move the apron to the side,' he gasped.

'I can't,' she groaned.

'Twist the string.'

'I've tried that... no... Don't. It's really digging into me...'

'One minute...'

'Ow! Ade, stop it.'

She lifted herself up off him, accidentally (on purpose probably) kneeing him in the groin. He winced.

'Cut it off. Go to the kitchen and get some scissors.'

Hesitation on her face. Doubt. Then: 'You won't do a runner will you? While I'm gone? I mean, I know I ain't much to look at, but a woman has *needs.* You have needs...'

'I'm going nowhere,' he said.

But then Brenda did something very strange. She walked over to the front door, turned the key in the lock and pocketed the key in her apron. Then she bent down – offering him a completely unrestricted view of her hay-bail arse – and slammed a second lock home. On her knees, she turned and offered him a fluttering smile. He smiled back, confused. And then became even more confused as she picked up his Adidas Originals trainers (by the laces, he noted; so she didn't have to put any of her rolling-pin fingers into the stinky interior of the shoes) and carried them with her into the kitchen.

Adrian lay on the couch in his paisley-print boxer shorts and listened to her fumbling around in the kitchen. His mind felt suddenly foggy and he wondered whether he'd drunk more Fairhurst's than he'd realised, or even whether she'd put something in the food to make him drowsy. He shot upright, shocked he was even considering such a possibility. But what had he said earlier about first dates needing to be on neutral territory in case the man was an axe murderer? What if the *woman* was an axe-murderer? He didn't know Brenda from Adam. All he had was her advert; all that crap about her wanting a real 'Man's man to take care of.' What if 'take care of' didn't mean serving him booze and feeding him up, perhaps scrubbing at the skid-marks at the rear of his boxer shorts? What if it meant *take care of,* as in with a swift axe-blow to the head, or crotch?

As if on cue, he heard the first scrape of one of the rusty knives against the butcher's steel. *Wrrrrappp-Zing,* it went. *Wrrrrappp-Zing.* And immediately Adrian knew she wasn't sharpening the blade in order that she could cut the string on her apron. She was sharpening the blade for him. In his mind's eye, he saw the *Tied Piper* headlines: LIMB ISLAND MAN LOSES THIRD LIMB, or ADRIAN 'BOBBIT' DEVONISH, THE EUNUCH OF THE CASTLE, or MAN GOOSED BY PIE, EMASCULATED.

Quickly he pulled on his jeans. Red-faced, he moved to the door, and as quietly as possible, tried the handle. He *knew* it was locked, he'd watched her do it, but something inside him told him he had to check; that he might have been imagining it all along. From the kitchen: *wrrrappp-Zing.* She was mocking him now, surely. Panicked, he tried the handle again. Tried one of his own keys, *knowing* it wouldn't work, but at a loss as to what to do otherwise.

Wrrrrappp-Zing.

53

The sands of time were starting to ebb for him. This was to be the last act in a life largely shaped by triumph. Death would be ill-deserved. People would mourn him as the visionary he was... Perhaps they'd erect a statue on the village green.

Wrrrrappp-Zing.

He didn't allow himself time to think. He moved over to the front window, picked up the still half-full goose pie dish and weighed it in his sweating hands. As his arm drew back to throw the dish through the window, Brenda came back into the room, now gloriously naked.

'What the...?'

The pie dish hit the window and time seemed to go slow-mo. The window wobbled like Rolf Harris's shuffle board. Gravy glooped across it. The pie dish smashed lackadaisically on the wooden floor. The window shook back and forth and for a moment; Adrian wondered whether the mad cow had bulletproof glass installed. But then the window gave, shattering like tears. Cold air plunged into the room. Then, silence.

'Adrian!' bellowed the wounded buffalo. For once she'd got his name right. But he didn't care. In his woollen grey socks, he climbed up onto the rickety table, senses so sharp he could even pick out the sound of the TV remote cracking under the leg it was supporting. Thrusting a victorious look over his shoulder, he dived through the gap and out onto the pavement. He landed on broken glass, but Ma Devonish's socks as well as being excellent at soaking up sweat were also so thick as to stop the shards from cutting through into his feet. 'Ha!' he called as he launched into a mad run to his car.

'Adrian!' shouted Brenda again, sounding like the broken, beaten Rocky calling to his missus. He ignored her, jumped in his car, gunned the engine. *Ride on Time* leaped out of the stereo speakers. He slammed his foot down on the accelerator and screeched out of her street, left her behind to wonder why she'd ever chosen to mess with Adrian Devonish.

His heart only started beating normally once he'd got out of her rabbit warren of an estate and joined the A24 somewhere near Charnley. His hands only stopped trembling once he'd turned off Black Box and replaced it with the more soothing tones of Bryan Adams. And he almost thought he'd got away scot-free until he saw the blue flashing lights in the rear-view mirror. His heart leapt once again. He glanced down at the speedometer, saw he was only doing forty or so in a sixty zone, but still eased his foot down onto the brakes. Carefully he indicated, pulled over into a layby, and only as the police car pulled up behind him did he remember he'd been drinking. Heavily.

The policeman approached and rapped on the passenger side window, gesturing for him to wind it down. Adrian acquiesced, but not before slipping a polo mint into his mouth.

'What seems to be the problem, officer?' he said.

'I'd like you to get out of the car please sir. And if you'd then like to follow me back to my own car and climb in the back, I'll explain everything to you there. Just be careful opening your door sir. Cars come down this stretch very quickly indeed.'

'I wasn't speeding,' said Adrian.

'No,' replied the policeman, thoughtfully. 'At least you weren't doing that, too.'

Christ! What else was the policeman talking about? Surely Brenda hadn't reported his breaking her window to the police? Surely she'd be too worried about protecting her secrets for that?

Wearily, he climbed out of the car, stepped around it, and faced the policeman. The policeman couldn't stop his face from collapsing into an amused leer. Adrian remembered his get-up; the frill-necked lizard brown shirt, the unbuckled belt, the lack of shoes.

'Been to a party, sir?' asked the cocky copper. 'Fancy dress was it?'

Adrian hung his head.

The policeman pulled out a breathalyser.

'Please!' begged Adrian. 'I've not been drinking... I've just had a terrible shock, that's all.'

The policeman rattled the breathalyser in Adrian's face. But suddenly a voice from the gods interrupted him. Or rather, a crackle from the radio which was attached to the rozzer's dark blue jacket (which seemed too long for him). Adrian heard the words 'wild animal on the loose' and 'just past the Limm turn-off on the A24'. He saw the policeman's hesitation before he turned around and answered the call and then gloriously, he heard the words: 'I'll be right there.'

The policeman clicked off the radio and turned back to face Adrian. Gave him a look which mixed contempt with pure unadulterated hatred, and then said, 'I could ask you to wait here, but you won't do that, will you sir? It looks as though you've had a lucky escape. My advice is park up somewhere safe as close as possible to here and call yourself a taxi home.'

Adrian nodded gratefully.

'Well,' said the policeman, 'what are you waiting for? The bloody fashion police?'

Adrian paused ready to give the mini-me rozzer a piece of his mind but then decided he'd be pushing his luck too far if he did. Instead he returned to his car, waited for the police car to hare off along the A24, and then he gunned the engine and followed, this time with Brian Adams on real low, just in case he drew any more undue attention to himself.

By the time Side A of *Waking up the Neighbours* had finished, he felt sober enough to look over the white lines onto the other side of the road to check for more police cars. By the time he passed the place where he thought the wild animal – most likely a bloody lost sheep or something - had been reported, and discovered it wasn't there, much less the flashing blue lights, he almost felt as though he could go another can of Fairhurst's. And even though darkness had descended in the blink of an eye, he found he was able to make the turn-off for the road down to the causeway without having to double-back on himself more than once (and even then he'd been distracted by having to fast-forward 'Depend on Me'.)

He was starting to feel good about himself, *captain of industry good, escaping the clutches of the law good,* until he crested the hill and saw that the tide was already halfway to blocking the road. It felt like a slap in the face.

He fiddled with the dials for the car stereo again, searching for 'Everything I Do', his great relaxant. *Rewind, rewind. Play.* Struggling to find the right place; the struggle making his foot twitchy on the accelerator. *Rewind, rewind. Fast-forward just for luck...* He clicked 'play' again and realised he'd fast-forwarded too far. *Concentrate.* Made a mental note to try and wrangle a CD player from someone down the Ship. *Rewind, rewind. Play.* And suddenly Adams' hoarse vocals cut through the night air like air-freshener. Adrian closed his eyes and belted out the chorus, imagining himself a Prince of Thieves. He'd make a good Robin Hood, he reckoned. He had just enough maverick (and beard) in him and just enough authority. Maybe he wouldn't give *everything* to the poor like Costner did in the movie, but he'd still give something back. He'd still be a *captain of forestry,* or whatever.

Man the chorus to 'Everything I Do' deserved another listen. It needed to be played at waking up the neighbours volume too. Adrian opened his eyes and fumbled for the dials and only then did he catch sight of the bloody red lights in front of him. The big looming shadow of a Combs' Mead truck. And then, in the same instant, he thought *too close*. If he was close enough to read the lettering on the back of the truck he was...

He rammed his foot down on the brake. Screeched to a steaming, ski-whiffed halt. Halted so fast the glove-box popped open and a spare pair of shoes he'd shoved in there for if ever the stink got too bad flew out. Smashed onto the passenger seat. He killed the radio. Pulled the key out of the ignition. And then sat breathing deeply in the front seat.

He didn't move. The only sound the flicking of his heart. Sounded like the *criiiiccckkk* of a thumb across the wheel of a lighter. He stared down at his spare shoes as though he'd never seen them before. They were brown, fake snakeskin. In fact, so snake-skinned were they, the laces looked as though they were made from a previous, shed skin. He'd bought them in Newcastle, was saving them up for a good, snaky day to wear them. Not many of those on Limm though... And what with his clubbing being somewhat curtailed recently, he had forgotten all about them. He started thinking about how much money he'd wasted on those shoes (that was the problem with going shopping after six pints) and then wondered what the hell he was doing. He looked up, peered into the darkness and watched the lorry gain the causeway.

The causeway... Now when he looked back through the front windscreen, he saw the tide starting to drag even further across the causeway. It had already claimed much of the middle part of the road and it wasn't just puddling there, but pooling. He saw his chance of getting home, getting some sleep, slipping further and further away. And suddenly home was most definitely where he wanted to be. Home was the only place he *could* be. Over here, out amongst the mainlanders, he didn't feel right. He had to be there. Where people didn't have to look at photos in his wallet to know he was kingly. Where policemen didn't stop him for swerving all over the road... Out here, off Limm, he was like a bairn had been off the teat too long.

Quickly, Adrian slammed his foot back on the accelerator and careered away down towards the sea, the causeway. He increased his speed, despite the fact he was now starting to feel decidedly queasy. He tried not to look at the dry stone walls on the verges, the way they swept past in a bumpy blur. Tried to focus on a set point, one of the lights in the village over the other side. But it was no good. Too damn bouncy. The light appeared as though it was attached to a hot air balloon or something.

He did see the luminous TALENT-STRAVANGANZA!!!!!! sign on the entry/ exit barrier to the little tourist car park. Couldn't miss it. It screamed out to be seen, like a flare. And Adrian felt the bile starting to churn in his stomach. He heard himself plea-bargaining in his head. Heard himself offering up all kinds of unlikely deals: *if I can only make it over the causeway tonight safe and warm and over on Limm, I'll go to that bloody thing... I'll become Mr. Community Spirit... I'll clap and cheer and I'll pretend like I'm just another Limm guy if I can just make it across...*

He gunned past the signs bearing the tide-tables, passed the 'This is the Point of no Return' sign, and began to believe that someone up there (or down there) had listened, mused over the deal awhile, and then nodded, allowing him to pass. But then he felt the back wheels starting to skid out, starting to move independently of the front of the car, starting to aqua-plane. For a moment, the steering wheel locked and he spun in a mad half-circle. He convinced himself the car was going to take a dive, a plunge, come crashing off the causeway and into the sea. He closed his eyes and upped the ante.

I'll cut down on the drinks... I'll cut out the fatty foods...

The car still streamed across the top of the water. The gear-stick rattled out of gear. The rev counter on the dashboard went through the roof as he slammed down both feet, one on the anchors, one on the accelerator. It felt like he was driving on ice. But it wasn't ice at all. It was water, most definitely water; he could feel it starting to seep in through the crack at the bottom of his door, soaking into his grey woollen socks.

I'll be nicer to people like Brenda if I can only get across...I'll call her and apologise...

He heard a clunking, grindstone noise from somewhere underneath the car. And then, somehow, he found traction. He forced it back into gear and then reached for the steering wheel. And now when he touched it, it responded. Sucking in a deep breath, he managed to right himself with an arm-clenched twist and then, giving himself no time to think about what he was doing, what he might be letting himself in for, he pressed on into deeper water.

Now he couldn't see through any of the side windows. The wheels were kicking up so much water it was as though he was Moses and he'd parted the waves. He had walls of water surrounding him on either side. And yet he pressed on, not allowing himself to think of things like coastguards or drowning. He pressed on, gritting his teeth, his beard bristling with hope. He pressed on, and he saw the central point of the causeway, marked by a wooden construction on stilts at the side of the road, a tower to which the coastguard could safely airlift the stranded tourists to safety. He looked over at the seat-well on the passenger side and saw there was a veritable rock-pool going on there. The seawater had reached at least six inches and was rising rapidly. Empty cassette cases, a laminated menu from the hotel, an empty can of Fairhurst's, an empty can of gin and bloody tonic (when the hell had he snaffled *that* down?) all floated on the surface like so much flotsam and jetsam.

The car was becoming Davy Jones' locker. Some sort of warning signal was flashing on the dashboard, but Adrian couldn't understand what it was. And then that pulsing light was joined by another one, and another one. And yet he pressed on past the stilted coastguard tower. The conditions were now so bad it was as though he was driving at thirty miles and hour through an elongated car wash. The windscreen wipers waved madly across the window but their efforts seemed futile. *Waves* were starting to crash against the front bumper, were breaking around him.

And then, just when it seemed all was lost, he felt the bumps in the road again. Suddenly, he could see the lights of Limm Island and not just the warning lights on the dashboard. Suddenly, he found when he touched his foot down on the accelerator, the car actually picked up pace. And then there wasn't a wall of water flanking him on both sides at all, just a small verge, and then a mound, and then a pool and then a puddle. And as though to confirm everything was going to be all right, the full moon winked out from behind a huge black cloud and the scene was suddenly bathed in light.

And he could now see the signs which bore the tide tables over the Limm side, dragging ever closer. He could see the road snaking up onto the higher ground of the island, and safety. He could see his route to redemption. Blowing out his cheeks, he clamped his foot harder on the pedals and aimed for that point in the distance which would mean he'd got through this, got through everything.

Adrian at last started to relax. Prized one, still half-locked hand off the steering wheel. Chanced a whistle.

And then he saw it. Full in the light of the moon a huge black shadow at the side of the road close to where the signpost had been hammered into place. A crouching, hulking, bent-over-four-legged *absence of light*. At first, Adrian was convinced it had to be some kind of aftershock from the trauma of the last few minutes. His mind playing tricks with him. But when he screwed up his eyes, shook his head, and then opened them again, the *absence of light* was still there. And it was moving. Stalking up to the edge of the sea and dipping a paw into it, before shaking off the wetness and then trying again. As though it was confused. As though it was trying to work out just how land which had been dry just moments before was now suddenly wet. The action reminded him of a cat. But this was like no cat Adrian had ever seen.

Correction: this was like no cat Adrian had ever seen *on Limm Island*. But he had seen big black cats like that before, on TV, on wildlife documentaries, in the zoo too, back in the mists of time. But it couldn't be something like that could it? Not here. Not on boring old Limm where the most exotic wildlife was the fuggin' fish. It looked completely out of place, this cat-thing, and clearly felt it too, judging by the paw-dipping. When it saw the car approaching out of the sea however, it didn't turn tail and run, as Adrian had been expecting it to do. Instead, it seemed to lock its eyes on Adrian's, and Adrian felt its power burning into him like judgement. And then, after the longest time, it stood up on all four legs, lifted its tail and released a jet of urine which rainbowed in the moonlight. And then it looked back at Adrian and he swore he saw it smile. Give this cockamamy, shit-eating grin which just about scared the helloutta him. Because he knew what this cat was doing. It was marking the edges of its territory, claiming the island as his own.

And then, everything got just that little bit worse. Because now the cat bucked back onto all-fours and faced him, and it seemed to draw its paw back and forth, as though gearing itself up for a run. Adrian eased off the accelerator, felt the car slipping again. Tried desperately to regain control. The cat clocked the car's stumble. Started to slink forward. And then, edge itself into a loping half-run, which became a gallop, which became a sprint. The cat, the panther, the *absence of light* was heading directly for him. Adrian gulped and then, without thinking, he changed gear. Shunted the car into reverse. After much grinding, the gears found a bite and the car jerked backwards, into deeper water. He didn't stop to think about what he was doing, he simply knew he had to drive. Drive away from this beast. Drive somewhere it wouldn't go. He had a vague idea it wouldn't like water. *Shouldn't* like water.

But it seemed to like water just fine. It plunged headlong into the waves and raced towards him. The car couldn't reverse quickly enough now. Water *was* starting to clog up the engine. He pressed down on the pedals harder and felt... Felt nothing, only that power had upped and left him. And now, suddenly, he felt the car lift. The water was picking the car up off the road, lifting it, *presenting* it to the panther.

And Adrian bargained harder now. *I'll marry Brenda. I'll make an honest woman out of her, I'll...*

The big cat leaped onto the bonnet. He heard the thump, then the creak of metal as it gave under its weight. Inside the car, water was now puddling in Adrian's lap.

This had to be a dream, didn't it?

The cat slammed a heavy paw against the windscreen, shattering it.

This wasn't real.

But he remembered the policeman's radio call. The talk of a wild animal on the loose. Claws, paws, teeth were now smashing further through the windscreen, cracking it like eggshell, coming closer. Adrian grabbed at the loose cassettes, the empty cans of Fairhurst's, *anything,* and chucked them at the animal's terrifying face. He even reached for his designer loafers and *launched* them at the thing.

The beast lunged through the windscreen. Adrian felt its hot breath. Smelled it too. It smelled bad. Sickly. Poisoned. He thrust out a hand, instinctively. Pushed it towards the beast's gaping maw, just wanting it away from him. The beast lunged again, its head cracking against the top of the steering wheel, and then it backed off.

The beast glared at him now. It had worked out, finally, that it was too big to get through the windscreen. Too excited to squeeze through the gap. Adrian stared back, with saucer eyes.

'Shoo,' he breathed, 'just get away...'

That was when he felt it. The pain. The agony. From his hand. He chanced a quick look down and saw...

He saw that one of his fingers was missing. All that was remaining was a stump. His finger had been lumber-jacked off at the knuckle. He cocked his head and studied it, awfully. How careless of him to lose a finger at a moment like this. At the time, when his fingers had touched the wetness of the beast's nose, felt the trembling warmth of its fur, he'd only been concerned with pushing away. Had been too desperate, to panicked, to realise it had taken something from him. And now he saw his own finger dangling, hanging off one of the beast's yellow fangs and he saw the wedding ring sparkling in the moonlight, the ring which no amount of lathering-up would remove – well, it was gone now; he was finally, properly *divorced* – and he thought now, now was finally the time he'd pass out. But he didn't. The pain was too great to allow him that. It jack-hammered in his brain, coursed through his blood. No amount of blue catering plasters would stem that flow.

And what's more, the taste of his blood seemed to have enlivened the beast, he watched as it recalculated, shifted its position, climbed on the roof and started trying to paw right on *through* it. He heard a sound a thousand times worse than nails on a blackboard as the panther's claws ripped against metal. The beast was growling in frustration now, breathing raggedly, desperately, hungrily. It shifted position again, tried to smash through the side window, and this time with its moving weight, it caused the car to skew off to the side into deeper water. The back of the car started to lag badly. The water now crept up around Adrian's neck.

And suddenly, the beast must have decided that *it* was in danger of drowning too. For it dived off the roof of the car, back onto the causeway and away, back to the island. Adrian would have heaved a sigh of relief were it not for the fact that the car was now sinking quickly.

Desperately, he fumbled at the door-handle, but the pressure of water wouldn't allow him to open it. And his hand with the missing finger was numb now. Dying. He tried his with his other hand, but it was too shaky to un-clunk, un-click him out of his seatbelt. He was too clumsy.

And now water washed through the smashed windscreen, punched into his face. It was cold. So cold it paralysed him. Pressed him back into his seat so all he could do was watch as the last of the space in the car was filled with seawater. Eyes wide-open in shock, that this could happen to him of all people, he wondered how long he would last. Whether the coastguard would come for him. Where his car would eventually wash up. Whether they'd be able to identify his body. Whether...

He felt his lungs exploding at last, and his eyes too. And he was almost glad, because that meant he wouldn't have to see that Dark thing ever again, or suck in his rancid stink.

4: The Suicide Note

The way Dr. Ray Shaw felt about his clinic was pretty similar to Stockholm syndrome, he supposed. Over the years he'd grown to love what was, at best an unlovable, nondescript building –The Bungalow, the locals called it, on account of it was a low, sprawling, single-storey building - but he also sensed that he'd become trapped by it. As though its rather poky dimensions had somehow restricted his personal growth. Once, he'd believed that a posting at a local surgery was just a stepping stone on the path to bigger and better things, but he'd long since admitted to himself that the Limm Island Clinic *was* the stone. The weight around his neck; he wouldn't be progressing any further up the ladder. He wouldn't ever see the megabucks which had showered so many of his fellow medical students. But then, that was the problem with General Practice; it just wasn't as specialised as surgery.

Shaw's job bordered on quackery these days; he couldn't remember the last time he'd had to use his medical brain. He simply listened, bored, as the lonely old women of the island told him their life stories and then he filled out the prescription dockets in his stereotypically spidery hand and sent them on their way to the chemist, where they'd pick up more of the mind-numbing drugs that made them forget who, when, or where they were, but which also stopped them from leaping off the causeway and into the high-tide.

The doctor's consultation room overlooked the sea. Builders had installed a large panoramic window which took up nearly the whole back wall of the room. It was supposed to offer him, and his patients, an almost picture-postcard perfect view of crashing waves, soaring sea-birds, bobbing fishing-boats. Shaw kept the blinds tightly shut at all times now but he could still feel its great, throbbing emptiness. Its loneliness. It called to him. It called to him like he figured it called to the islanders. Reminded them of their insignificance in the great, grand scheme of things. It was quite something to hate the sea on an island upon which, from virtually every vantage point, every promontory, every hidden nook or cranny, one could see it, waiting calmly for more prey.

Because loneliness was the Limm Island curse and the sea simply exacerbated the problem. Sea-salt loneliness pumped through the veins of his patients. Wasn't it strange that there were so few happy, surviving marriages on the island? Wasn't it strange that in virtually every family, there was a missing parent? And it was never a simple case of premature death or divorce, no; it was usually something deeper, something unspoken. And now, in those patients who still came to see him, usually under duress, because he was their only route to another fix of the old prescription medicine, he saw it in their eyes. The *remaining* parents, the ones left behind, were itching, scratching at the missing limb of their loss. He could see it in their eyes, could read it on their blood tests too.

Over the years, he'd felt it infecting his own blood. He wondered whether he'd still be *with*, if *with* wasn't too much of a euphemism, his own good wife, Felicity, if it wasn't for the fact her brain had gone so way out west that she didn't even know who he was any more half the time. Flick had always been a very introverted person, and he'd liked the silence in her once, but now she was so locked-inside herself she was almost spooky. The only time she ever showed any kind of enthusiasm for anything was when he let her have her knitting stuff. Let her get on with making her scrubby, lonely patchwork quilts, quilts which would have gone on forever had he not whispered them away in the night and locked them in the spare laundry cupboard at the clinic. He shouldn't have really let her do the knitting at all, if truth be told, but in his heart of hearts he knew why he did. Those needles had remarkably sharp points, didn't they? And *hadn't* Flick got ever so clumsy in her middle-to-old age?

He gulped down a throatful of now cold tea to wash down the guilt. It didn't work. He *was* guilty. Couldn't sleep the sleep of the just any more, as he had in college. Back then, he could have slept for two days solid and *still* been a little bleary-eyed. Back then, he hadn't been scared of his dreams and what they might whisper to him in the dead of night. Now he rose early; he got up before he'd even gone to bed sometimes (*what quick legs you've got, Shaw; all the better for avoiding your zombie of a wife with...*) He'd pass out in the armchair in front of the television for a dead hour or so and be woken up by the high-pitch monotone that told him there was nothing to watch any more. And instead of climbing the stairs *up to*

Bedfordshire (and to Flick) he usually forced himself into the shower and out the door, up to the clinic where he could pore over Excel spreadsheets illustrating emerging patterns and trends in the drugs he prescribed. Sometimes, he messed up the sheets on his side of the bed a little, just so Mrs. Bailey, the cleaner, wouldn't ask so many pertinent questions.

She was always asking questions, that one; demanding answers as though *he* was the one that worked for her and not the other way round. Constantly pressing him about why she kept finding those long pieces of wool on the arms of the chair or why she found lengths of twine on every surface in the kitchen. She didn't know about Flick and the knitting. Would scream like a tea-kettle at him if she did so... And if she'd be counted on to be like that about the knitting, then it was a good job she wasn't tasked to clean the shed, where the proper rope was, he thought. Because if his wife was, despite everything, a top class quilt-knitter, if she could pull together a quilt whilst at the same time soiling herself on *her* chair, *he* was a top class rope-man, and there were things he now knew that he could use rope *for,* whilst at the same time pretending it was merely a hobby, something to do with his hands.

Absently, he began running a long piece of cotton through his hands; dextrous fingers manipulating it; leading it a merry dance as they created knot after knot. Knots that were unbreakable. Knots that were capable of holding the heaviest of weights. Even when he wasn't concentrating, like this, he was always searching; searching for that perfect knot; feeling it out in the same way that his fingers had been trained to feel out the dangerous lumps and bumps under the skin of his patients. It had started when Flick had first showed an aptitude for the knitting. And at the time, he'd wanted to remain at her side in case she did herself a mischief (oh, those were innocent times). He'd held the wool for her, passing the different colours over when she needed them. Had started knotting then, without knowing why. He'd moved onto rope quickly enough.

After a while, he looked down and seemed surprised by the cat's cradle of string which he'd weaved about his fingers. Where had that cotton come from? He was sure that there'd been none in his pockets when he left the house. Sure that when he left the surgery at the end of yesterday, he'd removed every trace of loose fibre from every chair in the waiting room; every trailing piece of cotton from his shirt had been clipped short. He'd emptied the bins and taken them outside. He'd told himself that this fascination with the string and the rope had to end. And yet here he was with a length of cotton that was so long it could only have come from his grandmother's sewing box which was tucked away under piles of junk at the back of the shed. He'd avoided the shed for days now...

Shaw blew out his cheeks in frustration; stared at the cotton, willing it to disappear. But he felt his eyes becoming blurry, giving in before the cotton did. Tiredness was starting to make him do some very strange things. And tiredness could kill, even the motorway signs told him that; whether it would be him or one of his goddamn crone-patients, *or Flick,* only time would tell.

He needed time away from this place. Time away from the old x-rays on the walls which were only there to make him look good, or to remind him of a time when he used to actually practice medicine and not just become adept in the art of filling out forms. Time away from that horrid photograph he still felt he should display on his desk; him and Flick, before the curse of Limm Island took her. Time away so he could sleep the sleep of the just again.

Lack of sleep polluted the doctor's face; big black dustbin sacks hung from his eyes; so many years of missed-bits while shaving had given way to a half-beard which didn't suit him; angry tired-spots kept springing-up willy-nilly all over his cheeks. He'd never been conventionally good-looking - generally he thought his plainness made him the kind of person that goes unnoticed in a room – but now he was emerging out of invisibility and was becoming the kind of person that people would make whispered comments about.

Doesn't Dr. Shaw look ill *these days?*
Shaw he does.
Looks as though he's having some kind of breakdown...
Shaw-thing.
He's maybe trying a few of his own drugs?
Shaw-ly not...

Funny thing was, despite his name, he'd never been certain of anything. And it was surety he craved more than anything else. He was fifty-seven, approaching suitable early retirement age. Once upon a time he'd had plans for his retirement. Take up painting. Writing. Walking the coastal path. Now, he couldn't picture himself doing any of those things. He couldn't picture himself lolling by the fire, slipping into a Flick-style waking sleep either. Nor could he picture himself writing to the local health board and asking for a few more years. Hell, he couldn't even picture past the end of the day. Couldn't even picture past his next patient, no doubt another young mother with a screaming, snotty-nosed brats hanging off her arms, begging for free drugs he couldn't give. Begging and then railing at him for not acquiescing. None of them ever showed any trace of the politeness that was required, which used to be a pre-requisite, in conversations with their bloody doctors. And if it wasn't a young (single) mother, it would be one of the old birds that came cackling in through the door, fair rattling with the pills they already had inside them; they'd spend the first half hour of the consultation asking him about how his wife was, despite the fact that everyone knew she'd been Sleeping (Not So) Beauty for nigh on ten years.

He wanted to close the blinds in his head as well as those of the panoramic window. Wanted to not have to think, to picture, any more. Wanted to close his eyes and make like he was anywhere in England but this place, stuck out on a limb. But it was no good. He could smell the sea salting his nostrils. Could smell it seeping up into his brain. It felt as though an incredibly localised flooding was taking place. The sea must have over-shot the mark and now it felt as though it was pooling at his feet, damping up his shag-pile rug, blacking the edges of the wallpaper. And for a moment, it felt so real that he thought he'd better have a peek through the blinds to check whether the apocalypse he'd feared for so long, the apocalypse which Solomon had promised and which Shaw had *forced* himself not to give credence to (but which he believed in during the long night watches) was now coming to pass. Shaking the cotton from his fingers into the waste paper basket and shaking the fug of tiredness from his head, Shaw rose from his comfortable black swivel chair and stalked to the window. He rested his fingers on the dusty blinds. Took a deep breath. And then, giving himself no more time to think, he yanked the cord, tugged them open, blinking once, twice at the natural light which seemed so unnatural.

The sea hadn't overshot the mark. The Bungalow's car-park wasn't under feet of water. Locals weren't hastily depositing body-bags of sand around the doorways, across the village green. It was simply the same old sea view he'd turned his back on every day this past ten years. Empty, lonely, be-spotted with sadness. But not, definitely, definitively not apocalyptic. Sighing, cursing himself, he pulled the cord with a snap and allowed the blinds to fall once more. Now, once more, the dim glow from his computer monitor was the only light in the room.

He sat down. Began to scroll through a few lines of his master spreadsheet, juggling a few numbers. But no matter how many times he tweaked and massaged the figures, there was no way he could ever hide exactly how much Valium he pushed; how many Temaze-parties he'd unwillingly catered for. And there was no way that within Excel's impersonal grid, he could describe the sheer *need* for the drugs on Limm. Where, for example, was the column that allowed him to outline just how soul-destroying this island life actually was? On which row could he provide the salient information about exactly how much each and every person had lost over the years? How *everyone* had been abandoned and left here, castaway...

Castaway with the loneliness. It was the loneliness, he thought, which gave rise to that other drug which had swept the island ten years ago. Or was it the other way round? Which *did* come first, chicken or egg, the craze of a decade past or the loneliness? Certainly the loneliness had sowed the seeds, so that the Millennium cult could grow, but wasn't the ground fertile enough before that? So many lives ruined by hope. It was ironic. Bitterly ironic. That the cult should spring up here, promising its followers hope, and certainty. *Surety.* And yet all it did in the end was suck everything out of them and leave them husks. Like Flick. Like Flick who he should never have allowed to get so desperate that listening to all those hocus-pocus ideas actually made sense. Like Flick, who he should never have allowed to go *anywhere near* that man, that snake, that Solomon. Now, in no small way, he was the new cult leader, the new Solomon, keeping the masses stocked up on their hope-pills so they didn't have to face reality any time soon.

He sighed again, closing down the file, revealing a Word document he'd been working on, off and on, for the past couple of months. His suicide note. His eyes flicked over the lines. Occasionally he was embarrassed by the sentimentality that he'd shown, but mostly, it was exactly what he wanted to say.

> *To whom this may concern,*
> *Re: The things I have lost*
> *Pull at the rope. Pass its roughness hand-over-hand until what is lost is finally pulled out of the gaping maw of the sea. Hanging at the end of it are my self-respect and my dignity. My hopes and my dreams are also down there, waiting to be rescued.*
> *By settling here, and I mean settling as in 'settling for second, ninth best', I lost my wife, Felicity. I lost the children we may have had. I lost friends and colleagues and the discoveries we might have made. I lost relatives and I lost relativity. I lost them all, and what I got in return was Limm Island...*

Fingers hovering over the keyboard, he tried to formulate the next couple of lines. He wanted to say something about the pull of Limm being like the rope around the alcoholic's foot which means that he can never wander past a pub or off license. The impatient cursor flicked on and off; *come on,* it said, *get on with it.* But the right words just wouldn't come. He was on the right track, but not quite there yet. Of course, he had to continue with the extended metaphor of the rope. That would only be fitting. But was he making the whole thing just that bit too complicated for the police? It was his constant worry, that someone like Sam Bibby, the local beat bobby, would find him hanging, find the note, and would put it all down to madness or dismiss it as drunkenness; not even considering the weight that the words held for everybody in town.

Frustrated, Shaw clicked the little 'x' in the corner of the screen. *'Do you want to save your changes?'* it prompted.

'What bloody changes?' asked the doctor, out loud. 'Nothing ever changes around here.'

He slumped back into his swivel chair, feeling like he'd been wrung out. And it was still only afternoon. He had the whole of evening surgery to get through yet. He could barely imagine what he'd be like at the end of the day. He stared at the narrow streams of lights which slipped through the tiny gaps in the closed blinds. Unconsciously, he began to fiddle with yet another length of cotton that had miraculously appeared in his hands; twisting, knotting.

And as he continued to stare at the blinds, a picture began to emerge from them. At first, it was indistinct; just blurred shapes and colours. But soon, they began to achieve some form of lucidity. Eventually, the scene took on all the clarity of the view from the window earlier, when he'd thought the sea had over-shot the mark.

'Oh no. Not again,' breathed Shaw, and he tried to wrench his eyes away from the scene. But it had an almost hypnotic pull to it and he couldn't manage to stop himself staring into the blinds. Blinds which now felt like an abyss. An abyss which he *had* to plunge into… His eyelids felt as though they were being held open by matchsticks. Even if he'd tried, he wouldn't have been able to stop himself from looking on what Limm Island wanted him to see. The blinds played out the scene like an Imax cinema screen. And, over stereo speakers, he heard one, solemn voice, chanting over and again, *The tide of Darkness swells. The high tide of Darkness comes.*

He saw a slinking shadow of a beast. He saw The Darkness, and yet, at the same time, he felt part of it too. The slinking shadow of a beast was crouched down amongst some tall grass at the foot of a big old oak tree and Shaw could *feel* how alert the beast was. He'd never understood the expression *eyes-peeled* as he did now. For his eyes felt as though they'd given up blinking. They were raw, studying his surroundings. And as though Shaw half-recognised it, he felt that the beast didn't. The beast was alert. Out of his comfort zone. Watching. The beast felt hunted. Felt eyes on him from all sides. Despite the fact he'd marked his new territory – and Shaw could smell the acrid stink – it didn't feel like home.

It didn't feel like home at all. Things tasted different here. *Sourer.* Made him sick. Already he'd thought he was poisoned over the other side of the causeway. He'd eaten a big, stupid bovine animal. Ripped it apart. And had feasted. Feasted until he felt something like normal. And then, almost as soon as he was about to go for the choicest morsel, the eye, he'd felt the sickness come on him. Horrifying. He'd run, run as far away from the mutilated body as possible. Had staggered through a hedge and then *unleashed hell,* unleashed all the travel-sickness, he'd thought. And then, on shaky legs, he'd tried to beat a hasty retreat. To find a place to hide to wait out the waves. Lurked in the bushes, breathing raggedly as another predator – at least he'd first thought it was a predator – had approached the mutilated cow. But then this new predator must have heard him and had left, quickly, on wheels. Shaw felt the beast's confusion and its fear.

The beast watched and watched some more. It watched and it listened. Shaw could feel left ear twitching back and forth. A long reed of grass tickled its nose and the beast's massive paw described a lazy arc through the air as he half-absently tried to brush the grass away whilst at the same time never taking his eyes from his surroundings. His surroundings were the thing which had most disorientated the beast. Where the beast was from they didn't have oak trees like this. The long grass wasn't wet like this. Big bovine animals didn't make him sick. His prey didn't hide themselves away in big tin cans which then sunk into the sea... And mostly, there wasn't anything like the old house which was over to his left. The house was whitewashed. It had pretensions of grandeur too; two large columns flanked the door and there was a dilapidated fountain in the midst of the overgrown garden. It was unmistakably the Old Mason house. Unmistakably, it was the place that Limm Island forced him to look upon in his visions whenever they did occur. Solomon's old place... One of the oldest residences on the island, a place virtually swallowed up by woodland now. Solomon Mason's place, and The Darkness must have felt some of Solomon's old hatred towards it echoing up from the soil under its paws.

Paws. The beast was feline. Shaw could feel, see, it was feline. But he could feel in its loose musculature, its lithe body, its powerful jaws, that it was almost a different species to the common or garden moggies of the island. This beast... this *stranger*... was different. Was from somewhere else...

And this beast, despite his alienation from the landscape, despite the foreignness of the smell of the sea, despite the fact he didn't know yet what link he was in the food chain, and what larger predators might be out there, despite Solomon's hatred scoring the very geography of the land, was hungry. And even thinking about food was causing his stomach to bubble in anticipation. He needed to taste flesh again, even if it did make him sick. Surely some of it would stick inside him. Surely he'd get at least some protein.

The Darkness, the beast, wanted to feed. He wanted to feed so badly that when he first felt the slight, almost imperceptible rumbles of something moving, he figured he'd surely just imagined it. That it was his hungry mind playing tricks with him. But then he caught the *smell* on the breeze. A smell which was more subtle than that of the salty water, but at the same time more alive, more appetising. The Darkness sat up, more alertly, ears, nose twitching, mouth salivating, limbs making ready.

Past the oak tree was a large gap-toothed fence. Through it the beast saw something strange. Cocked his head. It looked like the predator he'd first seen over the other side of the road, before his retreat. Two-legs. Wheels. Through those same eyes, Shaw saw the same thing. Only he knew what it was. Instantly. Into the scene came a young, ginger-haired boy with a bike. He was wheeling the bike, not riding it, as though there was something wrong with it. The boy was, he thought, one of his some-time patients. Leigh? Luke? Was he the Dowsing boy? He couldn't be sure. The only thing he could be sure of was the sense of dread which was buoying in his bowels. He wanted to scream out to the boy, to warn him about what was over the fence, but he knew that he couldn't. For this was a silent movie; only Solomon's pasted-on commentary about the coming of the darkness could be heard. And Shaw wondered whether this was what Flick felt like every day, unless she had the knitting. Trapped. Silent. A bystander (though not an innocent one.) Shaw and The Darkness, the beast, watched as the boy stopped

71

wheeling his bike. Leigh or Luke or Lewis propped his luminous orange newspaper bag against the garden wall of the Old Mason house and started kneeling down, ready to fix it. The bike had a puncture, he saw. And was it fate, bad luck, karma, or was it The Darkness itself which had caused that puncture? Again, Shaw longed to be able to shout out; to warn the boy. But his mouth felt dry; his tongue had grown so big that it almost choked him. His pulse was frantic. Dreadfully frantic.

Shaw felt the beast's pulse rise too. In anticipation. Anger too. The Darkness was hungry, sure, but also his blood boiled and bubbled with tormented rage; it felt as though his face was well and truly being rubbed in the mud. Sure he was out of his natural surroundings and sure he still hadn't got his Earth legs, but still... Still he was a natural hunter, was powerful, fierce. And yet this orange boy, this little slip of a thing, was pausing so close to him, so nonchalantly close to him that it felt as though it was a challenge. He'd already let one two-legs get away and couldn't bear to think what would happen if he let another go... This poor bedraggled orange-furred creature was virtually begging to be put out of its misery, or else it was showing just how far The Darkness had slipped out of its comfort zone.

Unconsciously, The Darkness's paws begin to judder. His tongue clicked. It was that old feeling coming back to him; that natural urge. He'd feared it hadn't followed him across from... from the other side. He lowered himself into a crouch and watched, suddenly awake, more awake than he'd been since he'd first crash-landed on the island.

And at the same time, somehow, the orange haired boy's sixth sense had come into play. *Something* had told him of the danger he faced. Maybe Shaw's silent warnings had somehow carried through... Certainly, the more Shaw watched, the more he saw Lewis, or Lance's eyes starting to look around wildly, his neck jerking back and forth. Now he was starting to fiddle with the bike's chain with panicked haste. Spooked though, he couldn't seem to co-ordinate his fingers. They had nothing of Shaw's dexterity when he handled ropes. Lewis or Lance's fingers couldn't grip the chain properly. It was as though they were greased with fear, oiled with anticipation of pain.

The Darkness licked his powerful jaws. His majestic rear end twitched like a snake, building him up for his run. For Shaw

72

knew he'd run now. Shaw knew that the temptation, the implied mockery would be too much for him to resist...

He sprung forward out of the longer grass. He was now visible in the garden, a black streak. A black fingerprint of impending doom. He was visible to Lewis or Lance, who now, finally looked through the gap-toothed fence and saw death descending upon him. And, after a brief attempt at climbing aboard the still charley-horsed bike, a stumbling attempt at a run, Lewis suddenly became aware of his own fragile mortality. Shaw saw the moment it happened. Lewis simply flopped to the ground, to the pavement. Perhaps he'd given up. Perhaps he was playing dead. Perhaps he actually was dead – perhaps he'd had a heart attack at the sight of the charging Black Panther.

For the Black Panther was now leaping across the turf, swallowing up the distance between hunter and hunted in galloping, hungry strides. And somehow young Lewis managed to climb to his feet and started running too. Stumbling, uncertain, but running nonetheless. But Shaw knew that it was too late. The Darkness had already accelerated to full speed and was gaining on him every second. Was leaping the gap-toothed fence now, landing back down on the pavement, and then, in one fluid movement, picking up the chase.

Lewis stumbled again. And then The Darkness was on him. Jaws tearing into his whipper-snapper neck. Choking, snapping, punching him to the ground. Red. Red everywhere. Involuntarily Lewis's legs kicked and struggled, and the panther became even more intoxicated by his prey. Shaw could feel it cutting through his disgust, his terror; The Darkness was enjoying this. Like a domestic cat with a dead bird, the panther was now doing what every parent had told every child not to do; he was playing with his food. He wanted his buzz to continue. He'd not felt this alive since...

But now young Lewis had given up the ghost and was unmoving. The panther started to toss the boy about the pavement, trying to bring him back to life to prolong the fun. No movement; very disappointing. Shaw could feel the disappointment which the big cat felt. He could feel it in his throat, and somehow, that was the worst thing about everything he'd been forced to see. The sick, sick disappointment. And although the rest of the vision had been as silent as the grave, Shaw heard the scream as though it was coming from the waiting room. He wasn't sure whether it was Lewis, The Darkness, or himself that had made the sound...

He heard a frantic knock at the door to his consultation room. Terrified, he closed his hands over his face, over his eyes; pleading all the while for the visions to stop. The door opened.

'Are you all right, doc?' asked a shrill voice. 'I thought I heard something... Sounded spooky.'

Shaw peered through a gap in his fingers. Saw the reassuring, dumpy figure of Betty, the clinic's receptionist.

'Doc?' she asked.

'I'm sorry, Betty,' he said, clamping his trembling hands between his knees and raising his head, trying to control his ragged breathing. 'I've just got a headache, that's all.'

Betty leaned into the door jamb and gave him a quizzical look through her horn-rimmed specs.

'Really. I'm fine,' he said. 'Just the headache.'

'Well,' she smiled, 'you're in exactly the right place for that! How about I make us both a nice cuppa and find you some Aspirin?'

Shaw forced a smile and nodded his head. But Betty still lingered by the door, her large frame almost filling it. When he'd taken her on, she'd been as thin as a rope, but Limm Island had come for her. Now, she raffled down at least a packet of chocolate digestives every day. Ostensibly, she brought the biscuits for him, but he couldn't remember the last time he'd seen one, let alone been allowed to eat one.

'I did think I heard something from here,' she said, thoughtfully. 'Or maybe you'll just call me a mad old fool. Maybe I'm imagining things. My Alf used to tell me I was always imagining things...'

'You're not mad, and you're certainly not old,' said Shaw, dutifully.

Betty beamed. 'You always know the right things to say, doc.'

Shaw smiled. *Just go, woman. Just leave me alone.*

'It did sound a bit like a muffled scream or something though,' she said, half to Shaw, and half to the door which she swiftly closed behind her as she left.

The good doctor clamped a fist into his mouth and tried to stop himself from adding another scream to the one Betty had imagined. Or had she imagined it? Had the scream been real after all? He didn't know. All he knew was that the visions were becoming more and more regular and more and more real. They

74

were plaguing him. And deep down, he also knew that they weren't a result of the lack of sleep. They stemmed from something else. Something else which for years he'd managed to ignore.

For years he'd never acknowledged the fact that he had this inexplicable ability to *see things*. For years, he'd reasoned it away, using the medical knowledge he'd so carefully collated. For years, he'd convinced himself that he didn't take after his *goddamn ghoul* of a mother. But science could no longer explain what he saw. Reason couldn't compete any more. All he knew was that every time he saw the visions, they became more detailed. Like they were telling a story. And at the end of each story, he knew *oh how horrible but he knew,* that the end result was death.

That poor boy with the ginger hair... He *did* know him. He *was* the Dowsing lad. He'd treated his father way back in the day, when he'd drunk himself into such a state that he needed a new liver. The father wasn't on the scene any more – couldn't remember why; death, drugs, the Millennium cult, could have been any of them - and neither would the lad be if Shaw's sixth sense was correct, as it always had been. The only thing he didn't know was whether the vision was telling him what *had* happened, what *was going* to happen, or *what might* happen. The only question was when.

Outside, in the waiting room, he could hear the muffled sounds of the afternoon's patients arriving, full of complaints about the weather and their arthritis, full of pleading for more of the drugs and less of the pain. Dr. Ray Shaw took a deep breath, steeled himself for reality and decided that this was going to be the day that he made his final, perfect knot. Because, just like the chicken and the egg of the loneliness and the cult, he couldn't be sure which came first; did his visions *cause* The Darkness to wax, like a moon? If so, there was one sure-fire, tightly-knotted way of ensuring that the beast would forever be locked away and would never haunt the island like he'd seen it would. His hands didn't tremble as he opened the top drawer of his desk and pulled out a climbing rope. The hardiest rope he'd been able to buy at the outdoor pursuits shop in Charnley. Only by using that rope could he reassert the power of science over hocus pocus within himself.

5: Statues on the Beach

There was only one cranny into which Trevor Knox was going to spirit himself away; only one nook amongst a whole honeycomb island of them into which he'd retreat in order to wait out The Darkness. Sure, he could have chosen the thick woodland which crowned much of the centre of the island, but he sensed the woods weren't thick enough, sensed there were still great wide-open spaces into which The Darkness could seek him out. Or he could have chosen one of the old caravans in the abandoned Holiday Park, and made himself a little cosier than he was in here, but he knew that even if The Darkness wasn't to find him there, ensconced in a tin-can grave, one of the local teenagers would. They used the caravans as makeshift bike-sheds, or bus-shelters, or wherever it was kids went to do their exploring (in terms of bodies, drugs, booze, and ciggies) these days. He *could* have chosen one of the old boat sheds close to the jetty. Not many fishermen about these days, not since the quotas, and, this not being tourist season, he might have been able to crook himself away for a nice enough time. But there, he sensed, he'd be too close to the epicentre of what was to come. There, he'd not be far from Solomon's old place, and the rest of civilization; prey. He could also have plumped for a remote spot up by the monastery. But there, he'd have felt *too* out on a limb. Too much like the last man on earth waiting and watching as the end came to pass, just as Solomon said it would.

No, there was only ever one place Trevor was going to retire to in this kind of situation, and that was his hide. So aptly named. It was his spot for watching the wetland, the swathe of beachy ground which was left behind when the tide went out. An astounding variety of birds feasted on the rock-pool life - the molluscs, the crabs, the anemones – which the sea exposed, and in summer, the RSPB organised trip after trip out here. He'd have to teach fat retirees how to turn their binoculars the right way round, how they could mark off

76

the types of bird they spotted on their special-issue pink paper RSPB leaflets, as though it was an adult version of the I spy games he played as a child (and some of the visitors cheated like children too; he was sure half of them never saw three quarters of the birdlife they claimed to have) and how to tell the difference between a cormorant and a gannet (when they seemed more interested in pressing him on where the 'facilities' were, and why there wasn't a drinks machine on site.) In autumn and Winter nobody came, not even Ely Rhodes, which was why he'd come to think of it as *his* hide.

The hide was a concrete chamber sunk about four feet below ground-level. It was the size of a small family's tomb. If it wasn't for the strip of reinforced glass which spread the length of one wall, looking out onto the wetland, the place would have felt like a tomb too. Although the walls were concrete, Trevor sometimes thought he could hear the earth and sand around it compacting, compressing, *pushing,* ready to reclaim the empty space which had once belonged to it. The thought didn't scare him; he'd survived hurricanes in the hide. Hurricanes in which static caravans had been ripped from their bays in the Holiday Park and deposited on the beach. He'd sat in here as the small stream close by turned into an Amazon River, its cargo on the way to the sea including barrels from the cellar of The Ship, one of Limm Town's lifeboats, a bench from the village green, the odd car. He'd sat in here and waited the storm out, and could do it again. He'd been preparing for this for a long, long time.

He'd stockpiled cans. Had a deal going with a feller worked in the factory up in Charnley. He bought the rejects. Cans with no labels, with great whopping dents in them. He bought them and he buried them in another chamber next door to the hide. He bought the knock-offs because they were all he could afford in such large quantities, given the state of the wages he was getting for his National Trust job. Hours he put in, if he worked it out properly, he'd be well below the minimum wage, almost creaking down into slave labour territory. Which meant that when it came to buying his liquids, he'd struggled even more. Since Solomon, he'd had a great aversion to tap-water, and, having seen the three rotting sheep at the source of the stream up by the monastery last summer, he'd stopped drinking from the stream too. And L'O, the only mineral water they sold at either the newsagents or The Crab's Claws, was damn expensive. Which left him with mead. Solomon had never had any problem with mead, since mead was made from honey, and as such, he'd had crates of the stuff, kindly donated off the back of Joe Friar's lorry, lining the floor for weeks.

So he'd been prepared, like a good National Trust Boy Scout. But now the moment of truth had come, he realised he was prepared like a jaded, time-served office worker used to Wednesday morning fire drills on the dot of ten and not a minute later unless there was a fresh batch of admin work to finish off. He was prepared like the farmer who'd heard the boy who cried wolf too many times and now didn't go that extra mile to check whether his fences were secure or whether the gun was properly oiled. Hence, as Trevor sat down on the upturned box which he'd made his makeshift seat and struggled to pierce the lip of the can of – well, it could have been a can of anything, really – with the can opener, he realised too late how slack he'd been during the past couple of years. Time was he'd have performed fortnightly stock checks, rigorous testing on his equipment, but he'd grown lazy. The can opener, he saw, was rusty. Had no teeth to speak of any more, just this browning stump which reminded him of the one remaining tooth in his father's head in those two terrible years before he finally passed away.

Trevor started trying to increase the force on the top of the can. Put most of his weight on the opener and pressed down, hoping it would pierce the lip. Nothing happened. He cursed himself for his blindness. Cursed himself for losing sight of what was important. The job with the National Trust was only supposed to be a *tide me over* until Solomon's promise came to pass, but he now saw that it had become much more than that. He'd allowed the job to take over his life, and, regretfully, he'd done this because he enjoyed it so. Or, at least *most* aspects of the job. He loved animals. Loved their uncomplicated ways. Was constantly amazed by nature. The flora and fauna of the north east coast, the birds, the badgers, the foxes, the rabbits, the hares had seduced him. And he saw now that they were agents of The Darkness. Foot-soldiers in the war for the heart of Limm Island. And he'd let them in without even a whimper of complaint when he should have been making ready. He felt like the biggest fool now, because Solomon had proclaimed him a Keeper, and it was his responsibility to be prepared. And he wasn't. Loath as he was to admit it, he was scared. Like one of his rabbits.

He was scared. Perhaps that was why he couldn't work the can opener. Poor workman and all that. Despite the cold, his palms were sweaty. He wished Solomon were here now to tell him everything would be all right, but Solomon wasn't of course. Solomon wasn't a Keeper. Solomon was a sacrifice.

Trevor gave up with the can of whatever. Opened his rucksack and pulled out the Tupperware container which contained his emergency rations. Two Mars bars, some Kendall mint cake, his pills kindly supplied by Doctor Shaw. Also inside, wrapped in tin foil so as to negate the signals it gave off (least that was what he hoped the foil would do) was his mobile phone. He eyed it even more hungrily than he did the chocolate. Solomon could never have predicted the sign, when it did come, would come in something so small, so like a child's toy. Ten years ago, they weren't even heard of around these parts. They were like something from *Tomorrow's World;* one of their wacky, outlandish predictions which everyone knew would never come true, like flying cars. But the sign had come from the mobile despite everything. He longed to take the mobile out of its foil wrapper just to check the sign once again. He'd already listened to Ely Rhodes' answerphone message six, seven times and every time, after he'd returned the phone to the Tupperware box, he got that itch in his brain, that itch which said *are you sure you just heard what you thought you just heard?*

But that was The Darkness playing its tricks with him. Had to be. Ely's message was true. Righteous. And even though Trevor doubted, he could still recite it word for word. 'There's something very bad in the fields off the A24, something evil...'

No, there was no doubt was there? Doubt was The Darkness's tool and it was Unholy. Trevor just hoped Ely would remember his training, know what to do. He thought of Ely now. Yoghurt, they called him in Limm town. On account of his complexion. He was a tall, gangly lad. Stood out like a beacon amongst the rest of the Limm Island folk. Solomon had chosen wisely. Ely was different. Special. Over the years, Trevor had, as were his instructions, Kept him under his wing. Took him out in the National Trust Landie all over the north east coast. Made sure he was safe, even when that mother of his descended headlong into crackpottery. Back in Solomon's time Ely had looked like an angel. His hair shone like moonlight. Back in the day, they'd given him instructions as to how he should react when he first saw the sign. But now Trevor wondered whether the lessons, the teachings which Solomon had given to Ely, then an eleven year old boy, had really remained with him. Would he really know to come to Trevor now, as had been written? During their time bouncing over rutted tracks in the Landie, Ely had never once mentioned Solomon, seemed damn scared of the hide. It was almost as if he'd forgotten...

Though he'd still recognised the evil when he saw it. Had still seen the sign.

After the sign had been passed on, through the unlikely medium of the mobile phone, Trevor had done exactly as he was supposed to do. He'd abandoned the Landie over the other side of the causeway. Gone to the secret place he'd made ready. Had not passed go, had not collected two hundred pounds. But Ely should have been here by now, with him, and now this new doubt was starting to bite at Trevor, causing him to be twitchy. He couldn't sit right on the upturned box. He kept checking and re-checking the two sleeping bags he'd unrolled for them. He drummed his fingers on the lid of the Tupperware box and thought about calling Ely once more. Four calls he'd given him. Four *missed* calls. He'd gone one better than Peter as his doubt spread. Part of him wanted to go out and look for him, but he was a Keeper, and if he were taken by The Darkness now, there would be hell to pay.

He waited as the full moon slunk up in the sky, illuminating the thin spit of land which extended out towards the causeway. The tide was starting to drag and drop itself into the picture now. Soon the causeway would be covered. Water pooled by the sides of the road: black, oily. Closer, the white stones on the mostly shingle beach glistened like skulls. Somewhere distant, a sea bird cawed and trees buckled and creaked against each other in the wind. The high-tide of Darkness was here; ready to make the island their prison.

To numb the doubt, Trevor opened one of the bottles of mead. Forced himself to take a tidy sip rather than the hearty gulp he wanted to take. He stood, using the ledge underneath the hide's window for a bar, and he looked out onto the beach. And a distant memory prickled with him now. He recalled this very beach ten years ago, when Solomon's time came to an end.

There were twenty, twenty one people standing on the beach, feet wedged into the shingle. A score of silent shadowy figures arranged Canute-like against the incoming tide. In the low moonlight they stood like they were hewn from rock. In their midst, there was one group, a family, who were holding hands, facing the tide together, like it was all some game, but mostly the figures were standing on their own. Fighting their own personal Darknesses. The figures were the First Chosen. They spread maybe a couple hundred metres eastwards from where Trevor had been standing. Since that night he'd seen photographs of the Antony Gormley bronze statues on the beach at Crosby, near Liverpool. The figures reminded him of that. Their solemn obduracy. Their stubborn righteousness.

And Trevor had been jealous. Angry at the fact Solomon had not tapped him on the shoulder when they were all up in the circle by the monastery. He'd watched them, convinced they wouldn't have the moral fortitude, as he would have done, to remain standing.

At first as the tide rolled in, the figures had seemed clumsy. As though they were moonwalking on half-sunk shingle. He watched knees buckle, feet lose their grip. He watched a couple take a plunge into the ice cold waters which were pooling at their feet. But gradually, most of them found their strength. Stood rigid as the water crept up to their knees. Even the family group remained calm. Silent. Nobody cried out. Nobody tried to yank themselves away and dash away up the beach to safety.

They had found their strength by looking to Solomon. Solomon was the furthest out to sea. The only part of him which Trevor could make out was his bone white hair. But he could imagine the great man's face, fixed stern, eyes challenging whatever was out there. Solomon was the furthest out to sea and the waves were now quickly gathering at his waist, whilst it was still only cold-compressing the legs of the rest of his congregation. And now Trevor felt a great sadness in him which replaced the anger. Because he loved Solomon. Still did now. And all those people that said what they had was a silly, hocus pocus Millennium cult, that Solomon had brain-washed them all... Well, they would have shut up if they'd have seen the great man out there, first amongst the First, as the waves started to wash up over that great trunk of his, then over his chest, then up to his neck. And he never moved. At the time, Trevor thought Solomon would say something, give his final sermon. But there really was no need. Actions always spoke louder than words.

He remembered the moment Solomon's head first gulped under the water. He remembered his own legs had given, and he'd collapsed down into the grass, sobbing. He remembered that sinful Unholiness in him which made his eyes strain to see the great man's head bobbing back up again and then those big powerful arms of his beginning to stroke his way back to shore. Saying it had all been a test. But he didn't. His head never emerged again.

Through his hands, Trevor watched the same thing happen to the next figure. Again he experienced that same Unholiness, a strange desire in him to see the figure suddenly right himself and then start kicking for the beach. Again, the figure sunk, and rose. Further along the shore, the sea started to overwhelm the next figure. No... not figure. *Person.* He was starting to see them as proper, honest to goodness people again. The next person was the Shay woman. Mal Shay's wife. Cute little Kirstie's mother. Had two others too. Older. Long since flown the nest. Kirstie was what was commonly known as a 'mistake.' The Shay woman'd had a shine for Solomon all along, everyone knew it. And she succumbed to her fate just as he had. He gulped as she went down.

Simon Dowsing came next. He too was a parent of a young child. Lewis. Only four years old was Lewis. But Lewis would never experience going to that first football game with his dad, would never go out fishing the north east coast with him, would never... Trevor found himself sobbing harder now. So hard it felt like the grass around him was sodden with his tears, that the *grass* was drowning him just as the sea was drowning his closest friends, his blood-bonded fellow congregationists. He'd never hear Solomon sermonize again. He'd never hear the lustful singing of Si Dowsing again. He'd never help scribe Solomon's words with the Shay woman again. They were gone, and he was left, a Keeper.

The group of people holding hands, the family, came next. And at last he heard the children starting to shriek as the waves started to strangle them. Their parents' hands held them tight though. Held them as the waves drenched their faces. Held them as they tried to steal long, lingering breaths *between* the waves. Breaths which were meant only to give them the strength to shriek some more. And the sounds were so terrifying that Trevor found himself reciting the words from Solomon's book. *The high-tide of Darkness is coming. It waxes like the moon...*

He stopped reciting the words and found that the beach was silent again. Now the two parents were standing apart, their arms dragging into the water, still clutching on to their now surely drowned offspring like a chain with two broken links. Neither of the parents cried. Neither of them looked back. Both of them waited those final moments with terrible dignity, courage and pride. Horrible as it was, Trevor couldn't even remember their names now. To him, they were only amongst the First.

And then he heard a car on the coast road, screeching to a halt. Heard thudding footsteps through the undergrowth. Solomon had told him that if anyone came, Trevor was to hide away. Make himself safe because his role was not to come to pass for some time and he had to remain out of the clutches of The Darkness. He scurried back into the trees and waited. Expecting Dean Bibby, the town's policeman, a great hulking brute from fishermen's stock. Dean had two twin boys almost as big as him who he'd made into his unofficial deputies. Trevor imagined them coming down here mob-handed, spoiling the party. But it wasn't Bibby, or either of his bookend sons. It was, he was surprised to see, the town's doctor, Ray Shaw. Shaw bulleted past him, not three yards from where he was hidden amongst the trees. Bulleted past him with such a pace it was... Well, it was hard to credit it now that the man could once have been so sprightly, so desperate. Trevor remembered him plunging into the sea, hurdling waves, yelling. His voice was coarse, rough like sandpaper. Like he'd been yelling a long time all ready. Like he'd been screaming all the way along the coast road from town. He saw the moment the current started to strain against the doctor's legs and he saw the moment the doctor pushed into new reserves of strength. He saw him reach the closest of the figures. His wife, Felicity, only he called her Flick. At congregation she'd told them all she hated Flick, thought it flippant, Unholy. But now the doctor was screaming her name.

Her head was virtually under the water. Trevor thought she might have bent her legs as she heard her husband gaining on her, so that she could gain on her own death, and rise. But she was too late, or Shaw was too early. Or it was written that she should live out the day. Because he reached her and he boosted her up out of the black depths of the water. And then he started trying to breathe life back into her lungs. Trevor heard her cough, her splutter. She vomited all down the doctor's back like a winded baby.

And then the doctor was virtually dragging his Felicity out of the waters. Half-swimming, half-crawling, half-running. She was hanging limply at his side. She looked dead but Trevor had heard the cough, seen the vomit. Doctor landed her like a seal on the shingle and crouched over her, trying to breathe more life into her. But, what breath he had left evidently wasn't enough. She slipped into unconsciousness. Doctor looked in two minds whether to continue with his CPR or whether he should try to retrieve the last two Firsts, who'd yet to drown. He wrestled selfish desire to make sure *his own* was all right, he sinned against his Hippocratic oath. He stayed with his wife. And from where Trevor was hidden, he could see her glassy-eyes staring up to the stars, marking where she should have been. She survived, but only into a half-life, like the doctor's breath

83

wasn't enough. And ever since that night, it seemed, she'd remained unconscious, glassy-eyed. Waiting for the stars.

Trevor sighed, took a bigger sip from the bottle of mead. Felt its honeyed breath tickling down his throat. Felt it fluttering in his stomach. Felt it licking at his brain. He was glad Solomon had not seen what happened to the last of the First. Glad he hadn't had to live through what came to pass afterwards, when things got so black it seemed like The Darkness had already come. Glad too that he'd remained hidden all the while, as the blue-flashing lights of Bibby's police car had finally arrived and the three hulking brutes had started fishing for bodies like three steroided-up Neptunes. He was glad they never came a-knocking for witness statements from him. Glad that, despite everything, most of the details of what happened that night were brushed under the carpet. After all, what tourists would want to come to Limm after discovering *that?* What twitchers would come to watch birds feasting on the watery graves of so many locals?

The First Chosen's night hadn't gone properly to plan, but this new crisis was an even bigger test, Trevor realised. *Biblical* stuff. And the Ely was still out there, amongst the Unholy. At once, Trevor realised what he had to do. He had to make like Solomon. He had to stand. He had to trust that the waves wouldn't kill him, that they would only make him rise. He had to find the Diviner, whatever the cost. He upturned his rucksack, selected one of the more easily concealable hunting knives, the mobile phone, one of the Mars bars. Zipped himself up into a coat which was half-sleeping-bag. Tightened the laces on his walking boots so they bit into his feet, making him more alert. He took one last sip of the mead and then corked the bottle again, for later. And then he walked to the hide's back door. He keyed the padlock, unbolted the first couple of locks, was just about to slide out the bottom bolt when he heard it. Heard it as though it was in the hide with him.

Raggedy breathing. Rabid breathing, Hungry breathing.

Followed by a frenzied scratching. Large, steely claws *drrrrriiiinnnnging* against the cold metal of the door. Itching to get in. Itching to get to him.

It was too late. The high-tide Darkness was already here, smashing on the shore of his consciousness.

6: Out on a Limm

Manny Combs was perched on the edge of the desk with that all-too-familiar faraway look in his eyes. As though he was posing for a catalogue. Though Mike Ford couldn't think what catalogue on earth would use Manny as its model, nor what they'd be hoping to sell (or perhaps scare the customer into buying.) And if the way he was perched on the desk, so flabbily proprietorially, so arrogantly, was setting Mike's teeth on edge, then the way the wispy-haired mayor was talking was practically acting like a dentist's drill. Whining and burrowing into him. Poking and prodding around. Making him start to seriously think about giving that obituary he'd already got written and filed away about the *great* man the opportunity to see the light of day much earlier than expected.

They were in the cramped back room of the library. The unofficial offices of the town's weekly newspaper, *The Tide Piper*. Despite Mike's objections, the librarians seemed to have sneaked in more and more of their extra stock of celebrity biographies, Viking adventure tales and volumes on mead production and monasteries, leaving them in haphazard piles which stepping-stoned across the black and white chequerboard-tiled floor. A stack of red plastic kids' chairs was loitering in front of the small window, blocking the view. Everything else was papered with reams and realms of past issues of *The Tide Piper*. Even without Manny, the office was full to bursting point. With him in situ, it was becoming difficult to breathe.

Manny snapped out of his faraway look and held up a single finger. 'Don't you see, in writing those ruddy opinion pieces you're not doing the island any favours? You're inspiring negativity.'

Mike steepled his fingers, peered over the top of them, trying to keep a lid on his temper: 'Was that what you came in to say?'

'I just think people could do with a few more good news stories, you know? A few more funnies...' He picked up a copy of

85

the paper from the nearest pile. Started leafing through it. Paused, half-smiling. 'Here, like this. Amusing, informative, not at all hampered by any political viewpoint.'

Manny thrust the paper into Mike's face and jabbed at the piece in question. It was a puff piece, a filler, nothing more. A profile of the PE teacher from the local school, Carl Hamilton, a man who'd apparently got it into his head that he was on the verge of becoming the next Peter Sellers.

'Yes, well,' said Mike, firmly closing the paper, 'that was a piece I had to try very hard so as not to colour it with my own opinions.'

'What do you mean?' said Manny, narrowing his eyes. 'He's good. Could be a new star and God knows we should be shouting about him from the rooftops.'

'The guy's a moron,' said Mike, coldly. 'No. Not a moron, an *oxymoron*. Goes on and on about wanting to be a "serious comedian" and...' Mike paused, trying to face down Manny's new pursed-lipped, disapproving face, a face which said *don't go round using big words like that with me. If you're so good with words, how come you're still ruddy writing for a local paper whose circulation barely breaks into four figures...?* 'Well anyway...'

'Yes, anyway. Anyway he's a positive story and tomorrow, at the talent show, it could be his big break.'

'His big break,' mused Mike. 'The first real step up the ladder to Showbiz Stardom. Oh, okay, a Giant Leap towards an arena tour for his own, unique brand of stand-up comedy. And more importantly, his first Giant Leap *away* from being a bloody PE teacher at the local comprehensive.'

Manny Combs held up both hands in a surrender gesture. 'Whoah. Calm down, Mikey-Boy. You're getting far too hot under the collar. Maybe Hamilton won't win. Maybe someone else'll win.' He winked, then tapped his nose conspiratorially.

'What do you mean?'

'Nothing. Don't worry your head about it.'

'But what do you mean with that wink, that nose-tapping? Are you fixing the TALENT-STRAVAGANZA?'

Manny didn't answer. Instead he swung his short stubby legs off the desk and leprechaun-hopped down. He stole across the floor, picking his way through the leaning towers of books, and started trying to push the stack of red kiddies' chairs to one side in order that he could look out of the window. Not that there was much

86

to look at, simply a side-view of the town hall, which was now shrouded in darkness. If Manny was missing the place, he could quite happily trot on back there.

'I'm just saying,' said Manny, turning back to face into the room, 'we're the judges. We can decide what happens. We can write our own story for this one, and we can give it a happy ending.'

'Pick the cutest kid to win, that kinda thing,' sighed Mike. 'Fix it so...'

Manny slapped his hand down onto one of the red chairs. 'I'm not saying that at all. All I'm saying is...' A sad look clouded his features. 'We're cut off here. Isolated from the rest of the world. Set apart. And as far as the rest of the world's concerned, we're ruddy backwards. We're the place where the Vikings raped and pillaged, we're an ancient crumbling monastery, we're the place where all that crap with the hotels took place. It's time to look to the future, Mike. Not keep tugging on everyone on the mainland's sleeves and reminding them that they might not want us too close as neighbours. Do you see what I mean?'

Mike nodded warily, wanting to tug on *Manny's* sleeve and remind him that it was *his own* employee, Adrian Devonish, who'd been responsible for what Manny had rather euphemistically termed *the crap with the hotels,* but what was, in actual fact, a case of wide-scale libel and defamation of character. That Devonish hadn't been punished (yet) was not in any way down to the fact that he'd been clever in covering his tracks – he hadn't, he'd left his clodhopper trail so firmly printed it was impossible to blame *anyone* else – but rather because Manny seemed to have had at least some influence on the police investigation.

Ruth Sharp, the owner of the Seahorse had come to Mike with the story. She'd been flustered. He'd barely been able to understand what she was saying. In the end, frustrated, she'd gone over to his computer and sat down. Despite his confusion, he'd allowed her to use it (which was definitely not a Mike thing to do; usually he never let anyone *near* his computer). Something about her almost *total* anger convinced him to let her get on with doing what she wanted to do, in her own way. In fact, he pulled up his own chair and sat down and watched as she clicked on the internet icon on his desktop and then swiftly brought up three websites; Where2Stay.co.uk, DustyMantlepiece.com and TourismNorthEast.org. There she'd shown him the vicious reviews which had been posted online, for all to see, of her hotel. At first glance the reviews appeared wildly different, criticizing almost every aspect of her business, but after a while, she'd highlighted the similar phrases which kept cropping up. And then she'd shown him the pages for the Castle Hotel, the majority of which were overwhelmingly positive, and *all* of them praising the manager, one Adrian Devonish, to the high heavens. It was an obvious case of internet puppetry, barely even disguised. Trolling which was base and childlike, only, as Ruth reminded him, this was her *business*. And tourists did take notice of reviews, especially the positive ones.

In the end, the police investigation did nothing more than take away Devonish's computer 'for further analysis', which was at least embarrassing for him (people saw a computer being taken away by the police and immediately put two and two together and made one sick puppy) but not the final nail in the coffin Mike had hoped for. Mike's heroic expose story had had no real effect other than to reinforce some of the locals' existing attitudes towards this outsider, this 'tattle-tale', this Ruth Sharp, a woman who Mike had found very personable (once he'd bypassed her rage) and even friendly. She was the kind of woman who bristled at the thought of being helped by a man, and yet he'd wanted to protect her all the same. Ultimately though, his story had done *nothing* to help her.

Then again, he could think of nobody his writing *had* helped. It certainly hadn't helped him. All writing had done for him was build him up for a long career of yawning disappointment. He was no avenging angel. He wasn't even a very naughty boy (he'd never followed up on his interest in Ruth; there'd been no typically Mike, typically ham-fisted dinner invitations, no nothing. Just a full stop.)

He realised Manny was giving him a questioning glare. 'Look, what does it matter what I write? Nobody reads the damn thing. As I'm sure you'll remind me, we only keep going in the first place because of your contribution in terms of advertising fees...'

'Nonsense,' said Manny. 'The people here... they rely on the *Piper*. And it's time that we use it to paint a different picture.' The mayor started to stalk back to the desk. 'There *will* be changes here, on this island, Mike, whether you want to be a part of them or not. Big changes.' He picked up Mike's framed journalism diploma certificate off the desk. Made as though he was studying it intently, perhaps picking out how badly it was yellowing, becoming sepia tinted, perhaps also noting how the awarding college, across the causeway and up the coast in Sandham, was not even in existence any more, hadn't been for years now. 'We're not going to be *tin-pot* any more, you know?'

Mike wasn't sure whether Manny was referring to the newspaper, his diploma, or the island as being tin-pot; maybe all three. What he did know was the mayor had talked like this before. *Bridge-building.* Empire-building. Bringing Limm more in line with the rest of the north east of the country. Probably this was the second great story of his journalistic career; Manny's desperate grasping for his political legacy, as though he feared everything – the mayorship, the mead factory, the hotel – would all come crashing down around him if he didn't make that huge, last grand gesture of transforming the island, namely by replacing the causeway with a bridge.

'I know what you're thinking,' said Manny, 'you've got that inquisitive journalistic mind of yours whirring. I can almost hear the ruddy cogs... You're wondering why the hell I'd jeopardise my status as the biggest fish in this pond. Well, let me tell you. There's only so long a pond can carry on being a pond without becoming stagnant. And then the big fish dies anyway. All I've heard since the very beginning, since I first mentioned the bridge, is negativity. It's all "picturesque" this, and "spoiled landscape" that. The word "economic" hasn't even been mentioned once. And yet that's your story. Your positive spin.'

'Okaaaayy,' said Mike, as soon as he could get a word in edgeways. Once Manny started to talk, he seemed to get drunk off the sound of his own voice (a metaphor he would have loved to have used in *The Tide Piper* but knew he'd never summon up the requisite balls to do so, not knowing Manny's rather puritanical attitude to drinking.) 'We could run some features later in the...'

'The time is *now*, Mike. We're at the crossroads, as I told you. At the moment, Limm is a no-man's land. We're not close enough to either Newcastle or Edinburgh to make a difference. We're untroubled by decent mobile phone coverage and broadband connectivity. We're separate, a tidal island. We're battered by the North Sea winds to the east, and yet at the same time, we cling to the mainland like we're a ruddy child holding on to our mother's skirts to the west. We've got history, stacks of it, *ruins* of it, and yet, we're effectively ruddy hamstrung by being out on a limb. Haven't you ever wondered whether it was Limm Island that first gave rise to that particular phrase?'

Mike half shook his head, half-nodded; he felt as though he was being pummelled into submission by Manny's rhetoric. It was too late in the day to argue, to interject. The only thing he could do now, shaky on caffeine, was to look on, whey-faced.

'We've got forty, count 'em forty, different varieties of wild grassland and yet no decent restaurants, we've got unspoiled beaches and yet we can't get any proper tourists – ones who spend money and don't just bring their own picnics – to visit them. We're a bloody twilight zone. We're not Scots or Geordies, we're not Vikings or monks; we're a strange hotchpotch... Midway between one thing and another... But there's only so long we can go on, turning away from the modern world and everything within it. Yes?'

Mike found himself nodding vigorously. Whether he was agreeing with Manny, or with his own, internal monologue, the one which told him to open up the top drawer of his desk, rustle through all the unpaid stationery invoices to find the half-bottle of whisky he knew was stashed in there for exactly this kind of rainy day, he didn't know. He did know, however, that if he *did* happen to open the drawer, if he pulled out the half-bottle, and if he chanced to un-screw the top, he wouldn't get as far as pouring the liquid into his over-used coffee-mug, the one with the faded Newcastle United badge on the front worn from years in the dishwasher, before Manny would explode. He stayed his hand.

'And you understand the *idea* behind the bridge? No business can run effectively with their distribution channels cut off for fifty percent of every day. I'm not just talking about my mead factory here; I'm talking about all the businesses, even yours, eventually. Limm will *drown* without proper transport links. And if a business – yours or mine – is threatened, what do they do? They respond, they move. And if I were forced to have to move my factory off island, or if you had to produce your paper somewhere else, then what would happen to all the people I employ, or to your photographer, Yoghurt Rhodes? And yet still they complain. Still with the negativity. When we presented the architectural drawings in London, a couple of the most likely-looking idiots picketed outside the House of Commons...'

Manny got that faraway look in his eyes again. 'I don't know, Mike, I really don't. I mean, the drawings are *great*. There are tidal islands similar to Limm in Sweden; I know, I've visited them. And the *quality of life* of the residents has been improved massively after they had a proper lifeline – a bridge - to the mainland. What's more, the bridges themselves were these dramatic feats of engineering. You should have seen them; long, sweeping

90

sails; they looked like sails, glinting in the sunset. Beautiful. Things are going to change one way or the other. And if they don't... Well, don't quote me on this but, if there isn't a change soon, then I'll maybe see about leaving these no-marks to this cut-off, in-bred island if they want it so badly. Only, I'll maybe take my ruddy ball home with me. Sell-up the hotel and the factory. See how they like it then. Then it'll be picturesque all right. Then they'll be able to play at all the weird cult stuff they like when... well, you know...'

Manny's impassioned speech trailed off into something of a whimper. He looked slightly, breathlessly, surprised at himself. Certainly his cheeks had started to redden a little. Mike cocked his head and studied the mayor. It was the first time in his life he'd heard Manny even mention in passing the *weird cult stuff,* and Manny was in the newspaper office a lot, talking about all kinds of stuff (perhaps *the* biggest disadvantage of being so close to the town hall was Manny's constant 'just popping in to say hello'.) He'd stuck his beak into virtually every other story which threatened to run and run, but had steered clear of the *weird cult stuff* for ten years. This despite the fact the *weird cult stuff,* the island's own Millennium Bug, being *by far* the biggest story to have hit these shores for nigh on *sixty* years. Since the air-raid attacks on the munitions factory in the war, at least. If the *weird cult stuff* had happened now, there'd have been twenty-four hour coverage on the news channels, there'd have been news vans clogging up every car park in town, there'd have been reporters and presenters fighting over the available rooms in the Seahorse and The Castle Hotel. But ten years ago seemed a different era, and back then, Mike Ford had had almost exclusive access to the story. It was his own personal Waco and Pitcairn rolled into one, *THE biggie,* and it should have made his name. Won him untold journalistic prizes, bought him a ticket off the island. But it didn't. And the only reason it didn't, as far as he could see, was because the watching world on the other side of the causeway almost *expected* these things to happen in weird, liminal places like islands. If he'd stumbled on the story anywhere other than Limm, he'd have been a hero. As it was, he'd merely pointed out the obvious, as though he was a toilet attendant who'd just gestured to the lid of the toilet which was, of course, soaked with urine.

'Are you okay, Manny... Mr. Combs?'

Manny was starting to look decidedly *not* all right. In fact, his face had now turned purple. He spluttered something, something angry, which Mike could not properly make out. And then he reached a hairy-fingered hand up onto his shirt and looked as though he was going to start massaging his chest.

'Mr. Combs?' gulped Mike, imagining that Manny was about to have a heart attack right on his chequerboard office floor. Imagining that he was going to have to dig out that already-penned obituary...

Manny *growled* in response. And in that growl was a warning. *Don't quote me on that.* Then he turned on his heels and walked out of the office without even a 'see you tomorrow.'

And then Mike did open the top drawer of his desk and he did start fishing around amongst all the unpaid stationery invoices and he did discover the half-bottle of whisky. But instead of un-screwing the cap and pouring the amber liquid into the Newcastle United mug, Mike simply decanted it straight down his throat. He wasn't exactly sure what had just happened, but under all the rhetoric and the bravado and even the red-face, he understood that Manny Combs was worried about something far bigger than hotels and libel, he was worried about something which had wider ramifications than a bridge, too. And if Manny Combs was worried about something, that meant everyone should worry.

As he poured a second mouthful of whisky down his throat, he caught sight of the ever-watchful full moon peeping through the window. It was vigilant, not like him. Something bad was going to happen. He could sense it in his fingertips, just like he used to be able to when he sensed the right words about to pour out of him and he knew he should have been aware of it, that tingle of *wrongness* way before now.

And for a second, a millisecond, Mike saw something else. As he stared at the pasty-faced moon, he saw it suddenly glow red. Blood red, and then it was gone, as though it had never been there in the first place, but he knew it had. He remembered Solomon Mason's fateful words at the Millennium cult's woodland hideaway.

'The Darkness is gonna paint this town red, Mike. And there's nothing you can do. All anyone can do is pray, and be amongst The First. Hope that our Keepers see us through. Nothing you can do...'

And there hadn't been. There was nothing anyone could do about it. Only, Solomon had painted the town red, not The Darkness he was constantly spouting about.

Solomon.

7: Flipping the Bird

Laura Durrant was dead. Murdered. Cut down in her prime, and even the thought of it was making Sally Martin's mind go a little potty. Not whole-hog, kit-and-caboodle crazy of course because at the same time as staring down at her and performing a veritable Monty Python parrot sketch of alternatives for dead – Laura'd popped her clogs, the curtain had closed on her final performance, the fat lady (and Sal was *not* accusing Laura of being fat, wouldn't dream of it) had sung her swinging titties off – Sally could take one step back from herself and *understand* that this was the shock talking. Yes, just the shock. Or the grief. It had momentarily taken her, that was all, it wasn't stone cold permanent madness. But still...

But still, the very thought – the *sight* – of Laura dead was like some pesky, too-clever-by-half opponent had dropped a topspin return *just* over the net and no matter what Sally did, she couldn't bat it back and say *so what?* Sally gave a little shiver. Okay, a full on boneshaker. A teeth-trembler. And her only convenient excuse for this was that she was outside. It was dark, and it was cold. Okay, it was Baltic; a piercing wind cheese-grated her ears, making them feel thicker, longer than usual. Elf ears. Sally was an elf. *How's your 'elf, duck? Not 'arf bad.* The wind carried with it the foisty smell of ferns and of leaf mulch and clogged drainage systems and Sally realised this Elvin wonderland wasn't the romantic final resting place she'd have picked for herself or even for Laura. No, she'd imagined this place to be a haven of colour, a perfumery of scents, a paradise. Instead was just a rockery. A higgledy-piggledy rockery which seemed organised by no rhyme or reason in any language she'd ever heard of. It was a patchwork quilt of sludge-browns, oil-blacks, and suicide-reds. Too crushed in against the crumbling paintwork of the bottle green fence which separated them from Old

93

Man Poole's overgrown jungle of a back garden. This though, would have to make-do as Laura's grave.

Legs, hands, bottom lip trembling, Sally made herself *do* something. Anything to stop simply standing there like a statue in the garden. She told herself to get over herself sistah. And although her lips moved, she didn't actually say the words out loud. *I am only temporarily insane,* she told herself. And God knew, if anyone *did* happen to be watching – Old Man Poole perchance - they'd think she was muttering a quiet prayer (for the dead), wouldn't they? Old Man Poole had a habit of staring out at Sally from behind the curtains of the upstairs window in his house. She hadn't actually *seen* him watching her, but she'd felt his eyes on her on more than one occasion. Not in the way she used to feel men's eyes undressing her back in the city, in the spangly bars and the sprightly nightspots, but in a kind of relentlessly curious way, as though he was compiling some sort of dossier on her. The thought someone might be watching at least meant she steeled herself for action. And then, giving herself no opportunity to pull out, she hunkered down over Laura's limp corpse. And she observed. Clinically. As a CSI would. (Which in itself was a little mad, now Sally came to think of it; what'd be next? A *chalk outline* for her?)

Laura was at her feet. She was lying at right-angles to the toe of Sally's polka dotted wellington boot. She looked bedraggled, crushed, like she'd been through a wringer, or a flower-press. Sally's stuttering, but hopefully consoling finger reached out and brushed her. *Stroked* her. That same finger registered that Laura was bone cold. So cold it acted like an electric shock on Sally's nervous system. An electric shock which *almost* made her cry out loud. Almost made the tears come. But they didn't. Now she was down there, she felt like the woman with her finger in the dam. She knew one sniffle would burst the banks. She knew one cough would carry her off. *A coffin to carry her off in.* But she wouldn't let herself. She couldn't countenance crying out there again.

Instead of feeling the wetness spreading around her eyes, Sally felt it on her knees. Her knees were crying. It was the dew – did they have dew at half past eleven at night? - or the mud, or *Laura's blood* (don't be so goddamn stupid.) She changed position, though the damage was already done, and started in with the CSI stuff again. Though she'd already made up her mind. Had already made up her mind as soon as she stepped into the garden at half past ten on a cold February night, if truth be told.

There was a serial killer on the loose. A whole team of them, in fact. And Sally could tell the signs. Like Grissom, she considered herself an expert on creepy-crawlies – you had to know your enemies - and here, even to the untrained eye, the cause of death was fairly certain. Even Old Man Poole, from behind his musty curtain, could work this one out. Slugs. Snails. Sally had never known the difference really. Whatever, the vicious bloody *escargots* had got at Laura, just as they'd got at Rachel Dean a couple of days back – Thursday maybe. The slimy bastards had decapitated her, slivery-slivelled their snotty trails all over her leaves and choked the life out of her.

'Oh Laura,' whispered Sally, 'look what they've done to you.' Then she flicked her head round to check whether anyone was watching. *Because it was eleven o' clock at night and she was on her hands and knees bemoaning the death of a flower...* Her pony-tail slapped against her back and it felt like flagellation.

Laura was a young snowdrop. Fragile, beautiful. Cut down in her prime. Like all the flowers in the rockery, she'd been christened. Baptised too, with that first trickle of water from the can. Specifically, the flowers had all been christened with the names of Sally's old friends back in the city (when life was good and easy and she acted her age). It was company, see? Company other than the grubby brats she taught music at the local school. A way of hanging on to her memories. It was also tangibly mad. Mental. Christening *flowers*, for Christ's sake? But if she didn't have the flowers, she *would* go mad. Mental. Small town, island crazy. And that she didn't want. She didn't want to natter in the queue at MacAskill's or Buckby's Book-Buys about stuff as pointless as the new colour for the wheelie bins. She didn't want to grow old before her time working in some fucking office at the mead works. Most of all, she didn't want to start thinking that listening to that bloody PE teacher's jokes when they had after-works drinks at the Ship was the height of culture.

So she talked to the flowers instead. Price Charles would have approved. Oh, Old Charlie Boy would have been delighted at the way she treated them. Gave them little personalities of their own, which would match the ones of their counterparts in the real world. Laura, for example, had shared her namesake's dirty sense of humour and had – in Sally's head at least – also shared her blocked gutter laugh, something which hadn't exactly endeared her to Andrea, who was planted next to her. In Sally's head, Andrea would

95

always tut in that faintly condescending way of hers whenever Laura and Sal got going. Now, judging from her drooping head, Andrea felt faintly ashamed of her previous behaviour towards the younger snowdrop.

'You're right to be ashamed,' sniffed Sally. 'We were only having a bit of fun. For Christ's sake, there's little enough round here.' It was quiet (*too quiet. Like a horror film. Played on your imagination, which is why Rob had moved them out here, into the back of beyond, the tucked away, twice-removed heart of in-bred county, The Island of the Damned in the first place*) and Sally's voice sounded odd. Reedy. And yes, a little mental too. But, she told herself, she wasn't hurting anyone. What she was doing was pantomime. No more, no less. Rob should have been proud of her, as Old Charlie Boy would have been. But Rob would be far from pleased. He'd asked her to stop *with this craziness* on increasingly frequent occasions and had even started bandying the word 'psychiatrist' about, as in *you should go see one*. As in *your imagination's run away with you*. As in, *you're the dish, your imagination's the spoon. Do the math.*

But really he was just jealous. Jealous that it was her doing the imagining, not him. Not him who'd come here to the arse-end of the universe, the lip of the known world, the goddamn wormhole to another dimension because he thought it'd inspire him to write better screenplays. Well, from what Sal had seen, he had two hopes with that one: Bob and No. She'd hardly seen him write a word since they'd got here almost a year ago. Hardly seen him pick up his bank-breakingly expensive pen and his pretentious moleskine notebook. Hardly heard him battering away on his bloody typewriter (the same kind that Stephen King uses dontchaknow). Though for all he let her see of his manuscript, for all she saw of *him* these days, perhaps he *was* onto something. Perhaps he had written the new *Carrie* or the new *Shawshank*. Or perhaps instead, judging from the fact he always locked his papers away in the safe whenever he went out, he was aping another King work, *The Shining*. Her imagination told her this probably meant he was spending all day long going as stir-crazy as she was, writing stuff like 'all work and no play makes Rob a dull boy.' But no matter how much she tried, she couldn't get into that safe. She'd tried anniversaries, birthdays, *page numbers from his favourite King books,* but all combinations to no avail. Not even close. Certainly no cigar.

Irked by her thoughts, Sally dead-headed Laura without any of the usual fuss (and certainly no funeral). She made a mental note to get a hold of some new blue slug pellets around the rockery (*True Blue* they called them, like the pregnancy test). She'd have preferred to put down slug-sensitive land mines, but she wasn't sure you could get hold of such things in The Crab's Claws, even in Wagger's Secret Stash out back... More's the pity.

She creaked back up to her feet, grabbed the washing basket from where she'd dropped it in shock when she'd first seen Laura's corpse, and traipsed over to the washing line to collect the sheets in. To get back on with what she was supposed to have been doing before murder, serial killing and all things horrible (and slimy) distracted her. Which was mad enough in itself really. Who did their washing at close to midnight? It was no wonder Old Man Poole watched her.

She tried to whistle herself back into a good mood. Whistling had always been one of her fortes (that and French, and the piano of course) and she figured if she stayed out on Limm long enough, if she exposed herself to its radiation long enough, she'd end up putting her name down for the goddamn talent show one of these days, not just providing the musical accompaniment. Not yet though. Not while she was still clinging onto sanity with her fingernails. Not while her wellies were still the *good* type, the festival-going, young, fun and fulla cum type rather than the green, farming and fulla cow shit type.

She whistled. A shrill sound in the night-time quiet, but beautiful too, in its own way. She'd always had a rather large gap between her two front teeth (school nickname: Gappy) and this, she found made her mouth into a type of makeshift reed instrument. She crooned out the instrumental version of *I Predict a Riot,* by the Kaiser Chiefs. She'd found herself whistling that particular song more and more regularly over the past few weeks. There was a smell in the town, over and above the stink of the muck-spreading and the fish and the small-town desperation. A growing unease. The local paper, *The Tide Piper,* had reported a number of 'incidents' at closing time in the Ship. There was an ugly road rage attack up near High Loan Park. *Something* was *in the air* (wasn't that another song, by another group, who were around about the decade Limm Town appeared to be time-warped in?) and it was liable to snarl loose. Especially on days such as this, *nights* such as this, which would soon give way to tomorrows with their ridiculously named Talent-Stravaganzas.

Tomorrow, the whole town would be out in force. There'd be drinking. There'd have to be drinking, simply to drown out the racket from the various crappy choirs and, of course, the 'jokes' from the PE teacher-cum-Monty Python. And to warm the cockles of course. Who'dha possibly *thunk* of having an open air event on a day in February, when spring had most definitely not sprung? She knew exactly who. That lunatic, Manny Combs, who was the mayor, apparently (although that was like being king of nothing). Manny had tried to coerce her into running the local keep fit club down at the sports centre (in addition to her music stuff) when she'd just arrived. *On account of your good figure,* he'd said. He'd actually said that. And he'd actually presumed she'd be flattered, and would take him up on his admittedly tempting offer – teaching old ladies how to bend over without farting; what joy! - without slapping him round his chops or trying to tug out some of his desperately wispy hair.

She dragged a sheet off the line with far more force than was necessary and had to be quick to stop it from dropping into the muck. As she did so, she inhaled, thinking *for once,* the washing didn't stink of chimneys (or 'chimleys' as Laura used to say when we were kids), because it was past most people's bedtimes now and so the fires had been doused for the night. But really, chimley smoke, in this day and age; pretty much summed the town up. She'd grown sick of hanging the washing out because of the stink, but Rob insisted... Now at least, the washing smelled of the ten fluid tonnes (if there was such a measurement) of conditioner she habitually whacked in the machine.

As she was gathering in the sheet, the hunter arrived. People came up, arriving as if by magic, in a puff of decidedly-more-magic-than-chimley-smoke smoke from under the washing line, and started nosing round Sally's ankles. Not People as in Old Man Poole or Rob. Manny 'bloody doesn't need a' Comb(s) wasn't sniffing around her wellies (although come to think of it he probably did have some alarming fetish, and the combination of rubber and foot fetishism which wellington boots provided was probably right up his street.) People as in Sally's tortoise-shell cat. Her *petit chat lunatique.* Tiny little thing really, but a monster of a hunter. Shied away from strangers ninety nine point nine percent of the time, but somehow made allowances for Sally, which made People more important than even the flowers.

People wasn't always called People, of course. She used to be called Tommy, as in Tommy the Tortoiseshell. Sally had been left the cat in her aunt's will, and without telling Rob, had gone off and bought a cat-box and then driven right down to Cornwall to pick the poor little thing up. As soon as she'd got the cat home and out of that stinky car, Rob had started kicking up a fuss, citing allergies she'd never known existed as reasons she had to *call the League of Cat Protectors* immediately and have the thing taken away. And Sally had leaped upon his slip of the tongue and homed in on that, with an *oh, so they have a League now, do they, like the League of Extraordinary Gentlemen?* And the usual sniping had continued, even as the cat box with a whining Tommy the Tortoiseshell caged inside was promoted from porch to kitchen to front room. When finally she unhooked the gate and let the cat out, it immediately darted behind the bookshelves, in the tiniest of spaces, and stayed there for the best part of the next two hours. And every time she tried to entice it out with a *come on Tommy-kins, ch-ch-ch,* or a *Tommy, I'll give you tuna fish if you come out, there's a good boy,* Rob would snort with laughter. Until she finally had to ask just what the hell he thought he was laughing at, whether it was the sight of her on her knees, big arse in the air, and the know-it-all bastard couldn't help himself from telling her: according to him, Tommy wasn't a *he* at all. According to him, tortoiseshell cats could only be female (how? Why? Well, because Rob had said so, that was why.)

And so it came to pass, as things so often came to pass in the Martin house (i.e. a mutual loss of ground) that the cat could stay, but it had to be renamed immediately and forthwith and blah blah blah. Rob, bless him, had even come up with a few suggestions of his own: Carrie, Dolores Claiborne, It. But Sally wanted a name which would really suit her baby, one which would suit its burgeoning personality (and not one already thought of by Stephen King). Over a month, she toyed with a number of names: Dorothea and Cadeaux being particular favourites. But eventually, she settled on People. People *had* to be called People because know-it-all Rob was constantly telling her to *stop giving that damn creature of yours people-food.* And Sally discovered the best way of being able to continue to spoil People was to call her People.

Of course, although People had been on Limm for only around half the time Rob and Sal had, she'd settled twice as well.

Perhaps it was on account of being used to small-town, coastal life, having been born and bred in Cornwall. Whatever it was, whether it was farm-cat mousing genes or simply an innate fierceness in her, she'd proved herself the real hunter-gatherer of the Martin clan. She had acquired a habit of leaving her *petit cadeaux* - decapitated sparrows, disembowelled mice, D.O.A. frogs, and once a partially de-spined hedgehog – for the master and mistress of the house in the first place they'd find them when they woke; clawing open the shower cubicle and dropping them on the tiled floor in there, so they could bleed into the plug-hole. Nowadays Rob yelling, bellowing, *trilling* his five o' clock curses as he went for his morning shower was as good as any alarm clock for getting Sally out and about for the day, to do her own gathering from the washing line or from MacAskill's supermarket or her own hunting for one – just one – apt music pupil at the school.

As Sally bent down to give People a bit of attention, she was gratified to see the cat wasn't carrying any new horrorshow of a treat clamped in her jaws.

'Hello Peeps,' she said. 'And what have you been doing with herself today?'

People didn't answer. Of course she didn't answer. But she did kinda burrow her head against first Sally's wet knee and then her hand, begging for a good old head rub. People was quite partial to being stroked like this, like one would a dog, nice and hard, like Sal was *scrubbing* her almost. As usual, she started to purr along contentedly and even opened up her mouth a little so the scrubbing vibrations could kinda echo around inside her little tortoiseshell skull. But then, completely unusually, completely *rudely,* People suddenly swung her neck round and made to bite at Sally's fingers.

'*People!* What did you do that for?' said Sally, shooting her cat a rather wounded look.

People cocked her head questioningly and then let out one of her customary not-quite meows, a *meee,* Sally called it, because that was exactly what it was, this sound; *pay attention to meee, feed meee, stroke meee, play with meee.* But the cat didn't seem too concerned with any of these things and instead started to walk off into the rockery.

'Suit yourself; People by name, people by nature,' muttered Sally, starting in on the washing line again. But within an instant, People was back, nosing round her ankles like a regular foot fetishist.

'Well, I'm hardly gonna stroke you now, missus,' said Sally.

People *mee*'d again. A real long one this time. Sounded almost like keening.

'What's the matter, missus?' asked Sally, despite herself. She got down on her haunches once more and now cat and owner regarded each other with cocked, questioning heads. Then, without warning, People started to trot away again, back into the rockery, before turning, just as she walked over Laura Durrant's grave, and fixing her with such a people-look, such a human look, that it sent shivers running up and down Sally's spine.

'What is it?' she asked again, and this time, a daft recollection of her childhood, watching programmes such as *Skippy, the Bush Kangaroo* and *Lassie,* hopped, skipped, sprung into her mind by way of an answer. 'Do you... want me to follow you?'

Amazingly, People seemed to nod her head, or at least to duck it a little. But that was impossible, wasn't it? Nevertheless, Sal stepped up onto the rockery once more and now People was leading the way, clawing her way up Old Man Poole's fence before pausing again to look round.

'I can't climb up there, People!' But already, her wellie was seeking out a suitable foothold between the knotty planks which made up the fence. Already, her hand was pulling at the top of the fence, testing whether it would hold her weight. She'd not climbed a fence since... She didn't think she'd ever climbed a fence. She'd always been a bit of a girlie-girl despite the whistling and her love of animals. Hell, at school, she'd 'forgotten' her PE kit so many times, they ended up letting her take extra music lessons. And yet here she was, and it took her back to all those awkward moments trying to climb the high-horse which other girls could *vault* over. The fence could only have been six foot, only a foot taller than she was, and yet it seemed tall as a prison wall.

And yet she was already scrambling up it. Already finding a rhythm. She reached the top without allowing herself any more time to think and immediately People leaped down into the jungle which was Old Man Poole's garden. *Well, at least it looked like a soft landing. Over here the vegetation was so thick it could have been centuries old, like Old Man Poole himself.*

She jumped down and rolled to the side, so she wouldn't land on the cat. Already, as she tucked and bowled – Mrs. Smithwick would have been pleased – she found that she was laughing. Uncontrollably laughing. This was it, the final straw.

101

She'd gone mad. Her cat was communicating with her telepathically, was inducting her into a world of petty crime; trespassing, most likely scaring old men, muddying up her jeans and coat. Buried in the long grass, the leaf mulch, the accumulated junk of the years, Sally looked up and saw the black sky. And it looked unreal. Liquidy somehow. She reached out, thinking she could *touch* it and it would feel like a bubble, but she couldn't reach.

Somewhere off to the left, People *mee*'d again and Sally somehow stopped herself from teetering off the edge. She rolled over, hearing her leg *squelching* in the mud as she did so, hearing something else *crunching* too, an antique crisp packet perhaps, or brittle bones; she hoped it was the former. It smelled, however, like the latter. The whole of Old Man Poole's garden may as well have been a compost heap; the stink of rotten apples, dead plants and the sweat of live ones filled the air. The thought of all the spiders, serial killer slugs and other miscellaneous creepy-crawlies which might have made such a place their home (from which they launched their commando raids on her rockery) and which might, that very minute, have been considering creepy-crawling all over her, forced her to climb awkwardly to her feet.

She took a moment to look around. First checking Old Man Poole's top floor windows for signs of movement, and then, when there were none, studying the house in detail. It was the first time she'd seen the house from this perspective, without the big fence in the way. *With* the big fence in the way, Poole's place looked shabby but normal. A squat, dark-looking building whose drains could have done with a good clear-out and whose windows looked as though they might fall out of their flaky frames if anyone attempted to open them. But from here, Sal had a full view of the makeshift extension Poole, or a blind tradesman had fixed onto the back of the house. It reminded her of a shanty town. Walls which struck out at odd angles, a blue tarpaulin acting as a roof. Much of it looked open to the elements, and in fact, it appeared as though nature had started to reclaim it as its own. The hedge which flanked the garden now appeared to be eating in to one of the weaker walls, the one which looked as though it was supposed to be the wall of a greenhouse. She felt a twinge of sympathy for Poole. Clearly he couldn't cope, out here on his own. Clearly he needed someone to look in on him once in a while. Certainly anyone with a heart wouldn't have *left him trapped in such a place.*

102

And a trap was exactly what it seemed like. Sal looked with new eyes on the garden. Began to see the long grass as bars from a cage, the large, dark oak tree a gnarled sentinel, keeping watch. To People, however, it was a playground. At first she couldn't see the cat amongst the undergrowth, her tortoiseshell coat acting as ideal camouflage, but eventually she picked her out by her movement. She was up by the makeshift extension, looked to be running around in circles.

'*People!*' she hissed. 'Come on missus, we're going.'

But People didn't budge. Kept up the strange circular movements. Sally moved closer, and now she could see that People wasn't just running round in circles, she was *playing* with something. Something dead. She was tossing it up in the air to pretend the thing was still alive, trying to recreate the thrill of the kill. Sally steeled herself to go up, wrestle whatever it was from the cat's grasp, and then to drag People back over the fence by the ears if needs be. Anything to get them both out of here, because it felt bad. Despite the freezing cold, she felt prickly heat all over her.

'Come on,' said Sally, 'the fun's over. I've seen you've caught something, now we should...'

People turned round, faced her, and then arched her back, and for the first time since Sally had shoved her in the cat-box back in Cornwall, she curled up her mouth and hissed. Sal took a wary step back. People relaxed a little and tossed her catch in the air once again. And this time Sally saw what it was that her lovely little tortoiseshell was toying with. But it couldn't have been what she thought it was... Surely not.

People tossed again, scrabbled after it, and now the catch landed close to Sally's wellie. She saw the glitter of the gold ring on it as it caught the light. She saw the *nail* on it. Hell, she saw prints. But still she wouldn't admit to herself that what she'd seen was a human finger. But it was. It was a finger. And it was real. She could see the bone and gristle poking out the wrong end of it, the end which didn't have a nail on it. She could see... *Oh God.* She stifled a scream. She felt her knees starting to give way. People growled again, a sound remarkably similar to her satisfied purr, and then she picked up the finger and started to back away. Back into the makeshift extension. The finger seemed to be flipping her the bird...

'No!' shouted Sally, rediscovering her voice. 'No don't!'

But it was too late. People was gone. So was the finger. And Sally realised she had to see Rob *now* or else she'd be gone too.

103

Day Two

8: The Knowledge

The man had an easy air about him as he walked through the woods. He wasn't much concerned about being seen. There was nobody around *to* see him. Never was. The southern woods were no man's land. Had been for years. And yet he seemed to know them intimately. He knew just when to cut between the trees, where to start digging through the foliage, how to uncover the traps he'd laid. He had the knowledge, in a similar way to London cabbies; he'd become his own satellite navigation system. And his knowledge was the kind of knowledge which had been passed down from father to son since time immemorial. Checking on his traps wasn't so much his job, it *was* him.

He was wearing simple clothing. Camo-gear, others might call it, still others would say it was military surplus, and those who read the tabloids would call it the get-up of a lone psycho who had a rather unhealthy obsession with guns. But for him it was his everyday wear. A long black trenchcoat, fatigue trousers, water-proof gloves and black beanie, once-clunky hiking boots of the type you have to endure days of pain as you break them in, as they nibble at your toes, blister your ankles and saddle-sore your soles, before they eventually let you ride 'em like horses.

He walked with a brisk pace but never seemed out of breath. When he exhaled it briefly fugged the early morning air, but it was never the type of raggedy in-out, in-out which would suggest he was in any way exerting himself. He had a long, confident stride which yawned over hidden branches and tricksy patches of mud. A long, confident stride but a weird, bent-forward gait. As though he'd spent the majority of his life looking down and now his whole body was angled that way. He was tall, least for his family, maybe not in comparison to the rest of the world. But then, it was a long time since he *needed* to be compared with the rest of the world. Now, it was only him, and sometimes his pal, Copey.

The man cut through a clearing and paused a moment, removing his gloves. Listening to the stillness. This was his favourite part of the day. And to crown it, he scratched his arse through his fatigue trousers, then reached around front and unzipped. Flopped himself out and for once he leaned backwards as he released an arc of steamy piss into the air. This was freedom. The freedom to do whatever your body needed to do, whenever it needed to do it. And the man seemed so easy; he didn't even have the need to piss *against* something as most men do, even in public conveniences with the urinals, as though marking their territory. He just pissed, because he could. The territory was his already. Not in title or deed, but in spirit. He pissed, and as he did so he looked up for once, turned his gaze heavenward. The hazy early sunlight picked out a couple icicles hanging off the bare branches of the surrounding trees, like wind-charms. And then further up, the greasy grey sky, flecked with a reddish purple.

'Red sky in the morning, sailor's warning,' he muttered to himself, zipping up and wiping his hands on his coat. And he diverted his gaze downwards again, studying the yellow puddle he'd left behind in the clearing. It was still probably cold enough to ice-up in this weather. Hell, he'd already seen some ice a coupla traps back; the thin layer of slightly greenish crystal which topped the old stagnant pond not far from Coverley Bottoms. Yep, it was February, and still cold enough and mean enough to ice-up. It *smelled* icy in the atmosphere. Kinda grated at the lungs like there was glass in the air.

He rubbed his hands together, was about to slip them back into his water-proof gloves when he heard something. Rustling in the bushes about twenty, twenty five feet away, where the trees got a bit closer together and everything got just that bit darker. The rustling sounded too loud to be made by the usual woodland creatures he saw, and caught; it wasn't a rat or a rabbit, or even a badger or a fox.

'Copey!' he shouted. 'Copey, that you?'

No answer. Not even a rustle from the bushes. And the man started to feel a little silly. What was he, a stupid town-feller going about shouting in the woods? Shaking his head, he started walking back across the clearing. There was nobody out here. Never was. And he knew the place like the back of his hand. And there were *always* unexplained noises in the woods.

On to the next trap. So far none of them had turned up even a vole. He reached into his back pocket to retrieve his gloves, meaning to put them on this time, meaning to stop being a pussy-ass. But something stopped him. A lurching, belly-aching, neck-whispering feeling that there *was* somebody there, watching him. Someone or something. He started to move with a new purpose. Instead of the gloves, he reached into his back pocket and pulled out his father's long hunting knife, just to be on the safe side. He scanned the tree-line, searching out the glow of eyes, the bristle of movement, the blur of teeth. And for some reason, he remembered those old scare stories the old man used to tell him about these woods. That they hid things no man nor beast could credit. Things that could stalk you without you even knowing you were being stalked. Things that moved like shadows, which *were* shadows 'til their jaws closed around your neck like a trap.

The man shivered for the first time. And yet, at the same time, a sliver of sweat trickled down from underneath his beanie hat, started to run down his forehead. He reached up a hand to brush it away, and that was when he saw it. Not it, but the *suggestion* of it. The suggestion of where it had just been a coupla seconds ago, like the after-flash of a camera burning in your eyes. Quickly, he removed his hand and peered into the green.

But it wasn't quick enough. Quick enough would have been zipping up and moving on in the clearing. Quick enough would have been calling it a day after the last trap. Quick enough would have been staying a-bed when the alarm clock trilled at four that morning. The man didn't even have a chance to raise a hand in defence, let alone the hunting knife, which he promptly dropped as the great hulking shadow reared over him. He heard the jangling sound of the knife hitting some branch, some stray rock, at exactly the same time he heard the gristly *tearing* noise of the shadow's teeth tearing into his throat.

The Darkness was here.

9: A Doctor Calls

It was only seven o' clock in the morning. Sun hadn't yet crowned a new day. And still Ray Shaw had already been awake five hours. He reckoned it wasn't so much the psychosomatic effect of the coffee which was keeping him awake but the almost constant need to piss it had inspired in him. Mind, it wouldn't have mattered so much if he *had* made a Map of Africa on the sofa in the front room; Maps of Africa was the rather euphemistic term he and the cleaner used for Flick's 'little accidents' (another euphemism), and there were so many of them now that the whole pattern of the sofa's cover had been changed. Had Darwinned out of all recognition from the Rennie Mackintosh-style sofa they'd had couriered down from Glasgow, back when things could still have been rosy.

He was up because Flick was up and he had to keep an eye on her. He was *alive* because he knew Flick would get up and he'd need to keep an eye on her. He'd been asleep on the lounging chair as was his custom now, his only cover a broadsheet newspaper, weeks out of date, his only pillow an old towel which might, or might not, have been used recently to clean up another of Flick's Maps of Africa. He was asleep with his glasses on, and later, he'd wondered whether this was why his dreams seemed to be becoming ever-clearer, ever more visceral these days. He knew it wasn't. He was asleep, but only in the way that guard dogs sleep. With one eye, one ear open. Which was how he'd managed to catch her before she could cause too much damage... If he hadn't been here, if he had followed through on what he'd planned to do with the rope...

She wouldn't have lived out the night. Even in the time it took him to open his eyes, get them used to seeing reality again and not the horrorshow dream-time bonanzas they usually showed; even in the time it took him to thrust the broadsheet newspaper off his lap and then yank himself out of the cold, clammy clutches of the chair,

Flick had managed to turn on the gas on each of the hobs. Had located the kitchen knives he'd believed so well hidden. Had almost broken the freezer door off its hinges. And as he dutifully turned off the gas, and snatched the cleaver out of her hand and the bread knife from the side pocket of her pink dressing gown and somehow managed to wrestle the freezer door back on, he'd asked her, remarkably calmly, what she thought she was doing. And she'd fixed him with a hateful look, as though he really was her jailer, as though he did all of those things to wound her, and she'd said, 'I'm making fucking Sunday lunch, you fucking old cunt.'

And he'd not cried, no matter how much he wanted to. Because even though this wasn't his Flick – his Flick had never even said bloody to a goose – and even though it was still only two in the morning (though it *was* Sunday, to be fair to her) and no lunchtime in anyone's book, he still loved the bones of her. Which was good, because that was all she was now. Bones. She thought him and the cleaner were conspiring to poison her so sicked-up her food like a regular teenage bulemic. And he could have laughed at the irony, because she so wanted to die too, only not at his hands. Not at his fucking, cunting hands. Because in her eyes, in her Solomon-tinted eyes, through the haze his hands were Unholy.

He'd managed to Good Shepherd her out of the kitchen and into the front room. Set her up on the sofa with her knitting and the TV on for company. And then they'd lapsed into a warped kind of parody of his own parents. How they'd be on a Sunday at half past two (though for them it would have been two thirty in the afternoon). There was that same muffled silence between them, broken only by the clack of the needles. Occasionally there'd be a cuppa. Occasionally, one or other of them would react to something on the small screen in the corner. But nothing by way of interaction.

So Ray was quite surprised, taken aback even, when at 07.06, his wife addressed a comment to him. It was the cleanest, sanest, most Flick-like comment she'd made in over twelve months. 'Panthers are quite cute really, aren't they?' she said. And for a moment, Ray thought she'd somehow managed to wire herself into his embattled brain, had seen the things scored, burned, scarred on there from his Lewis Dowsing premonition. And he gulped. How could she have known? He looked over at her, saw her milky eyes fixed on him. She winked. Horribly, she winked.

'Panthers are quite cute really, aren't they?' she repeated. And then she thrust a knitting needle up, used it to point at the TV

108

screen. Where a nature documentary was playing. The good doctor had been so busy watching that his good wife wasn't trying to knit her own nostrils closed that he hadn't even registered what was going on on-screen. But now he saw, now he heard. The whispered, breathy tones of David Attenborough as he tracked a lone black panther through its habitat. Its *natural* habitat.

'The jungle chorus warns of the panther's approach. Howler monkeys howl, birds screech. Though the panther moves like a shadow, his prey are alert to his deadly presence.'

'Deadly presence,' said Flick, her voice becoming a low whisper just like Attenborough's. She slipped down off the seat, shoved her giant's tablecloth of a patchwork quilt to one side and crawled over, in a horribly feline way, to bask in the glow of the television. When the panther strode across screen again, she reached up and stroked it. And somehow, Ray thought it the most horrific thing about the whole morning; her stroking his nightmare. He creaked up from the chair again and went to her. Tried to pick her up, lift her away from the television. *Lying* to her. Telling her she might get an electric shock, when really the only one shocked was him.

It was difficult to lift her despite the fact she was only bones. It was hard to find purchase on her now. Her skin was slippery. And despite it all, she'd still managed to keep those long, muscular legs of hers, which kicked and swam against him like he was the tide. As he pulled, her dressing gown came loose, revealing her goosey, naked flesh underneath. As he pulled and she strained, he could see the outline of every knot and sinew (and bruise too) underneath her pallid skin.

Finally, she acquiesced, and allowed herself to be carried back to the sofa. She whimpered as she went, and Ray was at once sorry for his roughness, for treating his wife, his Flick, like a piece of meat, like a piece of panther-fodder. But once he'd sat her down again, she started talking again. But now there was nothing at all in those milky eyes. It was as though she was a puppet.

'The high-tide of Darkness is coming,' she said. And then louder, 'The Darkness washes in.'

Never had he wanted to slap her more. He wanted to leave a fiery red mark on her cheek in which the prints of his fingers were still distinct. He wanted to loosen teeth, draw blood, knock her out. Shut her cunting mouth up. And he felt his fist clenching by his side.

'The high-tide of Darkness is coming,' she said, again, chanting it now.

'Please,' he begged. Though whether he was bargaining with her, or with that bestial part of himself, he didn't know.

Finally, she stopped. Her tongue lolled out of her slack mouth. Her eyeballs rolled back in her head. She started to emit this low, moaning sound like an off-station radio. Ray forced himself out of the room, made for the kitchen where he found her bottle of pills in the padlocked cupboard. As he picked them up, he caught a glimpse of himself in the reflective surface of the oven; distorted as the image was, he could still make out the frustration which seemed to be seeping out of his every pore. He immediately felt guilty. From the living room, he heard Flick's moaning start to descend into a full-on tantrum.

'Come on Flick-Flick; take your pills,' he said softly, stepping back into the room. And, amazingly, she was good as gold. With the minimum of fuss, she swallowed those tiny red capsules, and within a couple of seconds, that familiar vacant look crosses her face again. No more chanting, no more tantrumming. Just emptiness.

10: The Old Mason house

Lewis Dowsing knew better than to linger by the Old Mason house. The words of his mother rang in his ears, not too subtly underscored by the voices of Mr. Buckby, the newsagent, Jabba Johnson, the headmaster of his school, his friends; the concerned of Limm Island.

'Don't get close to the Mason place,' they Dawn-chorused. 'Avoid it like the plague.'

And usually, Lewis listened to the voices like a good boy. Using the momentum gained from the steep slope of Dye Lane, he bombed past the Old Mason house every morning, barely even pausing to take a proper look at the place. But today was different.

The chain had come loose, and now that he was leaning in to inspect the damage, Lewis saw the clean break in the greasy chinks of metal. He'd been so rigorous in his checks, and his maintenance programme. For it to snap like that, so out of the blue, seemed a *very bad thing*. Like an omen. And now his ginger hair – definitely ginger, not strawberry blond as his mother so often contended – was shining out like a beacon for all to see. The only thing that his father had ever given him was now going to be the thing that got him into a whole world of trouble. And his mother had always warned him that trouble wouldn't be far away if he turned out anything like *him*.

But he couldn't help it. It was in the genes, just like it said in that biology textbook he stole on account of the photo of the woman breastfeeding. He'd seen the one photograph that his mother kept of that shadowman that haunted their every day. A picture from their wedding day; the lanky ginger brute downing a pint. His *first* drug, before the other; the Solomon Mason one. Mother had probably kept the photo just to remind her how bad he really was, case she ever felt like forgiving and forgetting. In the picture, Lewis's father wore the same frown of concentration that Lewis recognised in pictures he'd seen of himself. Same milk-white face too.

111

And now, Lewis felt himself growing paler. He felt the tremor in his stubby fingers as he ran the chain through his hands. And it wasn't just the chill of the wintery air that did it; he was wearing his big Parka after all. No: it was something else that made the hairs on the back of his neck stand on end, forced him to keep looking over his shoulder at the big old house and its tangled garden.

He'd always been *conscious* of the Mason house; remembered how his mother would grip his hand more tightly when they passed it on their round; subtly, but surely increasing her pace as she pushed his little sister, his little *half-sister,* in the pram, him being virtually dragged along at her side. Then there'd been the rumours at primary school. A *bad man* lived there once, went the playground tittle-tattle. A man that could still *do things* to you if you got too close, even though he was dead. Drownded (*yeah, but where was the body?*). And at first those fears, warped by an eight-year old's imagination, all revolved around a vague ideas of darkened rooms and of spiders being let loose on an unguarded face. Later, these ideas were translated into more fixed terrors; generally axes and chopping were involved. And finally, as Lewis hit puberty, he realised that the fears had become tangibly sexual in nature. He didn't know it yet, but the word that he was looking for, and the word on the lips of the *concerned of Limm Island* was cult.

The house was old; seventeenth century, or so the newsagent told him. It was one of two old manor houses on the island, a place where the rich folk lived and reaped the rewards of the countless people working *their* land, fishing *their* waters, and paying their rents and tithes. Built in the valley and surrounded by the southern woods it was not far from the edge of town but seemed *further away,* somehow. It also seemed about five shades darker than everywhere else in the town, despite the fact that it was painted all white. A squat building with a definite classical leaning, it had tiny windows like those of a castle. Or else they were like narrowed, menacing eyes, watching as boys like him passed. Judging. The eyes, along with the porch out front, whose ribbed roof tiles from a distance made it look like a wide, grinning mouth, added up to make the Old Mason place seem somehow alive. And it seemed to speak too. It spoke dire warnings about the consequences for one that got too close. One like Lewis, now.

Lewis screwed up his thin, freckled face and wondered how the hell he'd managed to get in this mess. He could barely even remember... He thought back to when he had heard the adults

112

talking once; Mr. Buckby downstairs with his mother. He'd been going on and on like he so often could about some boring and trivial matter that was just about torture for the young Lewis, perched on the stairs behind the locked door that divided shop and home. Sometimes, Lewis didn't know why he bothered listening to them, but then he always wanted to check whether Buckby would persuade his mother to get rid of him like his father had been gotten rid of back when he was a boy. But Lewis never seemed to hear those terrifying words. Instead, he got an earful of Buckby's complaints about slack newspaper delivery times, the petty pilfering of the schoolchildren (Buckby *hated* children despite the fact that he owned a shop which primarily catered to them) and the fact that the shop's meagre returns barely even put food on the table for him, let alone 'your lot'. Lewis listened on as the man his mother wanted him to call 'dad' described in great detail the lot of a humble shopkeeper. And his ears only pricked up when Buckby began to describe his journey to the cash and carry.

'It were weird, Jan, that's all I'm saying,' he said. 'Like an out of body experience. I don't remember anything from the minute I put the key in the ignition to the moment I was standing in front of the stack of 2p sweet jars. I was worrying about you lot... How I'd cope paying for this school trip you want your Lewis to go on... It was like I'd been on auto-pilot. I could have had any number of crashes on the way there. I could have killed someone... Anything.'

Lewis remembered how scary that idea had been; the idea that you could go ahead and do something as complicated as driving a car – okay, a scabby white van – and not even know that you were doing it. But, he reflected, *his* whole morning had been weird like that. Buckby had been lucky. Nothing had happened to the weaselly, stinky bastard, but Lewis sensed that he hadn't had such good fortune. He'd been ambushed unawares *when his mind wasn't properly on the job.* Punished for his terrible, terrifying thoughts.

He'd been thinking about the heavy newspapers – local ones in which all the talk was of the day's talent show, national ones in which all the talk was of bigger, televised contests - in his big, luminous orange paper bag; the one that he still got teased for doubling-up and using as his school-bag. Specifically, he'd been thinking about the red-top papers; the ones that his mother never used to have in the house before they'd gone over, lock stock and two biscuit barrels, to move in with Buckby above his filthy shop.

And more accurately, he'd been thinking of a certain page within those newspapers (or smut mutts as his mother still termed them).

Stealing glances at the page three lovely was an unexpected bonus of Lewis's round. Because he was nominally part of the newsagent's family now, he'd been given the longest, most torturous morning delivery route; the one that none of the other kids haggled for, despite the Christmas tips. And because his route was *expected* to take longer than everyone else's, he always factored in the time to shuffle through some of the seedier papers - the ones he delivered to the row of council houses which were rather optimistically called 'the estate' - and allow himself to memorise the images for later. Lewis's was the route that took in Summit Farm at one end of the town, and the mead factory way, way over to the other. The route took in countless hills – the monastery on Pate Hill no less – and couldn't have been done without the use of a proper mountain bike, and even then, any less than a good twenty, thirty gear one would have been useless. Luckily, Lewis loved bikes, and spent basically every penny he ever earned on 'souping up' his Trekker, with some help from Yoghurt Rhodes. In fact, there was only one thing that he loved more than his bike, and that was the page three stunnah.

That morning, he'd been thinking about his wonderful new plan. Up top of Pate Hill, not far away from the looming walls of the monastery, were some old abandoned huts. They'd once been a kind of National Trust visitor centre, but had long since given up the ghost and had gone feral. Recently, some local youths had busted-in the door to one of the huts and it had half-yawned, open to the elements for the past two, three days. Lewis's new plan involved creeping into that hut and allowing himself the freedom to take a closer look at Beth from Bath's bazookas, or Nancy from Nuneaton's nauks. Calling up into his mind the recollection of that picture was never the same as the thrill of actually having it right there in front of his eyes, he suspected. Sometimes, flicking through the paper, Lewis thought he'd just about explode, but he was always wary that Buckby would somehow *know* what he'd been doing. One of the customers would phone up and complain, or Buckby himself would catch him at it, on one of his *hush-hush drive-by checks,* which Lewis knew that the newsagent regularly performed on his delivery boys. But now there was the privacy of the National Trust hut, all those worries could be put to one side.

And Lewis had finally grown the balls to do it that morning. In that piss-stinking, insect-soaked, lager can-strewn freezing hut, he'd choked the chicken. He'd beat his meat. He'd strangled his one-eyed snake. In full view of the pretty Paula from Preston, whose puppies of the chest variety were almost full-grown rottweilers. Paula from Preston whose view of the conflict in Afghanistan was that it was 'stupid' and 'why can't we all just get along?' Lewis's splattered criticism may have showed that he agreed with that, although he wasn't sure about the bit where she said 'the only good thing about wars is that there's far more men in uniform, and everyone likes a man in uniform.'

Lewis's uniform was the pretty much standard paperboy-garb; the Parka for warmth, the fingerless gloves for dexterity; the tight jeans that wouldn't get caught in the pedals and would also negate the need for cycle-clips (Yoghurt was always telling him about the benefits of cycle-clips, but Lewis thought them stupid). And almost as soon as he'd finished, and the guilt set in, he realised that it wasn't the kind of uniform that someone like Paula would be impressed by. Certainly, she wouldn't have been impressed by the foolhardy, unprofessional way that he'd shot his muck all over the *Super Sport* newspaper he was now supposed to deliver to number 24 Groby Crescent. Certainly, she'd have had something to say about the way that he'd now coated the material of the fingerless love of his right hand in 'the gloop' as they all called it at school.

'What the bloody-hell am I going to do?' Lewis gasped, the weight of guilt now pressing even heavier into him. Gloop was now congealing onto Paula's prominent puppies like mayonnaise left out on a chip wrapper in the blazing sun. Black writing from page four could now clearly be seen, as though tattooed on her flat stomach. Quickly, Lewis removed both fingerless gloves and threw away the one that was already glooped-up beyond repair. With the other, he carefully tried to dab at the picture of Paula. He knew better than to scrub. To scrub now would be to tear the page. To make what he'd done even more obvious. To make the customer's call to Mr. *Fuck*by even more necessary.

With the wind rattling about the corrugated iron of the garage roof and fair battering at the mostly closed metal door, Lewis tried not to panic when he thought about the consequences of his horrendous, *warped* actions. But the image of his mother's disappointed face and her red-rimmed eyes wouldn't leave him. With a desperate sigh, he wondered how he could call his mother's face to mind so easily, when thinking of one of these girls was so difficult. But then, that was the root of all of his problems, wasn't it?

The gloop wasn't coming up properly. Although most of the *thick* part of it – the frogspawny bit – was now bunched up in the fist of his fingerless glove, the wet part was left behind, discolouring Paula's frilly knickers. And her nipples were smudged. Despite all of his efforts, the nipples didn't look right any more. It was as though they'd been horribly stretched now and were hanging onto the magnificent precipice of her boobs for dear life.

Frantically, he began to blow on the paper, thinking that he'd once had to dry out his homework in this way after his sister Grace had spilled water from the glass with her thick paintbrushes in it. Thinking that his mother's hair-dryer had worked then, but that the air that was pumped out then was warm, and he just couldn't get his breath anything above freezing, despite the fact that it *appeared* hot because of the fogginess or it in the hut's cardboardy coldness.

Finally, a quick look at his watch told him that he couldn't stay in the garage any longer. He could almost hear Fuckby's voice carrying on the wind, rattling on the old boards on the windows, 'We'll be sending out search parties if he's not back from his round in a minute. Boy's always dawdling. Always ballooning around.'

Lewis thought about simply removing the whole page and pretending that it had never been there in the first place. When in doubt, deny all knowledge. Make like Bart Simpson. But Bart Simpson had never wanked all over the Porters' *Super Sport,* had he? And Bart Simpson had never seen the size of Gerry Porter, had he? Gerry Porter looked like a man who could sit in the middle of his goddamn front room and drain the old main vein whilst staring-out Paula from Preston and not even care if his damn spotty wife came in and caught him at it. Hell, he probably got said wife to yank his chain for him when he couldn't be bothered, while *still* glaring at Paula from Preston as though he was going to rip her tits off because she thought that the conflict in Afghanistan was 'stupid.' He probably felt strongly about such things even though he couldn't get off his sweaty arse to join in and fight in the war. He would definitely feel strongly enough to come on down to Buckby's Book-Buys on main street and splatter his criticism all over Buckby's face, in blood if needs be. And then Lewis really would be out on his ear, mother or no mother, sweet little Grace or no Grace.

'Just leave ignore it,' he breathed.

It was a standard Dowsing reaction. Ignore what's right in front of you until you are blue in the face. Maybe it'll dry properly in the bag. Maybe nobody will ever know. Admitting to it, whatever *it* was, was simply inviting punishment which *might not* be required.

And yet, despite the powerful desire to simply forget all about it and trust to fate, Lewis found that he couldn't think of anything else. Despite the speed with which his legs pumped the pedals, he couldn't stop imagining the embarrassment of his discovery as an abandoned-National-Trust-hut-Tommy-Tanker.

'Shhhiiiiiiiitttttttt,' he growled, as he descended from Pate Hill at a speed which may well have been dangerous. But better to crash and burn than fade away into above-shop torture for the rest of his days.

Lewis remembered that thought now. It was the last thing he remembered about his ride. And now, his concern about the ruined newspaper only exacerbated the sense of fear about the Old Mason house over his shoulder. But deep down, some cowardly – like father, like son – part of him could reconcile himself with what might happen to him at the house. Some part of him secretly *wanted* to keep trying to fix the chain because if he was found dead, all butchered-up, then nobody would care about his masturbation, and certainly they'd all feel a little guilty about giving him such a hard time. He imagined even Buckby might say, 'Perhaps we should have cut him some slack,' as he stood over Lewis's decapitated corpse on a mortuary slab. Or Jabba Johnson might say, 'He was a good lad, despite robbing that biology textbook.'

But the biology textbook had taught him certain things about what pain looked like, as well as what was held beneath a woman's dress and bra. It had shown him what was *inside* the body. What could be damaged. And even the thought of his own heart, racing away inside of him, made Lewis feel a little faint. Even the thought of kidneys and lungs and muscle and bone made him feel somehow protective of himself. And he remembered the screams that his mother had made in the night, after what had happened to his father had happened, even though he'd only been very little at the time. He remembered how his mother turned *grey* for a while. Like a ghost. How she barely even mustered the energy to talk to him until one night, when her breath smelt sickly sweet and he knew she'd been sneaking drinks from the bottle in the locked cupboard in the kitchen. She'd her little boy on her shaking knee and asked him,

'Son, what do you know about pain?'

And Lewis had shown her a great whopping scab on his knee. He had been proud of that scab; it showed that he was now big

117

enough for big-boy's bikes; he'd never cried after that fall... But his mother had grabbed at the scab. Yanked it off his knee. Lewis had expected blood to spurt out all over the place and was shocked to see that it didn't. There was just fresh skin underneath.

'That isn't pain, son,' she said, 'that's just growing-up. Pain like I'm in can take over your life. Make you wish you'd never been born. He's left me. Left me with you and I just can't do it...'

Pain and the memory of his father's passing had always been inextricably linked for Lewis. And even the thought of what his father had been through made him stop and think. He couldn't just loiter here and invite whatever was in that house to come out and get him. He had to get away. Embarrassment, like that he faced over the *Super Sport* wankfest, would eventually go away; pain – real, *drowning* pain - was something you couldn't just walk away from.

He renewed his efforts with the bike. Took out the faulty link and then tried to knot the rest of the links back together. Nothing doing. He blew out his cheeks in frustration. The chain wasn't an easy-fix. Wouldn't have even been an easy-fix for Mister Bike himself, Yoghurt Rhodes. Certainly it was not an operation he could perform on the pavement, with his big orange paper bag leaning right up against the wall of the Old Mason house.

And inexplicably, he found himself becoming hard again, down there. Maybe it was the sheer powerlessness of the situation. Or some warped, background memory of Paula from Preston. Whatever, Lewis found his penis straining against his tight jeans.

And then he felt something else. He felt something watching him. Something watching him through the gap-toothed fence of the Old Mason House. He *felt* the eyes on him like a heavy weight on his shoulder. And then, as his erection quickly flopped, he started to move. At first wheeling the bike along with him and then simply letting it fall, and running full pelt. Running for his life. His lungs screamed for air. His breath rasped. He didn't dare glance back.

And then he tripped. His knee jarred against the asphalt of the road. His face came down on it hard too. A tooth chipped. He bit his tongue. Tasted coppery blood. Gurgled. Turned, tried to clamber to his feet. Couldn't. He was shaking too much. He flopped back down again, as though he was playing dead. And then, out of the corner of his eye, he saw it. His punishment. His pain. And it was worse than anything he'd ever seen in his life. Worse than war. And then he *could* scream.

118

11: Cinderella

The mobile phone was having a temper tantrum. It was vibrating so foam-at-the-mouth violently it had started to spin around on the desk like an angry breakdancer, scattering invoices and receipts every which way but loose. Somehow, it seemed even more insistent now Ruth had flicked off the accompanying ring-tone in one of the few brief respites from the calls. So far, she'd ignored seven - was it eight? - calls. All from a with-held number. And who had a with-held number but someone trying to mask their identity, someone trying to trick their way back into her life?

Vicar looked on questioningly, but seemed to sense the tension and didn't start barking as he usually did at repetitive sounds like the beeping of the microwave, the buzz of the alarm clock or the shrill call of the malfunctioning burglar alarm. Absently, Ruth reached down and scratched the back of his neck but he backed away deeper under the desk, confused. He was a shelter dog and Bowie knew what hell his previous life had been like, but the same went for her, didn't it?

She called him Vicar because of the little patch of white fur on his throat. Otherwise he was a hotchpotch of blacks, greys, browns. She'd picked him out straight away; the women at the shelter certainly knew how to tug on the heart-strings, telling her he'd been 'locked up longer than any other dog we have,' and that everyone usually took the 'cute puppies' instead. They said dogs looked like their owners, and if so, Ruth and Vicar were a perfect match; both were long-limbed and rather clumsy, both had that sliver of sadness in their eyes, both hoping against hope for a new start in life.

The phone continued to drill into the desk. 'It's okay, Vicar-baby,' she said, but the dog knew a lie almost by instinct and he

119

started to give off his habitual low, groaning sound. 'Singing', Ruth rather euphemistically called it. Now his ears were pricked back, the long mongrel fur on his back rose up like he was a descendent of the Spinosaurus, he bared his teeth. Ruth knew that no matter how many treats she gave him, how many times she neglected to punish him for traipsing mud all through the guest quarters of the hotel, this back-against-the-wall reaction would be the same every time he was confronted with something new or troubling. Sometimes he even reacted like that when he was dreaming; he'd be all tucked up in his basket in front of the lovely open fire and suddenly he'd start whining, scratching frantically at his collar, biting at *nothing, thin air* and then 'singing' that same mournful, hopeless Johnny Cash song to the moon which was still present in the early-morning sky.

She knew she should have simply turned the phone off, prized off the plastic cover (probably breaking a nail in the process), removed the battery and the SIM, destroyed said SIM, ordered a new one online with a new number attached, and started again. But something deep within her told her she couldn't keep running at the merest hint of danger. Couldn't go through this whole rigmarole every time a number she didn't recognise flashed up on the phone's display. It didn't have to be *him* calling. It could have been a tricksy telesales company who'd got her number from some database or other and were calling her over and over again, knowing *nobody* can resist a ringing phone forever. *But this early? Come on Ruth.* Okay, it could have been the police, or Bowie-forbid, a hospital; that at least would explain the urgency at this time in the morning. It could have been a disgruntled customer... but the Seahorse hadn't had many of those. Not *real* ones anyway. And the fact the phone was raging so, as though it were somehow channeling *his* relentless, white-knuckle energy, seemed to weigh more in her decision-making process than any other possibility.

The mobile froze, mid spin-cycle. Ruth sighed deeply, knowing it was only a matter of time before it started up again. She ran a trembling hand through her hair and sighed; soon, the hair-loss would become obvious, even to men. Already, women had noticed, she was *sure* they had. Not that they said anything, of course, but she could still tell. After they'd seen her in the right light (perhaps as she stood taking their order for afternoon tea, framed by the window with the merciless sun shining through, exposing her egg-shell pate) the women treated her with kid gloves. They acted overly kind (one woman even going as far as taking away her own breakfast plate and starting to wash it up). And when they left the hotel, as their husbands were negotiating the rickety credit card machine, they'd give her hand a squeeze as though to say *I hope you'll be okay.* It was clear they thought she was ill. Was on *the treatment.* What other reason would there possibly be for a woman in her late middle-age to be (go on, say it) going bald?

The mobile cranked itself into a spin once again and suddenly Ruth saw the phone's anger and raised it. 'Fuck you,' she seethed, picking it up, ready to toss it into the food disposal chute in the kitchen or to decapitate it in the shredder or to flush it down the loo. The list of ways she'd already murdered her mobiles was as endless as it was inventive. She'd once gone so far as replacing the battery with smelly crab meat and left it on the harbour wall, then watched through binocs as a monstrous seagull picked it up and then repeatedly dropped it back onto the concrete as though trying to break the phone/crab's carapace to get to the meat. The seagull had eventually given up, of course - it took the genius of an Einstein, the strength of a Hulk Hogan, the touch of a Phil Collins *Easy Lover* and the patience of a monk to open the cover of a mobile phone after all – but not before the screen had been smashed to smithereens. A swift toe-poke to the keypad had caused it to go spiralling off into the sea, where hopefully, a passing whale had sucked it up like the meaningless plankton it was, shitting it out somewhere even colder than Limm Island like the Arctic perhaps.

'Come on Vicar-kins,' she said, suddenly making a decision. 'We're going for a run.'

Vicar looked up at her, pleading: *you're not tricking me are you? Don't wind me up like this.* His tail banged manically against her leg; *please let this be the truth.* Swiftly, Ruth pulled her leg away. She didn't like the memories the dull, repetitive thudding dredged up; memories of the time she'd woken up in bed with Christian and found him masturbating furiously at her side, his fisted penis smashing into her thigh with each stroke.

She forced a smile. 'No joke, Vicar-baby. I need some fresh air. I need to get my head straight.'

Unable to contain his excitement any longer, the dog dropped to his haunches and started to drag himself along with his front paws, leaving his back legs *and other things* trailing against the wooden floor. Clearly, he enjoyed the friction. His face collapsed into a toothy, drooly, eye-lid curled gurn. Ruth tried *not* to think how much it looked like the doggy approximation of man's 'sex-face'.

He started to yip and gurgle; Ruth had to tear her eyes off him. She was uncomfortably aware of how *sexual* Vicar was. How, to him, every piece of furniture, every guest or member of staff he encountered, was simply something else to rub his crotch against. Sad thing was, she'd had him done, so all this was in vain, or else it was just a habit-thing, like Christian's masturbation was. She placed a hand on his horribly rigid back to calm him. His hair felt too wiry, too pubic. Still, she tightened her grip and then, as he slowed and she could feel a low growl echoing through his body, she attached the lead to his collar and secured him to the desk all in one swift, liquid move.

Despite the fact it was still dark outside, she pulled the curtains to and then started to get undressed. She pulled off her corduroy trousers and stepped out of them, uncomfortably aware that Vicar's eyes were still all over her. She tried to convince herself he was just looking at her, that there was nothing sexual in the way he was whimpering, but somehow, the only way she could continue was to turn her back on him, something she felt incredibly guilty about. She felt incredibly stupid too. Was this the kind of prude she'd become? Scared to be seen in her underwear by her bloody *dog?* What had happened to the woman who skinny-dipped in the lake out front of her university, in full view of the whole faculty, on the day her exams had finished? Whoever that woman was, she was long gone now, and she'd taken with her some of Ruth's most precious belongings; those key tenets of the women's magazines, self-confidence, pride and *hair*. That woman had unthinkingly (okay, not unthinkingly, quite maliciously, with the confidence of someone who hoped they'd die before they get old) ruined her hair with that constant dyeing. She'd shattered her self-confidence by reading too many books and then she'd run off with pride (run off to bleeding Gretna Green for a sham marriage which was always bound to go bust). And now Ruth had no pride left. If she hadn't lived in a hotel, she'd have removed all mirrors (*smashed them into submission;* she'd already taken the seven years' bad luck as it was).

She kept her running gear in the bottom drawer of the filing cabinet behind the door (underneath the terrible watercolour she'd tried to paint). Kept them so close, so handy, they'd become like her escape hatch, her coping mechanism. Tight-fitting black leggings of a scratchy material which made it very difficult to stand still comfortably in them. *Good; all the better; helps force that extra mile when the thighs were burning.* A Bowie tour t-shirt which had been washed so many times it was about as threadbare as her hair, and as grey too (once all the dye washed-out). A thick blue fleece which bore the Combs' Mead logo. The most expensive items in the whole ensemble were the running shoes. Good, hardy Rick Rogers' Nikes. Despite the battering they'd taken over the years, they were still in good condition. She took the time to clean them rigorously, much as her dad had cleaned his old football boots on the back step in the old days every Sunday afternoon after the match. The smell of Sundays for her had always been the greasy, oily smell of dubbin rather than Sunday roasts, and she supposed that had a lot to do with making her the woman she was today. Apart from the obvious, she looked after things. Looked after things so well she'd get an extra few years out of them instead of replacing them at the merest hint of trouble. And she'd never really bothered with Sunday lunches either, just like her mum.

She pulled on her gear with the minimum of fuss. Vicar knew better now than to interrupt her. He must have recognised the signs; the way she went over to that great lump of desk (a desk so knotted and gnarled it could have still been alive and living well as a tree) and unplugged a few wires and pulled out her Ipod. The way she checked through the track listings to make sure there was enough Bowie on there (there always was; tracks didn't just remove themselves from Ipods, no matter how 'lost' they appeared to be.) The way she paused, thinking... *anything else?*... and then went over to the mini fridge on the windowsill looking out over the bay, and pulled out the ribbed bottle of ice cold water – L'O - which she shoved in the pocket of the fleece. The way she reached down, calmed him once again, and then unhooked the lead and said: 'Come on boy!'

Yeaaaaaahhhh, sung Vicar, wagging his tail as though it was a demented wind-screen wiper. She led him out of the office, pausing briefly at the kitchen door, through which she could hear the first sounds of movement; the clattering of pan-lids, the fizz of the first oil in the frying pan, the slamming of the fridge door. Roberto the chef was here. She slipped past before he could ask another of his interminable questions about hygiene. 'We'll let him get on with it, hey Vicar-kins?' she whispered.

And then she stepped out onto the cold streets of Limm town and immediately felt calmed. It was strikingly cold still, but ever so delightfully quiet. So quiet she could hear the buzz of the streetlights and the soft rattle as the gentle sea washed against the shingle shore. So quiet, she could hear her own heart beating inside her head. It beat a tune of freedom; the same tune which had driven her here in the first place. She was free. Free to go for a run while it was still dark at 07.16hrs. Free to go out in a ridiculous blue fleece which was at least three sizes too big, and leggings which were two sizes too small. Free from Christian's constant digs.

Vicar was already straining at the leash, but Ruth reined him back in and allowed herself a moment to look out over the bay. Without people cluttering it up, it really was picture-postcard pretty. It *fitted in* with nature, not like cities which kicked nature into touch, laying claim to the land with a giant fist and saying, like Jonathan – *oh Jonathan* - once used to say whenever he touched *anything*, 'mine!' There were no high-rises staining the horizon here, no night-clubs, no vandalised cars, no dead bodies. It looked every inch like a small town in a child's picture book, or like *Heartbeat*. At this time in the morning she could imagine little wonderful small town-types asleep in their nightcaps in the rooms above the shops, all about to waken-up and marvel at the new day. She could imagine it a place full of quaint village fetes and dances on the village green (and not a place which thought a bloody TALENT-STRAVANGANZA!!!!!! was the height of culture). She could imagine the Ship being the centre of the community, instead of the doggerel, cranky place she'd discovered it to be. At this time in the morning, it seemed quiet and friendly enough for Postman Pat to deliver letters and for someone jolly like Mr. Benn to own the shops, like The Crab's Claws or Buckby's Book-Buys. It looked as though Bagpuss might reside in the lifeboat station. Hell, even the rival hotel, The Castle, looked, well, if not exactly pretty, it *scrubbed up nicely*. From her perspective, she couldn't make out the 1960's monstrosity which had been attached to the rear end of the Georgian manor house and stuck out like a sore thumb. In this liminal world, sore thumbs did not exist. That terrible man Adrian Devonish did not exist.

And then she swung round to look at her own place, the Seahorse. Sure, it had an unpretentious exterior, but that was in keeping with the rest of the village. It was a terraced row of low-slung, two storey buildings which had formerly been fishermen's houses. Four years ago, when she'd come here, the houses had fallen into disrepair and she'd been able to buy four of them for a song, or at most, as much as *three songs* on the karaoke machine in some London bar-stroke-eatery. She'd hired local contractors to knock the walls through to form one long building, and had assuaged local worries by keeping the traditional red sandstone exterior. What she'd done inside – turn it into a boutique hotel – was nobody's business but her own. Hers and her customers. Even in darkness, the place seemed inviting. All year round she kept the little star-lights in all the windows. One window displayed cakes and all manner of Roberto's goodies, another showed off a museum/ art gallery collection of *interesting* pieces of wood and shells; she'd always been a beachcomber and wanted to show the villagers she was one of them, despite her accent which said otherwise. She had a tasteful menu and wine list in a frame by the door, right next to the star from the local tourist board (it was far from her only recognition in the hospitality industry, but the only one she felt she needed to shove up people's – or one particular person's – nostrils.) She noticed she was still displaying a poster which advertised last month's charity event in aid of the lifeboats (and to celebrate the 1135th anniversary of the landing of the Viking invaders on Limm in 875). She chuckled at the arbitrary nature of the anniversary – were they going to celebrate the 1136th and the 1187th anniversaries? - and then set herself a mental reminder to have Jared take it down. Then made a second mental reminder to remind herself not to get him to take it down. She had to be very careful what/ when/ how she asked him to do anything...

She set off jogging and Vicar groaned with happiness. Ruth did too. As she ran, she thought about Vikings, and what she'd send them out to do if they ever happened to land again. She'd give them a list; first, she'd have them rape and pillage the 1960's extension to the Castle until nothing was left but a pile of miscellaneous breeze blocks, like some warped echo of the broken-down monastery on the hill. A symbol for all to see of the Ozymandian folly of fucking up her view from her top bedroom skylight. Next, she'd have them give Wagger John from the village shop, The Crab's Claws – why *did* they call him Wagger? She'd never seen him miss a day of work in four years – a warrior's funeral in order that he would stop selling her the cigarettes she clearly didn't want. And then, she'd get them to cut off some of their lovely long hair so she could make it into decent extensions. In return, she'd let them use her dining room as some kind of Great Hall, where they'd regale her with stories of the high seas. Maybe David Bowie could play the part of the head Viking. Over the Ipod speakers, Bowie's *Rebel, Rebel* suggested he might be a little difficult to persuade, just like dear Jared.

She ran.

It was still too early for sunrise, but already it felt like another storm was coming. Ruth was amazed how clearly she felt it, as though being here for four years was enough to tune her up with the rhythms of nature; it was like at university, when she and all four of the girls she'd lived with had all started to have the same menstrual cycles. She'd become a part of something bigger than herself. It was miraculous; once you turned down the volume of modern life, the kinds of ancient knowledge and experience which could be *just sucked up into the bones.* A regular barometer, she sensed thunder. Sensed a *proper* rainstorm (a Limm Island rainstorm, not one of your poxy city ones) was needed. Though the sea had been wild for the past few days, the harbour was all clammed-up with seaweed. It would come, the wildness, and hopefully it would wash away some of the tension in her (and in Vicar too, and, well, everyone on Limm.) Despite the cold, the past few days had seemed too full of electricity. Everything, it seemed, was on tenterhooks. Snappy. There needed to be a release. And not the goddamn talent show…

She ran. Already, her too-big fleece was sticking to her in all the wrong places; she could have wrung it out and given Vicar a drink if she so chose. But that would have meant stopping running, and she didn't want to stop running. When she was running, he didn't have to think about things. Oh sure, memories and thoughts nagged at her but she could pummel them into submission simply by slamming one foot down in front of the other. When she was running she didn't care what she looked like. Sinewy muscle flowed through her long legs as she pumped; her stomach tensed, for once spirit-level flat; her arms, flapping wildly by her side, spoke of inner *and* outer strength. Her face was a grotesque mask of concentration; she was determined to let her body breathe. Vicar was the same. He was *steaming,* such was the exertion, but his eyes looked somehow more alive than the doll-eyes which looked back at her in her office. This was his time too. They'd already left the town-proper in their wake; they'd vaulted over the rickety stile and onto the coastal path which they both knew so well that the near darkness didn't bother them. But she wouldn't have advised any of her guests to follow them. They wouldn't know about the parts of the path where the sea had eaten away at the cliffs so hungrily that the unaware runner could suddenly find herself on the edge of a mighty precipice. They didn't know about the always-slippy part near the old stream where a woman could turn her ankle, despite the fantastic support from the

126

Rick Rogers'. They didn't know the places where they might get dragged into the thick southern woods. But Ruth felt the contours of the land in her very bones. She knew when to dance around rabbit-holes and where to duck to avoid overhanging branches. It was second nature. She belonged.

She flung herself over ditches and through densely wooded patches and Vicar followed. Occasionally, she'd hear sounds from the bushes; nocturnal creatures escaping their mindless dash. Perhaps they sensed her single-mindedness and feared they'd be liable to be crushed underfoot without a second's thought. Or perhaps they saw in the mongrel Vicar the foaming jaws of a killer.

She zig-zagged up the slope of Brennan Mound and then back up to Pate Hill, where she weaved through the ruins of the monastery. Tumbledown archways, crumbledown halls, fallen stones; it was a wonder the National Trust hadn't fenced it off. It would come soon, this closure; health and safety was invading every aspect of everyone's lives, despite the fact that here, within the skeletal structure, things like government and local council seemed as far away as the monks who had once inhabited the place.

Every so often, as she rounded a pillar, she was met with the sweeping panorama of the sea, which almost gave her pause. The sea was both old and full of knowledge but new and threatening too. It told stories of old shipwrecks and of dashing pirates; of warships departing for battle and of wedding cruises. It held a million dreams and a million lives within it but couldn't speak of the mystery that lay deep inside; just a whispering as it brushed gently against the rocks at the bottom or the rattle of shingle on the shore. She imagined what the monks would have felt, busy brewing their mead one day 1135 years ago, when the sails from the Viking ships came into view. Back then, as the local guidebooks told her, the monks used to think if the soul was God's business, keeping the body strong and Milky Bar tough was the job of mead. She wondered whether, in those final moments, the monks hunkered down and prayed for their souls, or whether, like most men she'd encountered, they reached for their *other* God, the booze. She was pretty certain that when the Vikings did finally climb up the steep slope of Pate Hill, they'd have found the poor old monks sozzled, gourded, seven sheets to the wind. As if in denial of this, she thought she caught sight of a crouched figure – just a thin shadow – underneath one of the archways. Before the figure disappeared into the ether, she thought she caught sight of the pale, worried face of a very young monk. She thought she caught sight of his flowing brown robes. She almost thought she caught sight of his hands clasped together in prayer. But as her heart leaped, and as Vicar growled, the apparition faded and she told herself how stupid she was being. This was 2010, not 875, and *ghosts most definitely did not exist.* Hell, of the three; God, monks, and mead, only the mead remained.

Making sure that the body remained fortified with mead was now the job of Combs' factory, down the hill to the left. As yet, work hadn't started for the day and the chimneys weren't pumping out their meady smoke into the air, so she had a pretty clear view of the mainland. Only a mile or so away, a five minute run, and yet, if you missed the road, if the tide came in, that five minutes could stretch to eight hours. Unless you had a boat, or were friendly with someone who had a boat. Or had the patience to wait for one of Crabbie's boat taxis.

Yes, distances could be measured in *time* as well as space. It took her only a couple of minutes to reach Cawdor Head from the monastery, but it felt like a year on the calves. Even Vicar looked to be tiring now. She pressed on in a sprint until she reached the cliff edge and then she paused, the last person on the north east coast of England, the only person that far north east on the whole measly map.

On top of the cliff, she performed a few stretches and Vicar performed his ablutions. He seemed to wait to do it until the first signs of a pink glow started to float on the horizon, ruining the moment. As he shat, the sea basked in the sudden introduction of a new day as though it had never expected to see the sun again. Finished, Vicar wagged his tail, gave a couple of short, sharp barks and generally indicated he was raring to go again. Breathlessly, guiltily, Ruth turned her back on the sea, stole a surreptitious look around her to check whether the ghostly monk (or anyone from the dog-crap police) was anywhere to be seen, and started to run back down the path as it gently snaked down to the village; the village which nestled in the bay like it was trying to hide from something. When she saw the thousand-or-so little houses, she saw lights on in some of the windows. Finally, the rest of the town had decided to join her that February morning. She wondered how they could have missed out on so much.

Of course, she'd always been an early-bird; a 'lark' as her father used to say, usually while he was cleaning his football boots – it was about the only time he found time to talk to her. He thought she'd grow out of it in her teenage years, but if anything it had got worse. It got so bad that some days, her dad used to ask her whether when she got up of a morning, she met herself going to bed. He sat her down one evening and told her the diagnosis. 'There are two kinds of people, Ruthie,' he proclaimed, as though imparting the wisdom of the ages; a wisdom that had eluded other, much more lauded philosophers than him. 'There's night owls and there's larks; you're born either one or the other. You gets no choice in the matter. You're like your grandfather was. He always wanted to be first down to the factory in the morning, no matter how many he'd sunk the night before... drinks, I mean. He was up with the larks come rain or shine. Other folk are night owls, of course, and the two of them don't really mix. Night owls prefer to go to bed late and get up late; often they're only going to sleep when you're getting up to see the sunrise. If you were born late at night you become a night owl, but if you were born early in the morning, as you were, you tend to be more of a morning person and want to get up and go running at silly o'clock in the morning.'

In a place like Limm, old wives' tales – or rather, old men's' pub-tales - had a habit of seeming more real than in other places; places which ran to more artificially-defined clocks. In a place like Limm, Ruth could almost believe that her morning lark ways, and Christian's night-owl prowling had been the fundamental reason behind all the problems.

Ruth realised too late that she was thinking too much and plunged even faster downhill back into the town as though she was running away from the ghostly monk. The soles of her Rick Rogers' running shoes slapped against the concrete as she hit the road; the sound of Vicar's raggedy breathing filled the air. As the sun finally rose, she charged past The Ship as though hoping that this forward momentum could never be stopped. She'd run through the sea if she had to just so she could forget.

At the village, instead of turning left and circling back to the Seahorse, she turned right onto the coastal road. She'd already checked the tide tables that morning and knew the road would *just about* be released from its prison at this time in the morning, and part of her wanted to see just how far across to the mainland she'd dare to go. In four years, her record was halfway across, but getting that far had spooked her and she'd barely even set foot on the causeway since, let alone crossed it. It was as though, for her, the tide was permanently in.

129

But today she felt the need to keep running. And the coastal road was flat too, which meant it was easy to keep going. Keep going and going and going until all of the excess energy and worry was sucked out of her and replaced by the oblivion of exhaustion. Once she passed the last lagging house of the town she was left alone on the road. After that house, the road meandered around the western side of the island until it reached the causeway, and all she had for company were the gulls. When the tide was out, the causeway was flanked by mudflats, which provided a rich range of food for birds, making it a twitcher's paradise; the sheer variety of fantastically-named birds on display was staggering. Ruth knew; she'd been given the full list by the eager birdwatcher's who often took up residence in the Seahorse. They'd reel the list off their tongues as though they were reciting words from a play, or rather a pantomime or a cartoon, because the more she listened, the more she thought the mysterious birds sounded like characters from fairy tales; Merlin, Dunlin, Wideon, Pintail, Dopey, Sneezy and Bar-Tailed Bashful. They were the seven dwarves and a few friendly magicians to boot. Like in the stories she used to make up for Jonathan...

Up above, the birds cawed and shrieked and marvelled at the fact the sea had once again provided them with a mighty feast. Down below, on the road, the only sound was Ruth's Rick Rogers' trainers slapping on the pockmarked tarmac (if the coastal road had been a city road, the council would have been strung up, for Bowie's sake, but here, nobody seemed to mind the fact marram grass was growing through the cracks and sand got everywhere.) A lot of the birds seemed distracted today though. Many were gathered around the common area where one of the litter bins looked as though it had been attacked by a panther or something. The black bag had been torn from the bin itself and scythed open. Now crisp bags and empty cans of pop were scattered along the sides of the road. She *almost* thought about stopping and clearing up the mess, or about running back for a camera and taking photos, then emailing them to the local bigwig, Manny Combs, the owner of the mead factory and The Castle hotel (and also, wonder of wonders, the town mayor; wonder how he managed to get himself elected into that plumb role?) But she'd emailed Combs before, bent his ear on many an occasion, and he never seemed to listen. All he was bothered about now was building his damn bridge.

130

The bridge was this aging politician-cum-businessman's last grand but misguided gesture, an old man's need to leave his stamp on the world after he popped his clogs. His idea to bring Limm, kicking and screaming, into modernity. To put the islanders, the townspeople, within touching distance of the rest of the world and all of its benefits. But Ruth only saw the drawbacks for such a scheme. She didn't want to worry *he* might be able to pay her a visit twenty-four hours a day, just the hours when the causeway was open and fit for use was bad enough. And a bridge would have spoiled the environment, would have taken away the uniqueness of the island. Would probably ruin the hotel. Both hotels. All the bridge was was a nod to Combs' legacy. Women didn't need to worry about that sort of thing. Whatever happened, she still had Jonathan. Or, rather, she'd had Jonathan, and now he was somewhere else.

She needed to stop thinking about anything. If even non-existent bridges made her think of her son, then she had to clear her mind of everything. She ran harder. Faster. Threw herself into bends and plunged into the dips in the road. At her side, Vicar panted and wheezed but kept going. Finally she made the causeway and paused a moment to stretch. Peered under her viewfinder hand sailor-style at the other side, about a mile away. She thought she could pick out Trevor Knox's National Trust land rover parked up, the only vehicle in residence.

'What do you think Viccsy?' she gasped. 'Think that's Trev's landie? Think he'll come over and do something about all the litter?'

Vicar whined, scratched his ear. Let his tongue loll out of his mouth.

'Or is it David Bowie, finally come to help me run the Seahorse?'

Vicar flopped down onto his belly, still panting. His tongue rolled up, almost into a straw so as to suck in the air sharper and quicker.

'What do you think, Vicks Vapour Rub? Fancy having Ziggy Stardust doing your brekky in the morning and scratching your belly at night, eh? Do you reckon he'd carry a pooper-scoop?'

Vicar seemed to doubt it. Seemed more interested in sniffing at a small insect, or maybe a crab, which was crawling past his field of vision. He slapped a proprietary paw on top of it and then winced in pain.

131

'Come on, you great lump,' she said. 'No point letting the muscles relax. Let's get going again.'

Vicar looked disappointed but climbed to his feet anyway. His eyes seemed to contain all the sulkiness of a teenager. Jonathan would be a teenager now...

She started running again, yanking the lead and almost choking him, but eventually he came, bounding away on those great long mongrel legs of his. Running onto the causeway was strange. The first few times Ruth had run on it (not far, not even half-way then) she thought she'd never get over the weirdness of running on a road which was wet with seaweed and sand, which had rock pools instead of puddles and seafood roadkill rather than the usual rabbits, toads, cats and dogs. Talk about the difference between surf and turf... At the half-way point was a little hut on stilts. It was little more than an umpire's chair in tennis, used for the coastguard to deposit rescued tourists while they went back for everyone else in the car, but it had still proved, over the years, as mighty as a fortress to Ruth. *Thou shall not pass,* it seemed to say. *This road is not for thou.* And yet today she ran past it. She ran past it without even looking back to check whether there was anyone inside ready to leap out at her. She ran past it with the wind in her sails and determination burning at the soles of her feet.

It was getting lighter all the time, and as the other side of the causeway yawned closer she kept up her pace. She kept up her pace despite Vicar sniffing forlornly at a discarded can of gin and tonic. *A can of gin and tonic;* what class of litterbug were they dealing with here, for Bowie's sake? She kept up her pace despite the fact Vicar's breath was growing ever more raggedy. She kept up her pace right until the moment she found the man's shoe right in the middle of the road.

The shoe looked so out of place she just had to stop. It was positively sparkling new, a brown, snakeskin-leather thing which, though wet, looked remarkably intact. It didn't look as though it had been washed ashore after years at sea; looked as though it had simply been thrown onto the causeway overnight. There was a bit of seaweed poking out from the foot-hole, but that was about it. No limpets had attached themselves to the sole. No hermit crabs had nested inside. She stopped, crouched down. Vicar shouldered in to take a closer look, sniffing at it cautiously before backing away.

'What is it Vicks?'

He growled, not an uncommon reaction, but still, the shoe was unmoving, not beeping or vibrating like most of the objects he took against. Ruth picked up the shoe, sniffed at it as Vicar had. It smelled only of sea. She shook it, to see whether anything would fall out. It didn't. Then she looked *inside* it, to see whether there was any kind of name-tag on it (when Jonathan first went to school, she'd been asked by them – *she'd* been asked, not Christian, talk about assumptions – to sew little name tags into every item of clothing he possessed; even his towels, even his PE pumps). But then she realised how silly she was being. Vicar gave her a funny look. This was a man's shoe. Size nine it said on the sole.

She found herself tying the shoe by the laces around her neck. Vicar made a funny gurgling sound and it was almost as though it was laughing at her for her flotsam and jetsam ways.

'Oh, I know I'm being silly,' she sighed. 'But I don't know... I just think whoever lost this shoe would probably want it back. And you never know, that person might even be staying at the hotel... Oh, stop looking at me like I'm a complete idiot. I don't really think that this is David Bowie's snakeskin shoe. This isn't Cinderella. For one thing, if this was a fairytale,' she said, pausing to ruffle his pube-style hair, 'I wouldn't have a dog like you, would I? I'd have like... like a Great Dane or something.'

Vicar whined, choir-boy style. She rubbed his head again until he wagged his tail. And then she turned and started running back to the village and to the Seahorse. Back to reality. She would have forgotten the shoe completely were it not for the fact it consistently bumped into solar plexus while she ran, as though it wanted to remind her of something.

12: WTF

Everything about Sunday breakfast was making Kirstie feel decidedly nauseous. The pungent stink of the kippers, mixed in with burned toast and over-brewed tea sent her guts into an Olympic gymnastics routine; the exaggerated, visceral way her dad, Mal, clamped his jaws around the toast – *caaarrrrrruunnnncccchhhh* (loud as a hyena's vice-jaws crushing bones, as loud as the thing with the *chasing eyes* would have been) - made it seem as though she was performing said gym routine on a boat on the high seas in the middle of a thunderstorm; the way he stared at her as he masticated, rolling those overtly masculine jaws around as though they were on pistons, made her want to grab onto something just to stay afloat. She felt sick as a dog; green about the gills; *pregnant.*

Her dad was as prickly angry as he always was these days. She could smell the pub off him; the sickly sweet smell of last night's alcohol. It came off him in waves which were almost visible, like in a cartoon. It didn't take much for her dad to fill a room, he was a big bloke after all, looked like a rugger player, or as though he weight-lifted the barrels of mead at the factory of a lunch-time, just for fun. But here in the kitchen which was not much bigger than a ship's cabin – they had to fold up the table in order to open the washing-machine door – it was unbearable. He was wearing his usual work shirt and tie tight enough to choke him. Certainly his cheeks had become thunderclouds, ready to erupt at any moment.

They should have had the radio on; a bit of music or some DJ chit-chat would have filled-up all the tiny little spaces which fitted around her dad's moodiness. But the radio had run out of batteries and Wagger John's only sold the dock-off ones that went in the big ghetto-blaster things like they had in the eighties and didn't have any of them double-A sized ones which *every* device made since the dark ages used for power. So it was silence instead, interspersed occasionally with his crunching.

Caaarrrrrruunnnnnccccchhhh, he went, again. And she almost jumped out of her chair. He looked pleased by her reaction. A grey, lizard tongue poked out of his mouth and licked his lips. Missed a vital crumb in the crevice between his bottom lip and his chin. Kirstie tried to resist the urge to point it out. Instead she returned to her bowl of cornflakes which now looked more like wallpaper paste than cereal. She tried to spoon some of the gloop into her mouth, felt the sickness again (reminded her of Mammy Goose dead on the A24) and clattered the spoon back into the bowl. Wished she could just go back to bed.

'Well?' he said, through a mouthful of toast, spitting out crumbs, 'you going to explain about last night then?'

She hunkered down into her chair and tried to make herself as small, and hence as *not pregnant*, as possible. Pulled her dressing gown cord tighter around her belly. She felt it digging into her, but didn't stop. She winced... And her dad recommenced the crunching, the watching. Letting his eyes lazer into her like something out of *Star Wars*. She fiddled with the salt cellar, but soon Mal reached across the table, his eyes never leaving her face, and extricated it from her grasp, slamming it down so hard on the table some of his tea spilled out of the top of his mug.

'Not a word all breakfast,' he said, his voice rising in volume with every word. Getting so loud that it shook her mam's collection of ornamental teapots on the windowsill (neither her nor her dad had a collecting bone in their bodies). 'And you didn't eat your kippers neither. Looking at the state of you, you were out on the tiles last night. What have I told you about that?' He shook a head thick with the same dark hair Kirstie possessed. He'd always had longer than short, but shorter than long hair, her dad. Always in the same style. Sometimes, like now, it seemed to pop back into fashion for a while - *surprise!* - occasionally inspiring her friends to believe she had a *cool* dad for a while, until he had one of his explosions. Explosions which were generally sparked by something she said or did, or didn't say or didn't do. Or even her just being in the same room as him.

He jerked his chair back. The back legs screeched against the stone floor. The washing machine rattled in its too-tight space. Kirstie caught sight of herself in the reflective surface on the cooker (the only reflective surface left in the kitchen now neither of them cooked or cleaned like mam had: the over-used kettle's stainless steel surface now looked as though it was made out of plasterboard.) She saw how her dad had come to the conclusion she'd been drinking. The bags under her eyes made it look as though she'd taken a couple of hefty right-hooks in some dance-floor cat-fight, her hair looked as though it had been dragged through a rock-pool backwards, her chin was wobbling horribly. And she saw where the fat would go once the pregnancy showed itself properly. On the cheeks, on the chin(s), on the jaw. Pregnant, she'd look almost exactly like this lunatic who purported to be her dad.

'It's bloody ridiculous is what it is,' he yelled, standing over the table.

'I wasn't out-out,' muttered Kirstie. 'I was out, but not out-out... I was...'

'You were what? What were you doing?' His breath smelled like dragon-fire now, like God's fiery dragon-breath from on-high. She had to back away from him, almost back as far as the kitchen wall. Almost as far as the old height chart her mam used to update on Kirstie's every birthday. Pencil scribbles on the wall marking the back of her head as she grew. The last mark on the wall was only three and a half feet high.

'Nothing.'

'*Nothing?* Is that all you can say?' He slammed a fist down on the table. 'Your sisters were never like this...'

Kirstie felt a sudden, laugh-at-a-funeral style urge to scream back in his face, *Yeah, well, I was buying a pregnancy test... No, not one measly pregnancy test, as many pregnancy tests as I could afford, from bloody Salvadore's bloody Pharmacy in Newcastle because I thought that was just about far enough away so you wouldn't get to hear about it. Salvadore – greasy old bastard that he was - thought it was okay to feel me up buttercup while he was giving me 'the talk' about contraception before he gave me the tests. Thought it was okay because I was already, in his eyes, and yours too, probably, a fallen woman... Oh yeah, and before I forget, to get to Newcastle, I stole my boyfriend's car (the boyfriend you don't know about) and drove it without a license. On the way back, I managed to kill the mam of a family of geese, leaving the rest of the family to fend for themselves (sound familiar?) and not only that, I caused one of your trucks to jack-knife across the A24 and then we may or may not have been chased by a bloody great big bloody black panther thing. It's on the island now, probably gearing up for the hunt. How do you like them apples?*

'I just... I lost track of time, that was all,' she said in a small voice. 'I didn't mean to be late.'

Mal snorted so loudly the cutlery jangled. He kicked the table leg, tried not to wince at the pain. 'Don't be so obtuse,' he said, tossing in a complicated word just to prove how mad he was.

'It won't happen again,' she sniffed.

'And on top of everything else I've got to worry about, you're lying,' he said. Then he started to count his worries off on his thick fingers, this little piggie style (he used to play that with her way back when, laughing and joking all the while, but that had been before her mam had passed, before everything had changed). 'We got Dangerous Dan Dennison calling in sick *all week* so I have to work the weekend, Joe Friar rolling in late for the pick-up, almost missing the bloody road, Manny Combs on the warpath, apparently... I don't need you staying out all hours at the same time.'

She felt tears pricking her eyes. Tried to stop herself. But in her frazzled state it seemed a physical impossibility. Just like her dad's thundery anger required a release, so did the gradual water torture of the past couple of days for her. She felt a tear slide down her cheek. Felt her throat constrict. Screwed up her toes, clenched her fists, tried with all her might to make that the last one. But the effort merely drained the last of her resources and soon she was full-on crying.

The crying seemed to shake him out of it a little. He paused, ran a beef-joint hand through his hair. She sniffed. He cocked his head. She desperately tried to rub her eyes. His started to melt.

'Look, I know you think you're old enough to make your own decisions these days,' he said finally. 'I know you think you got it all worked out up here.' He tapped the side of his head. 'But while you're under this roof...' He paused again. Contemplated the destruction he'd inflicted on his usual neat pile of six slices of slightly burned toast. 'God what am I like? I sound like my old mam...' His face softened. 'I do worry, Kirst... All I ask is that you tell me where you're going. That sound fair?'

It sounded more than fair. She was lucky her dad's anger burned itself out so quickly. That he couldn't hold a grudge with her for more than a few minutes before remembering her mam... While she saw *him* in her face, he only saw her. Always had. It was the reason all of her photos from the local school were tucked away in the miscellaneous drawer in the kitchen (along with the blu-tac, sellotape, takeaway flyers for places which wouldn't deliver to Limm, and a few handy miniatures) and not on the wall or mantlepiece as in any normal house. She nodded her head. Wondered how he'd possibly react to the knowledge she was pregnant. Wondered just how much toast and tea (and later, miniatures) he'd destroy before that anger lost its spark.

'You working today or are you off to that talent show thing?' he asked, trying to change the subject, as though changing the subject was possible in their house. The words might change but still, underneath everything either of them said was the sorry subtext of her mam and what happened to her.

'Got a later shift today.'

'Oh. Right.' He stood awkwardly now, as though unsure whether to sit back down again or simply leave for the day. But leaving for the day five minutes early would go against his set routine. He *always* left at 7.48 because, right, it took him twelve minutes to warm the car up, fiddle with the radio, drive across to the factory and then sit in the car park and stare out into the sea for three minutes before clumping off into the factory for another day's grind. (Kirstie knew; she'd followed him and watched him do this on at least three separate occasions.)

'Do you want another brew?' she asked.

Mal considered the question a moment, then shook his head. He clumped over to the back door, a stable door, and opened the top part of it. A wet, gusty wind blew in. Kirstie had a flashback of when she was little, when it was her lifetime ambition to be able to see over that part of the door; her on her dad's shoulders looking out, pretending to be a race-horse waiting for someone to come along and groom her. Pin a ribbon on her blouse or something.

'There's a storm coming,' he said, quietly. 'I can smell it.'

Kirstie sniffed-up. Couldn't detect anything but fresher air, sweeping away the stale beer fumes he'd left behind. But perhaps he wasn't talking about a physical storm, perhaps he was talking about the storm inside her and him which was surely coming. Any day now. Her period still hadn't come and now the only thing for it was to do the tests. She climbed up from her chair and ambled over to stand with him by the half-open door.

The house was an old fisherman's cottage, and had seemingly been built back to front. While the front of the house led to a farm track which led nowhere the back of the house looked out

138

onto the bay. Kirstie had always wondered why they'd built the house like that, as though it was turning its back on the sea, but had come to the conclusion that it was because the fishermen worked the high seas all day, and hence wouldn't really want to be reminded of it at night as well. Above the bay, she could see the looming ruin of the monastery. Once upon a time her dad used to tell her stories about the monastery, how it was still known as the New Church, despite the fact it was over two hundred years old. It was desolate up there, like looking back through time. Even looking closer to home, into the town and its small row of touristy shops and arcades, the pubs and the Seahorse Boutique Hotel seemed like looking into a picture-book.

And if madam would care to look to starboard, she could pick out the other hotel across the shingle beach like the second bookend mirroring that of the Seahorse. The Castle Hotel, her place of work (and Rich's too). She didn't like to look at it now, just as the fishermen didn't like to look to the sea. Its awful 1960's extension reminded her of her perv-alert of a boss, Adrian Devonish, because it was ugly and stuck out like a sore thumb and everything. Even the land behind it, gently sloping grassland pockmarked with molehills, rising into undulating hills crowned with mist reminded her of pervy old Devonish; the deep purple heather at the top of the cliff thick like his Brian Blessed-a-like beard. Going to work there had been the start of all her problems.

No: it had come earlier than that even; quitting college had been the spark.

'Nice day for it,' she mused. Her dad shuffled, adjusted his tie and nodded, clearly not listening. It wasn't a nice day by any stretch of the imagination. It was typically grey February day. A mouldy-old-sock-stuck-behind-the-radiator day. Everything looked as though it needed to be wrung out, hung up to dry. The two of them stared out into the monotonous drizzle, not even wishing it away, just staring. Lost.

Mal snapped out of it first, slapping his hand onto the top of the stable door as though he'd just moved a chess-piece and was jabbing at the clock to say it was time for his opponent's move. 'Righto,' he said, taking a quick glance at his watch. 'I'll be off now then love.' He leaned over and gave her his customary peck on the cheek, ruffled her hair a little as he would have done had she been a boy, had any of them been boys, and then said, 'Look after yourself, eh? Take a bath or something.' He slipped on his work shoes and then he was gone, swinging out through the stable door and down to the car, head hung low, the weight of the world on his shoulders.

Kirstie watched him go and then slippered back to the table, started clearing away the plates and tea mugs, wiping the table. Performing her usual skivvy duties, getting everything shipshape again despite the fact her eyelids were starting to droop badly, despite the fact her legs were killing and she already felt as though she'd been on her feet for about a week. But she wouldn't be taking a relaxing bath as her dad had advised. Wouldn't be luxuriating in the bubbles eating a Galaxy. Wouldn't be getting her toe caught in the tap so she had to get the sexy firemen out to come see about rescuing her. No, she had a job to do. Once she'd tidied everything away into the sink, she tucked away the table and creaked open the door to the tiny pantry. Slipped inside. She ignored her work uniform which was hanging behind the door and instead reached in behind the mountain of tins (her dad always thought every storm was going to be a hurricane and hence stocked up far more than was necessary) and pulled out a plastic bag containing her filthy, wet clothes she'd been wearing last night. The bag was already giving off a musty, oily aroma. She held her nose as she carried the whole lot through, performed the usual rigmarole of positioning everything *just so* in order that she could open the washing machine, dumped everything in, whites and colours, and whacked it on boil wash. Then, after checking whether Mal's car had really left, she grabbed his big yellow rain mac from the coat stand and bolted out the stable door.

She planned to walk back across the causeway and up to the trucker's rest stop on the A24, to get Rich's car back. Should have done it earlier really, but she'd not dared go out while it was still full-dark and there was a chance she might bump into that rough beast she'd seen last night. Now she'd had a chance – all bloody night, in fact – to think about it, she'd come to the conclusion she'd definitely *not* been imagining those *chasing eyes*. And sure, she should have told someone about it, but she already knew what they'd say to her. They'd tell her she was being a silly wee girl. And they wouldn't pay her the blindest bit of notice. She'd also decided, during the long night of waiting, that maybe the beast was a *good thing*. Like, maybe if it did start hunting things on the island, it might act as a pretty good distraction, a cover-up for everything else that was going on in her life. She didn't want to meet it on a dark causeway, but if someone else did, and all the townspeople started

140

fussing around, like they had when that Manny Combs announced his plans to build the bridge and there'd been all sorts of protests, well, that would suit her fine.

She knew she was wrong to think such things, but then she was wrong in a lot of her choices these days. Coming to understand she was a plain bad person wasn't actually the shock it might have been. Her dad had been telling her it for years and now the perfect storm of the pregnancy (not even an if or a maybe any more, even though she'd not taken the tests; *couldn't*, they were still in the back of Rich's Gunner) the road rage and the great goose-massacre, simply confirmed it for her. All those lies. She hung her head as she walked, watching her feet squelch in the morning mud. As though she was performing penance.

She was still thinking about choices when someone crashed slap-bang straight into her, almost knocking her right over into *another* ditch. The other person gave a little yelp of surprise and then the other person's dog yelped too. Kirstie lifted her hood, a quip about people minding where they were going on the tip of her tongue. But she stopped herself when she saw it was Ruth Sharp, the woman from the Seahorse hotel. Ruth got a hard time from everyone on Limm, it seemed, and Kirstie felt a little sorry for her. It wasn't *her* fault she ran a hotel on her own as a woman and that the hotel she ran was actually miles better than the island's original hotel, The Castle. The other reason she stayed her tongue was because she was hoping she'd eventually be able to wangle a job there; surely Ruth Sharp would employ her pregnant or not; once she started to show, she doubted Adrian bloody Devonish would. Even if she did look as though she was on the way back from a night on the tiles Ruth would give her a job, surely. It was all women together, wasn't it?

'Oopsy daisy,' said Ruth, pulling a smile out of the bag. 'Are you all right, love?'

The dog, a funny mongrel rat of a thing with great long legs, made a funny gurgling sound in its throat.

'No harm done,' said Kirstie, reciprocating the smile. Now she could see past her embarrassment, she realised she had no need to feel bad about her appearance. Ruth looked far worse. She was dressed in running gear; nice trainers, sure, but woeful leggings, a tent of a fleece jacket and... And her hair. Kirstie suddenly realised she'd never seen Ruth without a hat or head covering of some description, but today she was bare-headed. Almost literally. Her hair was so thin it was barely even able to cover her scalp. There

141

was a bald patch right where her dad had one. What topped off the all-round tramp look for this season was the fact she appeared to be carrying a man's shoe dangling around her neck like it was a bouncer's ID lanyard. *WTF?*

Almost immediately, Ruth seemed to sense Kirstie's judgement and her hand started for her hair, as though trying to cover it. And Kirstie understood that there was something *wrong* with the woman. Something medical. Immediately she felt guilty for categorising her as a tramp. Felt she should say something kind.

'It was my fault anyway and I wasn't looking where I was going and... They're nice trainers I always tell myself if I got a nice pair of trainers I'd go out running... Do you like running I like running... and you've got that hotel looking very nice by the way.'

'Thank you,' said Ruth. She looked awkward just standing around talking, as though she wanted to get running again. But then she pulled a face as though she'd just remembered something, and said: 'You're up early for a Sunday, love. Are you going to do the talent show later? Can't you sleep? Nervous energy and all that. I do hear you're a singer.'

'How do you... No, I can't I have to work.' She pulled a face.

'Oh unlucky. I suppose the contest could have done with some genuine talent, otherwise it'll just descend into a cute kids competition. Or worse, that PE teacher from the school'll win with that awful comedy act.' Ruth smiled, then: 'Or what if that Devonish fellow chances his arm at juggling or something, eh? Wouldn't that be *awful?*'

Ah, thought Kirstie. *Another member of the Adrian bloody Devonish hate-club.* The two women flashed each other real smiles of understanding. '*Bloody* awful. A massacre,' said Kirstie, and then she realised she was probably tempting fate by saying such a thing, what with a mad, hungry, dock-off cat on the prowl. She gave an involuntary shudder.

Ruth Sharp must have read the sudden change in Kirstie, must have seen the clouding-over in her features or something. 'Are you okay? You look as though you've just seen a ghost?'

Kirstie rearranged herself. Offered up her best, blustery smile. And Ruth seemed to buy it, taking the smile as a cue to start chuntering on about nothing in particular, about the bridge, or about Manny Combs, or about her bloody dog. Kirstie gave up listening, just pretended again. She was good at pretending things. And especially good at pretending things weren't happening. At forcing herself to be as ignorant as people always presumed her to be because of the way she looked (or used to look.) Kept up the charade by talking as though she was just a common or garden Kirstie, unaware of stuff like consequences. She'd perfected the art to such an extent that she could even play ignorant with herself. When she'd walked out on college, for weeks she'd persuaded herself she was just on the extended sick, recharging her batteries, even though at the time, she couldn't imagine going back there again. It was easy; just ignore all the phone calls and letters and Mal's questions, keep her head down and weather the storm. Now, even while Ruth Sharp continued to blether on, all she could think about was the creature with the *creeping eyes,* and whether *it* could see through her pretence.

Ruth Sharp's mongrel dog yanked Kirstie out of her reverie. He was sniffing at her feet and scrabbling his balls across the floor at the same time. Ruth yanked his lead with a 'sorry about this,' and tried to get him to stop. 'I'd best get this one home. Vicks'll be hungry for his brekky-kins by now and I've taken him on a right royal ramble this morning.'

Kirstie was confused, but decided that she'd be best off not trying to understand the woman. She seemed a bit like one of those mad cat women only she didn't have a cat but a dog. Maybe she couldn't have children or something... Maybe that was why she had a dog she seemed to speak to it as though it was her little boy in them walking reins... Maybe she *needed* a child. Maybe Kirstie could *give* her *her* child.

Ruth started doing limbering up exercises at the side of the road. The dog did some of his own, trying to hump the poor woman's nice running shoes.

'I'll be off then, nice seeing you Mrs... Miss... Ruth,' said Kirstie.

'Ruth's fine... I hope I'll see you at the Seahorse soon, Kirstie... maybe you can sing a few numbers or something,' said Ruth, mid-stretch.

'Really?' said Kirstie, 'I'd love that.' (*And for an encore, you can have my baby...*)

'Okay, well nice chatting...'

'Uh-huh. Nice bumping into you,' said Kirstie, and instantly regretted it. It sounded like she was taking the piss. She walked on quickly, putting her hood up and slipping back into disguise. Her

143

feet starting to crunch on shells and pop on seaweed thrown up by the tide. The tarmac becoming gritty, sandy. Wet too. She reached the causeway without bumping into anybody else and was glad of it. She was starting to feel guilty again. About everything. And the only way to counter that was to walk faster, so her legs burned with lactic acid. A voice in her head piped up: *Why does the goose-killer cross the road? To get to the other side, to return to the scene of the crime.*

She fished around in the pocket of her jeans, desperately seeking the familiar plastic cover of her mobile, desperately wanting to call Rich, to hear his voice, to hear his usual irritation, because even that would be better than hearing the mocking voice in her head, the voice which told *sick jokes* like that. But she came up with nothing other than the new, familiar feeling of there being nothing there. It was strange; she wasn't like most of the girls she knocked about with in that the mobile was like a ball and chain in her handbag. She rarely used hers, only one or two of the mobile companies, Aircom and Walkermob, even got reception on Limm, and even then that reception was intermittent at best, collapsing into static in the middle of important calls, mislaying text messages... Hell, sometimes Kirstie *ignored* the calls that came through, like the ones from the college after she did her disappearing act, and when that got too difficult even switched it onto 'silent' and hid it away in her pocket. It was only a slip of a thing anyway. And yet now the phone wasn't on her, wasn't to hand, she craved it like she'd craved cigarettes last night.

She reached the other side of the causeway hardly remembering a single step she'd taken on it. She'd been so lost in her own head she'd not even registered the cold, but now she did. It seemed like one of those seeker missiles, finding the gaps in the coat and hood and exploding inside her, chiselling her cheek-bones, chapping her lips, making her wish she'd wrapped up warmer underneath. Still, she was here now, and after tapping the tide tables signpost for good luck, she stomped up the small B road up to the A24. From there, it was only a few hundred metres or so until she reached the trucker's rest point where she'd left the Gunner.

She could smell the greasy onions and shoe-leather burgers burning on the griddle of the JAX SNAX van even as she darted across the A24. And as she walked along the hard-shoulder she couldn't help but look down into the ditch, thinking *I've swum in that.* And also thinking, it's probably healthier than the crap from the snack van. Now, as she reached the lay-by, she could see exactly what the crap they served in decrepit-looking van with its runny-egg yellow paint did to a person. The customers, various assorted stony slabs of men were congealing on buckling white plastic garden-style furniture immediately in front of the van, looking as grey as reconstituted meat, sweating grease. Only a couple of these truckers even looked up from their frenzied shovelling of the food down their throats as Kirstie approached, but *both* of them wolf-whistled, as though it was an automatic response. One of the whistlers flashed her a gap-toothed smile, the other winked.

She walked past, breezily, holding her head high, determined that she wouldn't let them unnerve her. And she was doing a very good job of it too, thank you very much, until she suddenly *was* unnerved, only it wasn't the men doing the unnerving, no matter how many greasy comments they shouted amongst themselves. It was the sight of the horribly skewed bike which was leaning against the side of the snack van which got her. The bike which she recognised as belonging to poor Yoghurt Rhodes, the church youth club leader, cycling proficiency tutor and sometime photographer. Her bunch of friends had mercilessly teased Yoghurt throughout his school career, despite him being a few years older. But she'd always had a soft spot for him after what had happened with her mum. Not the kind of soft spot which inspired her to ask the bullies to stop with their tormenting him, but the kind of soft spot which meant, when she saw his familiar racer looking so badly smashed-up, *as though he'd been run over, like the Mammy Goose,* she stopped, turned back to the flabby customers of JAX SNAX and asked: 'Whose is that bike? Why's it here?'

One of the men, obviously designating himself as their official spokesperson, scraped back his chair. Got up. The chair remained bent at the knees. He rubbed his hands on a napkin which looked both oilier and tomato-saucier than his hands were in the first place, slurped from his polystyrene cup of dishwater tea, looked as though he was going to gargle with it too, but didn't. And then, finally, answered. 'Found it,' he said, waving a hand vaguely. 'Off up the road. Was sticking out the hedge. Saw it and thought I'd do it up for my lad. Why, is it yours, duckie?'

'No... I thought... But why's it smashed-up so bad?'

The man shrugged. His chequered shirt strained around his massive belly. 'Accident? Dunno.'

Kirstie couldn't think of what to say.

145

'Look, duckie, whosever bike it is doesn't want it now. Why else was it chucked in a hedge?' Then his face began to soften. 'I wouldn't worry about it. Looks like fairly small-scale damage to me. Nothing a few belts with the hammer won't fix. Wheels are warped, that's all. Whoever was riding the bike, well, put it this way, they weren't hit by no rig. Would've caused far more damage than that. Looks to me like it wasn't even a car. Just a minor accident, that's all. Probably whosever's bike it was just couldn't be bothered fixing it up, eh?'

Kirstie wasn't sure. Much as she wanted to believe the trucker, the evidence of the past twenty-four hours had her pretty much convinced that it was a shit, shit world, and in shit, shit worlds, people could get knocked off their bikes in hit-and-run accidents and all the driver would do is try and hide the evidence, chuck said bike away into the bushes and drive on, giving it barely a second's thought.

The man put a beefburger of a hand on her shoulder. She longed to shrug it away. 'Shall I fetch you a nice cuppa?' he asked.

Suddenly she felt exhausted. She wanted nothing more than to get away from here. Get in the Gunner and just do one. Without replying, she turned her back. She picked out Rich's car nestled amongst the larger lorries and she made directly for it, ignoring the trucker's shouts of, 'Oi, come back!' and 'You can take the bike if you really want it.'

She reached Rich's Gunner, his Millennium Falcon, and for an awful moment she thought she'd left the car keys in exactly the same place as her mobile (she could picture that place now so clearly it was frustrating: so close, so clear she could almost have reached up into her mind's eye and picked them up from the kitchen table.) But she found them in the back pocket of her jeans. She opened the car door and was greeted with the ripe smell of cigarettes which had been trapped inside overnight. She wafted her hands around a little, achieving nothing in particular, sighed, and then climbed in, wincing at the sight of the big white Salvadore's Chemists bag on the back seat. Slid the key in the ignition and whacked the heaters on full, both to warm her up and because the air-con always gave off a whiffy smell which might just cover up that of the cigarettes. She clunked the car into reverse and moved off, paying no heed to the trucker in the chequered shirt who was frantically waving to her as she passed.

13: The May Queen

They were playing knockout whist, sitting on fold-away plastic chairs behind the counter of the shop. Judging from the number of hands that Devon Buckby had already won, he was either cheating or Janice Dowsing's mind wasn't on the game. She sat shivering, despite her fleece, as Buckby slammed down yet another ace, trumping her pathetic leading three of clubs. Breathing heavily, he collected the cards and stacked them neatly in line with the others he'd won.

'And Buckby could be on for a white-wash here,' he said, mimicking the commentator's low tones from the Radio Coast's football programme. 'Dowsing just has no answer to his dashing card-play.' Then, more quietly, trying to inject an air of tension, he pulled his cards close to his chest and whispered, 'And now he can win it. What has he got up his magician's sleeve this time?'

Janice ignored Buckby's histrionics. She was used to them. She was more than used to the strange way that he commentated on everything he did. Like stacking the boxes of crisps in the store room; she fair shuddered when she heard him then: *'And Buckby goes for the big lift now. Gritting his teeth, he strains under the weight... Will he make it? Surely nobody could lift* that?'

There were times when she wanted to shake him out of his self-delusion. Times she just wanted to walk out that door, leaving him looking puzzled at the chime of that pathetic little bell which always rang just that little bit too late to warn them that someone had entered the shop. Once upon a time she'd been a somebody; Limm Island May Queen no less. She'd been swept off her feet by the strapping fisherman Collie Dowsing, sure that he was a man in her class; sure that they'd be seen as the island's equivalent of the prom king and queen. Only, she should have seen it coming that very first time she met him. When he fell off the big carnival float that was behind her official May Queen chariot. He'd been dicking around,

147

entertaining the crowd with his obscene gestures, but was clearly drunk too. Back then, it had been funny, but the joke soon wore thin.

Buckby placed his final card on the counter with an elaborate flourish, as though he was placing a sacrifice at the altar of the god of cards. *Here is my offering, ye mighty. Now, let me beat this damn woman as is written in Card Lore.* He looked up, tried to meet Janice's misty eyes. Tried to grasp the moment of victory. But she wasn't playing the game. She didn't even look at the card he'd played; simply tossed her own card on top of it and sighed.

'Hold up,' said Buckby, picking up her card. 'Was that a heart? Did you have a heart all along? If you had a heart, you had to play it when I led with a heart. You can't just…'

'Where's Lewis?' interrupted Janice. 'It shouldn't take him this long to complete his round, should it?'

Annoyed, Buckby looked at the stop-watch which was hanging from a knotted string around his neck, groaned in frustration. 'That's one hour, twenty three minutes, forty five… forty six seconds. An unwanted record for the lad.'

'Shut up, Devon.'

Buckby leaned back in the fold-away chair. It creaked in complaint as he spread his fat arms wide. 'Now hold on a minute here. He's your son. It's not my fault that he's performing so badly in the paper delivery time trials.'

Janice simply shook her head. She felt trapped in the poky little shop. Buckby's Book-Buys, he called it, but there were no real books in sight. 'Books' was the term her partner used to describe the smut mutts that littered the shelves; the red top papers she'd never have allowed to cross the threshold of their old house on Vale Row, the ridiculous cross-word mags and worse, the pornos on the top shelf. She'd *told* him to stop selling them so many times and yet he never listened to her. The whole situation was ridiculous. Sometimes, she'd wake up next to that great fat lump of a man and she'd wonder how the hell she'd got there. But then reality would sink in. He'd wake up too; sweaty hair all over the place, piggy eyes straining to see because he'd not yet put his glasses on. And usually, he'd say something like, 'Buckby limbers up for the morning rumpy-pumpy session. He's straining at the leash…' Fifty seconds, and much rolling about and cursing later, he'd say, 'Good morning dear. Have you parcelled up the papers yet?'

Catching a glance of her reflection in the shop window, between the postcard-adverts trying to sell *almost new* budgie cages and Subbuteo sets, she realised that these days she couldn't ask for much more from life. The whole thing with Collie had ruined her looks. Somehow, she could never get any life into her hair any more. It just hung limply off her head like it had given up. What had happened to that magnificent Hydra-head perm she'd had on May Queen Saturday? What had happened to her *eyes?* They had a look of defeat about them too, as though they'd cried too many tears way back when. Shocked, she peeled her eyes away and stared back at Buckby.

'Where is he? Can't you go out and look for him in the van?'

'Not in this mist,' he said, picking up a coffee mug and peering inside. He'd finished it *hours* ago now, it felt. Did he think that coffee mugs miraculously filled themselves up again? 'That would be plain stupid. Wouldn't see the end of the road let alone any other road-users. "Unless the journey is strictly necessary, don't go out"; that's what they said on the morning weather. And who am I to argue?'

'It's drizzle,' she said. 'I listened to exactly the same weather as you. There weren't no warnings.'

'Yeah... Well maybe there should have been,' he said, sulkily. '*Feels* like there's a storm coming on, eh? And just in time for His Majesty Manny Combs' talent sh...'

'Hush,' said Janice, 'don't mention the *you know what in front of you know who.*'

Their daughter Grace had been banging the TALENT-STRAVAGANZA!!!!!! drum for days now, *weeks.* She'd been up with the larks this morning too, like it was Christmas day, bouncing up and down on their double bed, pleading with them to take her down to Coverley Bottoms early so they could get a good spot. Buckby had said something about Grace being 'better than any alarm clock', and he'd said it in that charmless way of his which suggested, in a roundabout way, that Janice would have to make up for their daughter's shortcomings in one way or another that evening, when Devon auditioned her for her very own one-woman show. She stood up from the fold-away chair, started pacing the seven steps between front window and counter nervously. Looking for her son. Very much *her* son, not Devon's...

'You'll wear a hole in the carpet,' warned Buckby. 'How's about you put the kettle on? Me throat's as dry as a blinking desert.'

149

Janice pressed her forehead against the cold glass; feeling drops condensation start to run down her face. Or it could have been something else. How the hell had she ended up here? Well, for start off, she shouldn't have started delivering papers for the fat bastard when Collie had... Had walked into the sea like he did and she'd been left on her own with young Lew and she needed that extra cash. *Surely* she could have done something else for money. But she had nobody to look after Lewis, and at least when she walked the paper rounds, she could take him with her. And then, after a while, she started staying in the shop for a brew, just to warm her up, like. She found his strange way of talking rather sweet back then. Thought that he was too nervous to engage her in proper conversation; thought the verbal tics like the commentary and the child-talk were just a front. And she'd liked the company. But 'company' had a strange way of slipping its arms around you when you were parcelling up the papers in the store room. 'Company' had a way of brushing against your behind when you were straining to reach the tea bags on the top shelf. And she simply hadn't had the life in her to fight it off. And then Grace came along and she fossilized everything. Turned that runaway streak in her into cold stone. Cold, staying stone which would roll no more, would gather no moss. So she'd just settled. It was for the good of Lewis and Grace, as she constantly told herself. There weren't many two-parent families on the island at all any more, so it was a kind of head-start...

But where was Lewis now? Even fat little Ben Davis had finished his round now; he'd returned to the shop about twenty or thirty minutes back to collect his wages and had promptly spent it all on sweets and crisps and fizzy pop. She'd watched him wheel his bike away down the main street and wondered if he ever bothered cycling at all. The other boys had been much quicker, returning after only half an hour, steaming up the shop when they came in from the morning cold; all sly little digs at each other and wistful looks up to the pornos on the top shelf. At the time, she'd clearly thought *I'm so glad our Lewis is not like those boys. He's nice and polite and wouldn't ever want to look at the smut mutts.* But now, his absence was worrying her. He'd been distant for a few days and she'd kept meaning to have a word with him but just hadn't got round to it.

'He could be lying in a pool of blood,' she gasped, hardly even realising she'd voiced her fears. 'He could be praying for help... Anything...'

'Shall *I* put the kettle on then?' sighed Buckby.

150

'Give me the van keys,' she demanded. 'I'm going out looking for him.'

Buckby placed his hands on his womanly hips and slowly shook his head. 'You know you're not insured on that vehicle. What would happen if…?'

'Just give me the keys.' She stepped towards him.

Buckby backed away, against the counter. His shabby grey jumper rode up and his sweaty, fat belly was revealed. That trail of hairs that led down to his horrible sweaty penis. Disgusting. But she forced herself to stick her hand in the pocket of his brown trousers – the ones with the elasticated-waist – and started fishing around for the keys.

'Whoah,' he cautioned. 'A man could get ideas what with your hand down there.'

But before the scene could develop into something ugly – and by ugly it could have meant another of Buckby's misguided attempts at a little 'rumpy-pumpy' right there in the shop, or Janice clocking him one right on the end of his bulbous, penis-shaped red nose – they were interrupted by a small ginger-haired child holding a disfigured teddy bear.

'Mummy? What you doing mummy?' said Grace, through a mouthful of fingers. Seven years old and she was *still* sucking her fingers. Maybe Buckby was right. Maybe there was something wrong with the girl.

Janice swiftly extricated her hand from Buckby's pocket and turned to face her daughter.

'What you pulling that face for?' asked Grace. 'Why's mummy making a funny face?' she asked Bear.

Janice bent down to Grace's level and whispered in her ear, smelling the chocolatey, childlike scent of sleep and sweet sweat off her. Remembering when Lewis had smelled like that. 'Why don't we both go for a nice walk around the town? Would you like that?'

Grace nodded enthusiastically. Made Bear nod too. 'Are we going to the talent thing now?'

'Go get your coat.'

Grace scarpered off through the door that divided shop and home. Clattered up the wooden stairs.

Janice turned to face Buckby again. 'If you won't let us use your bloody…'

'Language!' he interrupted.

'If you won't let us use your *fucking* shit-tip van, then we'll walk Lewis's route. We'll find him.'

Buckby looked shocked. 'You're going way overboard. Have you been taking the pills that Dr. Can't Be Shaw gave you?'

Janice didn't answer. She grimaced instead, and listened out for Grace coming back down the stairs. Part of her hoped that Buckby would see sense and offer to drive them round, but she knew that if he did so, she was liable to wrestle the wheel off him. She didn't think she could handle his commentary on the driving conditions: *And then he takes a sharp left, negotiating the turn like a pro. Into the straight and then a hard-right. Mirror, signal, manoeuvre.* She'd manoeuvre him one of these days.

Absently, she picked up a bag of those Space Wrestler crisps off the shelf. The cheap and nasty ones that Lewis and Grace loved. Terrible for children of course, but good for a bribe.

'Jan!' gasped Buckby. 'You can't just go taking the stock, willy nilly.'

She shot him a weary look. He finally got the message, retreated behind the desk again, furtively picking up the big blue stock book and marking the crisp column with a thick '1'. Finally, Grace arrived at the bottom of the stairs again, and Janice immediately realised what had taken her so long. Instead of her warm duffle coat, she had taken the time to seek out her old princess outfit from its hiding place in the back of the cupboard in Lewis's room. *How had she known it was there?* It was too small for her now – left these constrictive marks on her arms where the sleeves bit in – but Janice was in no mood to argue. Instead, she took off her own fleece and wrapped it around Grace's shoulders.

'Mummy!' moaned Grace, but soon shut up when she realised that her mother was holding out a packet of the gaudily wrapped Space Wrestlers to her.

Without a word to Buckby, they stepped out of the shop.

'Where's Lewis?' asked Grace. 'Is he already at the talent thing? Is he saving us seats?'

'Don't put your fingers in your mouth, love,' said Janice.

'But I got all crisps stuck in there,' said Grace, sticking her whole hand in now, trying to pick at the stubborn bits in her back teeth. 'Did Lew get Space Wrestlers?'

'No. Lewis didn't get any crisps, because Lewis is making his mummy really worry about him.'

'He's prolly been caught at the monster house,' said Grace.

152

Janice stopped short. 'What did you say, young lady?'

'Nuffin, mummy.'

'No*thing,*' corrected Janice, before she could stop herself. 'What did you say about a monster house?'

'Well, that horrible monster house is on Lew's round, isn't it, mummy?' smiled Grace. 'Maybe the monster came out and got him. Can I have some more crisps then mummy?'

Janice didn't know what to say. She knew exactly which house young Grace was referring to. 'There is no such thing as a monster house,' she said, brusquely. 'Stop being silly.'

Grace's bottom lip quivered and she gripped Bear even more tightly. The poor thing was falling apart. It had been hers once, and she remembered the comfort it brought. But she also remembered a drunken Collie booting it around the front room like a rugby ball once, when his tea wasn't on the table on his return from the Ship. Janice ignored her daughter and walked on. Her head was starting to ache with worry. It felt like wild alarm sounds, klaxon calls of promised disaster were going off in there. She couldn't think straight. Suddenly, she realised Grace was tugging at her sleeve.

'What?' she snapped.

'*Ner-ner-ner-ner,*' Grace sing-songed, in almost exact replica of the sounds that were wailing through Janice's head. '*Ner-ner-ner-ner* mummy. *Ner-ner-ner-ner.*'

'What are you doing that for, young lady? Stop it now.'

Grace hid her face behind Bear's rump.

'Young lady?'

And then Grace lifted Bear's right arm up. Pointed it. Janice swung her head round to look.

Oh God. It's Lewis!

Grace put on her Bear voice. 'Because Lew needs annabulance mummy, see.'

Lewis did need an ambulance. Or a hearse. He was crawling, *crawling* along the pavement in this horrible lurching way. He looked drunk. He looked *green* with it.

'Stay here,' she hissed to Bear, to her daughter in her princess outfit. She had to go to her prince, her little boy, a boy who now looked half-Collie, half-drunk. Who now looked like any other male on Limm Island...

14: Cheryl Hammerstein

As the press cameras fizzed and popped, Manny Combs shot them what he liked to think of as his patented *Remember me, Cheryl Hammerstein?* look. Side profile. Staring off into the middle distance as though not quite concentrating on the present moment. Proud jawline but awkward smile as though he was unused to the cameras. As though he was saying *aw shucks, what do you wanna take a snap of an old snapper like me for?*

Each and every carefully choreographed press shot the same. From his poster-sized mayoral inauguration pic which had pride of place in the Town Hall corridors to the simple, supposedly off-the-cuff shots of him opening a new branch of MacAskill's SupaBuyz on the mainland or the extension to the Ship. Those same watery eyes. That same sense of wistful hope. A forlorn hope, sure, but hope nonetheless. Only slight flaring to the nostrils which suggested that deep down he knew why they were snapping his snapper. Because he was the big man about town. A man of power, but also a man with a great well of emotion inside him.

Of course, there was no Cheryl Hammerstein. But *most* people had someone like that. Some dreamboat who but for the will of fate could have been their soul-mate. *The one who'd got away.* And, in moments of triumph such as this, Manny wanted to project the image that he was just like everyone else. So he'd imagined up Cheryl. And she was the muse which he was counting on to inspire victory in his last, and most important election. Coming up in May, the Limm Islanders would go to the polls and they'd cast their votes on the single biggest issue which had reared its head on the island since the war (discounting the cult, and everybody discounted that, wiped it from the annals). They'd be at the ballot boxes in their droves, and their decision on whether to say 'yeigh' or 'neigh' to his vital, life-support line of a bridge was also a decision on whether they *got* his ever so humble face. Whether they could somehow go

154

for the appearance (that he was just another one of them) over the reality (he was a major landowner, the CEO of the mead factory, and majority shareholder in the Castle Hotel, and thus a good few social stratum above the fishermen, farmers, shopkeepers, teachers, boat-taxi drivers, and part-time National Trust men who formed the majority of the island's residents.)

So with Cheryl – *Chezza* as he sometimes called her when he was feeling particularly affectionate, which wasn't so often these days thanks to his dodgy ticker – floating somewhere on the horizon, perhaps reciprocating his smile, Manny felt able to get on with doing what he did best. Being a man of the people. And boy were there a lot of people. People, people everywhere *and not a drop to drink*. Used to be you'd only see numbers like this for Armistice Day, or for the speech days before the election, or the Viking festivals, or for May Queen, or when, for a few years, they'd run that godawful hippy One World Festival up at High Loan Park.

The people were here for the talent show. Here to be spoon-fed their entertainment. Here to watch the second-raters they queued with at MacAskill's or Buckby's Book-Buys or The Crab's Claws for their weekly shop, massacring pop classics on the old karaoke. Here to watch their colleagues at the mead factory knocking seven bells out of a tap dance routine. Here to watch the PE teacher from the school brutalising a comedy sketch. But mostly, they were here to watch the grand finale, the coup de grace; that same supermarket queuer, that same mead factory colleague, that same PE teacher being massacred, seven-belled, brutalised by the *judging panel*. They were here to boo and hiss. Here for the pantomime. Sometimes, Manny wondered why they didn't just cut to the chase and install a set of stocks on the stage. Or have done with it and bring back public hanging. Sure it was a modern world, but it was a medieval world too. It was like the second coming of the dark ages, he sometimes thought.

'One more, Mr. Mayor, sir,' called Yoghurt Rhodes, the rather over-enthusiastic part-time photographer from *The Tide Piper*. Rhodes was crouching low, in a sort of zigzag position, with one leg bent up on the second of the wooden steps which led up to the stage. He too was trying to project an image. An image of competency. He was aping *proper* photographers, had probably seen the way paps moved crab-wise around their targets. But despite his earnest efforts, Manny had already noted that the town photographer's (surprisingly muddy) high-vis bib was emblazoned with the legend CYCLING

155

PROFICIENCY INSTRUCTOR, his *other* part-time role; something which seemed to bring the whole composition into question. As did the rather gormless expression on his freckled features. As did the egg-shaped lump on the side of his head which made him appear even clumsier, even more cumbersome.

'All right, but be quick about it,' said Manny, a note of weary good humour in his voice. He shuffled into his typical side-on position and Cherylled his eyes. 'I'm sure you, and the guys from Charnley too, have got quite enough snaps of my ugly mug for one day.'

Rhodes, on his haunches, fired off a quickfire triple click and then obediently moved away from the steps. He'd always been suitably... submissive, had Yoghurt. Deferential. Manny liked that in his townspeople, though Christ knew few enough of them showed it these days. Perhaps that was why Manny always felt he could cut Yoghurt just that extra bit of slack. If it had been anyone else keeping him off the stage, where he was, any minute now, supposed to be giving the welcome (and housekeeping) speech, and later taking on the role of one of the judges, he'd have been liable to give them a piece of his mind. But Yoghurt was... Well, different. *Retarded,* Manny always wanted to say, but didn't, because one had to be *more* than careful about what one said these days. Hell, it was probably politically incorrect to call him Yoghurt even. But everyone did, even his poor old ma, so he was probably okay on that score.

He was called Yoghurt because his skin was so deathly pallid it seemed to glow. And because he was literally polka-dotted with freckles. And these weren't your common or garden freckles either. No, they were angry blotches. Manny had seen some of that horrible *Philadelphia* film once, and before he'd been able to find the remote control to switch it off, he'd seen those *lesions* on the Aids-boy's body. That was what Yoghurt's freckles looked like. Lesions. (Though they weren't of course; Manny had had a quiet word with Ray Shaw, the town doc, and had been convinced on that score.) To others, the rather more imaginative kids, the blotches looked more like the rather bedraggled pieces of fruit in a lumpy yoghurt, especially when set against his soupy-white skin, and so the name had stuck. So fast he might as well have been wearing it on his mustard bib which clashed so badly with his strawberry blond hair.

'You're a good lad, Yoghurt,' said Manny, slapping an appreciative paw onto his shoulder, taking care not to touch the

156

CYCLING PROFICIENCY INSTRUCTOR bib because now he could see it closer, he saw it was covered with some stains which looked rather more suspicious than mud. Rhodes visibly flinched at Manny's touch.

'Uh... tha... thank you Mister Combs, sir.' For a brief moment his eyes met Manny's, but then he dropped them resolutely to the floor, starting a staring competition with the muddy grass which had already be-spotted Manny's good shoes.

'Is that a new camera?' Manny continued, noting the rather fancy Nikon which Rhodes had dangling from a cord which stretched around his neck, probably so he didn't lose it.

At the mention of his camera, Rhodes suddenly gained confidence. He raised his head, grinning. 'Do you like it? It's a Nikon D40 Mister Combs, sir. I got it for my twenty-first last week. It's beautiful, eh? I... I dropped it yesterday and I thought it was a goner, but ...' And now he was becoming excited, the words were starting to tumble out of him. He turned the camera over in his hands, marvelling. 'But it's so well designed. Hardly a crack on it. And it's fast and easy to use. Bad cameras are ten-a-penny. Bad cameras shout about the megapixels and all that, but my Nikon, it just gets on with the job. And do you know what that job is, Mister Combs, sir?'

Manny didn't answer for a moment. He was still in shock after discovering Rhodes was twenty-one. *Key to the door twenty-one.* You were supposed to be a man at twenty-one. Rhodes still looked a boy, if admittedly a long, *streakapiss* gawky one.

'The job of a good camera is to *get out of your way*. To avoid becoming a chunky obstacle,' spat Rhodes. 'The job of a good camera is to *facilitate* your... your relationship with what you're seeing in your mind, and... and...' He stopped. Must have seen the surprise in Manny's face. The surprise which Manny had tried ever so hard to mask.

'I'm... I'm sorry,' stuttered Rhodes, his face suddenly turning raspberry yoghurt, his lesions seeming to seep into each other. 'Mam says... I get too carried away with my camera. I'm sorry Mister Combs, sir. I didn't mean to keep you. I know how busy you must be.'

Manny flashed him a luxuriant smile. Of course he was busy, but if he didn't have time to shoot the breeze with his subjects then where would he be? It was all about that personal touch. And besides, Yoghurt Rhodes was most definitely of voting age now.

And he needed every vote when the next election came around in May. Almost without thinking, Manny reached out an arm and scruffed Rhodes' hair. When he thought about this later, and admittedly this was *much* later, because a lot happened on the day of the talent show which took precedence over a simple, ill-advised touch, Manny cringed. At the time, he merely stopped smiling when he discovered Rhodes ginger hair wasn't as soft as it looked, but was, in fact, wiry, tough, and had the crinkly consistency of pubic hair.

Quickly, Manny took himself away, off up the stairs, to greet the rest of his public. When he stepped out onto the stage, he was still surreptitiously wiping off the *bad germs* from Rhodes' hair onto his trousers.

When he stepped out onto the stage, the first thing he noticed was the wind coming off the North Sea. *Christ* the stage was covered, but the cover had turned it into a wind-tunnel. It wasn't even windy off stage; was barely even breezy, the morning drizzle had given way to one of those dull lunch-times, even duller afternoons, but up here... Up here he just knew it would play havoc with his remaining wispy hairs. Just knew they'd be floating up in the air like strands of candy-floss. Just knew that the townspeople, the islanders would be nudging each other. Laughing behind their hands. He drew himself up to his full majestic height of five nine and *dared* them to laugh out loud.

In fact, nobody appeared to be laughing. As Manny stood at the microphone, some flunky adjusting its height for him, he realised nobody had even noticed he'd gained the stage yet. He looked out over that sea of faces, most of which he'd be able to put a name to if he let his gaze linger over them longer than a simple cursory, and saw they were all, to a man, woman and child, resolutely *not* looking at the stage. A lot of them were, of course, simply chatting amongst themselves, sharing gossip and the like. But still more had their heads dropped. Were engrossed in their damn mobile phones or their Ipods or their portable games consoles. And there were others whose eyes he couldn't see because they were so trussed up in their winter clothes. Big woollen, sailor-style hats pulled down low, or scarves dragged up high, Michelin Man coats which seemed to bubble over their faces. That was just about understandable given the conditions, but what wasn't understandable, what was pretty ruddy far from okay, was the fact that he couldn't see the eyes of some of them because they were wearing their damn hoods up, and if there was one thing Manny didn't like, with a passion which boiled hotter than even his hatred for mobile phones, it was hoods. The mayor in Charnley had run a successful campaign to get hoodies banned from the precinct in the sort-of next-door neighbour town and never failed to rub it in that Manny hadn't managed to pass a similar scheme through here.

'Sign of your waning power,' the snub-nosed chancer had taken great delight in informing him, accompanying his hurtful words with a jack-hammer prodding in Manny's chest. It had been all Manny could do to resist slapping the feller round the chops. That he hadn't was likely because he knew for a fact the Charnley mayor was right. His power *was* on the wane; certainly a few years back, he wouldn't have even needed to worry about the election. But now, he'd heard the mutterings at the bar of the Ship, read the letters to the editor in *The Tide Piper,* and he'd asked his occasional secretary, Mrs. Heggarty (Mrs. Higgledy-Piggledy, he called her, on account of her consistently messy hair and her piggish snout), what the word on the street was. And he'd not been expecting such an honest reply from a woman who usually made mice seem rambunctious. *Mousy* wasn't the word for her, but somehow she'd managed to rise above her usual shell-shocked whisper to inform him, in what sounded like a *delighted* voice, that the word on the street was that he was a dinosaur.

Well if he was a dinosaur, he was a ruddy T-Rex. And he was an *intelligent* T-Rex too. Hence the talent show on this day of all days. Hence he was going to be one of the judges. Hence he was going to play, he'd made sure of it, the *kind* judge, leaving it to newspaperman Mike Ford, to play the hard-man. Good cop-bad cop. All pantomime of course, but if he played it right, he might just improve his ratings in the polls.

The talent show was being held on the south side of the island, down at Coverley Bottoms (or Cover ye Bottoms as the town's kids called it, hell as everyone called it, apart from Manny, of course). It was pretty much the flattest piece of land on an island which was otherwise all hills and valleys and beach and harbour and had hence become, almost by accident, the mass meeting place for days such as this despite the fact it was a bit of an industrial no-man's land. Once upon a time, when Limm still had ideas above its station, a couple of factories had sprung up down here, right alongside the mead factory, due in no small part to the fact they could use the River Drey as a constant, free water supply. But those

159

factories had polluted the river to within an inch of its life and the new industry the town was counting on to secure its future never came. The new road they'd built down here was never actually completed, was given up as a bad job. The southern woodland they'd cleared to make way for the new factories just became a wasteland. During this term of office, Manny had campaigned to get a perimeter fence installed. He'd only narrowly won the vote, his victory only secured at the eleventh hour when a child had wandered off during last year's May Queen ceremony and fallen into the River Drey. The kid hadn't died, but had become very ill due to the chemicals which remained in the water. And Manny had won through on the child-safety vote. Today was the first day they'd be able to utilise the fence for its proper purpose, forcing people to have to pay to get in and not simply jib in through the woods which flanked the flat ground.

He looked out over all his *paying* townspeople and immediately started to feel better about the whole thing. Sure it was cold. And windy. Sure his hair was getting messed up and he'd have to sit through hours of water torture at the hands of the hopeless who thought they were the great and good, but soon he could be back at the town hall on Farne Street with his feet up, counting the takings into the coffers. The idea was a good one, he couldn't believe he'd ever doubted it. *In Manny we Trust.* They should have installed it as the Limm Island motto. Hell, they should have scrawled it on the huge banner, fluttering in the hardly-even-a breeze above the stage. The banner which actually bore the legend, TALENT-STRAVAGANZA!!!!!! Stupid name that, but that was what you got when you let schoolchildren choose.

He cleared his throat, prepared to speak. Out of the corner of his eye, he saw Yoghurt Rhodes hunkering down by the side of the stage, ready to fire off a few more shots. The other photographers, the ones from the bigger local papers, the ones run from offices in Charnley and Kirkby-le-Stag, and *not* from back rooms in the bloody library like *The Tide Piper*, were nowhere to be seen now. They had their shots. Could pass them off to their editors and pretend they'd been at Limm Island's TALENT-STRAVAGANZA!!!!! for the whole day when in reality, by now they'd be down the pub, getting *fine and dandied.* Which was what newspapermen did all the time. Was what *everyone* did all the time. Every day of their goddamn miserable excuses for lives. They cleared space so they could drink and drink and drink. It was no

160

wonder the world, the country, the county, was going to the dogs when only Manny Combs could keep a sober head on him.

He cleared his throat again, checked his mayoral chain was the right way round, and then he began. 'Ladies and gentlemen, boys and girls, Limm islanders and visitors, honoured guests and old friends, welcome to you all.' He paused. He could still hear the steady hum of conversation underscoring his words. Could still hear the dawn chorus of chirping mobile phones as text messages spread amongst the crowd like a virus. Turning phones onto silent was top of his 'housekeeping' list, but he knew he couldn't simply start shouting at them to do it now, not before he'd warmed them up.

'Ladies and gents, boys and girls, they said we were mad,' he continued, in a deep, confident voice. 'They said we were off our rockers, that we didn't know what we were doing. They said nobody in their right minds would come to an open air talent show in February.' He shot a pointed look to Mike Ford, the newspaperman, who was creeping up the back of the stage and pulling up a pew behind the long trestle table which formed the judges' panel. Ford shrugged, perhaps remembering his ill-advised headline *Rain's Got Talent,* and his even more critical sub-headline, *February Show Set to be a Wash-Out.* Manny carried on, finding his rhythm now, attaining a flow, getting in the zone. 'They said we were over-reaching ourselves...' He let the pause linger. He basked in the crowd's new found silence. Their submission.

He raised his hand, laid it flat across his brow as though he was straining to see something on the horizon. 'They said we were creating a white elephant, but I can't see any wild beasts on our island today, can you, boys and girls? I don't think the travelling circus has come to town today, do you, boys and girls? I don't think Coverley Bottoms has become a *zoo...'*

For a giddy moment, he thought he'd over-egged the pudding. Scores of excitable kids set about wriggling in their seats, craning their necks, and yelping as they looked around for Manny's wild animals. Some of them pretended to *be* wild animals. He heard a few 'oop, oop' chimp noises, a few tiger roars, a couple of bird whistles. But soon their mums started to get them back in order.

'All I can see is a great North Sea of faces. An ocean of faces. Faces which bear testimony to the fact that the Limm Island TALENT-STRAVAGANZA!!!!! is exactly what the town, the island, needs in order to banish those winter blues.'

161

The audience whooped and hollered (like Americans, Manny thought, with mild distaste.)

'The TALENT-STRAVAGANZA!!!!! is what we need to blow all the cobwebs away, good and proper.'

The audience whooped and hollered again. Manny held up a warning paw.

'But it's about more than that. This island has had a bad press over the years, even, in some cases from our own town newspaper,' he said, injecting his voice with a Cherylly sadness, casting a reproachful eye back at *The Tide Piper's* owner, editor, chief writer, sports correspondent Mike Ford, the man principally responsible for that awful opinion column *The Voice of the Sea*. 'I sometimes get the impression that *some people* would be happy if we hid our lights under a bushel. They'd be pleased if we never made any headlines at all. *Sure,* we all know we've been burned in the past, but being down here, at Coverley Bottoms, is surely the only reminder of that which we need.' He raised a finger. 'Back then, we had it wrong. Back then, we thought it was our natural resources – the bird reserve, the beach, the river, the hills, the monastery – which would finally elevate this town above the also-rans like... Well, you know who I'm referring to now, don't you, ladies and gentlemen...' Nods of agreement in the crowd. Face-cracking grins. A couple of teenagers lowered their hoods. Yoghurt Rhodes flashed off another couple snaps from his Nikon.

'Back then, we thought we could grow by dent of the fact we were different from everywhere else. That we were like a place set apart. But we were wrong. The powers that be, back then, were barking up the wrong tree. You see, ever since you kind folks voted me into power, I've been of a different opinion. I've been of the opinion that the thing we've got that nobody else round here does, not your Charnley's or your Kirkby-le-Stag's or your Barnwick's... The thing which makes us better than those other places... The thing that makes us *unique*... Well it's you.' And here he spread his arms as though he was embracing the whole crowd. He Cherylled better than he'd ever done before.

'Ladies and gents, boys and girls, *you* are the seeds from which this island, this town will grow. From which great things will evolve. You are the future. And *that's* why 'white elephants' like the TALENT-STRAVAGANZA!!!!! are so important. Because here today, we're going to see just how much wondrous talent we have here, and we're going to bring it out from under that bushel for all

162

the world to see. Ladies and gents, boys and girls, today we take our first small step in what we hope will be a giant leap for the town. And the best thing about it is that it's going to be great fun. We've got dance acts, comedy, singers, uh, a poet, a gymnast, BMX riders, a sheepdog trialler... We've got everything under the sun for your viewing pleasure. But always remember, the performers today are *our people.* Our sons and daughters, our sisters and brothers, our teachers, our dentists, our fishermen, our fishmongers, our hoteliers and our coastguard. Today, ladies and gents, boys and girls, I am but your humble judge, and I promise I'll keep you no longer than strictly necessary before we move on to the fun, but first, it falls to me to run you through a few housekeeping rules and general regulations for the show.' He shrugged. 'Some guys get all the luck, eh?'

There were a few groans, a couple of yawns, a noticeable increase in message-received beeps while Manny pulled a scrap of paper from his pocket and raced through the housekeeping, but generally, he was pleased to note, there wasn't much by way of disruption. People were seeing this as a necessary evil, something to be got through before the fun started. They didn't blame him for it. Hell, they probably blamed Mike Ford. All those well-timed digs about the press had reminded them all about *The Voice of the Sea's* demands that there be proper health and safety, his persnickety banging-on. *He* was the one to blame and it would only get worse for him when he had to play up to his pantomime villain bad-judge role. Everything was working out just as Manny had foreseen it.

When he finished, he nodded to Sally Martin, the school's music teacher, who was standing by the steps at the side of the stage. Sally was to be the presenter of the show (and also the musical accompaniment if any were needed; she'd got her piano set up in the equivalent of the orchestra pit). It was her job to announce the acts, ask the judges for their verdicts, and tell the contestants 'well done' after they'd finished their performances and were snail-trailing back off the stage and into obscurity. And yet, despite the fact she barely had any responsibility, the woman looked genuinely scared. Throughout Manny's grand speech, she'd kept removing her glasses with shaking hands and trying to polish them up. Every time she noticed him looking at her, she fiddled with her damn ponytail. Now, she'd lost so much colour in her cheeks she looked as though she was about to pass out. As she gingerly climbed the steps, Manny realised he should have gone for someone decidedly more glamorous. Sally was wearing this big, shapeless fleece coat thing which *drowned* her. She looked more like a dinner-lady than a presenter. He waited for her at the microphone and gave her an encouraging pat on the arm before she introduced the first act, hoping that would be enough. Hoping she'd also see the fiery warning in his eyes.

'Hello everyone, one and all,' she said, simply. 'Thank you very much for coming, despite the - *brrrrrrrrrr* – cold. Thank you for putting so much faith in the people of this fine town, this fine island.'

Manny was hoping she'd go on to talk more about why it was such a fine town, what set it apart from wherever it was she'd grown up - down south probably - but she didn't. She was straight into the business of the day. 'I'm sure you don't want to hear me prattle on; some of the kids here today hear enough of that at school...' She waited out the muted boos before concluding. 'And so, without further ado, I'd like you to give your very best Limm Island welcome to our first act of the day, a group of girls I know very well as they're in my fourth year class, and I'm sure everyone else will know them after today. Limm Island, meet Dancing in the Moonlight!'

Warm applause followed. A few wolf whistles; Manny hoped they were from the fourth year boys and not any of the older males in the audience. But as he caught sight of the fourth year girls' dancing troupe as they climbed the steps, as he *almost saw up their short, short glittery skirts,* he felt his heart give an involuntary flutter. He heard a wolf-whistle of his own *inside* his ears. Whether it was a wolf-whistle of appreciation or pain was open to some debate. Quickly, he pulled up a pew next to Mike Ford behind the trestle table.

'Ever seen *Donnie Darko,* Mr. Combs?' asked Mike.

Manny narrowed his eyes. What was this journalist fool playing at, distracting him like this? Doubtless this *Donnie Darko* was some kind of porno. Doubtless Ford was fishing, seeing whether he'd see the glimmer of recognition in Manny's eyes. Well, Manny wouldn't give him the satisfaction. Instead he stared directly ahead, at the girls as they arranged themselves in a V-formation, like vacationing birds. They were dressed like a cross between cheer-leaders and short-skirted Christmas trees, and if Manny had seen them on the street he'd have disapproved, but as it was, they were on stage, so he figured it didn't really matter.

164

The girls waited patiently, not a hint of giggling or anything – he'd mark them up for that - while Sally clip-clopped back down the steps, moved round the front of the stage, and then positioned herself behind the piano, as though she was going to play the tune to compliment a silent movie at the cinema. She was acting out her moves like a silent movie actress as it was, giving this big exaggerated nod to the girls on stage, and then counting them in with a sign-language a-one, a-two, a-one, two, three, four.

Manny immediately recognised the tune. It was from some supermarket ad. Mike Ford gave this wholly over-the-top groan and started writhing around in his seat as though he'd shat his pants.

'Grow up,' hissed Manny.

'I can't help it, I hate this song, I hate Toploader.'

Manny was about to give him a piece of his mind, but found himself transfixed by the fourth year girls' movement. The dance was rhythmically slow, not like those awful, regimented, slapped-thigh majorette routines he remembered his contemporaries dancing when he was that age. The dance was almost sensual. The girls hunkered down and then rose up from the stage like snakes being charmed. The girl at the front of the V, he'd find out her name later, was practically gyrating, swinging her hips in time to Sally Martin's piano, moving like a willo-the-wisp.

The crowd started chanting. Or something like it; certainly they were making a lot of noise, especially towards the back. He strained to see what was going on, tried to pick out any obvious ring-leaders, but it was hard to see exactly what was going on in the general commotion. Even Mike Ford appeared to have noticed what was going on. 'Trouble at t'mill,' he said, elbowing Manny rather too sharply in the ribs and pointing off in the direction of the disturbance at the back of the crowd. 'Still think this was a good idea?'

'It'll be a few drunks,' hissed Manny, 'that's all. Nothing to worry about. Soon as this act's finished I'll get Sam Bibby to go and have a word with them.'

Mike Ford pretended to be shocked. 'Sam Bibby? Are a few drunken buffoons enough to get the police in for? Are they going to cause a riot do you think?'

The idea had already crossed Manny's mind. For he could see that whatever was happening at the rear of Coverley Bottoms was getting worse. Now the muffled shouts had become something else, something wilder. Now he could see people back there starting

165

to push, starting to elbow each other out of the way. Even the dancing troup appeared to have noticed all was not well. In the middle of a slow, luxuriant pirouette, the blond girl at the front of the V gave a brief stumble, shouldered into her second in command, and for a beat it looked as though they'd all collapse like ten-pins, but Sally Martin's relentless piano accompaniment seemed to soothe them, and saved the day, for now at least.

Manny stood up to try to get a better view of what was going on off-stage. Mike Ford soon joined him. They looked on as the jostling for position turned into something of a bar-room brawl. They looked on as fists flew, as bodies fell, as women shielded children, as poor Sam Bibby tried to restore order. They looked on as Sally Martin finally realised something was wrong and stopped playing. They looked on as the fourth year girls' dancing troup froze, stock-still, as though they'd been playing at musical statues on a shingle beach. They looked on as the battling crowd started to part, as though a huge bowling ball had been sent tumbling through it.

Mike Ford shot Manny a look. Looked as though he was going to follow the look up with the actual words: *I told you so*. But he never got the chance. A scream pierced the wintry air. Then another. A third chilled through the whole assembly. Everyone stared at the yawning space of muddy ground where the crowd had been, where the disturbance had first occurred. And at first Manny could see nothing wrong. Later, he'd think it unbelievable that he didn't immediately recognise this as the terrible start of something, or the beginning of the end. But he genuinely couldn't see what the fuss was about. Couldn't see why Sam Bibby, along with a couple of fellers from the St. John Ambulance were now stalking carefully into that yawning space, stalking crouched low with their hands in front of them as though they were trying to catch, or ward off some kind of animal.

And then he saw it. Saw *him*. A battered, bloodied figure *crawling* across the wet, litter-strewn grass, dragging his half-dead body on. The crowd pressed back, away from him as though they didn't want to be infected.

'What the fuck?' said Mike Ford. 'The fight didn't look that bad.'

But Manny knew. Knew the man wasn't injured as the result of any fight. This was different. This smelled different. His nostrils flared and he sucked in the intoxicating aroma of *otherness*. Golden valve otherness. His right knee trembled as though it was going to give way.

'You need to calm the crowd, make some announcement,' said Mike.

But Manny remained as frozen as the fourth year girls' dancing troup. In the yawning space, the two St. John's Ambulance men had reached the crawling man and were trying to stop him crawling. They were quickly joined by Sam Bibby, who promptly set about ordering the crowd back, although there was absolutely no need for him to do so. Someone started to shout over the microphone on stage; out of the corner of his eye, Manny saw it was Mike Ford.

'Everybody remain calm! Stay away from the, uh, victim. Give him some room.' He paused, then: 'IS THERE A DOCTOR IN THE HOUSE?'

There was, and he was already stepping forward onto the grass which was already stained with blood from the mauled man. The town's one and only qualified doctor, Ray Shaw, stepped into the breach, accompanied by his able assistant, and Sam's twin brother, Mart, the part-time male nurse. The *fairy* male nurse; Manny hadn't credited the great hulking brute with that much bravery...

Suddenly he realised he needed to get in on the act. Needed to be *seen* to be getting in on the act. It was time for the mayor to take control. He forced himself to move. Creaked through the dancing troup and down the steps off the stage. Like Moses, he parted the waves of the crowd and he walked to the back of the field, breathing heavily. By the time he reached the medical men who were surrounding the mauled man, he was almost bent-double from the effort. By the time he reached them, they were already arguing about the best way to get the mauled man to hospital.

'We can't use the ambulance,' said one of the St. John's men, in a rather panicky voice. 'We couldn't get it through the perimeter so we hard to park it on the road... It's too far...'

'We could call Crabbie's Boat Taxis, get him to drive right up the river,' said the other.

'Don't be stupid,' sighed Sam Bibby, 'you know as well as me that Crabbie's are about as reliable as...' He looked as though he was going to say something derogatory about Manny, but stopped himself at the last minute, seeing the mayor on the outside of their circle.

'Well, whatever we do we need to move him quickly,' said Ray Shaw who was crouching over the body, 'he's already lost a lot of blood and we need to get those bites he's got seen to, properly.'

'Bites?' said Sam Bibby. 'I thought this was, you know, from a fight...'

'Shut up, all of you,' said Manny, shouldering though so he was standing over the body. For a moment, the sight of the mauled man's exposed flesh, the tears in his clothing, the gaping wounds, the pure, unadulterated terror in his eyes, gave him pause, but he managed to compose himself. Took another deep, restorative breath. 'Keep your voices down. The world is watching. Now, where exactly is that ambulance? We need this cleared-up as quickly and quietly as possible. Understand?'

The mauled man seemed to understand. He coughed, spluttered, vomited a torrential flood of blood all over Ray Shaw's overcoat. Shaw looked just about ready to vomit himself.

'The ambulance is parked-up on Dye Lane,' gulped one of the St. John's men. 'But it'll take a good ten minutes to walk up there and...'

Manny stopped him. Held up a traffic-cop palm. With his other hand he fished out his razor thin mobile phone, flipped it open, and pressed a single-button. He had his chauffeur on speed-dial.

'Mark? Yes, it's me. No, it's not over. Listen. I need you to do something for me. You're waiting on Dye Lane, aren't you? Good... What I need you to do is go-fetch the St. John's Ambulance... Yes, I know you don't have the keys, just *listen*... I need it *by hook or by crook,* understand? Bring it down to Coverley Bottoms... Yes, there's been a problem, but I'll tell you about it later. Just bring it down here, and then go back for the car... Yes, we're going to The Bungalow. Follow us up there.'

He snapped the phone shut. 'There. Sorted.'

'But... but...' stammered one of the St. John's men.

'Town'll cover any expenses incurred when my chauffeur *commandeers* your ambulance, don't you worry about that,' said Manny.

'I don't think he *was* worried about that,' said Ray Shaw, raising his blood-spattered head, turning to face Manny. 'I think what he's worried about is taking this... poor man back to my clinic and not to the proper emergency ward at Marwell. I mean, The Bungalow's not equipped to deal with something like this... It's only a clinic really.'

Manny hunkered down alongside the aging doctor. 'Remember what I said earlier about the people of this town being the seeds from which this town will grow? From which great things will evolve? Well this is your chance.'

Now it was Shaw's turn to stammer. He gestured to the mauled man. 'But...'

'Another thing, doc. The people of this town might be the seeds but they can also be poison. We take care of this in-house, you understand? This man goes to your clinic, to The Bungalow as you call it. And he'll receive the best Limm Island treatment.'

Prone on the floor which was slicked with his own blood, the mauled man gurgled again. His gurgle might have been an attempt at a scream. It was hard to tell, a large portion of his throat was missing. But what was certain was the fact he didn't seem entirely happy about receiving this *Limm Island treatment.* The man – Manny still didn't recognise him despite his close proximity – sucked in a deep, blocked-drain breath, seemed to be summoning all of his remaining strength for *something.* And then, with a tremendous effort, he raised both of his hands and gripped Dr. Ray Shaw's coat. Manny was surprised by how *clean,* how unmarked his hands were compared to the rest of his broken body. There were no cuts, no open wounds, all of his digits remained intact (which meant, Manny knew, that whatever had attacked him – and *attacked* really was the word, this was no accident – had moved with such stealth, such speed, the mauled man hadn't even been able to defend himself.)

Still gripping Shaw's coat with rigor-mortis force, the man let out a rasping breath, and then spluttered two words. Shaw leaned in closer, paying no mind to the blood which was continuing to rain down on him, and as he did so, the man *barked,* 'Help me!' before collapsing back onto the turf.

15: Knox the Stuffing Out of You

Trevor Knox couldn't remember leaving the hide. Couldn't remember walking through town either. Nor could he recall the struggle up Pate Hill or how he'd ended up sitting so close to the old monastery, staring into its skeletal archways, its ghostly pillars, its decrepit windows. He felt sick, was shivering-cold despite the thickness of his long, brown, sleeping-bag style coat. He vaguely remembered seeing a woman with a dog up here earlier, but then he'd been so wracked with illness he couldn't quite decide whether it had simply been a vision, a memory; his frazzled brain trying to tell him that there was something wrong with him.

What he did know was that the *something wrong with him,* The Unholiness, could be traced directly back to last night, when that thing, that scratching beast, had been waiting, out the other side of the hide's bolted door, ready to gobble him up. And it was as though the beast's raggedy breath had infected him. As though breathing in the *thing's* exhalations had knocked all the life out of him. Left him a husk. He'd left the hide once he was certain the thing had gone, of that he was sort of sure; he'd come out, into the open, to try to find Ely Rhodes, yeah, that sounded about right, but how long ago that was, and how he'd set about doing that, were a mystery to him.

He was coming to now though. And he reckoned what had finally brought him round was the smell. Like smelling-salts, the mouldy-old-sock, chemically- *bad* smell which seemed to fill the atmosphere up here had smacked some life back into him.

Funny thing about the smell: it reminded him of the underneath of Mikey Turner's oven, where once upon a time, plastic wrappers and discarded tin foil had accumulated alongside numerous mouse droppings and roach ends; there, they'd been cooked up into this unholy, unnatural brew which was surely not healthy. Once upon a time, Trevor had known all about the underside of Mikey

170

Turner's oven like as a young boy he'd known about hub flanges on a bike. Once upon a time, he'd passed out on the kitchen lino far too often and usually awoke from whatever trance-like state he'd descended to find himself staring into the abyss of cobwebs, oven chips and instruction manuals which also lay underneath. But that was a long, long time ago. Before Solomon had weaned him off the drugs, got him on some real hard stuff, like the truth.

But Mikey Turner's flat had burned down with Mikey inside it eight years ago. And still the smell. And, disgusting though it was, the miles he'd put between him and them, Trevor suddenly found himself craving a hit of drugs like he'd not done since the Millennium.

Oh he knew about temptation, and he knew about The Darkness. What he didn't really know about, he was surprised to find, was the monastery. This despite working up here two mornings a week for most of the last ten years. Why, for example, did he keep having to reach up with a lazy arm to brush away the millions of midges which seemed to congregate up here? Weren't midges supposed to come out in summer? But the Unholy bastards were all over him like cock-rash on an Unsaved STD victim now, biting with their tiny-weeny teeth at the unprotected skin of Trevor's face and his ankles, where his jeans had ridden up. Hell, some of them felt like they'd managed to crawl under the waistline of his boxer shorts now too; they were crafty like the desperate women at the end of the night up at the Cookie Club in Charnley once upon a different life.

'Fuck,' he breathed, wafting another swarm of the bastards away from him. Then he stopped, clamped that same hand over his mouth. He'd not sworn since... Since he wasn't tapped on the shoulder by Solomon to be one of the First Chosen, to be a founder member of the Millennium Club. He gulped. Soaped out his brain. Tried to remember the preachings. But up here, the preachings wouldn't come. Up here, in a place so stagnant with history, the atmosphere felt damp and oppressive. The air seemed thicker up here somehow than it had in the hide, and *louder*. Underscoring the faraway crash of the sea against the cliffs was another sound; a kind of ancient buzz. A kind of awakening.

Trevor knew he should leave. Make his way back to the hide. Or at least set out to find Ely. But at the same time, something deep within him was telling him he should stay, wait the sickness out. It told him that just maybe the sickness could infect Ely too... The longer he stayed here, away from Ely, the better.

171

16: Symptoms

When Lewis Dowsing woke up, he thought for one terrible minute that he'd wet himself. All of those awful memories washed over him; his mother, bleary-eyed stripping the bed while he stood naked on the landing, not knowing whether he should offer to help her turn the mattress. Her holding a trembling finger over her lips lest he wake the sleeping Collie.

But he hadn't wet himself. Not today. He felt the damp grass underneath his body and realised that *this* was what had soaked his jeans. Breathing a sigh of relief, he lifted his head. Tried to work out where he was.

He was lying on a patch of rough grass close to Vale Row. His mountain bike was a crumpled heap about three or four feet away from him. Further away, on the edge of the road, his luminous orange paper bag lay open, spilling out its contents like blood and guts. Pages from some of the newspapers were floating around on the breeze, scattering everywhere. It was like a ticker-tape parade. Like the May Queen. He thought he saw Paula from Preston go whirling past.

Nervously, he patted down his body, feeling for injuries, for cuts and bruises. Apart from a large, apple-sized swelling on his knee, he seemed to be okay. But he felt dizzy still. Light-headed. He tried to concentrate. He remembered being up at the garages. What he'd done there. And then he remembered his shameful, guilt-ridden dash away from the scene of his crime. How quickly he'd taken the steep slope of Dye Lane. Past that, he could remember nothing.

Lewis imagined how angry Buckby would be when he learned about all of the ruined papers. But he knew his mother would stick up for him when she heard what had happened. When he showed her the lump on his knee. She was better now. Better than she had been after Collie. She wouldn't go crazy and try to make it

172

worse like she had that time she'd yanked that scab off his knee. She was sympathetic now. She seemed to have forgotten all that pain business.

He needed to get back up there. Explain. He didn't know how long he'd been out. They'd be sending out search parties sooner or later though. Maybe his mother and Grace were already out. Maybe Buckby was scouring the streets for him in that crappy white van with 'cleen me' written on the back windows. Gingerly, he picked himself up from the grass and moved over to his bike. He examined the broken chain and realised that he wouldn't be cycling home. Not today. He picked up some of the papers and crumpled them into his big orange paper bag, but left the majority of them to float over the wall to the river, or into the jungle-like garden of the Old Mason house. There was *no way* he was going in there to retrieve them.

As he wheeled the bike along Vale Row, Lewis began to exaggerate his limp. Getting in practice for the moment that he stepped back into the shop. He wanted that moment to be as dramatic as possible. He wanted it slow motion; his mother staring aghast as he entered, dropping her coffee mug. It taking hours to fall through the air before smashing on the counter. Her hand going up to her face, trying not to scream. Then rushing to him, smothering him with hugs. Like he was a returning war veteran or something. Buckby would be off-screen somewhere, shaking his head wearily, knowing he couldn't complain about the papers. And – Lewis suddenly realised – he'd have absolutely no idea about Lewis's gloop being all over Gerry Porter's copy of the *Super Sport.*

Suddenly, Lewis felt good. Really good. Like he'd been offered a reprieve. Like he'd clutched victory from the jaws of defeat. Light-headed, he started to laugh, thinking 'clutching victory from defeat' sounded like something old *Fuck*by would say when he was doing that weird commentary thing in the store room, when he thought nobody was listening. He felt so good, it was almost as though he was drunk. It *was* like he was drunk, he decided; as though nothing could touch him; as though bodily things like pain couldn't get to him any more. His peripheral vision had gone all to pot; when he passed the graffiti under the bridge it seemed to draw him into its kaleidoscopic chasm; as though all he'd have to do was reach out and he'd touch another world. It was brilliant, but alarming at the same time, like when he woke up in the middle of the night

173

and it felt like he was the only person alive in the whole, blurry-eyed world.

But Lewis's good mood didn't last long. Only as far as the steep uphill slope of Dye Lane. As he began to walk up it, he began to feel tired. The light-headedness quickly passed, and when it did, his knee began to ache. Somewhere, far away, he thought he could hear the sea, but it sounded indistinct somehow, not real. And the further he walked, the further he pushed, the more tired he got. Only the fact that he was so very itchy kept him going.

Itchy. Why was he so itchy all of a sudden? It was as though he was having a delayed allergic reaction to the grass he'd been lying on. Sometimes, he got a bit of a rash when they did PE up on the football pitches. From the grass up there. It was a type of hay-fever, Dr. Shaw to be Wrong said. Really annoying. But this wasn't just annoying, it was like his skin was on fire.

'I'm burning up,' he muttered to himself. 'I must have caught a fever being knocked out in the wet grass so long.'

Deep down though, despite the easy explanations that he kept coming out with, Lewis thought that there was something badly wrong. Deep down, he feared that there'd been more to the falling-off-the-bike story than he'd first remembered. There was something else. Something his mind hadn't shown him yet. Something horrible.

He staggered on, thinking about crawling now, not walking. The orange paper bag felt like it contained lead weights. His bike felt as though it was stubbornly refusing to be wheeled.

Just get home. Don't think about the Old Mason house at all.

Lewis felt the paper bag slipping off his shoulder. He let it fall to the ground. Stumbled on. Someone could go back and get it later on. Buckby could bring his 'cleen me' van.

So itchy though. Can't scratch properly and wheel the bike at the same time. Easier to just leave it.

Giving in to the voices in his head, Lewis left his bike collapsed against the lamp-post. He didn't even bother to lock it. Didn't even know where the lock was, let alone what his combination was. The tingling sensation on his skin was plaguing him now. Part of him felt like ripping off his Parka and rolling himself along the loose stones on the pavement, letting their sharpness tear into his skin. Blessed relief.

He resisted the temptation, but only just. Kept going, but only just. He was bent-double now. Could barely see where he was

174

going. All he knew was that he *had* to get home. All he knew was that he had to push through that door and hear the welcoming ring of that little bell, and then his mother would make everything all right.

He made the village green. And now he was crawling. Not caring if anyone saw him. Not caring if even Tracy Bingham from the year above saw him like that. Not caring if someone like Deano saw him and threatened to kill him. The itchiness and the pain which came from his very bones was all that he knew.

But then he heard his mother's voice. His mother's *scream*. And suddenly, she was on him. Her hands felt like ice, her breath like a swarm of midges, biting, chewing on him. She was quarter-shouting, quarter-sobbing, quarter-telling him off, quarter-luxuriating in his return. But he couldn't make out a single word. It was as though she was speaking to him from the bottom of a deep well. Or as though he was at the bottom of a deep well. A well which was crawling with insects.

She dragged him some of the way back, but it hurt him to have her touch him. By the time they'd reached the shop, he was crawling again and she was somewhere behind him, whimpering. He nudged open the door with his head; flopped over the threshold. Heard the bell ringing to announce his arrival, about twenty seconds too late. Looked up; saw Buckby's sweaty, yellow-toothed, red-nosed face hanging over him.

'What the hell are you playing at, lad?'

Buckby's voice sounded like it was coming to him from Hell. Or maybe *he* was in Hell and Buckby was way up there in Heaven, looking down on him.

'Water,' gasped Lewis, like a man that had crossed the Sahara. 'Water…'

Buckby leaned in closer. So close that Lewis could smell the sweat on him. Even the man's breath was sweating. 'What are you saying, lad? I can't make it out. Your voice is all slurred…'

'Where… mother?'

And then Buckby groaned: 'Would you Adam and Eve it? The lad's drunk. Must be. Have you been drinking, lad? Lad?'

17: Cover Ye Bottoms

Despite the fact the TALENT-STRAVAGANZA!!!!!! had been aborted, nobody seemed to want to go home. One third of the judging panel, the mayor, Manny Combs, had gone off with Dr. Shaw and that male nurse in the St. John's Ambulance, another third, the bloke from *The Tide Piper,* had shot off somewhere else, probably to the office to get started writing up the days *real* news, and the other, Sally Martin, the school's music teacher was left with the unenviable job of organising the dispersal of the crowd. Yoghurt Rhodes knew he should go over and offer to help her, but he couldn't seem to summon up the requisite energy. For one thing, all of his exertions from yesterday were catching up with him and he was so very tired. For another, he had The Shirt on underneath his normal clothes. There, under his beige shirt and his luminous, muddy cycling proficiency vest, was her instrument of torture, and it made even hunkering down into his 'Z' photography pose difficult. Even talking had been difficult. Earlier, when he'd been with Manny Combs, he'd barely been able to breathe, and he was sure the mayor had registered just how uncomfortable he was.

But then, that was the whole idea of The Shirt in the first place, wasn't it? It was *supposed* to constrict him, was supposed to limit his movement. Was supposed to feel like he was wearing an all-in-one letterbox muffler so that if he ever, *ever thought about coming home so late and without his bike and covered in Unholiness again,* he'd dismiss the idea out of hand. And he had. From now on he was going to be a Good Boy. If only he could stop creeping into one of *his stares,* he was going to be a Good Boy.

Right now, he was trying to blink away the sight of Carl-Rhys Hamilton, the school's PE teacher and sometime comedian, going round trying to console the fourth year girls' dancing troupe, half of whom were still crying. He was trying not to stare as Phil

176

Simpson, the man who ran High Loan Chippy, attempted to drag a coffin on stage. Evidently, the coffin was supposed to be part of his act. Evidently the act was supposed to be some sort of magic show, though Simpson wasn't dressed like any magician Yoghurt had ever seen. *Hail praise Him,* Simpson was still wearing the same greasy white apron he wore every day when he doled out his chips. There was surely a joke in there which Hamilton could have used if he hadn't been so busy consoling the girls.

Yoghurt felt someone tugging at the arm of his tracksuit top. Snapped out of his stare. Swung round to see Michael Cleverley, one of the boys from his cycling proficiency class. Not the most able student. He did not cycle Cleverley at all.

'Did you see that man covered in all the blood? Is he dead?'

Yoghurt realised Hamilton was on the scene now. He sighed deeply. Luxuriantly. All-sufferingly. 'I'll handle this one Yog-lad,' he said. Then, turning to Cleverley, he spat, 'He didn't look very dead when he started rolling about on the floor, did he Michael? Didn't *sound* very dead either, come to think of it. I think we'd all have been a bit worried if all that screaming was coming from a corpse.'

Michael Cleverley shot Yoghurt a confused look. As though asking him to translate.

'What's wrong with you Michael? Were you born stupid or did you just grow that way? Stop looking at me like that...'

Cleverley bit his bottom lip. 'Sir, sir, but he might be dead now...'

'You don't need to call me sir now, Michael,' said Hamilton. 'We're not in school, are we? I can't see any corridors here, can you? I can't see any ties or any swing-ropes or any football kits. Mind you, half the time, most of you lot can't seem to see or even find your kits even if its football, eh?'

Despite The Shirt, despite the fact he should have been on Hamilton's side, Yoghurt found himself sharing the frustrations of Cleverley.

'Michael?' barked Hamilton.

Cleverley bit his lip again. 'Robert Heald says that the man who was covered in blood must have got bit by a big animal like a tiger or something and what do you think sir?'

Yoghurt moved away before he could hear more. He found himself walking over towards the X-marks the spot where The Darkness had slipped onto Cover Ye Bottoms. He hunkered down over the streaks of blood on the ground where the body of the mauled man had been before they'd packed him away to the hospital. And he thought about what Cleverley had said. A big animal. And he remembered the raggedy breathing from the bushes over the other side of the causeway. Not for the first time that day, he twitched for his mobile phone. Found himself tapping in Trevor Knox's familiar number. Somehow, it felt like a pre-programmed thing to do, like he could do it even if he was in one of his stares.

And this time, Knox answered. After only two rings. Yoghurt was so surprised he nearly dropped the phone. It took him a moment to compose himself and then he spoke.

'Trev... That you?'

A crackle, then, 'Yes, Ely. It's me. Listen though. We may not have much time. I need you to do something for me...'

'I will... Where are you, I'll come find you...'

Trevor snapped. Swore. Yoghurt shivered. Trevor *never* swore. 'Fuck. No. Ely, listen to me. What I need you to do is this: I need you to stay the fuck away from me. You hear me? I'm no longer my Brother's Keeper. You understand? I have been fucking...' The phone line crackled. Static interrupted. It kicked back in again. '...off the goddamn island, Yoghurt. Just get off the...'

The line went dead. For a long moment, three, four beats, Yoghurt simply stood there with the phone warming his ear. And then his knees buckled and he slipped down onto the ground, on top of the blood stains. He felt The Shirt prickling against him, telling him to get up, but he couldn't get up. Suddenly an old memory was thick around him like cobwebs. The big face of Solomon looming down to his. Smiling. Then pointing at a younger, fitter Trevor Knox. 'This man is your Keeper, Ely. Always remember that. And when the time comes, you must listen to what he says. For he will know what to do.' And Yoghurt had tried to grasp at Solomon's hand, had asked him, 'but won't you be looking out for me?' And Solomon had smiled, sadly. His eyes had flickered. And even though he'd only been eleven, Ely Rhodes had known what would happen.

'The Darkness is at high-tide,' he whispered to himself. 'The Darkness is at high-tide.'

And he would have gone on whispering to himself were it not for more activity up on the stage. Now a farmer had climbed up, had commandeered the microphone stand. There was a whoop as he brought it too close to the amplifier, but then he stepped forward, addressed the crowd.

'There is something loose on the island,' he bellowed. 'Something which is killing our livestock. You all know this to be true. My chickens...' The man choked back a sob. Clenched his fist. 'People, don't let this be another Millennium fiasco. Don't let *them* cover this up...'

Before he could say any more, a tag-team of Carl-Rhys Hamilton and Phil Simpson wrestled him to the ground. Used rather more force than was necessary. In fact, the way Yoghurt saw it, there was almost a madness upon the two men. A Darkness about them. He climbed to his feet, brushed himself down, and thought about how he could get off the island. About obeying his Keeper's command. But almost in the same instant, he knew he wouldn't. He knew his role was here. For, the way he figured it, he knew far more about The Darkness than any of his neighbours, acquaintances, cycling proficiency students, the bullies ever had. After all, he'd been living in its shadow most of his life.

He had to be able to think, and the best way of doing that was to get rid of The Shirt. And so, forgetting all about the crowd, Yoghurt Rhodes started the last act of the talent show. A completely and wholly unexpected strip-show which culminated in his removal of the dreaded, hairy instrument of torture. Flinging it down, he felt the cool breeze on his stinging flesh. And it felt righteous.

18: The Bibby Firm

Mart Bibby slammed down his pint. Amber liquid sloshed out everywhere as though there was an incredibly localised storm going down in the lounge of the Ship. Brass plates shuddered on the walls, a couple china dolphins jangled on the ledge above the fireplace. The electronic talking fish which had long since grown mute, gave a flicker of old life, *almost* looked as though it wanted to complain at the noise.

'They just told me I wasn't needed,' he growled. 'Or rather, that Manny Combs told me. Shaw didn't look as though he had any choice in the matter.'

'Shaw thing,' said Sam Bibby, chancing a smile, hoping it would help calm his brother. He'd not seen him this disturbed since the night they'd arrived too late, much too late, down at the shingle beach near the causeway two nights before the Millennium.

Mart didn't smile. Never smiled much any more. Not even at the old shared jokes which were like a secret language between them. He was looking tired. His big shoulders sagged. There wasn't much spring in him any more. He'd even, for the first time since he was about twelve, when their dad had bought them their first, shared, electric shaver, forgotten to present his usual, clean-shaven face to the world. He picked out his vacuum-packed carton of nicotine-replacement chewing gum and placed it on the table, glared at it accusingly, as though he wanted to do nothing more than screw the whole thing up and toss it into the fireplace. He looked as though he'd do anything for a Benson, or a Dorchester and Grey, a cigarette he could really get his lungs into. But, sighing, he popped one of the gums from the pack and slid it onto his tongue.

Sam Bibby took a heavy swig from his pint. He'd always liked things to be on a level playing field between the two of them. When one was up, the other was up, and when one was down, the other sunk low too. And Mart had already supped twice as much as

180

Sam had. 'Look,' said Sam, wiping the foam away from his mouth with a meaty paw, 'I'm as riled as you are. I should have been on crowd-dispersal. *Dad* would have been on crowd dispersal. Making sure that there wasn't trouble *after* the fact. Mind he always said it wasn't the darkness you saw coming that oughta bother you, but...'

'...The darkness you couldn't,' said Mart, solemnly. Still, it was a start. They were at least in the same book, if not the same hymn sheet. They called themselves The Bibby Firm when they were growing up. It was the two of them against the island, the north east coast, the country, the world. It was them two against all comers with their dad, the local beat bobby, as back-up. Their mam had been back-up too, but she'd got involved in a beef with a particularly vicious opponent in cancer and had not lived past their joint sixth year. Another Limm parent bites the dust...

'This place did for him in the end though, didn't it?' said Mart, staring forlornly into the fireplace, chewing as though the nicotine gum had no taste, had *never* tasted of anything. 'And it's come for us now too.' Suddenly he turned, fixed his eyes on Sam. 'I can feel it when I wake up, Sam. It's trying to get to me, suck me in. Trying to make me not care any more. And I can feel it when I go to bed too, when I know I've had too many of these.' He waved his pint glass, created waves. Mute fish on the wall once more thought about interjecting.

'It's just... We're coming up to middle-aged now. Maybe it's some kind of...'

'What? Crisis?' snapped Mart. 'Not likely. Midlife crises don't fucking bite at you like crabs. They don't make you take scalding showers three times a day just to wash away the filth... My flat above the Crab's Claws... I mean, they only serve the crab-cocktails in summer, when the tourists are about. But the *stink,* Sam.' He sniffed at his armpit. Said, in a half-sob, 'I can smell it on me now. I mean, I know what people say about me being a puff...'

'You're not...'

'I know... But I just give them food for thought. I have to douse myself in aftershave all the time. Like I've just stepped out of a brothel. Just so I don't have to smell fish. All. The. Goddamn. Time.'

Sam Bibby reached out a tree-trunk arm. He liked the way the muscles rippled in the firelight. Someone like Carl-Rhys Hamilton would mutter that he looked like a low-rent hen-night male stripper in his tight uniform. He'd say Mart looked like one too. But people like Carlo Hamilton were on the outside. They weren't part of The Bibby Firm. 'Three more months,' he said, clasping his twin brother's arm. 'Three more months and I swear I'll be able to put that bastard Combs out of office. If I can just dig something up on him... Anything... Well, the elections are in May. We can finish him. Leave with our heads held high. Like dad would have done.'

Mart shook his head, gave his gum a pensive chew. 'You've been saying that three years now. You've investigated the factory, the hotel, Adrian Bloody Devonish, for Christ's sake, and nothing will stick.'

Sam took another draught from his pint. In the bar room, the jukebox kicked in, and he listened to the first bars of *Sympathy for the Devil*. There were old men in the bar room, he knew, who went weeks without speaking to any of their companions, just drained pint after pint, stared at the scantily clad woman on the cardboard behind the peanuts, willing her to finally offer up her prizes to them. But they all, to a man, joined in on the 'woo, woo' chorus bits on *Sympathy for the Devil*. They were like a brainwashed cult... No. They weren't, Sam had seen what brainwashed cults were like.

'I'll find something on him,' said Sam. 'I can feel it.'

Mart finished off his pint, jangled some coins in his pocket. Looked as though he was going to say something like, *yeah right, that's if you get any time between cleaning up the graffiti on the bench on the green and liaising with the coastguard regarding yet more people stranded on the causeway.* But he didn't. He seemed too tired to even partake in his usual stock-in-trade barbed commentary on their shared disappointments at their lot in life. 'Another?' was all he said. And Sam got the distinct impression that Mart was going to keep drowning himself in beer for the rest of the evening. Suddenly he saw too much of their father in his brother. Their father at the end, when his fondness for one too many made his body finally give in to flab.

'Go on then,' he agreed. He watched his brother amble through to the bar room, heard him start ordering up another round without any of the usual chit-chat which would have once accompanied a visit to the bar. Mr. Mute Fish on the wall was more animated.

Sam pulled his mobile phone out of his pocket, absently started scrolling through the messages looking for a joke which he could maybe tell Mart to try and cheer him up. Dave Small, one of the PCs at the nick in Charnley, had a good line in blue jokes which would have made even the hardiest seaman blush. Close-to-the-knuckle stuff. But none of them seemed suitable. He was about to close the phone, return it to his pocket, when it vibrated to indicate he'd received an answerphone message. He received a lot of answerphone messages. Coverage on Limm was so patchy they sometimes came through as much as a week late. Doubtless it would be just another call about a lost cat or a stolen sheep or a vandalized boat. Or it would be Manny Combs telling him to make sure he was early for the talent show so he could check bags and coats for smuggled booze. But it *might* be that one call in a million which was important, so he pressed 'Listen'. Heard the terrified voice of Sally Martin, the school piano teacher, on the other end of the line. He listened to the message in full, and then pressed 'Repeat', dug out a pen, crooked the phone between his shoulder and his ear, and scrawled the details down on a decidedly battered beer-mat. By the time Mart returned to the lounge, clutching two pints and a couple of whisky chasers in his meaty fists and a packet of Mr. Pig's Pork Scratchings clenched between his whitened teeth, Sam Bibby was already off his stool, pulling on his jacket. By the time Mart had deposited his hoard on the table, Sam was already explaining that things on Limm Island had just got that bit curiouser. And before Mart could even complain that he'd have to drink the four drinks himself, Sam was out the door, making for his cruiser.

The call had him worried. Because what he had smelled on Sally Martin's voice, what had set his policeman's nose twitching, was panic. And the last time he'd heard a voice like that, so strained by madness, by fear, it had been in the days leading up to the Millennium. Solomon Mason had got his followers so riled up that they thought the end of the world was coming, or at least, the beginning of the end. They'd demonstrated on the village green and on the jetty, shouting their fears to every passer by. Causing more panic. Causing more trouble. Causing deaths at the beach. His father hadn't been able to handle the knowledge, after the fact, that so many members of the community had perished on his watch. Which was why Sam Bibby now liked to keep such an even keel. It was, he figured as he gunned the engine of his cruiser, the only thing he shared with his – *say it* – nemesis, Manny Combs. If only there'd been a replacement gum for Manny…

183

19: The Patchwork Quilt

The Limm Island A and E room, wasn't really A and E at all. More of a clinic, actually. A low-slung, functional building known as the Bungalow by most of the townspeople. People went to the Bungalow for their flu jabs in winter, or for their holiday jabs in summer. They went there for Mart Bibby's Fat Fighters club on a Monday, Tuesday's New Parents classes, Wednesday's old folks' coffee mornings. Thursdays it was closed. Fridays, and weekends, it operated with only a skeleton staff, volunteers mostly. There was only one bed, and that had been used more by the over-worked staff than patients, the aging doctor Ray Shaw – Dr. Shaw by name, Dr. Completely Uncertain by nature - often catching a few z's in between doling out cough medicine and lollipops to kids who'd done little more than pass their eye tests. There wasn't much by way of emergency equipment either; the life support apparatus they used was older than the building itself. Mostly, the medicines in the locked cabinet were off-the-shelf type stuff. Paracetamol. Vitamin tablets. Nicotine chewing gum. They no longer stocked morphine. There were hardly enough pain-pills to treat a bite from a Chihuahua, let alone whatever had mangled Dan Coffey so bad. And Manny had seen the man's wounds close up. And they *were* bite marks. And they were terrifying. And judging from the circumference of the bites, whatever had bitten him had one hell of a big jaw. One hell of a lot of sharp... *fangs*. Sabres.

And whatever had bitten Dan was still on the loose. And Manny wasn't the only one who'd seen the wounds. No, Dan Coffey had chosen to stagger right through the biggest crowd Limm Island had seen in many a year. He'd chosen to drip his no-doubt in-bred blood all over the biggest group of gossipers, washing-line rumour-mongerers, queue-at-MacAskill's muck-rakers... Hell, even though they'd whisked Coffey's broken body away from the scene as quickly as was humanly possible, people had seen. Taken photos or

184

videos on their damned mobiles too probably. And right about now, the word would be spreading quicker than the morphine-craze back in the 90's. Right about now, Manny was just about sure that panic would be starting to set in. And panic was just about the worst thing ever when it came to the voting public. Because panic caused muddy-thinking, caused people to form mobs, caused people to get itchy trigger fingers. Because Limm was a powder-keg island at the best of times, and right now definitely wasn't the best of times, no matter how many silly TALENT-STRAVAGANZA!!!!!! shows he organised in goddamn February in the goddamn open air.

Manny knew he had to get to the bottom of this mess as quickly, and as cleanly as possible. Which was why he hadn't sanctioned taking Dan across to Marwell, where they actually had a proper hospital – forty bed dontchaknow – and proper treatment facilities and medicines which were a little hardier than the stuff you could buy in Buckby's Book-Buys or The Crab's Claws, if you had a pound to rub together with your matchbook. Which is why he was hoping Dan Coffey would die, so he couldn't start in with what would be, inevitably an embellishment of the truth. Because Coffey was bound to lie. He had form. And, described in his twisted words, whatever bit him and was already, obviously *huge,* would start to take on dinosaur proportions.

Oh, Coffey had form all right. So Manny knew he had to get to him first if he did wake up. So Manny was keeping up a bedside vigil, just waiting for that first flicker of his eyelids, that first raggedy breath which wasn't a snore, that first growl of pain. Because then he'd be on him. Letting Coffey know the score.

The score, as it was, was one nil to Coffey. At least one nil to Coffey. Because Coffey and that damned Copestake kid were poachers. And not exactly secretive about it. No, they *flaunted* the fact they stole what was island property. There were plenty of partridges in the Coffey and Copestake's pear trees and, as yet, because they'd not been caught in the act, because they were only rumoured to be poaching, because they were crafty buggers (and Sam Bibby too damned stupid to catch 'em) they'd got away with it. But Manny had his eyes on them. And in a way, getting done over by an animal seemed to be just desserts.

'Any movement?' asked Ray Shaw, who'd stolen into the room without Manny hearing him, and when he spoke, it almost caused Manny to jump out of his muddied mayoral britches. He'd thought Shaw had found somewhere else to catch some z's, seeing

185

as though his usual bed was taken, but the crafty bastard had been off doing something else. Probably on the blower to his pals over in Marwell, telling them all about Coffey's animal bites, despite Manny's express instructions not to tell anyone about the mess.

Manny turned, slowly. Slapped on his Cheryl Hammerstein look just in case Not So Shaw managed to read the frustration which had been present earlier. He took in Never Been Shaw's wearied face. The doctor looked as though he'd fallen off his crest. His shoulders were hunched, his eyes haunted, his cheeks brushed with iron-filing stubble which made him look even older than he actually was. Manny knew for a fact Can't Be Shaw couldn't handle being the pressure of being the town's doctor any more. What's more, he thought he could catch the sniff of alcohol on the good doctor's breath. And sure, it wasn't distinct, no, he'd tried to cover it up with extra strong mints, but it *was* there. Now he came to think of it, Manny reckoned One Thing's For Shaw hadn't been off making banned phone calls at all. Probably he'd simply been topping himself up with a few sniffters of the old whisky, he'd released that old golden valve. The town was a veritable haven for drinkers. If it wasn't the morphine it was the drink. People slowly poisoning themselves, neutering themselves so they didn't have to fully comprehend the sad reality of their sorry existences. Sometimes, at town meetings, Manny would look around him and everyone in the room looked as though they'd pickled themselves in booze. Which was why, whenever he got the chance, *he* made the decisions, and let everyone else just wallow.

'Nothing,' said Manny, his voice a dull monotone. 'Dead to the world still.'

Are You Shaw looked as though he didn't like Manny's choice of words, but said nothing about it. Instead he strolled over to the bed and unclipped Coffey's file from one of the rungs. Manny saw the tell-tale shake in his hands as he started leafing through the papers.

'Will he wake up?'

There's Only Two Shaw Things in Life, Death and Crabbie's Boat Taxis Running Late raised his head. Fixed Manny with his tired eyes. 'I don't know. We should have...'

Manny held up a warning hand. 'Don't say we should have taken him to Marwell. We couldn't *risk* taking him to Marwell, can't you see that?'

186

Shaw Thing looked as though he was going to object. As though he was going to start kicking up a fuss again. Manny gave his shoulder a consoling pat. 'Besides, doc, you're better'n all of them chancers at Marwell. Here at the Bungalow, under your... careful supervision... Coffey's getting the best care he could hope for.'

Shaw-ly Some Mistake gave an awkward cough which was actually more of a bark. He shuffled his feet. Looked as though he wanted to get as far away from Manny's touch as was humanly possible. But Manny wouldn't let him. He increased the pressure of his hand on the doctor's off-white coated shoulder. 'You've seen the bites, doc. You've tried to dress his wounds. You've seen the mess whatever it is has made of this feller. Whatever it is is *big*. Whatever it is is out there, *stalking* our town. And whatever it is is brave. If it is an animal, and it's prepared to attack a feller like this, then imagine what it could do to a child. And now imagine you've got a child yourself. And you know there's something out there, *hunting* us. How would that make you feel?'

'But... What do you think it is, Manny? Mr. Combs, I mean...'

They both paused as the battered old life support machine which Coffey was hooked-up to – a machine which looked about as much use in a life or death situation as a goddamn *washing machine* – started to splutter and cough. As the steady bleep... bleep... bleep which told them it was, despite everything, still working, suddenly stopped. Bleep... bleep... nothing. One tick, two ticks, three ticks. And then bleep... bleep... bleep again.

Manny sucked in a breath which was half-relieved, half-disappointed and then answered, in a lower voice. 'It doesn't matter what I think it is. It matters what the *town* thinks it is. And if we can control what the town thinks it is, then we'll all be better off for it. Dan Coffey had an industrial accident. He got too close to some farm machinery. The machinery gobbled him up, not an animal. You got it?'

'But... People *saw* him, and people aren't stupid. Anyone with eyes would have been able to see that what caused his wounds was alive. Was alive and had... oh God... big jaws and teeth and...'

'It was an industrial accident,' repeated Manny. And even as he said it, he was starting to believe. And even as he said it, he saw how much Shaw-ly The Headline Writer's Dream wanted to believe too. And Manny immediately started to feel better about the whole situation. The thing with people was... The thing with people was

187

people was stupid. People wanted to be led. Ninety-nine percent of the town thought the world ended at the end of the causeway. Half of one percent of the town were like Dr. Shaw-t On Ideas. Knew there was *something* bigger than the town, but didn't dare think about how big that something might be. But there was only one person, so, approximately nought point six, six, six of a percent, who saw the whole, massive jigsaw which was the world at large. And that person was Manny Combs. And so, it was his duty to lead the blind. It was his duty to tell them what to believe. And Dan Coffey had had an industrial accident. End of story.

Shaw Me The Money returned Coffey's file to the bottom of the bed and the two men stared wordlessly down at the lump in the bedsheets who'd just had his status irrevocably changed. Coffey took up a lot of space in the bed. He was a big lump and that was for sure. Chubby bordering on fat. *Roomy.* They'd – Shaw and the fairy male nurse who'd carried him in – washed most of the blood off him before installing him in the bed, but now more of it was seeping out, from one of the many lacerations which covered his torso. Seeping out through the thick bandages. And the blood was black, not red. It had even started to stain the patchwork quilt which formed the bed's top-sheet. Manny reckoned Shaw-berry Jam would probably have to throw the damn thing out when they came to the end of this, when Coffey died, or woke up, or whatever. And Shaw-t Crust Pastry, for whom the big picture was still somewhat shrouded, for whom sentimentality was king, would probably be really upset by this. Because his dull as dishwater wife, his *insane* as dishwater wife, Felicity, had probably knitted the quilt herself. Manny, who had no time for quilts or wives, found himself staring so hard at the quilt it was almost as though he wanted it to spontaneously combust, carrying that lump in the sheets with it into whatever level of hell poaching got a feller into.

Bleep... bleep... bleep, said the machine, wearily.

'I feel so useless,' said That's For Shaw. 'All I can do is change his dressings. Mop up his blood.'

'You've done everything you can, for now. Got him on that machine and all,' said Manny. He slapped his paw on the top of the machine to emphasise his point. For a moment, it seemed as though it was going to finally give up the ghost, but then again with the bleep... bleep... bleep. The sound was starting to get on his nerves. Fraying them. Fraying them like so many of the loose threads which hung off Shaw To Be A Moose's wife's crappy patchwork quilt. He massaged his forehead, trying to steady himself. Then he had a thought. 'Actually, there is one thing you can do, if you fancy it?'

'Anything...'

'Witnesses.'

'Pardon?'

'Witnesses. Coffey usually didn't go round on his own, see? Coffey was usually in cahoots with that other reprobate, Copestake. And if Copestake *was* with Coffey, we need to track him down. Think you can make a couple of phone calls?'

'Try and find out if *that thing* went for him as well?'

'Sure,' said Manny. *Sure, Shaw. And to make sure he keeps his damn mouth shut too.*

Sure Shaw lingered. 'You'll come get me if anything changes. Even if his breathing changes... '

Manny made a dismissive gesture with his hand. 'Don't worry doc. This feller ain't going anywhere.' *'Cept for hell, of course.*

Dr. Shaw, I Presume, nodded and headed out the door, back down the hallway to reception. Manny went to check the old dithering doc wasn't going to come back, then closed the door behind him, wedging it with a chair under the knob. He allowed himself a brief whistle as he walked back to the lump in the bed. The whistle was pitched, approximately, in the same key as the bleeping old machine which was doing most of Coffey's breathing for him. Whistling Dixie for him.

'You can wake yourself up now,' he said, crouching low over Coffey's prone form. Crouching so low that when he talked, when he spat out his words, the spittle landed on the erstwhile poacher's chubby cheek and ran down it like a single, sad tear. 'And stop all this messing about.'

Coffey didn't move. His only answer was another mechanical *hoover* breath.

'Coffey. You need to wake up and smell the coffee before it's too late.'

Again there was no discernible change in the man's chubby-bordering-on-fat features. Manny wondered whether Coffey was somehow brain-damaged. Whether he'd been turned vegetable by that animal. Whether the minerals upstairs in his mind had gone off to cock.

'Coffey, if you can hear me, I'd like you to cough. One for yes, two for no. Can you hear me?'

189

Nothing. Not even a flicker of the eyes behind those heavy lids. Manny felt the frustration rising up inside him. He needed to know what Coffey knew. Needed to know just what size carpet he'd have to brush everything under. Before he knew what he was doing he'd reached down and had grasped Coffey around the throat. And before he could stop himself, he was shaking the man. Rattling him. As he did so, the breathing mask which covered Coffey's mouth got kinda loosened.

'Wake up, you fat fucker,' panted Manny.

But Coffey *still* wouldn't respond. And now Manny felt the rage bubbling on his tongue. Tasted caustic. Bloody, as though he'd chewed through his tonsils. He tried to gulp it back down inside him, but now it felt like a lump. Like a great lump of congealing mayonnaise in his throat. He struggled for breath. Thought about tugging the oxygen mask right off Coffey's great fat moon of a head and installing it on his own face. He gasped, wheezed, belched. Let go of Coffey. Let him flop back down, a dead weight, onto the bed. His dodgy ticker was beating a haphazard drum in his chest, like a drunken monkey. He gripped the metal bed-head with a white-knuckled hand. Forced himself to breathe in time with the steady bleep... bleep... bleep.

And gradually, his heart started to respond. Gradually, he felt the fire in his chest start to die down. Gradually the lump in his throat started to melt away.

'Look what you did to me,' he said, hoarsely. 'Look what you did, you ugly, poaching bastard.'

And now he felt the *good* part of the rage. The part which instilled a new kind of superhuman strength. The part which bypassed his dodgy ticker and worked straight into his big paws. He lashed out, his fist connecting with the side of Coffey's head. And it felt wonderful.

He punched him again, Coffey's head snapping back against the pillows. A long trail of drool flopped out of his slack mouth. And when his head snapped back into place, Manny saw, for the first time a flicker of something. His right eyeball rolling around in the socket. The eyelashes starting to dance, to creep open.

'I know you can hear me,' he said. 'So stop with this idiocy. We need to talk, and quickly.'

Finally, Coffey opened his eyes. And they didn't just open, they *saucered*. They flew open so wide they became an abyss. Coffey looked terrified. Manny crouched low over him. So close

190

now their noses were almost touching. So close Manny thought he could smell the tang of alcohol on the patient's breath. It disgusted him so much, he felt his hand clenching into another fist.

'Tell me what you saw.'

Coffey looked as though he didn't understand simple English. Didn't comprehend that this was a command. His bottom lip started to tremble and another long trail of drool slopped out. This time it contained a rich red seam of blood. Manny realised this was probably because he was now virtually lying on Coffey's chest. Was pressing most of his weight into him, into his chest wounds. It was almost as though he was *wringing* the blood outta him.

'What is it?' he barked. 'What is this thing in my town? On my island?'

Coffey sniffled. Blood was starting to appear in his nostrils now. And in his ears. His yellowing teeth were now *black* with it, as though he'd been drinking red wine. Hell, it smelled like red wine. And that smell almost seemed to be mocking Manny. *Everyone can have a drink but you Manny. Even this here half-dead poacher. Everyone in this godforsaken town can drink, a drink, a drink until the cows come home. Everyone but you, that is. And you know why, dontcha Manny?*

'What is it, Coffey? What are... ?'

Finally Coffey spoke, his voice a trembling high-pitched, *rodenty* squeal. He sounded drunk, goddamnit. 'It was a panther, sir. A black panther, Mr. Combs. It...' Coffey screwed up his eyes. Began to emit this eerie low keening sound. It was too loud. The sound would carry all the way down the corridor and into reception. The sound would bring that Shaw Is a Goody Two-Shoes doctor coming. The sound would bring Shaw and all his concern, and Shaw would see all the blood and Manny's face twisted in cold rage and he'd see the terror in Coffey's eyes and he'd think *this ain't no industrial accident. A man don't get so scared of a goddamn tractor or something.*

Manny thought he'd better give Coffey some space, so he climbed down off the bed and smoothed down the patchwork quilt a little. As he did so, he kinda knocked into the big old washing-machine style life support machine, and once again, it started to have palpitations just like the ones which his old ticker had been doing just a few minutes earlier, when Coffey had got him all riled. *Bleeee... Ble... B...*it went. Then nothing. And then, slowly, splutteringly, *bleep... bleep... bleep* again.

191

Manny thought he'd better hunker on down and have a proper look at the machine, just to be on the safe side. Shifting himself down into a position which roughly approximated the one Yoghurt Rhodes had been in what seemed like *years* ago, in some much older, more innocent age, when he'd been shooting off the old photies on his new Nikon, wasn't easy for a man of Manny's bulk, but he managed it somehow. He touched the plug. *I wonder what would happen if I... Surely, it wouldn't hurt if I...* It was weird, how something as simple as a plug was keeping the man in the bed alive.

'What are you doing, Mr. Combs?' groaned Coffey. Manny could hear him shifting in the bed, trying to get a better look.

'Nothing for noseys,' he said. And then, before he could give himself a chance to have second thoughts, he pulled the plug.

Bleep... bleep... Nothing. Silence. Beautiful, blessed silence.

And then Coffey spoke again. And Manny found himself surprised at the fact the man was still alive.

'Mr. Combs, why have you turned the machine off?'

Manny laughed then. A low rumble which must have sounded to Coffey like an earthquake. *Of course Coffey was still alive. The machine wasn't breathing for him now, was it? So he'd have to find another way of keeping him quiet.*

He climbed back to his feet.

'You must be very tired after all the... emotion of the day,' he said. He stroked a rogue strand of Coffey's hair away from his face. 'Must want to close your eyes and forget all about it, huh?'

'I... I don't think I could,' groaned Coffey. 'I think I'd... I might have a nightmare or something.'

Manny had never had kids. Never had a wife to have kids with. But at that moment, the feeling which washed through him could only have been described as paternal. 'I'm here, Dan, lad. I'm watching out for you.' He was going to add, *and I'll see that you come to no harm, not in my town,* but that wouldn't have been strictly true, and Manny had never been a liar. Not that he knew about anyway. Honest Manny, he could have been called, he supposed, if he'd ever followed up on those plans to open up a car showroom. But politics had got in the way. Duty and responsibility had got in the way. And the sacrifices – foregoing his own personal accumulation of wealth for the good of the island and its people – had started to stack up.

Now, of course, it was his admittedly sad duty and responsibility to make sure that the panic which all Coffey's talk of a black panther was bound to spread, was nipped in the bud, and quickly. And the fact that, in doing so, he'd well and truly even up those scores, definitely, *definitively,* make it one apiece, was neither here nor there. The only reason Manny was now gently lifting Coffey's head off the pillow, removing said pillow, and now – 'Don't Mr. Combs!'; 'I have to, son.' - holding it down over his face was to protect the many. The only reason he was making this small sacrifice, pushing the pillow down so hard he thought he could hear the crunch of Dan Coffey's nose as it crackled into so many pieces, was to ensure everyone else could sleep at night and not have to worry about the nightmares which were bound to plague Coffey's sleep forever, if he was allowed to live. The righteousness he felt as Dan Coffey's broken body started to kick and struggle, as he *launched* the patchwork quilt off the bed, as he flailed his arms about desperately, was something to savour. But there was a paternal sadness there too. And as Coffey's struggles began to die down, as he no longer had the power in him to kick out, as he stopped loosening up his bandages and spreading that black blood of his all about the place, he whispered, 'I'm sorry, son, I really am.'

Coffey was dead at least a minute before Manny finally moved the pillow away. He forced himself to look once. Just so he could remember the horror of his bloated, empurpled features, just so he could etch it in his mind as just one more thing he'd done for the town. And then he picked up the patchwork quilt and he draped it over him like a shroud. Then he turned his back, and walked over to the little sink. Above it there was a hand-written sign. NOW WASH YOUR HANDS. Manny did so carefully. Taking his time to scrub away at the black blood which had somehow gathered under his fingernails. Using a wire-brush which some kind soul, Shaw Runs a Clean Show perhaps, or else the fairy male nurse, had left on the side. Then, and only when every single spot had been washed away, cycling down the plughole, the water running at first a dirty brown, like the River Drey, then a lighter, toilet brown, until it became opaque, Manny went back to the door, removed the chair which was wedged under the knob. He pulled the door open, slapped on another Cheryl look, and he shouted down the corridor into the reception area, where he could hear the doctor talking animatedly on the phone.

'Doc!' he yelled. 'You'd better come. Quickly! I think the bleeping's stopped!'

Shaw sure came quickly.

20: Keep the wolf from the door

Though the fire was on in the front room, Sally was shivering, hugging the pint-sized coffee mug into the folds of her big blue towelling dressing gown as though it was a hot water bottle. She had her legs tucked in underneath her on the sofa, making herself as small as possible, using the big bean bag cushion on her lap for extra cover. And yet she was still cold.

By contrast, the policeman Sam Bibby, who was slouched, legs spread wide, on the armchair closet to the door which led out into the bracing hallway and was probably getting the draft from under the door full throttle, had already removed his not-exactly-standard-issue black Puffa jacket and was now in his shirt-sleeves. Looked as though he was seriously considering rolling them up too, if that were possible, if the thin material could actually stretch far enough to get over his bulbous, muscular arms. Jo thought there was something faintly obscene about his arms, and in particular, his hands. The way he picked up the tiny china tea cup she'd issued him with. The way he couldn't fit his fat – no, probably solidly muscular, like the rest of him – fingers through the handle. The way his fingers looked so dumb, the pinkie sticking out like a goddam T-Rex arm; useless. It wasn't Sam's fault; she was finding it hard to look at *any* fingers after what she'd seen.

She was trying to avoid his eyes, trying to avoid the policeman's judgement. But she could tell already he didn't believe her. Why else would he have waited full six hours since her frenzied call to come round, in practically the middle of the night, to take her statement? Stinking of pub too...

It had been Rob who'd answered the door; Sally simply couldn't after the rat-tat-tat shock of Sam's policeman's knock had shaken her out of an awkward half-sleep on the sofa. It had been Rob who'd answered the door, and he'd not even bothered hanging up on his call as he did so, remaining on the line on the cordless phone even as he ushered Sam into the front room, where Sally had been hastily re-arranging herself. And now, Sam was simply waiting for this to be over. So he could go back to the Ship most likely. That was why he was waiting for Rob to finish his phone call before he started in on the questions when he could have just as easily asked them in a different room now. He wanted Rob there, to keep them on the straight and narrow. He wanted Rob there because, Sally could see, he thought her mad. He thought she 'had form'. He'd probably heard her completely off-key rendition of *Dancing in the Moonlight* for the fourth-year girls' dancing troup at the talent show.

Rob was sitting by the desk in the alcove window, below the framed Alan Majchrowicz print of a raging sea which both men probably thought summed up her mental state quite accurately. Rob, infuriatingly, was dressed like a normal person, in his nice dark jeans and a polo shirt, and not in his usual trackie bottoms and hoodie (his 'writer's scrubs' as he called them.) He wasn't shivering. He wasn't wild-eyed and wild-haired; could never be wild-haired; a receding hairline at the age of twenty had seen him shave it all off forever, and now his bald dome shone like a *'pick me, pick me'* halo. And there was no doubting the fact Sam Bibby *had* already picked his side in the sanity stakes.

Rob was still on the cordless phone. It was crooked into his shoulder so he could scribble notes as he listened and talked. So he could show a heretofore unseen ability to multi-task. He was on the phone, Sally thought, to a potential agent in France of all places. Wasn't even bothering to attempt French.

'M.a.r.t.i.n,' he spelled. 'Robert Martin... No, Martin is my *surname*. Get it?'

On the armchair, Sam Bibby stifled a smile. On the sofa, Sally didn't bother disguising a sneer.

'Rob Martin. I sent you a manuscript... the first ten pages of my screenplay. Yes... *Oui*... The very dark one. It would be... somewhat troubling, too complicated to be made here in the UK, but with the sensibilities of the French... You've not received it? I posted it last Tuesday. Recorded delivery... Let me see if I can find my reference number...' He leafed through his moleskine notebook, licking the tip of his finger to turn the page. This tic reminded Sally of the librarian at her school, or of an accountant. Certainly it was a real *paper-pusher's* trait. She hoped Sam Bibby had clocked it and was now reassessing his previous opinion on Rob's good character.

'Here we are,' continued Rob, rattling off the eleven digit number. 'Yes, it was called *The Other World which Babies See.* Opened with a terrifying scene of a mother standing over a crib with the baby screaming. The baby could see...' Rob removed the phone from his shoulder, shook it, and then gave it an accusing glare. Then, by way of explanation, 'I don't believe it. The daft mare's only put me on hold.'

Sam Bibby nodded awkwardly, not quite knowing whether he was being addressed directly.

'And I am sorry to keep you waiting, um, Officer Bibby.'

Sam Bibby held up a Big Plate Special of a palm, signalling, *it's okay,* and then, in a low voice as though he feared the French literary agent, or the French literary agent's secretarial woman (sounded like a John Fowles novel) could somehow hear him through the hold music and across the channel, he said: 'And it's Sam. Call me Sam.'

'Play it again Sam,' said Rob pointlessly. Even he must have realised the pointlessness of what he'd said, because he had the good grace to look embarrassed. He raised the phone to his ear again – 'Still on hold!' - and then with a decisive flourish pressed the red 'end call' button. 'Honestly, those ribbits,' he said, giving this exaggerated shrug which was more Gallic than Asterix, Charles de Gaulle or Eric Cantona. 'Daft mare's probably gone out for a four hour dinner or something... Look, I'm sorry to have kept you, Sam, but I had to make that call, it was important.'

'Absolutely no worries,' said Sam. He was still using the soft voice as though he now feared the French literary agent's secretarial woman could hear him over a dead line. 'And I'm sorry it's taken me so long to respond to the call, but we were absolutely all hands on deck what with...'

'That daft talent thing?' interrupted Rob.

'Well... yes,' said Sam, and there was something furtive about the way he immediately averted his gaze; pretended to be looking at the rollicking waves on the Majchrowicz print. Rob, of course, completely failed to spot it; called himself a writer, an observer, and yet he couldn't even read the simplest of gestures, couldn't decipher the most rudimentary body language. Couldn't see that *something had happened* at the talent show. Something big. Something linked to the finger, perhaps. Certainly that was what Sally thought. 'Amongst other things... Anyway, I'm here now so I'd like you to take me through exactly everything that happened.

196

From the call, I believe you found a... Your wife claims to have discovered... A human finger...in...' He pulled a beer-mat from the pocket of his Puffa jacket. No moleskine for Sam Bibby, Sally noted. No, this was a Ship special. 'Discovered in the garden of a Mister Old Man Poole. That about sum it up, Mr. Martin?'

Rob's face beamed with the light of the sane. Sally thought he was going to crack some terrible joke about Bibby at least being able to pronounce his name right, not like them damn *ribbits,* but he didn't, instead, he reinforced the all boys together atmosphere by saying: 'Call me Rob, why don't you?'

'Okay... Rob. Why don't you tell me?'

Sally wanted to scream: *why don't you ask me? It was me found the finger... People actually, but People can't speak, only sometimes, and then it's not actual words but a kind of meeting of minds...*

'I'm a writer. Screenplays mainly, but I do some copywriting too. Everyone has to pay the bills.'

'Keep the wolf from the door, yes I know what you mean... Anything I might have heard of?'

Rob smiled. 'There was this one small series which, happily, some people watched. I suppose you could call it a cult thing really. You'll probably never have heard of it.'

'Try me,' said Sam.

'*Life on Mars?*'

'*Life on Mars?* The cop show, where he goes back to the seventies and all that? You wrote that?'

Sally bit her lip. Hard. *No of course he didn't write that. That's why we're not living in a chateau in the Dordogne. He was on a BBC mentoring scheme at the time and one, throwaway, two-minute piece of his dialogue somehow made it into episode seven of series two. Didn't even make it on the credits for the TV version. And yet he tells the story so many times he probably believes he wrote the whole goddamn script by now.*

'Not all of it,' said Rob, coming off all Uriah Heap humble. 'But you could say I was one of the key creative influences.'

'I love that show,' mused Sam. 'Sometimes I chat with fellow officers. Dave Small... We've got a social networking site you know; just for us lonely beat bobbies in small towns like this. And you won't find a bad word said about that show anywhere on the site. Wow, Mr. Martin, that's something special.'

197

'Rob,' said Rob, 'and I wasn't meaning to go all name-droppy on you, I was just setting the scene.'

'Like in a drama,' said Sam, edging forward on his seat.

'Like in a drama. So I was writing. I have a small office on the first floor. It overlooks the back garden, and Mr. Poole's property too, but I find staring out of the window can be a bit of a distraction, so I put up some of that thick black material which shuts out all the light. You know, like the old air-raid curtains? Well anyway, I was doing some draft work on my current work in progress. It's the psychological thriller which I'm in discussions with the French about, although don't get me started on their negotiating skills. So I was working on getting the dialogue just so, you know, trying to get it as authentic as possible, trying to make it how real people, like you and me and Sally over there, speak.'

For a moment, Sam Bibby looked confused as to who this mysterious Sally person was. Perhaps he thought Sally was the name of the cat. But he clicked when Sally slammed her pint-pot of coffee down on the coffee table. Both men shot her a wary look.

'And when was this?' said Sam Bibby after a beat of awkward silence.

'Last night... Anyway, I was tapping away, whittling down my words. Honing them. And from what I understand, my wife was outside bringing the washing in from the line,' said Rob.

'At night?' asked Sam.

Sally thought she'd better defend herself. 'I was doing the washing at night because otherwise it stinks of chimney smoke and Rob won't have that. I was bringing in the washing even though it wasn't properly dry, even though it was too cold for it to dry, and I was making sure I didn't put any socks in the peg bag and any pegs in the washing pile. Rob here was probably typing 'all work and no play makes Rob a dull boy,' over and over again, like in *The Shining.* Can we just get on to what happened?'

Icy silence chilled the room. Both men stared at the floor.

'I'm sorry about that,' muttered Rob.

'That's quite all right,' said Sam. 'I can see that...'

He left his statement hanging. Sally wanted to reach out and grasp it, shake it for all it was worth, *screech* in his face: *See that what? See that this is a cry for attention from a madwoman? Well maybe I do need some attention, but I found a finger. And I could describe it quite accurately. What I'm worried about is that the finger might belong to Old Man Poole. That maybe he's just lying*

198

*dead in that ramshackle house of his and nobody's even cared to go
see him... Or else maybe it's got something to do with the terrible
events at the talent show, the events Rob's not even bothered to ask
about yet.*

Rob cleared his throat and started again. Started with the
lies, the embellishments of the truth, playing his game, inventing
fictions which would make him come off as the sane superstar and
her as the whimpering mess. Nothing about his own stir-craziness,
the way, when she walked into his office soaked with mud, leaves
dangling from her pony-tail, screeching with terror, he'd not gone to
her, not put his arms around her. First he seemed more concerned
with covering his papers with his arm like he was a kid at school,
and then hastily depositing them in his drawer when he saw she
wasn't budging.

'It was a terrible shock, of course, seeing her come into my
office like that. She was *dishevelled.* Screaming like a banshee.
Blabbering all kinds of nonsense. It was all I could do to make her
sit down in a chair and take deep breaths. I have a Teasmade in my
office and I made her a hot drink and then she was calm enough to
tell me what she'd seen, or what she thought she'd seen, but
unfortunately she's not kept the evidence, have you dear? And now,
it appears our darling cat has run off with it, which seems...'

*Don't say convenient, don't say convenient, don't say
convenient.*

'...Frustrating. But I managed to calm her some more and
then I ran her a nice warm bath and laid out her dressing gown...'
Here he gestured to Sally, as though Sam might not know what a
dressing gown was. Sam acknowledged the gesture. *Thanks mate.*
'And she's been there ever since, apart from an hour or so earlier
today when she upped and left and went to that blasted talent
thing... And anyway, soon as she was back, I ran her another bath,
because she still seemed shaken, and I made her more tea and... And
it was while I was doing all of those tasks that she called you, I
understand. Which I'm dreadfully sorry about, because I'm sure
you've got enough on your plate as it is.'

For the first time, Sam Bibby asked her a direct question.
'Are you sure you saw a finger?'

Sally wanted to say something snappy like, *I'm so sure I
could even read the prints off it,* but instead, when she opened her
mouth, all that came out was a single, low sob.

'What do you think, Mr. Martin, uh, Rob?'

'Honestly?'

'Honestly.'

'Well the culprit, if that what she is, or the chief witness, is the cat. And we've not seen the cat since, have we, Sal?'

Sally shook her head. Tried not to imagine all the horrible new treats her darling People could now be pilfering from poor, rotting Old Man Poole's body.

'And has the cat got, um, form for killing small animals and such?' asked Sam. He'd now turned over a clean page in his cheapo notepad and was starting to jot down a few notes in a tiny, scrawled hand. A hand which didn't quite fit his real, satellite dish of a paw.

'Brings in creatures all the time. Even had a hedgehog once,' confirmed Rob.

'And do you think you could have mistaken this... uh... finger for a mouse or a vole or some other hedgerow thing?' His pen hovering over the beer-mat, expectant. Expecting to be able to wrap up the case in as little a time as drinking a china cup of tea. Expecting to be able to file it away as a 213 or something, whatever the code was for a madwoman who had nothing better to do with her time than make up stories. 'You see, as soon as I picked up the call from you, I came straight away... but as I was driving over, something occurred to me. After what happened this afternoon, I imagine all sorts of people are imagining all sorts of things...'

'What do you mean, *this afternoon*?' said Rob.

Sam Bibby told the full story of what had happened down at Coverley Bottoms. Rob's mouth flapped open and closed like a grounded fish. When Sam had finished his explanation, Rob blew out his cheeks, said, 'But... She never told me any of this...'

'I see,' said Sam Bibby.

'And you'll also be able to see what... what kind of a position this puts me in. I mean, after witnessing something like that... After the *shock* of witnessing something like that, you can understand that people's minds are liable to get a little... Mixed-up.'

Rob nodded.

Sally could see where this was going, but had to at least rescue *something* from the situation. She steeled herself to speak. Took a gulp from her now lukewarm coffee. Swallowed hard. 'Will you promise to check in on Old Man Poole?' she managed to gasp.

Sam climbed to his feet, sauntered across the dog-hair rug. Towered above her. For a moment, she thought he was going to pat her on the head – *atta girl* – but he didn't, he just lingered above her like a tall, bad smell, like a not quite properly erected ladder resting on the drains. After a moment, he said, 'I'll check in on him first thing in the morning. I'm not sure he'd appreciate being woken up at this time of an evening. I'll even go see the Father at Church. See about getting Poole's name put down on the community visit list.'

'Thank you,' said Rob. 'Thank you for being so... so understanding. She's...'

'I'm sorry too,' sniffed Sally, just wanting the ordeal to be over now, just wanting this Mister Po-liceman out of her front room. Just wanting People here, curled up on her lap, purring. Well, maybe not that... Not just yet.

'I'll see you out,' said Rob, shepherding Sam out the door. Closing it quickly behind them so they didn't let too much of the cold air inside (with the looney.)

Out in the draughty hallway, she heard the men talking. Whispering amongst themselves. *Whisper, whisper, whisper. Conspire, conspire, conspire.* Rob said: 'My wife's been a little *over-wrought* recently. I've spoken about psychiatrists and psychologists, but it doesn't make the blindest bit of difference. It's the move out here. It's being away from her friends and family. I tell her it'll be good for her, but...' She could imagine him shrugging here, then the two of them shaking their heads. Another dismissal. *She doesn't listen.*

She heard Sam Bibby's reply too. 'That's all right. Happens all the time. Look, if she needs to get out of the house, there are plenty of clubs she can join. My brother works part-time at The Bungalow. He runs dance classes and the like. Keep-fit. They're even doing French classes at the library. Adult education and the like. Why not get her involved in something like that?'

'Something like that would be... brilliant, thanks.'

She imagined the two men embracing on the front doorstep, their good deed done for the day. Sorting her head out was as easy as signing her up to an evening class according to them. Well it wasn't. *En coule* to that notion. Sally already knew more French than probably the whole town put together, and she already knew what she'd seen out back of Old Man Poole's place. And if the men wouldn't help her, or even see her point, then she'd damn well *prove it* to them. This was only the beginning.

21: Tell-Tale Heart

The sound was loud enough to wake the dead, but it didn't wake Manny. Despite the long night at the Bungalow, despite what he'd been forced to do there, he'd not as yet dropped off to sleep. Despite the fact the glowing red display on the bedside clock read 03.48, he was still as frustratingly awake, his mind as frustratingly *alive* as it had been at any point over the past, traumatic twenty-four hours.

When he'd left the Bungalow, leaving Dr. Never Been Shaw still snivelling and crying and alternating between complaining that they should have taken Coffey to Marwell and blaming himself for not having done enough, Manny had wandered out the door, out into the rain-slicked car park and had taken a moment, leaning against his car's cold, wet bonnet, in an attempt to slow his clattering heart. Then he'd climbed inside, climbing in the back seat first, as though still expecting there to be a chauffeur present. Only after a good minute did he remember he'd sent his driver away. Hadn't wanted him hanging around in case anything happened. And in this case anything *had* happened.

And as he climbed in the front seat and gunned the engine, as he listened to its delicious, well-tuned purr, he'd felt the tiredness washing over him. And as he flicked on the windscreen wipers and tried to clear the blurred screen, and discovered it wasn't the *screen* which was wrong, but his over-worked eyes, he'd decided he couldn't risk driving the two miles across town to his house. He'd decided the only thing for it was to take the much shorter trip onto Farne Street, to the town hall and his mayoral offices, where he had a bed, much like the one Coffey had died in (only *sans* the goddamn patchwork quilt) installed in a small adjunct room off his office.

Only, once he was tucked up in that bed, the sleepiness had suddenly evaporated. Once he was in the bed, and the lights were off, he'd started to feel haunted. Haunted by his tell-tale, non-conforming heart. As soon as he'd lain down he'd felt how bowling-ball heavy it felt in his chest. So he'd changed position, tried to balance out the weight. Tucked the pillows up behind his back as though he was a patient at Marwell Hospital. But even thinking about being in Marwell Hospital, even thinking of medical treatments, of open heart surgery, of himself being cut open, his rib-cage cracked apart to let their gloved fingers inside him, made him feel light-headed.

And in the silence of the town hall, all he could hear was his heart, beating a military tattoo in his chest. He'd thought he wouldn't last out the night. He'd started trying to second guess his heart. Tried to anticipate that moment when the crushing, suffocating pain would machete through him. Tried to anticipate just how bad it would be. Because if he expected it, it wouldn't be as much of a shock, and hence he could beat it. He tried to counteract the pain which hadn't happened yet by gripping his shoulder white-knuckle tightly. Tried to breathe deeper. *Surely more oxygen was good for the heart?*

But red wine was supposed to be good for the heart too, all the doctors said so, even old Never Shaw About Anything. And red wine, all alcohol was what had put him in this bloody mess in the first place, wasn't it? Because drinking alcohol, releasing the old gold valve, was akin to signing your own painful-slow death warrant.

He started seeing things in the shadows behind his eyelids. Slinking things. And then even they couldn't scare him, because every once in a while, just when he'd almost got himself convinced he could beat it, his heart would give a brief flutter, just to remind him it was there, just to remind him that it was *waaaay* out of his control. And with every brief flutter, Manny thought he was receiving the final broadcast, the famous last words, the warning that *this* was the one which would finally be the trigger for his heart, his whole body, to shut down.

So he was awake when the sound which was loud enough to wake the dead fire-crackered through the town hall. But he wasn't entirely compos mentis. At first he assured himself the sound was the black panthers of hell clattering down the corridors, coming for him. Then, when he realised it was coming from further away, he thought it could have been the, admittedly *un*ghostly, racket of Dan Coffey, come for his revenge, rattling his chains. But the sounds weren't jangly enough to be chains. Sounded more... more earthy than that. And more insistent.

It was the front door.

It was someone hammering on the door with all the urgency of the police on a drug bust. Hell, it *could* have been the police. Perhaps Ray Shaw had finally seen what was staring him in the face, that Dan Coffey hadn't suffocated himself to death at all, and had called them. Sam Bibby, the local Beat Bobby, would be there. But he'd have back-up too. He'd have a whole Bibby Firm team of bullet-proof vested back-up. And probably Mike Ford from *The Tide Piper* would be there. Just to make sure he could jot down Manny Combs remarkable fall from grace in that pathetic reporter's jotter of his.

Manny screwed up his eyes and tried to ignore the banging. But the banging wouldn't go away. It was relentless. It was going to send him over the edge. It was going to bring on the heart attack, finally. Wearily, Manny swung his legs out of the tight clutches of the bed's over-starched sheets. Gasped as his toes touched the cold concrete floor. Then forced himself to feel out his slippers which he'd tucked under the bed. Strangely, it seemed as though someone had moved them. Only a few inches or so, but they'd definitely been moved. But Manny hadn't slept. Had remained watchful throughout the night. So surely something or someone had moved them, or else...

...Or else his mind, or his heart, was playing silly beggars with him. Angrily, he yanked his dressing gown off the back of the door, pulled it tight round him, and padded out into the office, barely allowing himself time to reflect on how similar his slippered-feet sounded to the way an animal walked.

He stepped out into the icy cold corridor. The central heating was buggered again. Something to do with the pipes knackering themselves up when the water froze in them. He had electric heaters in his office, and in the adjunct, but out here there was nothing to ward off the night-cold. He reached for the light-switch, feeling a slight twinge as he did so.

The strip lights took a moment to flicker on. First the ones down the other side of the corridor, *blunk, blunk, blunking,* and then the power relaying from one to the other until, finally, his end of the corridor crackled into light. But the light didn't bring clarity with it. Manny's mind still felt clagged up with mud. He was dog-tired, he realised. He feel as though he'd starred in a reality TV experiment or

204

torture session in which the objective was to stay awake for the longest possible time.

As he tried to focus on the familiar things in the corridor, flickering tendrils of light danced in front of his eyes like cracks in ice; his brain, sorting through these images, felt as though it had been vacuum-packed. Now his whole body had started to ache and he was sure he was hearing voices.   'Let us in!' railed those voices. 'Let us in!' Each word stressed, underlined by another loud knock on the door.

Manny screwed up his eyes. Leaned against the corridor's wood-panelled wall for support. Forced himself to breathe properly. With each inhalation, there was another smash on the door, and a reciprocal, echoing one in his chest. He opened his eyes, to check whether he'd already been transported into a cold outer rim of hell. Immediately he fixed on the landscape painting on the wall opposite. A view of the skeletal rib-cage of the monastery painted by a local artist of some repute who'd also just so happened to be the mayor of Limm during the war-time (and was hence a hero, even though Manny *knew* for a fact the man had stock-piled rations right here in the town hall.) The painting was rendered in angry black jabs of the brush interspersed with a swirly purple which was supposed to represent the heather but which Manny had come to think represented the abandon which came through drinking, or through war. It was a kind of localised storm of wildness. *Release. It was like the golden valve of release had been tampered with...*

Sometimes, passing down the corridor after another terminable town occasion or other, Manny had looked at the painting and believed that, within its shapeless swirling darkness, he could pick out the furrowed brow of his father, back in the day. And he didn't like to be reminded of such things. Now when he looked at it, he saw something else entirely. He saw a gateway. A wormhole. A fucking tunnel to hell. He gave serious consideration to marching on over and ripping the damn thing off the wall, but then worried what damage the physical exertion might do him, but instead staggered for the door.

The door was a vast, two-leafed, ornate-looking thing which had, according to local folklore, been carved by a German tradesman. Which explained the *strangeness* of the carvings. Because, during the war, someone, most likely our mayor-stroke-artist-stroke-ration-hoarder-stroke-madman had gone at it with a chisel, had tried to smooth away the German's designs, replacing

205

them with some, rather less well-made ones of his own. Manny placed a large, still-trembling paw on this gateway. Felt the uncommon warmth of the wood. And then he felt the pulse of something *within* the wood. As though the wood was alive and had a heart. Then he touched the colder handle and swung the door open with a creak.

Four hulking yet shadowy figures were gathered on the steps, like sinister over-sized carol singers, under the town hall's stone-pillared porch. Though it was dark, Manny could see that they weren't police. Nor were they demonic representatives from Limm's *other* twin town, hell. Nevertheless, he could smell the rabid rage off them. Smelled almost bestial. He faced them down, flickering with a renewed anger of its own and an especially dry mouth.

'What do you want?' he croaked.

One of the men stepped forward. He was wrapped in a long Parka coat with the hood pulled up around his face. He looked like a bear, Manny decided.

'Answers, Mr. Mayor. We want answers,' said the man. He had a roughly hewn voice. Gravelly. Not well bred. He sounded the type who didn't speak much, but when they did, it was out of pure frustration. There were a lot of men like that on Limm. And, as though to prove that, the other three men stepped forward now too. All of them were identically raggedy dressed. Smelled of the earth. Though they all had their hoods pulled up around their faces, he thought he recognised one of the men.

'Toby Bull? That you?'

One of the men nodded, 'Aye, Mr. Mayor, sir.' Then he started fiddling with the zip to pull down his hood. Manny noticed red welts on the man's knuckles. *So it was him trying to beat the door in.*

'I knew your dad,' mused Manny, and then, deciding that embarking on the tale of *how* he knew his father was dangerous ground he didn't want to step on, he barked: 'What is the meaning of this... this rude interruption? What do you think you're doing, coming here mob-handed in the middle of the night?'

Toby Bull coughed an answer Manny couldn't quite hear.

'Another thing: how did you know I was here?' growled Manny.

'Dave Chester, your chauffeur. said you'd would be, most likely,' said Bull, who'd evidently elected himself spokesman of this rag-tag group. 'Said he'd followed the St. John Ambulance what you were in with Coffey down to the Bungalow and you'd told him to do one. So anyway, we saw your car outside, and...'

'All right, all right,' said Manny, holding up a warning paw. 'I don't need to know your bloody life stories. Now what is it you want answers *to*? As you can see from my attire, you've got me out of bed and I'm tired and tomorrow, I've got a lot of work I need to do.'

'We want to know what you're going to do, what the town's going to do, about this black panther what's...'

Manny narrowed his eyes. 'What do you mean, black panther?'

'The thing what got Coffey.'

'The thing what got Coffey was *drinking* near agricultural machinery,' said Manny. 'Getting so blind drunk he couldn't see what he was doing...'

The man who'd been standing at the back of the group stepped forward, speaking for the first time. 'Dan Coffey don't drink while he works, Mr. Mayor. And even if he did, he can handle it. And even if he was blind he'd be able to work his machinery...' Manny knew what machinery this man was talking about. Coffey's traps. For his poaching. And if this man knew Coffey as well as he *seemed* to, well, that made him none other than...

'You're the Copestake feller, aren't you?' said Manny. Brett Copestake. 'The other...' He was going to come right out and say it, accuse him of being the pheasant poacher, but a flicker in the lad's eyes stopped him. The lad looked as though he was going to cry and suddenly Manny realised he was at make-or-break point. He knew he had to get these men subscribing to his point of view and soon. And judging from what he'd seen, although the men were angry, they were also just a little bit scared.

'I don't know what you've heard about this black panther,' he said, his voice suddenly becoming rich, becoming his *speechifying* voice, 'but there is absolutely no truth to the rumour. There is absolutely nothing for the town to worry about and the tragic accident – for accident was what it was – which befell young Dan Coffey was...'

Just as he was getting into full flow, he was interrupted. He didn't like being interrupted. Especially by men like this. 'You can't play us for fools,' said Copestake. 'You can't just fob us off.'

Manny held up his hands in a surrender gesture. 'I'm not trying to do that. I know you men have far too much... *nous*... for that. I couldn't pull the wool over your eyes, even if I wanted to.'

For a tottering moment, he thought he'd over-egged the pudding. Had erred on the side of condescension. A muscle in Copestake's jaw trembled.

'Your friend, Dan Coffey was, I'm sad to say, killed in a terrible accident,' said Manny, and then, in a softer tone: 'I was there with him. At the end. Oh boy, he was brave.' He reached out, ready to place a consoling hand on Copestake's shoulder. And then, and only then, did he realise how badly he'd misjudged the situation. That he *had* over-egged the pudding.

Copestake squirmed away from him, *growling* like a wounded animal. The farmer, the spokesman, Toby Bull went to him, talking in a soothing voice. But Copestake was having none of it. Suddenly, in a loud voice which exploded into the night air, he roared, 'HE IS FUCKING WELL LYING! I'M NOT GOING TO STAND HERE AND HAVE HIM FUCKING LIE TO MY FACE.'

Manny was becoming decidedly twitchy. Despite the threat right on his doorstep, the volume of Copestake's rage had reminded him that there was a world out there, his town. And all this noise was likely to bring them out of their beds. The town hall overlooked a row of old stone terraced houses, what, twenty metres away? Right now, the residents of those houses would be rudely awoken from their slumber and they'd want to know what was going on. They'd shuffle on up here... A real crowd could develop. And crowds meant panic.

Another thought struck him: what if the residents of those houses were *already* awake? What if Bull's frantic banging on the town hall door had woken them? What if right now, they were already twitching their curtains, *and listening to all this talk of a black panther and of Dan Coffey's death?*

He appealed to Toby Bull, who at least was older than the rest of these farm men and poacher-types. Would have at least have developed *some* wisdom through the steady accumulation of years. 'We should go inside,' he hissed. 'We don't want to cause a scene out here. We can go inside and discuss this properly, like men. It's warm inside and light too.'

Toby Bull turned from comforting Copestake. Fixed Manny with judging eyes. Then, after a long moment, he nodded, and did the necessary, persuading the rest of them of the wisdom of the plan.

But then, another strange thing happened. Instead of simply following him over the threshold and into the corridor, two of the men hopped back down the steps, moved out of his view for a moment, and then returned pushing what looked like a tarpaulin-covered wheel barrow. Manny was, for once, lost for words as he watched the two of them awkwardly pushing and pulling it up the steps. Not for the first time, he reflected on the vast, gaping gulf which separated the different breeds in his town. On the one hand there was sane, dutiful, responsible him; on the other, there were these rambunctious working men. Men who probably showered in beer of a morning. Men who, apparently, saw fit to drag whatever it was they were taking to market later on, into the fucking town hall, where he'd allowed them a proper audience.

Wearily, he led them back down the corridor to his office. As he padded, he heard the squeaky wheel of the wheel barrow as it trundled across the tile after him, pushed by one or other of the gormless idiots. Toby Bull was walking alongside him, as though he thought that was his rightful place. They entered the office. It was rich with red leather and dark wood, mahogany mostly. Luxuriously lined with books; old town charters, map books, censuses going back to the goddamn Domesday Book. There was one of those library reading room lamps with a green shade on his huge, imposing desk. A computer on a smaller desk in the corner where Tuesday through Thursday mornings, Mrs. Heggarty (Mrs. Higgledy-Piggledy) took dictation. The office looked, Manny had always thought, rather like a mini courtroom. Suitably grandiose and legalesque. It reflected the fact that big decisions were made in here. And this ragtag bunch of farmers, dressed in their scruffs, looked like the accused.

If only they were. In fact, they were the *accusers*. Toby Bull started in on him almost as soon as he'd closed the door. 'We want to know what you're going to do about it, about this whole mess.'

Manny didn't answer. He walked over to the window and concertinaed opened the blinds. Gave himself a pensive, almost *Cheryl* look as he stared out over his sleeping town. In the town proper, the tea-light streetlights were blinking mustardly yellow. On the outskirts, the mead-works was still pumping out smoke. Further away, the dark looming shape of Pate Hill seemed to encroach on the Toy Town. To lace the whole image with threat. Something *liminal* was out there, from the world of the shadows.

'Look at the town, boys. Just look,' he said.

Toby Bull stepped up alongside him and looked. Manny caught his reflection in the window. His face had nothing of the right stuff about it. He didn't *see* what Manny saw. He simply looked, didn't interpret.

'Everyone but us hard working fellers safely tucked up in their beds, dreaming their little dreams. Perhaps some of them are a little sad, dreaming about the TALENT-STRAVAGANZA!!!!!! that never was. But they're safe in their little worlds. Do you really want to rock the boat, Bull?' Here, he placed his hand on Bull's shoulder, *made* the man look into his eyes and read the obvious care they contained. 'There has been one teensy-weensy accident, that's all. And believe you-me, I know it's cripplingly sad. I weep every time a single one of my townspeople gets *ill* let alone when one... perishes. But...' He lost the train of his thought for a second. Had to stare back through the window for inspiration. Saw it in the form of the fluttering flags which flanked the flowerbeds out front of the town hall. There were three flagpoles; one containing the Union Jack flag, the second hoisting the St. George's flag. The third, standing tallest, boasted the Limm Island crest. A majestic, brave stag with *huge* antlers, almost a *moose*. 'But one swallow does not a summer make. One accident does not mean we have some... some mythical beast stalking the town. But if people *believe* that there is, then we're all in trouble, aren't we?'

Manny was expecting Bull to simply nod, acknowledge he was wrong, and then lead the rest of his rag-tag troops – the men who were now slouching across Manny's own leather sofa as though they goddamn owned it – away to the markets or back to their farms. No: most likely to lead them to the pub where they could drink away their worries *like everyone in the town always did*. Manny was expecting Bull to apologise for disturbing his rest, to tell him that he'd never even contemplate such a thing again. He was, in fact, expecting anything but what Toby did next.

'Copey lad; Barney? Take the cover off that bloody wheel barrow, won't you? I think our Mr. Mayor needs to see what's inside there now.'

Copestake shot up from the sofa. Started untying some of the knots which fixed the tarpaulin to the barrow. And then, with a magician's flourish, he yanked the cover off, revealing what had been lying underneath all this time.

'Now do you see?' said Bull, shooting Manny a version of his own, *trademarked* all-seeing, all-caring pensive look.

210

And Manny did see. And Manny *smelled* too. For under the tarpaulin, drowning in blood and feathers, were at least six dead chickens. And a dead goose, *its goose well and truly cooked.* Manny thought he saw a duck in there too, and some other animal he couldn't identify. Usually he was good at spotting and naming animals, had been since he'd been a nipper. Growing up round here, a boy could hardly be any different. But this was like no animal quiz Manny had ever seen. The contents of the barrow looked like a slaughterhouse. It was difficult to tell one animal from another. Just when he thought he'd got a handle on it, *ah, that's a chicken's foot, has to be,* he'd see what was next to the foot, *a duck's bill,* and then a stray trotter, and then a leg and a wing and a rooster's plume and...

'Every. Single. One-a. Them. Neck's. Broken,' said Copestake, slowly. 'Every single one-a them fucking *played with.* And no industrial machinery likes playing with its food. Not even at the abattoir. They been played with, just as Dan Coffey was, so them's that was at your talent show tell me. Played with like a cat plays with its prey.'

'Only this isn't no house-cat, is it, lads?' said Bull. 'Not looking at the puncture marks. Creature what's out there fucking drained their blood... Creature must like the taste of fear. Like spice.'

'It could have been a fox. Yes, that's it. A fox!' said Manny.

Bull shook his head. 'This ain't no fox. This here's a panther, like we said before. And the thing is, Mr. Mayor, sir, this ain't the first morning we've all woke up and found *slaughter.* We didn't come to you yesterday, but it happened then, too. Alfie Grainger over the other side of the causeway. His cows... Butchered... And once we heard about Dan Coffey, we knew we had to come. It was our civic duty.'

Manny could have told them a thing or two about civic duty. But he didn't. He was too busy trying to gulp away the taste of dead animals in his throat. Trying not to vomit. He needed a nice, cool glass of water. Needed... *He needed a restorative whisky. Or a brandy to warm the cockles. He needed to sluice himself in the stuff. Use it to wash away all this badness, this evil. He needed...*

'Here, are you okay, Mr. Mayor, sir?' said Bull, another concerned look passing over his face. 'Do you need to sit down or something?'

Manny allowed the farmer to shepherd him over to his chair behind the desk.

'Sit down. Lean forward. Put your head between your knees,' ordered Bull.

Manny, meekly as a lamb (*a lamb confronted by a fucking black panther*) did as he was told. He stared down at the chequerboard tiled floor. All the black squares were swimming into the white squares forming this dull, swirling grey. Only, there was another colour too. Purple. That same purple which the wartime mayor-stroke-artist-stroke-ration-hoarder-stroke-madman had used for his heather in the painting in the corridor. The painting Manny hated so much.

He heard Toby Bull shout something over to Copestake, and his voice sounded faraway, lost in a hellish twin town somewhere. He wanted to scream, but wasn't sure whether his heart would let him.

Bull shouted again, 'Copey, chuck us your hip-flask. I reckon his nibs needs a nip. For the shock.'

Manny forced himself to raise his head, gasping, 'I'm fine, really I'm fine.' But then his stomach gave another lurch and he threw up the contents of his stomach all over his big mahogany desk.

Toby Bull was on him like a flash, trying to help. Manny elbowed him away, tears streaming from his eyes. 'I'm okay,' he gasped, *tasting sickness on his tongue.* 'I'm okay, please...'

'You're not, sir, you're...'

All the pressure from the past twenty-four hours crashed down on Manny at the same time. He reached up, grasped for Toby Bull's throat. 'Shut up! I am fine. Look at me, I'm fine!' He used Bull's Parka to drag himself to his feet. Not caring that his dressing gown was swinging open, he yelled into the dirty farmer's face. 'If I am ill, it's because people like you won't give me a moment's peace. Because I need sleep. Because I'm fucking relied upon, by every goddamn one of you to sort out everything, even your bloody non-existent panthers!' He ran out of breath, but continued to hold Bull in a rough clench while the rest of his rag-tag group stared on with gaping mouths.

Toby Bull's response though, left him even more short of breath. In fact, it surprised the life outta him, near enough. 'Okay, okay,' he said, with a look of *understanding* in his eyes. 'You're right, sir. And, goddamnit, I'm not usually the kinda feller that as soon as something goes wrong comes hammering on the town hall door demanding answers or compensation. None of us. We're – Dan Copestake aside... no, don't look at me like that Copey, you know

212

what you are – good honest hardworking fellers. We don't expect everything to get handed us on a plate. We do want answers, but we ain't gonna demand them if they're just platitudes, know what I mean?'

Manny nodded, not quite sure what he was agreeing to.

'At the same time,' continued Bull, 'I can see your... predicament... You don't want the townspeople rioting or anything like that. You don't want panic spread. Because once one cow in a herd starts panicking, they all do. So what I propose is this.' He held up his hand, counting down the fingers. 'One, we keep this black panther thing under our hats for now, just like you want. Two, we stay out your way and let you get on with doing what you think you should be doing, for the best of the town. And three, you let us hunt this thing down in our own way. Let us bring it down. What do you say?'

Manny still couldn't breathe through his nose. Not properly. And his mouth was still clagged up with the leftovers from his vomit-fest. But he allowed a satisfied smile to crack his face and dropped his hand away from Bull's coat. And when Copestake shouted over, asking whether he'd still like a drop of the old stuff out of his hip-flask, he *almost* nodded yes. But he didn't. He didn't want anything stopping his winning streak. Because that was what this was, when it came down to it. He'd won. He still had the old magic when it came to these *mano a mano* confrontations. If he had a drink, if he allowed himself that golden-valved release, he might put all of it, in jeopardy.

Day Three

22: Soberly Challenged

Manny Combs was thirteen and a half years old when he first got blottoed, Santa's Grottoed, Betty Booped, soberly-challenged. When he first painted the town red. When he first released the golden valve. Back then, he was called Brush, by pretty much anyone who deigned to speak to him, which was pretty much everyone under the school leaving age. Because for everyone else, Manny was the invisible child. His dad only noticed him when he himself was pie-eyed, and only then to clip him round the ear as he passed, ordering him to fetch another beer. His mam never spoke to anyone. Too damn shaky-scared to do so. Auntie Mabel was blind as a bat and couldn't see him anyway, and the teachers at school thought he was a lost cause, sat quietly at the back of the classroom simply staring out the window.

Not that he was without ambition, or even a kind of cruel intelligence, even then, but he'd still not had his growth-spurt and hence stood about two feet smaller than most of the lads in his class. And he was quiet around people he didn't know. People mistook his reticence as a kind of stupidity, but it wasn't. He was always working out the angles how he could stay ahead of the game, work himself an opportunity. And back then, for him, the opportunities he wanted were to be able to make money, look at nuddy pictures of girls, and smoke. And he had *certain ways* of getting hold of cigarettes which made him instantly popular with the lads he wanted to be popular with, namely stealing from his Aunt Mabel's newsagents (which had since been taken over by another of her nephews, Devon Buckby), right from under her crooked, witch's nose. Back then, in school, cigarettes were currency, just as they were in prison. And they afforded Manny several privileges, key amongst them being there was always *someone* who'd cover him when he and Roy 'Snakey' Sanderson bunked off.

The day Manny Combs first got tooth-floatingly, head-achingly, troll-eyed was a day they were supposed to be doing double-Geography (looking out the window), double-Maths (more looking out the window), double Art (trying to get a look down Miss Butterworth's top) and single Science (trying to burn things with the Bunsen burner and trying to avoid the desk rubber after Percy Pierce had flung it at their heads for talking). It was a good day to miss.

Manny met Snakey at the usual place, round the back of the new supermarket, MacAskill's, which had been built on the site of what had been a munitions factory in the war. It was a good place to meet. Sometimes, someone or other would leave the keys in one of the fork-lift trucks in the yard and there was a big, yawning gap through which they could sneak in order to have a quick go on one of them. They called going on the fork-lifts 'going on the Bucking Bronco', because usually it was only a matter of time before the Yardsman, a big bear of a feller who was clearly from farming or fishing stock, would come out of the back of the supermarket, yell at them, and then the game would start in earnest. The challenge was to stay on for as long as you dared before the Yardsman got too close. To stay on for as long as possible before jumping off and allowing him to give half-hearted, blubbery chase. To date he'd not caught any of them, but it had once come close with Richie 'Bones' Bonsall, who'd slipped on a patch of oil and the Yardsman had been *this close* to connecting with the back of his shirt as he scrambled to his feet. Manny himself held the record. He also held the watch.

Snakey was there first. Snakey was always there first. Every day, he was accused of malingering under his mam's feet, would receive a clip round the ear, and then he wouldn't have nowhere to go, nobody to see, until he either went to school or went round the back of MacAskill's. As per usual, Snakey looked delighted to see Manny. As though all his Christmases, birthdays, May Queen festivals had come at once.

'Brush!' he yelled. 'How's it hanging?'

Manny didn't answer at first. Instead took a moment to look his friend up and down, top to bottom. Top was his flood of greasy black hair, the rash of black heads and other miscellany pimples on the bridge of his nose and on his chin, his squashed nose, the permanently surprised look in his eyes. Bottom was his big – *canal-barge-sized* – feet. His mam could never find decent shoes to fit those flipper-feet of his and in the end, what he got looked like cast-offs from a clown school. Big flumping yellow things which turned up at the toes. And in between top and bottom, his get-up wasn't much better. His trousers looked as though they'd been patched-up so many times they were more patch than trouser now. His coat was an old military issue one and underneath, his shirt was dishcloth grey when it was supposed to be white.

'All right, chief,' said Manny, finally. 'You're looking every inch the scruff this morning.'

Snakey winced. Lowered his head. Kicked a stray pebble which bounced through the fence and into the yard.

'Ah, I'm only kidding,' said Manny, lightning up his voice.

'Fuckin-A,' said Snakey, putting on an American accent. He did that a lot since his mam told him his pops might have been an American serviceman.

'Ready for a day of adventure then, big lad?'

'Bucking Bronco again?'

'Maybe later. Supplies first.'

'Your Auntie's shop?'

'Mabel's shop. Affirmative,' said Manny, adding the last bit just to keep Snakey amused. He may have been a big man, with *almost* a man's body but he still acted like a child most of the time.

They stalked out from *their place* behind MacAskill's, keeping under the cover of trees. Not drawing any undue attention to themselves. At the wall which separated them from Peel Street, and civilisation, Manny made Snakey crouch down into the undergrowth while he performed a quick recce. He peered around the wall and then back to Snakey. Lifted up two fingers to indicate two civilians (pushing their wheeled tartan shopping trolleys) and then made a little wiggly-fingered move to indicate they'd have to keep low. Then balled a fist and pulled it into his chest. *Move quickly, now,* this was supposed to mean. But there was nothing quick or furtive about Snakey's movements. The lad crashed through the wet grass like a dinosaur and Manny shook his head wearily.

When they gained the road, the game was over. Manny had ended it by refusing to go into the low run himself. Snakey looked disappointed but didn't complain. He would, most likely, be gasping for a ciggie by now and knew better than to get into an argument just before the ration drop. Peel Street was blessedly quiet, apart from

216

the two old ladies dragging their shopping home. It was quiet, but it was also decidedly grey. When it rained on Limm, as it had the day before, it had a way of sponging into the houses and shops, giving them this sort of *wet dog* look which even the owner couldn't love. There were a few cars parked up, but not many. And the window displays were drab and unoriginal. Manny had already decided that as soon as he could, he'd leave this place in his slipstream. He wasn't entirely sure *how* he'd escape, but he knew he would. Already, and despite his diminutive stature, he sensed he was becoming a big fish in a small pond and Limm couldn't handle a shark in its midst.

As they walked, Snakey whistled. As they passed Dobbie's Bakery (now long since closed down), the whistling noticeably increased in both pitch and volume, in appreciation of the fine smell of fresh baked bread which was emanating from within. If Manny hadn't have been with him, Snakey would have had his snotty nose pressed against the window by now, squashing it even more than it already was. As it was, after the whistle, he tried to give himself an air of nonchalance. To cut to the chase, he copied Manny. Manny had this way of walking which he'd seen in the cowboy shows. It was a sheriff's walk, kinda bow-legged, kinda stiff, as though you were packin', but at the same time, loose too. As though you were cock of all you surveyed.

Walking like sheriffs they passed Coverley's Greengrocers (also long gone); they passed Dawson's Butchers (same story) and its horrorshow of hanging carcasses which for some reason never stopped people like his mam going in for chops for tea on Saturday nights. They passed Douggie's Home Shop (now The Crab's Claws), where you could buy every crappy invention known to man, and finally they reached Mabel's newsagents where they stopped and admired their reflections in the window.

Mabel's bookended the row of shops. Crossland's Shoes, which never had anything which would remotely fitted Snakey was at the other side. It was a poky place, almost an afterthought. As though it was that final, *have I forgotten anything before I slope on home? Oh yes, of course, my ciggies and my paper.* Mabel – well, her husband, of whom nobody was allowed to speak now – had owned the shop for nigh on twenty years now. Generation after generation of Limm's boys had grown up with her to thank for their work ethic after she employed them as paperboys. The only generation of Limm boys not represented was the one which was

217

just that little bit older than Manny. The generation who'd grown up under that great looming shadow of war, a shadow which still hung over towns like this, years after it had ended. The war had taken over half of the town's young men, and made widows of so many of the town's women. It had taken paperboys too; joining Boys Brigades and working the fields being given priority over the a few pence in the back-burner during those dark days. As though in sympathy, Mabel kept the shop as it had been before the war. At least it looked that way to Manny. As well as being the pokiest shop on the row, it was also, miraculously, given the competition, the drabbest. Only the fact she shifted the ciggies with all the enthusiasm of a regular dealer, kept her afloat.

They entered the shop, a tiny bell ringing to announce their arrival. Mabel, behind the counter, dressed in a gingham dress which might well have been made from the cut-off material from one of the sofas down at Allie's Home Store on Farne Street, made a big show of peering through her horn-rimmed glasses, trying to make out who'd come in. Failing, she asked, in a quivering voice, 'Who is it?'

For a moment, neither Manny or Snakey said anything. Snakey was too busy looking at all the lovely chocolate bars on the shelves, Manny was seeing just how long, he could push it.

'I said, who is it?' she asked, in an even more shaky voice. Her voice was as shaky as Manny's mam's hands. So shaky anyone would have thought they were Shakin' Sisters, but they weren't, she was Manny's *dad's* sister, which was why he had to be careful where he tread. She'd not shown that she had the same hot-blood temper as him *yet*, but there was a first time for everything, and Manny didn't want this to be the first time. Because, with the Combs family, the first time was the last time.

'It's Manny. Me and Snakey, just come to say hello.'

Her face broke out into a beaming smile. She made another big show, this time of removing her glasses and polishing them up on her dress, and then she stepped out from behind the counter and reached out her arms to give him a big hug. Neither he nor Snakey said anything about the fact she was holding out her arms to the wrong boy. In fact, for a moment, Manny thought that she actually was going to hug his friend, provide him with the first physical contact which was not a clip round the ear from his mam or a swift back-hander from a teacher since he was a primary schooler, but presently, she drew back her hands, giving a little giggle as she did so. 'Oh, forgive your Auntie Mabel, Manny. Happen you're too old for a hug these days, eh?'

'Weeelll...'

'Nearly fourteen, aren't you, lad?'

'December, yes.'

'And what'll you be wanting for your birthday?'

Manny thought about telling her he wanted a replica of a Browning pistol, but thought better of it. The woman was still a little funny around violence and guns as he'd found out when he was about four and he'd started waving a plastic gun about in her kitchen and she'd climbed on a bloody stool, as though she was trying to escape from a mouse. 'I was thinking some new football boots,' he said instead. And Snakey gave a little snigger in response.

'Football boots, that'd be nice,' she mused. Then she paused, thinking. 'Hold your horses a minute, lad.' Then she narrowed her eyes: 'Why aren't you at school?'

Manny thought on his feet. 'Haven't you heard? Pipes were leaking and they had to evacuate us.'

Mabel put her hands on her hips, cocked her head. When she did that, she looked like a pigeon, Manny thought. 'Is that right Snakey? *Were* you evacuated?'

Snakey cleared his throat, then spoke in that weird, stumbling Indian witch doctor voice he reserved for persons of authority. 'Oh aye, Mrs. Combs, there was, um, this big explosion. I'm surprised you didn't see it. It'll be on the news tonight.'

'He's exaggerating,' said Manny, jumping in quickly, before Snakey launched into a full-on description of how Jerry soldiers were hiding in the pipes and only he was able to save the day. 'But not by much. It was pretty scary. They said there could be gases in the pipes and we could have been poisoned by the fumes. They said... We should drink lots of tea to flush our systems out.'

Mabel seemed to consider this for a moment, but then she returned her glasses to her face, clapped her hands together, and said, 'Right then. I'll brew-up straight away. Are you boys going to be okay waiting out here? Or would you like to go upstairs and have a little sit down?'

Manny wasn't sure if she actually believed them or was just glad of the chat, but just to be on the safe side, he replied, 'We'll wait here. Watch the shop so you don't need to lock the door.'

'You are a good boy,' she mused. Then, hand resting on the jamb of the door which led up to her living quarters, she said, 'If

219

you're feeling woozy or light-headed or anything, just ring the little bell behind the door.'

'I'm sure we'll be fine,' said Manny, 'especially once we've had a cup of your famous tea.'

Snakey sniggered *again,* and Manny wanted to give him a clip round the ear. But Mabel didn't appear to have heard anything. She closed the door behind her and they heard her uncertain tread going up the stairs. By the time Manny had turned back to his friend, he was already behind the counter, starting to pick out his favourite cigarette brands.

Manny wanted to throttle him now. 'No. *Not from there.* Are you stupid or something? She'll see they've gone missing if you pinch them from the shelves. In here.' He showed Snakey another door, this one at the back of the shop, next to the battered old birthday cards. This door led directly into Mabel's store room.

Snakey's eyes lit up as though he'd encountered a dragon's hoard of gold. Boxes and boxes of crisps, chocolate bars, sweets from the toffeeworks over in Norsea. Crates and crates of returned glass bottles of pop. *Gold-dust* cigarette boxes. He whistled.

'Shut up, Snakes.'

Snakes shut up. They worked quickly, Manny a seasoned pro, Snakes a gifted amateur, loading up their school bags with Bensons, Capstons, Lambert and Scrutler, Dorchester and Grey. Not a word passed between them, but both, instinctively knew what to do, and exactly how many packs to take. Enough to see them through and a few which could be bartered in the school black market, not too many so Mabel would start to smell a rat.

Bags full, they returned to the shop, and when Auntie Mabel came back down carrying a tray with three steaming mugs of her famous sugary tea and a plate of pink wafer biscuits, both boys were safely standing behind the counter.

'Anyone come in?' she asked, clearing a space for the tray on the countertop.

'Only Mr. Fletcher, I think he's called,' said Manny, lying for no apparent reason. 'He said he was here to pay the papers, but he'd come back later.'

'Good boy.' She handed round the tea. Despite the fact it was scalding hot, Manny gulped it down. Snakey, however, hadn't noted his friend's urgency and cradled it to his chest, dunking pink wafer after pink wafer into the mug. Mabel, always one for the gossip, started in talking about the goings on in the town.

'There's all sorts of nonsense going around in this place at the moment. Honestly, it's like madness. And I blame that mayor of ours. Ever since the war, he's swanned about the place as though he's some kind of hero, which I suppose he is, but we're *fifteen years on* from the war. Baby boomers like yourself are nearly men now, aren't you? That shows just how long it is since he's done anything good for the town. I suppose he's like Churchill really, good in wartime, not really cut out for peacetime.'

Snakey couldn't stifle a lion's roar of a yawn, but Auntie didn't notice it.

'Gangs of lads causing trouble *every* Friday night. Lads running their motorcycles up and down the main street *at all hours*. They've got girls going round in short skirts. And the *music!*'

Snakey yawned again, this time his mouth was so wide he could have swallowed a large goat.

'And do you know that chap at Knoll Farm? Bull, they call him. I heard he was in trouble with the police because they think he's brewing his own liquor up in one of his barns. I don't know what this place is coming to. It's like the Wild West. The mayor *must know* all this is going on but he does damn all – I mean he does nothing – about it. Doesn't eye a batlid he doesn't.'

'That's funny, you said 'eye a batlid',' said Snakey.

Mabel gave him a funny sort of smile. The sort of smile Mrs. Cheevers was always giving Manny when she caught him in one of his dreamworlds, staring out the window. And then she collected herself and started in on more of the chat. 'I've not seen your dad for ages, Manny. How is he? Keeping his nose clean?'

Manny thought Snakey was going to laugh at the *nose clean* comment too, but he didn't. He was draining the last dregs of his tea; the ones which would doubtless contain a whole biscuit factory of pink wafer bits.

'He's fine, Auntie, really he is. Only, he asked us to run a few errands for him now school's out and we'd really better be getting on with them, hadn't we, Snakey?'

More Indian witch doctor: 'Oh yes, the, um, errands can't keep.'

Mabel looked disappointed, but after Manny had pecked her on the cheek, she let them go. They ran away from the shop as soon as the little bell had jangled to indicate the door had closed behind them. They sat on the bench on the village green to get their breath back after the run. Manny could hear a scary wheezing sound in his chest. Sounded like his dad's breathing when he'd had one too many drinks of a night. Like his chest was clogged with something which shouldn't have been there. He sparked up the first of the liberated cigarettes, hoping that would clear the blockage. Snakey looked on eagerly as he sucked in that first, sharp-sour drag.

'Paradise.' His chest was already starting to feel better.

He passed Snakey the lighter and Snakey lit up one of his own. Immediately started to blow smoke rings. There was a small part of Manny which was jealous of Snakey for being able to make smoke rings, but the majority of him pitied him. Because Snakey didn't seem to enjoy the taste of cigarettes as much as the tricks he could make the smoke do, and that, my friend, was fucking stupid and childlike, and just like the behaviour of a lad who'd end up here, on exactly the same bench, in fifty years time, still trying to amuse himself with silly tricks, whilst at the same time wondering what the hell he'd got to show for his miserable years on this planet.

They both sparked up second ciggies off their first ones and continued to smoke. Manny enjoying the peace and the fact the teachers weren't pecking at his head, Snakey was probably not thinking anything; he was probably just sat, dopey-dumb like, waiting to be told what he was going to do next. Manny's suspicions were confirmed within seconds.

'What shall we do now?' Snakey whined. 'I'm bored. And we can't stay on the green all day 'cos someone'll see us. We'll end up back in school with that bastard Pierce tanning our backsides.'

Manny was always the man with the plan, and, as usual, he already had an answer to Snakey's question. 'We go up to Bull's farm. Sample his home brew before it's too late.'

'Get drunk, you mean?'

'Well, yeah, maybe. But it'd be rude not to at least try it before the police come a-knocking, wouldn't it? And we're not rude, are we Snakes? Nobody's ever accused us of having a rude bone in our bodies to rub together.'

'I've got one rude bone,' said Snakey, a strange expression on his face. Moonish, almost. And suddenly Manny *got* what he was talking about, and was disgusted. He was talking about his cock, for Christ's sake. And it was all very well dopey old Snakey having a massive snake when you got the impression he had absolutely no idea what it was there for, but this, this *knowledge* he seemed to have, this boastfulness, this was something else.

222

'Have you ever got drunk before?' he asked. Hoping Snakey hadn't. Hoping that there wasn't *another* unwelcome development in his friend.

'Oh yeah, *hundreds* of times.'

And Manny was suddenly happy again, because he knew Snakey was back to his old, impressionable self. 'So have I,' he lied. 'It's fucking beezer, ain't it? We should raise a toast to Farmer Bull and his lovely farm and its lovely produce.'

'Farmer Bull's farm,' said Snakey, in his silly yank accent yet again. 'What's the feller on the next farm called, Farmer Sheep?'

They walked up the hill in silence. Manny would have usually sparked up a ciggie, but he was alarmed by how out of breath he was getting. He was having to suck up great lungfuls of air, which would have made smoking almost impossible. And, struggling along like that, for the first time Manny felt like he wasn't indestructible. That he wasn't bullet-proof. It was as though he suddenly became aware of the fragility of the parts which went to make up the whole of him. His frantically beating heart, his scratchy lungs, his screaming calves. And Snakey just walked on, as though they were strolling on the flat. Didn't even seem bothered by the slope.

Snakey seemed happy. Manny could see him getting all wrapped up in looking at the view. In the distance the sea, then, closer to hand the monastery, the southern woods, some of Farmer Bull's fields. They had their backs turned to the town, to Limm proper, but if they'd have looked round, they'd have seen the spire of the church, the small shopping street, the lifeboat huts, the village green, the school.

They reached a stile which took them off the rutted road and onto rougher ground. Manny seized the opportunity to have a breather, perching on the edge of one of the wooden slats and pretending that his shoe-lace needed re-tying. Once his breath had become a little less raggedy, he pulled out his cigarettes and was amazed at how shaky his hands were as he tried to flip the lid. He could barely even grip the ciggies. Snakey either didn't notice or pretended not to notice. But he noticed all right when Manny offered the pack round to him, greedily snatching at them.

'Cheers,' said Snakey, accepting a light. Starting up with the blowing smoke-rings again. Manny lit his own cigarette and noticed the sting in his throat as he first inhaled. It tasted bitter, raw, fleshy somehow. He thought about simply dropping the ciggie, grinding it

223

out with his heel, but saw Snakey was staring at him. It wouldn't do to have Snakey staring at him, not when he felt so weak. He forced himself to climb back to his feet, yanked himself up and over the stile. Dropped down into the longer grass on the other side.

There was a rudimentary path which cut through the grass and heather, skirted around the top of Pate Hill, and eventually led to the Bull Farm. Snakey knew it well. He came poaching up here regularly. Bagged himself at least a couple of coneys each time he came. Had to be careful so as not to wander too far into Bull land, but still, he knew it better than Manny. To Manny, stepping on the path felt like stepping back in time. It felt *years* away from school, from MacAskill's supermarket, *decades* away from things like the TV which the family had finally gotten around to getting.

They finished off their ciggies and were careful how they disposed of them now, stamping down three, four times on the cherries like they were having a regular hoe-down to ensure they'd properly been extinguished. The shaggy ground around them screamed *wildfire,* and wildfires were just about the biggest sin there was on Limm, once one got past the adultery, the petty thievery, the lying, cheating, worshipping false idols.

Eventually, the ground evened out and Manny started to find his breath much easier to catch. They passed through a wide metal gate. Once upon a time, Manny might have thought about leaving the gate hanging, allowing Bull's cows to go off cross-country, but now he had bigger mischief in his sights so he took his time making sure the gate was properly bolted shut again. They kept close to the hedges as they crossed the muddy field, in case one of the Friesians turned out to be a bull. Snakey assured him they kept Bull's bull in a field all of his own, only let him in when here it was breeding season, but even so, some of the great lumbering creatures looked big enough to be a bull. Certainly it wasn't worth the risk getting in a debate about it. Even Snakey lowered his voice as they pressed on.

As it turned out, the cows paid them little notice. A couple of them raised their heads, sniffed the air. Scuffed their hooves on the ground. One gave a low moan of a moo which sounded remarkably human to Manny. But most kept their heads bowed, chewing the cud. They were as passive as most of the kids in the school, as most of the townspeople. The bull would be like he was in a china shop amongst this lot, just as, one day, Manny knew he'd be kinda set apart from his contemporaries. On a higher plain. All it would take was some bullishness, some angle.

'How far is it now?' he asked, as they pushed the second gate closed, entering another field. This one was empty, pock-marked with patches of new grass. There was a big metal watering trough in one corner.

'Not far now, Mans,' grinned Snakes. 'Can't you smell it?'

Manny paused, wrinkled his nose. Now that his attention had been drawn to it, there *was* a distinct smell. But it wasn't the farmy, country smell he'd come to expect. Wasn't the ripe stink of muck being spread or the stink of death as animals were slaughtered. Wasn't the red diesel smell of tractors or the chuffy smell of wheat. It was something else. A smell he couldn't quite put his finger on. Somehow, it smelled desperate. And yet sharp at the same time.

Snakes nodded. 'Don't know what he's got up there but it allus stinks this way this time of year.'

'It'll be the bootlegging,' whispered Manny.

Snakes looked excited. Moved off, increasing his pace, lengthening his stride. Big and awkward he might have been down in the town, but up here, he was as nimble as a mountain goat. Manny performed a clumsy half-run in order to keep up with his friend, occasionally feeling the ground under his feet becoming uncertain, but keeping within Snakey's footprints all the while.

He was still walking behind Snakester as they cut across a third field. This one had a small dilapidated stone circle in the middle, six toothy statues which could have been there since the last Millennium. Snakey ran his hands over the stones as he passed them, as though it were some kind of ritual. As though he were touching them for luck, or for karma, or as a token gesture to whatever ancient religion governed this island before the monks and their Christianity. Manny didn't touch the stones, but he did feel, or thought he felt, a strange kind of thrumming emanating from the bare earth around the stones. For a moment, the circle felt like a gateway, a portal, like in one of the sci-fi comics he loved reading.

They walked on. Single-file still; Snakey for once in his life leading, path-finding, Manny following, walking with his head bowed, staring at the greenish stain of cow-pat which went all up his friend's heel. There was some on his trousers too.

They reached the foot of another hill, this one with an even steeper incline than Pate Hill. Snakey pressed on and Manny followed. At one point, he picked up a gnarled old stick to help him. Speared the earth with it, dragged himself up. Until finally, gasping, rasping for breath, they reached the summit. Manny felt like planting a flag. *I, Manny Combs - along with my faithful Sherpa, Snakester - have conquered this mountain, and now claim it for my own, under the Combs name.* He didn't plant the flag, because it was abundantly clear that other people had been up here before him. They'd reached the outskirts of the farm proper now. There was a big sign on a rusty metal fence which read 'Knoll Farm – Keep Out', and a couple of outlying farm buildings. Small animal pens too. A horse box. The ground was littered with debris. Farm debris, sure; there was a fallen grain silo, some clapped-out ploughing tools, a long strip of corrugated iron which had leaped off one of the roofs. But there was also military debris too. Amongst the molehills were mountains of what looked like old targets, tyres and even what looked like a crumbledown tank, a leftover from the time they had a munitions factory further down the southern side of the island. The tank would have occupied Snakey for hours, Manny thought, were it not for the promise of the booze.

Manny took over the situation again. Recalling their war games round the back of MacAskill's, he made a little wiggly-fingered move to indicate they'd have to keep low. Move for the cover of trees which flanked the perimeter. Snakey nodded. Tucked himself low. Manny balled a fist and pulled it into his chest. *Move quickly, now.* And the two of them scurried into the shadow.

The first of the out-buildings they checked was empty. There was no sign it had ever been used for anything apart from the large Map of Africa diesel stain on the stone floor. The second out-building had a door which was padlocked, which made it immediately seem more promising. Snakey slithered off to look for some implement amongst the many farm tools that he could use to break the lock, and Manny seized the moment to dart round the side of the building and take a good, long look at the farmhouse, a low whitewashed building with a tall chimney. No smoke was pouring out of the chimney so he thought it safe to assume the farmer wasn't home. Which meant he was likely out in one of his fields. Hopefully he'd remain there for the rest of the day.

By the time he returned to the door, Snakey was already there, wielding a large axe he'd found over his head, then, when Manny gave him the nod, bringing it crashing down on the lock. Sparks flew as metal connected with metal, but the lock wouldn't give. Manny nodded again, and Snakey once again smashed down the axe. This time, the crack echoed back off the hills, through the woods, around the skeletal rib-cage of the monastery. It *had* to have

226

alerted the farmer. Surely. It also broke the padlock. Not for the first time, Manny wondered whether Snakey knew his own strength.

'What shall we do?' said Snakey, dropping the axe and rubbing at his wrists. 'Scarper? He *must* have heard that…'

'We check inside first,' said Manny with the Planny. 'See whether Mabel's story was right. Maybe take a couple drinks too. If we go now, what was the point of that walk?'

Snakey bit his lip.

'Come on,' said Manny, shouldering the door. 'Follow me.'

It took a moment for his eyes to get adjusted to the darkness. The back end of the barn was shrouded in shadow and closer in, where the light from the door hit it, so much dust and particles of crap were kicked up that they could have been viewing the place through a hail-storm. But gradually, his eyes grew accustomed. About five full seconds *after* his nose had. Because even as his eyes were struggling to come to terms with exactly what was housed in the out-building, his nose had made up his mind.

'This is it,' he hissed. 'We found it.' Because that smell of desperation which had carried on the wind earlier as they were walking through the cow-fields was surely sourced here. It was riper here. Clogged the air. Seemed to slow the tiny particles of dust which were still sailing on the atmosphere.

He heard Snakey sniff-up, hawk up a greenie and then spit. 'Fucking stinks,' he muttered.

Manny ignored him. Slowly wheeled round, taking in the room. Despite the gloom, he could still make out the vast, almost unimaginable quantities of the old hooch, the old moonshine, which filled the place. There were shelves and shelves of the stuff. Whopping great demijohns of the foul-smelling liquid bubbling away. Tables in the centre of the room set up like Piercey's science lab producing yet more of the crap. Big Bunsen burnery type things heating it, fermenting it. Windy, snaky tubes filtering it. Corks stoppering it. Test tubes testing it. A great Belfast sink so big it could have been one of the watering troughs in the cow-field.

'Here, look at this,' said Snakey, tapping his knuckles on the wall. Someone had tacked a hand-drawn approximation of the 'Danger: Explosives' signs on the wall at a slightly lop-sided angle, suggesting he'd partaken in a few too many measures of his own brew. 'Looks like a kiddie's drawing,' he laughed.

Manny laughed too, because even though the smashing of the padlock might have alerted the farmer to their presence, now he was here, he only had eyes for the booze. He wanted to wallow in the stuff. He wanted to luxuriate in it like he was a Roman General and this was his Bath House. Romans never made it onto Limm, but they'd built their wall not far away from here. Manny felt that the Romans would have been with him in wanting to stay in here though. It would be foolish to scarper now when they were so close. Think of the stories they could tell at school after this. Think of how the drink would make them men. They'd be treated differently from now on. Least, he would. Snakey could do what the hell he wanted to do. Snakey could stay by the door, maybe pick up that axe again and get ready to strike Bull, the farmer with it should he stumble upon them within the midst of his dragon's hoard.

Manny went to one of the shelves, picked up one of the demijohns. A big bell of a thing. There was a label on the side which read 'MARCH'. Whether this meant the drink was made in March, or whether it was only drinkable in March, and *which* March was anyone's guess. He shook the demijohn a little, just to see what would happen, and the liquid seemed to foam as though polluted.

Towards the back of the room, Snakey found a crate of old milk bottles into which the liquid had already decanted. Through the clearer glass, Manny saw the liquid was greenish, like cow-pat. But, when Snakey lifted one of the bottles more into the light from the half-open door, he saw it now looked purple. An angry purple though, not like the softer tones of the heather outside on Pate Hill or Brennan Mound.

'Well?' said Manny, 'what are you waiting for?'

Snakey did the honours and unstoppered the bottle. Wrinkled his nose and gingerly sniffed at it. Coughed. Pulled a face. Scuffed his feet on the dusty floor, umming and ahhing.

'Drink,' said Manny. It sounded like an order.

And Snakey took it as one. He drank, and then screwed up his face. Looked as though he was about to throw up. But then, his pronounced Adam's Apple bounced up and down. He gulped. Then gasped. 'Aaaaah, that's the good stuff.'

Manny could already smell it on his friend's breath, this good stuff. It was a strange, unholy concoction of the dubbin which he used to rub into his football boots and the paint-stripper which they used on the boats down the harbour every spring, readying them up for a new coat. The smell turned his stomach. But, seeing a glimmer of *something* in Snakey's eyes, he snatched the bottle.

It tasted warm. Soggy rather than wet. Throaty. It wasn't sleek when it went down. It made him feel it every step of the way. Like burning. He gulped down as much of it as he could and then tried to stop himself from vomiting. Snakey cocked his head and Manny gave him a wink. 'Good eh?'

They both took another, longer draught from the bottle now, Manny already relaxing into the drink, getting its measure, Snakey drinking excitedly, so quickly he surely couldn't have even tasted it, which was maybe the point. They both wiped their mouths with the backs of their hands as they'd seen the fishermen do at the Ship.

'I think it's mead,' said Snakey.

Manny shook his head. 'No. That's based on honey. My dad brews it remember... This is like... barley wine or something.' Then, for no apparent reason, he started laughing. And now Snakey was laughing too. The two of them making more noise laughing like geese than Snakey had ever done smashing the padlock. Already they didn't care if the farmer found them or not.

They turned the out-building into their rough equivalent of the Ship. Snakey lined up the bottles from the crate across a low shelf and then they both perched on a couple hay bales underneath it as though they were regular bar-proppers. As though they'd done this every day their whole lives. They cheersed bottles. They clapped each other on the back, congratulating each other on their bravery, on their tremendous discovery. Snakey tried to tell a joke and got the punch-line dreadfully wrong but Manny roared with laughter anyway. Manny discovered that cigarettes and alcohol together were the best marriage since... Since year dot. He also discovered the drink, when it was poured on the floor and introduced to a lit match, was entirely flammable. So he warned Snakes to be careful. Snakes was too busy singing to himself.

After a while, they started to lose that immediate adrenaline rush, that spontaneous combustion of energy. Now they lounged on one of the hay-bales, both with a straw of hay tucked in the corners of their mouths like Huck Finn, both clutching half-drunk bottles of Bull's brew. Snakey's eyes had gone all liquidy around the edges. Manny was starting to see double. His arm was resting sort of close to the trunk of Snakes' body and he could feel the vibrations as his friend sung fishing songs. It made him want to rest his head on Snakes' belly. He almost did too, before he stopped himself.

They talked about school, about how they could get Piercey back for being a spiky-fucker and how they'd love to drench

Butterworth's titties in this brew and then lap it off like kittens or something. After a while, Snakey got up to take a piss. He started laughing, saying he was going to piss in some of the sciencey equipment on the tables in the centre of the room. Said it would make Bull's next batch taste better. He unzipped himself, flopped out his third bloody limb, started shaking it about, laughing that it was a fire hose. And Manny found he couldn't take his eyes off it. So like and yet so unlike his own. He was intrigued. He found himself adjusting his position on the hay-bale. So he could get a better look and also because he was stirring. Down there.

He found himself wanting to... He imagined the milk bottle a... He ran his tongue around the rim of the bottle. And then, suddenly he realised what he was doing. What he was thinking. What he was feeling. And he felt sick. Disgusted with himself. He screwed up his eyes and tried to force himself to think of something, anything else apart from Snakey's snake. But his mind was all over the place now. Vague ideas, half-formed thoughts, still-born memories mushed into one another. He lifted the bottle to his mouth, cracked his lips wide and poured the drink down. Self-medicating. Most of it dribbled down his front, but some slipped down his throat. He felt the tingle as it passed his tonsils.

He didn't understand why he'd felt like that towards Snakey. He didn't even know if it were possible to feel that way about another boy... Another man. There were rumours, oh there were rumours. About what some of the fishermen got up to on their long trips. About those navy boys up in the base at Norsea. What they got up to in their crisp white uniforms. But it was wrong. Against every law he'd ever been told about. It was wrong. Unholy. Not that he cared one way or another about that God crap but still... Still, they made jokes about those navy boys didn't they? Everyone did. He threw down another mouthful of the old booze, the old hooch, the old moonshine and tried to act like a cowboy. Taciturn. Masculine.

And gradually, his penis stopped tingling. He stopped having warped visions of bending down in front of Snakey like he was praying and... And he drowned himself in drink. His mouth was growing numb to the taste now. All he was aware of was how light his head was becoming. Which was good. He started to anticipate the new buzz which followed every swig. Started to look forward to the next one rather than the one he was having. Started to crave the loss of control each drink would bring.

He felt Snakey's weight again on the bale next to him. Heard his friend's voice. Snakey was trying to tell him something. Was shaking his arm now, calling, 'Manny? Manny?' But Manny had to ignore him. Couldn't look. Because of what he'd felt earlier. That intrigue. That tingle.

He might have blacked out for a while, because certainly he couldn't remember anything for the longest time. It was weird. One minute he had his eyes closed and the next, somehow, they both had fresh bottles now. Were both singing. Manny couldn't see straight at all now. He stared at the light which pooled around the half-open door, and as he stared at it the light kinda solidified. Became this floating, golden ball. Or not a ball, more of a button, a valve. A doorway. He front-crawled up from the hay-bale to go investigate. Heard Snakey shouting after him. He seemed so far away.

Manny approached the solid light. The Goldness. All around it felt warm, centrally heated. He felt himself basking in its glow. And then he reached out and touched it because that's what he felt the Goldness wanted him to do. It yearned for his touch. Was intrigued to feel his touch. It wanted to study his touch as though he was from a completely separate world to it. His hand shakily crawled across the chasm between worlds, between universes, *multi*verses. He touched it, and immediately he felt a pulse. Like the thing was alive. And the pulse carried, electrically, into his body. He started to feel as though he was melting from the inside-out. And then, just as the golden valve became scorching hot in his hand, he saw something, broadcasted, beamed-out from billions of miles away, from billions of years away. From a time where there was no clock and a place where there was no geography. A place which was at once old and new. He saw death, destruction, power. Nature, red in tooth and claw. He saw huge creatures with hungry eyes. He saw them and he felt like they sensed him too. One of the creatures, a giant black panther, growled.

And it was then Manny let go of the ball. He collapsed on the ground. Felt his insides still cooking. And that moment yawned into the rest of his life, or so it seemed, because from that moment forth, the golden valve had stolen some of his pulse, left him suffering from at first arrhythmia and then entering full-on heart attack territory as he got older. From that moment forth, whenever Manny Combs touched a drink, he'd receive that same fluttery feeling in his insides, and, in his mind, he started to call being drunk, 'releasing the golden valve.' And for a while Manny had to drink.

He began to release the golden valve with increasing regularity. Because, he found, if he did so, he could forget all about those terrible, terrifying *feelings* he'd had for his friend. And because he felt driven to release the valve. He felt those red, red creatures calling out to him. Calling him home. As he lay collapsed on the floor of the out-building, he saw how his life would be.

And then he rolled over and it was all streaming out of him. *Steaming* out of him. The poison. The Darkness. He bucked and groaned, prayed to the porcelain God, all the while bargaining. Promising he wouldn't even look at another drop.

But he would. He would and he did. Because when he looked beyond the scorched area of ground where the valve had floated, when he looked back, to the hay-bales, he saw a face which, were it not for the drink, would have haunted him the rest of his life. And though he had no recollection of overpowering Snakey, or of stringing him up from the rafters, or of hanging him, choking the life right outta him, leaving him green, cow-pat faced, puffy, dead, he knew that it had to have been him, or at least, if it wasn't him, if it wasn't directly by his hands, then it was the evil he'd momentarily released, allowed to cross-over between the worlds.

It was amazing how quickly Manny sobered up then. Amazing how steadily he could walk back out the barn, past the tank, down the hill, back to town. And pretend like none of it had ever happened. Pretend like none of it ever happened so that even when he was questioned by the young policeman, Joe Bibby, he could be as convincing as hell and so that one time, a couple years later at some kind of family function or other, and Auntie Mabel had come up to him, cornered him, whispered that she remembered he *had* been with the Snakester that day, that she remembered them being in the shop together despite, or in spite of what he told the police and the teachers, he'd even convinced himself (almost) that she was wrong, that she'd chosen the wrong day on which they'd lied about the pipes bursting at school. It got so he got so good at lying he was even able to cry when they had that silly anniversary for Snakey up at Knoll Farm and they had a big old bonfire and hotdogs and everyone told their favourite Snakey stories. Manny never told anyone his favourite Snakey story. Patched up his brain so he never thought of him again, and even when he did now, he called Snakey something else, something more acceptable politically, morally, lawfully. He called Snakey Cheryl. Cheryl Hammerstein.

232

23: Will

Trevor Knox was sick as a dog. Sicker. As one of the tourists who'd been forced to ride the waves on one of Crabbie's boat taxis. Sicker than that even. When he considered how sick he was, he remembered that old bar room joke, pulled it out from under Mikey Turner's oven, his cauldron of blue, and a gruff voice in the back of his head said, *you're sick enough to wake up fucked-up in bed with your goddamn sister and still fancy another go for old time's sake.* Trevor winced at the voice. At the language which was spiralling, kaliedoscoping around his head, unstoppable now. At the undertone of the joke too, which suggested Limm was the kind of place where people woke up with their sisters every day and still went back for more. He screwed up his eyes, tried to imagine the hallowed pages of Solomon's Book, his collected teachings. Tried to remember that he was one of the righteous. But it was no good. No fucking good at all. Because he'd allowed himself to get infected.

He'd seen his reflection in the window of the town's sometime art gallery as he'd stalked through it during the night, on his way back to the hide. And although some of what he saw was down to the weird lighting from the street lamps, he thought it was more than that. Over the course of twenty-four hours, the infection had feasted hungrily on his flesh, had hollowed out his cheeks, made caves out of his eye sockets. Had given him that hunched over gait when he walked too. Before this, he'd always walked like one of the righteous, head held high.

When he'd dared to look underneath his big, brown sleeping-bag of a coat he'd been shocked at the damage which the infection had inflicted on his body. His skin down there had erupted into scores of tiny and not so tiny lesions, strawberry birth-marks which reminded him somehow of Yoghurt Rhodes' complexion. Only, these lesions were far more sinister. They seemed to glow, pulse in the darkness. And they spread like mould. As soon as he

233

fingered one of them, he felt it bubbling up in his hand, then coursing up his arm. He was now wearing gloves because he couldn't bear to see what had become of that hand. It felt useless. Nothing more than a numb stump. When he tried to grip some railings which encircled the school's deserted playground to stop himself from stumbling over, his fingers wouldn't close around the metal. So he'd fallen. And for a moment he'd just lain there, on the pavement, and waited for oblivion to wash over him. But the midges wouldn't let him. They buzzed around his head, chewed at his ears, scurried through his hair-line, nibbled at his eye-lids. They didn't want him dead yet. They wanted him alive. And tasty.

Deep down he thought he'd always know it would end this way. And if so, he wondered why he hadn't made out a will. Devon Buckby sold DIY wills in the stationery section of his newsagency. He'd bought in a job lot of them apparently, after the Millennium, pissed off that he'd missed the real money-making opportunity when so many died, and was determined to never let something like that happen again. If he had made a will, on that too-heavy legal paper, he figured he'd have left most of his savings to the National Trust. Though animals weren't, according to Solomon, strictly amongst those who'd be Saved, they were still, as he saw it, innocents. Didn't deserve to get infected as he had, as the island had. But Ely Rhodes would get some too. By wire transfer or whatever. So he could pick it up wherever he was now that wasn't Limm. That he'd managed to warn Yoghurt before the infection had spread, was the one thing Trevor felt grateful for now, at the end.

The sea was rougher than it had been for a while. It had stirred up all the seaweed which for weeks had been clogging the harbour further up the shore. Here, almost in open water, it looked treacherous. Foamy. Nominally, it was going out, pulling up its skirts, but it was hard to tell. As Trevor walked deeper into its midst, he felt it sucking at him, felt it clawing at him, trying to drag him into the current which would wash him out past the spit of land which marked the very edge of Limm.

The midges were angrier now than they'd ever been. He could hardly see for them now. Had to windmill his arms about frantically just to check he was wading out in the right direction. If anyone on shore saw him, some dog-walking passer-by or maybe the Dowsing boy, the newspaper delivery kid, they'd think he was waving so madly because he wanted to be rescued. Perhaps they'd call out the coastguard or Sam Bibby. He'd have to make this quicker than he wanted it to be. Because the only thing he wanted now was to be able to pass on, pass up, as those statues on the beach had done at the Millennium. He wanted to be obdurate. He wanted to face the might of the sea and stare it down. But as the cold water fizzed over his testicles – greeted by a sharp intake of breath – the midges redoubled their efforts. He could now feel one crawling over his tongue.

He'd waded out past the breakers now. Underfoot, the seabed became smoother, less shingly. A big wave slapped into his belly, *sung* off the shiny material of his coat. The noise sounded like a scream, so loud he felt his ear-drums starting to rupture. Unless it was one of the midges had climbed inside, was now chowing down, eating its way to his brain.

It didn't feel far off, the end. Though the midges hummed like white noise on a TV in front of his eyes, he thought he could pick out the sun cutting through the clouds. Sneaking out to say hello and goodbye at the same time. And though he'd always believed that in staring directly at the sun he would make himself blind, he did exactly that. And he saw Solomon Mason's face. Those stern eyes. Those lips which spoke so many truths. And now, as the sea swelled around him, salting his lesions, cold-compressing his neck, he allowed himself to smile. It might have been ten years too late, but in doing this he was finally becoming one of the Chosen. Yes, that was it, he was the Second Chosen. He mouthed the words. Midges didn't fly past his lips now but the water did. He sucked in a great, fishy throatful of it. He didn't close his mouth, even though his lungs kicked, screamed, pleaded, accepted. He felt his body being weighed down by the coat. He let his knees bend. Now his head was completely subsumed. Now he couldn't see Solomon's face any more. But he could feel him. Getting closer.

And he felt the knowledge then. Solomon's ancient wisdom. His last thought; *There is another. Not just Ely, there is another. Another Seer. A female.*

24: Natural Yoghurt

Yoghurt Rhodes was trying to position his body so that he'd be able to see his back in the tiny bathroom mirror. There was an awful moment a while back he'd heard this clicking sound in his neck, like a seatbelt sliding home into its lock-compartment, and he'd thought he'd done himself some serious damage, unlocked one of his vertebrae, turned himself jellyfish. He'd waited for the paralysis to kick in, but it had never happened, and now he was twisting again, twisting like he'd never twisted before, any summer. If he wasn't so tall, maybe this would have been easier. If his mother had allowed any mirror in the house larger than a thumb-nail, maybe this would have been easier. If he hadn't lived with mother at all, maybe none of this would have ever happened. And even a couple weeks ago, such a thought would have struck him as so immediately blasphemous that he'd have Shirted himself up ready, issued his own punishment, but now he let the thought stand.

He cricked his neck still further, crooked his back. Tried to look past the pebble-dashing of freckles on his shoulders. Tried to pick out the actual marks, the bruises. Nobody who called on the house and encountered his mother would believe her capable of causing such pain. She looked as though she was pretty much incapable of *any* movement let alone swinging a great rope with a heavy knot in the end over and over again into her son's back. But that she had. Almost as soon as she'd discovered he'd disposed of The Shirt, left it lying down on the field at Coverley Bottoms. She'd whipped him so many times he'd blacked out. So hard that when he felt capable of movement again it was almost morning. His back ached now. But the anger seemed to make it bearable. Perhaps that was how his mother got through the long days since the Millennium.

He wanted to remember the bruising like a map, like his secret short-cut back here, should he ever need a reminder of why he

236

was finally going to cut the umbilical cord. He wanted to landscape photograph the topography of his back, to tattoo that image behind his eye-lids. He wanted the bruising to become like Braille so he could read all about how terrible his mother really was, should he ever doubt it. He wished he'd already left this sorry Lego-brick house behind forever. He wanted to bleach the poky bathroom right out of his head, he wanted to scour his bedroom – the one still decorated like a *child's* room, with the smiley faced sun and stars curtains and bedspread and the posters of north east coast wildlife on the walls and the big cross above his bed – out of his mind forever. He wanted to bludgeon all thought of his mother's stinking hole of a room, gloomy as a photography dark room, into his unconsciousness. Mostly though he just wanted away from here, and after this, he'd go downstairs and offer her his final goodbyes. She wouldn't come after him. Could barely even waddle over the front doorstep now, so that if he didn't bring the milk bottles in, they'd simply be left to be pecked away at by the robins and tits.

He pulled on a shirt. He'd bought it on a whim from a charity shop in Charnley. Liked the seventies style. There was a name scrawled on the label – BOYLE - and he'd thought at the time he could *become* Boyle when he wore it. Not Rhodes. But soon as he'd got it home, he'd spirited it away, still in the Oxfam plastic bag, right to the back of his chest of drawers, underneath the prayer beads and the tee shirt which had Solomon's face on it. Hadn't dared pull it on since. Until now. Now as he tugged the neck-hole over his head and as the material touched his weak-strong points, it felt like the right choice. He'd also selected baggy, flare-style jeans, *sans* cycle clips, and had forgone his Clark's in favour of some hiking boots which were fairly jazzy in design (certainly they wouldn't have been allowed had they been trainers, but as they were hiking boots, they were seemingly permissible.) He rounded off the look by manifestly refusing to comb his hair and leaving the toothbrush exactly where it was in the JESUS SAVES MORE THAN ANY GOALIE mug alongside his mother's. He took one last look in the mirror and then unbolted the door, stepped out onto the landing.

Where he paused. Already he could hear the sounds of his mother's chanting carrying up from the front room. He could picture her now; beached in front of the shrine to Solomon, surrounded by the remnants of more of the microwave meals she had delivered. Usually, she couldn't get back up again from such a position, would ask him. Maybe if he really was leaving, if this was his moment,

237

he'd install some kind of harness for her. Or maybe he wouldn't bother. Maybe he'd let her take her chances. Maybe he'd see if all her prayers, all her chants were answered instead.

He walked downstairs slowly. Aware of the jarring pain from his back as he trod on every stair. Every stair apart from the seventh one down, of course. Ever since he was little he'd bypassed that step. He didn't know why now. Perhaps it was the site of a particularly bad beating from his mother. Perhaps he'd slipped on it once, gone tumbling down like Unholy Jack and his Dark sister Jill. All he knew was it had become superstition for him. Now those cogs in his brain up there were a-whirring, he wondered whether religion was like that, like a tricky seventh step always to be avoided until eventually someone set it in stone, or in a great big book like Solomon. And then they started to be treated like laws. And then, to break those laws meant things like The Shirt and The Rope.

He reached the foot of the stairs, unlike Jack, with his crown intact. He'd have quite liked Jack as a first name. Sounded outdoorsy somehow. Jack Boyle. Could have been a private eye maybe. Or a star photographer, or distance cyclist. Sounded snappy. Snappier than Yoghurt, certainly, which glooped slow off the spoon. Yoghurt which was, when it came down to it, bacteria.

'Ely? That you?' screeched his mother from the front room. 'Stop lurking out there like a No Good and come help me up.'

Ely paused for a moment, said nothing. He stared at the front door. In particular at its dead-bolt. He could have made a break for it, slipped across that plastic covering which kept the stains off the hallway carpet, slid open the bolt, escaped outside. But if he did that, if he didn't fix this as *the* moment of his leaving – which meant words – then he knew he was liable to come back here. Something which was, in its own way, worse than The Darkness, worse than that rough beast which slouched through the fields across the causeway, which had followed him here.

'Ely? I can hear you *breathing* out there. Come in here *now*.'

He leveled his gaze at the picture of his father on the hallway wall. It was the one picture of that man that he'd ever seen in the house. It was a stock image ordered from *The Tide Piper*, from way back before Yoghurt had been born, or *cultured,* which was how yoghurt actually grew. His dad Thomas, whom his mother had only referenced as The Doubter for many years now, tucked low on a racer, his three-quarter length hair trailing in the wind. The speed Thomas was moving at, picked up on the long hill at Dye

238

Lane, meant that he appeared as a kind of blur, a stripe of suggested colour, and that was how Yoghurt had always thought of him, as an out of focus kind of chap. A race away before the going gets tough kind of chap. But now he thought about it, he wondered whether Thomas, Doubting or not, had simply found it impossible to stay. Because of *her*. After Solomon died, Yoghurt remembered his mother sitting him down on their big old Paisley-print sofa. Giving him what amounted to her version of the birds and the bees. Way she said it, she wanted Yoghurt to remember *Solomon* as his father now. Whether this was symbolically or literally, he wasn't wholly sure, and when he'd asked for clarification, he'd kindly been reintroduced to The Shirt. *Yoghurt, meet Shirt, Shirt meet Yoghurt.*

He sighed, lifted the photograph off the wall and left it underneath his coat and cycling proficiency vest by the door. Then he padded across the plastic mat, pushed through the doorway, and stepped into the front room.

The front room had once been two separate rooms. It had long-since been knocked through and had become a sort of reduced version of a church. The altar was where the TV would have been in any normal front room, the north and south transept were represented by the two-seater sofa and his mother's special chair (the one she ate, slept, *cultured* in), as well as, oddly enough, a foot spa. Down the nave, there were various smaller shrines and then at last, adjacent to the back patio windows, was the shrine to Solomon. It stood out within the sparsely decorated room. Was kept up to date with fresh flowers, newspaper cuttings from other Millennium cults around the world, as though Solomon often popped back because he quite fancied a read. There was also, in the centre of the shrine, the one surviving copy of Solomon's full preachings. This book his mother was absently stroking as he entered, looking at it with longing in her eyes.

He looked at her and felt nothing but disgust. She was wearing a red vest-style top which barely contained her bulk. Grey, overall-style trousers which would have fit someone in the land of the giants. She was surrounded by the microwave meals she'd already devoured. Slop. Her body looked like slop, too; grey porridge to be exact. Soon as she heard her son's approach, she instinctively lifted her arms, expecting to be helped to her feet. Yoghurt made no move to her and for a moment, the only sound was the whirring of the microwave at her feet.

Yoghurt stared past his mother, out the patio windows. Outside, pregnant clouds loomed ominously. He studied the old cat's footprint in the dried cement. Tiddles. That had been the cat's name. Long since gone now, of course, and perhaps at the brutal hands of his mother. Well, The Darkness was returning now, was already wreaking its revenge. And The Darkness came in the form of a cat.

'What are you doing standing there you great Unholy streak?' snapped his mother. 'Help me!'

Yoghurt shook his head. 'What you been praying for now?'

She pursed her lips. 'Do not take that tone with me, young man. You know as well as I do that this shrine, my prayers are the only thing that keeps the wolf from the door. And yet you look at me like... Like I'm useless. Like I just sit around here all day lazing. Would you like the Rope again, Ely?'

Yoghurt smiled at her then. Because there was no way she could hurt him low as she was. No way to hurt him now he'd made his decision.

'What are you grinning at, you Unholy fool? The high-tide of Darkness is coming. When the wolf's scratching the door, howling to be let in and...'

'It's not a wolf, mother, it's a panther. A black panther.'

She looked up at him. Gulped. Opened her mouth as though to speak. Closed it again. And for a moment, they simply stared at each other. There was fear and no little surprise in the eyes of Yoghurt's mother; in his eyes only that new-found hardness. They were torn from their reverie as the microwave *dinged*, causing his mother to utter this horrible yelp of shock, and then Yoghurt simply turned his back, walked out, picked up the photograph of the man he wanted to be his father, and left the Lego brick house.

All the way down the road, almost as far as the primary school playground, which he cut across in order to get to the old Holiday Park, he heard her screeching after him. But he ignored her. Fighting The Darkness after vanquishing his mother would be easy. He found the caravan he'd chosen, three to the left on the second row, cracked open the door, checked whether the door had been tampered with in any way, and then he checked his provisions. His Nikon, a few bits of food, a compass and a cagoule. Everything he'd need to go after the beast and capture it on camera. It would be like taking a photograph of God.

24: Swallowed a Fly

Brett Copestake zipped his Parka tighter around his face. Then checked his back pocket to see whether there was a handkerchief which he could use to practically choke his nose. Nothing doing. He dry-retched as he sucked in another noseful of air; tried to make himself breathe through his mouth only, but it seemed strangely impossible. Every time he stopped trying to breathe through his nose, his mouth wouldn't work and he thought he was going to pass out. Mind, passing out would have been preferable to the smell. Down by the River Drey, the fishy, kinda *off* smell was getting worse. And no matter how many times Bully told him the smell was likely on account of something going on at the mead factory, he still couldn't find it in himself to believe him. No. Something was rotten on Limm and it had absolutely nothing to do with the smoky belches which continued to pour from the tall chimney at the factory.

It smelled a bit like Davy Jones might have had, had he ever opened up his locker for inspection. It also smelled vaguely like the traps Copey laid out in the woodlands when the going was good; the kind of smell which would've made poor old Dan Coffey crazy with excitement because it meant there was something dead. And, for some reason Copey couldn't put his finger on rightly, he decided whatever was making that smell was big. Chunky.

'Honestly,' said Bully, 'anyone would think you'd never smelled the cellars at the Ship.'

Copey gasped. It was hard to talk and breathe through his mouth at the same time. 'But this isn't like off beer and that. This is worse... I mean, how can you stand it?'

Bully got this faraway look in his eye. 'I found a body once. When I was a wee feller. Up in one of the barns at Knoll Farm. I could only have been three, four maybe, and me da had told me on no account was I to go in that barn. Anyway, this one day, I remember it well because da was badly, and he was hardly ever

241

badly. Certainly never badly enough so he couldn't work.' He paused, brushed away a fly. That was the other thing about the stink; seemed to be attracting flies of all varieties like nobody's business; the whole gamut of them from big, fat bluebottles could barely fly they were that gorged on *something*, to little nibbly midges which went in for that ENT lark like they knew their hospitals.

'Anyway,' said Bully, once he'd collected himself, 'I was out playing in the yard, up by the old tank and I heard a strange noise from back barn, so I went to investigate. Turned out someone had busted the padlock see. Now, at the time, I was, how shall we say it, *intrigued* about that barn. On account of the fact I wasn't allowed in it. So I'd just got curiouser and curiouser, until finally I went that day, and it was like fate or something that the door was half-open. So I went inside. And it took me a while for my little eyes to get accustomed.' He brushed away another fly, as though he was brushing away the cobwebby reminder of that darkness.

'But even before I could see what happened, even though I was only wee, I knew what had happened straight away, Copey. Because of the smell. All the reports said later that boy hung hisself in that barn, but the smell said different. It was like he'd burned up inside. That smell, cooking liver and lungs... It'll stay with me rest of my life...' He sucked in his cheeks, spat on the side of the path, then unbuckled his water bottle from the side of his rucksack, cracked the lid and took a man-sized swig.

'Dirty' Den Fletcher and Andy Worcester (Sauce, as they called him) caught them up then, Worcester giving the older Bully a playful kick up the arse as they arrived.

'You telling Copey-lad more of your old war stories, Bully?' said Dirty. He accepted the offered water bottle and sucked from it greedily, spilling some down his chin. He flicked out a lizardy tongue to lick it away.

While they watered themselves, Copey watched Dirty clean his rifle. He was a stickler. So far, everywhere they'd stopped on their hunt that morning, Dirty had been there, cleaning off his imaginary spots. It got so that Copey thought Dirty had to be one of those ironic nicknames like Little John.

They were in what amounted to Robin Hood territory now, at least, they were deep within the southern woods. It felt like a long time ago Sauce had first picked up the trail. A long time since he'd lost it too. But they'd all seen the *size* of that damned print. And Copey had spared a thought for his old pal Dan Coffey. It was why he was here now, amongst these older men, these farmers. Outdoor men sure, but not exactly the type would have made him welcome even a week ago now. But the beast had changed everything. So much that even though they'd passed a couple loaded traps, they'd kept walking.

Two shots had been fired in earnest. First to unload was Andy Worcester, which was no surprise, seeing as though his finger had been itching on the trigger ever since they'd left the town hall last night. Sauce had seen movement, or 'the suggestion of movement' as he said later down near the Old Mason House, the place the kiddies called The Monster House. He'd fired first, asked questions later, like, why in the hell had he wasted a bullet on what was, as it turned out, nothing more than a house cat which needed a few weeks dieting. The second shot had also killed a cat, and that wasn't a surprise either. Copey figured a lot of cats would get killed while they hunted for the Big Momma of them all. No, the surprising thing had been that the shooter was Bully, a feller who'd seemed the calmest of the lot of them. But he'd seen his own *suggestion of movement,* and he'd fired almost without thinking and bagged himself a three-quarter size tabby with a fucking little bell on its collar to boot. There was a name too, Trixie, and Bully had said he wanted to bury the poor little thing, but then thought better of it.

Now, as Dirty and Sauce shared a chocolate bar, Bully was burying Trixie's pink collar in a shallow grave.

'Don't know why you're bothering,' said Sauce, through a mouthful of Biscuit Boost. 'Nobody'll miss a cat. Not nobody with no sense anyway. I've got three of the fuckers strung up on my porch. As a warning to the Big Momma.'

'You've shot three cats?' said Bully, sounding disgusted. 'Just what is the bloody point in that?'

Sauce smiled a chocolatey smile. It made his teeth look rotten, him simple. 'I never said I shot 'um did I?' He pantomimed strangling a cat. Copey looked away.

'Come on,' said Bully, evidently refusing to rise to the bait. 'Off we go.' He strode off down the path, his big green Barbour coat flapping behind him.

Copey fell into step with Dirty, leaving Sauce to hold up the rear. 'Do you honestly think we'll find the trail again?' he asked.

Dirty sucked his teeth, mused a moment. 'If it's left to us, yep. Why not? I mean we're all outdoorsmen. We've all hunted…'

'Not something as big as this…'

243

'Granted. But that's the point as I see it. It is big. And surely findable. I mean, for one thing, it'll need to be near prey which is big enough to keep it going. I think we'll find it. I just hope we're not too late. Mr. Combs is right in a way. If we get hundreds of people trampling through the woods, trying to get photos of it for their goddamn Facebook pages and the like, we're all in trouble.'

Copey sniffed. Added, 'I suppose some in the town might see the panther as an opportunity. Mind that Adrian Devonish, that bearded twat over at the Castle Hotel. He'll probably start running Panther Safaris or something. Upping the price of his rooms even though we're out of Silly Season.'

'Trevor Knox'll think all his Sundays have come at once. He'll be on at the National Trust to give him the money to build another hide so he can do panther-watching.'

'They'll ship that Attenborough feller up here to make a documentary.'

'It'll be worse than that fucking Millennium cult.'

'Aye, right.'

World set to rights, they walked on in silence now, crunching through the undergrowth, ducking under low branches, watching the shadows. They'd skirted the entire mid-section of the woods now and were following the river as it led them back towards the arse-end of the town, close to where they'd held the TALENT-STRAVAGANZA!!!!!! yesterday. The start of it all, as far as most of the public were concerned, but for farmers such as Sauce, Bully and Dirty, just another chapter. They'd all had livestock killed. They'd all had their farms turned into murder scenes. Copey hadn't, but then, he had other, stronger reasons for hating the beast.

They crossed the river close to Coverley Bottoms on a small, rickety bridge which, had Limm Island been a fairy-tale world, would have had a gruff troll living underneath.

'Cover ye bottoms, boys,' said Sauce as he passed through a gap in Manny Combs' all new, all-singing, all-dancing perimeter fence. Already the local lads had rendered the fence useless, puncturing at least five decent-sized holes in its defences.

'His nibs won't be pleased,' said Bully. 'Mind, I can't see them being able to charge an entrance fee for another wash-out of a talent show in future. All due respect to Coffey, of course.'

Copey thought about his pal now, thought that Coffey might well have used the very bridge they'd just crossed. Only he'd have crawled over it. He thought about the effort it would have taken to

244

crawl all that way when you were at death's door as it was. He didn't think he'd have been able to do the same. When his time came, he wanted to go on his own so that if he did piss and shit himself, like so many animals did at the end, it wouldn't be seen.

'Y'all right, Copey-lad?' said Bully, narrowing his eyes.

Copey nodded, stared back at the older man. There was yet another fly on him. Copey watched as it crawled down the farmer's cheek. The farmer hadn't even noticed. Hadn't made a move to brush it away. Or maybe, Copey reflected, because there were *so many* flies down here, Toby Bull had stopped bothering brushing them away. Watching him with that fly on his cheek reminded him of those pictures of famine victims in far-off places in Africa. There were always tons of flies. Always allowed to just go about their business. The starving people had no energy to brush 'em off. But Toby Bull had. Copey wanted to grab the farmer's beef-steak hand. *Make* him slap the fly off him.

For some reason, Copey was reminded of that old song: *I know an old lady who swallowed a fly.* They used to sing it at the primary school and he'd always thought it an unusually morbid little number. Especially the *Perhaps she'll die* part. He wondered whether the fly was somehow marking Toby Bull for the big cat. And then he shook his head, drove out the gloomy thoughts and squeezed through the fence after Sauce and Dirty. Bully squeezed through last. Which wasn't an omen. Omens didn't exist. It seemed nothing existed beyond the flies.

After they'd cut across Coverley Bottoms, they made for the old abandoned road, the road which had been made with industrial access routes in mind but which now played host to only the odd deer, badger or fox. There were clouds of flies down here. So thick that it was becoming hard to see properly. The sound of their buzzing was like a drill piercing through Copey's skull. The flies were so fat, so juiced up, it was as though he had to swim through the air. He noticed Sauce struggling similarly. Dirty frantically trying to keep the flies off his rifle. Only Bully seemed unaffected by them, which was strange. Strange considering his green Barbour coat now looked black there were so many of them crawling on him.

Loose gravel and now teems, *teams* of beetles were crunching under their feet. At the side of the road, they saw the oddly white, skeletal trees buckling under the weight of more insects. A branch cracked off one of the trees and sounded like a gunshot. Dirty swung round, fired in the general direction of the noise and it was as though his bullet went in slow motion.

Sauce Worcester muttered, 'I got a bad feeling about this.'

They saw something collapsed into the undergrowth at the side of the road. The old WELCOME TO LIMM ISLAND sign. It had been vandalized beyond all recognition. Welcome-matted into submission by the sheer weight of insects, or else something else had done for it. Yes, thought Copey, something else had done for it. The smell was so bad here it was as though it had fists, was punching him over and over again in the nose.

Copey was staring so hard at that old welcome sign that he never noticed Bully had stopped stock still on the road in front of him. The first he knew about it was when the side of his face connected with the carpet of flies on the older farmer's back. He shuddered, backed away. Bully made no move to suggest he even knew he'd been walked into. And now, as Copey watched, Bully raised a shaking arm, leveled out a finger, pointed off into the bushes. Where the dead shark was lying, ship-wrecked.

'Christ,' breathed Copey. And his first thought was that the damned thing had to be a fake, it looked so wrong out here that it could only be a fake. But it didn't smell fake. Nothing manufactured could stink so sewery-bad. Nothing manufactured could have suggested the sheer horror of its flanks, its broken dorsal fin. Great chunks had been bitten from its rubbery hide. Huge gorge-like tears had been made in its back. Its face was so alive with flies that, heavy as it was, outlandish as it was, it looked as though it might just take off and fly sometime soon.

Copey collapsed down onto his knees. Felt the vomit in his throat. Couldn't unzip his Parka quickly enough so that when the sickness came, he felt he was drowning in it. Right next to him, Sauce Worcester, a man who tortured cats for fun, was hunkered down throwing up Biscuit Boost after Ginster's pasty, sobbing, choking, gasping all the while.

Welcome to Limm Island, Twinned with Hell.

25: Life-Boat

The Bibby Firm were already down at the lifeboat hut when Mike Ford dragged himself in at around a quarter past nine. They were both down to their vests, elbow-deep in the lifeboat's engine. For a moment, he stood by the roller-shutter and simply watched the two Limm giants work, as wordlessly they passed each other tools, oil canisters, cloths, working with the precision of surgeons, working as though both were so attuned with what the other was thinking, they didn't actually need to formulate the words. He'd always thought the two of them... spooky. Which was a strange thing to say about two brutes whose obvious physical strength should have been their most ready defining factor.

Mart Bibby was notionally bigger than his brother (who was notionally – five minutes – older). As he twisted at something within the engine, Mike watched his bare forceps veritably thrumming with energy. As though he was picking up charge from the electrics in the engine. The back of his vest was wringing-wet with sweat despite the cold. Sam, at his side, was standing in a big black oil-stain on the floor. It looked as though he had grown out of the oil, as though his similarly brutal arms were machine parts cranking themselves up. Sam was tinkering with one of the filters, only, in his hands, it became more than tinkering, it became boa constricting the life out of the filter until it submitted to his will.

Mike could feel their collective wills heavy on the cold morning air. It was almost enough to send him scurrying back out through the roller-shutter and down to the back room at the library where he should be getting on with his other job. But he didn't leave. Instead he leaned back against the brass plaque on the wall, a list of all those brave volunteer lifeboatmen who'd lost their lives at sea, a list which included his own grandfather, and waited. Waited for them to swing round and notice his arrival.

The lifeboat hut was relatively new in Limm terms, had little over fifteen years on the clock. But still it buckled under the weight of history. There were the brass plaques on the walls which listed the names of the dead of course, but there were also the oil paintings of lifeboats on rocky seas throughout the centuries, and the framed articles from *The Tide Piper* recognising the rescues they'd performed over the years. Museum-style open chests which displayed the full gamut of sailor's knots lined the walls. Antique rudders tillers and booms littered the floor. And then, at the back of the hut, behind the current boat, was what amounted to a shrine to the woman who'd become the unofficial patron saint of lifeboat crews, Grace Darling, who, along with her father, had braved the seas not far up the coast to save a lucky thirteen, a blessed baker's dozen men, from the shipwrecked SS Forfarshire. Grace was a regular nineteenth century heroine, a woman who'd almost become myth. Mike had often wondered whether, if she'd been alive today, Max Clifford, or someone of his ilk, would have maybe tried to sign her up for the latest celebrity show in the jungle of Australia.

In their own little way, the lifeboat stations of the north east coast traded off the celebrity of Grace Darling. There was a tiny shop adjoining the hut; open two mornings a week and staffed by two women who looked as though they were formed from knots they were that old, that twisted. The shop sold the whole White Elephant of lifeboat-related miscellany, from trunk (lifeboat rubbers and pencil sharpeners, fridge magnets and teddies) to tail (lifeboat flasks, tea, and no doubt out of date biscuits). The only thing these items had in common was the name Grace Darling. That and the fact they had to work very, very hard, impossibly hard, to earn enough money to keep the current boat properly maintained.

The current boat was a rigid-hulled inflatable, a twenty-footer. Inside the hut it looked unweildly, but out on even the stormiest of seas, it could open up to around thirty knots. Mike had been on it when it was travelling that speed and it was some experience, the boat hydroplaning, slicing over the waves. Felt like flying. Or, more specifically, flying through some turbulence.

Mart Bibby finished up in the engine, hunkered down to wipe his hands on his knees, and then turned round. He didn't look surprised to see Mike lingering by the roller shutter, but he did seem disappointed. He frowned, creasing his forehead. Chomped down his big jaws on his customary nicotine replacement gum. Didn't make any effort to say hello.

'All right boys?' said Mike. And then, as though to explain his presence, he added, 'Saw the filthy clouds and I thought I'd come down. Make sure she's in good shape. There's a storm coming and I...'

'We can handle it,' growled Mart. 'As you can see, we got it covered.' Then he returned to his chewing.

Sam Bibby moved out from underneath the boat, smiled. 'Forgive Mart. He's like a bear with a sore head this morning.'

Mike nodded. He knew why. He'd popped his head round the Ship's door last night, just to see whether there was anyone in he could share a few late jars with. There'd been the usual old men, hanging limpet-like off the bar, but he'd also seen Mart Bibby, looming like a storm-cloud in the corner, close to the juke box. Though he and Mart went way back – they'd both volunteered for the life-boat crew since before they could even tie knots in their laces – he knew better than to interrupt one of the big man's funks. Because he could see even from the way he threw his pint down his neck that he was in a bad way, and when Mart was in a bad way, he was best avoided. When Mart was in a bad way, only Sam could get through to him. Mike had retired to his house, which was lonelier than the Ship, but safer. There, he'd indulged in rather too many whiskies as he tried to make sense of what he'd seen down at Coverley Bottoms.

'And besides,' continued Sam, 'we could do with all the help available this morning. I've been trying Trev's mobile a few times and there's no answer...'

'Perhaps Knoxy's scored,' sneered Mart.

Sam ignored him. 'So, how's it going Mike?'

Mike shuffled his feet, felt the pound of last night's whisky in his temples. He wanted to tell him things were going badly, that a whole shit-storm was coming and it wasn't necessarily the weather, but he held his tongue. 'What can I do?' he asked instead. 'Give me something to do. I need to get rid of a raging hangover.'

'Tell him he can put the kettle on,' snapped Mart, turning his back, returning to his engine.

Sam Bibby offered an apologetic shrug.

Mike Ford did as he was told. He squeezed down past the boat's starboard side until he reached the back wall where a small doorway led into the part-time lifeboat shop. Pushed through it. Rummaged through the bric-a-brac to find three fresh lifeboat mugs and a packet of lifeboat tea. Val, one of the crones who volunteered at the shop, was always playing hell with them for commandeering the stock, but when he looked inside each of the mugs, he saw they were so thick with dust they'd clearly been on the shelves years. He carried them through to the small bathroom, ran them under the cold tap until at least he could see white at the bottom, and then he slapped on the kettle. As he waited for it to boil, he looked out the window. Studied the roiling black clouds outside. The gloom. The wetness in the air. He'd studied English Literature as well as Journalism at college. Then, he'd had half a mind to turning his arm to writing a novel. But the English course had done little more than give him the tools by which he could pick apart a piece of literary writing, not how he could then Airfix it back together again. The course had merely left him with a locker-full of critical phrases through which he could deconstruct his world. This, he noted, was *pathetic fallacy*. The weather outside directly correlated with what was going on in his head. The swirling fug, the low-hanging clouds, the darkness, they were reflections of his state of mind, his doubts, his fears. It was a cheap authorial trick, he thought. He hoped that the shit-storm he knew was coming would be a sleight of hand too.

Kettle boiled, he poured three teas, sprinkled them all heavily with sugar to mask the taste of sun-bleached desperation which spiced everything in the shop. Still, dust motes floated on the top of the tea. He stirred extra hard to break them up, then carried them through to the Bibby Firm. Mart accepted his without a word of thanks. Sam though, looked pleased at the excuse to take a break and led Mike outside where they both took a seat on the edge of the ramp. The policeman took a gulp of the tea and swallowed, showing no signs that he'd even registered the drink was still scalding hot.

'So, he said,' wiping his mouth with the back of his hand. 'What did you make of it all yesterday then, Mr. Newspaperman?' He turned and fixed Mike with an unreadable expression.
There was a streak of oil on his cheek which looked almost like war-paint.

'The word farce springs to mind... I mean, it turned out to be the Manny Combs show, didn't it, but not in the way it should have been. I mean, it was me had to go up on the microphone, try to calm everyone down and...'

'The Manny Combs show,' mused Sam. 'Sometimes I get the impression this whole island is the Manny Combs show. Sometimes I think he only likes it when we're all backs-to-the-wall in crisis because then we all get a reminder he's the one in charge.'

250

He paused, took another hearty swig from his brew. 'What are you going to write about it in *The Tide Piper?* What's your angle?'

'I don't know yet,' said Mike. 'I just know...' His voice descended into a hoarse whisper. Last night's whisky seemed to have dried his throat out. 'I just know it *feels* bad. And the last time it felt like this was ten years ago. The Millennium.'

For a moment, neither man said anything. They both looked out past the Ship, past the village green, past the jetty and the small flotilla of boats bobbing in the harbour, their hulls coated with sea weed. They looked out at the sea and the sky, to the almost indiscernible point where both joined, that liminal place where it seemed the threat was being stored up, ready to explode.

'After the talent show, Mart and I went to the pub,' said Sam. 'There was nothing else for us to do. Manny wouldn't let us anywhere near the Bungalow. Anyway, I got this answering machine message. From Sally Martin. She's the...'

'The piano teacher at the primary, I know,' interrupted Mike.

'Yes well, she was in a right state. Could hardly make out what she was saying on the message, and at first I thought it was all to do with the Coffey lad. But then she started saying all this stuff about finding a finger and all and she seemed... It seemed as though it was the truth. So I buckled up, went over there to her place.' He stopped, sighed. 'Tell me, Mike, what do you make of her, that Sally?'

Mike remembered how the woman had been yesterday, when they'd been backstage before the show. Wringing her hands, muttering to herself, and that was *before* Coffey had announced himself on the scene. 'She's...'

'You trust her? Would she make something up like this, you know, for attention? See, when I went round there I played my cards close to my chest. And from what I could see she was... over-wrought. And her husband, bloody idiot he was, treated her like she wasn't there. So it all just seemed like a cry for help. I told her I'd go back there this morning, to look for this finger, but... But I haven't. And yet, something about the whole thing. It's wrong. Do you know what I mean?'

Mike nodded. 'I'd trust her more than some of the others at that school. Or in the secondary. That Carl-Rhys Hamilton for example.'

'I think that's what I think too,' said Sam. 'I think she's one of the good guys.' He looked back, over his shoulder at the lifeboat. 'Sometimes I don't think that boat's for rescuing people from the sea and returning them to the island. Sometimes I think it's the other way round... I feel like if things don't change soon, something terrible'll happen, but I also think that the changes themselves might be terrible.'

'So what do we do?' asked Mike. Suddenly, he wanted Sam to tell him what to do, even if it was to just go back to the lifeboat shop and make tea while the Bibby Firm manned the front-line.

'We make ready,' said Sam, jerking his thumb back, indicating the boat. And as he did so, a fat raindrop landed on that thumb and then hung for a moment, on the edge. Then that drop was followed by more. By the time the pair of them had covered the three paces back past the roller shutter, both were completely soaking.

The storm had started.

26: Shaw Thing

D r. Ray Shaw didn't like making house calls. Not since that awful time when Shirley Musson from the Holiday Park had called him out late one Friday night and had opened the door to him wearing this peep-hole bra and see-through knickers. His main problem with that had been the fact that Shirley Musson was sixty if she was a day, and her breasts drooped so much that they didn't so much peep through the bra as *plummet* through it.

'Ah, doctor,' she had said, 'so glad you came. I was wondering if you'd take a look at my pie.'

Pie, she'd called it; her vagina. And she'd shown him that too, opening her legs in what she'd thought had been a provocative fashion. And even then, even when the fishy smell washed over him, he'd managed to hold down his traditional Friday fish and chip tea. But when she said, 'I'd *love* to feel the bristles of your beard when you go down on me,' he'd lost control and vomited copiously into her roses. He'd not been able to eat a pie since, even though the Ship did a lovely Steak n' Kidney.

Up to the point that he received the frantic call from Janice Dowsing, it had been as uneventful a morning as Shaw could have hoped for. Flick had stayed in her room all night so he'd actually managed to get some shut-eye when he got back from the Bungalow (though he did suffer from a nightmare in which Dan Coffey had risen up in that patchwork quilt and had come after him with knitting-needle fingers). When he'd brought her an early breakfast in bed, as a reward for being good, and as a promise to himself that things weren't always as dark as they had been the past few days, she'd not thrown any of it at the wall, nor spat it in his face, nor tried to pull her own eyes out with the spoon. She hadn't actually eaten much of it, but, when she was placid like that, he could still pretend. And sure, he'd had the paperwork to complete and the coroner to placate when they came to pick up Coffey's body at about 8am, but the inquisition he'd been expecting hadn't been *all that*. In the end, the most insistent questioning had come from Betty, keen to find out any juicy tidbits she could broadcast over the washing-line telegraph and from his own prickled conscience. He didn't like the fact Manny Combs had made practically *every* decision yesterday, despite having no medical experience or training. His constant spouting that it was an Emergency Situation was all very well, but doctors like Shaw, close to retirement as he was, still had to be accountable for his actions.

But still, all so very uneventful morning for a Monday. The wash-out at the TALENT-STRAVAGANZA!!!!!! even seemed to have dissuaded a number of his more regular patients from visiting him that morning, as though not being able to see the conclusion to *Dancing in the Moonlight's* act had dropped them into a well of depression. The determined Mrs. Popplewell was a rarity in the fact she did pop in on her walk, just so she could drop in a cake she'd baked especially for him. She did it most weeks. At first, they'd been proper, home-baked marvels, just like Flick used to make on those occasional good days, but more recently, Mrs. Popplewell's health had taken a turn for the worse. She was dying. It was as simple as that. And no amount of medicines could alter that fact. One day, when he discovered a bit of cellophane wrapper under the cake, he realised that she no longer baked the cakes herself, but bought them in order to keep up that pretence that everything was okay. He knew how she felt; he'd been putting on that front that everything was hunky-dory for years now.

After Mrs. Popplewell had left, he pressed the buzzer to call Betty into the room. Betty knew the score. She was the human dustbin that was responsible for disposing of all such gifts nowadays. She seemed to expect the gifts too now, as though they were a part of her salary package; she took the cake without even a word of thanks and returned to the kitchen to make more hot drinks.

As he suspected, Betty kept the tea flowing all day; sometimes, he wondered if she ever did anything other than boil and pour, boil and pour. She didn't even collect the dirty cups. By half nine, four of them had accumulated on the corner of his desk, practically begging to be taken away on her wheeled trolley, but it seemed she had a blind spot for that part of the room.

He knew she was only fussing over him because she was trying to find out more about the casualty at the talent show. Trying

254

to catch him out while he was on the phone, in mid conversation with one of the 'peelers' as she called them. She seemed to have this notion that all policemen, doctors and teachers shared this communication hotline – like a higher-tech version of her own washing-line system – by which they all shared their information and juicy tidbits about the people of the town. And she probably wasn't wrong about that; he knew all about the Masonic presence on the north east coast. What she was wrong about was assuming that he'd be party to any of this information, and that he cared enough to listen to it even if he was.

By quarter to ten, the waiting room had emptied and he found himself at the blinds, peering through at the lingering morning mist which was still painting the whole island with its silent, black thickness. Shaw noted that he could barely see the sea. He couldn't even make out the village green. Even the houses on Rowbotham Row seemed like a ghostly apparition, flickering on the unstable, swirling currents in the air.

He clicked the blinds closed and returned to the black swivel chair, feeling that tingly feeling all over him again. He could feel another vision coming on. He could feel it like the mad, butterfly-flutter of the heart which warned of an impending attack. He didn't know if he could handle another vision, so soon after the first, so soon after his nightmare, so soon after he'd had to oversee the death of yet another of Limm's menfolk. He took a sip of tea, too late discovering that it was stone cold.

Suddenly, the computer screen fizzed a little and then clicked off. He pressed the 'on' button. Nothing happened. He pressed again, this time allowing his thumb to linger over the button. When he finally released it, the monitor was still blank. But he didn't care about any lost spreadsheets or suicide notes. Not now his fingers seemed to crackle and pop with static electricity. His right ear was burning up. What was it Betty always said: 'Left for love, right for spite.' Well, this was spite all right.

He felt his fingers reaching for the telephone on his desk before it had even started to ring. Felt his ear straining to hear what hadn't been said yet. He *knew* exactly who was going to be on the other end of the line. It was going to be Janice Dowsing. It was going to be something about her son. Something terrible had happened to her son. That had been what the early morning vision had been about two days ago. And although he knew the telephone was incontrovertibly going to ring, he still jumped a little when it did, vibrating against him twitching fingers.

He picked it up after two rings. 'Mrs. Dowsing,' he said.

'Oh! Erm... uh... Is that the doctor? Shaw?' she stammered.

'That's me,' he answered, feeling strangely numb. 'What can I do for you, Mrs. Dowsing?'

'H- how did you?'

'Got one of those new phones,' he answered, quickly, 'one of the ones that displays the caller ID.'

'Oh,' gulped Janice.

'Mrs. Dowsing?'

He heard a rustling noise, as though she'd momentarily lost her grip on the phone. Then, heavy breathing. Finally, her voice. 'Sorry about that... I'm trying to mop his brow while I keep talking... He lashed out a little bit, then...'

'Do you mean Lewis, Mrs. Dowsing?'

'Uh... yes. Sorry. I'm not being very clear about any of this, am I?'

'Just take a deep breath and tell me what the problem appears to be,' said Shaw. He was fiddling with the telephone cord now; knotting its twisted wire into the familiar shapes.

'It's Lewis. He's had a bad turn. I don't know what's wrong with him but it's bad. He was late back off his paper round yesterday... Grace and me went out searching for him. We found him but there was no reaching him... When we got back, Devon – that's my... uh... we live with him – he told us that Lewis had to be drunk because he collapsed over the threshold. He was slurring his words like he was a common booze-hound... But he's still like that now, and even if he had... had a drink spiked or something, it wouldn't last this long, would it?'

Shaw coughed. 'And what about the claw-marks?' He meant what he'd seen in the vision. The visionary black panther which surely now had to have been thing which had done for Coffey too.

'I'm sorry? Claw-marks? I don't know what you mean. I...' Janice started to sob.

'Where is he now, Janice?'

'He's in his bed,' she sniffed. 'One minute he's boiling up, the next he's stone-cold. We... I would have brought him in sooner, but it seems wrong to move him. He's got these *swellings*. All over him. Started off with one on his knee; like an egg it was. But now he's got some under his armpits... around his... his... groin. I don't

256

know what's wrong with him, doc. It's like inside his body is all poisoned by something. Maybe it's a bad allergic reaction, like with the grass and the hay fever.'

'That may well be the case,' sighed Shaw. 'But I wouldn't like to say. Not over the phone. I'll come out to your place and take a look at him. You're still above the shop on the main street?'

'Book-Buys,' she sniffed. 'That's right.'

'I'll be there in ten minutes.'

'And doc? Thank you…'

He replaced the receiver. Took a moment to collect his thoughts. He knew Manny would have wanted him to call him. He'd call it 'keeping him in the loop.' But Shaw had no intention in investing his trust with that charlatan again. He pulled on his long, grey mac and picked up his brown leather kit-bag; the staple doctor's uniform. He dressed that way simply to reassure the patient these days, he understood.

'Off out, doc?' asked Betty as he strolled into reception.

'House call,' he confirmed, still marching to the door.

'Erm… Dr. Shaw?' she called after him. 'I thought you said you weren't doing house calls any more. You made me print off that notice for the waiting room… Am I to take it down now? Honestly, how do you expect me to do my job if you don't tell me anything? Who are you going to see, anyway?'

Shaw paused with his hand on the door handle, sighed deeply. 'I think we can put this one down as the exception to the rule. Leave the notice up, will you Betty?'

'Is it Mr. Rennie? He's been awful with his piles.'

'No. It's not Mr. Rennie,' he said.

Betty looked put-out. It was a look she wore on a pretty regular basis when he wouldn't break the client confidentiality clauses just to satisfy her urge for tittle-tattle.

'Well doc,' she muttered. 'Considering it's ten now and you'll surely not be back until after twelve, and this is my half-day, I think I'd better go home… You can't leave me to cope with everything. You can't expect me to wait behind for you either. You know it's Sewing Circle on Mondays…'

Dr. Shaw had to force himself to remember that he didn't care any more. 'Okay Betty. Get your things and I'll lock up,' he said. 'But hurry please. This *is* an emergency.'

She made a big show of huffing and puffing as she collected the miscellaneous items to take home with her; most of them were items that she'd somehow slipped onto the clinic's order sheet without him knowing. The new issue of *Sixty and Sexy* magazine. The biscuits too. And the carefully-wrapped last slice of Mrs. Popplewell's cherry Bakewell. All of it went into Betty's cavernous, gaping maw of a handbag. *Let her take it*, he thought. *What does it matter in the great scheme of things?*

'I don't like being rushed, doc,' she said as she joined him, red-faced, at the front door. 'Not at my age.'

'Don't be ridiculous,' he smiled. 'You've got *years* in you yet.' Under his breath, he added the words *you busy-body old crow*.

She took the compliment with no grace. Instead, she looked eagerly at his sleek, black Mondeo, perhaps hoping that he'd offer her a lift.

'Bye then,' he said.

'Looks like rain,' she said, hinting. But she didn't need to hint. The clouds' bellies were now so low they were virtually perching on the roofs of the town, just waiting to be smashed like piñata.

He pretended to sniff up, like he was the type of person who went around claiming he could *smell* rain. 'You've got an hour or so yet,' he concluded.

She stuck out her bottom lip. 'See you Wednesday, doc,' she said, sulkily.

Shaw nodded. He locked up and watched her tottering away down the street on her silly high-heels – her one nod to fashion – and realised that he'd maybe never see her again. By Wednesday the darkness he saw in his visions may have spread too far.

He climbed into the car and chucked the bag onto the passenger seat, just in case Betty came running after him and dived through the closed window, demanding that lift. The only reason he was driving the short distance between the Bungalow and the main street was because he knew that there was rope handy in the boot. And he wanted it handy. He had no idea what the situation would be round at Book-Buys. No idea how long it might take to diagnose the problem. But what he did know was that if it was what he thought it was, he was going straight home afterwards. He wanted to make both of them safe before The Darkness reached high tide.

Traffic was scarce. No outsiders seemed to visit Limm any more. Once upon a time, tourists were here all times of year, and if it wasn't tourists it'd be locals going about their day. There were businesses to run, schools to get to. He hadn't even heard the usual clatter of a mead delivery truck as it passed through the too-narrow streets by the Bungalow on the way back, or to, the factory. He hadn't heard the chug of Trevor Knox's National Trust landie, usually a Limm town staple. *Something* about the today had put them off. It felt faintly post-apocalyptic. Like the storm they'd all been waiting for so long was already here and everyone had stocked up on tinned foods and bottled water, boarded up the windows, locked the doors, and prepared to wait it out. As he passed the Ship, he noticed even that was closed. The curtains were drawn and there was no candle burning in the top window to suggest one of his customary three-day lock-ins was in progress. If this was any normal Monday, people would have taken to the streets in protest. As it was, he picked out a parking space easily and was soon walking swiftly across the village green in the direction of Buckby's Book-Buys.

And as though it was fated, as soon as he un-clunked, un-clicked and climbed out of the car, the storm which had been brewing for days now started in earnest. He felt it on his shoulders first, like cold fingers caressing him. Rain drenched his face and left his hair desperately matted to his scalp. He made a run for it, splashing through puddles which were already pooling on the pavement, leaping over drains which were already gushing. The main street had already become a river.

By the time he reached Buckby's, he was drowned like a rat, like one of the unsaved. Janice Dowsing was standing in the shop doorway, holding it open for him with her back, arms hugged tight around her body as though to ward off unseen blows. He tried to step past her in as gentlemanly way as possible. Made it under cover and then stood there dripping, steaming, as she closed the door behind him and, strangely, he thought, bolted it shut. She turned to face him and even through rain-clouded eyes, he noticed how pale she looked. How washed-out she'd become despite the fact she'd not even set foot out into the rain. Her once-fine hair now hung lifelessly from her head, resembling so many of the cotton strings that he always seemed to find about his person.

'Mrs. Dowsing,' he said, gently touching her shoulder, aware that his hand was wet, but sensing she needed to feel his touch as proof of life. It was like that sometimes with Flick. And, just like Flick, she recoiled from his touch, as though it carried an electric charge. She dropped a balled-up tissue onto the floor, where it quickly became soaked with the water which had run off his coat.

'Dr. Shaw,' she said finally. 'You're here.' She said it as though she'd had doubts that it was actually him.

'I'm here,' he said, using that same reassuring voice he used with Flick.

'I'll take you up to see him straight away.'

Devon Buckby came out from the store-room. Looked with distaste at the fact there was a balled-up tissue littering his floor, that the doctor was simply standing there dripping onto it. He looked as though he wanted to complain, but eventually he lowered his eyes, picked out a copy of *The Tide Piper* from one of the shelves. Then he shuffled behind his counter and spread the paper carefully across the surface and pretended to be uncommonly interested in one of the articles. Apart from the *click-clack* of Janice's heels as she walked away to the back stairs, the shop was silent as a ghost ship. Shaw followed, aware of the noise his own shoes made as he crossed the floor. Squeaking like deserting rats.

'So, the symptoms only came on yesterday?'

'On his paper-round, it looks like,' confirmed Janice as she paused to open the plywood door. She led him through to a dimly lit stair-case stuffed full of children's coats, odd bits from a bike, and empty boxes of crisps. She seemed vaguely embarrassed as she prompted him to step over the mess and up the stairs; as though she'd once been a house-proud woman and had only now realised how bad she'd allowed things to become.

'He's sort-of sleeping now,' she whispered as they reached the top of the stairs. 'I've got his sister Grace keeping an eye on him while I was downstairs waiting for you…The swellings are getting worse… Before, when I was watching him, I could literally see them springing up on his chest and on his thighs.'

Must have been horrible. So horrible she didn't seem to even want to go in to her son's room. So horrible she remained out here, lingering by the closed door on the landing. It was as though she didn't want to let the doctor in now; didn't want to have her worst fears confirmed. Through the door, Shaw could hear the soft whisperings of a young girl; must have been Grace. She was whispering so frantically fast that it reminded him of how Janice had sounded on the phone earlier. Maybe she was trying to talk to her brother; tell him that everything would be all right.

'I think I'd better take a look at him then,' he said, as calmly as he could.

Janice half-smiled, half-grimaced as she opened the door. A waft of *bad air* emerged. It smelled like there was an old drunk in there, rotting away in his own bodily juices.

Shaw stepped into the cramped bedroom. Took in the posters on the walls; images of mountain bikes jumping off cliffs, extreme sports and the like. He hadn't had young Lewis marked-down as the sporty-type, not with his mild asthma and hay-fever. The lamp on the bedside table provided the only light in the room and as it had a blood-red shade, the whole room seemed *angry* somehow. Lewis was tucked up in the narrow bed; covers pulled up under his chin and appeared to be asleep. On a plastic fold-away chair next to the bed sat the young girl that he'd heard talking, Grace. And he now saw that she wasn't talking to her brother at all. Rather, she was engaged in an animated conversation with the battered teddy bear which she held tightly on her knee. She looked up at them as they entered the room.

'Is this the doctor, mummy?' she asked. 'Bear wants to know when we can go out and play. He doesn't like being in here with Lew after the monster got him.'

Janice looked more embarrassed now. 'She thinks that there's a monster in that Old Mason house,' she said.

And Shaw was uncomfortably reminded of that particular detail from his vision. The house. The big black cat, the beast, emerging from nowhere. Its claws.

'Dr. Shaw?'

Quickly, he reasserted his professional persona. The shock had got the better of him for moment, but he'd long grown used to covering up for his visions. Knew how he should react around normal people, especially people as worried as this. 'Ah, there's no such thing as monsters. Don't worry about that. I've come here to look at your brother because he seems to be ill... Maybe you should wait downstairs, Grace? With Mr. Buckby?'

'That would be a good idea,' said Janice. 'Grace go down and...'

'We don't like daddy, do we bear?' whined Grace. 'He tells us off for eating the Space Wrestlers.'

'Now, Grace,' snapped Janice.

Grace didn't move. 'Why is the doctor all wet? Has he been swimming? Mummy says we ain't allowed to go swimming until at least an hour after brekky, isn't that right Bear?' She made Bear nod.

'*Grace!*'

261

'That's all right,' said Shaw. He was embarrassed, always seemed to be embarrassed in front of kids. As though they could see right through him. 'Grace can stay if she wants.' Then, kneeling down close to Grace's chair, he said, 'It's raining outside, that's why I'm wet, I haven't been swimming. I suppose you could say I'm the real-life version of Doctor Foster.'

Grace looked at him blankly.

'*Grace!*' repeated her mother.

Finally Grace got up. She flounced out of the room with all the trapped-anger of a teenager. They heard her clattering down the wooden stairs and slamming the plywood dividing door behind her.

'Right,' said Shaw, clapping his hands together with rather more enthusiasm than he actually felt. 'Let's take a look at him, shall we?'

He moved over to the edge of the bed. Heard Lewis's sharp intake of air. *So he was awake...*

'Lewis,' he said, 'I'm going to pull the duvet cover off you so I can take a proper look at you.'

'No,' snapped Lewis, his voice strained, bestial.

'Now Lew, do as the doctor asks,' said Janice, softly, sounding close to tears again.

'No,' he called again. Louder this time. More desperate; he didn't want *anyone* to see what had happened to him. It was a voice full of pain and fear; a voice that should never be heard coming from the mouth of a young boy.

Shaw stepped back from the bed. Janice slipped in and started trying to tug the duvet away from her boy's body. But he gripped it hard, with all the ferocity of a cornered animal. The doctor helped after a while, joining in the horrible tug of war as though it was his solemn duty. Finally, Lewis let go with a mighty sob. His thin, lanky body was revealed. And Shaw knew immediately that things had probably already gone too far for the lad. His whole torso was covered in black spots, like lesions. Angry red marks scarred his arms and legs. Everywhere were those awful, egg-shaped swellings that Janice had mentioned on the phone.

'It's okay, Lew,' soothed Janice. But it probably wasn't.

'Lewis, I'm going to touch your face now,' said Shaw. 'Get a measure of your temperature.'

Lewis didn't react. He'd given up, it seemed, now that the terrible truth had been revealed. He didn't wriggle away from the doctor as he placed a hand on the boy's forehead.

262

'He's incredibly hot,' he said to Janice. So hot he had to pull his hand away. *Dangerously hot.*

'Should I call an ambulance?' asked Janice.

'Not yet,' said Shaw. 'Just let me…'

Lewis wailed incoherently, started thrashing about on the bed-sheets. One of the egg-sized lumps on his thigh ruptured, spilling foul-smelling yellow pus all over his leg and the once white sheets.

Shaw tugged his bag closer, opened it, pulled out a big needle. When Janice saw it, she let out a wail of her own. 'I'm just going to give him a little something to calm him down while I examine him further. Something which'll bring his temperature down too.'

Janice chewed her lip. 'What can I do?' she pleaded.

He needed her out of the room. So he could think. He closed the bag, hid the needle. 'I need some towels, a bowl of hot water,' he said, hoping it would buy him some time.

She nodded, looked as though she was going to get him what he'd asked for, but she paused, her trembling hand on the door. 'What's wrong with him?' she said. 'Please tell me what's wrong with him.'

'I don't know what's wrong with him,' said Shaw, which was the truth. 'I've never seen anything like it before. But I'll find out.' Which might not have been.

Janice left the room, quietly closed the door behind her. And Dr. Shaw thought about what he'd just said. He *had* seen symptoms like this, but only a long time ago, at college in the medical textbooks.

It can't be that! There's no way… Not in this day and age. Not in England.

Quickly, Shaw snapped open his brown leather kit bag again, pulled out a mask with which to cover his nose and mouth. Because diseases like the one Lewis had apparently contracted were air-borne. At least that was what all the research said, all the medical history from centuries back. Shaw shivered, and it wasn't necessarily because his wet shirt was cold-compressing his back.

27: King of the Castle

For the first time in a long time Rich Dailly had enjoyed the breakfast shift at the Castle. For the first time in a long time, salty, cloying smell of bacon which seemed to cling to him after he'd finished the cooking, didn't turn his stomach. For the first time in a long time he'd made like a regular Happy and he'd whistled while he'd worked. He'd made the kitchen porter, a Pole, laugh when he cracked that tired old joke – *give us this day our Dailly bread* – when he pulled the fresh batch of rolls from the oven. He'd pinched one of the waitresses arses, little caring whether she told Kirst. He'd whacked the radio on full and let Oasis blast out like he was back in his cooking heyday and anything was possible.

As he cracked the last egg of the day into the frying pan, he chanced a shell toss and for the first time in a long time, he managed to dispatch the egg right into the big food-waste bin like it was a basketball three-pointer. And as he spooned hot oil over the yolk, he allowed himself to drink it in, this new-old feeling, this freedom. He took a moment to remember just how much he loved the hotel and his role within it. Actually, forget his role within it. On a day such as this, he could truly pretend he was the lord of the manor. If he so chose he could have slept in any of the eight en-suite master bedrooms within it. He could have breakfasted in the courtyard out front, taken lunch in the private dining room and he could have suppered in the grounds overlooking the bay. All he had to do was clap his hands together and people would rush to clean up after him; all he had to do was point to his throat and the Czech bar man knew he quite fancied a pint of the old Fairhurst's or even a drop of mead. All he'd have to do is cough, and one of the Poles – no, make that *both* of the Poles – would be on hand, ready to bring him a clean frying pan, no matter that he hadn't finished with the old one. On a day like this, with Adrian Devonish AWOL (and for two mornings now), he was master of all he surveyed.

264

So much so that when the decrepit old tape player chewed up his favourite Oasis album, he took it with good grace. He simply wiped his hands down on his white chef's jacket and then ordered one of the Poles to stick the radio on. '*Ray-dee-oh,*' he said, just in case they hadn't understood. The Pole jumped to it, twisting the radio's knob through some of channels, turning, facing Rich every time she located one with this hopeful and yet expectant look on her fizzog. She discovered Girls Aloud.

'Twist,' yelled Rich. 'We're not having that shite in here.'

She discovered classical music next; the violins sounding to Rich like nails on a blackboard.

'Twist please Mrs. Croupier,' he shouted.

The Pole seemed confused, but finally got the message when he did the actions. She flicked past two or three stations which appeared to be entirely devoted to the music of Michael Jackson.

'Twist,' he bellowed, lifting the egg out of the pan with a spatula and depositing it on a plate which was already piled high, waiting for its coup de grace under the service lights. The plate was quickly taken away and that was it, breakfast service over. *Done,* as Ramsey would have said. Now it was the time for clean-up, and Rich had never minded mucking in with the clean-up (after all, it was what all good chefs, *like* Ramsey did, to foster the old team spirit) but still he needed something to listen to.

He plunged the greasy frying pan into the sink with a hiss. Then started cleaning the cooker, running a cloth round the still-red-hot hobs. His asbestos-hands had long grown used to the burns.

'Come on,' he yelled. 'Find *something* we can listen to, eh?'

And the Polish kitchen porter twisted again, and this time found a local radio phone-in and Rich decided to stick. He decided to stick because almost as soon as he started to listen, he recognised the voice of a loon-caller. He could tell by the caller's frantic, high-pitched voice. Radio Coast appeared to have more than its fair share of these idiots; people who'd get so apoplectic about their bins not being taken away that they'd gone all Michael-Douglas-in-*Falling-Down* crazy; people who'd take such offence at what some far-off celebrity was doing to another, they'd be damn near suicidal. Rich cleared down the surfaces and prepared to be amused.

'But you're not listening to me,' screamed the caller. 'I'm saying is it looked like a bloody...'

265

'I am listening, caller,' sighed the host. 'But we'll have to cut you off if we hear any more of that type of language from you. This is a family show, okay?'

'Um... sorry,' mumbled the caller. Rich paused, gripped the bottle of multi-surface cleaner too tightly and sprayed a load of its yolk-orange gunk all over the already-clean cooker. *Come on man; get mad,* he urged. It was funny when people went off the deep end. People did it more and more these days; aping Americans perhaps.

'That's okay. I can understand your being angry about what happened. I mean, by all accounts it was shocking. And I'd be mad too if *my* daughter had been up there on stage dancing when something like that happened, but here at Radio Coast, I'm not supposed to have an opinion...'

Well done host. Reel him in, thought Rich, handing the Pole a sweeping brush, indicating that she should get on with doing the floor now she'd found a decent backing-track.

'They won't even tell us why they had to cancel the show. All we know is that poor feller wandered in all covered in blood, and Jesus Christ, all they've said was it was an industrial accident...'

'Language!' interrupted the host. 'Hold on a minute, I'm hearing from the powers that be here at Radio Coast Towers that Christ is okay. Christ is officially okay... Carry on...'

Rich chuckled, scrubbed at a snail-trail of egg-yolk on the stainless steel surface. He knew what the call was about. Had been told about the fiasco at the talent show. Knew that the hapless parents of the hapless kids involved would want to be able to blame *somebody* for the fact their kids had been denied their one and only chance to be superstars, little knowing that the one thing which would actually make them superstars was unadulterated hard work.

'My daughter was in tears all night last night,' seethed the caller. 'We've had to keep her off school today because she's so shaken-up by it. And when she asks us why, there's simply nothing we can tell her. But there are rumours.'

'What rumours?' asked the host, sounding interested at last.

'About there being something loose on the island, something bad. There was talk in the Ship last night. And then that farmer got up on stage at the end and announced something was killing his livestock. And when that man crawled into the crowd he looked as though he'd been mauled.'

'You're not the first caller to tell me that,' said the host. 'Not by a long chalk. Just what *is* going on on Limm? I mean...'

266

The caller leaped in. 'I think it's a cover up. Just like with all that Millennium stuff. I know some parents are keeping their children off school today just in case. Until we know the full story. But we won't get the full story, not with a mayor like ours. I'd like to get hold of that mayor, that Combs and I'd like to give him a piece of my flaming mind. I think I'd like to do more than that...'

Rich gasped. The host gasped.

'Manny Combs is responsible. Make no bones about it. And he's covering it up. Has to be. Look at all the businesses he owns. All the property. And if there is something loose on the island, he'd stand to lose them all. And another thing...'

'Caller? I'm afraid we can't allow that kind of libellous statement on our show...'

'He's on the take. He must be. He's like them London MP's. He's only got his own interests at heart.'

'Coast Radio would just like to point out to our listeners at this point that not all Members of Parliament were involved in...'

'Oh you're just toting your typical liberal views,' blared the caller. 'You're afraid that in condemning Combs, you might lose your audience or your job. Just admit it, you know that I'm right.'

A radio jingle cut in. *Radio Ga-ga on Radio Coast; where talk is not as cheap as most. This is the Got Your Goat hour with your host, Clark 'Mad as a box of frogs' Sheldon.*

'I'm afraid that we've had to cut our caller off,' said Sheldon, wearily. 'As the whole of the audience knows, we're all about opinions, but when people start getting too hot under the collar like our Loony from Limm there, we have to take them off the air. So we'll ask for a new subject from our next caller... Mrs. Maguire from Limm... What is it with you Limm people, eh? Something really has got your goat today... Good morning, Mrs. Maguire; and what would you like to talk about today?'

Mrs. Maguire answered, in a screeching harridan voice. 'Is that me? Am I on?'

'You're speaking to the whole of the north east coast region, Mrs. Maguire... So, what's *really got your goat?'*

'Am I on air?'

'Yes Mrs. Mag...'

'Gerry... Gerry... turn the radio on. I'm on the radio... Sorry about that. I'm just telling my lad to listen to me in back kitchen. He's trying to get the tape player sorted to record me...'

'You're not supposed to be recording the show,' sighed Sheldon, but then he decided he didn't care enough to argue his point. 'But enough of that; you called the show. Tell me Mrs. Maguire, what's *really got your goat?*'

'What I want to talk about is that soap, *Beachcombers...*'

'You mean that Australian thing?'

'That's the one,' said Mrs. Maguire slowly. 'The very same. What I want to ask is what's happened to the lad on it? You know the one; Duncan. With the floppy hair. He was ever so nice but he went missing. Where is he, Mr. Sheldon?'

Clark 'Mad as a box of frogs' Sheldon was speechless for perhaps the first time in his life.

'Mr. Sheldon?'

'You're seriously asking me where a *made-up character* in a daytime soap opera which is filmed over the other side of the world has disappeared to? Oh hold on a minute, Mrs. Maguire; he's here, under my desk with that missing kangaroo and the koala bear who makes the tea. He's told me to tell you that he's pig-sick – pig-sick I tell you – that he can't be on the show any more, but he's decided to come over here and work in a bar like every other Australian under the age of twenty. That answer your question?'

The only answer was the long monotone buzz of a dead phone. Sheldon sighed and whacked on the jingle yet again. Rich clicked the radio off. Made to leave the room. The Polish kitchen porter stood in his way. When he threatened to step round her, she moved the brush so he couldn't.

'What is it Agn... Ang...' He always struggled with her name. Perhaps it was because she was aggressively tall, and her height almost made him ill at ease. Certainly she towered over him so that he always found himself at eye-level with her small breasts.

'*Anastazja,*' she said. 'What about Mr. Devonish? Maybe he is missing like the Duncan on the *ray-dee-oh.* Is not like him. He always here, watching...'

'Sticking his beak in.'

'Beak. Yes, his beak. But where is he now, Mr. Rich...'

'*Dailly,*' he corrected, 'Mr. Dailly.'

'Should we not look for him? Check his room? Call police? The *ray-dee-oh* say there is something bad on the island. What if something bad has got him?'

Some hope. He shook his head, tried to step past her, desperate not to let anything spoil his mood.

She stepped in front of him. '*Please,* Mr. Day… Dailly?'

He sighed. 'Okay. We'll go check his room. But after I've had brekky. You understand? *After.* You mop the floor, wash up the rest of the pots, and then come find me.'

She nodded slowly.

He walked out of the kitchens, betting his bottom dollar it wasn't in Gordon Ramsey's job description to go off forming impromptu search parties on the hunt for notoriously drunken hotel managers. Went off to get his breakfast. It was safe now, the few guests the hotel had had now vacated the breakfast room. The fat Elvises had left the building.

He settled down with a coffee and some toast. It was due to bitter experience that Rich always placed himself at least two breakfast tables away from the double-doors which led through to reception and the stairs. Every day without fail, at least one of the guests would let rip with a gut-wrenching tear-jerker of a meat-fart which would congeal in the air right by the doors like black pudding, lingering at least as long as it took him to start preparing some new smells for lunch. It was as though the guests had too much reserve to simply drop their bombs at their breakfast tables, but as soon as they reached the no-man's land of the double doors, they just couldn't resist. And besides, once their unholy smell started to curl up the ends of the breakfast room's tired wallpaper, the guest would already have vacated the scene; gone back to their room or darted out through reception and escaped into the Limm Island streets.

In a way, these arse-led mustard gas attacks were understandable. Most people, in these hundred-mile-a-minute, health-obsessed times, didn't have time to eat a cooked breakfast every day. But when they came away on a weekend break and their defences were down, nine out of ten would plump for one of his Full Englishes. And their bodies simply couldn't cope with the sheer amount of meat at that time in the morning. The boa constrictor sausages squeezed at their guts, the flapping surrender flags of bacon fluttered in their stomachs, and what the black pudding did to them, nobody even cared to think about.

And the meat-farts by the double-doors were getting worse. The more awards which eluded the kitchen, the more food Adrian Devonish ordered Rich to heap on their breakfast plates. He'd doubled, then trebled the sausage count, included scrambled *and* fried egg, and even at one point, went to the dramatic length of including steak. Quantity not quality ruled the day, which was probably the reason why the Seahorse down the road had so easily carried off the last couple of North East Breakfast of the Year trophies, and why the Castle's residents were leaving trophies of their own by the double-doors. Sometimes, the chorus of bubbling, broiling bellies in the breakfast room got so loud, it started to drown out the sounds of the interminable Lighthouse Family, whose CD they *always* played because Devonish ordered it. Rich didn't mind about losing out on the awards, but having to take orders from Adrian Bloody Devonish was what *really got his goat.*

Even though Devonish was AWOL, there was still something of him in the breakfast room. Two framed prints above the fireplace which contained newspaper reports from Adrian's fabled glory days. Both were now becoming rapidly faded now and Rich knew for a fact that Adrian had called up *The Tide Piper* direct a while back, asking for fresh copies, but Yoghurt Rhodes had told him they didn't store back copies from 'so many years ago.' And besides, those prints had been the work of his predecessor, Mikey Turner, and everyone knew what had happened to him.

Rich glared at the prints. The first of the cuttings trumpeted the headline 'King of the Castle'. Rich also knew for a fact that Devonish loved that headline; that he thought Mike Ford had really earned his corn with that one. Underneath the headline was an image of the younger Adrian, looking every inch a Limm Henry VIII outside the Castle's front doors. The sheer barefaced confidence in his face was astounding. The fact he really believed himself a King obvious to all. He was posed like the King of the Hotels, the Limm VIP, like 'The man who *invented* the tourist trade on the island' as the second headline read.

'Where are you now, Devonish? King is dead long live the King, is that it?' breathed Rich, and then almost choked as the stink of musty farts started to clog at the back of his throat. After collecting himself, he wondered how he'd like it being the new King if, as he suspected, Adrian really had *done one* before Manny Combs worked out the full extent of their losses. One thing Adrian was good for was handling the guests, keeping them out of Rich's way. On the occasions Rich had been confronted by guests, he'd always ended up wanting to punch them in their pampered faces. They'd come up to him, full of their stories of what they were going to do with their days as though they were doing him a real favour by telling him. And from it, he'd learned that there were a finite number of times he could hear some cagoule-clad idiot say, 'oh, we're going

270

to bip on up to the monastery today' (*bip on up;* what the bip did that mean?) or, 'Johnny and I are going to attempt the clifftop walk this afternoon, but we shan't be looking down shan't we not, Johnnykins?' ('No dearest,' cringed Johnnykins, 'but I might fucking push you off. Dear.') Or, 'the whole family have been looking forward to sampling the sea air over at Norsea,' before his still wearisome, still-throbbing-from-last-night's booze head exploded all over the panoramic window.

Worse were the guests he bumped into in the bar who talked-up their lives 'back home'; the ones who seemed hell-bent on talking down to him as though 'hotel chef' was somehow not a patch on 'IT Coordinator' or 'Drag Queen'. And worse still were the ones who brought their snivelling kids along with them and expected him to smile indulgently as the brats crayoned on the white tabletops, attempted to put great cracks in the panoramic window as they smashed their heads into it like caged animals, or, in one terrible case, when one little fucker tied his shoelaces together.

At least all the guests had now all finished up their breakfasts and left; even the new couple who'd turned up late expecting to be fed, despite the fact Rich had long since switched off the ovens and started the clean up. After a long think, and a spit in the pan before he applied that final cracked egg, he'd decided to serve them. If Adrian had asked him to do it, he'd have refused, said something like 'it would contravene my human rights to get that cooker on again; a man has to have a break, you know.'

And a man did have to break, and with Adrian away, this was the best damned break he could remember. He luxuriated into his chair while the 'serving wenches' (a Devonish phrase) clucked around him, collecting the remaining plates and cups for the Polish kitchen porter to wash up. He supposed he was nominally supervising, occasionally pointing the wenches to a table he believed deserved attention, or advising them on the best way of carrying plates. The wenches complained when Adrian did that. 'Don't teach us to suck eggs,' he remembered one old-stager (Muriel) saying to him. But for him they were good as gold.

Nominally Rich was supervising, but in actuality, he was only giving the waiting staff the beans/ tomato portion of his concentration, preferring to spend the sausage and bacon of his time on scouring the local papers for write-ups of the talent show, or to see whether there was anything about the animal which was supposedly on the loose. But the early edition of *The Tide Piper* said

271

nothing about either, which was strange. In fact, most of the paper seemed to be made up of re-hashed articles from the past few weeks instead of anything new. They'd re-issued an article on Carl-Rhys Hamilton, one of Rich's sometime drinking buddies, in which he 'told all' about his desire to be a top comedian (they'd tormented him mercilessly down the Ship and refused to laugh at any of his joke for days.) Underneath the newspaper was a pile of countryside house and home magazines which had been delivered that morning. Adrian Devonish had been becoming more and more obsessed with hotel reviews. Never used to be. Never needed to be. Once upon a time, the Castle had been the only hotel/ guest house establishment on the whole of Limm Island. Once the tide washed in every day, it was *always* left with a new batch of tourists who'd missed their window to get over the road and back to the mainland until the next day and needed somewhere to stay. Now Rich knew that at least twenty of the Castle's rooms were unfilled. Absently he wondered whether he'd want to take the step up into Devonish's place if the chancer never came back, and, if he did, what he could possibly do to get the numbers looking a bit better.

As he was thinking, he took a slurp from his coffee, realising realised it was bone cold. All of the serving wenches had now absconded. Into the kitchen where they were supposed to be helping the Polish girl washing-up, but doubtless they would be engaged in their usual rigorous bout of smoking out the back instead. He played a little game with himself. Played Devonish for a Day. Clapped his hands together loudly and called 'Service!' in a trilling voice, but there was absolutely no response. He counted six... seven big waves creeping into the bay through the panoramic window before there was even the least sign of movement from the kitchens. They were probably locking themselves in the walk-in fridge just so they could avoid any real work.

'Service!' he called again. He'd go hoarse at this rate, but there was *no way* he was going to allow the waitresses the satisfaction of marching on into the kitchens himself. That would put him well and truly out of his good mood. Outside, in the bay, another few more waves crashed in. Rich couldn't tell whether the sea was going in or out. What he *could* tell was that the waves were noticeably rougher than they had been for the past few days. For the past few days, frogspawny seaweed had been malingering around the jetty but now it was getting stirred-up good and proper, tossed about all over the place. What's more, now he was looking, really looking, he noted that the *sky* looked rough too. It looked as though it was going to rain at any moment, and not just rain, but suicidally-leap down at the island. Which was not a good thing. Because if it did rain like that then the caravan was liable to leak, and the caravan was just about the only place Kirst would allow him to get his oats. Least until he got his divorce.

'Service!' he called, and finally he heard someone step on the creaky step between kitchen and breakfast room. He swung his head round to see the girl in question, Kirstie Shay, the rose amongst the thorny, bushy serving wenches. Kirstie always seemed to pull the short straw and did more work than the rest of them put together, Rich knew. Perhaps that was why she was universally known as 'Kirst'. She was cursed with her youthful good looks. Cursed, at least Rich thought, with a destiny beyond the island, where maybe he could follow, once the divorce came through, *if* the riches of a promotion here weren't possible. She wasn't model class, no matter how much time she spent practicing her sulky pout in front of the mirror, or her hoity-toity runway-style walk along the main street between the Holiday Park and the shabby little house in which she lived with her old dad, but she was a looker enough to perhaps work in 'promotions' or 'hostessing' or carrying the boards round the ring before each round in the boxing down in Newcastle. So cursed was Kirst that the other wenches had instantly shunned her, as though her beauty was an insult to them. She was cursed, and that meant she needed rescuing, and that's exactly what he'd done, jumping in there before Devonish even got a chance to butter her up.

Bloody Devonish. He couldn't seem to get away from thinking about him. Still, at least the beardy chancer had done well with the new uniform. Kirst looked damn hot in that new, shorter skirt and the low neck-line of the white blouse. Adrian, he had to admit, had done good, even if the drawback of the uniform was that everyone also had to look at good old Muriel's legs. And man, Muriel's legs were truly a thing to behold; pasty white below the knees, but bright, sparkling around the thighs. It was as though she spent her breaks practicing to become a majorette, constantly slapping herself as majorettes do, in between tossing big sticks off.

'Yes, Richard?' asked Kirst, playing it cool even though there was nobody about. Even though she could have broken the intra-employee relationships law and come sat on his knee, she kept her distance. Still, she blushed when she spoke, wouldn't meet his eyes, and he liked that. He liked it that she seemed... unaware of her

273

Beauty Curse. He reached up and tucked an unruly strand of her luscious coal black hair behind her ear. She flinched away from his hand, immediately looked over her shoulder.

'What's the matter, love?' he said. 'There's nobody about. Why don't you come give me a kiss?'

She hung her head. 'I... I don't...'

'Are you free to come up the caravan his afto?'

She blushed several shades darker.

'The weather? It'll be all right. You'll be wet enough anyway when I've finished with you.'

She fixed him with fiery eyes for a second, but then lowered her gaze. Outside it had started to rain and it was as though it was warring against the sea. Stray arrows, cannonballs of rain smashed into the roof of the breakfast room. It could have been a percussion backing track to their stilted conversation.

'What's the...' Suddenly, a thought struck him. 'Say, seeing as though the Bearded Wonder's away, we could use one of the rooms here.'

'No,' she snapped. 'No *way.*'

'Nobody would need to know, Kirst.'

She sighed, 'What would you like?'

He played along. 'A nice bit of slap and tickle followed by a side order of how's your father.'

'*I meant...*' She lowered her voice. 'I meant to drink. You called service like Devonish does.'

'Don't be like that,' he said. 'Can't we have a bit of fun?'

She looked out of the window, into the rain. There was a wistful look on her face.

'Come on duck,' he said, 'I'm *busting* here.' He gestured down to *The Tide Piper* which was now sitting on his lap, covering a real morning glory of an erection. 'It's been weeks since we...'

'Had sex? I can't have sex with you today,' she hissed.

He shook his head. Eased back in his seat, moved the newspaper away, edged his crotch forward so she could see the decent sized lump in his tight Portfolio chequered chef's trousers. *Here, love, take a look at my Portfolio. I'll stock and share you up any day...* 'On the blob is it? Or are you playing hard to get? You forget, Kirst, I've already *got* you.'

She made a little noise in her throat. Might have been a sob; maybe she was on the blob.

274

'Aw, come on my lovely! Cheer up, it might never happen.' He flashed her his *winning smile.*

'Oh God,' she moaned. 'It already *has.*'

He blew out his cheeks. Did this mean what he thought it meant, that she'd fallen for him? That this was now about more than a nice bit of slap and tickle followed by a side order of how's your father? If so, then he wasn't sure it was a good thing. For a start, the divorce proceedings were nowhere near the stage he'd told Kirst they were at. No, they were only at 'trial separation' stage at the moment; there'd been no talk of making it official. He frowned stared out at the veritable storm which had already developed out there. Wind had picked up now and it was whipping up the sea.

He bit the bullet, method-acted the caring, sharing *boyf,* like in the crappy rom-coms she insisted on bringing round the caravan whenever she stopped the night. 'Is there something wrong, love?'

She looked as though she was going to say something, something serious (like *I love you*) but she didn't. In the end, she simply said, 'I'm okay, Chef Dailly. Just a little tired. I was...'

'Out painting the town red over the weekend while I was working,' interrupted Rich. 'Is that it? I thought you'd have at least popped in to say hello... Did you go to that talent show thing?'

He watched her fiddle with the string of her apron, she looked as though she wanted to say that important thing again. But the words wouldn't come. 'I just couldn't sleep was all,' she said, finally, staring off through the panoramic window at the storm, as though she was mesmerized by it.

'Do you know,' he said, 'I saw Carl-Rhys at the weekend. He told me he'd seen you in Newcastle. In a bloody chemist's of all places. I told him he had to have been even drunker than usual.'

He saw how Kirst's face now blazed red before she twisted it away from him.

'*Were* you in Newcastle?'

She hung her head in shame. 'I... I...'

'Well thanks for fucking telling me. I could have driven us there in the Gunner, we could have had a night out, seen the sights... But if you want to go without me, that's fine and fucking dandy.'

She stood, slowly shaking her head. 'It's not like that.'

'It bloody is,' he said. 'Now, don't just stand there stuttering. Get me a fresh coffee.'

Kirst bowed to him. She actually bowed. Then she sort of curtseyed too, went the whole kit and caboodle, and started to walk away, back to the kitchens, head lowered in due deference.

'And a roll too, and some bacon if there's some left!'

He tried to return to his flicking through the various magazines, to his good mood, but was too distracted. He'd been sure Carl-Rhys had been mistaken about his sighting of Kirst in Newcastle. Sure of it. He'd thought it a poorly-planned comeback on Carl-Rhys's part for all the stick he'd given him for the article in *The Tide Piper*. But now. What the hell had she been doing there? And not just in Top Shop or whatever but in a chemist's…

He heard movement from over by the kitchen door again and looked up expectantly. Thinking it would be Kirst back to explain. But it wasn't Kirst. It was the bloody Polish kitchen porter.

'We go to Mr. Devonish room now?' she asked.

'No. Not yet. Go back in the kitchen,' he said, impatiently.

The tall girl paused and then manifestly ignored him, carried on walking into the room. Walking with a purpose, as though she was late for a boat taxi.

'Later!' he repeated.

The tall girl carried on walking. Striding. Eating up the ground between them and then towering above the table. Her long legs were *built* for this, for ignoring his express instructions.

He shifted back in his chair. 'I'm sure Devonish will turn up. I don't think there's any need search and…You should be on a break now, Ag… An… *Duck*. We can do this any time.'

She reached the table. 'We go now.' She tapped her foot on the floor. 'I have already check the car park and his car is missing.'

Rich smiled. 'So that's good, isn't it? He won't be here. He's away in his car.'

'But I have check the roster book and he was scheduled to work today.'

'It's an emergency then. He's been called away. A family member is sick and…'

'He has no family. And I took liberty of calling his mobile. The line is dead.' She *mimed* dead, pulling an imaginary rope taut on her long neck.

'Well then, he was called away urgently and he's run out of juice.'

'Mr. Devonish never lets his mobile run out. We must check his room. Natasza has given me key.'

Natasza was Anastazja's equally tall sister. One of the chamber-maids. She too unnerved Rich. Probably it was all that whispering they did when they got together to smoke their Polish cigarettes.

When he didn't move, Anastazja jangled the room key in his face. He thought the room's fob, a big wooden thing with a rendering of the Limm monastery cut into it, would have made a good murder weapon. It was certainly chunky enough to do some damage. He didn't want to test the Polish girl's mettle any longer when she had this in her hands. She had an air about her which told him she could club him with the fob and then quite happily go back to washing dishes.

He slapped his palms down on the table, onto the newspaper article about Carl-Rhys Hamilton, and then climbed to his feet. 'Come on then, no time like the present.'

Anastazja led the way up the stairs to Adrian's room. Since time immemorial he'd had the pick of the rooms at the Castle and, unlike the rest of the staff, had stationed himself in the old Georgian manor house part of it rather than the crappy extension, the Arse. He'd picked an en suite too, which was a rarity at the hotel. He waited patiently as the Polish girl unlocked the door. When she did so, a terrible musty smell emerged. Both of them took a step back, took a moment to collect deep breaths. Rich watched the rise of her small breasts under her apron as she sucked in the *Summer Breeze* scented air in the corridor. For once in her life, or, since she'd come to work at the Castle at least, Rich saw that she was perturbed. No, beyond that she was scared. Must have been the smell. She must have immediately thought *body*. And it was ripe enough to be a body too. Perhaps Anastazja had left Poland because of some war or other. Perhaps there the stinking bodies had mounted up. He wasn't exactly sure of the geography, politics or history of Eastern Europe, but he did know there were wars going on there all the time.

Anastazja stood to the side to let him enter first. Her one nod to his masculinity, his professional superiority. He hesitated. Only for a beat, but it was enough for her, he knew, to register that he too had thought the worst. That his mind was now percolating the worst, making it a headier, richer brew. That he was now imagining Devonish's bloated body hanging from the rafters or drowned in the bath or slicked with blood on the Castle's custom made sheets. He forced a hand over his nose and squashed his nostrils together. And then entered the King of the Castle's chamber.

277

It was a big room. Spacious, airy. Cats could have been swung in it, no danger. Even that fabled beast, the one they'd talked about on Radio Coast, the one which was apparently loose on the island, could have been used as a lasso and not troubled the sides. It was the kind of room a feudal master would wake up in, and when he did, he could have pressed his trousers until the cows came home if that was his bag. He could also have signed-up to the adult channels on the huge flat screen TV (which Rich assumed Adrian frequently did), made the most of the tea and coffee facilities (which he knew Adrian *never* did; not when there were Polish serving wenches downstairs who he could pull off important service and kitchen portering duties in order to hand deliver him a filter coffee whenever he wanted one) and dashed open the curtains and enjoyed a prize view across the whole of the Limm harbour, taking in Brennan Head, Pate Hill, the monastery.

It was the most up-to-date of all the rooms. All clean-lines and classic furniture rather than the fuzzy flat-pack crap they stocked in the Arse. As well as the flat screen TV, there was a huge sleigh bed, an executive lounge area containing a chaise longue and a very low coffee table, a well-stocked mini bar, and a plush rug on the floor. The room was generally tidy; certainly not suggestive of a wild animal being loosed in there. The bed was still made, corners still turned down. There were no signs of recent activity; no half-drunk cups of coffee on the table, no dirty plates stacked by the door. The TV remote was still in its slot on the wall, which meant it hadn't been moved since the chambermaid had last been in.

But at least they'd not discovered a body. Now, as he relaxed, Rich realised how tightly-coiled his body had been. It felt like the time when his wife had almost caught him and Kirst up at the caravan. He looked over at Anastazja. Shrugged. Was about to tell her *I told you so,* but then he caught another whiff of the bad smell and he stopped himself.

Anastazja hunkered down and looked under the sleigh bed, so Rich thought he'd better make busy pretending to look in the executive section of the room. For some reason, he found himself fingering the spines of the books on the shelves by the TV. There wasn't much choice; crime-thrillers all the way; Adrian must have *loved* crime-thrillers, he thought, because the reader was guaranteed a bit of racy sex, there was always a bit of slap and tickle followed by a side-order of how's your father which involved the wizened old cop and his younger, boobier pardner. Absently, Rich wondered why

278

he kept thinking of Adrian in the past-tense. He supposed it was desire, on his part.

He moved on, studied the faintly annoying Joan Miro print on the wall as though he was trying to pick out Adrian Devonish in the multi-coloured blobs. He imagined Adrian standing in this exact spot, thinking, *Call that art? Any Tom-Dick could have rushed that off with about six strokes of a brush. And he wouldn't have even had to use a proper painter's brush. A roller would have done. It looks like something produced in the bottom-set art class; the one in which the students had to make pictures by dabbing half-potatoes into the paint...*

Funny how he seemed able to summon Adrian's distinctive voice at will. Funny how, despite the fact the two of them didn't get on any more, he was becoming more and more like the erstwhile King of the Castle.

Anastazja called him, interrupting his reverie. He swung round. She was holding up a manky, grey woollen sock with tweezer-fingers. A couple fat lazy flies buzzed around it. 'I find the source of smell,' she said. Then, she walked over to the window, dragged open the rich red curtains, pulled the latch and tossed he sock out. Done, she wiped her hands down on her apron.

There was only one place left to try. The en suite bathroom. The door was closed, but Rich could see through the narrow gap under the door that the light was on and... And surely the bathroom was the most obvious place. Surely someone, somewhere had done some kind of study and worked out that most suicides took place in bathrooms, perhaps because they were easiest to scrub down afterwards; the suicide's one nod to those who'd have to pick up the pieces after he'd gone. He looked at Anastazja. She nodded. *Go. Check it.* And so, on feet which felt like the half-potatoes with which Joan Miro had painted the picture on the wall, Rich headed directly for the en suite. He mash-potatoed his way into the bathroom and tugged on the light-pull even though the light was already on. Force of habit. He tugged again. Too hard. For a moment he thought it was going to bring half the Castle's roof crashing down through the ceiling onto his Chicken Licken head.

Why the hell was he thinking of Chicken Licken, he wondered? Perhaps it was because the bathroom was so overwhelmingly *chickeny*. Smooth eggshell tiles, yolky soap, omelette facecloths, chickenfeed bath-bombs, feathery towels; a man could *nest* in that bathroom, and he imagined Adrian frequently did.

He imagined Adrian loved nothing more than sitting on the king-sized toilet and whiling away the hours reading his kingly crime-thrillers, even though guests probably wanted seeing-to downstairs.

The spotlights in the bathroom were harsh, unforgiving, like those of a battery farm. They seemed to pivot and turn to follow Rich's movements as he went to the bath, peered over the side, making sure his egg-head was always warm. They also took great delight in showing him the fact that Adrian Devonish was hidden nowhere in the room. He stalked over to the long mirror. Ran the tap hot, scalding hot. He was about to plunge his head under the water-flow when he caught sight of his profile. And he looked... He looked like Adrian Devonish. *Sans* beard of course, but there was definitely a Devonish in there somewhere. The harsh lights picked out the red fissures and cracks in his eyeballs in unnecessarily microscopic detail. He stuck out his tongue; it looked furry and yellow. Must have been on account of the whisky he'd slipped in his coffee that morning. Absently, he found himself reaching for a toothbrush and he'd almost applied some toothpaste before he realised it wasn't his own. He shuddered. Replaced the toothbrush and paste. Picked up another of the condiments which were scattered around the sink. A medicine-style bottle. He read the label, hoping that it would show him Devonish was suffering from some incurable disease. But the label didn't tell him that at all. The medicine was foot-treatment ointment apparently. To be applied twice a day. The ingredients of the potion, he'd seen it contained, amongst other things, formaldehyde, with which they embalmed dead bodies. Seemed fitting. Tied in with the stink from the grey woollen sock the Pole had found.

He walked back into the executive section of Adrian Devonish's room, thinking *there's an explanation for everything, even Kirst and her secret visits to the chemist, even Adrian's absence; he'll turn up, and soon, tail between his legs most likely.* And that's when he heard it. From downstairs. The rip-snorting, knee-trembling, gut-wrenching scream. And he could have sworn it was Kirstie Shay.

28: Twinned

The sign was now buried under the weight of so many insects that it no longer read, WELCOME TO LIMM ISLAND. TWINNED WITH ALSFELD, GERMANY. The only legible word was now TWINNED. There was a large dent from where the great white shark had hit it, and inside it, insects were spawning more insects. Insects were born and immediately started to crawl across the bodies of their dead parents. Insects twinned and twinning. Sinned and sinning. Growing. Feeding. Over-populating. There were so many flies they'd managed to alter the shark's position, so now it was looking out directly onto the road, at the swarm of other flies which pooled around the other body. The dead man. The dead man whose green Barbour jacket was now so shredded it was virtually unknowable as what it once was.

The flies were mainly attracted to the gun-shot wounds. The wounds were clean; the bullet had coursed straight through his ear, continued through his brain, and had exited out the other side, thudding into the grass verge on the other side of the road where, as it landed, it threw up a cloud of dust. The wounds gave a whole new meaning to *in one ear, out the other,* a joke which the man in the Barbour coat might have found funny once. Though both sides of the wound were now so thick with flies it was hard to tell, at certain angles it was possible to see clear through the man's head: the mushed pink-grey of his dead brain, the inner-workings of both ears. Cerebral veins were sliced and being feasted on, the frontal lobe was quivering as eggs were being laid, hatched, fried by other flies.

The man had been dead only an hour and yet, the activity of the flies had hastened his decomposition now so that he seemed as though he'd been dead weeks. Or as though he'd just been washed ashore having been buried at sea. He'd been shot because of the flies. *For* the flies. Though individually they hadn't been aware of what they were doing, there was a kind of throbbing, collective

281

consciousness which pulsed through them as the four men had arrived. A consciousness which came directly from the golden valve. They'd felt compelled to overwhelm the men with the sheer weight and scale of their numbers. Surround them. Blind them. Blind especially two of the men, two men twinned in deadly destiny. First the man in the green Barbour coat so that he couldn't get away. So that he was dragged down by them. Second the man who had been so obsessively cleaning his rifle. The flies hadn't pulled the trigger but they'd made the Dirty man so frantic he'd started waving the gun about, trying to protect himself from larger predators. They hadn't pulled the trigger, but they'd been crawling up his nose, into his ears so that he felt he was drowning and that the only option left to him was to fire, because the crack of a gun-shot might well clear the flies a little. They hadn't pulled the trigger, but they'd seen all. They'd seen all as the bullet had smashed through the head of the man in the green Barbour coat. They'd seen all as the three surviving men had been allowed to escape. To carry word of what they'd seen back to their own swarm so that, in the end, their swarm would simply limp away, limp off this island, leave the golden valve to its own devices.

And now the flies sensed a new danger. On the ground, their six-legged foot-soldier cousins sensed it too. And it wasn't only the rain, which had been threatening all morning now. It was something else, something which would perhaps threaten their ownership of the two bodies, of the sign. It was something which would follow in the footsteps of the Black Panther and the great white shark. Another *big* predator. From the twin-world. From beyond. And this predator would be stronger, rawer, fitter. Redder in tooth and claw. This predator would leave a trail of death and destruction behind it like nothing which had been seen before. And they wouldn't be there to pick up the pieces because *everything* would come to an end.

The golden valve then, was to be their originator, their protector *and* their destroyer. And that was the way it was supposed to be. And when the valve started to vibrate, to strum with energy, to screech, like two huge cranes rubbing together, the flies cleared a path for it, because that too was the way it was supposed to happen. And as the valve started to shudder and splutter, the sheer force generated, the devastating interruption to the atmosphere caused the black clouds overhead to finally split. The rain started, the waters broke. Soon a new birth would come to pass. The Darkness was rising.

29: An Umbrella

The rain was assaulting the top of his golf-style Combs' Mead umbrella so powerfully it was difficult for Manny to retain his grip on the handle. The noise of it was making it impossible to hear anything which was being discussed at the water's edge. Such was the force of the gale, if it wasn't for the fact the umbrella had been designed to be windproof it would have long-since turned itself inside-out like the cheap MacAskill's standard-issue umbrellas which had been wielded by most of the other people on the beach.

Even with the umbrella his face was wet. The wind carried the sea-spray most of the way up the shingle shore, so that the watery attack was taking place from all angles. It was impossible not to come over all *drowned rat*. But Manny kept the umbrella erect. Hoisted it like a flag. So that the townspeople would see the Combs' Mead logo and know he was here despite the storm; the reliable, the trustworthy, the eminently electable Manfred Combs.

From the outside looking in, it was a show of strength then. From the inside looking out, it was something completely different. Manny felt the shingle shifting under his wet feet. He felt the ache in the back of his legs from standing up too long. He felt the beginnings of a familiar fluttering in his heart. And from inside the umbrella looking out, everything seemed *wrong,* upside down, back-to-front, turned inside out. It was wrong, all wrong, had been all morning. And it started with the car on the beach. Cars weren't supposed to be washed up on shore, not two minute's walk away from the village green. Cars weren't supposed to beach themselves, like confused whales, in full view of the lifeboat hut and the Ship.

But that's what had happened. And by the time someone had thought to call him, the whole damned town knew the whole story. Before he'd even replaced the receiver after Mrs. Heggarty's

283

warning call, a crowd scene had already developed. By the time Mrs. Heggarty had replaced her own receiver, her bloody kids had 'liked' the photographs which had already appeared on Facebook. By the time Manny had changed out of his dressing gown and slippers and dressed himself in full mayoral garb, *including* chain, even those families who'd kept their kids away from school and had busied themselves calling Radio Coast phone-ins telling all and sundry about the mysterious beast which was stalking the island, had packed up their picnic baskets and, despite the rain, headed down to the beach. By the time Dave Chester turned up with the limo, a veritable One World festival had developed. Rich Dailly from the Castle, had set up a covered stall selling hot buns whose queue was only rivaled by that of Neal Chase, the ice cream man, who was now selling tea quicker than his kettle could boil, from his van.

By the time Manny Combs arrived at the beach, the Bibby Firm had got the lifeboat Land Rover and towed the car fully out of the sea. By the time Manny arrived, there was such a circle around the car, watching Sam do his CSI stuff, that Manny couldn't press through it. And all the while elbows would shoot up in his face as more and more of his townspeople jostled for space with which they could rattle off a few shots on their camera phones, and then, no doubt, upload those same images directly onto the internet.

And despite his hatred of such things, he could see *why* people were taking camera phone snaps of the car from the depths. It was streamered with long strips of sea-weed so that it looked as though it had just carried away the bride and groom at an underwater wedding. The windscreen was smashed-out, missing. The bride was nowhere to be seen, but the groom was in the driver seat, dead, his face clenched into a mask of pure terror as though he was already regretting his vows.

Mrs. Heggarty filled him in on the details he'd missed, all the while trying to shuffle in under his umbrella with him because her own had been ripped apart by the wind. 'There's some debate as to who saw it first,' she sniffed. There was a great globule of liquid on the end of her nose; it was almost forming stalactite proportions. 'There's some say it was that Kirst Shay girl what works at your hotel. They say she saw the car surfing in on one of the waves like a sea monster, through the big panoramic window you have in the breakfast room. You know that window?'

He nodded impatiently, *of course I know it, it's my hotel.*

'Anyway, they say she saw it and that she recognised it immediately as you-know-who's. They say she screamed so loud she almost brought the house down. Fell into a dead faint afterwards, but most of the other waiting staff had seen by then.' She wiped her nose with the sleeve of her sodden raincoat, tried to wheedle some room under the umbrella once again. Manny allowed her an inch, but no more. 'Or there's some that say it was the men in the lifeboat crew what saw it first. The Bibby brothers were down there anyway, apparently, seeing about maintaining the boat before this storm took a proper hold, and I mean, they'd have been expecting if anything was to be swept ashore, *shipwrecked,* it would be a boat, but... But anyway, Mike Ford was down there too and...'

Manny's heart sank that little bit lower. It was floating in his puddled shoes now, wriggling like a dying fish. 'Ford?'

'The very one; after all, he's in the crew and all and...'

'Where is he now? I couldn't see him with the Bibby's down by the car.'

Mrs. Heggarty pointed a long bony finger off in the general direction of the queue for Rich Dailly's hot rolls. Manny looked, and he saw the newspaperman scurrying up and down the line, getting his vox-pops in, taking down notes he could use for *The Tide Piper.* He sighed. Things were spiralling ever more out of his control. And the scary thing was... The scariest thing amongst many scary things, was the fact that most of the people seemed to be *enjoying* this. When he looked at Rich Dailly, a man who'd only half an hour earlier learned the news his boss had been washed ashore dead in a car, he saw a man who was revelling in the moment. Rich Dailly, he saw now, was trying to impress him. As though a few hot rolls would make him think he was trustworthy enough to be put in charge of his hotel. But what people like him didn't understand was the bigger picture. That there might not be a hotel at all if bodies continued to pile up like this...

A wind-blown plastic bag slapped into Mrs. Heggarty's face. Manny helped her peel it away from her mouth and then, soon as he'd cast it into the wind again, resumed the questioning.

'So,' he said, 'how widely known is it that the body in the car is Devonish's?'

'Common knowledge,' she replied. There was a streak of blue on her forehead which had been transferred from the plastic bag. It made her appear marked in some way. 'It was Richard Dailly who, uh, identified the body. And now he's telling everybody who'll buy a roll off him.'

'What about cause of death?'

'I'm not a CSI person,' she said, 'but I'd have thought that was obvious. Washed off the causeway. No two ways about it.'

Manny allowed himself a smile. If it really was as simple as a misjudgment on the causeway, a stupid, idiotic, *touristy* mistake, but a mistake nonetheless, then everything might still be okay.

'Mind,' said Mrs. Heggarty, 'there is the problem about the missing finger on the body. That just about sticks out like a sore thumb, that one. And of course, there are some that say it's probably been bitten off while he's been in the water, by a small shark or something, but Sam Bibby has said them marks on his knuckle are consistent with what he saw on the body of poor Dan Coffey at the talent show down at Coverley Bottoms and...'

'Shut up,' growled Manny. 'I don't want to hear any more.' He shouldered her out of the way, walked awkwardly onto the beach proper, where the shingle was terribly slippery. He looked left, to where he needed to plug the leak which was his own employee, Rich Dailly. Then right, another leak; Sam and Mart Bibby, who seemed to be giving a running commentary on their investigations to the watching crowd. And then he saw leaks all over. Camera phones. Text messages. E-mails. People gossiping to each other along their washing-line telegraph. Leaks everywhere. Too many to plug.

And the sea broiled and bubbled, waves crashed onto shore, rattling, rattling on the shingle. And it was almost as though the sea was laughing at him. Suddenly the mayoral chain felt too heavy around his neck. For a moment he buckled under the weight of it. Tucked himself into an inverse 7 so that to anyone watching, he must have looked as though he was going to throw up. From somewhere faraway, he heard a shout. He dropped the umbrella. Felt the water battering down onto his back. He collapsed down onto the shingle, immediately feeling the cold water soaking his great mayoral arse. He looked at his upside-down Combs' Mead umbrella. Already it had filled with water. *Water, water everywhere, but not a drop to drink.* He craved a drink. He yearned for a drink. His *Kingdom* for a drink. He dropped his head in his hands and moaned.

He heard the crunch and squeak of feet on the shingle around him. Heard people asking him questions. Always with the fucking questions. Always looking to him...

'Mr. Combs, are you all right, sir?'

'What's wrong with you?'

He moaned louder, hoping he could make his voice so loud it would drown theirs out, and more importantly, drown out those other voices which had now started rabbiting away in his head. *Drink-a-drink-a-drink-a-drink.* Like a goddamn train. *Let drink be your umbrella, your shelter, your saviour. Your golden valve. Do it, do it, do it, do it do it, do it...*

'Should we call an ambulance?'

'Have you got Dr. Shaw's number on your moby?'

Manny was shouting now. Shouting into the wind, into the rain, into the sea. Shouting. Singing nonsense words over and again.

'He's drunk, he has to be.'

He felt hands clutching at him, tucking under his arms. At first it felt as though the sea was reaching out for him, pulling him into its raging clutches. But then, somehow, he registered that it was human hands. Wrenching, dragging him to his feet. He tried to stagger out of their grip. Kicked, windmilled his arms. He felt his big mayoral chain swing up, clunk him in the face. Clunk into his teeth. Heard a crunching sound. Tasted blood. He struggled again, but the hands remained firm. He couldn't escape. And so he swung round, clutched the lapels of one of the men who was assaulting him. He didn't recognise the face. It could have been any old demon. And he screamed into that face, pleaded with that face. 'Where's Cheryyyyyyyyyyyl? Where is she?'

The man opened his mouth to reply. His mouth smelled of death and black panthers and seawater and mead. 'I don't know any Cheryl, sir.'

'Not Cheryl then, *Snakey.*' And then finally he passed out, let oblivion wash over him, let himself be released.

Manny finally came to and his face hurt. Felt like the time, *donkeys* ago when he and Snakey had been cycling down the steep slope of Dye Lane and he'd hit some loose bit of gravel or a patch of oil or a goddamn twig and he'd careered arse-over-tit, body-over-handlebars, into the tarmac, landing face-first. The bruising, the grazes had taken weeks to go down, but the pain teeth had stayed with him for *months.* For months they chewed off-key like a warped piano. Only the golden-valve heart fluttering had remained with him longer.

He cranked open an eye. Saw he was on his own sofa in his own front room in his own house, which was a relief. He saw the

287

mayoral chain draped across a big fluffy towel on his coffee table. He saw the dirty pile of his mayoral clothes on the floor. Discovered, embarrassingly, that he was naked. That whoever had dragged him off the beach and home, had then stripped him naked as the day he was born and covered him with a blanket. Only one thing was worse than one or all of his townspeople witnessing him going King Lear on the heath crazy n the beach, and that was one or all of his townspeople witnessing his crooked, scarred naked body. His un-birthday suit. And there was no doubt that even if it had been only one, two people who'd brought him back here, because of damned camera phones, *everyone* would see eventually.

The room was mostly shrouded in darkness. Only one of the table lamps was casting out any light, and what light it did give was weak. The curtains were drawn. He couldn't tell whether it was day or night, how long he'd been out. He wondered what had happened to whoever had brought him back here. He got the distinct impression that they – whoever they were – were still here somewhere, perhaps in the kitchen. Certainly it would be just like the interfering busybodies of Limm town to remain here uninvited, no doubt helping themselves to his superior brand of scran while they were at it.

He felt a pang of the old anger rising in him, but only a pang. Mostly what he felt was sadness. Post-apocalyptic desertion. Like he was the last man left on earth with any sense. Like there was nobody, *nobody* left for him. He tried to summon up his Cheryl Hammerstein look and only succeeded in making himself cry. Because she, *he*, was long gone. Had been hung from the rafters at the barn up Knoll Farm. Had been taken by the golden valve.

And through the sadness, Manny felt the pull of the golden valve, reminding him of that familiar release it could offer him. Now he remembered what else was in the kitchen cupboards (behind a padlocked door) waiting for him. Gingerly, he tried to lift himself up into a sitting position, making sure that his wasted body was kept entirely covered in case anyone should step into the room. Moving took him a long time, as though his brain had only just re-booted itself and was still only working at half-capacity. It took him another few moments before he could summon up the mental strength to turn his seating into standing. Eventually he managed it, using the armrest for leverage. And once he reached full-height, it felt for a moment as though he was suffering from vertigo. His knees knocked, his thighs wobbled, his heart lurched. But then he managed to compose himself, and, walking in a half crouch, with the blanked draped around him like a toga, he padded towards the kitchen.

Mrs. Heggarty met him half-way. 'Oh... Mr. Combs sir... You should go back to the sofa before you do yourself a mischief,' she said, linking his arm as one would a senile old man, one who'd somehow wandered out of his home and found himself in the supermarket fruit and veg aisle. 'We don't know what's, uh, wrong with you and we should wait 'til Dr. Shaw gets here. I can make you a cup of...'

Manny felt the golden valve spasming through him. Involuntarily he flapped his arms. He didn't feel it as his fist connected with the side of Mrs. Heggarty's Higgledy-Piggledy face, but he heard the gunshot crack. Nor did he feel it as his leg kicked out at her as she went down, but he saw the look of surprise on her face. She went down, and the back of her head connected with the sharp edge of a shelf which had been affixed to the wall. Manny couldn't remember having affixed that shelf to the wall, nor could he remember getting a man in to do the fixing for him, nor could he remember why there'd ever been a need for it. Certainly there was nothing lining the shelf. It was as though the shelf's only purpose was to provide the final, jarring contact with Mrs. Heggarty which would send her into the next life.

She landed on the carpet a dead weight and Manny only had eyes for the shelf. For its sharp corner. It seemed purpose-built for braining someone. He touched the edge and felt it prick his finger, drawing blood. His own mixed with that of Mrs. Heggarty. And as the blood pumped into his finger, he felt it pulsing, throbbing, *itching*. That finger seemed now more powerful than his whole body, his mind too. It led him into the kitchen, helping him to walk fully Homo sapiens erect now. It guided him to the locked cupboard which contained the booze he should, by rights, have thrown out. It found the key to the padlock. The one he'd long told himself he'd lost. And the tea-total Mead Baron, the non-drinking mayor of the island surrounded by liquid, opened up the cupboard and saw all those lovely bottles full of that lovely drink and that lovely release.

And the golden valve told him *yes, now is the time.*

Down by the WELCOME TO LIMM ISLAND sign on the old abandoned road, two billion flies shuddered as Manny Combs creaked open the bottle of Jack and sucked hungrily on the golden valve's golden teat. The end was beginning.

289

30: Breaking the Caricature

Slumped over the bar, Mart Bibby resembled a caricature, or so thought Mike Ford. An artist could achieve a reasonable likeness to Mart's face by simply sketching, in a hard pencil - say a 9H perhaps - the figure eight on blank piece of paper. Now the artist could start to add some detail. The rocky outcrop of his chin lent him an air of aloof, but pride-wounded masculinity. In fact, his strong jaw-line, which the artist could emphasise with, say, a 2B pencil, had only been strengthened by his relentless chewing of nicotine chewing gum. He could have probably crushed a large animal in that bear-trap jaw of his now. He looked outdoorsy, but equally at home in the informal pub atmosphere into which he had descended. Indeed, the artist would have been sorely tempted to use a little artistic license, perhaps adding a cowboy hat to his closely cropped head, just to make sure that the audience appreciated this man as a quiet, but effective force of nature. But a cowboy hat, Mike decided, would have been a little *YMCA* for Mart Bibby. Instead he simply *wore* the pub, like it was a second skin, or his new clothes.

The Ship that evening resembled the result of some infantile scribblings on the part of some caricaturist who dealt in the simple, face-value facts. This caricaturist had shaded in the yellow stains of many years of cigarette smoke seemingly blown straight at the walls. He'd scattered the tables out in order that nobody had to sit close to anybody else, and daubed the carpets with a healthy coating of grime. He'd pictured the ruddy-cheeked barman, Kev, as a man whose laboured, rheumy-eyed struggle to even get from one side of the bar to the other was about as healthy as the pipes which held his beer. There was some kind of blockage in his internal organs, and liquid was seemingly seeping out of his every pore; his system was obviously overloaded with the stuff. He'd turned into one of his drinks.

290

The Ship wasn't a place for the faint hearted; it was a place for those who wanted to take a long hard look at themselves in the reflection at the bottom of their glass, and then order another pint to forget about what they'd seen. And on Limm that day, that description applied to just about everyone. The Ship was any port in a storm, in *the* storm, and the residents were out in force. They wanted Mart Bibby to explain it all for them, in terms even a child would understand. Seemingly, this throng of still-wet people who'd retired from the beach to here, had appointed him their Explainer in Chief. It was up to him to tell them what they were all going to do about the bodies. And this was because Sam Bibby was otherwise engaged, and because Manny Combs was AWOL, in body and mind, and somehow, despite everything, despite his 'dubious sexuality' and his inability to give up cigarettes like a man (no, Mart had to rely on the gum), *somehow,* Mart had been appointed third in command. He was shunning that responsibility for now, preferring to *wear* the bar. Despite the fact there were increasing cat-calls for him to take the floor and talk, Mart Bibby was barely moving at his stool at the bar.

Mart's shoulders coiled in snakes of tension, eyes only for his drink. But even he could not resist the temptation of turning to look once he heard the buzz from the other drinkers at the arrival of somebody new in the pub; judging by their reactions, it had to be a woman.

Stick to the plain, the simple, Mike. Make like a journalist. Like a *local* journalist with a story on his hands. Lose the artistic, English Literature degree shit...

Okay, woman entered bar. Mart Bibby turned awkwardly on his bar stool, and was greeted by the sight of Ruth Sharp, the woman from the Seahorse, standing by the front door like something out of a Western movie. *Enough with the metaphors...* All that was needed to say was that Ruth Sharp was standing, one hand on her cocked hip, looking for someone. She was wearing an expensive looking cream trouser-suit with high heels; clearly she wasn't embarrassed or self-conscious about her height, despite the fact that she dwarfed just about everybody in the pub. Clearly she wasn't self-conscious about her head either, despite the bandana she was wearing which made Mike Ford believe she looked like someone from *G N' R.* She was carrying a log-lead but no dog.

Nobody moved, nobody said anything.

291

'I'm looking for Mart Bibby,' she announced. 'Your brother said I might find you here.'

Mart raised a hand. Identified himself.

'Congratulations,' said Ruth Sharp. 'You win first prize. You and I need to talk.'

Everyone watched to see how Mart would react. He didn't fly out the back door as many had expected, nor did he roar at her to fuck off.

Ruth Sharp strode into the bar room. Mike Ford wanted to ask her why she was carrying a dog-lead but had no dog, but he thought better of it. She *made* him think better of it. Still, he stayed close to the bar so he could hear their exchange.

She reached Mart. Picked up his pint pot. Sneered at it. 'So you're drowning your sorrows are you? Like men always do.'

Mart said nothing to contradict her.

'Big feller like you, feeling sorry for yourself. *Sulking*. When there's jobs to be done.' She tried to catch the barman's attention. The barman, however, was studiously trying not to meet her eyes and was studying the image of the woman on the cardboard behind the packs of peanuts.

'As I said, I've just been speaking with your brother. He's taken my dog, Vicar. They're out patrolling. Vicar'll be sniffer-dogging. They could do with a hand, Mart. The *island* could do with a hand. I was out there today and... People don't know who to look to. They need someone. Which is why we've called a meeting. Tomorrow. First thing. What I need is someone to help me put the posters up around town. Sam said you'd be just the man.'

'Hmmm,' grumbled Mart, slurping from his pint glass. 'Maybe.'

'It's okay,' said Ruth, 'you can finish your drink first. Hell, *I* could do with a drink before I go back out on those streets again.'

And now Mike Ford was *sure* Mart Bibby would tell her to fuck off, but he didn't. Instead, he simply said, 'What'll it be then?'

While Ruth had almost had to climb over the bar and hit the barman in the face to get his attention - in fact she looked as though she was seriously contemplating this - all it took was a slight inclination of Mart Bibby's head, and the barman was straight over to take their order. Mart, it seemed, was fluent in the language of pubs; a mysterious hotch-potch of gesture and sounds which was intended to confuse your average customer. Pub language contained many subtle gradations which could be suggested by miniscule inflections of a local's head. For example, by cocking his head slightly to the right, a man could have implied that he was indeed interested in another drink, but that his wife at home would have been none too pleased with him if he had that drink. A slight nodding of the head over a nearly empty glass meant that the customer was ready for another drink, but was quite prepared to wait for the barman to serve other, less practiced pub-speakers first.

The barman puffed and panted his way through the taking of their orders, becoming confused over whether soda water was, in fact, the same as lemonade, or was it mineral water? He loaded the Ruth Sharp's drink with ice and even clattered about in the fridge for a while searching for an elusive lemon which he could shove into the glass as well. Maybe he wanted a glace cherry to put in there too. Finished, the barman returned to his staring at the peanuts, his misery clinging to him like the pith on an orange. Mart was a bitter lemon though. He led them away from the bar and the two of them cleared the lounge area before sitting down, close to the fireplace.

And Mike Ford found his curiosity getting the better of him. He poked his head round, aware that it was liable to get shot-down by Mart Bibby; that he might get chewing-gum spat directly into his face.

'What do you want, newspaperman?' barked Mart.

And Mike said, 'I want to help you.' And it wasn't necessarily because he thought he might get a story out of it.

293

31: Sick Shadow

The black panther was shivering. The day's rain had soaked everything, including it, and now its fur was slicked back, pressed down against its body. It wouldn't dry no matter how much it tried to lick the moisture away. It knew that it made him look smaller. Bedraggled and small in a place it still didn't know, no matter how much scent it sprayed on the strange trees.

The panther could smell sickness and it knew that it was coming from its own body. That the days of vomiting-up everything it had caught must have caused it some serious damage inside as well as out. Its musculature was wasting away. Its fur was molting. There was a bald patch on its neck where it had scratched and scratched at an itch it just could not reach. Its eyesight wasn't what it once was. Smell still remained, but the benefits of that were negligible. One smell overwhelmed almost everything else. The smell of the other animal from the other place, the shark.

The panther had found a nest for itself in one of the trees towards the thick centre of the southern woods. Had crooked itself into a branch and tried to wait out the wave of sickness. And it knew something was *really wrong* when it spotted three more two-legs setting up camp not far away from his tree. The three men seemed as disorientated as the panther did. One of them was walking with a pronounced limp, another was sobbing constantly, and the third had something mentally wrong. Kept flapping its arms about as though to swat at imaginary flies. In another time and another place, the trio would have made easy prey, wounded as they were. And the panther had tried to get itself geared up for the attack, but after a while, after they'd lit a fire and settled down for the night it had realised that even then, it couldn't summon up the requisite energy to attack.

It sensed its time in this new place was coming to an end. Sensed that it had done whatever duty was expected of it – by what, it wasn't sure – and so it flopped its tired head down onto its paws, closed its eyes, and allowed itself to drift, to dream. And it dreamed of the other place, the not-quite twinner place. It dreamed of home back beyond the golden valve. It dreamed it was an early morning, just as the sun was rising. Still dark enough to see the twin moons, but light enough to see all the rich prey coming out to feed. Hunting time. It dreamed of full stomachs and happy limbs and the pleasure of a chase. It dreamed of the taste of still-flapping prey, when its blood was spiced by fear. It dreamed of the other place. Where its disease did not exist. Where its disease was not borne by blood, spread into the two-legs and the animals it had seen. It dreamed, and didn't even hear it as the golden valve finally, finally released its replacement onto the island, fully-formed, claws extended, wings spread. Ready to hunt.

Day Four

32: The Super-Hero's Alter Ego

Manny Combs had finally run out of lies. Excuses had deserted him too, slippery, nibbling rats that they were. He was now immune to the subtle art of misdirection. The persuasive power of another drink would no longer help. The pull of the golden valve was gone, for now, and guilt was on him like a rabid dog. He woke up on his sofa in front of the blaring television, piss-soaked jeans cold-compressing his thin legs, an axe wound of terror slap-bang in the middle of his forehead and his heart feeling *too soft*.

'Bastard,' he said, shifting his position, feeling the crick in his neck, *hearing* the click as it settled back into place. 'Bastard,' he repeated when he felt the first shiver rip through him. It was Arctic cold in the front room and his sodden jeans hardly helped. He couldn't even remember putting on jeans, that's how drunk he'd been. He tutted at himself, and the sound of his dry tongue slapping against the roof of his mouth sounded like someone dropping a penny to the bottom of a deep well.

Automatically, he reached down to the side of the too-low sofa, where, in his drinking-phases he was usually in control enough to leave a restorative bottle of whisky or mead or a can of Fairhurst's waiting for him, but his fingers closed around nothing. His heart fluttered. He looked over the edge of the sofa, into the abyss, and saw the bottles. Everything from the high-end Tallisker to the low-rent Bacardi, finally, which was lying on its side, shaking out its final pissy drops onto the already badly stained carpet. He'd polished off everything.

PAINT THIS TOWN RED

'Bastard,' he said and tried to think of nothing. Tried to let oblivion take over again. But already he knew it wouldn't. Bitter, urine-soaked reality told him that. He'd been off the drink ten years now, ever since the Millennium, that party to end all parties when his madness had infected everyone else so much there'd been a whole beach-full of bodies. After that, somehow, he'd sought help. Gone to Dr. Shaw, a man so wracked with guilt after what had happened to his own wife he was Shaw not to relate anything Manny said to the *wrong kind of ears*. Shaw had listened to his various sob stories and had concluded that Manny was what was known as a *functional* alcoholic, because he was able to hold down his powerful position and influence whilst throwing enough of the hard-stuff down his throat that he could drown out his past. But there was nothing functional about waking up like this. Waking up like one of the tramps around the markets in Charnley, bleached with piss and oozing with booze. Not when he was in his fifth decade. Not when he was supposed to *know your limits,* i.e. *your limit is none, because one is too many and a thousand is never enough.*

No. There was nothing functional about yesterday. Hence the guilt. Hence the dry bed where once a river of lies and excuses would have flowed. Hell, even from where he was sitting he could see Mrs. Heggarty's feet, clad in their awful workaday shoes, poking out from round the side of the sofa, where he'd left her.

It didn't have to be like this. He should have left Limm when he was still young enough to do so. It was *Limm's* fault, not his. If Manny had been born *anywhere else* in the world, he could have been a prime minister or a president and not just biggest fish in a small pond of no-hopers. *Limm's* fault that he had to grow up in a man's world where the only choices were fishing or farming, where he was truly out on a limb. It *wasn't his fault* that he didn't know about things like how to roll out a net or how to shear sheep. It *wasn't his fault* that when he'd been younger, he could only feel like a man when he smoked, when he released the valve.

He ran a trembling finger through his greasy hair. Images, sounds, impressions, smells came back to him, but he couldn't remember, not for the whole sorry life of him, what the hell he had done last night after killing Mrs. Heggarty, after releasing the golden valve. He couldn't even remember if he'd left the house or not. Certainly he didn't seem to have, judging by the fact his shoes weren't covered in mud. But he could never tell. Sometimes his black-outs took him far and wide (though never to the toilet).

297

'Shit,' he snarled. He picked up the remote control and started to flick through the channels on the TV. Even static would be better than what was going on in the ninth circle of the hell which was his brain.

'I'll never drink again,' he told himself. But even as the words passed through his horribly cracked lips, he knew he did not mean them, not fully. There was still some part of him which believed life wouldn't be worth living, hadn't been the past ten years, without the booze. He'd once written a list of all the things he'd lost because of alcohol – Snakey, the Millennium Cult, a sorry handful of girlfriends as well as countless other potential girlfriends all in the Seventies (no wonder he hated that decade), a copy of his father's will, bank cards, cash, hair, his self-respect – and what had he gained? Misery, a paunch and a few cuts and bruises. And yet he still thought he could cook the books to make drinking seem a reasonable thing to be getting back into.

He continued absently flicking through the channels, barely registering what was on screen now. Suddenly though, something on screen gave him pause. A blurry image. A scene he recognised. It took him a full minute of staring at the screen for him to realise he was actually looking at the car on the beach. On the national news. Manny ratcheted up the volume a notch.

The north east correspondent was talking over the images, explaining them. 'Images and video like this have swept through Facebook, prompting some observers to ask whether privacy and decency settings should not be improved. Children as young as thirteen can use the US-originated website and could have received full access to these horrific images of the dead man in the car. And this, remember, is Limm Island, the same community where ten years ago, *eighteen* bodies were washed ashore. A place where there were rumours of a mysterious cult. One thing's for sure, the eyes of the world will be on Limm now, especially given the other rumours which have circulated about the island. Those which tell of a wild animal on the loose, slaughtering livestock.'

And then the TV footage cut away to a long-shot of the island. 'Today, the world's media is expected to descend on the island by hook or by crook. And while the island is unreachable now, and will be for another eight hours, you can be sure that some in the media will find a way, by hook or by crook.'

The camera zoomed in on two men crouched in the back of a rowing boat, tugging their oars against the waves. The reason they were so cramped in the back was immediately obvious; two big cameras and a huge boom microphone filling the rest of the boat.

Manny gulped, felt the world turning under his feet. He checked his watch. Five in the morning now; still a good six hours until the rest of the media could get across the sea's moat. Still another six hours until he could legitimately get served with a pint at the Ship (much as he would have dreaded going in there). It was both too long and too short a time to wait. He decided to go for a walk. Taking care not to fall over, he reached for his trusty umbrella (miraculously rescued from the beach by Mrs. Heggarty, he presumed) and for his coat (which thankfully covered his wet crotch). He gurgled some water straight from the tap in the kitchen and then took a quick look in the small basket by the door which usually contained his keys and his mobile. The keys were there, but the mobile wasn't. *Fuck's sake, where was it?* He tried to lower himself to his knees to look on the floor – maybe he'd missed the basket or something – but it made his head spin too much, so he decided to worry about it later. He slipped out of his room, trying to tell himself that losing the mobile was *a good thing.*

Despite a few problems with the lock on the front door, he managed to gain the dark street. He stumbled past the row of small shops, the village green and the small lifeboat hut. He paused for a moment to try to peer through the windows of the Ship, but saw nothing beyond the thick curtains and so he pressed on for the beach.

The sorry excuse for a beach. It used to be said that no Limm Islander would ever be seen dead on it unless it was strictly necessary, which was ironic given what had happened yesterday. But still, every year, the stupid tourists flocked to it. *We're on holiday,* they seemed to be saying. *We have to go on the beach.* So they'd set up their windbreaks and their tents and their barbecues and their picnic hampers and then the children would ask: 'Where's the sand? I thought beaches were supposed to have sand?' So the parents, to prove one could still have fun on a beach *sans* sand, would attempt to sunbathe, or something equally stupid. In time, they'd discover that even the seemingly passive act of lying down was made into an endurance test by the sharp stones of the shore and their seeming desire to roll back into the primal-soup sea from whence they came. Through the panoramic window at the Castle while he breakfasted, Manny had watched countless numbers of them as they tried to find a way to position their bodies which would minimise the parts of it which actually touched the shingle. They

299

tried to *streamline* themselves, as tobogganists and swimmers did. Why would anyone want to do that? And besides; wasn't shingle the name of some awful disease?

Once, Manny used to love the oldness of the stones; the possibility of fossils. But he was not that boy any more. Hadn't been since he released the golden valve. What's more, he couldn't imagine *being* that boy any more. Couldn't imagine feeling so interested in anything that didn't come in bottle shapes with alcohol percentages written on the label. But then again, since he'd been that little boy, every one of his skin cells had been replaced. Every memory he had, every worry he had was now replaced. Now cursed the stones on the beach, taking them as a personal affront. He hated how awkward they made him look as he walked over them, how they exaggerated his drunken lurch. He looked, he decided, like some weird marionette being operated by his own shaking hands.

He decided to sit down and he worried at his already ripped fingernails with his teeth as he looked out into the bay. In the darkness, he thought he could discern rolling, spiralling shapes. Flickering lights. Strange fish-like creatures and giant seals whorling through the air. He screwed up his eyes. Tried to persuade his addled brain to get a *little* more sober. Sober, he was at least a little bit more like the mild-mannered alter-ego of a superhero (or villain).

It wasn't working. Which meant there was only one thing for it. A walk back into town. Now he was fully awake, he felt restless energy starting to rattle through him like a London tube. It was always the same with these off-the-scale hangovers; nervy boredom, seething misanthropy, the need to do *something*. He wondered whether he'd be able to wake Wagger John at The Crab's Claws, what the chances were of getting his hands on a quick sharpener before the official licensing hours started.

Although all the lights were off at The Crab's Claws, Manny tried the door. It was locked, so he shook the handle so the door rattled in its frame for a while. His heart rattled reciprocally in his chest. Ignoring it, he pressed his face against the glass and stared through, checking for movement, though surely it was too early for that. Through the rapidly fogging glass, he saw everything remained still. In fact, it looked as though *nothing* had moved, no shelves had been emptied, cleaned and then re-stacked for a good few years. Nothing ever seemed to be purchased. Nothing was ever removed for being out of date. There were still Marathon bars and Loggers in the chocolate rack, still copies of magazines on the rack which hadn't been seen anywhere but a dentist's waiting room since the 1980's. There were cardboard signs everywhere: 'No more than 2 school children at a time,' 'This is not a library – please buy magz before reading them' and Manny's personal favourite: 'This is not a phone box – do not make your personal calls in here.' Problem was, the place looked about as big as a phone box and smelled about as fusty as a library, and there probably weren't even two school children on the whole of Limm that would be seen dead in there. The worst part was the 'tourist section', which was cordoned off in the winter months like an exhibit in a stately home. Only, even the most stuck-in-a-timewarp stately home wouldn't have displayed the stained Birds of Limm tea towels, sun and dust bleached 'Go out a Limm!' baseball caps and the rack-loads of windbreaks.

Manny rattled the door again, and finally, Wagger John emerged from the back of the shop, still buttoning up his grey cardigan. The cardigan was a key part of his uniform, along with his ragged tartan slippers and his slacks which were held up by two belts for no apparent reason. Funny thing was though, he *could* be arsed. The nickname was a throwback to his school days when he was a regular absentee from primary school; his dad always pulling him out on impromptu fishing expeditions. Far as Manny knew, John had not missed a working day in his life. Nevertheless, at places like the Ship, the name had stuck, much to Wagger's chagrin.

Everything was to Wagger's chagrin. Even opening the door to what would be his first customer of the day. He jangled a gaoler's set of keys into various locks, and finally prised it open, but not open fully enough for Manny to bluster past him and into the shop.

'Mr. Mayor, sir,' said Wagger, blinking. 'What's to be the problem? I heard the knocking and I thought it was the police and...'

'I come on important business,' said Manny.

Wagger only nodded solemnly.

'Yes, *island* business.'

'Oh aye?'

'Can we discuss this inside?' said Manny, affecting a bone-shuddering tremble. 'It's important...'

'Important enough to get me out of my bed at five thirty?'

'Important enough.'

Wagger nodded. Manny breezed past him into the shop, hoping that breeze didn't give off too much of an ammonia stink. He needn't have worried; Wagger busied himself with creaking down to check whether the morning papers had been delivered yet before following him back through the door. The bell on the door croaked.

'So?'

'So how are you, John? Okay?'

'Not really, to tell you the truth Mr. Combs,' he said. 'My bunions are giving me gip and the school kids keep ignoring my signs and...'

Manny tuned him out. Wagger had the easiest job in the world and yet he talked it up like it was some mournful duty he was compelled to perform, like reading a passage from the bible at his best mate's funeral *every day*. The way he went on, it was as though he thought he expected a bloody tip.

'...And someone robbed my doorstop the other day as well. What's the world coming to when someone will rob a doorstop? And I wouldn't mind, but it was a lovely doorstop. Antique...'

Yeah, bet it was antique, like everything else in here, thought Manny, picking a path through the tight shelves to the beer and wine fridge at the back of the shop, hearing the sing of his coat as it caught on some of the health hazards which were sticking out; probably poison-tipped spears or screaming skeletons or any number of other Indiana Jones style traps in this Limm Island Temple of Doom. He opened the fridge, reached in to its glorious coolness and picked out a can of Fairhurst's. Then, to be on the safe side, he picked up a bottle of wine too.

'Here! It's too early for me to serve you *that*. Mayor or no mayor, I could get in...'

'Too early? Who's going to care?' said Manny, turning to meet Wagger's ghostly stare. Challenging him by tossing the can from one hand to the other. Pocketing the wine. 'Have you not seen the news this morning, you fool? Do you not know that all hell is descending on Limm in... ?' He consulted his watch. 'About five and a half-hours.'

'Um... I can't do anything about the licensing laws.'

Manny felt the anger rising inside his belly. He felt like grabbing Wagger by his wispy lapels and lifting him off his greasy linoleum floor. Perhaps shutting him in the fridge for good measure. His heart was racing. 'Tick-tock, Wagger, tick-tock... The island as we know it is going to come careering to a halt in five and a half hours and who then'll give two shits about the damned licensing laws? All I want is a can of beer and a bottle of wine,' he said, through a clenched jaw. 'And with all this shit-storm on the way, I just need something to take the edge off. So I can feel okay again.'

There, he'd said it. Come out with the truth. No wonder he was always feeling the pull of the sauce. It was the only way he could feel okay; the Okay Sauce.

'Can't do nothing about the law, no matter what you say about *sheesh-storms,*' said Wagger, with a shrug.

The shrug and the not-quite swear simply enflamed Manny further. He stepped forward, snarling. 'Look, you!' Then paused. He felt his heart skipping violently in his chest. *Thu-thud, thu-thud. Thuddity-thud, thud.* Irregular, like monkeys attempting to play a military tattoo. Angry monkeys. As loud and wriggly as gaggles of fifteen year old girls on the top deck of the bus. He'd felt his heart playing similar tricks over the past few days but this was worse. Worse because after the initial race came three, flickery, not-quite beats. *Thu-thud, thu-thud. Thuddity-thud, thud. Flutter.* The world suddenly felt gooey at the edges. For a sickening moment, Manny thought he was going to collapse. Wagger John evidently thought the same; a rare, concerned look crossed his shadowy features. But then, the skipping stopped, as quickly as it had started, and the two men were left staring at each other, rather too close for comfort between the too-tight shelving and the dog-eared birthday cards.

Wagger John reached out to take the can of Fairhurst's out of his hand. At first, Manny's fingers remained tightly curled around it, but with a bit of wiggle, Wagger managed to extricate it from his grasp. Then he went for the wine. Took it no problems. Manny couldn't *move.*

Wagger John cracked open his fridge and replaced the can on the top shelf, the wine on the bottom. 'Wanting anything else today, Mr. Combs, sir? A nice birthday card, perhaps. A windbreak?'

Manny found he still could not speak. His heart had started playing its tricks again, and now it was so insistent. He didn't care how he looked to the shopkeep. All he cared about was the flutter, every two, three beats. The way it seemed like the trigger for his heart to shut down. His heart which now felt so big in his chest it was about to make him topple over. Doc'd warned him about this, just as he'd warned him about the functional alcoholism. Manny wished he'd listened.

'Are you all right Mr. Combs, sir? You look faint.'

303

He wasn't all right. He was leaning, arse-first against the bereavement cards now, trying to anticipate the missed beats, trying to second guess his own heart. With every flutter, it felt as though blood was draining from his extremities; his feet had turned into sheer shingle, his hands Scotch eggs. To counteract the vibrations, he was now clutching his chest, as though expecting lightning pain to strike at any moment. It was how his dad had gone, after all, and these things were hereditary. Like the drinking.

So he wasn't a super hero after all. Wagger John had him by the arm now, and was trying to lead him away from the cards but Manny wouldn't budge. He opened his mouth wide to suck in air. The sound of his heart exploding was now ringing in his ears. Manny felt himself slipping to the floor.

He landed, and three or four new job cards floated down on top of him. He curled himself into a foetal comma and from somewhere, he could hear Wagger's moans. 'You can't do this here. Oh, this is terrible, as if I haven't got enough on my plate. Manny?'

Manny rolled over so he wouldn't have to see the look on Wagger's face. And as he rolled it felt as though his massive heart was rolling out of him, landing like a brick on the linoleum floor. Spinning, vibrating, still angry at him. It took him a moment to realise that what had dropped out of his chest – or more correctly, from the pocket in the chest of his coat – was his lost mobile phone. A brick of a thing, but then, he couldn't work the decent ones. For a moment, he simply stared at the phone. Tried to work out whether his heart was still in place. Whether he was still alive, or had entered some purgatory full of shit mobiles and *concerned* shopkeepers who wore tartan slippers.

He was alive. He could smell the tartan and years-old polish on the lino. He could *feel* the lino sticking to his cheek as though it didn't want to let him go. He could hear Wagger John droning on and on, about 'ambulance' this, and 'Dr. Shaw' that. He could see the crap underneath the shelving unit; dust, old sweets, screwed up balls of paper. Probably crabs and mice too. He could feel the blood pumping round his body, suddenly animating those Scotch egg hands of his. *It had been the mobile phone vibrating in his pocket all along. Not a heart attack. Not death.* Suddenly, he was light headed from the elation and not from the fear. He reached out for the mobile and pressed the answer button, ready to bellow his delight down the line at whoever was calling.

'That you, boss?' said a voice at the other end of the phone, before Manny could even find the words to express his gratitude.

'Boss?'

'It's me, yeah.'

Whatever the caller said next was drowned out by the sound of Wagger John's patience finally snapping: 'This is not a phone box! This is my shop. I have to make a living. If you want to make a personal phone call make it outside. Now please. Will you get off my floor?'

'Excuse me,' said Manny into the phone, 'you'll just have to bear with me, I seem to be stuck inside a...' - he commando rolled onto his back, lifted his head and stared into Wagger's eyes – '*lunatic* asylum. Just let me get outside so I can hear you properly.'

'You haven't even bought anything,' sobbed Wagger, as Manny levered himself back to his feet using a handily placed postcard dispenser.

Manny shouldered past him. 'End of the fucking world,' he said, 'just remember that,' as the bell jangled to jubilantly proclaim he'd managed to escape the Temple of Doom *just about* intact. He went over to sit on one of the benches which flanked the village green and returned the phone to his ear. 'Sorry about that... Just went in to buy a paper and I get all kinds of nonsense. Who is it anyway?'

A deep breath: 'It's Dave Chester. Your chauffeur? Where've you been? I've called your mobile over and over. Since about ten last night...'

'Whoah there, Dave. You're not the one to go demanding to know where *I've* been, are you? That is not your role. Now, what's the problem?'

Dave sighed again; his breath whistled as though he'd chain-smoked too many ciggies.

'What's up, Dave?' asked Manny, already starting to grow bored of sitting still. For one thing he was very hungry. Call it the sea air; plays havoc with a man's stomach, especially after a shock.

'Well, after your *turn* yesterday... Some things have been happening on the island. Things I know you won't be happy with.'

'What is it? More calls to the phone-in on Radio Coast?' said Manny, absently picking at a flake of paint on the arm of the bench. He was alive. And yet he still had to deal with fucking no-mark idiots almost as soon as he'd escaped the clutches of death. He should have been celebrating. Or finding a way of escaping the island before the cavalry came. The media. Before they too realised

305

he was to blame for all of it. 'Oh, just spit the fucking thing out,' he snapped. He felt like saying *oh, just spit the fucking thing out already,* like they did in the American films. 'Already,' he added.

'Already what?'

'Doesn't matter. What are you trying to tell me?' He stared out to sea, past Cawdor Head, where yesterday's storm was already forgotten, where it was millpond-calm.

'Well... It's the townspeople. That Ruth Sharp from the Seahorse, Sam Bibby, the gay lad Mart Bibby, and Mike Ford to be precise. They've been, uh, plotting, while you were, uh, *out*. And they've arranged a town meeting for nine today for, as it says on the posters, *a full and frank discussion of everything that's been going on on the island over the past few days...* '

'Posters?' said Manny, suddenly feeling ill again, suddenly seeing the once-solid mental picture of his bridge starting to become ghostly. He wiped a trembling paw across his brow and it came back looking greased-up with a slug-trail of cold sweat. 'Where?'

'Everywhere, boss. You said you were out on the town already. Look around you!'

Manny looked over his shoulder. There was a small glass-fronted community noticeboard on the village green. Inside, where the poster for the TALENT-STRAVAGANZA!!!!!! had been only days ago, there was a new sign. Even from here, he could read the fateful words, EMERGENCY GENERAL MEETING. He gulped.

'What do you know about this meeting? Any intel?'

Now Dave's voice was so low, Manny had to press the phone hard against his ear, just to make out what it was he was trying to say. What he heard made his heart flutter as badly as in Wagger John's. 'Now you listen to me, Mr. Combs, sir. I'm going against all my principles even telling you what I've told you already. What I need are assurances. I need to know that I'll be rewarded for this after it's over.'

'You cheeky...'

'Enough. See, the way I see it is there's two sides in this now. At least two, actually. And at the moment, I've plumped for your side, because your side has the most chance of winning. But things could still go either way. Way I see it is, if you can promise me a decent reward, it'll be in both of our interests for me to keep helping you. To keep quiet about the body in your front room.'

Manny gasped.

306

'That's right. Mrs. Heggarty, I believe. Two children, I believe.'

'You won't...'

'I won't say anything. We can have the whole thing cleared up before the media even get here. If you promise.'

'I...'

'And it's not just Heggarty, is it?'

Manny felt his body dribbling through the slats in the bench. He was *so sure* Dave Chester was going to mention Snakey. Dan Coffey too.

'There's also that doctor. Shaw. He came a-calling at your house last night. He's... I spun him some cock, some bull, got him convinced you'd gone off-island for some proper medical attention. But he's suspicious. He knows there's things going on which are bigger than him, us, most of the people on the island. So I fobbed him off. But you're not going to fob *me* off, are you?'

'Where are you now?' said Manny, quickly.

'Do we have a deal?'

Manny winced. 'Yes... Yes whatever you want. I'll...'

'Good. I'm parked up just past Dye Lane, near the Old Mason House. Quiet down here. You know, I like it so much maybe I'll buy the place, do it up. With my reward like.'

'Fine. *Fine,*' said Manny. 'Just come get me. I'm at the village green. What say you we'll collect us up as many of those posters as we can before sun-up?' With that he clicked off the phone and heaved a huge sigh. In the far beaches of his brain, he knew the next few moments were a make-or-break time for him. And he thought he might just be able to pull it off, especially now he'd been warned about the meeting, the body. But when he stood up, ready to make a move, he felt a sudden wave of tiredness wash over him. The kind of tiredness which could only be assuaged by a good long lie-in or a soak in the shower or a few nips of whisky. He dropped back onto the bench and allowed his head to slip into his hands. He tried to massage the desire to drink out of his head. Tried to concentrate on something, anything else. Listened to the waves clattering up the beach. He was nearly asleep by the time the sleek limo purred to a halt in front of him.

33: Vultur gryphus

It was still full dark. Yesterday's storm had cleaned the atmosphere. Washed it, brushed it, toweled it dry. At least up here, high above the remaining clouds. Down there smelled rotten. Down there, the predator had already done its job, had left carrion littering the island, just waiting to be picked off. Down there, disease was acting ever more aggressively, laying a trail of destruction which Vultur gryphus would eventually feast on too. Vultur gryphus was circling. Waiting. Its time would come. Soon.

Every once in a while, it flapped its massive six-metre wingspan. They made a satisfying *whump* as they cut through the air. Because of the sound, the vulture was reassured it was the largest thing for miles around. Top of the food-chain certainly, now it sensed the predator, the panther, which it had followed here had passed. And though the vulture had no conception of where *here* was, its native cunning, its beady-eyed intelligence told it that it had nothing to fear here. That here, it was godly. Awesome, in the old traditional sense of the word.

The vulture felt majestic. Though it knew on the ground, hobbling around on those big flapping talons it had, it looked faintly comical, like it was playing dress-up as a drunken medieval king, complete with a black cloak and a roll-necked ruff of white feathers, up here, soaring, it was majestic. The most animated of its parts was its bald pate. It was constantly flicking back and forth, watching, waiting for the right moment. Tick, it looked south, to the lower reaches of land, to the pathetic plume of smoke which was emanating from a factory down that way; tock, it looked north, to another end of land, to a place which almost looked as though it was being eaten away at by the sea. As though the sea shared its scavenging nature. And the sea too looked bald. Unmasked somehow by the pale moonlight. Absently, Vultur gryphus wondered whether that too was for hygiene purposes. Vultur

308

gryphus wondered whether, like it, the sea was always sticking its head into all sorts of bloody crevices, all kinds of rotting wounds, and hence needed to be *wipe-clean.*

It circled closer to the centre of the island, above the monastery, and then back down to the coast again. Limm Island's one town lay spread below it like a patient on a hospital bed giving its final kicks of life. Limm was a terminal case. And the vulture circled, waiting to strike. Its hooked beak clacked in anticipation. It almost couldn't wait to get started on tearing into dead, dying flesh. To feel the rip as he pulled. To taste the spice of fear. It had arrived now, and like a fat lady, it was about to sing. As it circled once more, it let out a piercing cry which encompassed all the power, the longing, the rage it felt.

34: The Ghost and the Caravan

The only way Rich could extricate himself from the caravan's tight little toilet cubicle without shouldering the door off its hinges was to bow his head and kinda juggle his bulk sideways through the doorway. Watching him step back into the room like that, all crouched like a monkey, Kirstie wasn't entirely convinced he'd made the relevant steps up the evolutionary ladder as she had. He had a long, proboscis nose like a monkey, and his ultra hairiness didn't help either; he was rug-backed, carpet-fronted, and in his boxers, as he was, he didn't seem much to look at at all. But at least he had a good job with solid prospects, and he wasn't quick with his fists like some of the other men on the island. In fact, over the past few days, he'd showed himself to be a rather entrepreneurial kind of chap. He'd already shown her the takings from his make-shift roll-stall on the beach yesterday.

He sweated his way across the three paces back to the fold-out bed in which Kirstie was trying desperately to catch up on missed sleep and aimed a wet kiss for her forehead. It actually hit home somewhere between her exposed breast and her neck. Rich was drunk, stumbling, shambling, in a way that seemed exacerbated by the fact her watch read 05:46.

'What you lookin' at me like that for?'

'Just looking, that's all,' said Kirstie.

'You know it's me one day off, and if a man can't have a few bevvies on his day off, then what's the world coming to? Especially after yesterday...'

Kirstie cast a forlorn glance over to her handbag, slumped in the corner. The handbag that still contained the ten pregnancy tests they were supposed to *do together* today. She needed his support after the disasters and the lies of the past couple of days. But she could hardly blame him, could she? She'd not told him of her plans

310

for the day, and when she woke up and found him still drinking through the night, still half-cut, she knew today *wasn't* to be the day.

She'd woken up aching all over. Half of her was convinced her period was finally on the way, but when she finally located the main source of the pain – that shoulder again – she'd realised it had been false hope. And when she found herself actually wanting one of Rich's grease-laden bacon butties, she was ever more convinced the results of the tests could only be positive, or negative, depending on how one viewed the whole thing.

Rich cracked open another can of Fairhurst's Super Strength. Foam fizzed out of the top and he wedged his whole mouth against it and supped in the fashion of a victorious Grand Prix racer at the brew. 'Gaahhhh,' he said, delighted. 'You sure you won't join me in a few tipples?' He was putting on his pretend posh voice, and Kirstie rewarded him with a pretend laugh before shaking her head. 'Some people have to work tonight.'

'Aye, well, now I'm the boss... and now Devonish has popped his clogs... Don't go thinking you can... Fanny about, eh?'

Kirstie winced.

'And don't let any of the punters get an eyeful of your legs either,' he warned. 'Your pins are for my eyes only.' He gurned a grin in her general direction. Unconsciously, Kirstie pulled the duvet cover up over her breasts. He flopped down onto the fold-out bed next to her, breathing deeply, as though going to the toilet had been a real effort for him. Drinking whilst lying down wasn't the best idea however, and, when he lifted the can to his lips, much of the contents poured down the sides of his mouth and dribbled on the pillow. She couldn't help the disgusted look which crossed her face.

'Whassup with you babe?' he drawled. 'You're not still thinking I should be... How did you say it? More *considerate* about the whole thing? The man was a fuckin' perv, no two ways about it. You said so yourself. He won't be missed and it would be, ah, what do you call it... Hypocritical to say that you did miss him now. I said the same to them Abba twins. The Polish girls.'

Kirstie grimaced. She didn't like it when Rich talked to the other girls at the hotel, especially when she wasn't there. Not that the two Polish girls could seriously have been considered rivals; they were just too weird. Too much like those conjoined twins they featured every other week on some Channel Five freak show documentary. When they'd first arrived, she'd been really interested in them. Asked them all kinds of questions about what it was like in

311

Poland, what they ate there and what the word for 'boyfriend' might be. She'd taken great pains to convince them she wasn't like most of the people on the island, and especially not anything like the Castle's longest standing employee, old Muriel, who refused to speak to them and always said things like 'watch your pockets' whenever the girls entered the room, and worse when they left it again. Kirstie had determined the Poles at the Castle would become her exotic friends, only they'd simply not been interested. All they ever seemed interested in was their cigarettes and their little whispered conversations. She doubted they'd care either way whether Adrian Devonish had died or not as long as it didn't affect their fag-breaks.

And another thing. Rich's refusal to understand that the Abba Twins was actually a nickname which demeaned *him* rather than *them*, on account of the fact they were from Poland, not Sweden... Well, it made her think how stupid, how thick-headed he was. How *Limm.* And yesterday, he'd thrown his hat in the ring for Devonish's job... She was worried that even if the tests did show negative, *Rich* might turn out to be the stick-in-the-mud who kept her here, despite all his ambitious talk...

'I would have liked to speak to Mr. Combs yesterday, see what his plans for the Castle were,' continued Rich, scratching at his balls through his boxer shorts. 'I mean, now I'm... the person everyone will look up to... Well, I'd have liked to at least be able to let everyone know what was going on with the place.' He shifted position. 'But you saw what happened to him too. *Everyone* on this whole island's gone mental. I feel like I'm the only one sane.'

'You might be sane, but you're not sober,' said Kirstie slowly, trying not to look through the gap at the front of Rich's boxers.

'Aw come on babe, what was I supposed to do? You were asleep after all... Babe?' His hand reached for her under the duvet. She flinched away from him, thinking *stop it with the babe, why don't you? As if I need a reminder?*

'Come on. We've not done it in *days...* '

She screwed up her face.

Rich tutted and immediately she felt guilty. She knew she should have been grateful, that he'd stayed with her despite the fact she'd been so... so *infected* with the sulks for the past few days. 'I'm sorry,' she breathed. 'I just...'

312

He sucked at his can. More of the stinking liquid dribbled onto the pillow. 'Yeah, well, he said... Can't blame me for boozing, can you? Can't get at me for painting the town red if you're...'

'I'm sorry...'

'And here's Muggins letting you go off in *my* car. To Newcastle of all places.'

'I'm sorry... You're...' She felt her face flush. She was so lucky there was no damage to Rich's darling Gunner. So lucky he'd been lazy enough to believe her hastily concocted story about needing some driving practice.

'And?' prompted Rich. 'Are you going to tell me what you were doing in Newcastle?'

Kirstie hid her face. 'Not yet... Just bear with me, please.'

Rich sulked. 'That's what I feel like. A bloody bear. I have to do some much bearing-with, that I've turned out all Yogi.'

'It'll be okay... I promise...'

Rich's hairy fist closed around the now empty can. He started to crush it. 'It better had be,' he said. 'That's all I can say.'

Kirstie lowered her eyes.

'Is it the divorce, is that what this is? I *told* you about that. *She's* the one playing silly-beggars. If I had my way, it'd already be signed, sealed, delivered.'

'No, no. It's not that...'

'And you know what she's like. She's a fucking... Harridan. That's what she is. A *vulture*. Hell, once she finds out I'll be getting a promotion, she'll be after getting her talons into me for more money. She'll get that great hooked beak of hers and she'll try and tear her pound of flesh from me. She's...' He paused, struggling to contain his anger, spluttering for words. 'She'll try and finish me off. I bet Ramsey never has to put up with someone like her.'

He shot up from the bed, collected another can from the side and cracked it open, fuming. She could almost see the poisonous fumes coming off him. He drank angrily, hungrily, and then said, 'And once she finds out about us? Well, there'll be hell to pay. She'll be all like, *you must've got her knocked-up you stupid fool*, or *you've done the deed, now you pay the price* and... and all that.'

Kirstie held her breath. *Knocked-up.* He'd said it. In that stupid whiney voice he always reserved for when he was taking the piss out of his wife, but he'd still said it. It felt like testing the water, seeing what he really thought. *Knocked-up,* and the way he sneered around the words made her think...

Rich took a long, contemplative sup and then wiped a thick paw over his stubble. He'd shaved before work yesterday morning, so this doormat's growth on his chin was *twenty-four hours* or something. He truly was a hairy one (just like Devonish). Kirstie couldn't help but wonder whether she'd give birth to a spider monkey rather than a human baby...

'She's a cheeky get,' Rich concluded. 'Gotta watch for her.'

Kirstie bit the bullet. 'But what if, like... What if I did get pregnant? What would we do then?'

Rich finished another can, slammed it down onto the small table and climbed unsteadily to his feet. 'Fuckin' hot in here,' was all he said as he stumbled over to the buzzing fridge to grab another. Kirstie decided she'd better not question him any further.

As he bent down in front of the fridge, staring in as though confused by its contents, he let rip with a wheel-rocker of a fart. When the smell hit her, Kirstie almost gagged, but managed to keep the meagre contents of her stomach in check. Nevertheless, everything about the caravan was making her feel sick. Rich was right, it was too hot in here. In summer, it would become virtually unbearable, like climbing inside a tin can. As it was, they were squashed together like baked beans with too little tomato sauce, and the smells emanating from Rich were enough to strip wallpaper. Lucky then, that the caravan didn't have any wallpaper. Didn't have many decorations or home comforts to speak of at all. Just the fold-away bed with the damp-smelling duvet; she had provided a cover, stolen from her dead mum's linen cabinet after three occasions of sleeping 'bare-back' as it were. She had also provided the set of candles which littered the small table (also fold-away) and the white sheet which she'd fashioned into makeshift curtains. But the real problem about the one-room *slum* was the rust. Rust was everywhere, and its reddish-brown colour reminded her uncomfortably of the colouring of the dead Mummy Goose in the middle of the A24, and that was a day she wanted magically tipp-exed out of her mind for good.

'Let's go out,' she said. 'I know it's early, but let's go to the beach. Take your cans if you want...'

'What you want to go out for?'

'You said it yourself, it really is hot in here...'

'People'll see us on the beach, Kirst,' said Rich. 'This is an island of curtain-twitchers... And I'm not fit for driving us anywhere. And I'm *definitely* not letting you drive. You'd leave the bleedin' car over the other side of the causeway again... Hey, that Joe Friar fellow didn't try get it on with you, did he?' He narrowed his eyes. 'Some of the fuckers on this island are as bad as Devonish.'

'No. Joe was a... proper gentlemen. Took me straight home like I said. I was a bit embarrassed to have to explain to my dad, like, but everything worked out okay in the end, didn't it?'

'S'pose,' said Rich, still staring at his can of beer as though hypnotised by the dancing, clearly lagered-up tiger on the front. 'Good job you never attempted to get across that road in me Gunner though. If anything had happened to that car...'

She tried to feel for her knickers in the bed with her bare foot, touched something which felt cold and hard. Jerked away, certain it was bones; certain it would be the bones from the dead Mummy Goose come back to haunt her. Rich had once prepared a special Chinese banquet at the Castle – back in those heady days before they were an item, but it seemed written that they would be – and he'd showed her the frozen chicken's feet in the walk-in, nearly scaring her sick. They were a speciality, according to him, and *this* was how she imagined they would feel. Only these would be bones from a goose not a chicken. She hadn't told Rich anything about the goose, didn't want to, but the whole incident was still playing on her mind. She told herself she was bring stupid and reached down under the duvet and pulled out the cold, hard object, which turned out to be something everyday, something familiar. Keys. She dragged them out and jangled them. 'Lost something?'

Rich sat on the edge of the bed and frowned. 'They ain't mine,' he said.

'Well, they definitely aren't mine,' said Kirstie, regarding the key-ring with contempt. It was a metal tag with a Christian fish carved into it, like the ones on too-slow cars. She tried to think back to the old juffer who'd first hit the goose. Had he had one of those fishes on his car? Wouldn't have surprised her if he had. Kirstie saw that terrible image of the goose's neck billowing reedily in the wind, and then how it had snapped. That jolt as her wheels had crushed its brittle bones...

These weren't bones. These were keys. Get. A. Grip.

'They the keys from the Castle?' she asked.

Rich reached out to her, rather as a mountain gorilla would for technology way beyond its comprehension. His curled fingers brushed her cheek. 'They ain't from the Castle; the bearded wonder doesn't – *didn't* - trust *anyone* with them. No; there's been something I've been meaning to tell you.'

And suddenly she knew why he'd been so forgiving about the stolen car, why he'd not got jealous – not properly – about her rescue by the man from the brewery and his big truck – and why he'd not even pushed that hard for sex that morning. He was feeling guilty. He was seeing someone else on the side. Using *their* caravan to do the dirty deed. Before she'd given up on college, she'd been studying *Othello*. In that play, all it took was a goddamn handkerchief to convince the hero of his wife's guilt. Here, in the caravan, it was a set of keys. Rich was seeing someone else. She shot up from under the covers as though emerging from a treacherous sea. Rich gave her a questioning look.

'What you doing? I was...'

'You were *what*? Rich? What *was* you doing?' She was off the bed now, yanking up her knickers with one hand, frantically waving the set of keys around with the other.

'Gonna tell you about how, the other night, I noticed someone had jimmied the lock. And someone has eaten a coupla cans of me beans. And then there's them keys. They ain't mine, they ain't yours. Whose are they?'

Kirstie looked at him blankly. That answer wasn't the one she'd expected.

'Weird though. They never touched me beers,' continued Rich, shaking his head.

'What are you talking about?'

'Someone's been coming in here when we're not here.'

'Why would someone want to go and do that?'

Rich shrugged. 'Dunno. Didn't want to tell you 'cos I knew you'd go all mental like this.'

'How am I supposed to react?'

'Come on,' said Rich, grabbing her arm rather too forcefully. He dragged her to the door, opened it, and then showed her some marks which surrounded the lock. 'See?'

Kirstie somehow managed to wrestle the front door shut while still keeping her arm draped across her naked breasts. She pulled away from her boyfriend and glared at him. 'You mean to tell me *we slept* here while this axe-murderer could have been doing anything to us?'

'Calm down,' said Rich, shepherding her back over to the bed, then stretching over to the cupboard and pulling out a cloudy-

316

looking glass and pouring her a half of Fairhurst's from his can. 'It won't be some axe-murderer or owt like that. It'll likely be one of the lads from down the Ship. Cheeky get mind, whoever *is* coming in here uninvited. So what I'm gonna do is set up some traps in the long grass. That was why I needed to tell you about it, in case you stumbled over here one night and had your leg cut off...'

Kirstie drank from the cloudy glass, not caring about the germs. The beer was strong, almost mead-strength, and it immediately hit her between the eyebrows like an ice-axe. She massaged her brow. 'You're going to set traps?' she said, softly. 'That legal?'

'About as legal as you going off taking the Millennium Falcon on your little trip,' he said, slyly. 'But look where we are, for God's sake.' He swept his arms around to take in the view of Cawdor Head through the gap in the sheet-curtains. 'Nobody really gives a shit what happens on Limm... We're off the radar as far as the law's concerned. Here, we have our own version of justice...'

Kirstie wanted to laugh. Who was this hairy Urangutan sitting next to her, talking like he was some Wild West gunslinger?

Rich was getting into the flow now; he had that excited look in his eye (like a new dad.) 'Bear traps,' he said. 'Trip-wires. Glue-boards. I could electrify that fence, maybe.'

'Why don't you just put a sign up behind the bar at the Ship or in the Castle saying *Has anyone lost a set of keys with a Christian fish symbol on them*?'

'Oh aye. And then have people find out about us? You know what gossip's like round here. And if Denise gets a whiff of this, and I mean a whiff, then she'll have me for everything I own.'

'Oh. She not notice you coming out of your half of the house every other night coming up here? She not figured out you only sleep in your bed three times a week?'

'Denise and I keep ourselves to ourselves. We may share a house, but our paths do not fuckin' well cross,' snarled Rich. Kirstie took a sip of her beer to stop herself from saying anything else.

Rich changed the subject again. 'You know what I'd like to get my hands on? Land-mines. I could scatter loads of them round here, so only we knew where they were. And I know for a fact we'd never get blamed. Even if someone did end up getting their legs blown halfway off Cawdor Head, or into the monastery or something, then people'll just think it was another leftover from when they had that military factory place on here...'

Kirstie sighed, fearing now he was on a roll, he'd never stop. In a way, he was just like a little boy. And now she didn't want him like that, dunderheaded, drunken, *little boy* Rich. She wanted someone decisive, strong, supportive. She wanted someone, in fact, who was rather like the chef persona he projected in the kitchens at the Castle; the persona she'd first fallen for.

Since the dawn of the hard-man celebrity chef, Rich had treated cheffing as though it was manual labour, as though trying to make double-sure people didn't keep thinking of it as a woman's job. He was an inveterate pounder of meat; he smashed steaks into submission with his fists. He *processed* cheese onto functional, but uninspiring cheese boards; he manhandled salads; he strangled geese. No, he didn't strangle geese. But he was a sight to behold in the kitchen nonetheless. A caged animal raging, swearing, chest-beating his way through dinner service and then doing it all over again come breakfast. He was, she'd thought then, an attractive alpha male, the real King of the Castle, despite mad Adrian Devonish's claims to the contrary. That first kiss, pushed up against the frozen pasta dishes in the walk-in fridge had been frantic, breathless, sexy, despite his stubble. The way he brushed against her, reached long Urangutan arms around her under the guise of stretching for the red sauce had been wonderful. And the first sex, in the courtyard where he usually went to smoke had been quick, sweaty, memorable. But they'd not moved on from the caravan. They were still playing at this; beans and toast and bacon butties rather than Chinese banquets. Where were her Chinese banquets? He hadn't so much touched a spice in the caravan, let alone attempted any of the dishes from the Castle's over-priced menu.

'Hey,' said Rich. 'Looks like you're getting the taste for it. Fancy another bevvie?'

Kirstie looked down at her cloudy glass and realised he was right; she'd drunk the whole lot. Swallowed it all down like the 9% bitter medicine it was. 'Go on then,' she said, tilting her glass so Rich could pour in some more of the amber loopy-juice. 'Just a small one though. Can't have my new boss sacking me, can I?'

'Don't worry. I'll see you right,' grinned Rich, who was swaying alarmingly on the end of the bed. At some point in the last five minutes, he'd suddenly crossed over from drunk to very drunk. His eyes had gone all glazed-over and he had this moonish, buffoonish grin on his face. He'd be bloody singing to her in a minute. One of those old sea-shanties all the old fishermen sung down the Ship at closing time.

Suddenly, her mobile chirruped, alerting her to the fact she had a text message. She reached for her pink-covered mobile. 'It's dad,' she said, staring at the screen.

'Sending out the search parties, is he?'

She opened the message. It was the usual text-speak gobbledegook. She had to read it aloud just to try and make sense of it. What was it about dads and technology like mobiles? Why did they think they had to *get down with the kids* and write like that? Every one of her friends, even Emma, used ninety percent perfect grammar in their texts. *No* kids wrote like her dad did.

'R U COMIN OME 2NITE AFTA WRK OR STAYIN @ EMAZ? ID LIKE 2 HAVE A CH@ WIV U PLEZ. DAD XXXX'

'What's he writing it like that for?' said Rich, through a burp. 'He fuckin' thick in the head?'

Kirstie ignored him. She had the sinking feeling her dad must have finally spoken to Joe 'The Charnley Kid' Friar and found out a little more about his daughter's nocturnal habits. 'I'd better go,' she said, pushing the glass of beer away from her and reaching under the bed to find her top. 'My uniform's at home anyway. And if I go now, I can be there before...'

Rich started to get all-clingy, jokily stopping her from pulling her top properly over her head and running sweaty, monkey fingers over her breasts. 'Don't go yet, darrrrllllliiinnnn,' he drawled. 'We haven't fu... Chri... Christened the bed today and I'm getting horny.'

'You've got enough to be getting on with setting all your traps,' said Kirstie, resisting his advances. Somehow.

'I can do me traps anytime,' he said, wheeling his arms around as though it was the universal sign for *any time*. His arm connected with the half-empty can of Fairhurst's and sent it spiralling off onto the linoleum floor, where its contents drained away like blood. 'Fuck,' he said, as they both got up at the same time to get the cloth, banging their heads together. 'No, you siddown, I'll clean it.'

He stumbled over to the sink and then tripped over her handbag in the corner. 'Fuck!' he said again, this time more loudly as he came crashing down like a wounded buffalo right into the toilet door. When he picked himself up again, he was standing right in the middle of a pile of pregnancy tests which had leaped out of the

319

handbag like lemmings. He kicked one of them away, but then looked more closely. It seemed to take him a while to get his eyes to focus. Then came his gasp of recognition, or rather a mewl, like that of a young kitten. He sunk back down to his knees and for a moment, hung his head.

Then he asked, 'Is there something you should have told *me*?'

Kirstie stared at him unhappily.

He picked up one of the tests, started waving it. 'Was this what you were in the chemists for? Christ...' For a moment, it seemed as though he was reading the label, but then she saw he wasn't. He was simply muttering the word 'no', to himself over and over again.

'I haven't done the tests yet,' she said quietly. 'I was waiting for the right moment.'

'The right moment to trap me,' he groaned. 'The right moment to drag me back down to earth... Kirst, I've never been as happy as I was yesterday... On the beach. And now this. You're trying to...'

'I wanted us to do the tests together.'

'Women wanting a piece of me from every side. Vultures. Every single last one of you.'

Kirst opened her mouth to speak. Found the words would not come. Quietly she slipped on the rest of her clothes. Rich made no move to stop her, even when she swung open the caravan's creaky door. Even as she gathered the rest of the pregnancy tests together and stuck them back in her bag. Even as she pulled the door closed behind her and entered the cold full dark of a new morning on Limm. She walked four, five paces and then stopped. Something was rustling the long grass just in front of the next caravan, close to the big sign which read LIMM HOLIDAY PARK. FUN FOR ALL THE FAMILY. CARAVAN'S FOR HIRE PER WEEK OR PER NIGHT. She paused, ready to retrace her steps, thinking of the black shadowy thing she'd seen on the causeway. Thinking it was her punishment here, finally.

If so, she didn't want to turn her back on it. Didn't want the first she knew of its approach to be the claws tearing down her back. Didn't want to feel its hot, raggedy breath on the back of her neck. She peered into the long grass. Tried to pick out eyes. Cat's eyes glowed in the dark didn't they? She looked harder. Sniffed too. Sniffed at the post-storm breeze.

The *something* in the long grass rustled some more and then finally, as Kirst thought she could bear it no more, the something emerged. And she saw it was a seagull. A fat seagull. It cocked its head and looked at her, then started absently running its beak through its feathers. Kirstie felt a wave of relief coursing through her. She made to step around the bird, but when she did, it hissed. She hadn't been aware that birds could hiss, but this one clearly could. It hissed again and then it *ka-kaaaed,* stepped menacingly forward. Like it was a guard dog, trained to stop her from leaving. She shivered. Tried to step around it the other way. Again with the hissing, the *ka-kaaa*ing.

This was a particularly *avian* form of revenge. For the goose what got cooked. Because it was decidedly *big,* this seagull. Decidedly arrogant. Wasn't scared of her at all. And she knew that some of the gulls on Limm, fed-up by ice-cream and hot dogs, and the crab chowder served from The Crab's Claws in summer, had become sort of mutant breeds, but this one was special. Every time it cocked its head and looked at her it was as though it was saying, *oh yeah, and what you gonna do about it?*

Despite everything, she wanted Rich. She wanted him to save the day, to throw open the caravan door, launch a can of Fairhurst's at the bird's head and then carry her back inside to safety. But he was probably already passed out drunk now; snoring, scratching at his balls with a great wide grin on his face, thinking about how he was now the new King of the Castle.

The bird edged forward. Kirstie pressed herself back against the caravan. She started to drum her fingers on the metal, hoping it would wake Rich. Hoping it would Morse Code out her distress to him. Hoping he wouldn't think it was just the storm starting up again. It seagull hissed once more and then it *ka-kaaaed,* stepped menacingly forward.

'Shoo,' she whispered. 'Go away…' She plunged her hand into her bag, hoping there was some kind of snack inside which she could use to distract it. A choccy bar, some chewing gum… Hell, judging from the size of the thing it was probably omnivorous. She held out one of the tests as though it was a tasty treat. 'Here boy,' she said, waggling it, 'have a look at this.' She feigned throwing it off over the bird's head a couple times, checking its response. Both times it jerked, as though following the imaginary throws. It was going to *work.*

This time she threw. The throw was pathetic. The pregnancy test almost hit the bird square on the beak. It flopped into the grass at its feet and the gull *ka-kaaaed* at it. And then ignored it.

'Go away,' she pleaded. 'Leave me alone!'

And suddenly the gull stopped. Flapped its wings. Gave a far less confident-sounding hiss. It flapped again. And then, without warning, flew away. As it went, it left behind a sickly white trail of poo, and, of course, the pregnancy test. Kirstie was just about to heave a sigh of relief when she heard something else. Something far more worrying. She heard the crash of something on top of the caravan. Something heavy. She heard buckling metal. The crack of glass. She heard the *whump* of wings much larger than those of the seagull.

Then the caravan door opened. Rich poked his head out, rubbing his eyes. 'What the hell's going on out here?' he said. 'What the...'

He wasn't allowed to finish his sentence. A black shadow seemed to slide off the roof and envelop him. The black shadow tarred and feathered him in one fell swoop. And the movement was so swift, Kirst couldn't really get a handle on what she was seeing. She saw talons. A hooked beak. A ruffle of white feathers. She saw beady, hungry eyes. She saw a bald head. She saw something which was, with wings spread, bigger than the damned caravan.

Rich screamed once before his throat was torn out. Kirstie did not scream at all. She found herself stumbling backwards, away from the beady-eyed thing. She found herself stumbling, falling, half-running and then stumbling, falling all over again. She heard the *criiiiccckkk* of flesh being stretched, of bones being broken. She heard a little scuffle as Rich kicked his last. But she knew he was dead, knew she was yet another statistic, another Limm Island one parent family, before she'd even crashed through the fence. She might have been upset, but mostly, mostly, she wanted to protect herself and the new life which she was now nearly a hundred percent sure was growing inside her. Later, much, much later, she'd maybe tell the baby that its daddy had been killed trying to protect them, diverting the beady-eyed thing's attention for a few crucial moments. In her heart of hearts, she knew that wasn't true. But from her own bitter experience, she knew that sometimes a lie was better than the truth. A white lie to protect from the black badness. It would do. It would have to do.

35: White-Dark

Over the past twenty-four hours Ely Rhodes had been chalking up sins as quickly as the poor student, more concerned with playing Xbox than learning the do's and don'ts of biking, collected fails on the cycling proficiency test. He'd played Russian Roulette with the Cardinal Vices and had come up trumps, bullet-wise on virtually every single one. And the *tricksy* thing was, he didn't really know what he felt about it.

He'd been wrathful to leave his mother there, in the house, stewing in her own juices. He'd been gluttonous too, waffling down nearly all the food in the cupboards at the Holiday Park caravan so that it couldn't have been more obvious he'd been squatting in there, waiting for his moment. A moment which should have come sooner, much sooner, of course, but he'd been slothful, and so had out-stayed his welcome, so that he was nearly caught when the two people – Rich from the Castle he thought it was, and some girl – had staggered up to the caravan yesterday evening. He'd had to climb out the window sharpish while they fumbled for the door. But still, they'd have seen the marks from his Swiss Army knife around the door when he'd pried his way inside.

The next of the dominos to topple had been pride. He'd been too proud to walk after that beast on his two *God be praised* feet. And when he'd seen the mountain bike outside the Ship *not even chained up,* he'd been envious. So he'd taken it for himself, to be his steed. It was the first thing he'd stolen in his life and he swore it wasn't *really* stealing, because once this was all over he'd return it. But he hadn't exactly gone into the Ship, prayed silence, identified the bike's owner, and then settled a hire fee. He'd simply taken it. Because it was the kind of bike he'd always wanted. Because he was twenty-one years old and for most of his life it had been all about the things he *couldn't have,* the things he was sacrificing, just to prove he was a worthy, Holy person.

323

And now, he was feeling lustful. He lusted for this all to be over and, when he looked on the body of the dead panther, he could almost believe it was. His joy at this discovery was only tempered by Solomon's words. Words which remained cobwebby thick around him, despite the draught of the intervening years: 'The Darkness shall come, and it shall come in multitudinous guises. It shall come large, but with the aspect of a shadow, stalking, hunting. It shall come small, in germ and disease, spreading its wickedness so that the Unholy should become infected. Finally, it shall come as a winged beast, soaring, ready to pick off townspeople as prey.' Yoghurt would always remember how Solomon had trilled the word 'winged', emphasising the second syllable, turning it into an antique word. *Wing-ed.* Somehow, it had made the word more terrifying to the young Ely. Like The Darkness was as old as language. Older.

There'd always been debate about the meaning of some of Solomon's more obscure preachings. Yoghurt's mother, for example, believed that it automatically meant all animals were the agents of the Unholiness, but Trevor Knox had disagreed. Perhaps it was his time in the National Trust which had shaped his opinion, but Trev had subscribed to the theory that the influx of animals, as suggested by Solomon's apocryphal speechifying, was due to the island being turned into a type of Noah's Ark. Yoghurt wasn't sure which of them he believed. What mattered was *one down, two to go.*

He'd found the body after a long cycle across much uneven terrain (praise be, then, for the mountain bike.) He'd been following some new, fresh-looking prints he'd picked up close to the River Drey, tracking them as they cut through into the thicker woods, where at least the overhanging branches would have offered the panther some protection from yesterday afternoon's tempest. He'd lost the trail somewhere a couple miles back and had been simply trusting to instinct since. And it seemed instinct had served him well. Instinct *and* a good, Castle-breakfast-sized portion of luck too. Because he'd stopped here, in a small clearing, only because he'd seen the signs of a recently doused fire. Like Trevor Knox had taught him, he'd stirred the ashes, discovered the fire had only just been doused. And then he'd had a look around just to see who else was stalking the woods, looking for The Darkness, presuming it would be some of the farmers, or even... He even dared hope that his luck was so well and truly in that Trevor Knox was close, perhaps performing his morning ablutions in the bushes somewhere, before setting out on the hunt again. He'd shouted for his friend, but had

324

received no answer from the gnarled old trees and the thick, rain-clogged leaves.

He'd been about to retrieve his bike from where it was propped up against the largest of the trees, a real old one with a trunk whose girth had to be wider than tractor wheels, when he'd caught a whiff of something on the breeze. He'd taken the light from the front of the bike and gone to investigate further. Because something about the smell most definitely did not smell right. Somehow, the beam from the bike-light only served to make things in the clearing grow ever more spooky. It gave just enough light for the shadows to come out to play, but not enough to explain away what those shadows actually were. Yoghurt's over-wrought, over-tired brain came up with all kinds of explanations. He kept seeing, or thinking he was seeing, a great shadowy beast lurking, ready to pounce. But then he'd stumbled across the body. Literally stumbled across it. It seemed to have fallen out of one of the trees and was buckled into a rather unlikely angle, its neck and one of its legs broken.

Excited, he hunkered down next to the body and studied it. The Darkness had definitely come large with this one. Even in death, it looked heavy. Brutal. He performed rough guesstimations in his head. Had to be three metres long, not including the tail. Which was larger, much larger, than any panther he'd ever read about. Its head seemed unnaturally big. Weighty. He reached out a hand, gingerly, and touched it. Thought for a moment that he felt a pulse. Jerked his hand back as though he'd been electrocuted. Tried again, and this time felt nothing. He leaned in closer, picking up more and more of that *off* stink. He held the light over it now, tracing it over the beast's body. Now he could see better, he decided it wasn't the fall from the tree which had killed it. No, the beast looked as though it had been gravely ill. Much of its fur had molted. Its long tongue flopped out of its mouth, sluggish and yellow.

He thought about taking a souvenir. Something which would prove to the townspeople, beyond a reasonable doubt, what had been stalking them. Thought about cutting off a huge paw with his Swiss Army knife. But then thought better of it. He found his camera in the ruck-sack and rattled off a few photographs instead. Then he clambered aboard the bike again and headed back to the town. Already, a thick morning mist was starting to descend. Yoghurt didn't want to be trapped out here if one of Limm's famous Hoar's Blankets occurred. Because then he'd never find his way back. And

325

even though one of the beasts was dead, the other was surely here now, the wing-ed one.

He pedalled furiously. Even with the light re-affixed to the handlebars, visibility was becoming very poor. Icy air hung like a blanket over everything. Fog curled around the branches of the trees and choked the life out of the plants. Steam seemed to wrench at the pedals on his bike and grow thick around his wheels. It clagged the air so that breathing became a luxury rather than a right. It got like this in the mornings on Limm sometimes, after storms, when new, colder air passed over warmer water. The sailor's had christened the phenomenon, and, just as with most of their sayings, it had originated in the blue, in the Unholy. The gruelly mist had first been named for the dense, scratchy blankets prevalent in the whore houses which populated the north east coast, blankets which were laced with crabs and lice. Going out in an itchy Whore's Blanket was as foolish as going *down there* with a whore, without protection. Going out in a Whore's Blanket was only for fools or landlubbers. Over the years, the name had changed, had become a *Hoar's* Blanket so as to become more acceptable for the less sea-minded of the Limm population. There were some who now claimed Hoar's Blanket stemmed from the Old English *haw,* as in *haw*thorn, as in ancient. Certainly that was what Yoghurt's mother had claimed. But Trevor Knox had told him the real truth.

He wished Trevor was with him now, perhaps waiting at the bottom of this latest slope in his land rover, ready to bip him off back into town. Safely ensconced in the passenger seat of Trev's landie, he'd have quite happily listened to Trev telling him exactly how Hoar's Blankets came to be formed, *geographically,* rather than feeling it practically, as it iced his cheeks, bit at his hands on the handlebars. He couldn't be sure which direction he was travelling in. All he knew was that he was descending into the deepest, most haunted part of the fog. Which felt right because surely it was thickest over water, so, if he kept going, he'd eventually reach the sea, and then he'd be able to follow the shore round until he got his bearings. But it was tough going. Now the whiteness was so thick, so noisy, he couldn't see branches as they speared out of the nothingness, reached for his eyes. He couldn't see the tree stumps on the ground, lying in wait for him, ready to send him over the handlebars and onto the floor. And when he heard, or thought he heard, the screech of something big, something hungry from up above, it was all he could do not to simply fly off into a panic.

Somewhere close, he thought he heard the mighty flapping of huge wings. *Whump,* went the sound. *Whump.* It sounded like the door to a tomb being slammed shut, like the end of things. Yoghurt felt his hair uncurling itself, standing on end; something even the best hair-straighteners couldn't have achieved. He found his eyes freezing wide open. He almost came off the bike when he reached the foot of the slope, as he felt the front tyre catching in mud, stopping, mid-cycle. The back of the bike lurched out, sending himself into a terrible tail-spin, but somehow, he managed to right himself. He didn't allow himself pause, even though the backs of his legs were starting to shudder and shake.

He entered a climb now, and his legs burned hotter. His breath caught in his throat. His fingers felt like they'd splinter away at any moment. Some deep, dark part of him screamed at him to just give this up. Stop pedalling. Stop changing gear. Just let himself fall. Lie on the ground and let whatever was up there – the wing-ed creature – come for him. But, as he drove onwards, upwards, a new pain came to him. The pain from where his mother had scarred him with the Rope. He felt it and it energised him. He gritted his teeth, forced himself to plunge deeper into the dense, wet fog. It slicked his hair, dripped off his nose and then pooled around his crotch, but he pushed on.

He reached the crest of the hill. His heart plunged when he realised he still couldn't see where he was, but from somewhere close, he heard the call of a gull. *Ka-kaaa.* And his heart leaped back up again, as though it was attached to a bungee rope. The gull had to mean he was approaching the shore-line. He kept cycling. Head down now, racer-style. And it got so he felt as though he was pedalling through the sky, that there was nothing under him but cloud. It was a terrifying, freeing feeling. For a moment, he was sure he'd been lured out, over the edge of the cliff, that at the moment, and with a sickening pull, he was going to feel gravity. That he'd crash to his doom amongst the soupy water, head-cracked in by one of the jagged rocks jutting out from the sea. But then he felt the surface change. He felt the jarring bumps as he cycled onto loose shingle. As he made the beach.

Now, as well as discovering the full range of the sins he was chalking up, Yoghurt Rhodes understood that at the same time, he was unearthing virtues in himself. Virtues he'd never known he possessed. Like bravery, like determination. Like commitment. He felt a wave of pleasure washing through him. For a couple beats, all he wanted to do was throw himself off the bike and into the sea. Let it cleanse him. But he knew he couldn't rest at all now, because now, one of the most misinterpreted of all Solomon's passages was coming true.

'When the day shall become white-dark and the sun shall be put out, then, thou shall know that The Darkness is so close thou shalt hear it saltily banging upon the door.'

'But we shall not let it in,' whispered Yoghurt. 'We. Shall. Not.'

And he pedalled on. Though the mist was still thick, and the going across the shingle was not good, he pedalled on. Into the white-dark he pedalled on. Head-down he pedalled on. The bike's speedo said he'd covered five miles since the densest part of the southern woods now, so he had to be back, close to the town now.

In fact, he was past the town. When Yoghurt finally realised where he was, it was only because he cycled headlong into the big, lumpen body of one of the Limm farmers. 'Dirty' Den Fletcher, he believed the man was called. Fletcher manhandled Yoghurt's twitching handlebars as though he was wrestling a bull, and brought him to a halt, with a breathy, 'whoah there soldier, where do you think you're going?' Yoghurt, still attempting to pedal, answered only with a gasp.

'Here,' said the farmer-type, shouting over his shoulder, 'Sauce, mate, there's someone here trying to get through the blockade.'

Yoghurt, who was now, finally, no longer pedalling, heard the crunch of boots across shingle. Saw the shadow of a man approach. Finally picked out the face of Andy Worcester.

'Well I never,' said Worcester, narrowing his eyes, 'if it isn't our old village idiot, Yoghurt Rhodes. Where do you think you're going?'

Yoghurt wiped cold sweat off his brow with the sleeve of his coat. 'I'm just...'

Worcester smiled. Two of his teeth were coal-black so it looked as though most of the top-front row of his teeth were missing. 'It don't matter where you're going, or where you *thought* you were going, lad. What matters is where you're going now. You're going back to the town, all right?'

Yoghurt nodded, uneasily.

'There's a good lad. See, we've got a road-block here, so as to keep those beasts on the other side of the causeway from coming over once the tide goes out.'

For a moment, Yoghurt thought Worcester was talking about the panther and the wing-ed beast. He was about to tell him that he was too late, that the beasts were already here, already hungry. That road-blocks wouldn't do any good now that the white-dark was here. But Worcester must had misread the fear on his face for incomprehension.

'You not seen the news, lad? Fucking media are here. Waiting like vultures. Soon as the tide's out they'll be wanting over. Only, we don't want that, do we? Why, only a couple of hours ago, Len Chipchase caught two of them trying to row over in a boat. Crabbie's got 'em now in his boat taxi hut.' He laughed, a deep grumble. His friend, Fletcher joined in.

'Heave-ho,' said Fletch, finally. 'How do you like them apples?'

Yoghurt only gulped. The pair of them seemed half-crazy. Now he'd studied them a moment, he saw both of them were flicking and swatting at the mist every few seconds as though it contained hundreds, thousands of tiny flies, or stinging insects.

'You know the score,' said Worcester, suddenly stopping laughing, suddenly fixing Yoghurt with piercing eyes. 'This is Limm Island. We sort out our own problems here. We don't need no outsiders. Now scarper. Before Crabbie or Chipchase thinks you're another they can add to their prisoners of war.'

Yoghurt waited while Fletch let go of his handlebars and then immediately set off. He had to pick a path through a veritable elephant's graveyard of farm machinery before he made it onto the coastal road. There, packed closely together, were about the island's whole population of tumbledown tractors, crumbling combine harvesters, rusted old cars, a woebegone caravan and even what looked like an old, old tank.

36: The Seahorse

E ven though Manny Combs and Dave Chester had gone a good job of removing some of them, the signs advertising the meeting were still everywhere about town. Sally Martin would have been delighted to see they hadn't used the same sign-writer as they had for the TALENT-STRAVAGANZA!!!!!! Or if they had, they'd at least told him/ her to go easy on the exclamation marks. Indeed, there seemed a sense of weary resignation to the posters. Instead of the *roll up, roll up* circus-style language of the talent show ads, these ones had more a *come on down if you feel you have to* resignation to them. They promised a 'full and frank debate regarding the going's-on on Limm.' They promised 'everyone who feels the need to speak will be listened to,' and 'all (sensible) queries considered.' The word 'answers' was nowhere to be seen.

Nor did *The Tide Piper* seem to have anything by way of actual, verified news. *The Tide Piper* had been delivered very every that morning, apparently by a paperboy who watched too much American TV and thought it was okay to simply launch the paper over the front wall *in the general direction* of the front door rather than posting it through the letterbox. Sally generally shunned it, fearing the meaningless stories and the boringly functional photography would steal her youthful soul, turn her old and small-town overnight. But she read it this week, hoping to uncover even the smallest snippet of a story which might go to some way to explaining what she'd seen in Old Man Poole's jungle and the events which had taken place down at Coverley Bottoms on Sunday. Taken together the two horrible happenings made her feel ship-wrecked. That there could have been a raging inferno, an outbreak of deadly disease, a mass murder since then, and nobody had thought to come round and let them know; that it had to fall to *The Tide Piper*, nearly a full day after the fact, to tell her something else had

330

happened, that a body had been discovered on the beach during the storm, made her feel overwhelmingly, Old Man Poole lonely.

Sally read the paper cover to cover, read even Mike Ford's irritable opinion columns searching for a definitive explanation of what had happened, but it seemed the whole story was confused by the clamour of voices, many of which seemed to hold opposing views as to what they'd witnessed. The lead story, under the headline 'Alas Poor Copey; Tragedy at the Talent Show' was a purple prose piece full of references to the drama of the injured man crawling right into the middle of the crowd. Only on page four was there any kind of attempt to look into the reasons why it had happened, and even then, it was a lot of guff about industrial accidents. Ford kept quoting from a key source at the Bungalow, a key source who sounded a lot like the doctor, Ray Shaw. Ray Shaw, apparently, had a lot to say about working with agricultural machinery when under the influence of alcohol. Another piece seemed to claim the man's injuries may, in fact, have been as a result of a fight which had broken out in the crowd (again as a direct result of drinking alcohol.)

Then, on page eight, a reprint of the posters which were all about town; the open invitation to the town meeting. Apparently, it was to be held at the Seahorse. The advert advised people to 'get here early, to avoid disappointment.' Getting there at all presented more of a problem for Sally. When she'd first indicated a desire to go to the meeting, Rob had been far from keen on the idea. Since Sam Bibby had been round, it seemed her hubbie barely wanted to let her out of his sight. Thus he'd set up his prized typewriter on the fold-away table in the window alcove in the front room, and set her up on the sofa under a billion-tog duvet. Apparently, he wanted her to sweat out her madness, like it was a fever.

'But I'm not ill. I'm not bloody contagious,' she said, after the rattle of his fingers across the typewriter became too much to take. 'I think we should go to this meeting. There's more to this than the *Piper* is letting on. I mean, why would they call a town meeting just because of an industrial accident? And what about this new body on the beach? They found him washed up in a car, you know?'

For a moment, she thought Rob hadn't heard her. He continued to slump over the typewriter, picking out the keys in his plodding, single-finger style. Then, he pressed the carriage return – *ding!* – and turned to face her, his bald head catching the light which speared through the window. It looked especially shiny that

331

morning, as though he'd buffed it up with Brasso. His expression was one of muted impatience. 'Did you say something?'

'We should go up to the meeting.'

Rob seemed to consider this a moment. He picked up a stack of papers, tapped the top as though he was about to perform a magic trick, as though he was tapping them with a wand, but in the end, the only magic which interested him was clumping the papers against the table so they'd have a uniform straight edges. The dishwater dullness of this gesture seemed to sum Rob up; the hoped for magic never arrived, no matter if he did look mysterious as a magician in some lights. His tricks were always ones of monotony, or of neatness. Never of wonder.

'I don't think our presence there will be required.'

Sally wanted to explode. All over his bloody neat papers. 'Why not? Aren't you interested to find out what's going on? Does it not pique your professional curiosity? I mean, what if there's some great story in there? And the storm's over now anyway. We *are* allowed to set foot out of the house, you know.'

'I've got a story already. I've already written most of it. I'm re-drafting now. The one the French are interested in, remember?'

'But you might get ideas for *another* screenplay, and besides, I'm sick of lying in this room.' 'I'll make you another Cup-a-Soup then. Cheer you up a bit.'

'I can't think of anything more depressing than a cup of soup. I want to get out of here…'

'You sound just about as moany as that cat of yours,' sighed Rob. 'Here I am making all these sacrifices. Working down here, bringing you hot drinks, keeping the fire on despite the fact I'm *roasting* hot. Cutting your toast into little triangles. All these sacrifices and all you can do is moan.'

'I'll get out of your hair then. Go up to this meeting. Leave you to your precious work.'

Rob slammed his hand down on the table, scattering his neat piles of papers. 'You're not going anywhere. Don't you understand? You're *ill*..'

Sally knew she couldn't win. Closed her eyes and pretended to be asleep. Even when People came in and climbed under the duvet with her and lying across her feet, she didn't flinch. And eventually when sleep did wash over her, she dreamed of fingers. Pointing, accusing fingers. She should have been getting to the bottom of this mess.

As she woke, cricked into an unnatural position on the sofa, her body rolled into a foetal comma, a punctuation mark which separated her from People who was relaxing across the whole cushion he'd commandeered for himself, she could hear Rob talking urgently on the phone. And in that moment before she could properly brush away the cobwebs of sleep, she thought his voice was echoing from that twin-town dreamland she'd crossed over from.

'There are a number of different universes which exist at the same time,' he was saying. '*Multiverses,* they're called. And the film's about the liminal areas which exist when these multiverses overlap... Let me ask you a question; why do babies always cry?'

Sally creaked open one eye. Snapped back into the singular universe which was her mundane front room. She heard the tinny, scurrying sound of a voice on the other end of the line. She could imagine that other voice answering Rob's question, full of exasperation: *Babies cry because they are hungry... tired... too hot... too cold. Bored. Want attention. Only a man would seriously write something which explored why bloody babies cry...*

The agent's dampening tactics, if that was what they were, didn't work. Rob again: 'What if they are crying because they are somehow attuned to some other level of consciousness. What if they can see across the multiverses? What if they are crying because they see ghosts...? *Non,* Madame Pelettier. Not like in *The Sixth Sense...* I mean something more profound. What if we are all born with this fully-developed kind of understanding of the world... and the worlds, plural? What if, once we start to acquire language and get involved in all the rubbish like school and nursery and toys and then college and work and bosses and pensions we lose the ability to see across the multiverses? And what if there is something, some valve or something, which can be released and... Yes, I know you said you didn't have time, but... But do you not see how exciting that would be? Cracking through the normal dimensions, reaching a new understanding? Madame Pelettier? *Damn it.*'

'Bad line?' asked Sally. She knew how testy he could be when people didn't recognise his *talent.* Both of them were well-versed in what she liked to think of as *the aftermath of rejection.*

'Oh, hello. I didn't realise you were awake...'

'I was just napping. People woke me up.'

'Do you want another brew?'

She shook her head.

333

'No, no, I didn't think you would.' He went back to the typewriter. She watched him. Saw the anger, the disappointment, the complete and utter incomprehension, all of it encapsulated in his one finger, his ring-finger, which hovered over the keyboard. Would he take the plunge back in?

Evidently not. He pushed back his chair, let it crack back against the wall. He stood up, ran his hand over his bald dome. Sighed extravagantly. Stretched. Then said, 'You're right, you know. We should get out of here for a bit. Get a bit of fresh air. Looks a bit misty out, but the storm's passed now.'

Even People looked a little shocked.

Their truce was uneasy, but it was a truce. Rob didn't do his usual *dit-de-dit*-ing as she took a long, lukewarm shower; there was no pacing up and down the upstairs hallway, no drumming fingers on the banister, no shouts of 'aren't you done yet, you're wasting water?' She left the bathroom door open so he could wander in if he wanted, and it had been a while since she'd done that. In the end, he slipped inside and skulked around by the sink, shrouded in steam. For a while, he just stood there, drawing on the fogged-up mirror, or writing perhaps. But eventually he talked. And she did too. They kept things *level*. And she could almost remember why she'd married Rob in the first place when he offered to go downstairs and leave some food out for the cat.

People had come back Monday morning after being out all weekend, and despite trying to see her in the same light as she always had, chiding her with a 'well, well, well, where have you been, you dirty stop-out?' as soon as she'd loped into the front room, Sally still felt wary of her former darling. Especially when, on Monday morning, Rob had yelled out his customary complaint about People leaving one of her *petit cadeaux* for him in the shower, and she'd been absolutely *sure* it was going to be a finger (it wasn't; just a barely-old-enough-to-be-out-on-its-own field mouse.) This hadn't stopped People cuddling up to her, demanding head-rubs, at every available opportunity, of course, but still, it was as though everybody in the damn house was treading on egg-shells. Still she was glad that Rob had volunteered, for once, to feed her. Even though she could hear he was struggling with the task. As soon as she shut off the shower, she heard him downstairs, opening and closing cupboards, seeking out the cat food. *Under the sink,* she wanted to shout down to him, *where it's always been.* She didn't.

334

Arguments could break out in the most random places; since they'd lived on Limm, they'd rowed about just about every nook and cranny in the house. She didn't want to try the cupboard under the sink out for size. There were all kinds of plumbing things down there, pipes, water-tanks and the like, and *under the sink* might well have been a gusher.

She moved quickly, grabbing a towel and slipping into her slippers. Padding across the hallway into the bedroom. Already her teeth were chattering. Already her arms were loaded with goose-bumps. She rigorously toweled herself dry, trying to massage some warmth back into her body. Whacked on the hair-dryer, but not for too long, just in case Rob *did* start with the dit-de-dits. Opted for a functional pony-tail so it could dry out over the course of the afternoon. She picked out her good jeans and slipped them on, her toes coming out the other end of the denim almost blue it was that cold. Found some thick socks, rolled them on. Then, to finish, she dug out a warm roll-neck jumper from the back of the cupboard. Used to be Rob's but she'd ended up borrowing it so much it had eventually become hers. The way she got ready now bore absolutely no relation to the way she used to. It wasn't even a *step*-child, or a cousin three-times-removed to how she used to put herself together, but, as she stepped down to the kitchen, she realised there was a lot less of herself *to* put together now.

Still, Rob seemed pleased to see her when she walked into the kitchen. 'Nice jumper,' he said.

And she said: 'Thanks for feeding the cat.'

They were both surprised by how thick the fog actually was when they stepped outside. Sally muttered something about People not being able to find any more little presents in this kind of weather, and Rob muttered something about having *told her* that staying off work this past couple of days was the right idea. And she supposed it was, though it left her feeling isolated. Usually, she could have counted on the fourth-year girls' dancing troup to fill her in on every level of gossip which was spreading around the island like muck.

They'd decided to walk, and, almost as soon as they reached the coastal road, they realised what a good idea that had been because, almost as far as they could see, which admittedly wasn't far, given the cotton-wool quality of the air, the traffic was backed up on both sides of the road. Which was understandable in *one way,* in the direction of the town proper, but the other? Well, that took some explaining. What also took some explaining was the fact that all the traffic going into town was cars, four wheel drives, land rovers, and all the vehicles heading *out* of town, in the direction of the causeway, were farm vehicles. Big rusting heaps of junk which creaked and moaned like dinosaurs.

'Maybe there's some kind of farmer's market we've not heard about,' said Rob.

A big tractor coughed past them, only adding to the fug which surrounded them, and Sally tugged herself deeper into the folds of her coat. 'Maybe the farmers are having their own meeting.'

'Maybe something's really gone down here,' said Rob, finally sounding excited.

'Maybe you can write about it,' smiled Sally, hoping that he would. Hoping he'd write so much about it he'd get the whole damned island out of his system. Hoping he'd unblock himself well enough to finally admit, that they were better off, had always been better off, in cities, where a procession of farm vehicles like this would have been treated with the blasé dismissal it really deserved. Not that there was much island to see. No, it seemed to have become remarkably drawn in on itself. As though it had made a ball out of itself due to the mist. She couldn't see Pate Hill or the monastery.

Rob gripped her arm. 'Sal? What's wrong? I was asking you a question. You were miles away.'

I wish...

'Nothing,' she said. 'Just thinking, that's all.'

Rob seemed satisfied with this answer. Only a writer who spent half of his life inside his own head could have been satisfied with such a measly bite-size chunk of an answer. But then, that was Rob. They walked on in a silence which only he could have described as companiable. For Sally, it was as though the fog had a voice all of its own and was shouting in her ear, filling up the space between them with its white noise. The fog made it so it still seemed like the middle of the night. They passed a row of old fishermen's houses and Sally thought they looked as though they were tinted with sepia. They passed the Castle and even its eyesore of an extension seemed old. As they walked onto the main street, more and more people joined the footpath. She waved at a couple girls from the second year. Lowered her head as she walked past Carl-Rhys Hamilton who was perched on a wall outside the Ship, looking rather confused at the whole world. When they walked past The Crab's Claws, an old man came out the door, almost walked straight

336

into them, and in that instant where she gasped, readjusted her footing, and walked round him, she could have sworn she recognised him. She asked Rob.

He smiled. 'That's your Old Man Poole. Here, have a look.' They paused for a moment, pretended to take a rest on the bench at the village green. Watched as Poole walked past. *Walked* past. He didn't hobble or creak past. He walked past, looked surprisingly sprightly. He had a walking stick but didn't seem to be relying on it at all. Merely seemed to use it through habit. Neither of them let on to him, and he didn't let on to them. They let him get a good few yards up the road and then followed.

'Full of beans,' said Rob. 'I told you so. Not exactly a lonely old man, is he?'

He wasn't. Old Man Poole had now paused, was talking to a group of similarly white-haired oldsters. All of them seemed to look to him, as though his opinion really counted. And whatever he was saying, it really was an *opinion,* not platitudes. Indeed, something seemed to have got him so riled that he was waving his walking stick about now, *conducting* with it.

They walked past and Sally peeled her ears.

'There's a storm coming!' he railed.

One of the oldsters dared to contradict him. 'We had the storm yesterday, Pooley, or have you forgotten yesterday already?'

Poole ignored the interruption. 'There's been a storm coming for over thirty years... There's a storm coming and we've left the window open. We've not battened down the hatches. Things are getting in. Damp, dark things.'

'Calm yourself down, Mr. Poole,' said one of the old dears.

But Poole wouldn't hear any of it. 'Not that kind of storm. Mark my words. This is the divil's work.'

'The *divil,'* sneered Rob as they walked past, as they gained the Seahorse, as they joined the queue which was lined up outside. 'He calls it *the divil.* Isn't that sweet of your nice old man?'

Sally shook her head. There was nothing sweet about today. On a day like this, the divil really did exist and he came with great clomping cloven hooves and huge horns, all the better to scour you with. On days like this, town meetings were probably as much use as chocolate teapots, as pissing in the wind. She was starting to get a bad feeling about this.

37: Chopper

F reddie Livermore's phone was already red hot to the touch and it wasn't even half eight. It was already running out of juice; during the last frantic call from the studio in Newcastle, he'd heard the warning beeps. He'd have to borrow Charlotte's phone, but his assistant was already involved in her own calls, trying to source the chopper which they so badly needed. He drained the last of the oil-slick coffee he'd bought from the tragedy of a caff – JAX SNAX – up at the trucker's rest stop, crunched the plastic cup in his fist, and then searched his pockets for his cigarettes. He'd find them if his brain wasn't so all-over-the-place, if he hadn't had to get up so early, if he hadn't had to stay over at the bloody earthquake disaster zone of a B and B over in Charnley. Charlotte had told him they were lucky to get that, that most of the hotels as far down as Newcastle were already booked up by the news crews, but sometimes he wasn't sure whether Charlotte made his life difficult for him on purpose just because *he* made *her* life difficult.

He watched her on the phone. She was playing with a ringlet of her hair, twirling it around her finger like it was a ribbon. She was on to the airfield at Kirkby-le-Stag, trying her feminine whiles on the feller on the other end of the line.

'But if you *do* have a helicopter and you take us up in it, we'll be able to get lots of footage of you, lots of stuff about your *brand*. Of course, we can't *do* advertising, but we'll get some good ground shots of Freddie in front of the chopper. It'll be great publicity. Uhuh... No, I do realise that you usually hire these things out... No... What I'm suggesting is we come to some sort of a deal... Sir, do you know how much money it costs to advertise on TV these days?'

Freddie made a *wind it up* gesture with his hand. They had to get the chopper first. Had to beat all the other news crews. He felt as though his whole reputation depended on it. He'd have been willing to do anything to get the exclusive. But what with the causeway impassible and the news of what had happened to the brave souls who'd attempted to row across to the island spreading like wildfire - apparently they'd been captured by some lunatic, country bumpkin-types; sounded like something out of *Deliverance*. Freddie shuddered at the thought, clenched his butt-cheeks – it wasn't the low-hanging fruit of a story he'd hoped it would be.

'Yes,' said Charlotte. 'I do understand your, uh, predicament.' She tucked the phone between her ear and her shoulder and made a very familiar gesture. She rubbed her thumb and forefinger together, suggesting *this* was the predicament the man from the airfield found himself in. 'Yes, I do realise Coastguard is warning that all unnecessary trips should be put on hold at least until the... The what, sorry? Pardon? I thought you were calling me a whore... No, no I do understand. Completely.' She put her hand over the speaker. Spoke to Freddie. 'He says the sea mist, the fog thingy means Coastguard won't let us go up. He's playing silly buggers.'

Freddie made a beckoning gesture. 'Let me speak to him.'

Charlotte obediently handed over the phone. He felt it was just as hot as his own when he pressed it against his ear. 'Hi there, this is Freddie Livermore. Northumbria Tonight. Hadrian's-North correspondent. Who am I speaking with please?'

The man on the other end of the phone had an alarming stutter. So much so that Livermore, Mister Professionalism personified usually, almost found himself bursting out laughing as the man struggled manfully to say his own name. As he listened, he looked out into the fog, tried to pick out anything through the white-darkness. It was strange; from here, on the rise near the tourist car park on the right side of the drowned causeway, it looked as though the mist covered only Limm. As though it had sent up its own smokescreen to shield it from prying eyes. Closer to hand there was still mist, but it was nothing like as thick as it was over there. Here, he could pick out how painfully *full* the car park was. 'Lovely to speak to you sir,' he said, as soon as he was reasonably sure the stutterer on the other end of the line had finished. 'Look, I'm speaking man to man here, right?' He looked pointedly at Charlotte, who looked away, sparked up her own cigarette. He'd bum one off her later. That was the good thing about having assistants like this. Sure they came and they went, sure as soon as a bigger thing came along, a thing which actually paid, they'd jump ship quicker than he

339

could beg them to stay, but every one of them seemed cut from the same mould, they all lived these thousand mile an hour lifestyles which meant *hell yeah they smoked, hell yeah they'd stay up all night drinking with the crew, hell yeah, they put out.* 'What I mean is this. I know you're a businessman. I'm a businessman too. News is business these days, just like any other. It's all about returns, being there first, getting that story before any of our rivals. Now, I don't know if you know this, but I've an occasional slot on *Countryfile.* I'm kinda like their roving reporter. They let me do stories all about the north east coast and its people. And its *businesses,* sir. Do you understand me? If you were to let us have the chopper today, there'd be absolutely nothing stopping me from doing a full fifteen minute slot on your airfield.'

He winked at Charlotte. *Master at Work,* said the wink. Charlotte's phone beeped impatiently to say that there was a call waiting. He briefly lifted the phone away from his ear and saw that it was his producer, calling from the studio. Freddie supposed he felt similarly towards his producer as front-line troops used to feel about their supposedly superior officers in the war. He thought Rog (as in Rog the Dodge, as in *he'd dodge everything that looked, smelled, tasted like hard work)* was gone-to-seed.

He returned the phone to his ear. Listened to some more of the interminable stuttering. He made a grab for the cigarette in Charlotte's mouth and she shot him a filthy look but then let him have it. He sucked at it hungrily, then interrupted the airfield man in full flow. 'Look, is it a yes or a no, because I can't be here, pissing into the wind any longer. Yes or no, sir?'

A long pause. Then, 'well fuck you very much then.' He slammed a thumb onto the 'End Call' button and sighed. 'What now?' he said, hoping somewhere in her Charlotte's big satchel, she'd have the answer. Certainly she seemed to have everything else in there, including, he'd been amused to discover, a couple of miniature vodkas, pilfered from the mini-bar back at the hotel.

She shrugged. 'We've tried everything. Even that feller from the local paper over there,' she jerked her thumb back, indicating Limm, the back end of beyond, the ghost town, 'but he's not answering his calls, or even responding to texts. I tried that boat taxi place like you said, but Christ, the feller answered the phone sounded like a *right nut.*' She showed him screw-loose, twisting a finger at the side of her head. She was always talking with her hands, Charlotte, like she was French in a former life. Wasn't a bad thing. She did *some things* very well with her hands. Hence the sleepless night in the Charnley hotel.

'Crabbie, they called him,' she continued. 'Crabbie by name, crabby by nature. Right old weirdo. But then I suppose they all are, over there, aren't they? Know what he said to me? He said, *This is Limm Island. We sort out our own problems here. We don't need no outsiders.* '

'You said. And then he told you about,' he lowered his voice, 'the road-block.' He hadn't told anyone else in the car park about the road block. It was his ace in the hole.

'Uh-huh,' said Charlotte. She pulled a little mirror out of her satchel and adjusted her make-up. Expensive stuff it was. Even when she'd been crying last night, begging that she could come live with him, it hadn't run like the cheap mascara did. He wondered whether money ran in her family. Certainly she couldn't have afforded the good stuff on the wages Northumbria Tonight laid on for her (i.e. nil but expenses). They got around all the sticky legal stuff by calling it an 'Internship'. Freddie himself would never have been able to start in the journalism game if he'd have had to pimp himself out for free for the first couple years of his working life. Still, he wasn't as good-looking as Charlotte. She was weather-girl good-looking. He was... He supposed he looked clean. And people – his nan especially – said that they liked *clean* people reading the news. As though a bit of grime and dust got in the way of their telling the truth. He scrubbed up well, he reckoned. And had a good head of hair. Which put him in a different league to the producer who, for years, had been wearing a 'syrup' which was so obvious it hurt.

'So, any other ideas?' He was going to add *in that pretty little head of yours,* but he didn't. The thing about Charlotte's was, no matter how they behaved in hotel rooms, they always liked to pretend it was all just professional during the day. She had this pout about her. And this flicker of tension which showed around her eyes whenever he attempted to pinch her arse as she climbed out of the van or hunkered down to mess around with the boom-mic. Even Pete, the cameraman, had noticed. Pete had said *watch out what you're getting yourself into with her. She's a vixen.* But generally, as with everything Pete said, he'd ignored the fuck outta it and then laughed it into nothingness.

'Well,' she said, biting her lip. 'We could...' She opened her satchel again. Pulled out a dog-eared Yellow Pages. 'What I was thinking was aerial photographers.'

He was disappointed. He ground out the cigarette under his heel and let himself shrug down onto the back lip of the van, picked at a splash of mud which he'd just noticed on his jacket. But it wasn't in Charlotte's nature to get mad at such setbacks, and she didn't want to just get even either. No, Charlotte got *animated*. She started dancing around on the spot in her designer, posh festival-style wellies.

'No but, do you understand? Aerial photographers like? There must be some in here...' She waved her Yellow Pages like it was a flag. 'And you know what they do, don't you though?'

'Take photos,' said Freddie, disconsolately. The muck on his jacket wasn't moving. He'd have to get the whole thing dry-cleaned, and Northumbria Tonight were getting antsy enough with his expenses claims as it was.

'No, but...' She was so excited now, she was bouncing. 'But where do they take the photos from?'

'From the...' Suddenly he cottoned-on. 'Ah. Clever girl. Good idea. Right, you start calling them up, there can't be too many of them along this coast, can there?'

Charlotte nodded, rested the Yellow Pages on the lip of the van and started flicking through it. As she did so, Freddie's mobile buzzed once again. He looked down and saw it was the producer, *again*. Thought he'd really better answer it this time.

'Hello chief... Can't talk long. I can hear the beeps...' He hadn't really heard the beeps. But he had seen something interesting. A couple of the guys from the rival programme, North East News, were lingering with intent by the big sign which showed the tide tables. One of them, his counterpart, Bruce Howitt, was crouching down, sticking his hand in the water, as though he was seriously considering *swimming* across. Perhaps *his* assistant had sourced wet-suits. Perhaps *his* assistant was going to carry him across on her back. He narrowed his eyes.

The producer continued to talk about unimportant things, as producers were wont to do. Then Freddie had to grit his teeth, admit that they hadn't managed to source a chopper yet, though they had some leads.

'Sounds like you need my help,' said the producer. 'I can be up there in... An hour, tops. What time does the tide go out?'

Freddie gulped. 'Chief... Chief? The beeps are going, I can't hear you... I can't...' He clicked off the phone. The last thing he needed was *him* up here, sticking his beak in. He'd never hear the end of it from the other news crews. He returned the phone to his pocket and looked down at Charlotte. She was now sitting cross-legged on the loose gravel of the car park, the Yellow Pages spread across her knees, phone clamped to her ear. She was using both hands to type something into her lap-top which she'd just fired up and had propped on the lip of the van. Always resourceful, that girl, she'd managed to set up a field office no hassle. He thought about asking her whether he could take a couple of the numbers for the aerial photographers but then decided against it. He found his cigarettes crushed in the back pocket of his jeans, fished one out, tried to re-roll it back into shape. Sparked it up. Inhaled deeply. He knew he already reeked of smoke, but that didn't matter. All that mattered was that he *looked* clean. This was TV after all.

He watched as Pete high-hurdled back from over the farmer's fence. He'd been over to take a piss. Couldn't risk it any closer to the rest of the news crews for fear of being filmed (cameramen were like that, Freddie had found). He exchanged brief hellos with a couple of technicians from other crews and then skirted back to the van. Somehow, he'd managed to pick up a packet of crisps and a sandwich along the way. He was always eating, was Pete. It was some kind of minor miracle that he managed to stay so fencing-post skinny.

Pete looked vaguely put-out that they'd opened up the back of the van without him. That they might have touched some of his precious equipment. When Charlotte had outlined what had happened to the two brave newsmen who'd hired that tiny boat and rowed over to Limm, Pete had seemed more concerned by what might have happened to their equipment than he was about their skins. He poked his head round and looked inside the van, performed a quick inventory of the parts inside and then, satisfied, he popped a handful of crisps into his mouth. Crunched loudly. Booted up his own lap-top. This was how news crews rolled now, for better or for worse. Not so much on the seats of their pants any more, rather, on the battery life of their computer equipment and mobile phones.

'Have you got anything useable from all the Youtube footage?' asked Freddie, before dragging so hard on the ciggie that the heat nipped at his fingers.

Pete grinned. 'Quality's poor. The people on that island couldn't keep a steady camera hand if their lives depended on it... But I did find a couple of useable clips of the beach yesterday.

Though you can't see much for the squalling wind and the torrential rain, you can still pick out the car. You can still pick out there's a body inside the car. I've already spliced them in, for after you do your *to camera* bit. Have you tried contacting any of these amateurs, you know, see if they'd agree to be telephone interviewed? We could use what they say over some stock-images of the island or something.'

'Sounds like you're trying to do the whole thing without having to actually go over there,' observed Freddie.

Pete nodded, hammered the keys to his lap-top, looked up again. 'That's what a lot of the other boys are doing at the moment. Boys from Newcastle Nightly News have already got signed, sealed contracts with three of the girls from the dancing troup. They contacted them over Facebook, apparently. The girls have all agreed to talk about their harrowing ordeal as that wounded feller crawled into that talent show of theirs. Radio Coast has already blocked out a whole morning for a phone-in about what's going on over there. It seems nearly everyone who lives there wants to go on, spouting their opinions...'

'Way of the world,' said Freddie. 'But it's lazy journalism. We need to get over there.' He paused, looked down to the water's edge to where Bruce Howitt and his buxom assistant were still stationed. He pointed. 'Say, you haven't happened to find out what they're doing down there have you?'

Pete looked very pleased with himself. He grinned, then tucked back his head, poured the remaining crisps into his mouth. And then spat out his answer through a fug of cheese and onion breath and crumbs. 'They're after the big dog. That mayor of theirs. Feller who thinks he's some kind of feudal lord or something...'

'Combs,' said Freddie. 'Manny Combs. There was a spell a while back when the rumour mill was flying. They said he was going to die. Dodgy ticker. I had Charlotte – or the Charlotte which we had then – compile a full dossier on him. You know, that we could use for an obit if we needed it... Anyway, he survived... I'll ask Charlotte if she can dig it out when she's finished on the blower. Maybe if we get over there first, we can steal Howitt's thunder. Dodgy fucker though, that Combs. From what I read...'

'There is one good thing about him,' mused Pete, opening up his service station sandwich.

'Oh aye, what was that then?'

'The bridge,' grinned Pete. 'He wants to build a bridge. Instead of the causeway. Has a real bee in his bonnet about it. If we had the bridge, we could be over there now.'

Freddie saw his point. But he also saw that all the other crews would be over too. And if news was a business now, it was all about the key differentiating factors, the Unique Selling Points. And the USP of *Northumbria Tonight* was going to be they got to the news *first and fast.* By hook or by crook. The helicopter. They *had* to get it. He looked back down at Charlotte. She was deep in conversation with someone on the phone. He heard her mention *Countryfile,* and he wasn't sure whether that was a good or bad thing. He heard her repeat the same lines about getting some good ground shots of him (Freddie) standing in front of the chopper, so they could see the logo. He heard her mention that they could also show some still images (which would of course mean that they had to credit the aerial photographer in question.) He waited impatiently for her to finish, drumming his fingers on the van door, smoking, stealing more surreptitious glances at Howitt and his glamorous assistant. Finally Charlotte clicked off her phone. He stared at her hungrily. She frowned. Bad news. But... But wait. What was that twitching at the corners of her mouth?

Charlotte lifted her hand. Gave him the thumbs-up. 'We're on,' she said, her voice kinda going up and down, such was her excitement. It was exactly how she'd sounded last night, when she was riding him, asking him all those questions about how she could make a better impression. 'There's a field he says he can use just down the A24 a bit. Says he'll be there in forty-five minutes.'

Freddie couldn't stop himself from reciprocating her grin. And the best part, the best part of all of it was seeing the faces of all the other news crews as they quickly packed up and climbed back in the van. Freddie could see that they all thought he'd simply given up, that he was going back to the studio to cobble together something from all the Youtube footage. And even better than that was the moment they drove out the car park and Howitt himself clocked them as they made the turn. Howitt grinned. Then raised a hand and waved. But that hand might as well have been giving a victory salute. He thought he'd won.

345

38: The Hopeful and the Hopeless

Ruth Sharp had never seen the Foxglove room so busy. Staff like black waist-coated bees buzzed from table to table pollinating them with hastily-printed flyers, cut-outs from *The Tide Piper*, bucket-loads of pens, and the ubiquitous clipboards. Each clipboard contained a petition, and each petition had already been signed by at least one name, just in case the islanders who would later arrive would somehow feel funny about being the first to sign-up. Ruth had already thrown away four petitions, spoiled as they were by fake names, so when she found the name Robbie Williams on a fifth, she was less than happy. All morning, she'd felt as though she was being mocked behind her back. She'd run a gauntlet of funny looks and smirks since coming down, dressed in a freckly red bandana. In a way, she could hardly blame them, but she'd at least hoped the jokes would be more 'in her face' than it had turned out. Nobody had mentioned *Pirates of the Caribbean* at all yet. There'd been no 'arrrrs' and no 'me hearties' either. It was all making her very uncomfortable. She wasn't used to hats. And the bandana seemed to be worse than yesterday's beanie hat for making her head itch. Already, she'd started carrying a pen behind her ear which would serve as a scratching stick when needed.

'People!' she called, slipping the pen under her bandana and worrying at her scalp, 'we have to be above board with everything we do in this campaign. Funny as they are, we can't be seen to be forging petitions. Can we please just use our own names on them? No more Robbie Williamses.'

Roberto, the chef, who was moonlighting as a bar-polisher paused from his task, smiling. 'Uh... I think you'll find one of the temps we got in this morning *is* actually called Robbie Williams. Lives on Dye Lane. That's not a fake.'

As Ruth tried to compute the information, there were a few titters from over the other side of the room, the stylish piano bar area which Ruth had modelled on a scene from *Casablanca*. Just to make sure guests got the reference, there was an old poster of the film on the wall, next to the Pony Tail Palm. This was where they were setting up the morning's feast, on a long trestle table borrowed from the Ship. She raised an eyebrow; knew she had to improve at this thing called banter. It seemed to be the secret currency behind every single work transaction which took place. 'And I suppose the other lad is Michael Mouse or something, is he? I'm not falling for that.'

Roberto's smile extended into a full-on grin now. It made his whole face light up. And in that instant, Ruth made a promise to herself she would banter like she'd never done before from now on. 'Honestly,' he sniggered. 'He *is* called Robbie Williams. Saw his time-sheet this morning, with his name on it. I was going to put him in kitchen, but maybe our Rob would be better off doing the music.'

'That'd get the people in,' said Ruth. Then, putting on a silly announcer's voice, she continued. '*And now, live on stage from the Seahorse Boutique Hotel, performing his hit Limm Island protest song 'The Town Needs Answers', Misterrrrrrr Robbieee Williams.*'

Roberto gave a weak smile. The titters in the piano bar area were barely audible. Ruth wondered what she'd done wrong. She thought she'd pitched her banter just right; topical, amusing, using a silly voice, and yet nobody seemed to be rolling about in the aisles. She gave her scalp a good long scratch with the end of the pen again and tried not to look too downcast. But Roberto caught her eye again and gave a faint nod in the direction of the doorway which led into the bar from the kitchen. And before she even turned her head, she knew what she was going to see. She turned her head just as the temporary Robbie Williams was affecting a sulky exit from the room, clearly having heard all of her 'joke'.

'Oh dear,' she said, to nobody in particular. She stood in the middle of the room for a moment and then clapped her hands together and followed the Robster back out into the kitchen. But now, Robbie wasn't in the kitchen, not unless he had decided to freeze himself to death in the big walk-in fridge rather than face the indignity of another jibe about his name. He wouldn't be in there would he? She levered open the door, poked her head round it, and breathed a sigh of relief when she saw nothing but the usual boxes of fruit and veg, the crates of cream and milk, the sauces and stews in tupperware containers. She shivered and then backed out. As she turned, she spotted what she thought was a thin plume of smoke in the back window of the kitchen by the bin store.

347

'Robbie?' she said.

She'd found him. He was crouched down beneath the windowsill, leaning against the kitchen's outside wall, smoking. There was something pathetic about the way he smoked. Sucking it in with an audible hiss as though trying to emphasise how much he needed it. He lifted his head to face her, shaggy ginger hair flopping as he did so. And she couldn't help but think what a disappointing version of the ex-Take That popster she'd contrived to hire.

'Uh... Please don't take the Robbie Williams stuff to heart.'

He hung his head again, grunted something, wiped a greasy paw on the white coat Roberto had specially provided him with for the day. Despite it being XXL, the coat was unbuttoned and the lad's flab hung out. He was very much Fat-Stage Robbie.

'Uh... Robbie? The scheduled break is at ten. We've still got a lot of work to get through... Would you please finish off your cigarette and come back inside?'

He grunted something from behind his windbreak of ginger hair, picked at his ear with a stubby finger. Then he took another drag from his ciggie and said: 'I get the Robbie stuff everywhere the agency post me. Once they even booked me for a wedding at the Castle and when I got there I found out I was supposed to sing not do the washing-up, which is what they hired me for. When I went on stage, they booed me off.' He sniffed and took another drag.

'Why don't you put your name down as Robert Williams on the forms? Or Rob? Or go mad and change it to William Roberts?'

William Roberts looked at her as though she was mad. He was as untouched by her banter as he was by her desire to get him to work. She reckoned that if there were another Ruth Sharp - a famous Ruth Sharp; a famous, good-looking and not lanky at all Ruth Sharp (who *never* wore bandanas) – she'd have taken great pains to make sure everyone addressed her as Roo Sharp or Ruthie Sharp or just changed her name by deed poll.

'Robbie Williams is my name,' he sighed. 'I keep hoping the other Robbie Williams just decides to call it a day... Honestly, it's like a knife to the heart every new song he does...'

Ruth decided she'd better go back inside. Already laughter was starting to bubble up inside her stomach. She tried to convince herself she wasn't laughing *at* him, but that wouldn't strictly be the truth. She picked up one of the vast urns from the kitchen floor and started to brew some coffee, wondering if there was still a way they could shoehorn the Robbie Williams story into their campaign.

There wasn't. Nobody, not even Robbie Williams, was mad enough to back it. Getting the Limm Islanders here, when there was free food and the promise of answers, was one thing, but getting them to actually listen to the big cat expert who Sam Bibby had spirited onto the island yesterday was quite another. And accepting outside help on getting rid of the problem? Well, that was tantamount to heresy here. Still, at least she was *doing* something.

Roberto entered the kitchen just in time to stop her from overfilling the urn.

'Thanks.' Then, remembering an old cracker joke, she added: 'How much does a Greek urn?'

Roberto scratched his head. She couldn't resist reciprocating, scratched her own.

'It's a joke.'

He looked embarrassed. 'What's the punch-line?'

Robbie Williams stepped back into the room, reeking of smoke. 'That's the joke,' he said, 'how much does a Greek urn, as in *earn*, as in money.'

Ruth gave a fake laugh. Roberto looked at her as though she was crazy. 'Neither of you should give up the day jobs then,' he said, 'especially you, Robbie. Stick to singing. I like *Angels*.'

Robbie flounced straight back out of the kitchen.

'You've got to be able to take a bit of banter in this game,' said Ruth and Roberto at exactly the same time. The two of them shared a laugh at the way their thoughts had crossed. Then, all of a sudden, Ruth started to feel incredibly lonely. She'd almost forgotten that warm glow of synchronicity when someone else's thoughts exactly matched her own; she'd forgotten in-jokes and family catch-phrases. But moments like the one she'd just shared with Roberto somehow tugged her back so she could almost smell the Micro Chips and ice cream and the well thumbed aroma of a children's book in which the child could recite the words she was reading even before she'd read them herself. She felt very much like following Robbie Williams back out the back door. She felt very much like driving onto that causeway and never coming back.

'Everything ready then?' she asked, in a husky voice.

Roberto grimaced. 'It is… But Ruth… This is all starting to smack very much of bribery. All this food…'

She nodded; she'd been thinking the same thing. But it was too late now. She couldn't think of anything else to say, so she lumbered out of the kitchen, carrying the urn with her, wondering how much a woman of approaching fifty would earn for all of her freely given community spirit. Probably not much more than a few sneers from the locals who already treated her with a mistrust which bordered on the obsessive. She stepped back into Foxglove and was almost immediately shouldered out of the way by the second temp, the one she'd not even bothered to learn the name of. He was a very red-faced young man and he tottered past carrying yet another tray of appetising cream buns. Robbie Williams followed, the smell of smoke still clinging to him like a bandana. He was carrying the scones and triangle-cut sandwiches, which he'd mixed together on one tray. Ruth gave him a wink of encouragement and tried to think of some other, less taxing jobs she could ask him to do. Once he'd deposited his tray on the bar, she handed him the huge urn of coffee and asked him to take it over to the seating area over by the grand piano. He nodded, looking pleased to be asked, but as he took the urn from her, she caught sight of something in his eyes that she didn't like. It was a Boy Scout *I'm doing a Good Thing* gleam. And Ruth immediately knew why; he thought she was ill. He thought that explained the bandana.

'Not there, there,' she shouted, out of spite. He was carrying the urn awkwardly between his legs as though it were somehow attached to his balls which didn't quite contain the right Williams genes. He waddled over to the grand piano, usually the centre-piece of the room, and then rested a moment, pretending he didn't understand where she wanted him to put it.

'The trestle table!' she shouted.

The Robster looked confused; as though he really were a millionaire pop star and he'd never worked a proper day in his life. As though he only entered hotel rooms such as this one once everything was already set up and ready to go. Jared Forrest, the kitchen-porter-cum-odd-job-man, was slumped across two of the tables, putting the finishing touches on a rather over-elaborate drawing gave a rather over-elaborate sigh, as though the Person from Porlock had just ruined his majestic dream.

'Sorry to disturb the masterpiece!' she called.

He shook his head, returned to the drawing. Within seconds, he had the tip of his tongue poking out of the corner of his mouth again. Such was his concentration, it was as though the fate of the whole world depended on whether he could complete his drawing. She wondered how she'd ended up working with a bunch of people who more or less redefined the term 'artistic temperament'; Jared with his angry art, Roberto with his obsessive eye for detail in his cakes, the temp with his *tonight Matthew, I'm gonna be* sensibilities. The silly, troublesome part of Ruth wanted the fake Robbie Williams to deliberately nudge Jared's table as he staggered past, straining under the weight of the urn. The silly, troublesome part of her wanted the Robster to spill the coffee all over the drawing, or to misguidedly ask Jared whether there weren't better things to be doing than rendering an artist's impression of the beast which was supposed to be stalking the island.

There was a clatter and jangle of piano keys as Robbie half-dropped the big urn on top of the grand. Jared twitched dangerously again, and for a moment, she thought he was going to climb out of his seat and give the ginger temp a real piano lesson. To diffuse the tension, she called over. 'Please don't put it on top of the piano, Robbie! On the trestle. The long table... Everything okay, Jared?'

Jared shook his head and continued with his drawing. Robbie sulkily removed the urn from the top of the piano, now placing it on the floor at the foot of the large Pony Tail Palm as though he wanted to give it a mini jungle safari. She decided to leave the pair of them to it. The sad thing was, she already knew that nobody would be coming along because of her and Mart's rabble-rousing antics yesterday or Jared's artist's impressions. No: they'd be coming for the free grub. And they'd make no secret about it. She just knew people would come and fill their plates and then slip away back into the morning mist as though they were *part* of that mist as soon as they'd finished.

When the first person arrived at the meeting, announced by the jangle of the small bell on the door, he almost walked right back out again. A whippet of a man wearing a flat cap and a luxurious moustache who couldn't have looked more northern if he'd been chewing on a meat pie and had mushy peas for a beard. He took one look at the expectant faces of the five people who were arranged on the high-stools by the bar, sighed, and then made out he'd entered the wrong premises. Ruth decided that the old man was probably right; they did look like a jury up there and must have been a bit of a shock to him. But Jared rescued the situation, bounding off his stool like a well-trained gymnast and covering the expanse of polished wood floor between bar and door in a matter of three long strides.

'You here for the emergency meeting?' he bellowed.

351

The man stole a wary glance over his shoulder, then at the big clock above the piano. Then he decided to study the film posters - old movies like *Casablanca* and *The Magpie Trap* – and strangely, they seemed to put him at his ease. But not as much as Jared, who took him by the arm and led him up to the expansive buffet which was spread out on the trestle table by the piano. The old man's eyes widened in awe as though he'd just seen a dragon's treasure hoard.

Soon more people started to arrive. Apparently there was a queue outside. And now the staff had stopped behaving like a jury and started pretending to mingle, there weren't any *Should I stay or should I go* moments. Jared was sitting in the corner by the piano with his drawing pinned to the wall behind him. Roberto was wringing his hands by the buffet, carefully watching the faces of everyone who tried one of his cakes to check for the slightest twitch which suggested it wasn't the best thing they'd ever tasted. Robbie Williams, who she'd told to look more relaxed, was now draped over the piano stool as though he were performing a life drawing pose. But at least they were trying.

The food was the real ice-breaker; she saw old women who never even deigned to pop their heads round the door of the hotel even when it was new and gossip-worthy, wolfing down Roberto's cream buns, not caring that they were getting whipped cream in their moustaches. *Everyone* seemed to have a moustache; they should have been collecting hair samples rather than signatures; it would have been easier. She saw late middle-aged men who'd probably never eaten much beyond the realms of chips, crisps or baked potatoes, now tucking into the onion bhajis and the quiche as though it was manna from heaven. She saw old fishermen shunning the tuna sandwiches she'd put out especially and instead plumping for the goat's cheese and rocket on rye.

She saw a couple teachers from the school educating themselves with the Mexican wraps and a murder of Goth-style girls flocking around the breadstick-and-dip combo platter. Mike Ford and Mart Bibby were over in the corner, whispering in each other's ears furiously, but still wolfing down the home-made crisps. Sam, of course, was somewhere else, keeping the special guest company. But everyone else was here. Conspicuous by his absence though, was the mayor, Manny Combs. But then, she'd kinda expected that.

'Right,' she said, when she was finally satisfied that everyone had a full plate. 'Shall we get this show on the road?'

Her announcement barely cut through the hum of conversation, but it did reach Mike Ford in his corner, who looked mightily put-out that it wasn't *him* making the announcements. Promptly he stood up and she watched him barrel, head and shoulders above the crowd of wizened old pensioners, over to where she was standing at the bar. 'Don't you think I should be...uh... chairing the meeting?' he asked. 'I'm not trying to be mean, but what we have to say... Might sound better coming from me...'

'Course Mike,' she said, trying not to sound annoyed. 'I just thought I could do the boring, mundane stuff like getting people to sit down...'

'And the housekeeping,' interrupted Mike. 'Telling people where the bogs are and that.' He nodded, then slammed his fist down onto the bar. A couple of people looked as though they were about to drop their plates in shock. Robbie Williams almost fell off the piano stool. 'Right?' Mike bellowed. 'Shall we get this show on the road? First up, I'd like to thank you for coming. I know it takes a lot to give up your mornings, but if you're anything like me, the events of the past few days will have left you needing answers. Yearning for the return of your security... And I know it takes a lot to even leave the house on a day like today, what with the Hoar's Blanket... So thank you...' He paused, glared at an old woman who was still talking. He glared at her for longer than was strictly comfortable. When finally she realised she was being stared at, she hid behind the biggest slice of chocolate cake Ruth had ever seen.

'Where were we?' continued Mike. 'Ah yes. Our *situation*. Now, I know there have been a lot of rumours flying about the place over the past few days. And that's why this meeting is so important. We want to do things by the book, so everyone who has anything at stake knows exactly what's going on and can make an informed choice, a collective choice, as to where we go from here. There are some on this island... There are some people WHO DON'T WANT YOU TO KNOW ANYTHING. There are people here who WANT TO COVER THIS ALL UP...'

Ruth tugged on the sleeve of his pullover.

'What?' he bellowed in her face.

Ruth made a gesture which was supposed to mean *turn down the volume*. Mike misread it: 'Oh. Right. Yes, without further ado, I'd like to introduce you to Ruth Sharp who will run you through the procedures when you want to go for a piss.'

353

The gasps from the crowd were almost as loud as the crash of Robbie Williams as he finally slipped off the piano stool and landed in the pot which contained the burgeoning Pony Tail Palm.

'Uh, sorry about the language,' said Ruth when the din finally died down. 'But Mike's anger on this subject pretty much sums up how we all feel, I'm sure?' Ruth counted one... two nods from the crowd. She started again, nervously touching her bandana. 'I'm not sure how many of you have been in here before, but I'd like to welcome you all. We hope to see you again sometime.'

Mike made a *hurry up, get on with it*, gesture with his hand. She chose to misread it. 'We've been open a couple of years now, you know, and we'd really like to be taken seriously as part of the community. Which is why we decided to host this meeting here today. We believe that if we get the whole community singing from the same hymn sheet, then we'll have a fighting chance. But before we get on to the nitty gritty of the meeting, I've been asked to go through a few housekeeping rules.'

There followed a few, prolonged groans from the men as though it had finally dawned on them that the reason they'd had their no-such-thing-as-a-free-lunch was because they'd have to help out with the dusting and the ironing in return. Ruth fingered the edge of her bandana again. 'Don't worry, I won't be asking you all to help clean the hotel!' No laughs. Bad sign. 'I mean I need to tell you about the fire escapes and where the toilets are located.'

She decided to cut out the jokes entirely and get off that stage as quickly as possible before she scared these people enough that they'd *never* come to the Seahorse again. She described the route to the toilets and that everyone should gather on the village green if the fire alarm went off, and then handed back over to Mike. The newspaperman was in his element; he paced through Foxglove as though he were a politician, giving his rehearsed speech which took in everything they knew about the threat, and the three bodies which had so far turned up. When he mentioned the bodies, there were a few whimpers. Someone, towards the back of the room was crying, but it was hard to tell who it was.

'There's something here,' continued Mike, 'on this island, and there's nobody here qualified to say exactly what it is, or what we should do about it...'

'I told you. It's the storm,' shouted Old Man Poole.

'People found a finger! In my back garden!' called Sally Martin.

354

Suddenly everyone was calling out their own horror stories through mouthfuls of the free food.

'Our Sophie said she thought a big cat was stalking her as she went to Buckby's store.'

'Lee Froggatt says that there were cat footprints near his pond.'

'It's all over the internet. It was even on the news this morning.'

Mike Ford slammed his fist down on the bar again. 'Order! This meeting is supposed to be about answering questions, not rumour-mongering. Yes, there is stuff on the internet. Yes, the media have sniffed out a story here. But there are some here, on this island, who still want us all to turn a blind-eye to it, while *something* picks off people and animals. But people, although there are some…'

Mart Bibby coughed 'Manny Combs!'

'There are some, who think this island is run like a dictatorship, it's actually a democracy. *We* get to decide what happens to us. Our mayor does not necessarily have to be author to our fate.'

Suddenly Ruth realised what Mike Ford was doing, he was beginning his campaign for office. This was his first speech. She'd wondered why he'd been so keen to help down at the Ship last night. And she realised that his congregation would see through his rhetoric straight away, that they'd surely see this as a bid for power of his own. All this *we* business and what he really meant was *me*. The meeting was just a chance for him to continue with his own personal vendetta against Manny Combs.

'People,' he said, 'I am now about to utter those dreaded words. Words which most of us thought we'd never hear on this island. We need outside help.'

'No way!' shouted someone.

'No flaming chance,' shouted another.

Mike Ford smiled. Just like Combs did, Ruth thought. 'I thought you might all say that, but hear me out, please. That's what we've got the petitions here for, so you can register for or against.' He held up a clip-board. 'Like a proper democratic process. We haven't got time for a proper vote, but once this is all over, I'd like to be able to count up those names and know we did the right thing.'

He paced the front of the room, hands clasped behind his back. 'What we're asking for is your permission, folks. To *act*. To stop shoving everything under the carpet like the Combs regime.

And let me tell you a little bit about this outside help we're looking for. We're not looking for the type of outside help which will burden us with fishing quotas so we can't make a proper living like we've always done here. We're not looking for the kind of outside help which will *interfere,* when no interference is needed. We're not looking for the type of outside help which will come up with new rules and regulations all the way down in London... We're not looking for a bridge, or a motorway or a twenty-four hour Tescos which will cover the entire eastern seaboard. We're not looking for CCTV cameras on every corner and a McDonald's in place of The Crab's Claws... We're looking for *qualified* people who can come here, and in proper conditions, get rid of this menace.'

There were a few shouts of opposition. But only a few. Mike Ford held up a finger. 'And what we propose is this. As soon as the causeway opens this morning, all families with young children, all elderly residents, everyone who *can,* should calmly and without panic, leave the island. Go to visit relatives for a few days. Go to stay in Edinburgh or Newcastle. Anywhere but here... While... while the job is done.'

The dissenting voices piped up again. None of them, apparently, could even conceive of being off the island, even *if* there was a beast stalking them. There followed another debate as to whether there actually was a beast at all and Ruth found herself tuning out. When she tuned back in, Mike was blithely discussing the importance of organising an event committee, and that was when she realised the whole thing was in danger of running out of steam. A committee, experience told her, was a very good way of making it look as though you were doing things, when you really weren't. Mike needed to get the people mad, not entice them with the promise of more interminable meetings. They needed to *do* things not just sit around wolfing down pastries, quaffing wine and tea. People were already growing bored.

She decided she needed to up the ante and quickly. She needed to find her Quartermain. As she exited stage-left, through the door which led to the back section of the hotel, Mike Ford continued to remind everybody just how important it was that they jot their names down on the petitions.

39: A Quartermain

The big cat expert wasn't what Sam Bibby had been expecting. He'd been expecting a rugged, H. Rider Haggard-style hero. A Quartermain. Someone who looked as though they could handle the more... unsavoury... aspects of nature without even wrinkling his safari suit. A man with keen-eyes, a well-trained nose and a lantern-jaw. A man who'd treat the animal with the respect it deserved once it was dead, perhaps by mounting its head on the wall; there was an ideal spot for it in the lifeboat hut.

The man who was slouching across the chair in Ruth Sharp's office was something of a disappointment. He didn't seem to have the requisite gravitas. Certainly didn't look like a hero. Heroes didn't demand en suite accommodation on the evening prior to the meeting. They didn't demand a slap-up Full English before they got started for the day. They didn't, as this poor-quality Quartermain had, take one sniff of the fog outside and then decide they'd prefer to stay in the warm for a few moments longer. Heroes, at least in Sam Bibby's book, weren't *Yanks*.

Earlier, the Yank had dropped his bottle of L'O off the desk and then looked at Sam as though expecting *him* to retrieve it for him. After a momentary impasse, Sam had bitten the bullet and slid off his chair, reached for the rolling bottle and then something horrible had happened. The Yank had thrust out his crotch a little and as Sam turned his head, the feller said: 'while you're down theyah,' before roaring with laughter. Which definitely didn't sound like the sort of thing a hero would say.

The man had introduced himself as Rick Fallon. He'd placed an ad on the Beat website. According to the ad, Rick would work anywhere in the UK. Apparently he specialized in the investigation of escaped exotic animals. He had links with customs, had good references from a couple forces down south, and his CV had checked out; on it, he'd been listed as *Doctor Richard Fallon,* which

357

sounded one helluva lot more professional than Rick, which sounded too close to *Slick*. He'd driven up last night. Sam Bibby had been out with Ruth Sharp's dog Vicar anyway, and so he'd gone to meet him at the end of the causeway, just in case there was a problem. He'd been baby-sitting him ever since.

This morning, he seemed an even less likely saviour. Rick was dressed in a big thick Puffa jacket with a T-Shirt underneath which advertised 'Adult Material Downstairs' with an arrow pointing down to his crotch. He had shoulder length hair and what must have been a weeks' worth of stubble on his chops though Sam knew for a fact that last night he'd been clean shaven. He could have been anything from twenty-five to forty, Sam reckoned, but he erred on the side of caution. Thirty-odd. Only, slightly immature with it, as was often the case with people who didn't go out and get themselves a proper job. Fallon was still *attached* to the University of Manchester's Zoology department apparently. Which meant he'd never entered the real world. Which meant he still dressed like a kid. Soon as he'd got him going on *animals* though, which was after all, the reason he was here, Rick was a regular professional.

'You said you had an image?' said Rick. 'Of the paw-print?'

Sam nodded, but made no move to open the file which lay in front of him on the desk.

'Well, can I see it then?' he continued, stretching his hand out across the desk expectantly. In the manner of someone who'd lived off hand-outs all their life. The Bank of Mummy and Daddy had doubtless put him through his undergraduate degree. Government grants or sponsorship had most likely set him on the path to being a doctor, or, more correctly, a vet. Doubtless he was *surviving* on some six figure salary at the university now; doubtless with a favourable pension scheme to boot. And still touting for private work on the police Beat website.

'Patience,' he said. 'I need to know I can trust you first.'

'You've already seen my CV... We talked... last night.'

'Tell me a little more about yourself,' said Sam. 'Tell me about your methods.'

Rick paused. Took a moment to look around the office as though hoping there'd be something in it to give him inspiration. There wasn't much for him to go on; just Vicar's dog bowl and a big rusting filing cabinet.

'What do you want to know?' said Rick.

'I want to know how you plan to kill it.'

Rick coughed, as though embarrassed. 'Well, I'm not entirely convinced there *is* an it at this stage. All we have at this stage is hearsay.'

'There is an it,' said Sam, slapping his paw down onto the desk. 'Inside this room there is an it. Outside this room, in the bar-room, my friends are right now explaining to the whole town that there is an it...'

Rick narrowed his eyes, spoke again, seeming to ignore everything Sam had said. 'It's my job to find out exactly what is living on the land around this town. To find quantifiable, scientific evidence. Tell me, did you ever hear about the Beast of Bodmin Moor?'

Sam didn't like where this was going, 'This is nothing like that.'

'Oh but it is,' said Slick Rick. 'I was called in on the investigation down there too. By the AFF – that's the Ministry of Agriculture, Fisheries and...'

'I know what it is, *Rick.*'

'Yes, well. There'd been reports of panther-sized creatures on the moors, just like Limm. Talk of livestock mutilated or killed, just like here.'

'But we have *photographs.*'

'So did they. We went down theyah in ninety-five. Team of seven of us, three of whom were responsible for gathering *non-specific* data, which was what we classed as the rumour and hearsay and all that. It was their job to go round interviewing the locals, hearing their stories. I was called in as the authority on all-things big cat related. They called me back all the way from Kruger, where I'd been working with white lions.'

Sam felt a yawn coming and did nothing to hide it when it did. Slick Rick was momentarily knocked off his stride, but he soon regained his composure and continued.

'We were theyah three weeks. We put down more motion-triggered cameras, studied more video footage, investigated more footprints, went elbow deep in more scat samples, than I'd ever had the money, or the time to do out in South Africa. And we found nothing. *No verifiable evidence.* Which is exactly how we concluded the report. Foxes could have mauled those farm animals. Badgers. Stray dogs. There was no big cat on Bodmin Moor. I combed every freaking blade of grass in the place and...'

'And it didn't pop up and say hello, is that it?'

359

Now it was Slick Rick's turn to cut-in. 'This one you think you got doesn't hide itself away, does it? According to you, it's attacking people. Do you know how rare it is for a big cat to behave like that?'

Sam sighed. 'I'm not going to get into a pissing contest with you, *Rick.* You're the so-called expert. If you say it's impossible for it to be a big cat, then I'll take your word for it. But there's something out there. And I want you to tell us how to help us catch it. If you don't want to help us, don't. I just need you to tell me how.'

Rick nodded. Scratched his stubble. It made a rasping sound which *grated.* But now he was showing signs of submission; staring down at the floor, refusing to meet Sam's eyes.

'Why all the attitude-bullshit, Sam?' asked the Yank finally. 'Do you really want my help or are you just crossing me off your list, saying you've contacted the *so-called* big cat expert and he wouldn't help so you could get on with solving problems like you island-people normally do? Offof your own backs. That it?'

'I'm sorry,' said Sam. 'I don't know why I'm being like this, I really don't.'

Rick Fallon gave what looked like a genuine smile. 'That's alright,' he said, 'I see exactly *why* you reacted to me like that. You forget, one of the biggest aspects of my role is the study of behaviours. Your behaviour was exactly how a cornered animal would behave. You see an outsider coming onto your territory and your back's up straight away.' Sam tried to interject but Fallon raised a hand. 'I'm not trying to tread on no toes here, Sam. And I *can* help. But we can't just do what you want, what everyone wants, and go out on the hunt for this thing. We have to be take precautions. We have to have a proper plan.'

'How about we take a look at that photograph we've got now, eh?' said Sam, meek as a house-cat now.

Fallon took the photo, studied it. 'Certainly looks like an exotic feline print,' he mused. 'But I'd like to see for myself before I make any rash decisions. That okay by you?'

'Okay,' said Sam. 'We do it your way... But... But there's one more thing I'm going to have to ask you to do. I'm going to have to ask you to go out there...' He jerked his thumb back, indicating the Foxglove room. 'I'm going to have to ask you to go in there and kinda outline the do's and don'ts as far as big cats are concerned.'

'Do make them leave the island, don't let them stay, playing the hero,' said Fallon, solemnly.

'You try telling them that,' said Sam.

There was a rap on the door, and before it opened, Sam remembered distinctly thinking, *that's Ruth Sharp, right on cue.* And even when the first of the men entered the room with a scarf wrapped round his face, Sam was so prepared for it to be Ruth that he at first took the scarf to be simply an extension of her usual head-cover. Like maybe she'd got so antsy about how her head looked now that she'd gone for the full-on Burka. It took the entrance of the second man to convince him otherwise, but even then he wasn't really aware of what was happening.

Slick Rick Fallon was though. He let out a shocked, 'the *fuck'*, before attempting to climb to his feet, finally coming over all Quartermain. Sam saw the rifle butt heading in the direction of Fallon's face in slow motion, but there still wasn't enough time to stop it from connecting. Wasn't enough time to try and catch the big cat expert before he collapsed back down into his chair, a pool of blood already collecting at his temple. The first man, the one who'd hit him, quickly pulled back his gun and started cleaning the butt with his sleeve, as though he was afraid of the germs. Cleaning it *obsessively.*

'I thought you'd have known better, Sam Bibby,' growled the second man through his scarf. 'I thought you'd have known that outsiders aren't welcome here.'

'He'd actually made that...' *Sniff.* 'Abundantly clear,' groaned Rick Fallon. 'You guys don't exactly roll out the red...'

The second man lowered his scarf for a second, spat in the Yank's face. Slick Rick let it snail-trail down his face. 'Shut up. *You* don't speak here. *You* don't have a voice,' the man said.

Sam Bibby tried to place the voice, racked his brains to think of who in the hell would do such a damned fool thing. Problem was, on Limm, there were *plenty* of people who might.

'Who is it?' he said. 'Show your faces.'

A gravelly laugh from the second man. 'You think we'd tell you that, you're more stupid than we thought, Bibby. More stupid than even that big gay brother of yours.'

'He's out there,' hissed Sam. 'In the other room. All I have to do is shout and...'

The first man, the man who'd been obsessively cleaning his weapon since he'd first hit the Yank, suddenly turned it around, cocked it. His thumb twitched at the trigger. 'Yeah?' he said. 'That right? He get in here fast enough to stop a bullet, can he?'

Sam gulped. He felt his Adam's Apple bungee up and down in his throat. His tongue felt dry. Like it would be too painful to speak now. So a whisper. 'You working for Combs?'

The two men shared a look. One of them laughed again. And then, once again, the rifle butt came down. This time it connected with the side of Sam's head, sending it rocking back against the back of the chair and then whiplashing forward again. By Christ it hurt. If he hadn't have come over all *wounded pride* with the big cat expert this morning... If he'd have just taken him on the hunt last night instead of waiting... If he'd have only trusted an outsider... Who was the real one working for Manny Combs?

'We're working for the *island,*' said the first man, finally. 'For our way of life.' He reached out, placed a hand on Sam's shoulder. Sam automatically flinched. 'You know how it is. You've always known how it is. People like this...' He nodded over at the Yank. 'They think being out here, on Limm makes us people insular, suspicious of outsiders, stuck in our ways. And I can see fellers like him's point. But being here, removed from everything. It's what makes us a proper community. We got a culture of our very own. And that's a rare thing nowadays. They talk about the world getting smaller. About things like...' He spat. 'The internet pulling everyone closer together. But maybe we *don't wanna* be closer together. Maybe we're happy out here, on a limb, doing our own thing. Maybe it's the best thing for us. Do you *understand,* Sam? I know you do. Your daddy understood...'

Sam groaned.

'So, you see, I'm sorry for all the rough stuff, but well, if that's what I gotta do, that's what I gotta do.' The second man passed something forward and the first man grasped it. 'And I'm sorry we've got to do this too, my friend. Awful sorry about it. But them's the breaks.'

Sam barely had the time to react to the fist as it plunged forward into his unguarded face. And he barely had the time to stick out his hands to stop his fall from the chair. He felt unconsciousness slipping over him like shaving foam or sea weed. All he remembered later was the hot sticky feel of the burlap sack which had been applied to his head. The smell of it. Smelled like one of the big farms. Bull's maybe. Or Worcester's. Yes, more grain on Worcester's. Worcester's it was.

40: The Nightmare

In Janice Dowsing's dream, they'd come into the shop like the government officials at the end of *ET*, wearing radiation suits and masks over their faces so she couldn't see their eyes when they were talking to her.

In the dream she asked them, then begged with them, then screamed in their faces for them to tell her what was going on. One of them came to her, placed a gloved hand on each of her trembling shoulders. She felt the heat of those hands. They were telling her to pipe down. And to get out of the way.

'But why?' she demanded. 'He's my son!'

But they ignored her. Set about the task in hand; unloading the sleek black, government-style vehicles outside, bringing in their terrible machines and containment tents for Lewis's bedroom. Clomping up and down the stairs. The way they did this, without a word passing between them, did their talking for them. Whatever Lewis had caught had got these big people worried. Worried enough to forbid taking Lewis to hospital lest it spread before they could make a proper diagnosis.

Dream mixed with reality then, because Dr. Shaw was still there just like he was in real life. In real life, he'd stayed, but was about as effective as Buckby was; he might as well have not been there judging by how little he did to stop the spread of those lesions. In the dream Shaw and Buckby tried only not to get in the way of the men as they set up their machines. Both of them wore masks of concern, although for different reasons; while Shaw's was probably genuine, even in the dream, which was merely the projection of her own prejudices, she understood that Buckby's worried look was probably more on account of his fear of lost revenue than anything else. He probably feared what the whole scene would look like to the people on the main street. He probably feared that it looked like the Environmental Health coming to pay a visit.

Even in the dream, Janice wished that it could have been something as simple as the Environmental Health. That would be something within the realms of possibility, something everyday, and not *this*.

Even in the dream, Janice didn't know what to do with herself. She'd boiled the kettle over and over again, but nobody wanted tea. She'd put out a plate of biscuits, but the only people interested in them were Buckby and Grace. She'd picked up the telephone on a number of occasions, but never seriously got past the point of dialling. The sad truth was that there was nobody she *could* call.

In the dream, she felt so helpless she barricaded herself in the bedroom. Shoved a chest of drawers behind the door so it couldn't swing open. And in the dream she'd felt the weight of those drawers, as though they contained the weight of all her dreams. And she'd prayed then. Hunkered down on her knees at the side of the bed like the good little girl she'd once been. And then, miraculously, she felt a presence in the room. A presence which hadn't felt the need to announce itself, or scare her. It simply *was*. It was as though some valve had been released inside her. She unsteepled her fingers, unclenched her eyes, untucked herself from her kneel. Sat on the end of the bed and waited for the presence to announce why it was there, why it was haunting her.

It turned out to be her mother. She should have known it right from the off. The reason she'd been alerted to the presence in the first place had been the slight, lingering smell of lavender. And her mother had always smelled of lavender (always sung that song, too *lavender blue, dilly-dally*). Her mother dilly-dallied onto the bed next to her and took her hand. And her mother's hand felt strange. Plasticky. Janice wanted to yank her hand away, but in the dream, everything moved too. Damn. Slowly. So instead, she had to sit there whilst this plastic version of her mother stroked her hand.

'It'll all be okay, Jan-Jan, you'll see,' whispered the plastic woman. 'Just give in to it, don't let it pain you. There's nothing you, nor anyone else can do now.'

Janice hung her head. Sweat dripped down her forehead. Suddenly it had grown very hot in her dream-room. When she looked up, looked into her mother's eyes for the first time, her first instinct was that the woman was crying. But then she saw that it wasn't tears rolling down her cheeks, but blistering, burning plastic.

Only, it didn't smell of burning plastic, it smelled of lavender. Janice looked away again.

'Jan-Jan, *Jan-Jan,* look at me when I'm talking to you. You want them to think I taught you no manners? *Look* at me.' She dug her fingernails into Janice's flesh. Janice yelped, jerked her head around.

The plastic woman gurgled with laughter. Some of her face dripped off like candle wax. 'Thought you were better'n everyone else, didn't you, Jan-Jan. Thought you were better'n *me.* You with your May Queen crown and your long legs... But look at you now. You'll burn, just like I am. Just like everyone will. *It will find you.'* Janice looked on, horrified, as her plastic mother reached inside her own body, and pulled out a battered, gunk-coated but instantly recognisable May Queen crown. She dripped up from the end of the bed and walked to the window, tossed the crown out, into the trash.

'Oh, please, G- God,' Janice stammered.

The plastic woman pivoted back round. Fixed her with a doll-eyed look and then shook her head. Globules of burning plastic took flight off her forming shooting stars in the husky bedroom air. 'Not God. The Divil,' she said. 'The Darkness.' Then she started cackling, tipping her head back and shouting out the laughs. Laughing so hard some of her plastic teeth started to pop out of her mouth, like corn. Laughing so hard more of her face started to slip, slide away, pooling on the floor. Laughing so hard...

...That Janice woke up. She woke up and immediately felt relief. But then, as she sucked in the lavender scent of his room - lavender with a savage undertone of burned plastic - then, as she felt the sticky, electric heat, she felt the scream building inside her. And then, when she felt someone reach out and touch her arm, she did scream. She screamed and rolled over, so her face was in the pillow. She tried to chew it instead of screaming, but it was no good. Her scream, as it echoed back to her from the walls, off Buckby's stupid built-in wardrobes with their stupid mirrors, sounded as though it was coming from the depths of an asylum for the criminally insane. Or else hell.

The hand started to stroke her arm, and she bit down once again on the pillow. 'Hush now,' said a gentle man's voice, a *gentleman's* voice, certainly not Buckby's. 'Hush. You must have had a dream. Quiet now, you'll wake the children.'

She dared to look up from the pillow. Saw Dr. Shaw perched on the chair at the side of the bed. Though it was dark,

365

though she was still brushing away the cobwebs of the nightmare, she still felt a flicker of concern for the man. There were great big body-bags under his eyes. His hair seemed to have turned from a distinguished salt-and-pepper to a shocked grey while she'd been asleep. His eyes looked bloodshot, told all kinds of horror stories which were worse, much worse than the nightmare.

'You're still here,' she gasped. And then, almost in the same breath. 'How's Lewis?' And then, 'Grace? Is Grace okay?'

Dr. Shaw continued to stroke her arm. 'One question at a time. First, Lewis...Lewis is...'

'Oh God, doc, is he all right?'

He leaned forward and clasped her hand, tightly, and for a moment, she was convinced Shaw was going to tell her Lewis had died in the night. And she decided she didn't want to hear that. She wrenched her hand away from him, clamped it over her ear. Did the same with her left hand, and then, like the girl who'd so wilfully prayed to be May Queen every night, sinfully neglecting those poor, starving Africans she was *supposed* to be praying for, she started to shout, *'la, la, la, la, la. I'm not listennniinngg.'*

With gentle, yet forceful hands, Shaw removed her hands. 'You need to be quiet, Janice. Lewis is sleeping now and he needs his sleep.'

'*Sleeping,*' she gasped. 'Not...'

He shook his head. 'Alive. But not necessarily kicking.'

'Have you worked out what's...'

'He's ill. I might say gravely ill, but I wouldn't want you to get the wrong idea.' He tapped his doctor's bag which was on the floor next to the chair. 'Old trusty here carries a lot of things, but what she doesn't carry is my full medical dictionary. That spans twenty volumes. Not even the Bibby Firm could lug all that around.'

She wanted to scream at him. *Just get on with it.* She knew why he was talking to her so slowly, so calmly, as though he was trying to hypnotise her into that same calm. But in an emergency like this it felt like too much. He opened his bag. Pulled out a small notepad. 'I went home during the night. Just to check on the... Just to look at the books. I think I might have at least made some sort of breakthrough as to the, uh, symptoms.' He opened the notepad. 'Let me see now. Ah, here we go. Right, from what you've told me, and from what I myself observed yesterday, Lewis is in the first stage of, uh, infection. He's developed a rash – lesions, as we both saw – and when he can talk, he's spoken of pains all over his body. He's

366

immensely tired all the time and yet he can't sleep, and so, a kind of delirium has overtaken him.' He skipped a couple pages. 'Temperature high. So high it has started to adversely affect the nervous system. Brain too...'

'He's... he's *brain damaged?* '

Shaw coughed. 'No. Not yet. Though there isn't much time. You mentioned that when you'd seen him coming back to the shop, you, or Mr. Buckby, or both, thought he was drunk.'

'Yes. He was crawling. Incoherent... He looked...'

'And that got me thinking. About something I'd once read about, a long, long time ago.'

'*Just tell me, doc,* ' Janice pleaded.

'I'm getting to that,' he said, softly. 'I'm just trying to prepare you. You see, since I've come back here, I've been looking for the *secondary* signs of the disease to take hold. According to the books, this should come after five to six days, but it appears that in Lewis this process has been much accelerated. Those lesions we both saw. They were mainly in the, uh, *dampest, darkest* places of his body, weren't they? Around the neck, the groin. The armpits. Now, the second stage of infection announces itself as swelling in all of those aforementioned areas. Buboes. Have you ever heard the word before?'

Janice shook her head.

'No reason that you should have,' he said, evidently taking her silence as a no. 'Of course, you might have done were you a historian.'

'A *historian?* What are you talking about *now?* '

'I'm talking about...' He lowered his voice. 'I'm talking about the plague.'

'The... plague? Like the thing that killed everyone in medieval times?'

Dr. Shaw spoke more urgently now. 'No, even in those days it didn't kill everyone. Between twenty-five and fifty percent of those who contracted the disease survived...'

'You're telling me he has a one in two chance of survival. Less than that?'

'I can't say. It seems... Accelerated in Lewis, as I said. Though the books told me to be cautious for blood in his urine and stool and black boils and spots all over his body too and there's no sign of them... So maybe that means he's got a less virulent strain. Or maybe...'

'But *how?* How's he got it?'

Shaw could only shrug. Dr. Permanently Unsure.

'And anyway,' she said, her thoughts going a mile a minute now, 'they got rid of the plague, didn't they? They invented a cure... Can't you just get the cure?'

Shaw winced. 'It's not as simple as that...'

'Yes it is,' she said, swinging her legs out of bed. 'It's as simple as a quick phone call to the mainland, surely. *I'll* make the call. They can airlift it over in a helicopter or something or they can take Lewis over there or... *I* don't know. You're the doctor. What are you doing for him?'

'Everything I can,' said Shaw, gripping her shoulders. 'Everything humanly possible. I've got him on antibiotics and we've got, as you might have noticed, the heating on full-whack. I've read the books and one of the old cures was to leave a bowl of vinegar at the end of the bed and...'

She snarled. 'A bowl of vinegar. Fucking antibiotics. The goddamn heating? What's that going to do? It sounds like quackery, doc. You're out of your depth. Get out of my way. Let me get to the phone.'

He wouldn't budge. Kept his hands pressed on her shoulders. It reminded her, uncomfortably, of the man in the radiation suit in the nightmare. Only, in the nightmare, her reactions hadn't been as sharp as they were now. In the nightmare, she'd not had the presence to lift up her knee and jab him in the balls with it, but she did now. She did it so hard, Shaw kinda squeaked and then collapsed over to one side. She barrelled over to the door. Saw it was locked from the inside. With angry, trembling fingers, she unlocked it.

'Don't,' gasped Shaw. 'Please don't...'

She ignored him, started to swing the door open. Immediately, weight hit it from the other side. She was sent flying back onto the floor by Grace, who landed on top of her. Grace, her daughter. Madly, breathily, hungrily, she sucked in Grace's sweet scent and then overpowered her with kisses. She kissed all along the top of her forehead. Kissed that sweet button nose, those rosy-red lips.

'Grace!' she said.

Dr. Shaw pulled them apart. For the first time in her life, she saw the mild-mannered doc was angry. *Beyond* angry. He picked up Grace and deposited her over the other side of the room, then stood over Janice, panting. 'I said *don't open the door*,' he barked. 'I told you, didn't I? I didn't just caution you, I made it explicitly clear you were not going to answer that door.'

'Dr. Shaw said I shunt come in here,' said Grace from the other side of the room. 'He says you're ill, mummy. Isn't that right, Bear.' She made Bear nod his assent. Bear nodded solemnly, *I concur.*

And suddenly, Janice felt like the plastic woman. She felt herself melting into the carpet. Parts of her puddling, pooling away, tearing away, streaming away. 'Is it true?' she moaned.

Dr. Shaw nodded. 'I was trying to bring you round to it as carefully as I could...' His anger seemed to have drifted away now, instead she saw only disappointment in his slumped shoulders, his wrinkled brow. 'Lewis must have passed it on to you... Hence the, uh, quarantine conditions. Grace... Well, until now, she'd shown no signs of it. But I'll have to check her over again now.'

'Oh God... I'm sorry.' She found she couldn't get up from the floor now, even if she'd have wanted to. This wasn't just passing on the herpes germ so your kid got coldsores, this was something far, far worse. This was murder. Or if not murder, manslaughter. She'd put her daughter in harm's way, *death's* way, through her own rash actions. She looked over at Grace and she saw that even now, the girl was starting to itch, using Bear's button nose to get at a scratch in the small of her back. 'Oh God... What can we do? There has to be more we can do than simply place a bowl of vinegar at the end of the bed. It's the twenty-first century, for Christ's sake.'

Dr. Shaw sighed down on the end of the bed, looking defeated. 'I'm afraid that's where you're wrong... You see, quite a lot's happened over the past twenty-four hours. On this island. And I suppose you could say that, to all intents and purposes, we're back in the Middle Ages. There's a Hoar's Blanket outside and no amount of wind will shift it. Coastguard, Flying Doctors, they wouldn't risk coming out here, not on a day like this. And by road... Well, there's a bit of a situation there too. Some people have set up a road-block, see? They won't let anyone on or off the island.'

Every new revelation felt like a mournful bell tolling. She wanted to beckon Grace, make her come over here, so they could both lie together and wait out this storm, no matter how long it might be. But she knew she couldn't. She knew she couldn't even *touch* Grace. Couldn't even breathe on her. She looked over at her daughter, clutching that big daft Bear of hers and cracked a smile,

369

hoping it would seem encouraging. Hoping Grace wouldn't be able to read the fear in her eyes.

'It's okay mummy,' said Grace, 'Bear says it'll all be over soon, isn't that right, Bear?' Bear nodded. 'Bear says that he'll watch out for us, even though the white-dark is here.'

'What do you mean Grace?'

'Bear says that The high-tide of Darkness has come, and it has come in multitudinous guises. It shall come large, but with the aspect of a shadow, stalking, hunting.'

Janice tried to climb to her feet. She was looking at her daughter with horror. 'This has to be the... the plague speaking... Is that right, doc?'

Dr. Shaw looked as though he'd swallowed his own tongue.

Grace continued. 'The Darkness has come small, in germ and disease, spreading its wickedness so that the Unholy should become infected. Finally, it has come as a winged beast, soaring, ready to pick off townspeople as prey.'

She then placed Bear carefully on the pillows at the top of the bed. Said, 'Bear needs to rest now. It makes him tired when he sees things.'

Dr. Shaw and Janice looked at each other. Both gulped. They waited for further revelations but none were forthcoming. While Bear flopped on the pillows, Grace flopped down onto the foot of the bed and within seconds, she was snoring, softly.

'What the hell was that, doc? That was the disease, right?' She wasn't sure now whether she *wanted* it to be disease. Was daemonic possession worse than disease?

Only after Dr. Shaw had tucked her back into bed and served her a steaming hot tea did she ask the two remaining questions, questions which had remained almost afterthoughts throughout the whole hellish episode. First, 'And are *you* all right, doc? Are you infected?'

He shook his head. Said something strange. 'No. Ironically, I am not.'

Second, 'And Devon? Mr. Buckby? Is he okay?'

The doctor looked away, awkwardly. 'He's, uh, gone, I'm afraid. I tried to tell him my diagnosis just as I did you, only, before I managed to say the word *plague,* he left. Don't know where. I'm sorry.'

'No, *I'm* sorry,' said Janice. And she was. For all of it.

41: Bird's Eye View

T he aerial photographer didn't turn out to be the owner of the helicopter. Which, when Freddie Livermore thought about it, made sense. Otherwise, why weren't all the cameramen in the news game quitting their jobs and moving into this new field if it paid well enough to buy a chopper? It had been Pete who'd wrung the information out of the photographer, almost as soon as he'd arrived. Indeed Pete had been so keen to find out this information he'd run under the rotors while they were still revolving at quite a pace, while they were still beating the long grass down into what looked like a crop circle just off the A24. He came back to them looking satisfied.

'It's his *brother's,*' he said, with a relieved smile, as though he'd just found out the grass was definitively not greener on the other side. 'Brother's an, uh…' He shot a sheepish look at Charlotte. 'Well, let's just say he's in the TA game, and when I say TA I don't mean Territorial Army.'

Charlotte smiled helpfully. 'It's all right, Pete. I already know.' Then to Freddie, she said, 'His brother's Norman Brewer.'

It was all she needed to say. Everyone knew who Norman Brewer was, and the game he was in. Tits and Arse was only the start of it. His north east coast porn empire covered the full range of sexual fetishes from feet to prosthetic limbs. The brother however, the aerial photographer, wasn't what they were expecting and they wondered how two peas could have been raised so they seemed not only to have come from different pods but from different *planets.* After the pilot switched off the engine, the photographer finally opened the door, climbed out, and shuffled across the beaten grass to meet them.

'Nice day for it,' said Freddie, extending a hand.

The photographer responded, offering a clammy handshake which Freddie, usually a man whose rule for handshakes was *hang*

371

on for dear life until the other man let's go, was only too happy to pull out of. 'Archie,' said the photographer. 'Archie Brewer.'

'What's that then, a bit like James... James Bond?' said Freddie, for some reason trying to leaven the situation with some humour. Perhaps because it all felt so very awkward. Archie Brewer seemed to inspire awkwardness like his brother seemed to inspire girls to shed their clothes. He stood about six two but seemed ashamed of his height. So much so that he kinda bent his back in the middle, crooked himself smaller. Unless he spent so much time running under rotor blades the wind had stuck and he'd remained like that. He had great wispy eyebrows, whose stray hairs sprouted every which way but loose. The beginnings of a gruff beard. In fact, everything about him seemed fuzzy, hairy, and a little damp too. Apart from his eyes. Piercing blue they were. Freddie, when he felt those eyes on him, felt an unconquerable urge to look away.

'Ah,' said Archie, cracking an ill-advised smile made up of nicotine-yellowed teeth, 'the aerial photography game's not all fast girls and cars.'

Charlotte laughed rather too shrilly at his 'joke'. Freddie felt the need to talk over her. 'Look, Arch. You're a brick for letting us go up in your bird.'

Archie shrugged. 'S'alright. I'm not that busy at the moment. There's not much call for a good aerial photographer any more. Not now every man and his dog's got Google Maps on their computer. Not now everyone can zoom in on it and pick out their own houses and...'

'Every man and his dog,' mused Pete, 'wasn't that the name of one of your brother's, uh, special pictures?'

At the mere mention of his brother Archie hunchbacked himself, deckchaired himself into something smaller. *Sharper.* 'Very droll,' he sneered. 'Have you been thinking of that ever since you came up and asked me about the chopper earlier?'

Freddie thought he'd better step in before these two men started arguing, before Pete started making wild claims that video was more of an art form than photography because it was more naturalistic, or somesuch. 'We ready to roll?'

'Not yet,' said Archie, through gritted teeth. 'Pilot's just got to make a few checks first.' He looked round at the chopper. Inside the cockpit, the pilot, dressed in ubiquitous aviator sunglasses despite the fug, and a white shirt which looked *navy jets* and was sure to get Charlotte hot under the collar, gave a friendly salute.

Archie saluted back, rather raggedly. He'd have been given fifty laps of the parade ground had he made a salute like that on active duty.

'She's a... lovely looking bird,' said Freddie, aware of the double entendre. *Highlighting* the double entendre, hoping it would cover up his true feelings about the chopper, which were that it immediately looked too small, too flimsy. Too *bird-like*. Sure he'd felt the power of those rotors (they'd mucked up his hair) but he'd also seen it pitch and yaw as it dragged in to land. He'd seen how the wind, and it was only a *slight* wind at that, had buffeted it.

His second impression of the helicopter was that Brewer had gone rather over the top with the branding. As though, as soon as Charlotte had given him the green light, he'd had someone, perhaps the pilot, perhaps that wasn't a *navy jet* white shirt at all but rather a painter's overall, daub the entire left side of it – or should that be starboard side? Port side? – with sickly green paint which read BREWER INC. The lettering reminded him rather of JAX SNAX up the A24. Such an expensive toy and they'd ruined it.

'So, can you drive... *fly* this thing?' said Freddie, when it was clear Archie was going to make no response to his earlier, *she's a lovely bird comment*. Archie smiled. 'I've learned... But I'm... Both of us, my brother and me, we're more *behind the camera* kinda guys. We're both serious about the composition of our pictures, despite the difference. It's all about artistic integrity and...'

Good girl Charlotte. He watched how she read the situation, led Pete away by the arm before he could get involved in a debate about the semantics of imagery. Led him away with promises of more food, by the looks of it; as soon as they were a safe distance, she opened her satchel and pulled out a Biscuit Boost which he looked delighted to receive. Then, the pair of them started unloading the van. Selecting which equipment they needed to take with them. No boom mic, Freddie noticed. He didn't go over and help though because now, his uneasiness was spreading. He felt it in his bowels, in the manifest need to shit. He felt it in his knees. He felt it, finally, in his shoulders, when the pilot came out with a life-jacket and slipped it over his head. He was about to protest, ask *why* he needed a life jacket, but realised he didn't want to hear the answer.

He supposed there was a very real possibility of crashing. Visibility, even on this side of the causeway, was poor. Over there, it looked like someone had opened the biggest sack of flour in the world and had then shaken it up and let it form a cloud. Over there, it looked dangerous. Not that Charlotte seemed bothered. No.

373

Charlotte seemed excited, more animated than he'd ever seen her. The pilot could barely hold her still enough to put on *her* lifejacket. And when he pulled it over her head she gave this little squeal, which sounded identical to the noise when she orgasmed.

Even Pete was excited. Asking questions constantly. 'Hey, do you have to give one of them safety demonstrations before we take off, like in a plane?'

'No man,' growled the pilot. 'Just strap yourself in and enjoy the rode.'

And, 'How long do you have to train to fly one of these things? Is there a test, like a driving test.'

'Yes. Yes there is.'

And, 'How far can you go in these things?' And, 'How high can we go?'

The pilot gave up answering. Freddie wanted to ask a question of his own; *are there toilets, because I think I might shit myself if not,* but decided against it.

They climbed aboard. The pilot had to give Freddie a hand-up and the whole thing felt very undignified, like the time when, for a feature, he'd had to step onto a boat and pretend he was sailing it, only, whenever he finished his to-camera speaking part and made to step on the boat, it kinda shifted on its mooring, drifted further off the jetty. They'd had to do about fifty takes and it ended up being the moment which most people stopped him on the street about. 'Say, aren't you the guy off *TV Presenters Do the Funniest Things?* The one who couldn't climb on that boat?'

Once they were all safely on board and buckled up, the pilot clambered into the cockpit, affixed one of those strap-headset things to his face, adjusted his aviators, and then started the rotor blades. Freddie felt a lurch as the helicopter immediately tried to take-off, perhaps buffeted by a gust of wind. He *almost* lost control of his bowels. Archie turned round in his seat and shouted something over his shoulder, but the noise was already so loud whatever he said was lost.

Loud, and getting louder. It was almost as though noise was the power flying the chopper. He felt it in his feet, in his knees. He felt it exploding in his ears. And then, in an instant, he forgot all about it because the pilot lifted the helicopter off the ground. It bounced upwards, briefly bounced back down again, and then gained height. Charlotte looked over at him. There was a kind of madness in her eyes. He tried to fix himself an adventurous mask of his own, but feared it came out strained. Pete elbowed him in the ribs, trying to rearrange himself on his seat so he could look out the window, but really, there was no point. So close to the ground, visibility was still so poor they couldn't see beyond the fence at the end of the field. The trees next to it seemed like reflections in a calm lake; reflections of some other world.

The chopper gained height, pushing through some alarming turbulence and into calmer air. Freddie at last released the breath that, until that moment, he hadn't realised he'd been holding. Charlotte shouted something over at him and he couldn't hear. He wanted to lean over, so she could shout in his ear, but he didn't feel like the floor was solid enough beneath him, like, maybe if he shifted his weight he'd cause the floor to fall out entirely, and then all that would be between him and crashing to the ground was his seatbelt. Charlotte unbuckled hers and stretched over.

'I *said*, this is *brilliant*. This is *sexy*,' she said, her hot breath tickling his ear. For some reason this made him need to shit even more. Perhaps his erection was taking up too much room down there and his bowels had decided on the ejector-seat to release some space.

To his right, Pete started unpacking one of his small, handheld cameras. Clicking it together, assembling its parts, like it was a gun. And if it had been a gun, Freddie would have wished there was a silencer fitted. Still, at least the noise covered up the bubbling, broiling turmoil which was going on inside his stomach.

The chopper climbed some more, seemed to hang for a moment, which almost caused him to lose the contents of his stomach from *the other end*, and then banked left. Into, amazingly, clearer skies. They were high enough that they were above most of the fug, but low enough that they were under the clouds. Pete gave a shout of delight and immediately started filming. Charlotte pressed her nose to the glass like a little girl taken on the bus for the first time. And at first, Freddie only concentrated on the glass, wondering whether it was reinforced, whether it was strong enough to hold Charlotte's weight pressed against it, wondering whether, if it wasn't, it would crack and she'd plunge out and then some kind of hoovery-suction thing would be created like in films when they opened the doors on planes while they were still too high in the sky. The glass was greasy. Looked as though it was streaked in ice-cream, vomit, dust and dirt. But eventually, he trained himself to look *past* the glass.

There was a tremendous view of the north east coast stretching up into Scotland; a land of rolling hills and crashing cliffs, of battered bays and skeletal trees hunkering down against the wind. He dared look down and he saw the A24, glistening with oil which had most likely been slicked from JAX SNAX. The road ran parallel to the high-speed rail line which joined Edinburgh with Newcastle and the east coast; for a while and he looked down on a Toy Town train which rocketed past them like something out of a science fiction movie, too sleek to be part of this hard-bitten environment. A Virgin, he thought. Probably hadn't been many of them in anything owned by a Brewer for a while, unless Brewer the Lesser, the aerial photographer, was one. Soon the train passed, bucking and weaving through the many level-crossings which pockmarked the farm roads, pressing onward to the comforts of civilisation.

Freddie sucked in a breath. Smelled the sea - a salty-fresh, crabby and *open* odour - and then picked out the dark shape of Limm Island through the white noise of the denser fog over there. From this perspective it looked as though Limm wasn't even an island at all but just the furthest eastern part of the coastline. A rockier, foggier, altogether darker part, sure, but part of the same mainland. He couldn't see the dividing line but he knew there was one. If it wasn't for the fog, he'd have been able to see parts of the causeway slowly starting to emerge as the tide started to disembark. The causeway; the thing which at once acted as the umbilical chord and the choking-noose for all on Limm.

He'd just about managed to convince himself that the journey wouldn't have been much better had they been going by land. He knew from bitter experience how hard it was to drive over the causeway, crunching over the sand, through great anchor chains of seaweed and around some small and some rather less small pieces of driftwood. He knew that the van would jolt and buffet him almost as much as the helicopter was, because down there, there were huge potholes in the tarmac, brought on by over-use of chains on the tyres in snow.

Outside, a flock of sea-birds started to fly alongside the chopper for a while, like an air-borne version of the dolphins which swam playfully around speed-boats in the Med. He watched them as they ducked and dived through the air like the great cockney chancers they were. He was sure the birds were cockney, even though he wasn't sure what specific type of bird they were. It was because the birds had a big-city confidence to them, bred from the

376

knowledge that they were protected by the National Trust and the RSPB. They had a wide-boy strut which meant there was never nothing that would get them down.

After a while, the birds flew off into the clouds and it was almost as though they'd seen what was coming, because suddenly, the chopper slammed into another load of turbulence. First, it felt as though the helicopter was travelling fast, downhill, on a cobbled street. Then if felt as though it was travelling fast, downhill, on a cobbled street and the suspension had gone. Soon though it become like the helicopter was trying to plot a course over a gigantic Toblerone. Freddie screwed up his eyes.

He felt Charlotte's hand wrapping round his. Least he hoped it was hers. If he opened his eyes to check, he was going to throw up. He tried to imagine himself on solid ground. Tried to imagine himself on a sunbed, topping up his tan ready for the next *Countryfile* job. Tried to imagine himself comfortable. But now it felt as though he'd never been comfortable in his life. And the strangest thing was the noise. It didn't sound like the whirr and chop of rotor blades any more. It sounded like hundreds and thousands of flies buzzing around his head. A couple times, he reached up, using the hand Charlotte wasn't gripping, and tried to swat them away. The third time he attempted this, Charlotte leaned over and whispered into his ear. Even the pressure of her breast against his knee didn't excite him now though.

'Are you okay?' she whispered. 'If you feel sick, I think you're supposed to tuck your head between your knees or something.'

No, he thought, *tucking your head between your knees is the Assume Crash position. So your teeth are protected. So you can be identified even if the plane... helicopter... explodes you into smithereens.*

'Freddie?'

The turbulence continued.

'Freddie, do you need a sick bag or... Or something?'

He groaned. He felt green, like a landlubber set sail on stormy seas. He felt full-up with bile. He felt like he'd sacrifice the story just to feel steady ground beneath his feet again. Hell, if he was on solid ground now, he'd untie his shoes, roll off his socks, go gamboling across a farmer's field, cow-pat or no cow-pat.

After a while, Charlotte said something else. 'Pilot just said we've crossed into the fog up above Limm now. He says he'll start looking for somewhere to land now. Isn't that something?'

He groaned. What was something was the fact he could taste vomit on his tongue and he'd not even been sick yet. He needed something, anything to take his mind off this... This agony. He pulled her into him. 'Help me, Charlotte... Please... I can't...'

'Yes you can,' she said, firmly.

He sniffed.

'Pull yourself together, Fred.'

He couldn't. Surely.

'This is work. This is the job. Calm the fuck down, okay?'

He clawed at her top, touched breast. She pushed his hand away like a mother who was trying to ration her kiddie off her milk. 'No. Look, Freddie, we're nearly there now... Not that I can tell because it's so white-dark, but... Stop it.' She pushed him away again. From somewhere off right, Pete sniggered.

Freddie felt a wave of anger tiding through him and at once it seemed to drown out the sickness. After a few moments cursing behind his teeth, he felt right enough to move. A few moments more and he dared look through the glass again. He looked out and saw white. Snowdrift-white. It felt like they were floating on the thick, cotton-wool air which was surrounding the helicopter. 'Where are we?' he said, his tongue thick in his throat.

Pete rolled his eyes. Pointed down. 'Somewhere down there, at least according to the co-ordinates, is the Limm monastery.' He pointed a little left. 'Somewhere down *there,* is Limm town, and Manny Combs.' He waved the hand-held camera.

'Why haven't we landed yet?' asked Freddie.

Charlotte bit her lip. Glanced at Pete. 'Pilot says we can't. Yet. On account of this... mist. He calls it a Hoar's Blanket though.'

'What we gonna do?' said Pete.

Freddie narrowed his eyes. 'Now? We contact this Manny Combs. Now we get our source. Straight to the top. And as soon as we can land, we set up a meet. Okay?'

Charlotte was already reaching for her phone.

Absently, Freddie brushed away a fly. Saw another crawling across Charlotte's cheek as she turned her head, ready to speak into the phone. There was another one too, crawling on the headrest of the pilot's seat. And another, he now saw, on the control panel. Fucking flies. Nothing but an irritant.

378

42: Mary Celeste

They could have spontaneously combusted. Or evaporated into the ether. More aptly, they could have been swallowed up by the thick, gaping maw of the Hoar's Blanket, never to be seen again. As the breeze caught the door and slammed it shut behind her, Ruth Sharp echoed the sound by letting her head clump against the wall. She screwed up her eyes, opened them again and saw once again they weren't here. That she wasn't going mad. That she wasn't seeing things that weren't there, or blanking out the things that actually *were* there. Ever since her fleeting vision of the monk in the ruined remains of the monastery a couple days ago, she'd felt haunted by visions, but this, flagrantly, wasn't one of them. Sam Bibby and the big cat expert had disappeared. And it wasn't exactly like they were *small objects* which could simply get lost behind the desk or roll behind the filing cabinet. They'd gone, and the only thing they seemed to have left behind was the bottle of L'O water, which was lying on its side on the desk, dripping out its remaining contents onto the floor.

She flopped down at the desk, dropped her head into her hands. When she'd first moved here, she'd imagined sitting at this desk with a good obedient dog at her feet, and being inspired to write the one novel which she knew lay within her. Something about the call of the sea and escape from mind-crushing mundanity perhaps. She'd had similar dreams about painting; sweeping seascapes, the majestic monastery ruins, Cawdor Head; the landscape bent over backwards for her, but the rather crude watercolour on the wall behind the door was as far as she'd got. Even in her own private space, she'd gone to some lengths to ensure it was hidden, just in case anyone happened to pop their head in and laugh. Now the paints were on the top shelf, half hidden by her *How to Write* books like a guilty, pornographic secret. The easel was being used to prop up a big calendar which showed bookings for months in advance. Before his OCD really set-in, Roberto had once borrowed one of the brushes to brush pastry in the kitchen and Vicar used the paint-mix pot for his water when his other bowl was in the wash. As far as she knew, this was the last time anyone had used any of the equipment. One day, of course, she'd take on someone else to run the place for her; a manager giving herself the time to actually learn to paint or to write or to photograph. But now, the island had taken over. Was commanding her every thought, was in tune with, and dictating the very rhythms of her body.

This was a problem. She thought about calling Sam's mobile, but knew for a fact that its signal was intermittent at best, and besides, it *felt* wrong. The island made her sense it was wrong, that they'd gone somewhere, someplace where phones didn't matter. She drummed her fingers on the desk. It used to be that her office was her problem-solving place. She could sit at this desk, whack the Bowie on full, and let that part of her which had seemed so painfully dormant when she was a housewife revel in the minutiae of running a hotel. In the logistics, and even the boring stuff like the accounts. At the age of (through gritted teeth) forty-nine, she felt as though she'd finally grown up; learned to stand on her own two feet, and had evidenced that by entering the Ship last night, all-guns blazing, so to speak. But now it felt like the rug had been yanked out right from under her and... And for the first time in a while, she thought about leaving Limm's people to their fate like she'd left Jonathan to his fate with Christian.

But she forced herself to remain in the chair. She forced herself to pick up the phone, prepared to call the emergency number Sam Bibby had left for her. Now, Ruth was a sixties child. Her best years were the late seventies, early eighties, and she'd been heavily into the music scene (i.e. she'd smoked a little pot, occasionally tried acid) and had tagged along on numerous ban the bomb demonstrations, marches and protests. Having to stoop to the level of calling the police (and she didn't necessarily class Sam Bibby *as* police, he was more of a local do-gooder, but his friends, they were *definitely* police) was not in her make up. She still had a deep distrust of them which stemmed from a particularly violent demo when she happened to be caught on the back of the head by a policeman's baton. She wasn't worried about 'being a grass'; she didn't care that 'outside help' was frowned upon; she didn't live by the rules of Limm Islanders after all, she wasn't one of them, as they were constantly reminding her. But still, to even consider taking the step of appealing to the police for help seemed to be another nail in the coffin of the old, young her. Bowie wouldn't have called the police. But then again, David Bowie's sole source of income wasn't a hotel on an island which seemed to be sinking, by the accumulated weight of all the disasters, into the very sea from whence it had come.

As she was dialling the number for Northumbria Police – the nearest station on the mainland was about twenty miles down the coast in sunny Norsea – Vicar ambled into the room with an accusatory look chalked across his jowls. Ruth almost didn't make the call. Her finger hovered over the red button on her mobile. Vicar continued to stare.

'I have to do this,' she breathed. And to her eyes, his eagerness to creep back under the desk, where he started to lick at the sliver of exposed skin between her socks and the bottom of her corduroy trousers, seemed like grudging acceptance. She hammered in the last two numbers and then tucked the phone between her shoulder and ear and waited out the twenty or so rings until someone answered.

'Hello?' said a surprisingly young-sounding voice.

'Err, yes, hello. I was wondering whether you could help me... Is this the Norsea Police Station?'

A pause followed, as though the speaker was unsure. Ruth half-expected him to shout something like *sarge? Is this the cop shop or what?* through a mouthful of chewing gum. Then: 'Yeah. Who's this? This is a private line, you know. There's a non-emergency help-line. Number's in the Yellow Pages.'

'This is Ruth Sharp,' she said, in her best, most authoritative voice, the one reserved for such grand occasions as informing Christian she was leaving, and telling Adrian Bloody Devonish she didn't want to hear another of his opinions about the workings of the hospitality industry on Limm. 'I don't need the number for the non-emergency help-line... I was given this number by a...' She'd been about to call Sam Bibby a friend, which was stretching the point somewhat. 'One of your officers gave me this number in case I needed to call in... He said you'd be able to help me.'

'Who said?'

'Sam. PC Bibby. Limm Island.'

A whistle. 'Sam Bibby. Well I never. I didn't know he was going round giving my number out. What seems to be the problem, duckie? Is Sam there? I'd like to speak to him.'

'Sam's, uh, not here... That's why I feel *forced* into calling you.'

'Who's forcing you, like?'

'I mean, I feel duty-bound. There's nothing else I can do. This is a last-resort kinda thing,' said Ruth. Under the desk, Vicar finally stopped licking at her leg and started rolling around like he did when he was randy. She shot him a warning look.

'R-i-i-i-ght. And who, or what seems to be the problem, duck?'

Ruth was flabbergasted. Surely *nobody* went around calling women *duck* these days, let alone desk-jockeys at the police station. Surely even up here, in the middle of nowhere, in the lonely old north east, they'd had training courses on stuff like political correctness and how to speak to the general public? To make things worse, under the desk, Vicar was making ominous signs that he was about to start shagging her leg.

'Vicar!' she warned.

'You want to make a complaint about a vicar?'

Vicar *did* start shagging her leg, wooing her with his version of the Johnny Cash classics, throat-gurgle style. 'Stop it, Vicar!' she hissed, trying to shake him off. In response, the dog went all Spinosaurus and bared his teeth. From where Ruth was sitting, it looked as though he was bloody grinning at her.

Another pause, and then: 'Look, is this a joke? If so, it in't funny at all, duck. And...' Ruth dropped the mobile phone on the desk and missed the next part of the conversation. She seized the opportunity to push the randy dog off her with both hands and then tucked herself firmly behind the desk, so there was no room for him to get back under there. Then she picked up the phone again, half-expecting the young policeman to have put the phone down. He hadn't. He was still moaning. Evidently, this wasn't the first crank call he'd received in the line of duty (even though it wasn't *supposed* to be a crank call). '...and the chief's off up to the borders leaving me manning the fort all on my tod. It was someone pulling our legs about a wild animal on the loose last time. Up the A24.'

'Oh,' said Ruth. Really, it was all she could say. 'Sorry... But this isn't a crank call... My dog, Vicar, was playing-up, that's all. Shall we get on with my what I need to tell you?'

Vicar must have heard his name from where he was skulking over the other side of the room. He started making more of the Johnny Cash noises and then scratched at the back of her desk chair. Resolutely, she ignored him.

'You have a dog called Vicar?'

'Yes. But he's...'

'I bet that gets you into all sorts of funny situations... Like, say you were walking your dog past a Church and you happened to shout *c'mere Vicar,* and what if the actual vicar came out 'cos he thought you was calling him, like?'

'Yes, it's a name fraught with dangers like that,' sighed Ruth.

'Or what if you were walking past a Church and there was a Christening ganning on and the vicar never turned up and the guests were all like *call the vicar,* and someone called the vicar and then your dog showed up... Madness. I mean, would your dog even know all that stuff about putting the kiddo's head in the watter and that?'

'Thankfully, the scenario's never occurred, but if it does, I'm sure he could wing it.'

'Oh aye? He a clever 'un, that dog of yours? Me mam's dog, Albert; she reckons he can say proper words, like that dog on the telly what says *sausages.* I told her, she wants to borrow a video recorder, get him on *Animal's Do the Darndest Things.* She could get herself two hundred and...'

'I'm sorry to interrupt, but can we please get back to the matter at hand?'

Sulkily: 'Yeah...'

She felt like asking whether he had a pen, but reckoned that any questions, or in fact deviating from the course of her story at all, was liable to lead them down yet another dead end. 'I'm the owner of the Seahorse Boutique Hotel on Limm,' she began, before rattling off the full story of how Sam Bibby *and friend* had apparently gone missing off the face of the earth from her back office. When she finished, she took a deep breath and prepared for the barrage of questions the young desk-jockey would doubtless have for her, like whether Sam *and friend* would have been able to slip out the hotel's back door, and whether, more importantly, that door was green or blue, because his mam had a green door, but were blue ones better, or perhaps he'd go back to the dog, ask whereabouts Vicar slept, *like, does he have a hotel room all to hisself, like?* But he surprised her by saying: 'That doesn't sound like Sam. Sam Bibby's usually careful. Always punctual. Least he was in college, like. That's where I know him from. But listen, I'm hearing all sorts from that island today.... That's where my boss really is, over the other side of the causeway, only I'm not supposed to be giving that kind of information out to the general public. My advice? Stay indoors. Keep the doors bolted. I have a few other ways I can try to get in touch with Sam which I'll give a go, and if I have any luck, I'll call you back... I'll call you back if I don't have any luck too. How's that suit?'

'Thank you,' gushed Ruth. 'Thank you so much... I just... Well, it might seem like a trivial matter, nothing to concern the police, but Sam *did say* he'd be here and it's important and... Well, as you say, it's not like him and...'

The desk-jockey cut in: 'You're preaching to the choir here, like. Hey, preaching to the choir. I imagine your Vicar does some of that, doesn't he?'

'Well, he does sing sometimes,' said Ruth, aware that she was veering dangerously into uncharted territory again, but she was just so grateful. And the desk-jockey seemed nice. Harmless. Under a different set of circumstances, she would have found his old-mannish jokes rather funny. So she stayed on the line rather longer than she was expecting, telling him all about how she got Vicar from the shelter and how he could sing Johnny Cash when he was angry, confused or randy. And when they finished the call, she'd got herself another customer for the summer season. Desk-jockey, or PC Nick Webb, said he'd definitely be coming, once he checked with 'her indoors' of course, and definitely *after* all the 'malarkey' on the island was over, to stay for at least a couple of nights, and maybe, just maybe, she'd let him walk the dog. She didn't tell him the price of an overnight stay, didn't want to in fact. She didn't want it to sound like bribery when she offered him the Snowdrop Suite for less than half-price.

Soon as she replaced the handset in the cradle though, Vicar started growling, as though he was annoyed he was no longer one of the most talked-about things in the room. A couple beats later, she realised the real reason why, when Mart Bibby blundered into the room, almost filling the entire doorway. He looked as surprised as Ruth had been that Sam and *his friend* weren't in situ. Paused for a moment, scratched his great, bowling-ball head.

'They've gone,' said Ruth. '*Puff.* Vanished. Just like that.'

Mart Bibby shook his head. 'Shit... So's everyone else in the front room. And I mean everyone. Mike Ford was still banging on at them to sign the petition but then one of them kids got word on their mobile... Apparently there's been a road-block set up on this side of the causeway. And everyone just upped and left. Headed down right for it. I'm not sure whether they wanted to join in with the block or whether they wanted to break through it, all I know is when I tried to shout after them to come back, nobody listened... Mike's gone after 'em to try to pull them back but...' He shrugged. 'You saw him out there, giving it all the big I-am, like he's the next politician. And folk don't want to hear that. They want action. So either they've thrown their lot in with the farmers, or else they've gone to fight 'em. Either way, the emergency meeting's turned into an emergency all on its own. I should have bloody known.'

He slumped down into one of the chairs. 'What do we do now?'

Vicar sniffed at the big-man's crotch. Mart wafted him away. Vicar sniffed again. And suddenly Ruth had an idea.

'Is Sam's coat still hanging in the corridor?' she asked.

Mart nodded, sadly. 'It is. Why? You cold or something?'

She didn't answer, she walked out into her silent hotel, retrieved the coat, balled it up, held it under Vicar's nose. 'Come on boy!' she said, putting on her excited voice. 'Come on Viccsy. Where's the man who wears this coat? Where's Sam Bibby?'

Vicar buried his nose in the coat, sniffed. Sniffed some more. And then his body tensed. His tail stuck up like the pole at the back of a dodgem car. He gave one, gruff little bark and then dashed out of the room. Ruth was on his tail quickly, Mart was a little slower off the mark, but once he saw what they were doing, he was mustard-keen.

43: Prometheus

Across the water, three sets of would-be interlopers looked set to descend on the island. There was a traffic jam cresting the hill over the other side of the causeway and then trailing down the B-road towards the tourist car park. But the tourist car park was already full and the causeway was still impassible, so in the end, all the vehicles simply buzzed around the edge, helpless and hungry as flies.

There were three sets of would-be interlopers and, despite the Hoar's Blanket, or even because the Hoar's Blanket *wanted him to see,* Manny Combs could easily pick out who was who even from this distance. First there was the media, a slick of ant-like vans which each carried their satellite equipment on their backs as though they were trays of dinner-party tidbits; offerings to their queen, the rolling twenty-four hour news networks. Then there were the vehicles belonging to the hunters, those who'd sniffed out, through the wires of the ruddy internet, the promise of a real, live exotic beast on the loose, one which they'd be able to trap, or hunt. Gun down and win a prize. The vehicles of the hunters were defined by their council estate chic. They were souped-up Fords and Vauxhalls with exhaust pipes as big as trees and super whoofer sound systems which would scare any right-minded big cat into the middle of next week. These north east coast heroes were here to make their names, hoping a reality TV career would follow their slaying of the beast. Manny had some doubts over which was the more blood-thirsty of pursuits. The final set of vehicles were those belonging to the animal protection idiots. Those who wanted to throw themselves in front of the panther and stop the bullets. These people came in their camper vans and their Beetles and their bloody skip-like Skodas. They were all of them a scourge, and as soon as the tide pulled up its skirts far enough, they'd all finger their way across the wet causeway onto *his*

386

island. The only saving grace was the road-block, set up by some of the more dunderheaded farmers.

So far, the dunderheaded farmers looked as though they'd hold firm, but what would happen when even they were dazzled by the TV lights? What would happen when some smarmy exec promised them their very own Andy-Warhol fifteen minutes? The TV crews, of course, would just lap up those dunderheaded farm-types. They loved NIMBYs, especially when they didn't really appear to have any clear agenda and were simply acting up. TV was always showing madcap NIMBYs like the idiot Fathers Against Justice and the lunatic BNP. That kind of guff filled great ruddy chunks of the news networks. For them, Limm had become one part an *and finally* story, one part docu-soap, one part freak show.

Village idiots waving placards and bedsheets which said the things they couldn't possibly form a sentence complete enough to speak. Gurning, buck-tooth, inbred yokels stuttering barely comprehensible responses to TV's questions. And in the end, they'd all stand aside. They'd let the three sets of interlopers onto the island. And that really would be that. He couldn't rely on any of them. Could only rely on himself.

They were parked up in the limo some way back from the coastal road, in the gateway to one of the fields. Manny was leaning forward in his seat, gripping the furry headrest of the seat in front. He was imagining what all the other local mayors along the north east coast would be thinking. Shadrack or Addam, or another of those interminable local bores would make every effort to call him on the blower as soon as the TV footage was shown. He could almost hear Shadrack, trying to control his voice through the guffaws and wheezing and fug of Addam's whisky breath as they crammed their truck-like bulks into the phone box by the Tyne Bridge. 'You've lost it, Manny!'

'You okay, sir?' asked Dave Chester, the chauffeur, who had pivoted on the front seat and was now staring at Combs. Chester was a slight man with a boyish body. The chauffeur's cap, which Combs still forced him to wear at all times, even though the balance of power between them had inexorably shifted, looked too big for his head. Big as a cowboy hat. And that was rather fitting, considering the man *was* a cowboy; insisted on being paid in cash, despite the problems thrown up by last year's expenses row. He'd also been rather negligent when it came to stocking the mini-fridge which divided the back seats, and in his more suspicious moments,

Manny was *sure* the man was helping himself. That would explain the cross-hairs of burst blood vessels on his thin nose and the constant shake in his long fingers.

'Sir?' pressed the chauffeur.

Manny had the urge to thumb the button-thingamajig which powered the dividing window contraption but couldn't seem to summon the requisite energy. Until very recently, he would have revelled in the opportunity for a good old scrap but now - now the media were sicced on men like him; now they wanted to uncover shaggers and alcies and shysters at every misplaced moral turn – he found the old back's-against-the-wall bottle seemed to have deserted him. Perhaps that was why the pinched-face, long-fingered chauffeur was looking at him so strangely.

'I'm okay,' gruffed Manny. 'Tip-top, my boy. Nothing I like more than a challenge.' He rubbed his hands together for added effect but found his palms too sweaty and swiftly stopped with that malarkey. Instead, he smoothed down his camel-hair coat, smoothed out his brow, and offered him his beaming TV smile. He caught sight of himself in he rear-view mirror and was astounded by how Blairy-fake the smile seemed. How showing his teeth in such a fashion made him appear like some cornered animal; some dark, creeping, predatory animal tainted by madness. Only, this predatory animal was now becoming jowly and his once jet black hair was now salt and pepper grey and had started receding badly; it was, in fact, a wholesale retreat, reflecting the tidal flow around Limm Island.

He sighed luxuriously, and let himself relax back into the soft leather seat, opening the mini-fridge at his side. He rummaged around a little, but found nothing to his complete satisfaction, and so opted for a can of gin and tonic. A *can* of gin and tonic. Was this how far he'd stooped? What happened to the Bombay Sapphires and the Rummy Gins of a decade back? What happened to tonic so smooth it could have been rolled on the thighs of virgins? Eh? What? Eh? Next he'd be drinking whisky and milk on trains like tramps who need something to simultaneously line their stomach and make themselves throw up. *Trains.* That was another thing the local government watchdogs were trying to *encourage.* They wanted him to give up his chauffeur-driven limo and resort to cattle-class. Luckily, in the most recent witch-hunts, he'd been able to argue his case very well. After all, no trains stopped near Limm Island any more, and this was almost the whole of his constituency. In some ways, it suited him that Limm was so remote.

'Chin-chin,' he said, cracking open the can. Foul-smelling, stagnant toad-broth fizzed up over the lip of his can and soaked into his coat. He didn't bother wiping it away. Instead, he rooted around to find his old-faithful crystal tumbler for that added touch of class. Found it in the seat-well amongst his papers, where he'd left it earlier. It still contained sad, shrivelled lemon from his last early-morning drink.

'Want me to drive you back home now, sir?' asked Chester, hopefully. 'So we can sort out that little *problem* behind your couch before someone finds it?'

Manny shook his head. He was very much inclined to sit it out and wait for the end out here. And besides, going along on those windy roads back to the town Limm would be suicidal if he was trying to drink a good old G and T at the same time.

'No thank you,' he said, and then took a sip from the glass. The bitterness made him wince but he took his medicine. 'Pass me the binocs there will you? I'll see if they can pierce through this milk-gloom a bit more... The binocs... There's a good boy.'

Obediently, Dave Chester reached over to the passenger seat and then handed over the binoculars. 'Doing a bit of bird-watching, are we sir?'

'No, I am ruddy not,' said Manny, testily. He hated the seabirds which flocked around the mudflats here when the tide was out. They were part of the reason his plans for the Manny Combs Memorial Bridge hadn't simply been rushed through without any public consultation. They were the reason the wildlife wallahs had got so up-in-arms about the plans. As if birds counted as much as humans. Birds were ruddy *pests*, that was what they were. Why, already, since they'd been parked-up, one feathery bastard or another had taken it upon themselves to shit on the limo's windscreen not once, not twice, but *thrice,* like the ruddy cock-crowing three times to signal Peter's denial of Christ.

He trained the binocs across the gradually falling tide and onto the crowd over the other side, and he had to strain his eyes to pick out the individuals. He couldn't believe they were still there despite the fact there was quite clearly a road-block. *Nothing better to do.* But it was too late now. All too late. And the fug around them seemed to be drawing closer. In the white-darkening sky, seabirds bobbed and weaved and made their ruddy mating calls or whatever

389

they were. He felt his temperature rising and had another long draught of his G and T to dampen it somewhat.

He winced at the bitterness of the last few drops of G and T and reflected on the mess which lay in front of him, through the binocs. 'Look at them,' he seethed. 'What do they possibly hope to achieve?'

Dave Chester, clearly unaware whether an answer was required, simply grunted by way of response, before twitching uncomfortably in his chair. He was a real fidget was Dave; something which Manny saw as the unmistakeable mark of his lowly upbringing.

'Why are they here?' he asked again. 'Do these people really think collective action works?'

Dave Chester was clearly lost.

'Go on,' said Manny, 'tell me.'

'I... I...' Reeves blinked once, twice. Scratched his chin. Glanced at the back of his hand as though the answer might be written there in his scrawled red biro. It wasn't. All that was there was the edge of a tattoo which stretched halfway up his arm. A tattoo! Talk about marking yourself out for the menial for the rest of your life. Even if he had contained the vaguest sense of intelligence, Dave Chester would never have been able to hold a public office with that thing on his arm. The tattoo was, Dave had informed him, a black and white rendering of the former Newcastle striker Andy Cole. Apparently, Reeves had been down to the tattoo parlour every day for a week to get the detail right. When the masterpiece was completed, one January day, he'd gone straight down to the pub to show it off to his mates. Who immediately showed him the headlines in the tabloids; Cole had that morning been sold to Manchester United. Dave Chester had used the story as a ha-ha to illustrate his bad luck in life so far; Manny knew it was more than that. Someone like him would never had *considered* such a stupid thing in the first place. It was yet another example of *these people* being wholly incapable of being able to help themselves. And yet, Manny felt as though he had to help. It was one of the major reasons behind his move into politics, into the whole mayoral game. He felt it his *duty* to keep prodding away at dumb proles like Dave Chester, if only just to open their eyes a little.

He decided to make it easy for him. 'Take your football team, for example. You've got that Mike Ashley feller runs the club, but you, none of you, want him there. And yet, the only collective action which would ever make him sit up and take notice would be if the fans stopped spending all their money on the season tickets or the new home strip or their subscription to the club's TV channel. Collective action is only powerful when it comes in note form with the Queen's head on the front.'

'Aye, but Mike Ashley... Well, we don't exactly make him feel welcome when he comes to St James' Park, do we?' He started rummaging around in the passenger footwell, where his important papers were kept; porn mags, football fanzines, old fast food wrappers and empty cans of pop. Manny had tried, on many occasions, to get him to tidy this mess up, but Dave seemed incapable of properly responding to what were, to all intents and purposes, *orders*.

'Here,' he said, head popping back up between the seats like a seal's. 'Have a look at this.' He passed over a dog-eared copy of *The Mag*, the Newcastle United fanzine. The front cover featured the famous picture of Mike Ashley in the stands wearing a tight Newcastle replica shirt which strained against his belly as he bravely downed a pint of beer from a plastic pint pot. The headline read: 'Is this a Fit and Proper owner for our Club?'

'But this is just background noise,' said Manny, wearily. 'Ashley'll sell if he gets a good deal, not if the...' - he made the sign for rabbit-ears – '...fans tell him they aren't happy with him. What the fans think is of no concern to him. No, it's more than that. Think of the fans like those ruddy little birds in wildlife documentaries which you always see hitching a ride on the backs of rhinos. Egrets. You'd think the egrets were an annoyance, pecking and tweeting away as they do, making a nuisance of themselves, but they're not. They're actually part of a delicate ecosystem *around* the rhino. They get rid of all the nasty tics and bugs and whatnot, preventing the rhino from getting all the diseases associated with them. They're ruddy...' - more hand-cycling as he searched once again for the right phrase – '... ruddy... They're keeping the rhino going, that's what they're doing.'

Dave Chester looked confused. He thought for a bit; Manny could almost see the cogs and wheels inside his head moving as he twisted his nose, rolled his eyes and then, finally started to smile. 'He does look a bit like a rhino, like. A bit lumbering beast.'

'I was speaking metaphorically,' sighed Manny. 'All right. Take that new supermarket which opened in Norsea a few months back.'

'That big-massive thing which looks like a flying saucer?'

'The very one. Remember all the protests and petitions and letters to the council when the plans first came out for that one?'

'I remember I was always getting flyers popped through the door saying I needed to write letters of my own, like. And I remember there was always loads of people there on a Saturday morning with their banners and that.'

'Yes. They were a pretty organised bunch,' mused Manny. 'Went down there a couple of times myself... Anyway, those protesters, that twittering, vocal majority, all they ended up doing was raising the publicity for the new store. Sure, there were public consultation exercises and the like, but never anything...' - he thought for a moment – '...never anything which seriously put the plans in jeopardy. In fact, all their twittering drowned out all the proper objectors, and in the end, many of the locals stopped listening. I think the silent majority got sick of listening to them, and in the end decided a new supermarket would actually be good for them...'

'But didn't the council block the plans at first?'

'At first,' said Manny, 'but then the supermarket appealed, and we managed to rush the appeal through on the hush-hush. The first anyone got to hear about the new decision was when we sent a letter to all Norsea residents, politely informing them that the supermarket would be going up, and there was nothing they could do about it. Funny thing was, I was there a couple of weeks after it opened, and who should I see there at the till, trolley stacked full of produce, but one of the main leaders of the protesters, some ruddy local solicitor or something. Of course, he had the good grace to look sheepish about it, but he didn't go and put his shopping back as I suggested he might. He didn't *pollinate the local shops* instead. He just queued up at the till next to me, and racked up his points like a good little egret.'

'A good little egret,' repeated Dave Chester. 'I like that. Here; are you cold, sir? I can whack on the heating if you like?'

'*Whack* away,' said Manny, raising his glass to his lips and then remembering he'd finished off the G and T a while back. Dave didn't notice the faux pas, busy as he was fiddling with the air-flow system as he was. There were so many controls in the front of the limo it was like a cock-pit, and Dave didn't seem to be able to find the one which regulated the air in the back. Not for the first time, Manny thought about hiring another chauffeur. One without Andy

392

Cole tattoos decorating his arm like it was the Sistine Chapel (or *sixteenth chapel* as Dave had referred to it one fateful day.) He'd thought finding the stray 'L' plate a few weeks back nestled between the seats had been the final straw, but evidently it wasn't. Evidently, he *could* stand Chester's moonlighting, petty pilfering and sheer imbecility. He constantly surprised himself with his kindnesses to his fellow man. He cracked open another can of gin and tonic by way of a reward for his magnanimity, finding that now he'd drunk a can of the stagnant brew, he'd acquired the taste. All he was missing was the *clink, clink* of ice in the glass – and surely there was no sweeter sound in the whole world than that; it was more pure than even the most wonderful arias – and perhaps a fresh slice of lemon.

But it would do. He settled back into the seat. The leather creaked and then submitted to his weight. Bubbles fizzed delightedly in the glass as he raised it to his mouth. Dave Chester gave him a hopeful look in the rear-view but Manny ignored him. They wouldn't be leaving. Not yet. Not while the good glow from the golden valve was on him. Only now did it occur to Manny that he was starting to feel drunk and that this might explain in some way his mellowing. But in talking with Dave Chester, he'd managed to talk himself down from a cliff of depression, and now everything seemed somehow softer, furred like Dave's headrest. This crisis would be overcome. Thrice-crowing doubters of his mayoral abilities would be cast aside. And despite the fact many old truths were now crumbling, his certainty that the bridge would come to pass, that the bridge would be his final hurrah, not dead Mrs. Heggarty on his carpet or some... some ruddy beast, would carry him through. And his name would last. Would echo through the ages. Would stand testimony to the fact that Manny Combs knew what was best. More and more, he was starting to think about what legacy he would leave behind, and more and more, the bridge seemed... symbolic. And if, when he was gone, some egret like Mike Ford or Sam Bibby chose to name the it 'The Combs Link', or 'The Manny Combs Bridge over Troubled Water', then it would be fitting.

He was snapped back out of his reverie by the sudden, almost overwhelming need to relieve himself. *Christ* it came on fast these days; yet another reason for him to think about that legacy. He looked out of the window to check whether there were any public conveniences about. Of course there weren't. *Used* to be. A few years back, but he'd had them closed down, just like the ones in the tourist car park over the causeway. Graffiti.

'How far to that little garage out at MacAskill's?' he asked.

No response from Dave Chester. He had his head slumped right down and for a moment, Manny feared the man had fallen asleep. But then he noticed a small black wire extending from his ear. An earpiece. If he hadn't known better, he'd have thought the man a secret service spy, like in the Dick F. Choker novels he always devoured on quiet nights on Limm *sans* booze, but he clearly wasn't; Chester didn't have the *right stuff* to be a secret service spy. No, Manny decided; he was clearly trying to tune into the radio without being noticed; trying to find out the team news for the evening's football match. Manny already knew who would be playing; number one, hopeless; number two, gutless; number three, talentless... He rapped on the top of Chester's cap with rather more force than was necessary and the chauffeur shot up about a foot from his seat. His small black earpiece clunked out onto his shoulder.

'What?... Uh... Sorry, sir,' gasped Dave, whilst simultaneously trying to hide the headphone. 'Just... checking the weather conditions. See if this Hoar's Blanket'll lift.'

'I said, how far is that self-serve petrol place over by MacAskill's?'

Reeves coughed: 'Ten minutes... Fifteen minutes... Given this white-dark, I'm not sure. We'd have to take it careful-like... But we don't need petrol. We're on almost a three-quarter tank as it is.'

'Not talking about petrol,' said Manny, 'I'm talking about... I need to visit the little boy's room.'

'They not have the public bogs just round here like, aye?' said Chester, making a big show of peering off into the white-darkness.

'They don't... Ah *fuck* it,' said Manny, cranking open the side door. 'The whole of nature is my private pisser.'

His suede loafer crunched down onto gravel. He tried to climb out without spilling a drop of the G and T, but ended up wrestling with the door when his camel-hair coat got stuck on the window-winder and some liquid slopped out right at the last onto the leg of his trousers. He cursed under his breath, placed the glass carefully on the roof of the limo and then started rooting around in his pockets for a hanky. Only after a wholly unsuccessful rummage did he start to comprehend how fuggy it had become so suddenly. It was the kind of cotton-woolly white-darkness one forgot whilst

394

living in the city with all its twenty-four hour neon, its strip-lighting and its Duracell Bunny energy; it felt as though a white air-raid blanket had been draped over everything. The only spatters of light now, came from the assembled farm vehicles on this side of the causeway, and, of course, from the interior of the limo. 'Christ,' he said, tugging his coat tighter around him.

'I might have a torch in here somewhere, sir,' called Dave from a half-open driver-side window. Manny ignored him. Fog like this might have been unsettling, but he was a Limm boy deep down. He'd been born into this liminal world. Nothing it could throw at him could hurt him.

He set off walking across the car park, hearing his loafers splashing into puddles and then feeling the wetness seeping in and getting between his toes. He just about heard Dave Chester shout something like: 'I've found the torch,' and then, he was sure he heard him say something like: 'you old bastard.' He ignored the sploshing in his shoes just as he ignored his chauffeur, but something made him walk a little bit farther before he unzipped and let rip with what now felt like it was going to be a torrential downpour of urine. Who knew what new-fangled gadgets people had on their phones nowadays? Dave Chester could have a ruddy infrared camera on his and might right now be filming his stuttering progress in the dark across the wet gravel ready to post up on Youtube. Just another thing he'd have to hold over his head. It was the type of thing the media *lapped-up.* Nowadays there was no such thing as old school respect. Respect meant something else entirely. Respect now wasn't awe or gratitude, nor was it something earned. No, it was like a ruddy raffle-prize.

Thinking angry thoughts helped bring a new sense of purpose to his stride. Before, as he'd just set out from the limo, he could well imagine he would have looked like Jodie Foster at the end of *Silence of the Lambs,* walking as though blindfolded, palms outstretched in front to save himself. Now, he was walking like a mayor again. And he thought his eyes were starting to adjust to the whiteness. Thought he could pick out soft, furry shapes that were shaded differently to the rest of the gloom. Also, he could smell. He could smell that strange mix of freshness and staleness, sweetness and sourness which was unmistakably the sea. The trees and grass. The farmland. The animals. Limm. The mainland. The lemon-tonic on his breath. He could smell the fog.

He saw a shape rearing up out of the gloom in front and for a moment, hesitated, but then realised it was the sign on which they tacked the tide tables in order that nobody got caught out on the causeway. It didn't work. Not completely. Every year, a handful of tourists who'd been indoctrinated into the modern way of thinking – exception will be made for me – didn't take the tables seriously. Every summer, tourists idled in the cafe or the pub, finishing off their cream teas or draughts of mead while the North Sea edged its way around the headland. *The sea'll wait for us,* they seemed to be saying. Unfortunately for them, and fortunately for Manny, whose hotel grew fat off the revenue pumped from stranded tourists, the sea didn't give a shit about anyone, or whether they'd planned to drive home that afternoon. It was urgent, deaf to all protest. And when some foolhardy tourists *did* chance the road, believing their luxury, tank-like 4x4's could get through anything, even the sea, they soon discovered themselves marooned. They had to climb on the roofs of their whimpering 4x4's and wait for sea rescue from the coastguard, or air rescue from one of the helicopter squads down at Norsea. Above the tide tables, these signs had the photographs to prove it. Manny smiled to himself in the darkness as he reminded himself of the fact that the iron-rod governance of the sea would soon come to an end. Soon, his bridge would rule in a proper, democratic way. He gave the sign an almost superstitious pat as he passed it, or perhaps he was simply saying goodbye to the old way of doing things. He didn't care. Another gut-clenching wave of urgency passed through him and he knew he'd have to relieve himself soon or else his bladder would explode.

He made out a low dry stone wall just in front of him and he decided it was good a place as any. As he unzipped, he wondered at himself, at how he'd been indoctrinated. Why was it he had to go for a piss *against* something? And why had he carried himself all the way across that field, soaking his feet in the process, on the hunt for it? Was it because of the ubiquity of urinals, or was it a more primal instinct, like marking territory? Well this was his territory all right. In a few years time, huge concrete struts would be plunged into the ground here. Steel girders. Somewhere, about twenty feet above him would be a toll booth and next to that, with pride of place, would be the plaque, 'The Sir Manny Combs Lifeline', and next to that, perhaps a statue. He smiled at the thought, pulled out the old man and prepared to christen his own plaque.

Only, now the old man was out, being gently tickled by the breeze and rubbed by the thick darkness, the waterfall of piss just wouldn't come. He strained, gritted his teeth, thought of the tide and flows and waterfalls and still nothing came. He ran his hand over the dry stone wall, felt the subtle movement of the rocks, but could sense no movement from within himself. He tucked himself back into his trousers and zipped back up again, half expecting that he'd need to go almost as soon as the zip was back in place. That would be more of that thing called irony. Like the toilets being closed down. Like him dreaming of bridges passing water when *he* couldn't even pass water.

He started to walk back to the car park, using the dry stone wall as a guide. He figured it ran parallel to the coastal road and soon he'd find the gateway, and find the limo tucked inside it. He'd walked for a good minute before he understood that he'd obviously missed the turn-off. Mind on other things, like his prostate, and what condition that might be in. He retraced his steps, trying to stop the dull note of panic from rising in his ears. He walked about twenty paces and then realised that no matter how far he stretched out his arm, he could no longer feel the dry stone wall.

'Come on, where are the lights?' he muttered, and then, more loudly: 'Chester! Where are you?'

No answer. Nothing but the sound of the waves brushing the shore somewhere off to the left. Or was it the right? Suddenly, Manny was unsure of the veracity of what his senses told him. He thought he could hear the thunder-pitch sounds of movement of large animals, cows perhaps – horses? - not far away. Thought he could sense it *through* the ground. But it might, just as easily, have been the sea he felt. And still his eyes couldn't get past that first, slightly blurry stage of just becoming accustomed. Still it was too black to see anything further than half a yard in front of his face. The fog was quilted, treacly, dangerous. His heart started beating faster. Panic crept up to his throat, choking him.

How was it possible, in this age of satellite navigation systems and mobile phone tracking – the thought of a mobile made him reach for a pocket, but he already knew it was not there - and money and the internet, to grow truly lost? How was it possible Chester was not already out looking for him? How was it possible, in this world of certainty and solid ground, to feel such disarray, such *moving* ground. It was definitely moving, the ground. Like shingle. It was shifting and reforming and trying to fool him.

'Chester!' he bellowed.

No answer. Just the wind whistling off a sign somewhere. But if it was a sign, it could be the sign bearing the tide tables and the photographic evidence of other people who had similarly underestimated nature. He headed towards it. In the direction his nose told him, because his eyes were telling him nothing. And in a few moments, his outstretched, Jodie Foster hand touched wood. And his heart leaped. He fumbled around, much as though he were trying to pin the tail on the donkey, hoping to touch the thin plastic sheets which they used to cover the tide tables. Familiarity. But he lost touch with the wood again. Until he bumped his knee against it. Sharp, hard pain. He felt himself buckle, almost fall, and then he forced himself to climb up again. And he remembered the story of the blind men in the room with the elephant. The one who had the tail described it as a rope; the one who touched the leg described it as like a pillar; and the one who touched the tusk described it as like a branch. What part of something was he touching now? Was he touching wood, even? He climbed up what felt like a step and felt wooden slats criss-crossing in front of him. It *might* have been a stile, or it might have been something else entirely. And if he crossed the stile, what then? What if there was a bull in the field? A bull wouldn't let him get a good feel of its horns before it gored him...

'Chester!' he bellowed.

And this time there was an answer. A mad screech and a flapping of wings in his face. Felt bigger than a seagull, but then, seagulls were always bigger than expected. It continued to flap and Manny continued to try to ward it off, without quite knowing where its next attack was coming from. But then he lost his grip on the wood and his slip-on loafers couldn't provide the purchase to keep him upright. And then he felt himself falling. He couldn't tell how far, but he hit the ground hard on his back. From above, the gull, if it was a gull, cawed. Victoriously. And then, finally, Manny's bladder chose to erupt. He felt the warmth which spread around his crotch as he still searched for something which his eyes could focus on. And then, Manny Combs became his own statue as the vulture – for a vulture was what it was – plunged down into him, burying its hooked beak into his side, into his liver, as though he was Prometheus, and this, finally, was his punishment for his over-reaching.

44: Welcome to Limm, Twinned with Hell

Vicar ran far as the edge of the woods, with Ruth in hot pursuit and Mart panting behind them, but then, abruptly he stopped. Hunkered down on his haunches and growled. Ruth pulled up next to him, tried to stroke him. And he dragged his lips right back and showed her fangs. When Mart Bibby arrived, Vicar offered him a *keep back* bark and then continued to hunker down, front paws first, as though he was trying to dig himself a hidey-hole in the ground.

'Vicar-baby,' she soothed. 'Calm down love, for Bowie's sake.'

Mart Bibby raised an eyebrow, as though to say, *what, David Bowie is your God?* And she tucked her hand on her hip and stared right back at him as though to say, *yeah, so what? He's better'n your God.*

Vicar's hair was completely standing on end. He was glaring into the woods, into nothing, it seemed like at first, but Ruth's eyes had been wrong on a couple other occasions over the past few days and as such she peered into the white-darkness too. And at first, all she could see was the ghostly trees. But then, as she continued to stare she saw that the air *around* the trees was moving like static on an untuned TV. White noise. And as she continued to stare some more, like a magic eye picture, the truth suddenly hit her, like a train, between the eyes. Suddenly she saw what Vicar was getting so upset about.

It was the flies. Hundreds of thousands of them. *Millions* of them. Surrounding the edge of the southern woods like they were forming a forcefield.

'Do... do you see that, Mart?' She swung round. He looked very red-faced from the strain of the run. Perhaps he was one of those body-builder types whose hearts were so highly strung all it took was a little of the wrong kind of exercise and they simply exploded. He was *more* than red-faced. His cheeks were purple. Veins pulsed in his temples. He spat on the floor over and over again.

'Mart?'

'I see 'em,' he coughed. 'Hell, I can *taste* them. Thicker than the smell of crab at The Crab's Claws. I can feel them trying to crawl down my throat.' Soon as he said that, one fat fly landed on his chin. Another on his cheek. A third on his neck. They were washing themselves in his sweat, having a grand old time. Even when he flapped out a big paw to try to waft them away, they stayed.

'What do we do?' gasped Ruth. 'I mean you... *we*... can't carry on, like this. Do you think Sam's really gone into those woods, with those *things?*'

No answer from Mart. She addressed the same question to Vicar, holding Sam's coat out in front of his nose again. Vicar's answer was non-committal. His ears twitched madly as the flies descended on him, too.

Without warning, Mart gave a bestial roar, flung his arms out, windmilling them through the white noise of the air. He looked like King Kong on top of the Empire State Building. He started walking backwards, slowly, surely away from the edge of the woods, still wafting, still swatting, still bellowing.

Ruth dashed after him. 'We can't just leave your brother in there, with the flies. I mean... This is unnatural, isn't it? This is...'

Mart nodded grimly. 'I'm not fucking leaving him, love. I'm going back for my landie.'

The three of them approached the edge of the southern woods again. More cautiously this time, despite the fact they were inside the lifeboat crew's land rover. They approached it as carefully as the sea, feeling their way closer, closer, lapping their way up to the tree-line. They approached it as *inexorably* as the sea, as though they knew they had to draw back in. As though some moonish force which was stronger than the brotherly bonds of The Bibby Firm, which was more desperate than Ruth's desire to prove herself capable of standing on her own two feet, and more determined than Vicar and his drive to protect his mistress, was pulling them.

As they approached the trees, Vicar started growling, arched his back. Flies like hail started to kamikaze into the windscreen and in a matter of seconds the wipers were so heavy with them that they stopped moving.

'Are you sure the landie'll make it?' said Ruth. 'I know it's an off-roader, but this is so far off any beaten track we might as well be on another planet.'

Mart grinned. Somewhat madly, Ruth thought. 'I've made some modifications,' he said. 'For Limm. I mean, this thing has to tow a lifeboat, a big 'un too. So I added a little something under the hood. Some extra power, shall we say.'

She didn't feel relieved. She continued to rub at Vicar's back, trying to calm him, wondering whether the dog could feel the tingle in her fingertips, the agony in her heart, the doubt in her mind. The land rover pulled off the dirt track and made its first break inside the tree-line. Angry branches smacked on the roof like so many protesters on the top of a van which was taking a killer away from court. Heavy things thudded into the underside of the vehicle. Ruth thought that any moment, one of those things might rip right through. Unconsciously she lifted her feet off the floor. On her lap, Vicar whimpered. His ears were pressed down flat against his head. His eyes were wide, panicked. For the first time, she saw what he might have looked like as a new-born puppy. She felt his paws twitching against her, as though he wanted to get away. She saw the new resignation in his eyes as he knew he couldn't.

So far, the masking tape they'd stretched over the tops of the windows seemed to be working. No flies had gained entry. But it was only a matter of time before they worked out they could crawl up through the engine, out through the air-vents, and a home delivery feast'd be right there waiting for them.

Mart Bibby seemed to be driving on instinct. Trees loomed out of the white-darkness so fast it was all he could do to avoid hitting them, so most of the time it felt like *reactive* driving rather than *proactive* driving. They weren't exactly following a scent any more, just trusting that the pull of whatever it was which had dragged Vicar out of the Seahorse, that had dragged them all to the woods, that had made them back-track and bring the landie, had been right.

They ducked onto a steep slope and Ruth felt herself pressing her body into the seat so as not to roll onto Mart or the gear stick. Vicar pressed down too, his claws digging in to the seat cover, and her knees. She winced, but chose not to pull him up on it. For a moment, the landie tipped onto two wheels, and she thought they were going to flip over, make like a tortoise, but somehow Mart managed to do something to stop it. They hung, for one beat, two, as

401

the wheel *screeeeeeeed* round, as they heard it searching for purchase, and then they jolted forward. Too fast really, as Mart couldn't avoid the next tree. They heard it rip off the front bumper as they passed.

They hit the Drey. It was thick with water and the banks were steep, slippy. Mart took the descent at a dog-leg angle – Vicar would have been pleased, if only he'd have opened his eyes – and got them down safely. In the river, they felt the swell of the water, its desire to take them off, to make Adrian Devonishes out of them. But they also felt the pull of that other thing, which kept them on course, which took them around the sharpest of the rocks, which took them, finally, up the other side.

Everything was denser over the other side. The gaps in the trees here were filled with bushes, long grass, dead logs. The spaces in the air were filled with a murderous number of flies. The white-darkness closed in around them. Even before the flies found their way through the air-con system, the white-darkness did, and now it was blowing around the landie's interior. It tasted weirdly plasticky, and yet fishy too. Outlandish, like that first taste of an entirely foreign country as you step off a plane.

More branches tried to stop them, more stumps tried to rugby-tackle them into submission. The *thud-thud-thud* as they crashed over them was providing a steady, boy-racer soundtrack to their proceedings.

'I'm sick of that bloody racket,' said Mart. His voice sounded thick too. He twiddled with a few knobs on the dashboard radio which until then Ruth had thought too antique to be in full working order, and eventually she heard music creaking tinnily out. She recognised it immediately.

'Bowie,' she whispered. 'It's Bowie.'

Mart gave an elaborate, but not unfriendly groan.

It was *Life on Mars*. Her favourite ever.

'Shouldha called it *Life on Limm*,' observed Mart, after listening to Ruth murder the first verse-chorus. 'All that stuff about cavemen and beating up the wrong guy. That's life on Limm, warts and all. Might as well be Mars now though, eh?'

He was right. The ground was cratered now, dusty. Strangely it seemed to glow red. Now, when they smashed into branches and low-lying trees, those same branches snapped meekly away, threw themselves down, submitted. They passed close, almost too close to a tree on her side, and Ruth saw that the tree was brittle, white, skeletal now, like disease had gotten hold of it.

'What happened here?'

Mart shook his head.

'Where are we anyway?'

'Doesn't matter,' said Mart. 'We're getting close, I can feel it.' And as though to kill all conversation then, he cranked up the radio onto full volume.

Ruth tried to peer out through the windscreen but it was becoming increasingly difficult to see anything. Flies had nested across the glass, had compacted then, formed another layer, fossilized themselves under the pressure of more and more flies landing. The metal roof sagged under their weight. A murder of them had caused the wing-mirror to fall off. They lounged across the bonnet. And Ruth thought the flies would clog the engine, would soak up the fuel, would eat the exhaust pipe. She thought they'd lay waste, like locusts, to the doors, to the wheels. She thought it'd be flies in the end, small insignificant flies which would do for them, not a big, lumbering feline. And as though to let her know she was thinking along the right lines, the first of their number started buzzing angrily behind the air-vent. She fished in the glove-box, tried to find something, anything to wedge against the vent, to keep it closed. Eventually settled on the log-book. She pressed against it with her fingers, with all her might. Her fingertips went white with the force. But then she felt something horrible. She felt the flies, through sheer weight of numbers, pushing back. Vicar shifted position on her lap.

'Mart,' she hissed. '*Mart!*'

He turned his head, took his eyes off the road. Didn't really matter; it was negligible how much he could actually see through the flies anyway. He turned off the radio. 'What?'

She nodded down at the air-vent. Lowered her voice still further, to a whisper, as though the flies could hear her, as though they could understand her. 'They're pushing,' she said. 'I can't hold them much longer.'

Mart frowned.

'Mart,' she hissed again. '*Mart!* If they start coming in here, I don't think we could carry on. They'll go for our eyes... I can feel it.'

Mart nodded solemnly. 'I was thinking the same thing.'

Vicar was evidently thinking it too. He stood up, for the first time since he'd been in the landie, started circling on Ruth's lap. And then, horribly, he started to bite himself. All the while whimpering away in the back of his throat. And Ruth thought, *that there is an animal beyond distress. When I took him from the shelter, I told those women I'd be giving him a better life, but look at him...*

She couldn't look. Blindly, she tried to push his snout away from his side, tried to make him stop with the biting. He gave her a warning growl. She continued to push, to shepherd, to harry. To *annoy.* Christian always said, in that oh so very Christian, oh so very charitable voice of his, that she was annoying. That it was no wonder he snapped at her, sometimes with his mouth, sometimes with his fists. Thankfully, his bark was worse than his bite. But Vicar's wasn't. When the second of the three males in her life inflicted violence on her, first nipping at her fingertips and then full-on sinking his teeth into her wrist, she felt the world collapsing. She jumped back in the passenger seat, pushing him off her, kicking him down into the foot-well. At the same time, she let go of the log-book which she'd had wedged against the air-vent. It flapped down in the foot-well right beside Vicar. And for a moment, nothing happened.

For a moment. Then it was as though the air became flies. Flies flowed up her nose, stung into her eyes, loaded her face. She heard Mart Bibby's agonised cry, his cough as the flies started to enter his mouth. Flies prevented her from reaching out, helping him steady the wheel. The landie slid into a stomach-churning spin. She heard it crack through trees, smash through rocks, career over dead things. She tried to hide her face in her hands, tried to suck in a breath, but more flies came. So she thought she was going to *drown* in flies. She felt her heart beating heavy in her ears. She heard her lungs wheezing. She heard Vicar going mental in the foot-well. The sounds Mart Bibby was making were very similar.

And then, suddenly, the land rover hit something which was not a skeletal tree or a crumbledown rock or a stump or a bush. It hit something massive, and for a moment, it sunk *into* that thing, but then it sort of bounced back out again, as though whatever it was had taken a taste of the vehicle, and, not liking it, spat it out. Ruth's head crashed back against the seat's headrest, and then forward again, so that her nose connected directly with the dashboard. She tasted blood. Her lungs squealed. And she knew she had to take a breath. She knew she had to, despite the fact her body would probably fill up with flies. She opened her mouth. And she was sure that what

404

slicked down her throat with the pungent air she sucked in, was a carpet of flies. She was sure this would be her last breath, and she was sure these would be her last thoughts, so she saved them for Jonathan, her son, her little boy. She remembered the first moment he'd been placed in her arms at the hospital. That lop-sided smile of his. That one tuft of hair he'd had at the front of his head. Like a Superman curl, it was. Her Superman. She mourned him now as though he was the one who'd died. She mourned him, and it felt somehow unholy, unrighteous that she should still be breathing, which she was...

She opened her eyes. She hadn't even been aware they'd been closed until now. And she saw the cloud of flies had lifted. A few still buzzed around, but they had nothing like the numbers they'd had before. She opened her eyes and she saw Vicar, at her feet. He was looking up at her with mournful eyes, *sorry* eyes. She smiled at him. *Water under the bridge. My fault anyway.* And then she looked round at Mart Bibby. His big head was resting on the steering wheel. There was a thick trail of blood trickling from his nose and for a moment, she thought he was dead. The thought that she could be out here in the deadlands with only Vicar for company scared the hell out of her.

But then Mart cracked a smile. Spat out a fly, and some blood too. 'I know an old lady,' he said.

'Swallowed a fly?' said Ruth.

Mart winked. 'Few of the nasty fuckers actually.' He lifted his head off the steering wheel. His hand immediately shot up to his nose. He touched it gingerly, but he still winced. 'Broken.' Then he nodded over at her. 'How 'bout you?'

She touched her own nose, or rather, the bloody, grizzly mess which had been her nose, which was now just a series of lumps and bumps and gristle. 'Snap,' she said. 'Mind you, it'll hardly ruin my looks, will it? What with me being bald and all.'

Mart looked unsure whether to laugh, but then added, 'S'pose mine'll make me look like a brawler. Maybe people'll stop saying I'm of 'dubious sexuality' now.'

They both laughed for a moment and they both stopped laughing at exactly the same time. For their laughs sounded shrill, lonely, like the laughs of interlopers in some secret place. Again at exactly the same time, they both looked forward, through the windscreen, and they both gulped at what they saw.

'We'd better get out,' said Mart.

'Yes,' said Ruth. But neither of them moved. Both of them continued to stare forward at one of the most unlikely, most outlandish spectacles they could have hoped, or dared to see. They were looking at the body of a full-grown great white shark. It had been what they'd hit, and the grille had left a tattoo of lines on the shark's dead flank. There were great chunks of flesh missing from the shark in other places, huge islands of its bulk had been eaten away. Many of the flies which had been inside the land rover were now floating, like a layer of smog, above the body, as though they were just waiting for their moment to tuck in.

'Kiffs like a bastard, eh?' said Mart.

'Good job we've got a pair of broken noses then. 'Magine what Vicar can smell.'

She looked down at the dog. His nose was wrinkling, but he was no longer growling. He seemed as intrigued by this new discovery as them. As though the dog had finally made the decision for her, Ruth reached for the door handle. As it opened, she heard the *scriiiiiiiicckkk* of the masking tape coming loose. She stepped down, not even sure what the ground would feel like under her feet after the journey they'd had. It felt normal. A little crunchy, a little charred, but normal. She heard Mart Bibby climb out the driver side, similarly testing the ground. Vicar jumped out last, but he was the first to investigate the shark. He sniffed at it a while and then barked over at them, as though to say *hurry up, it won't hurt you.*

'Oh, that right mister?' said Ruth. 'It won't bite eh? Maybe its not the shark I have to worry about, maybe its you.' But when she reached him, she still gave his head a rub.

She hunkered down next to the shark and took a good look. Saw the rot which had already set in. 'Thing's been dead a while,' she said, which surprised even her, because what she'd been thinking was *what the hell's a shark doing here?*

Mart Bibby remained standing. 'I think... I think I know where we are,' he said, in a slow, trance-like voice. 'Over there... There was a sign. It used to say *Welcome to Limm.* They put it up by the road they built for all the new industrial places they were hoping would come up in the valley. Road's abandoned now.' He whistled through his teeth. 'No wonder.'

Ruth clambered to her feet. She looked over at what might have been the old sign Mart was talking about. Whatever it was, it was buried by flies now.

'*Welcome to Limm Island,*' repeated Mart, '*twinned with Alsfeld, Germany...* More like, *Welcome to Limm Island, twinned with Hell,* eh?'

He was right. This place had much the same kind of geography as she'd imagined for hell. Sparse, lonely, dead. Brittle, uncertain, foggy. Hot. She was surprised to find herself sweating. Even Vicar seemed hot, his tongue was lolling out of his mouth like he needed to bury his head in a margarine tub full of water. She watched him as he trotted off, thought he might be on the hunt for that very thing, doubted there'd be any around here. And then Mart Bibby gripped her arm. She swung round. He was pointing off up the road.

'I... I think that's another body,' he said.

Vicar was heading straight for it.

'Come away from it now!' called Ruth. 'Vicar!' For some reason, she felt more concerned about him approaching this second body. Perhaps because the first had seemed so unreal, so outlandish, but this second... It looked human. Looked like any other Limm islander. *The first,* a voice inside her head corrected, *was from another world, the second is from yours. That's the distinction you were looking for.* Indeed it was, but she wondered where that voice had come from. What *universe* it had come from.

'Maybe we should go back to the jeep,' she whispered. 'Mart, I think we should get out of here.' She whistled for Vicar to come heel. Vicar as per bloody usual paid her no mind. Neither did Mart Bibby. Mart Bibby was too busy looking back, towards the land rover.

'There's someone coming,' he said. 'Oh my God there's someone coming.'

45: Medusa

Yoghurt Rhodes thought he might have remained in one of *his* stares for the rest of eternity if it wasn't for the arrival of the land rover and all the hubbub it brought with it. Certainly part of him would have liked to remain staring at the thing for the rest of eternity if that was his fate, because it certainly was beautiful. Had to be Holy. Or that was what he'd thought when he'd been staring at it. Now he'd finally torn himself away it felt Unholy. He could feel it pulling at him, tugging at the sleeves of his coat, screaming in his ear, *come back to me. Come look on me again.* And only God could be so arrogant, couldn't He. Only God or maybe Solomon. So either the golden thing was God, or else it was a False Idol. He couldn't make up his mind. Trevor Knox would have known. His mother, of all people, would have known. But he didn't. He could have stood there, trying to come up with an answer to its Sphinx-like riddle forever, then, if it hadn't been for Ruth Sharp and Mart Bibby.

When he first saw them, he thought there probably wasn't an unlikelier combination of people on the whole island. After he'd blinked, and the afterburn of their bodies silhouetted against the white-darkness had become scarred on the back of his eyelids, he thought that perhaps they were now the last people left on Limm, so maybe it was the *only* combination. Certainly both looked as though they'd been through a fight. Both had broken noses. There was blood all over Ruth Sharp's arm, and so, naturally, his first question to them was, 'Has the wing-ed creature come?'

And he was rather put out that both looked at him as though *he* was the mad one who'd just come blind-driving straight into the body of a great white shark which could hardly be missed.

'What are you doing out here, Yoghurt?' said Mart Bibby.

Ruth Sharp cocked her head and studied him. He looked down, kicked at a few dead leaves with his feet. Couldn't decide how to answer.

'CAN YOU HEAR ME LAD? ELY?' shouted Mart Bibby. He turned to Ruth and said, 'Always been a strange one, him.'

'I can hear you,' he said, finally. 'Loud and clear.'

'Right then,' said Ruth, 'any chance you can explain just what in the hell's gone on here?'

Yoghurt shook his head, swung his arms. Dallied. She walked up to him. Tried to still one of his arms. He let her. For now. 'Yoghurt? Ely? Is that your name, Ely?' she asked.

He nodded, slowly.

'How did you get out here?'

He shrugged. 'I felt it.'

'Felt what?'

'The call.'

'The call?'

'The call.'

'I don't know what you mean. You're going to have to explain it to me...'

Just then, Ruth's dog, a mangy thing, a stray from a home most likely, came bounding back to them. He started dancing around Ruth's feet, yapping excitedly.

And Yoghurt knew, suddenly, that he had to protect the poor little thing. 'You can't let him see it,' he said, breathlessly, lifting his eyes up, meeting Ruth's, *imploring* her. 'Shut him up in the land rover, do anything, but don't let him near it.'

'Near what, love, the shark? Don't worry, Vicar here's already had a good sniff of the shark and he's not interested... Oh! Do you mean the *other* body? Yes, yes I know, I'll keep him away from that one... Did you, did you know him?'

'Know who?'

'The dead man?'

Yoghurt was getting angry now. 'I'm not talking about any shark or any dead man, I'm talking about *it*. The golden valve.'

Mart Bibby sneered. 'I think he's the one what wants locked-up inside the landie.'

Ruth Sharp pressed though. 'What do you mean, a valve? Where is it? *Show* it to us.'

He bit his lip. 'We shouldn't. Should leave. Not supposed to be here. Feels bad. Like trespassing.'

409

'Nobody owns this land, Yoghurt-lad,' said Mart. 'Not even Combs. We can go as we please.'

'But…'

'Just show us,' said Ruth. 'And don't worry, if anything *happens,* we'll answer for it.'

Yoghurt wanted to ask her how many links up the food chain she'd go, in her answering. Would she, for instance, answer to The Darkness, the divil himself, and say, *yes, it was me, your honour. I persuaded Ely. It wasn't his choice.* Would she say it to the winged thing as it swooped for her? Would she tell it to the golden valve? He wondered what Solomon would have done in the same situation, and for the first time in his life, he came up with a complete blank.

And so, he led them through the trees to the golden valve.

The three of them had been staring at it for a long time now. Hypnotised, Yoghurt thought. The golden valve was all of their questions and all of their answers rolled into one. It told truth about the origins of life, it told truth about other universes, the *multiverses.* It waxed lyrical on the future of the island. The future for them was to stare at the valve. At first he'd heard Ruth mutter, '*beautiful',* and Mart something blasphemous. And he'd felt a swell of sinful Pride that he'd led them here. Let them look on it. And despair. But now neither of them were saying anything. They were in one of *his* stares.

He could feel its pulse. It carried through the ground. Usurped his own heartbeat, so that it was the pulse of the golden valve he felt in his ears and not his own. He felt it thrumming through his legs, energizing them, which was a good thing, because otherwise, given that he was being asked to stand stock-still-rigid for so long, his muscles might have given in, sent him tumbling forward *into* it. And he felt that if he touched it, that would be the end.

The spell was broken when Vicar, the dog, entered the scene. He immediately growled at the thing, and then started tugging at his mistress's corduroy trousers with his teeth, trying to pull her away from the valve. When she remained statue-still, Vicar went for *Mart's* trousers, or at least that was what Yoghurt thought he did. He couldn't swivel his head far enough round to see exactly what was going on. And then Vicar started in on Yoghurt's trousers. He could feel the dog's hot breath on the hairs on his legs, could feel the tug. And he wanted to look down, he really did. He wanted to scuff the dog's collar, or scratch its head, or let it lick his hand. But he couldn't move. And Vicar must have recognised this. The dog must have somehow sensed what was going on, because he finally let go of the trousers, turned to face the golden valve. Crept towards it, growling. *Singing*, almost. He crept into Yoghurt's eye-line and crept further. Crept so that he was now directly underneath the valve. And Yoghurt immediately smelled burning. He could see the dog's fur curling at the ends, charring.

The dog bared its teeth and then, in a moment which was frozen in time, it leaped up, caught the valve between its jaws, and started to shake it. Furiously, righteously. As though it was trying to make amends for something it had done with one, last heroic act. It shook and shuddered the valve, rattled and rolled it too. And there was a moment he swallowed the valve whole.

Yoghurt seized the moment and snatched his eyes away from it. For a moment, he thought he'd gone blind. He couldn't even make out the hand in front of his face. *How many fingers am I holding up? Fingers, I thought you were holding up a great vacuum. Nothingness. I thought you were holding up hell.* But then he could see. He could see, but he didn't dare look back at the fight between dog and valve. Though it soon became pretty clear which was the winner. He heard a terrible whimper, then a coughing sound, like cat trying to rid itself of a hairball. Then he saw the poor dog drag itself past him and make for Ruth's feet. It was bald now, just like its owner. Its nose had been smashed, tenderized, burned beyond submission, again like its owner. Yoghurt saw it take one last, loving look at Ruth before it finally bowed its head. Ruth didn't look back. She was still entranced by the valve.

Mart Bibby wasn't though. Mart Bibby was still a functioning human being, and not an Unholy zombie. The two of them met each other's eyes, taking care not to look anywhere near the direction of the valve, whose pull they still felt. Mart jerked his head back. Growled, 'The landie. Come on. Let's get rid of this thing before it takes us, too.'

Yoghurt nodded, though he wasn't exactly sure *how* Mart Bibby proposed to dispose of the thing with the landie, much less what they could do about Ruth Sharp and her poor, dead dog. Still, he followed Mart as they staggered away from the valve, and as they staggered, they felt the shackles on their legs gradually loosening, they felt their sight returning to normal. Would never be 20:20 again, but at least they could walk without falling over every few paces.

411

When they got back to the landie, Mart Bibby gripped him by the shoulders. 'Stay here,' he spat. 'If I do get through this, I don't want to have to patch you up down at the Bungalow. I think I'll have enough on my hands already.'

Yoghurt nodded, pretending like he was still the good boy who always did what he was told by *everyone,* by preachers, by teachers, by policemen, mayors, male nurses... He watched Mart gun the landie's engine, roll down the window. 'She's still in decent condition,' he shouted. 'Took on a shark and she's still in full working order. That's Limm engineering for you.' He wound the window back up again and, as he drove off, Yoghurt heard him give a huge, terrible cry. It sounded like a Knight going into battle. Sounded   kinda   like   he   was   shouting, 'chaaaaaaaaaaaaaaaaaarrrrrrrrrrrge.'

Soon as the dust had cleared, Yoghurt followed. And as he did so, he felt the valve not just pulling him in anymore, but *calling* to him. And it didn't only have just one voice, no, the valve had many voices, all clamouring for attention. One of the voices could have been Solomon, another Manny Combs, a third his mother. Fourth, fifth and sixth could have belonged to those who'd walked into the sea before the Millennium and stood, still as statues, as it washed over them. The seventh might have been his father. The daddy he'd not seen since he was small. The daddy who'd been effectively scrubbed out of his life save for the one framed image in his ruck-sack.

And Yoghurt found himself answering. 'Yes,' he said. 'I can hear you, but who are you?'

Amongst the valve's countless voices, was one which recited the poetry of Walt Whitman. Trevor Knox had kept a book of Whitman's poetry in the glovebox of the National Trust landie. Claimed that it gave him inspiration. And when Yoghurt asked this new, Walt Whitman voice to identify itself, it answered, 'I am large, I contain multitudes'. Which sounded about right. Oblique, but right.

He heard the land rover too. Heard the clunk as Mart Bibby changed gears, heard the crunch as its tyres passed over some of the bodies of the fallen insects, heard it wheel-spin a little, and almost stick, in the stagnant water which had seeped out from the shark's belly. Yoghurt tried to remember where he'd left his bike, his ruck-sack, but everything seemed cloudy now. It was as though normal narrative pathways had been blocked and this big absence had taken their place. It was difficult for him to move forward, or back. The

412

valve was making him sluggish, both physically and mentally, the closer he got to it. He felt the power being drained out of his legs, felt his chin drop to his chest, felt his feet like they were encased in concrete blocks. It was all he could do simply to shuffle.

By the time he reached the dead shark, he had to reach out, prop himself up by holding the broken dorsal fin. The valve whispered to him that he should just maybe lay down and give in to sleep for a while, because as well as containing multitudes, it contained eternities too, so Yoghurt's stopping at the shark would be nothing but the blink of an eye compared to a lifetime of looking. He paused, breathed a couple husky, rasping breaths. The sound of his own breathing reminded him of the Black Panther over the other side of the causeway. And he remembered what had happened to the Black Panther too. How he'd seen its diseased and broken body. How *it* had maybe given up and allowed oblivion to wash over it. He forced himself to walk on.

In the distance he could hear the land rover reversing. The engine whined in complaint. Yoghurt plunged forward, managing to find a stumbling rhythm now, somehow. Perhaps, he thought, the valve was distracted. He seized his chance. Despite the burn in his legs, his lungs, his throat, he started to run. And as he did so, his head started to clear. And like backed-up text messages, just waiting for Limm's shaky signal, suddenly, the answers to some of his questions came to him, as though in a camera flash. He clearly *saw* the bike, with his ruck-sack draped over the handlebars. He clearly saw how to get to it. And he knew that he *had* to get to it too. It was as though he'd read the story in advance. It was as though he already knew that Mart Bibby would fail.

The bike was propped up against one of the skeletal trees close to the old WELCOME TO LIMM sign. But unless he'd had his flash of inspiration, he wouldn't have seen it. Because it was as though the valve was trying to *hide* the bike. Three, four large branches had crashed down on top of it from the tree above. Flies formed a protective barrier around it. The bike itself seemed to have changed colour. Had become, chameleon-like, a kind of dusty, white-noisy colour which was almost impossible to pick out. But Yoghurt wasn't relying on the vision in his eyes any more. He was trusting to the vision in his head. The vision which led him directly to the bike. Quickly, he shifted the branches, climbed aboard, started to pedal. He looked down once, as he careered down the old abandoned road, and when he did, he saw the bike slowly changing colour again, back to the red and green it had previously been.

Yoghurt reached the valve at the exact same time as Mart Bibby. He skidded to a halt and watched as Mart's land rover came crashing through the undergrowth, heading directly for the valve. There was a single-minded intensity to Mart's driving which suggested he wanted to ram straight through the valve, crash it off the face of the earth. He was driving in a low gear and the landie seemed to scream as it entered the clearing, the charred ground which surrounded the valve. Time seemed to buckle, bend back in on itself so that Yoghurt saw the final moments in slow motion. He saw the dust kicked up by the landie, so thick it could have been the start of another Hoar's Blanket. He saw the front of the vehicle bouncing up and down as it smashed through the uneven terrain. He saw strips of masking tape flapping from the windows like streams of fly-paper, catching flies as they went. He saw the windscreen, slicked with more flies. And through it, he saw a little toy lifeboat on the dashboard, crashing around like it was on the high seas. He saw Mart Bibby's face, contorted into a paroxysm of rage. He saw the man's big paws, white-knuckled on the steering wheel. He saw the moment, those fingers started to release themselves from the wheel, one by one, so that, for a moment, he thought Mart was going to dive out of the moving vehicle and roll to safety, like a stunt-man. But then he looked back at the big man's face and he saw only absence. Mart, he understood, had now looked on the valve and been hypnotised again. So too, it seemed, had the engine. Suddenly it coughed, spluttered, and then gave out completely. But the land rover sailed forward on auto-pilot, as though caught in a tractor beam. He couldn't see exactly what happened because his land rover blocked his view of the valve as unstoppable force and immovable object collided. He heard it though. He heard the terrible screeching sound of tearing metal, a grinding sound too. The land rover continued *past* the valve, only, as it did so, it seemed to split itself into two, *divide* itself, *twin* itself so that, as it finally came to a halt, its front grille pressed into the trunk of a tree, the top half of it, and the top half of Mart Bibby, carried on, skewing off to the side, slamming down onto the charred ground. Before Yoghurt could tear his eyes away, he saw Mart Bibby, *sans* legs, *sans* half of that great trunk of a body, cough up a seemingly never-ending stream of blood, and then, finally, he was stilled.

414

Yoghurt gulped. Screwed up his eyes. Then opened them again. But he didn't know where to look now. He couldn't, *wouldn't* look at Mart again. He couldn't, *wouldn't* give in and look at the valve either, because now, after what he'd seen, he thought that if he did, he'd be turned to stone forever, like in the Medusa myth. And there was nobody left to save him now, nobody to break the spell. Vicar was dead. Ruth Sharp was statuesque. Stock-still, despite the fact Mart's decapitated landie had come within a hare's breadth of her after it had been torn apart by the valve.

And now he felt the valve's full attention swinging back onto him. He felt it calling to him. Using just one voice now, Solomon's. *Come to us, Ely. Come to us.* And he wanted to. He so wanted to. He *envied* those voices within the valve, because they were safe, secure. He lusted after being with them. He was greedy for it now, he realised. Gluttonous for the end. But still he wouldn't look. Still he wouldn't give in to it. He forced himself to look at Vicar instead, for hope, for inspiration, but it *hurt.* It itched like he was wearing the Shirt and being battered by the knotted Rope. He couldn't hold out much longer.

But then he smelled it. Tangy on the breeze. *Petrol.* He'd always been rather enamoured by the smell of petrol, especially when it was tar-pit-thick at the garage down the A24. For it had always reminded him somehow of freedom, of getting away. Of the sweet smell of otherness. They'd never had a car, or any sort of vehicle, when he was growing up. His mother had banned all talk, or thought of them, which, of course, had made him secretly obsessed. Before he could even recite one of Solomon's verses, he'd been able to name every car on the road. It was probably one of the reasons he settled for a bike. Just so he could get a little bit closer to freedom. Now, as he wrinkled his nostrils, the petrol told a different story. He looked back at the truck and saw the gas waterfalling out from the underside of the landie. And he knew that he had to get out of here. Because all it would take was a single spark and...

He corrected himself in his head. He had to get out of here. And he had to take the valve with him. Somehow, he knew that was what he was *here* for, what all the trials and tribulations of his life had been building up to. He had to take the valve with him. Make it safe. And somehow, he knew he could do this, while even a gorilla of a man such as Mart Bibby couldn't. Because Mart Bibby hadn't been preparing for most of his life for a moment like this. Mart Bibby didn't have the right tools.

415

Yoghurt knew what he had to do and he knew how he could achieve it. Actually doing it was another matter. For he found that now he had a plan, now he was full of a new-found determination, the valve was becoming tricksy. Though he couldn't, *wouldn't* look at it, he sensed it moving above the clearing. Dancing. Teasing. He felt it drawing close to him, so close he could feel the vibrations from it, vibrations which he seemed to be able to translate, vibrations which tried to seduce him with their breath tickling the back of his neck, vibrations which begged and pleaded with him, *cajoled* him like an ice-cream hungry child. *Take your hands off the handlebars,* they said. *Feet off the pedals. Inch your head around. And look.* It would get so close he could have almost swatted it away like a fly, and then it would shimmer away from him again.

He had to fix it. Stamp down its position. And then he had to capture it. He had to use his camera. Quickly, he tugged it out of his ruck-sack, draped it around his neck. He would use it as the shield it had always been for him. He would use it to reflect the valve's golden light back in on itself so that for a beat, two, he could grab it. He forced a hand over his eyes and started to slowly but surely walk the bike forward, so that he was as close as possible to the valve. And even though he wasn't looking at it, he felt sun-blindness. He felt leggy, tired. He wanted to be still. But he forced himself on. He forced himself so close the valve was almost touching the handlebars. And then he lifted the camera. Removed the lens cap, let it tumble to the ground. Flicked the flash on full. And pressed the button.

The valve seemed to cry out. For a moment, all Yoghurt could see was light. Dazzling, golden light. And for that moment, the valve might have disappeared, gone back to where it had come from. But he knew it was still there. Wounded, but still there. He looked down at the fading image of the shot he'd just taken was replaced on the viewfinder by a view of his feet. And for just a second, the valve's cat's eye light remained. An after-image. He dropped the camera, unstrung the top of his ruck-sack, turning it into a gaping maw, a hood, a trap. And then he lassoed it over the valve. And then he started to pedal. And for a moment, he thought the valve was too heavy, like a microcosm of a whole universe whose weight was too much to bear. He could hear it humming inside the ruck-sack, burning through the fabric. He could smell fear. Whether it was his or the valve's fear, he had no idea. Didn't care. He plunged his foot down on the pedal and the bike creaked forward.

416

Now he could see the valve glowing inside the bag, throbbing. He pressed his left foot down, edged forward some more. It was wobbly, it was uncertain, it was as though he needed stabilizers, but it was progress.

He started to pedal. Fast. He tuned everything out but purpose. He was heading for the cliffs, he thought; ready to ride straight off them and into the sea. He was heading for the cliffs, to finish what he'd been born to do. And yet, as he cycled, he heard the valve shouting, yelling, calling. Only, it wasn't calling to him any more. It was calling to someone, some*thing* else. It was calling in a language he didn't understand, in a language which seemed older than the island itself. It was calling in a language which *wasn't* a language at all. But Yoghurt still knew it was calling for help.

He barely registered the changes in the geography, as he cycled up from the valley of the southern woods, past Coverley Bottoms, through the River Drey and then up. Up, up in the direction of the monastery. Up Pate Hill, towards Cawdor Head. He barely noticed the Hoar's Blanket had now, suddenly lifted, leaving barely a trace of it behind. He barely noticed that he was no longer swatting away flies. But the valve was getting heavy again. So heavy, Yoghurt had to forgo the steeper slope which led up past the monastery, and instead head up past Knoll Farm. So heavy that his legs started to wobble again. It was *too* heavy. Too loud. Now, the valve was screeching *constantly,* like a bird left behind in a nest by its mother. Like a bird. Almost as soon as Yoghurt had registered the thought, he felt a shadow from above pass over him. And then, dreadfully, he heard a reciprocal screech from the skies.

It was the wing-ed beast, come for him at last. It was the wing-ed beast, and it was here, sharp in beak and claw. Red. Now, all Yoghurt could see was red. Red all over. It was as though the whole island had been daubed in it.

46: Exodus

The pilot hadn't been able to find anywhere he could land the helicopter. According to Archie, the Hoar's Blanket was playing havoc with the controls, so that the pilot couldn't even judge how far they were above ground. So that the pilot couldn't even judge whether it was *land* below them or sea. Freddie Livermore, now that he was over his air-sickness and his almost overwhelming desire to take a shit, was feeling a clenching sensation in his bowels still, only it was for another reason. It was for frustration.

It was getting sticky in the back. Close. What's more there seemed to be a whole recon squad of flies which had found their way inside now. He was just glad Pete didn't have the camera switched on, because this was another moment for *TV Presenters Do the Funniest Things*. Him fair apoplectic in the back of a helicopter, while his story was down there, just waiting for him. Charlotte was having to field more and more calls from the studio. Was having to resort more and more, to the old Livermore excuse; 'Sorry, I can't hear you, the reception's bad... You're breaking up.' Charlotte was also putting in numerous calls to Manny Combs' mobile, but was getting nothing from that. It was all so very annoying. He could picture Howitt and his buxom assistant, down there safe on the ground, like the tortoise, ready to steal a march on their hare.

He clenched a fist. Felt like punching it through the window. If he had a parachute, if he'd been sure it would unfold properly, he might have done, and then followed that fist with his whole body. Maybe he could ask Charlotte to try it first.

The helicopter pitched, yawed. His stomach lurched a little as it dropped. And then he felt Pete dragging on his arm.

'Fred... look.' He was pointing down into the fug, and for a moment, Freddie had no idea what he was supposed to be looking at. But then he saw it. The shadowy, ghostly shapes of huge,

Bracheosaurean farm vehicles all lined up in a row across Limm's coastal road, close to the causeway. Behind the vehicles were a number of burly, farmer-type men, all standing with their arms folded across their chests, as though they were bouncers. And behind them, separated by about fifty metres of road, was a crowd. The helicopter swept over them and Freddie saw that there were *hundreds* of people. Had to be the whole population of the island. Women, kiddies, blokes. All just standing there as though they were waiting to be processed. As though they were solemnly waiting to be allowed off the island. It looked like an evacuation. Like exodus. Only two people within the crowd raised their arms and waved to the helicopter. Most kept their heads low, tucked into their chests. Seemed resigned to something. Or scared.

'Can't you land further up or something?' he breathed.

Archie shouted and the pilot shook his head. Then turned to Freddie and made a cut-throat gesture. 'Try to land down there, we're dead. There's air currents which are too strong and…'

'I don't care. That's our story right there,' cried Freddie. He looked down forlornly at the last of the crowd, a bunch of five, maybe six people standing huddled together. They appeared to be singing. One of them was waving a placard which read, 'The End is Nigh'. It was like the whole place had been overtaken by madness. *This* was *the* story. The one he'd been waiting for all his life, only… Only they were heading in the wrong direction.

And then he felt the chopper spring upwards. Pulling against the Hoar's Blanket and the wind. 'Where the fuck's he going now?' he yelled. 'Why are we going *up* not down?'

Archie smiled infuriatingly. 'He's looking for a safe place to land, like you asked. Higher ground. Maybe the Hoar's Blanket won't be as thick there.'

Freddie Livermore didn't want to deal in maybes. Maybes weren't hard currency or TV journalism prizes. Maybes were fucking goddamned white lies. The pilot didn't want to land at all. He saw it now. He saw they'd been fed a line, all of them, and they'd taken it, hook, line and sinker. A fly buzzed onto the end of his nose and he virtually punched himself in the face trying to get it off. Charlotte gave him a funny look. Charlotte could fuck off. Charlotte could find herself another internship once this fiasco was over. There was always another Charlotte.

The helicopter continued to climb. Flies continued to buzz round the place. Even the pilot was starting to get annoyed by them

419

now, and the way he was waving his arms about surely wasn't a good idea. Charlotte gave him a different kind of funny look and he felt the tiniest twinge of sympathy for her then. At least, when this fiasco was over, he'd get a good blow-job out of it. That was the least she could do for him after she sourced this shit-tip of a helicopter. He looked over at Pete, but Pete was now almost comatose on the seat, just lolling there bored. Perhaps he'd gone for too long without food. Perhaps his metabolism had conked out on him. Was Freddie the only one could be professional around here?

'Are we nearly there yet?' he said, punching the back of Archie's chair to get his attention.

'Oh. My. God,' was Archie's only response.

Freddie shook his head. 'Christ's sake. All I did was whack your seat a little...' He leaned forward. 'Archie? Arch?'

Archie wasn't concerned about the seat. That much was clear as soon as Freddie saw his face in profile. Archie was only bothered by something he'd seen, out there in the cotton wool air.

'Oh. My. God.' His mouth flapped open, closed like a runway wind-sock.

And now Freddie looked too. Peered out into the gloom, the white-dark. And he saw, amidst the swirls and tendrils of fug, that there was something else moving out there. Something *huge*. And he saw that the story back down there was nothing compared to this, because this felt like... It felt like he'd seen something prehistoric. Mythic. Like a dragon. He saw wings. Mighty, powerful, *awesome* wings. Span had to be something in the region of six metres. He saw a horrible, wrinkly, scaled head. He saw a vast hooked beak. He saw a flash of white feathers forming what looked like a neck-brace. He saw talons. He saw each of these things as individual snapshots, never quite the complete picture, and part of him was glad, because he knew that if he had, the image of that wing-ed beast in full would haunt him for evermore.

'What the hell is that?' he gasped. 'I mean, what *is* it?'

Everyone turned to look, even the pilot. And the bloody bird looked straight back at them. Beadily. And then it opened that vast hooked beak, opened it wide, and it released a screech which chilled Freddie's bones. Only, the screech wasn't the only thing the bird's mouth released. No, it also released flies. Thousands and thousands of flies. And each and every one of them stormed the helicopter. Blanketed the windscreen. Slowed the rotors.

Freddie felt the chopper start to fall.

47: Knoll Farm

Almost as soon as Yoghurt had felt the wing-ed creature's shadow on his back, he'd lost control of his bike. Had skidded into an old metal feeding trough, bouncing off it with a great *brrrunnnkk*. His bike went skittering off back down the hill and he landed away from it, on a patch of new grass which immediately soaked into his back. Though it might have been blood. The ruck-sack flopped down on top of him, winding him. For a moment, blinding him too. He could tell that the valve would inch its way out of the fabric soon, and then he'd be made to pay.

Or maybe he'd be made to pay sooner, because as he looked up and saw the vulture circling, he could pick out the exact moment when it chose to swoop. It dropped like a stone through the sky, its wings tucked into its back, its talons extended. Stream-lined. He felt its eyes on him. Already feeding on him. It would go for his liver first, he knew. For a while, he'd remain alive, feeling, *hearing* as it tore flesh from his bones. It would go for the fatty parts next, though there weren't many on him, all the cycling had seen to that. It would save the choicest parts; the tongue, the cheek, the ears, the eyes, until last, almost as though it still wanted him to be able to speak all evil, hear all evil, see all evil, right to the end.

He couldn't move. He was frozen to the sodden ground. He couldn't breathe now either. The ruck-sack was pressing down on his lungs as though it was part boa constrictor. His eyes were blood-shotted. Saw red once more. Red everywhere. Everywhere save the silhouette of the swooping bird, come to take him away, *ha-ha*. He didn't want to look any more. Didn't want to see, but the valve forced his eyelids open. Pinned them back with invisible matchsticks. His eyes felt as though they were being cheese-grated.

Tears streamed down his crimson cheeks, spilled onto his claret neck, dribbled onto his painted chest. He felt like a sacrificial virgin. He felt like he was paying the price for everything that had

421

ever happened on the island. For now it was the island's life which flashed in front of his eyes, not his own. He saw Vikings arriving on the north east coast, near Brennan Head, in their longships. He saw the red they spilled. He saw the monks destroying the forest and the red they spilled. He saw fishermen draining the sea of its fish. Tomato sauce on plates. He saw Manny Combs rinsing his hands over a sink. The water gurgling down the plughole was apple red. He saw Solomon and the rest drowning off the spit, the sea turning pink. He saw Trevor Knox and Adrian Devonish and Rich Dailly and Vicar and Mart Bibby and... And countless more. All red, all dead.

The bird was close now. He could feel its wind, the stench of death it carried with it. It was so close it was blocking out the milk-white sun. It was so close it was freezing.

And then he saw something else falling from the sky. Something which didn't make any sense to him. Something which didn't compute with the images of Vikings on their longships and monks with their mead. He saw a helicopter. A helicopter which looked to be crawling with something oily-black. He saw a helicopter with one of its rotor blades shorn off, so that it fell at a lop-sided angle. He saw a helicopter, and he thought he could pick out the ghost-white faces of the crew inside.

He saw the helicopter as it plunged close to the vulture. Saw the moment as the two impacted. And then he saw how the two became tangled, so that it was hard to tell what part belonged to which. He saw how the vulture tried to adjust itself, how it finally unfurled its wings and tried to flap away from the heavier helicopter which would drag it down. He saw how the two remained stuck, fast, and how the bird panicked, re-gathered its strength and then...

And then it was like the retina-defying moment to end all retina-defying moments. It was as though the valve's will coursed through the vulture and sent it flying upwards, still tangling with the helicopter. He saw the unlikely pair rise high as the clouds, and then he saw them drop again. Plummeting this time. Only, they weren't plummeting down onto him any more, they were going down somewhere else. Even though he knew it was impossible, he thought he heard the almighty splash as bird and chopper smashed into the sea. And then there was silence.

And then there was nothing. And then there was despair. He'd survived, but for what? The golden valve remained in the ruck-sack. It didn't seem in any way diminished by the end of the wing-ed beast. It continued to try to wriggle out of the bag, continued to pulse, continued to burn, continued to whisper to him.

He heard the sound as it was released. *Riiiiiiiiiiiiiiippppppppppppp.* And then he looked away. He saw its shadow though. He saw its shadow and even its shadow scorched the grass. And it was as though the valve was taking one long, last look at him, because after a while, he saw the shadow starting to float away from him, up the slope, entering Knoll Farm. And though he didn't know what he was doing, why he was doing it, or even what he could do if he caught up with the thing, he followed the burned earth up there too.

By the time he reached the top of the hill, the valve was already gone. Its trail led away into one of the old decrepit barns. He dashed after it, hurdling over rusting farm machinery, antique ploughs, discarded mowers, abandoned tractors. He made the door and took in the smashed padlock, as though someone else had been here before him, and not only the valve. Already, he thought he could hear voices from inside. He pushed through the door.

Inside, there were shelves and shelves of bottles, test tubes and brewing equipment. There were two boys, about fourteen, fifteen, sitting on a hay bale, laughing. They couldn't see him, it seemed. And at first he couldn't see the valve at all, nor could he feel it. But then, as the bigger of the two boys got up from the hay to take a piss, he saw it. He saw it glowing directly above the head of the smaller of the boys, the one who looked like a remarkably young, remarkably thin version of Manny Combs.

Manny Combs seemed to sense his presence then. Looked directly at him. And there was wonder in his eyes. He climbed up from the hay bale and started out in the direction of Yoghurt, his hand outstretched, his fingers grasping. And as he walked, Yoghurt became aware of this strange ticking sound, which he at first put down to the boy's feet scraping across the ground. But as Manny's hand reached out, seemed to pass through a vertical pool of liquid, and then *touched* Yoghurt's cheek, he realised what the ticking actually was.

And then, there was light. Across the multiverses, there was light.

48: Things Fall Apart

Grace Dowsing-Buckby was standing at the window of her mother's bedroom when light burst into the sky. She was so unnerved she nearly dropped Bear, but Bear clung on. She'd already been prepared. She knew this was coming. For Bear, it was the sound she would remember more than the light, the sound which, she knew, was unlike one any of the witnesses have heard before. Bear knew that although they wouldn't mention it in any of their statements later, some of the witnesses would describe it to themselves as a bit like a giant's sneeze, or an island's fart. It was as though they felt the need to resort to fairy stories in order to describe the cataclysmic events, because at least fairy stories had happy endings. But Bear knew that even then, even in the deepest part of the night, when they couldn't help but remember, when the sound seemed to echo back to them through the thickness of their pillows or in the thud of their strumming hearts, they'd know that even the way they described the sound to themselves didn't quite capture it.

In fact the sound was *absence* of sound, it was sound being sucked in to something else, something larger, darker than itself. The sound was an unearthly, hellish vacuum. And it was felt in the very crust of the earth. The witnesses felt the sound more than they heard it. It carried up to them through shaking legs, echoed into their vital organs, rattled off kidney, lungs and heart. And the witnesses were, thank goodness, away from the epicentre. Over by the causeway, already trying to mount their escape. The witnesses were standing in worried groups behind the cordon of farming vehicles, about two miles away from the blast. Even in town, less than a mile away, this absent sound, pitched so low only the hounds of hell would respond to it, caused all hell to break loose.

Anything and everything the absent sound hit, it transformed. It subsumed. It devoured. And the first thing the sound hit was reality. It *bent* reality, curling it back in on itself like a boomerang. It shook, rattled and rolled the fabric of the earth. Pavements wobbled. The jetty catapulted up into the air. It was like the start of an earthquake, but at the same time nothing like an earthquake. It was a different kind of force this, one which definitely felt unnatural. *Unearthly.*

And then, as the absent sound finally relented, the witnesses by the causeway heard a different sound. For some, this secondary sound took the place of the first sound. When they were asked later, 'what was it like?', they'd describe the primeval, tar-pit yell of the collapsing buildings. It was an easy mistake to make and besides, nobody later wanted to contradict them, but if you really wanted to know what that moment was like when the blast went off, it was as though the whole world sucked in a heavy breath... *Wahoooom...* Held it one, two beats... And then exhaled.

Ground zero, Knoll Farm, was devastated almost immediately. The whole place started to concertina in on itself, then buckled, then snapped. Pressure caused the barns to explode. Glass shattered. Other, newer farm-buildings staggered, stooped, dropped. Inside the buildings, their very foundations were smashed. Steel poles bent like reeds of grass. Girders snapped. Joists turned jelly. The noise now was immense. Older witnesses compared it to the Blitz, when Jerry came to bomb the munitions factory. Younger ones said it was like hundreds of planes taking off at the same time. It was a cacophony.

Black smoke belched into the air. Flames too. On the unfortunately named Dye Lane, it was as though everything simply decided to live up to its name and rolled over and died. On Cannon Street, it was as though a huge cannon had been fired. This wrecking, cannon ball careered indiscriminately from building to building, from house to house, on its single-minded path of destruction.

The extension behind the Castle started to suffer from erosion. On fast forward. Great chunks of its facade sheered off, crumbing down onto the rumbling ground below. It was *un*architectured, *un*constructed. Many of the witnesses up by the causeway had for years hated the very existence of the extension. They'd called it all the names under the sun. It was a scar on the landscape, they'd said. A monstrosity. An Arse. But now something huge had picked at that scar, now something more monstrous had emerged.

425

To the south west, the Combs mead factory, that great cathedral of a place, exchanged solidity for something far more liquid. It crashed like a wave, whirlpooled in on itself. It was pulled in different directions by unearthly tides, and the centre could not hold. Things were falling apart, as that great visionary, WB Yeats wrote. And Yeats' rough beast had slouched right onto Limm's shores, smashing everything in his wake.

Chaos. Chaos everywhere. *And not a drop to drink,* as another famous poet didn't (quite) say. And as a less famous mayor once misquoted. Chaos, in fact, was exactly what this was. In its classical meaning, chaos was an abyss, was *dark matter,* was the state of the universe. Right now, it seemed as though Limm was slipping off the face of the earth, slipping into that abyss. This was the apocalypse, the second coming. The end.

The air smelled coppery, like fresh blood. To Bear, it also smelled of something else. Something completely unearthly. The reek from something deep inside the abyss rose, pumped into the atmosphere. It was a fug of desperation and guilt, and of anarchy and broken dreams. It was a slaughterhouse stink of overflowing passionate intensity, a pitiless brewery's malodour puffing into town when the wind changes.

And the wind had changed. The witnesses' faces, though they'd only heard the destruction, were frozen, solidified into masks of shock. When the wind changed, it really could make a face *stay like that,* just like in the old wives tales. The faces of the witnesses had become rough rock, had been carved by some devilish sculptor, had been chiselled into, *nothingness.* Bear could see them. That man, a former fisherman, though now he was wearing one of those high-vis vests, perhaps he'd been working on the drains or on the bins, was bent double nearly. Looked as though he was readying himself to throw up. Except when Bear looked at his face, his eyes, mouth, nose even, had all become great, fat zeroes.

That besuited woman, the one who had to prop herself up against one of her colleagues in case she fell over (or apart; everything was falling apart) was grinning. A great, whopping abyss of a grin cracked her face. But Bear looked at her eyes. Saw the blind panic. Saw that single tear which slug-trailed down her powdered cheek.

Next to her was the newsagent. Buckby had given up smoking a long twenty years ago, but now his mouth was clamped firmly shut around a cigarette. A long trail of ash dangled

426

precariously from the end of the cigarette but he didn't move to flick it away or even spit it out. In that moment everything was precarious.

A farmer had now started to marshal the crowd. Big mustachioed feller. Shoulders broad as roof beams, feet wide as drums. But even his face was frozen. It was frozen into a contorted version of the very face he had when he was a child, when he was forced to go and stand in Trouble Corner, usually for stealing too many biscuits from the barrel. Then, as now, he screwed up his face, wrinkled his nose, surrendered his eyes behind his big jutting brow. *Not fair,* his face said. He'd frozen into the post-watershed moment, just before he was going to burst into a massive *waaaaaaaah.*

Limm Island lurched, sloped, buckled under the pressure. Centuries old buildings gave up their ghosts. Birds, even the gulls, half of whom barely bothered flying these days, took flight as one. They'd lost their perches, their nests, their babies. Even the rats deserted the sinking ship. Bear could hear them. It was that *other* sound, the one none of the witnesses wanted to think about. In seaside towns, Bear thought, you were never more than three metres away from a rat, or so they said, but now they were closer. Close enough to make skin crawl. It was them making that scratching, yelping, *terrified* noise as they scurried through the sewers, or openly through the streets, leaving their piper long behind them in their desperation.

Everything was ruined. Bear could hear the creak of buildings as they coughed their guts up, as they tried, forlornly to follow the rats. Everything was ruined, had been turned upside down, shaken up, and then righted again. But Bear also knew that this would not last, that right now, the world, *this* world was correcting itself. Putting itself back on the right axis. She knew that soon, all the people would remember of the explosion would be the sound. And she also knew that when they found the land rover which had been dripping oil up by the old WELCOME TO LIMM sign, they'd put it down to that, even though they'd get the nagging feeling that it wasn't that at all, that it had been something far more momentous than a simple gas explosion, that this had been the rubbing together of two Tectonic plated universes.

Bear allowed Grace to stroke her head rather too roughly.

'It's all right,' she whispered into her ear. 'It's okay. Everything will be fine soon.'

427

And Grace looked straight back into her button-eyes. 'Will everythink go back to the same?'

Bear didn't know how to answer that one. Because Limm would never be the same from now on. Things would always be that little bit lop-sided, that little bit changed from how people remembered them. And they'd stop, look at *that thing* which they'd remembered seeing all their lives which suddenly looked wrong, and they'd think *that wasn't like that before,* or *how did that get there?* But then they'd get on with their days again, and only in the middle of the night, in the quiet, sleepless parts, would they hear the echoes of that sound which had accompanied the blast, and they'd think, *what if?*

Epilogue: Six Months Later

Ely

Ely had been hoping for a sunny day. One of the crisp, clean, endless ones he remembered from his childhood. But they never seemed to come around any more, even in the height of summer. He'd been hoping for a sunny day, a *cidery* day, a day so unlike the time of the white-darkness it was as though it belonged to an entirely different universe. He'd been hoping for one of those days which reminded him why he still loved Limm, but he reckoned he'd have been waiting an eternity for that. Already six months had passed. And so now was the time.

It wasn't ideal though. The clouds above the beach looked vaguely post-apocalyptic; through screwed-up eyes, their shapes resembled destroyed buildings, tumbledown churches and bus stations, abandoned cityscapes. It looked a lot like Charnley on a Friday night when the pubs were chucking-out and the cavemen had nothing more to look forward to than a fight; a rolling, gargling, snarling, half-blind fight on the cold concrete floor amongst the greasy chip-wrappers and the lost handbags. Sea birds cut through the clouds, spinning in over-elaborate, sling-shot circles seeking out their aerial photo prey in the rabid, foaming-at-the-mouth sea. *Ka-kaaa*, they called, menacingly, but most shied away from plunging down into the depths. And the sea click-cracked stones by way of response; click-cracked them with the enthusiasm of a north east coast Fonzie clicking his thumb and finger in appreciation of something or someone of exceptional beauty. Only, this Fonzie was end-of-the-night drunk. It was lurching, belching, kebab-on-the-way-home drunk. So drunk was the sea, it was still throwing up more of the flotsam and jetsam from the wrecked helicopter out there in the big black distance. Of course, it had long since gone past

429

the point of vomiting solids – there were none of the *real treasures* now, hence the lack of a crowd at the water's edge - but still there was something to retch-up, the occasional spool of tape or mobile phone or an old news script or a pair of pilot's aviator shades.

Yoghurt waited on the uncomfortable shingle, occasionally shifting position so as to try to fit himself into the stones more properly, but generally he was as still and silent as the alcoholic who sat and stared at his tumbler of whisky, daring himself not to take a sip. He was wedging himself into place, as though he still felt the need to hold himself down, as though he still felt the need to try to stop himself from slip-sliding off the edge of the country, off the edge of the universe, and into oblivion. For a moment, Yoghurt looked like the sum total of humanity, stuck here with nowhere else to go and unable to drag himself away anyway. Nearby, the wind whipped the red flag so that it flapped crazily on the bent pole, as though trying desperately to attract the attention of someone over the other side of the beach. A police officer to help him perhaps. Or a lifeguard. But still Yoghurt waited.

Behind the rolling clouds, red sky seeped in; sailor's delight. Or was it warning? Yoghurt had never known which way round it went, but certainly, he didn't seem delighted or warned in any way. His makeshift fire had almost burned itself out, despite the fact he'd tried to guard it from the wind by digging it deep into the stones. He didn't seem bothered about trying to find more firewood. Occasionally, he fingered the scar on his cheek. An angry red blotch from where a younger, thinner Manny Combs had reached across time-zones and touched him. Occasionally he looked over his shoulder, back to the Seahorse, where they'd already erected the FOR SALE signs. Occasionally he listened out for the sound of the new lifeboat land rover. But mostly, he just looked out at the island which was him. *He* was the island, he reckoned. That poet who'd said no man is an island had been stone-cold wrong on that score.

Poor Vicar was an island too, and a mongrel one to boot. So maybe *he* was wrong. Maybe they were twins. Like the earth and the moon. And then there were the others, the other survivors. The few who still remained who knew – in *kind* – what had happened. So maybe they were a bit like an archipelago. But they were certainly separate. It was the knowledge, he supposed. Those terrible images which had been scarred into their retinas. Images which made it seem as though everything in the town was subtly changed. Like some evil tricksy spirit had crept onto the island overnight and *altered* things. Made everything different. As though a full-scale replica of Limm had been built, only every 'I' hadn't been dotted and every 't' hadn't been crossed. Whenever Yoghurt went into town with his eyes open he'd notice something else which had changed, like, the clock on the town hall, would be about half a foot lower than he remembered it from times past. Or, there were two benches on the village green, not one. Or the Castle hotel was now two storeys not three, and its extension was not as much of an eyesore as it used to be. Other people, he was sure, *must* have registered these changes, but they didn't pay them any mind. They were happier remaining blinkered.

Yoghurt was no longer blinkered. He knew how fragile even this reality was, even this moment was. And he knew that he was changing. Becoming someone wholly different to the Yoghurt he'd once been. And yet, at the same time, he knew that somewhere else, in some other reality, the old Yoghurt would still remain. He was starting to think deeply about how time and space weren't flat at all, weren't linear, like a narrative. Life, he thought was like one of those *Choose Your Own Adventure* books he'd sneaked out of Limm Library when he was a kid. Every time he turned the page, every time he picked a different fork in the road, each change, each decision he made would bring about scores of other alternate endings which were played out in a different universe. In one universe, he was sure, he'd have failed. The Darkness would have taken over. In another, perhaps he wouldn't have been the hero, perhaps he'd have shied away when push came to shove. Perhaps someone else would have stepped up to the mark. Perhaps even now, he'd still be that unchanged, undeveloped character who thought only of cycling proficiency and whether, if he was late for his tea, he'd have to wear the Shirt. And somewhere, *all* of those things were happening, *had* happened, were about to happen.

Best way he could put it was this. It was as though every moment was captured in a photograph, frozen in time. It could have been one of his action shots, say, of a dog leaping up to catch the ball in the air. Once the flash had gone off, the moment would be allowed to play itself out, but it was allowed to do this in myriad ways. Myriad places. In one time and place, the dog would leap, catch the ball in its mouth and land, gracefully. Be rewarded with a treat from its owner. In another, the dog would miss the ball. The ball would bounce, roll, slink off into the bushes. *Flash.* Another camera shot. Another world of possibilities would open up. In one

431

time and place, the dog would crash into the bushes after it, see a flash of red amongst the long grass. Retrieve it, be rewarded with a treat and maybe a pat on the head too. In another, the dog would sulk back to its owner and *not* be rewarded with a treat. And yet at the same time *all* of the stories were splayed out, like a hand of cards, ready to be dealt, so that, at the same time as the dog was being rewarded in one narrative strand, in another, it was being berated for losing yet *another* ball, and in another, it caught the scent of another dog in the bushes, got distracted, and loped off, with that strange running style of his. In one strand the dog was alive, panting, tongue lolling out of its mouth, ready for a Full English breakfast and a margarine tub full of water, in another, it was dead, fried by a camera flash of energy as it tried to swallow the golden valve. The question was, or so Yoghurt perceived it; was it the same dog on every card, in every photo? Didn't even the slightest fractions, the minutest gradations of difference *change* the dog? Didn't experience alter it? And that wasn't even taking into account the bigger differences, like, say, between live dog and dead dog…

Thinking about it all made Yoghurt's brain hurt. He thought that if there could just be one photograph, like the one he'd kept of his father, one moment frozen in time, then that would have been more… satisfying. But then, perhaps life wasn't supposed to be satisfying. Perhaps the photograph of God which he'd been endeavouring to shoot most of his life, at least before the valve, wasn't just one photograph. It was the full deck of them, splayed out, all playing at the same time. All those little twists and turns at the same time.

He sighed. Checked his watch. Nearly time. He stood up, brushed himself down, and kicked stones over the fire, dousing it out. Started to stroll off the beach, or at least, stroll as best he could; it wasn't easy on the shingle, everyone on Limm knew that, in *whatever* universe, whatever reality they belonged. Or did they? Was there one Limm which, due to a geological quirk, had a sandy beach? Was there one Limm which wasn't even an island? Was there…

He stopped himself. Shook his head to clear it. Stepped onto the village green. Kirstie Shay was sitting on one of the benches. She was wearing a big, baggy University of Newcastle hoodie which covered her bump. When she saw Yoghurt, she winked.

He walked over to her, beaming 'You got in then, did you?' he said, nodding down at the hoodie.

432

'Well... Sorta... They've accepted me on a foundation course for next year. Once I've had a year getting used to this wannabe footballer I got inside me.'

'You're leaving as well then?' he asked.

'Uh-huh.'

Yoghurt felt the blood rising in his cheeks. He wanted to say more. In the end though, all he could say was 'congratulations', and then go about his business. He looked back at her, once, on the bench and thought she looked... She looked happy. The world behind her like that, looked as though it was stretching out for her, making room.

He stepped onto the pavement, almost straight into Dr. Shaw and his wife. They were taking a morning stroll. 'Mind yourself, Yoghurt-lad,' said Shaw.

And Felicity, his wife, gave him a playful nudge in the ribs. 'Mind *your*self, Ray. You know he calls himself Ely now.'

And Shaw looked over the moon that his wife was telling him off, right there on the pavement.

'Off anywhere nice, Ely?' said Felicity.

Yoghurt bit his lip. 'Sort of,' he said. 'Off to see a woman about a dog.'

Felicity narrowed her eyes. Pretended to tap the end of her nose. 'Oh, I see, it's like that is it? Well, you mind how you go, young man.' The pair of them started to walk off and then she paused, tugged her husband back. 'And Ely,' she said, 'Ely, I feel like I've got to thank you. I don't know why, but I just feel like I have to.'

Dr. Shaw rolled his eyes. 'Come on Flick,' he said, 'let's get you home. I think this sea air is getting to you.'

They walked away, both of them laughing. Yoghurt laughed too. But quickly stopped as he walked past the big cairn at the end of the jetty which was there to mark the passing of the people who'd died in the storm. He crouched down and read the names hewn into the stone. Traced his fingers over the letters.

ADRIAN DEVONISH, TREVOR KNOX, GILLIAN HEGGARTY, RICHARD DAILLY, MARTIN BIBBY. And then, at the bottom, in smaller letters, as though an afterthought, MANFRED COMBS.

Did it make things worse that the cause of these people's deaths was being brushed under the carpet yet again? Was it somehow bad karma for everyone to have forgotten about the Black

Panther, the wing-ed beast and the plague? Or was it better, *safer,* that people simply believed it a storm, a terrible Hoar's Blanket which had done for five of the population? Was it somehow more respectful that suddenly all the Youtube videos, the Facebook groups, the *horror* had disappeared into the ether, into some other universe? Right now, in some other place, had Limm Island become a ghoul's playground, a place where blood-hungry tourists stopped off to see where a whole island had been ripped apart, limb from limb?

A small bicycle bell dragged him out of his reverie. He looked up to see Lewis Dowsing on a very new-looking Raleigh, complete with all the bells and whistles. 'What do you reckon?' said an obviously proud Lewis.

'Brilliant,' said Yoghurt. 'It'll definitely get you round your paper-route quicker.'

Lewis bit his lip. 'Erm... I'm not exactly doing that any more...' He looked lost for a moment as *something* washed over his face, whether it was remembrance of knowledge, Yoghurt wasn't sure. Yoghurt wanted to reach out for him, to tell him everything would be all right. But he saw there was no need. Lewis's face soon collapsed into a grin again, and he said, 'Righto, best be off then, see ya mate.'

Yoghurt watched him cycle off along the pavement. Then he watched as the boy performed a dangerous-looking skid and then bunny-hopped off the kerb. He thought about shouting over to him, gently reminding him that skids and bunny-hops – and oh, no, what was this; a wheelie? – weren't part of any cycling proficiency code *he'd* taught him, but then he remembered how long, even in this reality, Lewis had had to spend cooped up in his room, getting over the sickness. Whatever that sickness was, nobody ever seemed to say. Whatever that sickness was, surely recovering from it was just the excuse he needed to perform a few show-offy bike tricks.

Yoghurt climbed to his feet, started to walk. He passed the village's community news board, where all the usual adverts for all the usual bake sales and coffee mornings were displayed (nobody in this reality had even considered a TALENT-STRAVANGANZA!!!!!!). He spotted a sign for the Fat Fighters Club which was being run by Sally Martin down at the Bungalow, Tuesday and Wednesday mornings. Yoghurt's mother had joined *both* classes, and was taking to it with the same religious zeal as she had Solomon's words. Now, when he called in for his tea on a

434

Friday – a salad, always a salad – the whole downstairs of the house had been turned into a shrine to healthy eating. There were calorie counters on the wall near the patio windows. She'd covered the patio, with the cat's pawprint, with a big trampoline. Ely thought it was a little close to the house, that she might do herself a mischief with one, off-key bounce, come crashing through the French windows, but he chose to say nothing. Always he said nothing. He preferred his foresight at much less than 20:20 nowadays.

He passed the town hall, where Mike Ford, the new mayor, had set up shop. He'd only got in by a whisker in the voting in May (against no less an opponent than Carl-Rhys Hamilton; a *comedian)* and there'd been some doubt as to how he'd fare. But so far, he seemed to be shaping up well. He'd immediately scrapped all plans for the bridge, already blocked plans for a fast food franchise which wanted to take over the never-open art gallery. He'd kept the local bus service running. Liked to dress up as mayor a bit too much, liked the high-falutin' life a bit too much, but then, Limm Islanders had come to expect that of their mayor.

Of course, what with all his mayoral duties, Mike had been forced to give up his role at *The Tide Piper.* For the last couple months, Yoghurt had taken over the reigns. He was Acting Editor in Chief, but it really was Acting, like he was playing at it. In truth, he remained the chief photographer. Rob Martin, Sally Martin's husband, had taken on the vast majority of the writing duties. And it turned out he wasn't at all a bad writer. His prose was a little too purple at times, his world-view a little *harrumphy,* but then, that seemed to tie in well with how most *real* Limm islanders outlook. When Yoghurt left the island at the end of the day, the paper would be in safe hands.

The takeover down at the Castle had been far less smooth. With Adrian Devonish *and* Rich out the way, there was a vacuum at the top. Even its remaining open was in some doubt after Manny Combs' death was discovered too. In the end it was taken over by a chain, Premier Hotels, about which there was much grumbling, but at least it remained open. There wasn't much grumbling about the two new bosses however, the pair of Polish girls nicknamed the Abba Twins, for no accountable reason. Everyone knew they worked so much harder than everyone else. *Four pairs of hands and all that...*

Ruth Sharp was waiting for him outside the Castle's former rival hotel, the Seahorse. She was examining the FOR SALE sign with great interest. She was wearing a fisherman's woollen hat, rolled down so low it almost covered her eyes, but when she saw Yoghurt, she pulled it off with a *taaa-daaaahhh* flourish and showed him her freshly-shaven head.

'Finally bit the bullet,' she said. 'Did the whole Sinead O'Connor thing. Not that there was much of it to shave off anyway.'

Yoghurt didn't rightly know who Sinead O' Connor was, but he *did* know who David Bowie was. Couldn't *not* know if you hung around Ruth for long enough. And yet again, when he looked at her, he was struck by how much like her hero she now looked. It was all in the eyes. Looking at the valve so long seemed to have done funny things to them, so that, in some lights, it looked as though they were different colours. One sea blue, one forest green. Although sometimes it was one Vicar-brown, and one a white-dark as though there was no colour at all.

'Looks nice,' he said, finally.

She nodded. 'I've already been up there, done a recce. It's safe. Everything's gone. When the landie blew it must have taken everything else with it.'

When the landie blew. A likely story.

'But I did find this,' she said, opening up the ruck-sack which was at her feet. She pulled out the rather battered, rather dusty remains of his Nikon camera, *sans* lens cap of course.

'Bloody hell,' he said, and then clamped a hand over his mouth.

Ruth laughed. 'Tried it. Works. The photos...' She fixed him with her strange multiversial eyes.

'I know.' He thought back to what was on that camera. Images of the panther print, of the dead panther, of the valve... He could blow the whole cover story sky high if he wanted to.

'It's up to you, of course,' said Ruth, 'but I think you should destroy the film. Keep the camera, obviously. But destroy the film. What do you say?'

'I say we bury it. We're digging a hole anyway.'

Ruth smiled.

In the end, the camera was the only thing they did bury. They covered it with a large piece of driftwood Ruth had found on the beach. On it, she'd marked the names:

MART BIBBY

436

And VICAR. Next to Vicar's name she'd placed a small asterisk. It referred to one of the other names she now knew her former stray by: THE DIAMOND DOG. They both shed a few tears and stayed longer than they should have done, trying to talk what had happened into some kind of sense. They both sung along to a Bowie number Ruth played over the small speakers of her Ipod, Yoghurt just humming really, but Ruth belting out the words. And then, finally, she clapped him on the back.

'We ready then soldier?'

He nodded. He nodded happily, and for him, the best bit was yet to come.

Ruth

He followed her, almost bumper-to-bumper all the way up to the A24, swerving from one side of the road to the other, flashing his lights every few hundred yards. Feeling shaky enough as it was, it was all Ruth could do to maintain control of her car, a lovely red Hotspur of the type driven in the late 70's film *What got Garry Gorman's goat?* which she'd bought with some of the proceeds of the sale of the Seahorse. Although the car was in near-mint condition, she noted it did not handle as well as modern cars. Not like Christian's company Merc which had once upon a time given her such smooth rides. No, in the Hotspur she felt as though she really was driving, and not being driven; any miscalculation of the bends on her part and she was likely to drive straight into a ditch. The Merc, back then, had cushioned her to the outside world. It wouldn't have ever let her move out from the perfect driving line it had settled itself into, and would probably have decided to steam away from the Shay Mead truck rather than suffer the indignity of holding up a queue.

Nevertheless, the Hotspur reached the turn-off for the A24. It was on the crest of a hill, so it was only when she was almost upon the junction that she realised the traffic was at a standstill. She slammed her bare foot down on the brakes and felt pistons groan and motors whirr. The car gave off a sound like a bike chain which had come loose. Claggy. Grinding. Not soundless like the Merc had been. The Merc would have ice-skated to a halt. The Hotspur *Eddie the Eagled* to a coughing, spluttering collapse, its nose poking out onto the A24 *just* between two other cars, both of which issued her with beeps of warning.

Welcome to the mainland.

She edged back behind the white line of the junction and clicked on her indicator. Behind her, the mead lorry beeped in complaint. It wanted her to move forward. The cars on the A24 wanted her to move back. Ruth made herself ignore them all and instead stared off into the middle distance, pretending everything was okay. But it wasn't.

The queue stretched back as far as the eye could see in both directions. Nobody else seemed to care that they were most likely queueing because of an accident. Instead of taking the time to reflect on their luck that it hadn't happened to them – perhaps they'd forgot to feed the cat that morning and hence were a few minutes later than usual in reaching the A24, or perhaps, as she had, they'd had to stop off and pick up a couple passengers for the ride - they were getting increasingly angry at the delay. They didn't seem to care that life was so random, so fragile.

They did things differently here. She chanced a look into some of the cars; despite, or in spite of the recession, men shouted into mobile phones, gesticulating wildly, whilst simultaneously stuffing sandwiches into their mouths and trying to gain an extra few feet in the jam as they rushed towards staff restructuring meetings in Newcastle, or alarm call outs in Charnley, or job interviews in Middlesbrough. Teenagers texted, and turned up their music loud so nobody would try to edge in front of them while they weren't looking. Sharp-suited women checked their make up in their rear-view mirrors, eyes quivering with suppressed rage. Ruth simply breathed. Deep-breathing was her gift; the one thing she was very good at.

The truck behind her beeped angrily for the seventeenth, or was it eighteenth time. Ruth shot a dirty look into the rear view mirror, catching sight of the driver, a hulking baseball-cap wearing

438

brute of a man who had seemingly christened himself 'The Charnley Kid' judging by the Christmas lights arranged at the back of his cab, amongst various football scarves (and doubtless there'd be a copy of the *Sport* in there too, folded into a crook in the dashboard so the tits were still on show.) She considered flicking him the V's, but decided against it. The driver was liable to climb out of the truck and come knocking at her window. He'd have time to do it too, because although the lights had changed, there was still no gap in the traffic. As it was, he was leaning half out of the window now, waving manically.

'It'll be all right,' said Yoghurt, from the back seat, where he was buried under a mound of Kirstie Shay's seemingly endless *stuff.*

'I know him,' said Kirst, 'he's all right. The driver, I mean.'

Ruth sighed. He didn't seem *all right.* Clearly the man was Kellogg's Honey Nut Loops. And she thought she understood why he was so irrationally annoyed with her. It wasn't because she hadn't found a gap, nor was it because she was a woman in command of a fairly decent condition Hotspur.

She edged forward The driver of a sleek black Nevada (a funeral car if ever she'd seen one, with that elongated back as though to fit a coffin in) finally deigned to look out of his cockpit window, spotted her, *winked,* and then let her ease into place behind the 4x4. *Winked.* The cave-man winked at her. Sexism was alive and well when it came to traffic jams; if she'd been a bloke with a Bowieish tinge to her hair, he'd never let her in, but he had, and so she flashed her lights to say thanks. She felt her cheeks flush with embarrassment.

Still, a wink was a wink was a wink. When would men stop winking at her, she wondered? Never, she hoped. The only other time she'd been off the island in the entire time she'd owned the Seahorse, she'd been to see her mother in those last, dreadful days at the nursing home and *even then,* a cheerful old fella with a yellow stain around his crotch had perched on a bench opposite them and tipped her mother a wink of epic proportions. So epic was that wink, it had almost brought her mother out of her catatonic state for one final hurrah. It hadn't, but it had come so close. She'd felt the twitch in her mother's hand; the *consciousness* which was there... and then not there. She imagined that same old fella would have been the type to lift his flat cap in salute as the black funeral cars went by a couple of weeks later, but she'd not been able to attend the funeral and so

439

couldn't be sure. That was the way she imagined it though; a day full of the old-fashioned paying of respects; old men with the traces of tears in their eyes as they tucked into sausage rolls; no hint of a scene if... no, *when* Christian turned up on the search for her because she wasn't there...

'Can we put the radio on instead of David Bowie?' said Kirstie from the back.

Ruth tried not to sneer. 'What do you think, Ely?' she asked, hoping he'd plump for the Bowie, hoping he'd be on her side, especially after the ceremony for Vicar. But of course he wasn't. He was hanging off Kirst's every word.

'Errr... Errr... Radio, I reckon,' he said, blushing.

She turned the damn thing off altogether. It was frustrating, this never quite getting going, never quite getting away; being forced to stare at the quivering brake lights of the 4x4 in front. Ruth prided herself on being a very level-headed driver, but if there was one thing which was bound to shift her into road-rage territory it was people being over-enthusiastic on the brakes, *dab-dab-dabbing* at them constantly, whereas if they'd kept to a steadier pace in the first place they could have simply cruised along somewhere between five and ten miles an hour and had the time to look out of the window.

She'd had about enough of the whispered complaints from the back and so finally clicked on the radio, wondering whether they still bothered with traffic reports, or whether the country's arterial roads were now so clogged-up there was no need; perhaps the mainland was now so close to a heart attack - brought on by its far too busy, monochrome, recessionary existence – it wouldn't survive much longer and all that was left was this bloated, brain-dead corpse. The radio fizzed, popped and then tuned in. Some awful europop was vomited up by the speakers. Was it europop? ASBOpop? Ruth didn't know the proper terms, but she knew that the hypnotic drum beat and *Alvin and the Chipmunks* style singing made the song the kind of diversionary nonsense which might as well have been pumped out by the government to placate a disaffected youth, and to distract them from what really mattered.

Kirstie in the back immediately cheered and clapped her hands together in a faintly *simpleton* manner. 'Cheesemonster!' she cried. 'Yes! I love this one.'

Ruth groaned. Opened the window, hoping to get rid of some of the sound. Wasn't good. Too *gassy.* So she unbuckled her seatbelt and leaned over, wound down the passenger side window instead. And that was when she saw the big, Shay Mead lorry which had been bearing down on them all the way up the B-road off the causeway pulling onto the hard shoulder right next to them.

She felt her heart beating fast in her throat. Even though Kirstie claimed to recognise this lunatic; even though this lunatic now *worked* for Kirstie's dad, she was still wary. Something didn't smell right. She tried to look straight ahead, tried not to attract the man's attention, but it was no good. From the back, Kirst gave him a cheery wave. And now Ruth was seriously thinking of K-turning it, cutting into the traffic on the other side of the road and simply returning to the island, taking down the FOR SALE sign, re-listing the Hotspur, and pretending like none of this had ever happened. That it had, like, happened to another *version* of her.

She tried to edge the car forward, tried to put some distance between her and the lorry. It was no good. The lorry-driver was now opening his cab door, stepping nimbly down those tiny steps down the side, and then pausing to reach up for something, which he tucked under his arm. Her first thought was gun. She thought he had a gun, that he was going to shoot her for going so painfully slowly across the causeway. For stopping. For shaving her hair. For surviving, when maybe she shouldn't have.

Kirstie wound down her window, shouted, 'Hi Joe!' And Ruth thought, *that's it, missy, that's your ride to Newcastle gone, out the window. That's your free lift to the hospital when the baby's due gone too.*

The man was walking out onto the road now. There were a few half-hearted beeps at him, but he carried on, still clutching something tightly under his arm.

Go away, go away, go away, go away.

He reached the car, slammed a big paw down on the roof. Ruth jumped. Was still jumping when he crouched down by the window, grinned at her, and said, 'Aren't you forgetting something?'

And Ruth wanted to smash into the car in front, cause them all to domino into each other, cause the police to come, just so this *man* wouldn't keep crouching by her window, talking in riddles. She scratched her head.

'I said, aren't you forgetting something?'

Ruth blew up at him then, 'Am I forgetting my highway code by going too slow for you? Am I forgetting *nobody leaves Limm Island alive?* Tell me, what am I forgetting?'

441

He grinned. 'I've been trying to stop you since Limm town, woman. Here, have a look.' He lifted the thing which had been tucked under his arm up to the window. And Ruth closed her eyes, expecting it to go bang. But it didn't go bang. It went woof.

She creaked open an eye. Dared to hope.

Joe Friar was still grinning, though Ruth only had eyes for the dog. It looked like Vicar, it smelled like Vicar, hell, it *wriggled* like Vicar, so surely it was Vicar...

'Vicar?' she breathed.

The dog barked, once, as though she'd carefully instructed it that one bark always meant 'yes'. As though he'd ever let her train her.

'Saw the little bleeder running after your car, didn't I?' said Joe.

Vicar jumped through the open window and made himself comfortable on the seat.

Yoghurt Rhodes met her eyes in the rear-view mirror. 'Welcome to the mainland,' he said. 'They do things differently here.'

THE END

A .J. Kirby is the author of four novels; *Perfect World* (2011); *Bully* (2009); *The Magpie Trap* (2008), and *Paint this Town Red*. His published fiction also includes two volumes of collected short stories, *Mix Tape* (2010) and *The Art of Ventriloquism* (2012), and three novellas, *The Haunting of Annie Nicol* (2012), *The Black Book* (2011) and *Bed Peace* (2011).

His prize-winning short stories have featured in a wide number of publications, both in print and online. Award recognition has come from Huddersfield Literature Festival, Ilkley Literature Festival, Mere Literary Festival, the H.E Bates Short Story Competition, and in writing competitions run by Cinnamon Press and People in Action. He received an honourable mention in the worldwide Best Horror of the Year 2008/9, judged by the esteemed editor, Ellen Datlow and in 2011, he was shortlisted for the Paperbooks 'Tale of Two Halves' competition, and was awarded runner-up in the Dog Horn Publishing Fiction Prize. He also won the genre fiction prize in the Big Issue in the North's Short Issue.

Andy lives in Leeds, UK with his girlfriend Heidi and his lucky black cat, Eric. He started writing after losing out in a game show hosted by Les Dennis. To find out more, visit Andy's website: www.andykirbythewriter.20m.com.

443

PAINT THIS TOWN RED